D0908725

SUE GRAFTON

THREE COMPLETE NOVELS

"J" is for Judgment

"K" is for Killer

"L" is for Lawless

Also by Sue Grafton from Wings Books®

SUE GRAFTON: THREE COMPLETE NOVELS

"A" is for Alibi

"B" is for Burglar

"C" is for Corpse

SUE GRAFTON: THREE COMPLETE NOVELS

"D" is for Deadbeat

"E" is for Evidence

"F" is for Fugitive

SUE GRAFTON: THREE COMPLETE NOVELS

"G" is for Gumshoe

"H" is for Homicide

"I" is for Innocent

SUE GRAFTON

THREE COMPLETE NOVELS

"J" is for Judgment

"K" is for Killer

"L" is for Lawless

Wings Books

New York

This edition contains the complete and unabridged texts of the original editions.

The contents of this omnibus were originally published in three separate volumes under the titles:

This 2007 edition published by Wings Books, an imprint of Random House Value Publishing, a division of Random House, Inc., New York, by arrangement with Henry Holt and Company, Inc.

Wings Books® the colophon is a trademark of Random House, Inc.

Random House
New York • Toronto • London • Sydney • Auckland
www.valuebooks.com

A catalog record for this title is available from the Library of Congress.

ISBN: 978-0-517-23075-6

Printed and bound in the United States of America

10 9 8 7 6 5 4 3 2 1

CONTENTS

"J" IS FOR JUDGMENT

For Torchy Gray,

in honor of a friendship that began
with a green bean collage . . . hers, not mine.
Western Kentucky State Teacher's College
Bowling Green, Kentucky
1958

ACKNOWLEDGMENTS

The author wishes to acknowledge the invaluable assistance of the following people: Steven Humphrey; Jay Schmidt; B. J. Seebol, J.D.; Tom Huston, Seacoast Yachts; Chief Deputy Richard Bryce, Sergeant Patrick Swift, and Senior Deputy Paul Higgason, Ventura County Jail; Lieutenant Bruce McDowell, Custody Division, Ventura County Sheriff's Department; Steven Stone, Presiding Justice, State of California Court of Appeal; Joyce Spizer, Insurance Investigations Inc.; Mike Love and Burt Bernstein, J.D., Chubb-Sovereign Life; Lynn McLaren; William Kurta, Tri-County Investigations; Lawrence Boyers, Virginia Farm Bureau Insurance Services; John Mackall, Attorney-at-Law; Jill Weissich, Attorney-at-Law; Joyce McAlister, Associate Attorney, Legal Bureau, Police Department, City of New York; Diana Maurer, Assistant Attorney General, State of Colorado; Janet Hukill, Special Agent, FBI; Larry Adkisson, Senior Investigator, Eighteenth Judicial District Attorney; Peter Klippel, Doug's Bougs Etc.; Frank Minschke; Nancy Bein; and Phil Stutz.

With special thanks to Harry and Megan Montgomery, whose boat, *The Captain Murray,* plays such a central role in both the novel and jacket photograph.

1

On the face of it, you wouldn't think there was any connection between the murder of a dead man and the events that changed my perceptions about my life. In truth, the facts about Wendell Jaffe had nothing to do with my family history, but murder is seldom tidy and no one ever said revelations operate in a straight line. It was my investigation into the dead man's past that triggered the inquiry into my own, and in the end the two stories became difficult to separate. The hard thing about death is that nothing ever changes. The hard thing about life is that nothing stays the same. It began with a phone call, not to me, but to Mac Voorhies, one of the vice-presidents at California Fidelity Insurance for whom I once worked.

My name is Kinsey Millhone. I'm a licensed California private investigator, working out of Santa Teresa, which is ninety-five miles north of Los Angeles. My association with CF Insurance had been terminated the previous December, and I hadn't had much occasion to return to 903 State. For the past seven months I'd been leasing office space from the law firm of Kingman and Ives. Lonnie Kingman's practice is largely criminal, but he also enjoys the complexities of trials involving accidental injury or wrongful death. He's been my attorney of record for a number of years, stepping in with legal counsel when the occasion arises. Lonnie is short and beefy, a body-builder and a scrapper. John Ives is the quiet one who prefers the intellectual challenges of appellate work. I'm the only person I know who doesn't express routine contempt for all the lawyers in the world. Just for the record, I like cops, too: anyone who stands between me and anarchy.

Kingman and Ives occupies the entire upper floor of a small building downtown. Lonnie's firm consists of himself; his law partner, John Ives; and an attorney named Martin Cheltenham, Lonnie's best friend, who leases offices from him. The bulk of the day-to-day work is attended to by the two legal secretaries, Ida Ruth and Jill. We also have a receptionist named Alison and a paralegal named Jim Thicket.

The space I moved into used to be a conference room with a makeshift kitchenette. After Lonnie annexed the last available office on the third floor, he had a new kitchen built, along with a room for the copying equipment. My office is large enough to accommodate a desk, my swivel chair, some file cabinets, a minirefrigerator and coffee maker, plus a big storage closet stacked with packing boxes untouched since the move. I have my own separate phone line in addition to the two lines I share with the firm. I still have my answering machine, but in a pinch Ida Ruth covers incoming calls for me. For a while I made a pass at finding another office to rent. I had sufficient money to make the move. A sidebar to a case I was working before Christmas resulted in my picking up a twenty-five-thousand-dollar check. I put the money in some CDs—the bank kind, not the music—where it was happily collecting interest. In the meantime I discovered how much I liked my current circumstances. The location was good, and it was nice to have people around me at work. One of the few disadvantages of living alone is not having anyone to tell when you're going someplace. At least now at work I had people who were aware of my whereabouts, and I could check in with them if I needed any mothering.

For the past hour and a half, on that Monday morning in mid-July, I'd sat and made phone calls on a skip trace I was working. A Nashville private investigator had written me a letter, asking if I'd check local sources for his client's ex-husband, who was six thousand dollars in arrears on his child support. Rumor had it that the fellow had left Tennessee and headed for California with the intention of settling somewhere in Perdido or Santa Teresa counties. I'd been given the subject's name, his previous address, his birth date, and his Social Security number with instructions to develop any lead I could. I also had the make and model of the vehicle he was last seen driving, as well as his Tennessee license plate number. I'd already written two letters to Sacramento: one to request driver's license information on the subject, another to see if he'd registered his 1983 Ford pickup. Now I was calling the various public utility companies in the area, trying to see if there were any recent hook-ups in the guy's name. So far I hadn't hit pay dirt, but it was fun anyway. For fifty bucks an hour, I'll do just about anything.

When Alison buzzed me on the intercom, I leaned over automatically and depressed the lever. "Yes?"

"You have a visitor," she said. She's twenty-four years old, bubbly and energetic. She has blond hair to her waist, buys all her clothes in a size 4 "petite," and dots the "i" in her name with a heart or a daisy, depending on her mood, which is always good. Somehow she sounded as if she were calling on one of those "telephones" kids make with two Dixie cups and a length of string. "A Mr. Voorhies with California Fidelity Insurance."

Like a comic strip character, I could feel a question mark form above my head. I squinted, leaning closer. "Mac Voorhies is out there?"

"You want me to send him back?"

"I'll come out," I said.

I couldn't believe it. Mac was the man who supervised most of the cases I'd worked for CF. It was his boss, Gordon Titus, who'd fired my sorry ass, and while I'd made my peace with the change in my employment, I could still feel a flush of adrenaline at the thought of the man. Briefly I entertained a little fantasy that Gordon Titus had sent Mac to offer his abject apologies. Fat chance, I thought. I did a hasty survey of the office, hoping it didn't look like I'd fallen on hard times. The room wasn't large, but I had my own window, lots of clean white wall space, and burnt orange carpeting in an expensive wool shag. With three framed watercolors and a leafy four-foot ficus plant, I thought the place looked very tasteful. Well, okay, the ficus was a fake (some sort of laminated fabric tinted with accumulated dust), but you really couldn't tell unless you got up real close.

I would have checked my reflection (Mac's arrival was already having that effect), but I don't carry a compact and I already knew what I'd see—dark hair, hazel eyes, not a smidge of makeup. As usual, I was wearing jeans, my boots, and a turtleneck. I licked my palm and ran a hand across my shaggy head, hoping to smooth down any stick-up parts. The week before, in a fit of exasperation, I'd picked up a pair of nail scissors and whacked all my hair off. The results were just about what you'd expect.

I hung a left in the corridor, passing several offices on my way to the front. Mac was standing by Alison's desk out in the reception area. Mac's in his early sixties, tall and scowling, with a fly-away halo of wispy gray hair. His brooding black eyes are set slightly askew in a long bony face. In lieu of his usual cigar, he was smoking a cigarette, ash tumbling down the front of his three-piece suit. Mac has never been one to plague himself with attempts at fitness, and his body, at this point, resembles a drawing from a child's perspective: long arms and legs, foreshortened trunk with a little head stuck on top.

I said, "Mac?"

He said, "Hello, Kinsey," in a wonderful wry tone.

I was so happy to see him that I started laughing out loud. Like some great galumphing pup, I loped over to the man and flung myself into his arms. This behavior was greeted by one of Mac's rare smiles, revealing teeth that were tarnished from all the cigarettes he smoked. "It's been a long time," he said.

"I can't believe you're here. Come on back to my office and we can visit," I said. "You want some coffee?"

"No, thanks. I just had some." Mac turned to stub out his cigarette, realizing belatedly that there weren't any ashtrays in the area. He looked around with puzzlement, his gaze resting briefly on the potted plant on Alison's desk. She leaned forward.

"Here, why don't you let me take that?" She removed the cigarette from his fingers and took the burning butt directly to the open window, where she gave it a toss, peering out afterward to make sure it didn't land in someone's open convertible in the parking lot.

Mac followed me down the hall, making polite responses as I filled him in on my current circumstances. When we reached my office, he was properly complimentary. We caught up on gossip, exchanging news about mutual friends. The pleasantries gave me time to study the man at close range. The years seemed to be speeding right along for him. He'd lost color. He'd lost about ten pounds by the look of him. He seemed tired and uncertain, which was completely uncharacteristic. The Mac Voorhies of old had been brusque and impatient, fair-minded, decisive, humorless, and conservative. He was a decent man to work for, and I admired his testiness, which was born of a passion for getting the job done right. Now the spark was missing and I was alerted by the loss.

"Are you okay? You don't seem like your old self somehow."

He gestured peevishly, in an unexpected flash of energy. "They're taking all the fun out of the job, I swear to God. Damn executives with all their talk about the bottom line. I know the insurance business . . . hell, I've been at it long enough. CF used to be family. We had a company to run, but we did it with compassion and we respected each other's turf. We didn't stab each other in the back and we didn't short-change any claimants. Now, I don't know, Kinsey. The turnover's ridiculous. Agents are run through so fast, they hardly have a chance to unpack their briefcases. All this talk about profit margins and cost containment. Lately I find myself not wanting to go to work." He paused, looking sheepish, color coming up in his face. "God, would you listen?

I'm beginning to sound like a garrulous old fart, which is what I am. They offered me an 'early retirement package,' whatever the hell that means. You know, they're maneuvering to get some of us old birds off the payroll as soon as possible. We earn way too much and we're too set in our ways."

"You going to do it?"

"I haven't decided yet, but I might. I just might. I'm sixty-one and I'm tired. I'd like to spend time with my grandkids before I drop in my tracks. Marie and I could sell the house and get an RV, see some of the country and visit the clan. Keep making the rounds so we don't wear out our welcome." Mac and his wife had eight grown kids, all of them married with countless children of their own. He waved the subject aside, his mind apparently focused on something else. "Enough of that stuff. I got another month to decide. Meantime, something's come up and I thought about you."

I waited, letting him get around to the subject in his own good time. Mac always did better when he set the stage for himself. He took out a pack of Marlboros and shook a cigarette into view. He dried his lips with one knuckle before he put the cigarette between his teeth. He took out a pack of matches and lit up, extinguishing the match flame with a mouthful of smoke. He crossed his legs and used his pants cuff as an ashtray, leaving me to worry he'd set his nylon socks ablaze. "Remember Wendell Jaffe's disappearance about five years back?"

"Vaguely," I said. As nearly as I remembered, Jaffe's sailboat had been found, abandoned and adrift, off the coast of Baja. "Run it by me again. He's the guy who vanished out at sea, right?"

"So it appeared." Mac seemed to wag his head, casting about for a quick narrative summary. "Wendell Jaffe and his partner, Carl Eckert, put together limited partnerships for real estate deals to develop raw land, build condominiums, office buildings, shopping centers, that kind of thing. They were promising investors a fifteen percent return, plus the return of their original investment within four years before the two partners would take a profit. Of course, they got in way over their heads, taking off big fees, paying huge 'overhead' expenses, rewarding themselves handsomely.

When profits failed to materialize, they ended up paying old investors with the new investors' money, shifting cash from one shell company to the next, constantly soliciting new business to keep the game afloat."

"In other words, a Ponzi scheme," I inserted.

"Right. I think they started with good intentions, but that's how it ended up. Anyway, Wendell began to see that it couldn't go on forever, and that's when he went off the side of that boat. His body never surfaced."

"He left a suicide note, as I recall," I said.

"That he did. From all reports, the man was exhibiting all the classic symptoms of depression: low spirits, poor appetite, anxiety, insomnia. He finally goes off on his fishing boat and jumps overboard, leaving a letter to his wife. In it, he says he's borrowed every cent he can, pouring it into what he now realizes is a hopelessly failing business. He owes everybody. He knows he's let everybody down and he just can't face the consequences. Meantime, she and his two sons were in a hell of a situation."

"What ages were his kids?"

"I believe the older boy, Michael, was seventeen and Brian was about twelve. Jesus, what a mess. The scandal left his family reeling and forced some of his investors into bankruptcy. His business partner, Carl Eckert, ended up in jail. It looked like Jaffe jumped just before his house of cards collapsed. The problem was, there really wasn't any concrete proof of death. His wife petitioned for a court-appointed administrator to manage his assets, or the few he had left. The bank accounts had been stripped and the house was mortgaged to the hilt. She ended up losing that. I felt sorry for the woman. She hadn't worked in years, since the day she married him. Suddenly she had these two kids to support, not a cent in the bank, and no marketable skills. Nice lady, too, and it was rough on her. Since then, we've had five years of dead silence. Not a whisper of the man. Not a trace."

"But he wasn't dead?" I said, anticipating the punch line.

"Well, now I'm getting to that," Mac said with a touch of irritation. I tried to silence my questions so he could tell it his way.

"The question did come up. Insurance company wasn't anxious to pay off without a death certificate. Especially after Wendell's partner was charged with fraud and grand theft. For all we knew, he was a skip, taking off with the bucks to avoid prosecution. We never said as much, but we were dragging our feet. Dana Jaffe hired a private investigator who initiated a search, but never turned up a shred of evidence pro or con," Mac went on. "Couldn't prove he was dead, but you couldn't prove he wasn't, either. A year after the incident, she petitioned the court to have the man declared dead, citing the suicide note and his depressed mental state. Presented affidavits and whatnot, testimony from his partner and various friends. At that point, she notified CF she was filing a claim as his sole beneficiary. We launched our own investigation, which was fairly intense. Bill Bargerman handled it. You remember him?"

"Name sounds familiar, but I don't think we ever met."

"He was probably working out of the Pasadena office back then. Good man. He's retired now. Anyway, he did what he could, but there was no way we could prove Wendell Jaffe was alive. We did manage to overcome the presumption of death—temporarily. In light of his financial problems, we argued successfully that it was unlikely, if Jaffe was living, that he'd voluntarily appear. Judge ruled in our favor, but we knew it was only a matter of time before he reversed himself. Mrs. Jaffe was plenty mad, but all she had to do was wait. She kept the premiums on his policy paid and went back into court when the five years were up."

"I thought it was seven."

"The statute was changed about a year ago. The Law Revision Commission modernized the procedure for probate in the estate of a missing person. Two months ago, she finally got a finding and order from the superior court and had Wendell declared dead. At that point, the company really had no choice. We paid."

"Ah, the thick plottens," I said. "How much are we talking?"

"Five hundred thousand dollars."

"Not bad," I said, "though maybe she deserved it. She sure had to wait long enough to collect."

Mac's smile was brief. "She should have waited a little longer. I had a call from Dick Mills—another retired CF employee. He claims he spotted Jaffe down in Mexico. Town called Viento Negro."

"Really. When was this?"

"Yesterday," Mac said. "Dick was the agent who sold Jaffe the original life insurance policy, and he went on to do a lot of business with him afterward. Anyway, he was down in Mexico, dinky little place, midway between Cabo and La Paz on the Gulf of California. He says he saw Wendell in the hotel bar, having drinks with some woman."

"Just like that?"

"Just like that," he echoed. "Dick was waiting for the shuttle on his way out to the airport and he stopped off in the bar to have a quick one before the driver showed. Wendell was sitting on the patio, maybe three feet away, a little trellis arrangement between the two of them. Dick said it was the voice he recognized first. Kind of gravelly and low with a south Texas accent. Guy was speaking English at first, but he switched to Spanish when the waiter came over."

"Did Wendell see Dick?"

"Apparently not. Dick said he never was so surprised in his life. Said he sat there so long he nearly missed his ride to the airport. The minute he got home, he picked up the phone and called me."

I could feel my heart begin to thump. Put me anywhere close to an interesting proposition and my pulse accelerates. "So what happens next?"

Mac tapped a length of ash into his pants cuff. "I want you to go down there as soon as possible. I'm assuming you have a valid passport in your possession."

"Well, sure, but what about Gordon Titus? Does he know about this?"

"You let me worry about Titus. This thing with Wendell has been sticking in my craw ever since it happened. I want to see it settled before I leave CF. Half a million dollars is nothing to sniff at. Seems like it'd be a nice way to close out my career."

"If it's true," I said.

"I've never known Dick Mills to make a mistake. Will you do it?"

"I'd have to make sure I can clear my schedule here. Can I call you in an hour and give you an answer then?"

"Well, sure. That's no problem." Mac checked his watch and stood up, placing a thick packet on the corner of my desk. "I wouldn't take much more time if I were you. You're on a flight leaves at one for Los Angeles. Connecting flight's at five. Tickets and itinerary are in there," he said.

I started laughing. California Fidelity and I were back in business.

2

Once my commuter flight landed at LAX, I had a three-hour delay before the Mexicana flight took off for Cabo San Lucas. Mac had given me a folder full of newspaper articles about Jaffe's disappearance and its aftermath. I settled myself in one of the airport cocktail lounges, sorting through the clippings to educate myself while I sipped a margarita. Might as well get into the spirit of the thing. At my feet I had a hastily packed duffel bag, including my 35-millimeter camera, my binoculars, and the video recorder I'd given myself as a thirty-fourth birthday present. I loved the impromptu nature of this trip, and I was already feeling that heightened sense of self-awareness that traveling engenders. My friend Vera and I were currently enrolled in a beginning Spanish class through Santa Teresa's adult education program. So far, we were confined to the present tense, short, mostly declarative statements of little known use—unless, of course, there were some black cats in the trees, in which case Vera and I were prepared to point and make remarks. *¿Muchos gatos negros están en los árboles, sí? Sí, muchos gatos.* I saw the trip as an opportunity to test my language skills, if nothing else.

Along with the clippings, Mac had included several eight-by-eleven black-and-white shots of Jaffe at various public functions: art openings, political fund-raisers, charity auctions. Judging by the events he attended, he was certainly one of the select: handsome, well dressed, a central part of any group. Often, his was the one blurred face, as if he'd pulled back or turned away just as the camera shutter clicked. I wondered if even then he was consciously avoiding being photographed. He was in his mid-fifties and big. Silver hair, high cheekbones, jutting chin, his nose prominent. He seemed calm and self-possessed, a man who didn't care much what other people thought.

In a curious way, I felt a fleeting bond with the man as I tried on the idea of changing identities. Being a liar by nature, I've always been attracted to the possibility. There's a certain romance in the notion of walking out of one life and into another, like an actor passing from one character role to the next. Not that long ago I'd handled a case in which a fellow, convicted of murder, had walked away from a prison work crew and had managed to create a whole new persona for himself. In the process, he'd shed not only his past, but the taint of the homicide conviction. He'd acquired a new family and a good job. He was respected in his new community. He might have continued pulling off the deception except for an error in a bench warrant that resulted in a fluke arrest some seventeen years later. The past has a way of catching up with all of us.

I checked my watch and saw that it was time to go. I packed away the clippings and grabbed my duffel bag. I moved through the main terminal, cleared security, and began the long trek down the concourse to my posted gate. One immutable law of travel is that one's arrival or departure gate is always at the extreme outer limit of the terminal, especially if your bag is heavy or your shoes have just begun to pinch. I sat in the boarding area and rubbed one foot while my fellow passengers assembled, waiting for the gate agent to call our flight.

Once I was seated on the plane with my duffel stowed in the bin above, I pulled out the glossy hotel brochure Mac had enclosed with the tickets. In addition to my flights, he'd booked accommodations for me at the same resort where Wendell Jaffe had been seen. I wasn't convinced the guy would still be in residence, but who was I to turn down a free vacation?

The picture of the Hacienda Grande de Viento Negro showed a three-storied structure with a stretch of dark beach faintly visible in the foreground. The blurb under the photograph boasted of a restaurant, two bars, and a heated swimming pool, with recreational activities that included tennis, snorkling, deep-sea fishing, a bus tour of the town, and complimentary margaritas.

The woman in the next seat was reading over my shoulder. I nearly shielded my paper as if she were cheating on a test. She was in her forties, very thin, very tanned, and sleek. She wore her black hair in a French braid and was dressed in a black pants suit with a tan shell underneath. There was not a hint of color on her anyplace. "Are you headed for VN?"

"Yes. Do you know the area?"

"Yes, I do, and I hope you're not planning to stay *there,*" she said. She was pointing at the brochure with a little moue of distaste.

"What's the matter with the place? It looks fine to me."

She pushed her tongue along the inside of her cheek as though she were checking her gums. Her brow lifted slightly. "It's your money, I guess."

"Actually, it's someone else's money. This is business," I said.

She nodded, clearly unconvinced. She occupied herself with her magazine, a look on her face like she was trying not to butt in. After a moment I saw her murmur a comment to the man on her right. Her traveling companion, in the window seat, had a wad of Kleenex hanging out of one nostril, stanching a nose bleed that had apparently been induced by increasing cabin pressure as the plane prepared for takeoff. The twist of tissue looked like a fat hand-rolled cigarette. He leaned forward slightly to get a better look at me.

I turned my attention to the woman again. "Really. Is there a problem?"

"I'm sure it's fine," she said faintly.

"Depending on how you feel about dust, humidity, and bugs," the man interjected.

I laughed . . . heh, heh, heh . . . on the assumption that he was kidding. Neither one of them cracked a smile.

Belatedly, I learned that *viento negro* means "black wind," a fair description of the blizzard of dark lava soot that swirled up from the beach late every afternoon. The hotel was modest, an upside down U-shape painted apricot yellow with little balconies across the front. Alternate patios had planters affixed to the railings, with bougainvillea tumbling down in a waterfall of magenta. The room was clean but faintly shabby, looking out across the Gulf of California to the east.

For two days I cruised both the Hacienda Grande and the town of Viento Negro, looking for anyone who even halfway resembled the five-year-old photographs of Wendell Jaffe. If all else failed, I could try to quiz the staff in my amateur Spanish, but I worried that one of them might tip him off to the inquiry. If he was there, that is. I hung out by the pool, loitered in the hotel lobby, took the shuttle into town. I tried all the tourist attractions: the sunset cruise, a snorkling expedition, a bumpy, ass-agonizing jaunt on a rented all-terrain vehicle, roaring up and down dusty mountain trails. I tried the two other hotels in the area, local restaurants, and bars. I sampled the nightly entertainment at the hotel where I was staying, all the discos, all the shops. There was no sign of him.

I finally managed to get a call through to Mac at home and filled him in on my efforts to date. "This is costing a lot of money if he's already blown out of here . . . assuming your friend actually saw Wendell Jaffe in the first place."

"Dick swore it was him."

"After five long years?"

"Look, just keep at it for another couple of days. If he doesn't turn up by the end of the week, you can head on home."

"Happy to oblige. I just like to warn you when I don't get results."

"I understand that. Keep trying."

"You're the boss," I said.

I learned to like the town, which was a ten-minute taxi ride from the hotel down a dusty two-lane road. Most construction I passed was in a state of incompletion, raw cinder block and rebar abandoned to the weeds. A once stunning view of the harbor was obscured now by condominiums, and the streets were filled with tots selling Chiclets for a hundred pesos apiece. Dogs napped in the sunshine, sprawling on the sidewalks wherever it suited them, apparently trusting the local citizens to leave them unmolested. The storefronts that lined the main street were painted harsh blues and yellows, bright reds and parrot greens, as gaudy as jungle flowers. Billboards proclaimed far-flung commercial influences from Fuji color film to Century 21 real estate. Most cars were parked with two wheels on the sidewalk, and the license plates suggested an influx of tourists from as far away as Oklahoma. The merchants were polite and responded with patience to my halting Spanish. There was no evidence of crime or civil rowdiness. Everyone was too dependent on the visiting Americans to risk offense. Even so, the goods in the market stalls were shoddy and overpriced, and the fare in the restaurants was strictly second-rate. Restlessly, I wandered from one location to the next, scanning the crowds for Wendell Jaffe or his look-alike.

On Wednesday afternoon—day two and a half of my stay—I finally gave up the search and retired to the pool, where I lathered myself with a glistening coat of sunscreen that made me smell like a freshly baked coconut macaroon. I had donned a faded black bikini, boldly exposing a body riddled with old bullet holes and crisscrossed with pale scars from the assorted injuries that had been inflicted on me over the years. Many people seem to worry about the state of my health. At the moment I was faintly orange, having recently applied a primer coat of Tan in a Can to disguise my winter pallor. Of course, I'd missed in places, and my ankles were oddly splotched with what looked like tawny hepatitis. I tipped my wide-brimmed straw hat down across my face, trying not to think about the sweat collecting on the underside of my burnt umber knees. Sunbathing has to be the most boring pastime on the planet. On the plus side, I was disconnected from telephones and TV. I hadn't any notion what was happening in the world.

I must have dozed because the next thing I became aware of was the rattle of newspaper and a conversation in Spanish taking place between two people on the chaises to my right. Here's how a conversation in Spanish sounds to someone with my limited vocabulary: blah, blah, blah . . . but . . . blah, blah, blah, blah, . . . because . . . blah, blah, blah . . . here. A woman, whose accent was clearly American, was saying something about Perdido, California, the small town thirty miles south of Santa Teresa. I perked right up. I was in the process of lifting the brim of my hat so I could see who she was when her male companion responded in a rift of Spanish. I adjusted my hat, turning by degrees until he came into view. Shit, it had to be Jaffe. If I made allowances for aging and cosmetic surgery, this guy was certainly a distinct possibility. I can't say he was a dead ringer for the Wendell Jaffe in the pictures, but he was close enough: the age, the build, something about the man's posture and the way he held his head, characteristics he probably wasn't aware were part of the image he projected. He was scanning the newspaper, his eye moving restlessly from one column to the next. He sensed my scrutiny and flashed a cautious look in my direction. His gaze held mine briefly while the woman rattled on. Emotions shifted in his face, and he touched her arm with a warning look at me. The flow of talk was halted temporarily. I liked the paranoia. It spoke volumes about his mental state.

Smoothly I reached down and retrieved my straw tote, fussing in its depths until his attention was focused elsewhere. And me without my camera. I was kicking myself. I pulled out my paperback, which I opened to the middle. I flicked an imaginary bug from my calf and then inspected the site, conveying (I hoped) a complete lack of interest. They took up their conversation in lowered tones. Meanwhile I was running a set of mental flashcards, comparing the guy's face to one in my folder. It was the eyes that betrayed him: dark and deep-set under platinum brows. I studied the woman with him, feeling reasonably certain I'd never seen her before. She was in her forties, very small and dark, tanned to the color of polished pecanwood. She had breasts like paper weights in a halter made of hemp, and the arc of her bikini bottom indicated she'd been waxed where it hurt.

I settled down on my chaise with my hat across my face, eavesdropping shamelessly on the escalating conflict. The two chattered on in Spanish, and the nature of the dialogue seemed to shift from simple upset to intense debate. She broke it off abruptly, withdrawing into one of those injured silences men never seem to know how to penetrate. They lay on adjacent chaises for much of the afternoon, hardly speaking, interaction at a minimum. I would have loved to snap some pictures. Twice I considered a quick run up to the room, but I thought it would look weird if I came back moments later loaded down with photographic equipment. It seemed better to wait and bide my time. The two were clearly guests of the hotel, and I couldn't imagine them checking out this late in the day. Tomorrow I could take some pictures. Today I'd let them get used to the sight of me.

At 5:00, the wind began to rattle through the palms and a haze of black dust spiraled up from the beach. I could feel the sand blow against my skin like talcum powder. I tasted grit and my eyes were soon watering in response. The few hotel guests within range of me started packing up in haste. I knew from experience that the gusts of soot would abate automatically once the sun began to set. In the meantime, even the towel boy working the concession stand closed his booth and fled for cover.

The man I'd been watching pulled himself to his feet. His companion waved a hand in front of her face, as if to fan away a cloud of gnats. She gathered up their belongings, ducking her head to avoid getting dust in her eyes. She said something to him in Spanish and then moved off toward the hotel at a rapid pace. He took his sweet time, apparently undismayed by the sudden shift in weather. He folded the towels. He screwed the lid on a tube of sunscreen, tucked odds and ends in a beach bag, and ambled toward the hotel as she had only moments before. He seemed in no hurry to catch up with her. Maybe he was a man who liked to bypass confrontation. I gave him some leeway and then stuffed my belongings in my beach tote and followed.

I entered the lower lobby, which was usually left open to the elements. Bright canvas sofas faced a television set. Chairs were arranged in small conversational groupings for the smattering of guests. The ceiling rose two floors to a railing above that marked the upper lobby with its registration desk. There was no sign of the couple. The bartender was bolting tall wooden shutters into place, barricading the room against the hot, stinging wind. The bar was immediately bathed in an artificial gloom. I went up the wide, polished stairs to the left, checking the main lobby which was located on the floor above. I headed for the hotel entrance on the off chance that the two were staying somewhere else, perhaps retrieving their vehicle from the hotel parking lot. The grounds were deserted, people driven indoors by the mounting fury of the winds. I moved back to the elevators and went up to my room.

By the time I secured the sliding doors to the balcony, the sand was being blown against the glass like a sudden summer rainstorm. Outside, the day was shrouded in a synthetic twilight. Wendell and the woman were somewhere in the hotel, probably holing up in their room just as I was in mine. I pulled out my book, tucked myself under the faded cotton coverlet, and read until my eyes closed in sleep. At 6:00, I woke with a start. The wind was down and the overworked air-conditioning had made the room too cold for comfort. The sunlight was fading to the mellow gold of late day, brushing my walls with a pale wash of maize. Outside, I could hear the maintenance crew begin its daily sweeping. All the walks and patios would be cleared and the piles of black sand would be returned to the beach.

I showered and dressed. I made a beeline for the lobby and

began my circle of the premises, hoping to catch sight of the couple again. I scanned the hotel restaurant, the two bars, the patio, the courtyard. Maybe they were napping or having dinner in their room. Maybe they'd taxied into town for a bite to eat. I snagged a taxi myself and headed into Viento Negro. The town, at that hour, was just coming to life. The sinking sun briefly gilded all the telephone wires. The air was thick with heat and laced with the dry scent of the chaparral. The only contribution from the gulf was the faint, sulfurous smell of wharf pilings and gutted marlin.

I found an empty table for two in an open-air cafe overlooking a half-completed construction site. All the weedy cinder block and rusted fencing didn't dull my appetite in the least. I sat on a rickety metal folding chair with a paper plate of boiled shrimp, which I peeled and dipped in salsa, forking the accompanying black beans and rice into a soft corn tortilla. Canned music played, jittery and tuneless, brass harmonies blasting out of the speakers overhead. The beer was ice cold and the food, while mediocre, was at least cheap and filling.

I went back to the hotel at 8:35. Again, I scanned the lobby and then toured the hotel restaurant and both bars. There was no sign of Wendell or the woman I'd seen with him. I couldn't believe he'd be traveling under the name Jaffe, so there wasn't much point in asking for him at the desk. I hoped they hadn't decamped. I roamed the place for an hour and finally settled on the sofa in the lobby near the entrance. I rummaged in my handbag for my paperback novel and read inattentively until well after midnight.

Finally I gave it up and returned to my room. Surely the two would resurface by morning. Maybe I could find out the name he was currently using. I wasn't sure what I'd do with the information, but I was certain Mac would take an interest.

3

The next morning I got up at 6:00 for a run on the beach. The morning after I arrived I'd timed out a mile and a half in each direction. Now I reduced that to quarter-mile loops so I could keep the hotel in view. I kept hoping I would spot them . . . on the terrace above the pool, taking an early morning walk on the sand. Unlikely as it seemed, I was still worried they might have checked out in the night.

After my run I went up to my room, took a quick shower, and dressed. I loaded film in my camera and hung it around my neck by its strap, returning to the sunroom off the upper lobby, where breakfast was being served. I chose a seat near the open door, placing my camera on the seat of the chair next to mine. I kept a restless eye on the elevator doors while I ordered coffee, juice, and cereal. I stretched out the meal as far as I could, but neither Wendell nor the woman made an appearance. I signed the check, grabbed my camera, and went downstairs to the pool. Other guests had appeared. A pride of prepubescent males pushed and shoved each other in the water while a pair of newlyweds played Ping-Pong in the courtyard. I circled the hotel and headed back inside, passing through the bar in the lower lobby as I went up the stairs. My anxiety was rising.

Then I spotted her.

She was standing near the elevator doors, with a couple of different editions of the newspapers in hand. Apparently no one had told her how seldom the elevators worked. She hadn't yet applied makeup, and her dark hair was still tousled and asymmetrical from sleep. She wore rubber thongs and a terry-cloth beach coat loosely belted at the waist. Through her gaping lapels, I caught sight of a dark blue bathing suit. If the two were scheduled to depart that day, I didn't think she'd be dressed for the pool. She glanced at my camera but avoided my eyes.

I took my place beside her, looking up with blank attention as the indicator light moved haltingly from the third floor to the lobby. The elevator doors opened and two people emerged. I hung back discreetly, allowing her to get on the elevator first. The woman pressed 3 and then flashed an inquiring look at me.

"That's fine," I murmured.

She smiled at me vaguely, with no real intention of being friendly. Her narrow face looked pinched, and dark shadows under her eyes suggested she hadn't slept well. The musky scent of her perfume filled the air between us. We rode up in silence, and when the doors slid open I gestured politely, allowing her to get off first.

She turned to the right and headed for a room at the far end of the corridor, her flip-flops slapping against the tiles as she walked away. I paused, pretending to search my pockets for my key. My room was one floor down, but she didn't have to know that. I needn't have bothered with my wee attempt at deception. She unlocked the door to room 312 and went in without a backward glance. It was then almost ten, and the maid's cart was parked two doors away from the room the woman had entered. The door to room 316 was standing open, the room empty, stripped of occupants.

I headed back to the elevator and went straight to the front desk, where I asked to have my room changed. The clerk was most accommodating, possibly because the hotel was nearly vacant. The room wouldn't be ready for an hour, he said, but I was gracious about the wait. I crossed the lobby to the gift shop and bought myself a copy of the San Diego paper, which I tucked under my arm.

I went up to my room and packed my clothes and my camera in the duffel bag, gathering up toilet articles, shoes, and dirty underwear. I took the duffel with me to the lobby while I waited for the room change, unwilling to give Wendell the opportunity to skip. By the time I went up to claim 316, it was almost eleven. Outside 312, someone had set a room service tray stacked with dirty breakfast dishes. I scanned the toast crusts and coffee cups. These people needed to include a fruit exchange in their overall meal plan.

I left my door ajar while I unpacked. I had now placed myself between Wendell Jaffe and the exits, as both the stairs and the elevators were several doors to my right. I didn't think he could pass without my being aware of it. Sure enough, at 12:35 I caught a glimpse of him and his lady friend as they went downstairs, both now dressed for a swim. I moved to the balcony with my camera and watched them emerge on the walkway three floors down.

I lifted my camera, following their progress in the viewfinder, hoping they'd alight within zoom range of me. They passed behind a splashy screen of yellow hibiscus. I caught a glimpse of them arranging their belongings on a nearby table, seating themselves with some attention to comfort. By the time they got settled, stretching out on their chaises in preparation for sunning, the flowering shrubs obscured all but Wendell's feet.

After a decent interval, I followed and spent the bulk of the day within a few yards of them. Various pale new arrivals were establishing their minikingdoms, staking out their turf between the bar and the pool. I've noticed that resort guests tend to be territorial, returning to the same recliners day after day, reclaiming bar stools and restaurant tables in hastily improvised routines that would rival all their old, boring habits at home. After one day's observation, I could probably predict how most of them would structure their entire vacations. My guess was they went home feeling ever so faintly puzzled that the trip hadn't generated the kind of rest they were looking forward to.

Wendell and the woman had parked themselves two loungers down from the spot they'd occupied the day before. The presence of another couple suggested they hadn't been quite quick enough for the location they really wanted. Again, Wendell occupied himself with two issues of the news: one in English from San Diego and one in Spanish. My proximity attracted little notice, and I made a point of making no eye contact with Wendell or the woman. Casually I took pictures, feigning interest in architectural details, arty angles, ocean views. If I focused on anything in range of them, they seemed to sense it, retreating like exotic forms of sea life recoiling in self-protection.

They ordered lunch by the pool. I munched on some wholesome chips and salsa at the bar, nose buried in a magazine but keeping them in view. I sunbathed and read. Occasionally I went over to the shallow end of the pool and got my feet wet. Even with the oppressive July temperatures, the water seemed nippy, and if I lowered myself into the depths by as much as six inches, I suffered shortness of breath and a nearly overwhelming desire to shriek. I didn't really relax my vigilance until I heard Wendell make arrangements to go deep-sea fishing the following afternoon. Had I been truly paranoid, I might have pictured the outing as a cover for his next big getaway, but at that point what did he have to get away *from*? He didn't know me from Adam, and I hadn't given him any reason to suspect that I knew him.

To pass the time, I wrote a postcard to Henry Pitts, my Santa Teresa landlord. Henry's eighty-four years old and adorable: tall and lean, with a great set of legs. He's smart and good-natured, sharper than a lot of guys I know who are half his age. Lately he'd been on a tear because his older brother William, who was now eighty-six, was having a geriatric fling with Rosie, the Hungarian woman who owned the tavern down the street from us. William had come out from Michigan early the previous December, fighting off a bout of depression that descended on him in the wake of a heart attack. William was a trial under the best of circumstances, but his "brush with death" (as he referred to it) had exacerbated all his worst qualities. I gathered that Henry's other siblings—Lewis, who was eighty-seven, Charlie, age ninety-one, and Nell, who turned ninety-four in December—had taken a completely democratic family vote and, in Henry's absence, had awarded him custody.

William's original two-week visit had now expanded to seven months, and the personal proximity was taking its toll. William, a self-absorbed hypochondriac, prissy, temperamental, and pious, had fallen in love with my friend Rosie, who was herself bossy, neurotic, flirtatious, opinionated, penny-pinching, and outspoken. It was a match made in heaven. Love had turned them both rather kittenish, and it was nearly more than Henry could bear. I thought it was cute, but what did I know?

I finished the card to Henry and wrote one to Vera, employing a few carefully chosen Spanish phrases. The day seemed interminable, all heat and bugs, kids shrieking in the pool with ear-splitting regularity. Wendell and the woman seemed perfectly content to lie in the sunshine and brown themselves. Hadn't anyone ever warned them about wrinkles, skin cancer, and sun poisoning? I retreated into the shade at intervals, too restless to concentrate on the book I was reading. He certainly didn't behave like a man on the run. He acted like a man with all the time in the world. Maybe after five years he no longer thought of himself as a fugitive. Little did he know that officially he was dead.

Around five, the *viento negro* began to blow. On a nearby side table, Wendell's newspapers gave a rattle, pages riffled into snapping attention like a set of canvas sails. I saw the woman snatch at them with annoyance, gathering them together with her towel and her beach hat. She slid her feet into her flip-flops and waited impatiently for Wendell to collect himself. He took a final plunge in the pool, apparently washing off the sunscreen before he joined her. I collected my belongings and left in advance, conscious that the two of them were not far behind. As anxious as I was to maintain a connection, I thought it unwise to be any more direct than I'd been. I might have introduced myself, striking up a conversation in which I might gradually bring the subject around to their current circumstances. I'd noticed, however, their scrupulous avoidance of any show of friendliness, and I had to guess they'd have shunned any overtures. Better to feign a similar disinterest than excite their suspicion.

I went up to my room and shut the door behind me, watching through the fish-eye until I saw them pass. I had to assume they'd hole up the way the rest of us did until the winds had died. I took a shower and changed into a pair of dark cotton slacks and the dark cotton blouse that I'd worn on the plane. I stretched out on the bed and pretended to read, dozing intermittently until the corridors were quiet and no noises at all filtered up from the pool. I could still hear blowing sand slant against my sliding glass door in gusts. The hotel's air-conditioning, which was fitful at best, seemed to drone off and on in a fruitless attempt to cut into the heat. Sometimes the room would be refrigerator chilly. The rest of the time the air was merely tepid and stale. This was the kind of hotel that generates worries about exotic new strains of Legionnaires' disease.

When I woke it was dark. I was disoriented at first, unsure where I was. I reached out and turned the light on, checking my watch: 7:12. Oh, yeah. I remembered Wendell and the fact that I was dogging his trail. Had the pair left the premises? I got up from the bed and padded to the door in my bare feet, peering out. The hall was brightly illuminated, empty in both directions. I slipped my key in my pocket and left the room. I moved down the hall, passing 312, hoping a crack of light beneath the door might indicate that their room was occupied. I couldn't tell one way or the other, and I didn't dare risk plastering my ear to the door.

I went back to my room and slipped my shoes on. Then I went into the bathroom, where I brushed my teeth and ran a comb through my hair. I snagged a shabby hotel towel and took it out on the balcony, placing it on the railing near the right-hand side. I left my room lights on, locked the door behind me, and went downstairs with my binoculars in hand. I checked the coffee shop, the newsstand off the lobby, and the bar downstairs. There was no sign of Wendell or the woman who accompanied him. Once outside on the walkway, I turned and lifted my binoculars, skimming my sights across the hotel's facade. On the top floor, I spotted the towel on my balcony, magnified now to the size of a blanket. I counted two balconies to the left. There was no sign of activity, but Wendell's room lights were dimly visible and the sliding glass door seemed to be halfway open. Were they gone or asleep? I found the house phone in the lobby and dialed 312. No one answered my ring. I returned to my room, tucked my room key, pen, paper, and my soft-sided flashlight in my pants pocket. I doused the lights.

I went out onto my balcony and leaned my elbows on the railing, staring out at the night. I kept my expression contemplative, as though I were communing with nature when I was really trying to figure out how to break into the room two doors over. Not that anyone was watching. Across the face of the hotel, less than half the rooms were lighted, bougainvillea trailing like dark Spanish moss. I could see an occasional guest sitting out on the balcony, sometimes a cigarette ember glowing in the shadows. By now it was fully dark and the grounds were plunged in gloom. The exterior walkways were lined with little low-voltage lamps. The swimming pool glowed like a semiprecious stone, though the filtering system was probably still laboring to remove all the soot. On the far side of the pool, some sort of social event was just getting under way—music, the buzz of conversation, the smoky scent of grilled meat. I didn't think anyone would notice if, chimplike, I swung from one balcony to the next.

I leaned forward as far as I could and peered right. The adjacent patio was dark. The sliding glass door was closed and the drapes were drawn. I had no way of knowing if the room was occupied, but it didn't seem to be. I was going to have to risk it in any event. I swung my left leg over the railing and tucked my foot between the pales, adjusting my position before I swung my right leg into place. The distance to the next balcony was a bit of a stretch. I grabbed the railing and gave it a preliminary yank, testing it against my weight. I was aware of the yawning three-story drop, and I could feel my basic dislike of heights kick in. If I slipped, the bushes wouldn't do much to cushion my fall. I pictured myself impaled on an ornamental shrub. Not a pretty sight, that one—a hard-assed private eye, punctured by a sticker bush. I wiped my palm on my pants and reached across again. I extended my left foot and inserted it between the pales on the next balcony. It's never smart to give a lot of thought to these things.

I made my mind a blank and hauled myself clumsily from my balcony to the next. In silence I crossed my neighbor's patio and went through an identical procedure on the other side, only this time I paused long enough to peer around the corner and satisfy myself that Wendell's room was empty. The drapes were pulled back, and though the room itself was dark, I could see a rectangle of light slanting out of the bathroom. I reached across to his railing, again testing my weight before I ventured the distance.

Once on Wendell's balcony, I took a little time to catch my breath. A breeze touched my face, the chill making me aware that I was sweating from tension. I stood near the sliding glass door and peered in. The bed was a king-size, the cotton spread pulled down. The sheets were atangle, showing the tousled imprint of a little predinner sex. I could smell the lingering musk of the woman's perfume, the damp smell of soap where they'd washed up afterward. I used my little pocket flash to amplify the light seeping in from outside. I crossed to the door and secured the chain, peering through the fish-eye at the empty corridor beyond. I checked the time. It was 7:45. With luck, they'd taxied into town for dinner as I had the night before. I flipped on the overhead light, trusting providence.

I did a visual survey of the bathroom first, since it was closest to the door. She had covered the counter on either side of the sink with a profusion of toiletries: shampoo, conditioner, deodorant, cologne, cold cream, moisturizer, skin toner, foundation, blusher, loose powder, eye shadow, eyeliner, mascara, hairdryer, hairspray, mouthwash, toothbrush, toothpaste, floss, hairbrush, eyelash curler. How did the woman ever manage to leave the room? After doing her "toilette" every morning, it'd be time for bed again. She had washed out two pairs of nylon underpants, which she'd hung over the shower rod. I had pictured her in black lacy bikini briefs, but these were that serviceable, high-waisted style favored by lingerie conservatives. She probably wore bras that looked like corrective appliances after back surgery.

Wendell had been accorded the lid to the toilet tank, where his Dopp kit sat, black leather with a monogram in gold that read *DDH.* That was interesting. All he carried with him was a toothbrush, toothpaste, shaving gear, and contact lens case. He probably borrowed her shampoo and deodorant. I checked my watch again. The time was 7:52. I peered through the fish-eye with caution. So far the coast was clear. My tension had passed, and I suddenly realized I was enjoying myself. I suppressed a quick laugh, doing a little dance step in my tennis shoes. I love this stuff. I was born to snoop. Nothing's as exhilarating as a night of breaking and entering. I turned back to the task, fairly humming with happiness. If I didn't work in behalf of law enforcement, I'd be in jail, I'm sure.

4

The woman turned out to be the sort who unpacked all her suitcases, probably within minutes of checking into a room. She'd taken the right side of the double dresser, and she'd filled the space neatly: jewelry and underwear in the top drawer, along with her passport. I scribbled down her name, which was Renata Huff, passport number, birth date, place of birth, the passport agency that had issued the document, and the date of expiration. Without searching further among her personal effects, I checked the top drawer on Wendell's side of the dresser, hitting pay dirt again. His passport indicated that he was using the name Dean DeWitt Huff. I made a note of the data and checked the fish-eye again. The corridor was empty. It was now 8:02, probably time to scram. With every additional minute, there was an accelerating risk, especially since I had no idea what time they'd left. Still, as long as I was there, I thought I'd see if anything else turned up.

I went back and opened the remaining drawers systematically, sliding my hand under and between the neatly stacked articles of clothing. All of Wendell's clothes and his personal effects were still in his suitcase, which was propped open on a stand. I worked in haste, with as much care as I could muster, not wanting them to discern my presence after the fact. I lifted my head. Had I heard a noise or not? I checked the fish-eye again.

Wendell and the woman had just emerged from the elevator and were heading in my direction. She was visibly upset, voice shrill, her gestures theatrical. He was looking grim, his face stony and his mouth set, slapping a newspaper against his leg as he walked.

One of the things I've learned about panic is that it inspires gross errors in judgment. Events take place in a blur in which the instinct for survival—winged flight, in this case—overrules all else. Suddenly you find yourself on the far side of a crisis in worse shape than you were to start. The instant I spotted them, I tucked all my personal items in my pants pocket and slid the security chain off the slide track. I reached for the bathroom light and flipped it out, flipped out the overhead light in the bedroom, and then moved speedily to the sliding glass door to the balcony. Once outside, I glanced back to assure myself that I'd left the room just as I'd found it. Shit! They'd left the bathroom light on. *I'd* flipped it out. As though with X-ray vision, I could picture Wendell approaching on the far side of the door, room key at the ready. In my imagination he was moving faster than I was. I calculated rapidly. It was too late to correct. Maybe they'd forget or imagine that the bulb had burned out.

I crossed to the edge of the balcony, swung my right leg over, secured my foot between the pales, swung the other leg over. I reached for the railing on the next balcony, crossing the distance just as the light in Wendell's room came on. I was acutely aware of the adrenaline that had juiced my pulse rate up into training range, but at least I was safe on the adjacent balcony.

Except for the guy standing out there smoking a cigarette.

I don't know which of us was more surprised. *He* was, no doubt, because I knew what I was doing there and he did not. I had an additional advantage in that fear had accelerated all my senses, giving me an exaggerated awareness of his persona. The truth about this man began to flash through the air at me like the subliminal messages suddenly made visible in a sports training film.

The man was white.

The man was in his sixties and balding. What hair he had was silver and combed straight back from his face.

He wore glasses with the kind of dark frames that looked like they'd house hearing aids in the stems.

The man smelled of alcohol, fumes pouring from his body in nearly radiant waves.

He had blood pressure high enough to make his flushed face glow, and his pug nose had a ruby cast that gave him the kindly look of a K mart Santa Claus.

He was shorter than I and therefore didn't seem that threatening. In fact, he had a puzzled air about him that made me want to reach out and pat him on the head.

I realized I'd seen the guy twice in my constant cruising of the hotel in search of Wendell and his lady friend. Both times I'd spotted him in the bar—once alone, his elbow propped up, his cigarette ember weaving as he orchestrated his own lengthy monologue, once in a party of bawdy guys his age, overweight, out of shape, smoking cigars, and telling the kinds of jokes that inspired sudden martini-generated guffaws.

I had a decision to make.

I slowed myself to a leisurely pace. I reached over and lifted his glasses gingerly from his face, folding the stems so I could tuck them into my shirt pocket. "Hey, stud. How are you? You're lookin' good tonight."

His hands came up in a helpless gesture of protest. I unbuttoned my right sleeve, while I gave him a look of lingering assessment.

"Who are you?" he asked.

I smiled, blinking lazily as I unbuttoned my left sleeve. "Surprise, surprise. Where you been all this time? I been lookin' for you since six o'clock tonight."

"Do I know you?"

"Well, I'm sure you will, Jack. We're going to have us a good old time tonight."

He shook his head. "I think you've made a mistake. My name's not Jack."

"I call everybody Jack," I said as I unbuttoned my blouse. I let the flaps hang open, revealing tantalizing glimpses of my maidenly flesh. Happily, I was wearing the one bra not held together with safety pins. In that light, how could he tell if it was faintly gray from the wash?

"Can I have my glasses? I don't see very well without them."

"You don't? Well, now that's too bad. What's the deal here . . . you nearsighted, farsighted, astigmatism, what?"

"'Stigmatism," he said apologetically. "I'm kind of nearsighted, too, and this one eye is lazy." As if to demonstrate, the gaze in his one eye drifted outward, following the flight path of an unseen bug.

"Well, don't you worry none. I'll stay real close so you can see me good. You ready to party?"

"Party?" The one eye drifted back.

"The boys sent me up. Those fellows you hang out with. Said today's your birthday and everybody pitched in to buy you a present. I'm it. You're a Cancer, is that right?"

His frown was slow and his smile flickered on and off. He couldn't quite comprehend what was happening, but he didn't want to be unkind. He also didn't want to make a fool of himself, just in case this was a joke. "It's not my birthday today."

Lights were being flipped on in the room next door, and I could hear the woman's voice rise in anger and distress.

"Now it is," I said. I pulled out my shirttail and peeled my blouse off like a stripper. He hadn't taken a puff of his cigarette since I arrived. I took the lighted cigarette from his hand and tossed it over the railing, and then I moved closer, squeezing his mouth into a pout like I intended to kiss him. "You got something better to do?"

He laughed uneasily. "I guess not," he said in a little puff of cigarette breath. Yum yum.

I kissed him right on the puss, using some slurpy lip-and-tongue stuff I'd seen in the movies. It didn't seem any sexier when other people did it.

I took his hand and drew him into his hotel room, trailing my blouse along the floor like a feather boa. As Wendell came out onto his balcony, I was in the process of closing the sliding glass door behind us. "Why don't you relax while I clean myself up. Then I can bring a little soap and warm water and we'll clean you up, too. Would you like that?"

"You mean just lie down like this?"

"You always make whoopee with your shoes on, honeybun? Why don't you take them old Bermuda shorts off while you're at it. I have to take care of a little something in the other room, and then I'll be right out. I want you ready now, you hear? Then I'll blow out that big old candle of yours."

The guy was unlacing one sturdy black business shoe, which he pulled off and tossed, peeling off a black nylon sock in haste. He looked like somebody's nice, short, fat granddaddy. Also like a five-year-old, prepared to cooperate if there was a cookie in the offing. I could hear Renata, in the next room, begin to shriek. Then Wendell's voice thundered, his words indistinguishable.

I gave my friend a little finger wave. "Be right back," I sang. I sashayed toward the bathroom, where I set his eyeglasses by the basin, then leaned over and turned on the faucet. Cold water gushed out with a vigorous splashing that masked all other sounds. I shrugged into my blouse, eased over to the door, and went out into the hall, closing the door behind me with care. My heart was thudding, and I felt the cold air in the corridor wash across my bare skin. I moved swiftly to my room, pulled my key out of my pants pocket and jammed it in the keyhole, turned it, opened the door, and shut it behind me. I slid the burglar chain into place and stood there for a moment, my back to the door, pulse racing while I rebuttoned my blouse as quickly as I could. I felt an involuntary shiver run down my frame from head to toe. I don't know how hookers do it. Yuck.

I crossed to the balcony and closed my sliding glass door, which

I locked with a snap. I pulled the drapes and then I moved back to the door and looked out through the spyhole. The old drunk was now standing halfway out in the hallway. Mr. Magoo–like, he peered right, squinting without his glasses. He was still in his shorts, one sock off and one sock on. He'd begun to eye my door with interest. Suddenly I wondered if the man was as drunk as he'd first appeared. He glanced around casually, making sure he couldn't be observed, and then he moved over to my fish-eye and tried to peer in. I pulled back instinctively and held my breath. I knew he couldn't see me. From his side it must have been like looking down the wrong end of a telescope.

He gave a shy little knock. "Miss? You in there?"

He placed his eye against the spyhole again, blocking the little circle of light from the hallway. I swear I could smell his breath through the wood. I saw light in the fish-eye again, and I approached with care, pressing my eye to the tiny circle so I could peer out at him. He had backed up and was looking down the hall again with uncertainty. He moved to my left, and after a moment I heard his door close with a thunk.

I tiptoed over to the sliding glass and took a position just to the left, my back against the wall as I peered out. Suddenly . . . slyly . . . the top portion of the old guy's head appeared as he craned around the wall between his balcony and mine, trying to get a glimpse into my darkened room. "Ooo-whooo," he whispered hoarsely. "It's me. Is it time to party yet?"

This guy's blood was up. It wouldn't be long before he'd paw the ground and snort.

I held myself motionless and waited him out. After a moment he withdrew. Ten seconds later my telephone rang, a room-to-room call, if you really want my guess. I let it ring endlessly while I felt my way into the bathroom and brushed my teeth in the dark. I fumbled back toward the bed, peeled my clothes off, and laid them on the chair. I didn't dare leave my room. I couldn't read because I didn't want to risk turning on the light. In the meantime, I was so wired I thought my hair might be standing straight up on end. I finally tiptoed to the minibar and extracted two small bottles of gin and some orange juice. I sat up in bed and sipped screwdrivers until I felt myself getting sleepy.

When I emerged in the morning, the drunk's door was shut with a DO NOT DISTURB tag hung over the knob. Wendell's door was standing open and the room was empty. The same cart was parked in the corridor between rooms. I peered in and caught sight of the same maid patiently damp-mopping the tile floor. She set the mop aside, leaning it against the wall near the bathroom while she picked up the wastebasket and carried it into the hall.

"¿Dónde están?" I said, hoping that I was saying "Where are they?"

She must have known better than to pepper her response with lots of past participles and pluperfects. I wasn't going to get it unless she kept the meaning down to a minimum.

What I believe she said was, "Gone . . . they leave . . . not here."

"¿Permanente? Completely *vamos?"*

"Sí, sí." She nodded vigorously and repeated her original statement.

"Mind if I take a look?" I didn't really wait for her permission. I pushed my way into room 312, where I checked the dresser drawers, the night table, the desk, the minibar. Goddamn it. They hadn't left me *anything.* Meanwhile, the maid was watching me with interest. She shrugged to herself and moved back into the bathroom, where she tucked the wastebasket under the sink again.

"Gracias," I said to her, and backed out of the room.

As I passed the cleaning cart, I caught sight of the plastic bag attached to one end, filled with newly accumulated trash. I snagged it off the hook and carried it back to my room, closing the door behind me. I moved over to the bed and dumped the contents on the spread. There was nothing of interest: yesterday's papers, Q-Tips, used tissues, an empty can of hairspray. I picked through with distaste, hoping my tetanus shots were up to date. As I gathered the detritus and stuffed it all back in the bag, I caught sight of the front page, which was splashed with news of a crime spree. I unfolded the section, flattened the newsprint, and studied the Spanish.

Living in Santa Teresa, I've learned it's almost impossible not to pick up a smattering of the language whether you take a Spanish class or not. Many words have been borrowed, and many simply mirror their counterparts in English. Sentence construction is fairly straightforward and pronunciation is consistent. The story that was spread across page one of *La Gaceta* had something to do with a homicide (*homicidio*) in the *Estados Unidos.* I read aloud to myself in the halting style of a kindergartner, which helped me decipher some of the meaning of the text. A woman had been murdered, her body found on a deserted stretch of highway just north of Los Angeles. Four male inmates had escaped from the juvenile facility in Perdido County, California, fleeing south along the coast. Apparently, they'd flagged down the victim and commandeered her car, shooting her in the process. By the time the body was discovered, the escapees had reached the Mexican border, crossing into Mexicali, where they'd killed again. The *federales* had caught up with them, and in a wild exchange of gunfire, two youths were killed and another was severely wounded. Even in black and white, the photograph of the shooting scene seemed unnecessarily lurid, with ominous dark splotches on the shrouded bodies of the deceased. The four juveniles were pictured in a row of sullen mug shots. Three were Hispanic. The fourth was identified as a kid named Brian Jaffe.

I booked the first flight back.

On the plane coming home my sinuses seized up, and during our descent into Los Angeles, I thought my eardrums would burst. I arrived in Santa Teresa at 9:00, bearing with me all the symptoms of an old-fashioned cold. My throat was scratchy, my head ached, and my nasal passages stung like I'd sucked a pint of saltwater up my nose. I couldn't help but rejoice, anticipating the use of NyQuil in fully authorized nightly doses.

Once safely home, I locked the door behind me and hauled a stack of newspapers up my spiral stairs. I emptied my duffel into the dirty clothes hamper, stripped off my travel clothes, and added them to the mix. I donned my sweat socks and flannel nightie and tucked myself into the hand-stitched quilt Henry's sister made for my birthday, settling in with the accounts of the jailbreak in the Santa Teresa paper. The story had already been moved to the second section, page three. I got to read it all again, only this time in English. Wendell Jaffe's younger son, Brian, along with three confederates had made a daring daylight escape from the medium-security juvenile commitment facility called Connaught. The dead inmates were identified as Julio Rodriguez, sixteen, and Earnesto Padilla, whose age was fifteen. I wasn't sure what extradition agreements the United States had with Mexico, but it looked like Brian Jaffe was being sent back to the States as soon as sheriff's deputies could be dispatched. The fourth escapee, a fourteen-year-old, was still in critical condition in a hospital in Mexico. His name was being withheld from the local papers because of his age. The Spanish-language paper, as I recollected, had listed him as Ricardo Guevara. Both the murder victims had been Americans, and it was possible the *federales* were anxious to relinquish responsibility. It was also possible that a great whack of cash had been passed under the table. Whatever the circumstances, the escapees were lucky not to find themselves permanently incarcerated down *there.* According to the paper, Brian Jaffe had celebrated his eighteenth birthday shortly after his capture, which meant that once he was returned to the Perdido County Jail, he'd be kept and charged as an adult. I found a pair of scissors and clipped all the articles, setting them aside to take with me for the office files.

I glanced at the clock on my bedside table. It was only 9:45. I picked up the phone and called Mac Voorhies at home.

5

"Hi, it's Kinsey," I said when Mac picked up on his end.

"You don't sound like yourself. Where're you calling from?"

"Here in town," I said. "I just came down with a cold and I'm feeling like death."

"That's too bad. Welcome home. I wasn't sure when to expect you back."

"I walked in the door forty-five minutes ago," I said. "I've been reading the papers, and I see you had some excitement while I was gone."

"Can you believe it? I don't know what the hell is going on. I haven't heard a word about this family for the last two, three years. Now all the sudden the name's cropping up everywhere."

"Yeah, well, here it comes again. We hit pay dirt on Wendell. I spotted him right where Dick Mills said he'd be."

"Are you sure it's him?"

"Of course I'm not *sure*, Mac. I never laid eyes on the man before, but judging from the photographs, this fellow comes damn close. For one thing, he's American and he's in the right age group. He's not using the name Jaffe. It's Dean DeWitt Huff, but the height's on the money, and the weight seemed close enough. He's somewhat heavier, but he probably would be in any event. He's traveling with a woman, and the two kept themselves very isolated."

"Sounds pretty sketchy."

"Of course it's sketchy. I could hardly walk up to him and introduce myself."

"How sure are you on a scale of one to ten?"

"Let's put it this way: adjusting for age and some surgical tampering, I'd say a nine. I tried to get some pictures, but he was very paranoid about attention. I had to maintain a very low profile," I said. "By the way, what was Brian Jaffe in jail for, has anybody said?"

"As I understand it, some kind of burglary. Probably nothing sophisticated or he wouldn't have been caught," Mac said. "What about Wendell. Where is he at this point?"

"That's a very good question."

"He got away," Mac said flatly.

"More or less. He and the woman took off in the dead of night, but don't start screaming yet. You want to know what I found? This was in their room after they checked out. A Mexican newspaper featuring Brian Jaffe's capture. Wendell must have spotted it in the late edition because the two of them went off to dinner at the regular time. Next thing I know, they're hightailing it back, and they're both upset. By this morning, they were gone. I found the newspaper in the trash." Even as I played out my recital of the facts, I realized something about the situation was bothering me. It was too coincidental—Wendell Jaffe ensconced in that obscure Mexican resort . . . Brian breaking out of jail and heading straight for the border. I could feel a spark of insight connect the two events. "Oh, wait a minute, Mac. I got a little flash here, catch this. You know what just occurred to me? From the moment I spotted Wendell, he was skimming through the papers, five or six altogether, and he was checking every page. What if he *knew* Brian would be making that escape? He could have been waiting for him. It's possible Wendell even helped set it up."

Mac cleared his throat with a skeptical hum. "That's pretty far-fetched. Let's don't jump to conclusions until we know what's what."

"Yeah, I know. You're right, but it adds up in a way. I'll table it for now, but I may check it out later."

"Any idea where Jaffe went?"

"I talked to the desk clerk in my rudimentary Spanish, but it didn't produce much except a half-concealed smirk. If you want my opinion, I think there's a good chance he's heading back in this direction."

I could practically hear Mac squinting through the telephone lines. "I don't believe it. You really think he'd step a foot in this state? He wouldn't have the *nerve.* The man would have to be nuts."

"I know it sounds risky, but his kid's in trouble. Put yourself in his place. Wouldn't you do the same?"

There was silence. Mac's kids were grown, but I knew he was still protective. "How could he have known what was going on?"

"I don't know, Mac. It's always possible he kept in touch. We don't have a clue where he's been all these years. Maybe he still has contacts in the area. It's probably worth pursuing if we're trying to get a line on his current whereabouts."

Mac cut in. "What's the game plan here? You have a scheme in the works?"

"Well, I think we should find out how soon the kid's being brought back from Mexicali. I can't believe much will happen over the weekend. Monday, I can talk with one of the deputies at the county jail. Maybe we can pick up Wendell's trail from there."

"Sounds like a long shot."

"The long shot was Dick Mills's spotting him in the first place."

"True enough," he conceded, though he wasn't happy about it.

"I've also been thinking we should talk to the local cops. They have the kind of resources I can't touch."

I could hear him hesitate. "Seems early to bring the police into it, but I'll let you use your own judgment. I wouldn't mind the help, but I'd hate to scare him off. *If* he shows, that is."

"I'm going to have to get in touch with old friends of his. We'll just have to run the risk of somebody warning him off."

"You think his pals will cooperate?"

"I have no idea. I gather he ripped off a lot of folks back then. Surely there are some who'd like to see him land in jail."

"You'd think so," he said.

"Anyway, we'll talk Monday morning, and in the meantime, don't fret."

Mac's laugh was bleak. "Let's hope Gordon Titus doesn't get wind of this."

"I thought you said you'd take care of him."

"I was picturing an arrest. Lots of public glory for you."

"Hold on to the thought. We may get there yet."

I spent the next two days in bed, my vacation extending into a lazy, unproductive weekend by virtue of my affliction. I love the solitude of illness, the luxury of hot tea with honey, the canned tomato soup with gooey grilled-cheese sandwiches. I kept a box of Kleenex on my nightstand, and the wastebasket by the bed was soon filled to the rim with a puffy soufflé of used tissues. One of the few concrete memories I have of my mother was her salving my chest with Vicks VapoRub, then covering it with a square of pink rose-sprigged flannel, secured to my pajama top with safety pins. The heat of my body would envelop my nasal passages in a cloud of heady fumes while the ointment on my skin conveyed a mentholated contradiction of searing heat and biting cold.

I dozed fitfully during the day, my body aching with inactivity. For two hours each afternoon, I staggered down my spiral stairs, dragging my quilt behind me like a wedding train. I curled up on my sofa bed and flipped on the television set, watching mindless reruns of "Dobie Gillis" and "I Love Lucy." At bedtime I stood in my bathroom at the sink and filled my little plastic cup with the vile, dark green syrup that would ensure a good night's sleep. I've never once downed a hit of NyQuil without shuddering violently afterward. Nonetheless, I'm aware that I harbor all the incipient characteristics of an over-the-counter cold medication addict.

Monday morning I woke at 6:00 A.M. only moments before the alarm was set to go off. Once I opened my eyes, I lay in my rumpled nest and stared up at the domed Plexiglas skylight above my bed, trying to gauge the day ahead. The morning sky was thickly overcast, bright, white clouds forming a dense ceiling probably half a mile thick. At the airport, the commuter flights to San Francisco, San Jose, and Los Angeles would be stalled out on the runways, waiting for the fog to lift.

July in Santa Teresa is an unsettling affair. Morning dawns behind a cloud bank that lingers just off the coast. Sometimes the marine layer clears by afternoon. Other times the sky remains overcast and the day stretches on in a nebulous gloom, creating the illusion of storm clouds hovering. The local citizens complain and the *Santa Teresa Dispatch* reports the temperatures in a chiding tone as if the summer season weren't always this way. Tourists, who arrive in search of rumored California sunshine, spread their paraphernalia on the beach—umbrellas and sunscreen, portable radios and swim fins—waiting patiently for a break in the monotonous gray skies. I see their little children hunkered in the surf with toy buckets and shovels. Even from a distance I can sense their goose bumps and pale blue lips, teeth beginning to chatter as the icy water surges around their bare feet. This year the weather had been very strange, varying wildly from one day to the next.

I rolled out of bed, pulled on my sweats, brushed my teeth, and combed my hair, avoiding the sight of my sleep-smudged face. I was determined to run, but my body thought otherwise, and after half a mile I was beset by a coughing fit that sounded like the mating call of some wild beast. I abandoned the notion of a three-mile jog and contented myself with a brisk walk instead. My cold, by then, had settled in my chest, and my voice had dropped into that wonderful, husky FM disc jockey range. By the time I reached home, I was chilled but invigorated.

I took a steaming hot shower to loosen my bronchial passages and emerged from the bathroom feeling somewhat restored. I changed my sheets, emptied trash, ate a breakfast of fruit and yogurt, and went into the office with a file folder full of clippings. I found a parking space down the street, hoofed the block and a half, then hit the stairs. My usual pace is two stairs at a time, but today I had to pause at every landing on the way up. The downside of fitness, which takes years to achieve, is how quickly it vanishes—almost instantly. After three days of inactivity I was back to square one, huffing and puffing like a rank amateur. The shortness of breath inspired a renewed round of coughs. I entered through the side door and paused to blow my nose.

As I passed Ida Ruth's desk, I stopped for a chat. When I first met Lonnie's secretary, I found the double name unwieldy. I tried shortening it to Ida, but I found it didn't suit. The woman is in her mid-thirties, a robust outdoor type who looks as if a day of typing would drive her round the bend. Her hair is white blond, combed away from her face as if blown by a strong wind. Her complexion is sun-scrubbed, her lashes white, her eyes an ocean blue. Her clothing is conservative: straight medium-length skirts, boxy jackets in muted tones, her blouses a boring succession of the long-sleeved, button-down sort. She looks like she'd prefer to be paddling a kayak or climbing the face of a rock in some national park. I've heard that in her spare time she does precisely that—backpacking trips to the High Sierras, fifteen-mile day hikes in the local mountain range. She's undeterred by ticks, steep inclines, venomous snakes, poison oak, sticks, sharp rocks, mosquitoes, or any of the other joyous aspects of nature I avoid at all costs.

She flashed a smile when she saw me. "You're back. How was Mexico? You turned orange, I see."

I was in the process of blowing my nose, my cheeks suffused with pink from the climb to the third floor. "Great. I had a ball, picked up a cold on the plane coming back. I've been in bed for two days. That's my faux tan," I said.

She opened her pencil drawer and took out a mint dish filled with big white pills. "Vitamin C. Take a handful. It'll help."

Dutifully I plucked up a pill, which I held to the light. It was easily an inch long and looked like it would require surgical removal if it got lodged going down.

"Go on. Help yourself. And try zinc if your throat hurts. How was Viento Negro? Did you get up to see the ruins?"

I picked up another couple of vitamin C's. "Pretty good. A little windy. What ruins?"

"You're kidding. The ruins are famous. There was a huge volcano that blew . . . oh, I don't know . . . in 1902? It was something like that. In a matter of hours, the entire town was buried in a blanket of ash."

"I saw the ash," I said helpfully.

Her telephone rang and she took the call while I continued across the hall, pausing at the water cooler to fill a paper cup. I tossed down the vitamin C, adding an antihistamine for good measure. Better living through chemistry. I moved on to my office, unlocked the door, and opened one of the windows, letting in some fresh air after the week away. There was a pile of mail on my desk: a few checks for accounts receivable and the rest of it junk. I checked my answering machine for messages—there were six—and I spent the next thirty minutes getting life in order. I made up a file for Wendell Jaffe and tucked in the newspaper articles about his son's escape and recapture.

At 9:00 I put a call through to the Santa Teresa Police Department. I asked for Sergeant Robb, belatedly aware that my heart had begun to thump. I hadn't seen Jonah for a year by my calculations. I'm not sure our relationship could ever have been classified as an "affair." At the time I first met him, he was separated from his wife, Camilla. She'd walked out on the marriage, taking both their daughters, leaving Jonah with a freezer full of home-cooked meals that she'd placed in recycled TV dinner trays. In roughly three hundred foil-wrapped tins, she'd assembled an entrée and two vegetables. The directions, taped to the top, always said the same thing: "Bake in 350 oven for 30 minutes. Remove foil and eat." Like he was really going to try to eat with the foil in place. Jonah didn't seem to think that was weird, which should have been a clue. In theory, he was a free man. In truth, she kept him on a tight rein. She'd come back at intervals, insisting that the two of them see a therapist. She'd find a new marriage counselor for each reconciliation, thus assuring that no real progress was ever made. If they came anywhere close to working out a relationship, she would split again. I finally decided that I had troubles enough, so I removed myself from the situation. Not that either of them seemed to notice. They'd been together since the seventh grade, when both were thirteen years old. One day I would read about them in the local paper, celebrating the wedding anniversary where etiquette suggests gifts made of recycled aluminum.

In the meantime, Jonah was still working the missing persons detail. He came on the line abruptly, using his businesslike policeman's manner. "Lieutenant Robb," he said.

"Oh, wow, it's 'Lieutenant' Robb. You've been promoted. Congratulations. This is a voice from your past. It's Kinsey Millhone," I said.

I enjoyed the moment of startled silence while he computed my identity. I pictured him suddenly sitting back in his chair. "Well, hey there. How are you?"

"I'm fine. How are you?"

"Not bad. You have a cold? I didn't recognize your voice. You sound all stuffed up."

We went through the formalities, exchanging basic information, which didn't take that long. I told him I'd left California Fidelity. He told me Camilla had come back to him. I could see it wasn't any different from missing fifteen episodes of your favorite soap opera. Tuning in again, weeks later, you realize you really haven't lost a beat.

Like a plot synopsis, Jonah began to fill me in. "Yeah, she got a job last month. Working as a court clerk. I think she's happier. She has a little money of her own, and everybody seems to like her. She thinks it's interesting, you know what I mean? Helps her understand my job, which is good for both of us."

"Well, that's great. It sounds good," I said. He must have noticed I didn't press for additional details. I could feel the conversation stalling like a biplane about to crash. It's disconcerting to realize how little you have to say to someone who once occupied such a prominent place in your bed. "You're probably wondering why I got in touch," I said.

Jonah laughed. "Yeah, I was. I mean, I'm glad to hear from you, but I figured there was something up."

"Remember Wendell Jaffe? The guy who disappeared off his sailboat. . . ."

"Oh! Yeah, yeah, yeah. Of course."

"He's been spotted in Mexico. It's possible he's on his way back to California."

"You're kidding."

"No, I'm not." I told him an abbreviated version of my encounter with Wendell, omitting the fact that I'd broken into his room. In talking to cops, I don't always volunteer information. I can be a dutiful citizen when it suits my purposes, but this wasn't one of those occasions. For starters, I was secretly embarrassed that I'd blown the contact. If I'd done the job right, Wendell never would have known anyone was on his tail. I said, "Who should I be talking to? I thought I ought to notify someone, preferably the detective in charge of the case back then."

"That'd be Lieutenant Brown, but he's gone now. He retired last year. You'll probably want to talk to Lieutenant Whiteside in Major Frauds. I can have you transferred if you like. That Jaffe was a bad-ass. Neighbor of mine lost ten grand because of him, and that was *peanuts* compared to most."

"I gathered as much. Did they have any recourse?"

"They put his partner in jail. Once the scam came to light, all the investors brought suit. Since there wasn't any way to get Jaffe served, they ended up publishing the summons and complaint, and finally took his default. Of course, they got the judgment, but there wasn't any way to collect from him. He stripped all his bank accounts before he disappeared."

"So I heard. What a bummer."

"You got *that* right. Plus, he was mortgaged to the eyeballs, so his house wasn't worth a cent. I know people who'd love to think he's still around someplace. He ever showed up, they'd enforce the judgment in ten seconds flat, whip his ass into court, and take everything he had. *Then* he'd be arrested. What makes you think he'd be dumb enough to come back?"

"He's got a kid in big trouble, according to the papers. You know those four inmates who escaped from Connaught? One of them was Brian Jaffe."

"Shit, that's right. I didn't make the connection. I knew Dana in high school."

"That's his wife?" I asked.

"That's right. Her maiden name was Annenberg. She got married right after graduation."

"Can you get me an address?"

"Shouldn't be too hard. She's probably in the book. Last I heard she was down around P/O some place."

P/O was the ready reference locally to the two adjoining towns—Perdido and Olvidado—on Highway 101 thirty miles to the south. The towns looked just the same, except that one favored shrubs along the highway and the other did not. Usually the two were referred to in the same breath—P/O with a hash mark mentally inserted between the initials. I was making notes like crazy on a legal pad.

Jonah's tone underwent a shift. "I've missed you."

I ignored that, conjuring up a piece of fiction to extricate myself before the conversation turned personal. "Oops. I better go. I have a client due in ten minutes, and I want to talk to Lieutenant Whiteside first. Can you have me switched over to his extension?"

"Sure thing," he said. I heard him depress the plunger rapidly several times in succession.

When the operator picked up, he had the call transferred to the detective bureau. Lieutenant Whiteside was away from his desk but was expected back shortly. I left my name and number with a request to have him get back to me.

6

At noon, feeling punk, I walked up to the corner minimarket, where I bought a tuna salad sandwich, a bag of potato chips, and a diet Pepsi. I figured this was no time to obsess about being nutritionally correct. I went back to my office and ate sitting at my desk. For dessert I sucked on some cherry cough drops.

Lieutenant Whiteside finally called me at 2:35 with apologies for the delay. "Lieutenant Robb tells me you may have a line on our old friend Wendell Jaffe. What's the story?"

For the second time that day, I went through an abbreviated version of my encounter. From the nature of the silence on his end, I had to guess Lieutenant Whiteside was taking notes.

He said, "You have any idea if he's using an alias?"

"If you don't press for details, I'll confess I did get a wee tiny glimpse at his passport, which was issued in the name Dean De-Witt Huff. He's traveling in the company of a woman named Renata Huff, who must be his common-law wife."

"Why common-law?"

"He's not divorced, as far as I've heard. His first wife had him declared dead a couple of months ago. Oh, wait a minute now, can dead men remarry? I hadn't thought about that. It's possible he isn't really a bigamist. Anyway, according to the data I saw, the passports came out of Los Angeles. He may well be in the country by now. Is there any way to track the names through the passport office down there?"

Lieutenant Whiteside eased in. "Not a bad idea. Spell the last name for me, if you would. Is it H-o-u-g-h?"

"H-u-f-f."

"I'm making myself a memo," he said. "What I'll do is check with Los Angeles and see what passport records show. We can also notify customs officials at LAX and San Diego so they can keep an eye out in case he comes through either port of entry. I can also notify San Francisco just to cover that base."

"You want the passport numbers?"

"Might as well, though my guess is the passports are forged or counterfeit. If he skipped—which is what it looks like—Jaffe may have ID in half a dozen names. He's been gone a long time, and he may have set up more than one set of documents in the event things get tight. That's what I'd do if I was him."

"Makes sense," I said. "I keep thinking if Wendell contacted anyone, it'd be his old partner, Carl Eckert."

"Well, it's possible, I guess, but I'm not really sure what kind of reception he'd get. They used to be close, but when Wendell pulled his little vanishing act, Eckert was the one left holding the bag."

"I heard he went to jail."

"Yes, ma'am, he did. Convicted on half a dozen counts of fraud and grand theft. Then the investors went after him in a class action suit, claiming fraud, breach of contract, and who knows what else. Not that it did any good. By then he'd filed for bankruptcy, so there wasn't much to collect."

"How much time did he serve?"

"Eighteen months, but that's not gonna stop a sleazy operator like him. Somebody was telling me they ran into him not too long ago. I forget now where it was, but he's still in town."

"I'll have to see if I can scare him up."

"Shouldn't be that hard," he said. "Meanwhile, what are the chances of you coming by and working with our police artist on a composite? We just hired a kid named Rupert Valbusa. He's a whiz at this stuff."

"Sure. I could do that," I said. Mentally I was calculating the worrisome issue of Wendell's likeness suddenly being plastered everywhere. "California Fidelity doesn't want him scared off."

"I understand, and believe me, we don't either. I know a lot of people with a vested interest in seeing this guy picked up," Whiteside said. "You have any recent pictures of him?"

"Just some black-and-white photographs Mac Voorhies provided, but those are six and seven years old. What about you? There's not a mug shot, is there?"

"No, but we had a photograph that went out when Jaffe first disappeared. We can probably adjust that one upward for age. What kind of cosmetic work has he had done, could you say?"

"I'd guess chin implant and cheeks, and he's maybe had his nose refined. From the pictures I was given, it looks like his nose used to be broader across the bridge. Also, his hair is snowy white now, and he's bulked up to some extent. Aside from that, he looks pretty fit. Nobody I'd want to tangle with."

"Tell you what. I'll give you Rupert's number and you two can work out your own arrangements. He doesn't come in on a regular basis, just when we need him to work something up. Soon as he's done, we can issue a 'be on the lookout.' I can contact Perdido County Sheriff's Department, and in the meantime I'll call the local FBI offices. They may want to distribute a bulletin of their own."

"I'm assuming there's still an arrest warrant outstanding."

"Yes, ma'am. I ran a check before I picked up the telephone.

The feds may want him, too. We'll just have to see what kind of luck we have." He gave me Rupert Valbusa's telephone number, then added, "The sooner we can get this in circulation, the better."

"Got it. Thanks."

I tried Rupert's number and got his machine. I left him my name, my home telephone number, and a message, encompassing the bare bones of the case. I suggested an early morning meeting if his schedule permitted and asked him to get back to me to confirm. I hauled out the telephone book and checked the white pages under Eckert. There were eleven of them listed, along with two variations: one Eckhardt and one Eckhart, which I didn't think were correct. I tried all thirteen numbers but couldn't stir up a "Carl" among them.

I dialed Information in Perdido/Olvidado. There was only one Eckert listed and that was under the name Frances, whose tone was one of polite caution when I told her I was looking for Carl.

"There's no one here by that name," she said.

I could feel myself cock an ear, like a dog picking up a signal pitched beyond human hearing. She hadn't said she didn't *know* him. "Are you related to Carl Eckert, by any chance?"

There was a moment of silence. "He's my ex-husband. May I ask what this is about?"

"Sure. My name is Kinsey Millhone. I'm a private investigator up here in Santa Teresa, and I'm trying to track down some of Wendell Jaffe's old friends."

"Wendell?" she said. "I thought he was dead."

"Looks like he's not. In fact, I've been trying to contact old friends and acquaintances on the off chance he might be getting in touch. Is Carl still in the area?"

"Actually, he's up in Santa Teresa, living on a boat."

"Really," I said. "And you're divorced?"

"You bet. I divorced Carl four years ago when he started doing time. I had absolutely no intention of being married to a jailbird."

"I can't say I blame you."

"I'd have done it if anybody blamed me or not. What a smooth-talking skunk he turned out to be. You find him, you can tell him I said so. There's no love lost between us."

"Do you happen to have a work number for him?"

"Of course. I give his number to everyone, especially his creditors. It gives me great pleasure. Now, you'll have to catch him during the day," she went on to caution me. "There's no telephone on the boat, but he's usually there by six every evening. Most nights he has supper at the yacht club and then hangs around until midnight."

"What's he look like?"

"Oh, he's very well known. Anyone could point him out. You just go on over there and ask for him by name. You can't miss him."

"What about the name of the boat and the slip number in case he's not at the club?"

She gave me both the marina and the slip numbers. "The boat's called the *Captain Stanley Lord.* It was Wendell's," she said.

"Really. How did Carl end up with it?"

"I'll let him tell you that," she said, and hung up.

I did a few odds and ends and then decided to pack it in for the day. I'd felt crummy to begin with, and the antihistamine I'd taken earlier was knocking me for a loop. Since there wasn't much else going on, I thought I might as well go home. I hiked the two blocks to my car and headed over to State Street, where I hung a left. My apartment is tucked away on a shady side street just a block off the beach. I found a parking place close by, locked the VW, and let myself in the front gate.

The space I now occupy was formerly a single-car garage, converted into a studio, complete with a sleeping loft and spiral staircase. I have a galley-style kitchen, a living room that serves as guest quarters on occasion, one bathroom down and another one up, all of this fitting together with amazing efficiency. My landlord redesigned the floor plan after an unfortunate explosion two Christmases before, and he'd infused the "day-core" with a nautical motif. There was a lot of brass and teak, windows shaped like portholes, built-ins everywhere. The apartment has the feel of an adult-size playhouse, which is fine with me, as I'm a kid at heart.

When I rounded the corner, moving toward the backyard, I saw that Henry's back door was open. I crossed the flagstone patio linking my studio apartment to the main house on the property. I tapped on the screen, peering into his kitchen, which looked empty.

"Henry? Are you there?"

He must have been in cooking mode. I could smell the sautéed onions and garlic that Henry seems to use as the basis for anything he makes. It was a good indication that his mood had improved. In the months since his brother William moved in, Henry had ceased cooking altogether, in part because William was so finicky about what he ate. In the most self-deprecating manner imaginable, William would declare that a dish had a little bit too much salt for his hypertension or just that wee touch of fat he wasn't permitted after his gallbladder removal. Between his fussy bowels and his temperamental stomach, he couldn't handle anything with too much acid or spice. Then there were his allergies, his lactose intolerance, and his heart, his hiatal hernia, his occasional incontinence, and his tendency to pass kidney stones. Henry had taken to making sandwiches for himself, leaving William on his own.

William began to take his meals at the neighborhood tavern his beloved Rosie had owned and operated for years. Rosie, while paying lip service to William's maladies, insisted he eat according to her personal gastromedical dictates. She feels a glass of sherry will remedy any known debilitation. God only knew what her spicy Hungarian cooking had done to his digestive system.

"Henry?"

Henry said, "Yo," his voice emanating from the bedroom. I heard footsteps and he came around the corner, his face wreathed in smiles when he caught sight of me. "Well, Kinsey. You're home again. Come on in. I'll be right there."

He disappeared. I let myself into the kitchen. He'd pulled his big soup kettle from the cupboard. There was a bunch of celery in the dish rack, two large cans of crushed tomatoes on the counter, a package of frozen corn and one of black-eyed peas. "I'm making vegetable soup," he called out. "You can join me for supper."

I raised my voice so he could hear me room to room. "I'll say 'yes,' but I gotta warn you you're risking a cold. I came back with a real doozie. What are you doing back there?"

Henry reappeared, bringing a stack of fresh hand towels into the kitchen with him. "Folding laundry," he said. He tucked the towels in a drawer, keeping one out for current use. He stopped and squinted at me. "What's that on your elbow?"

I checked the skin on my forearm. The self-tanning lotion had darkened decidedly. My elbow now looked as if it had been swabbed with Betadine in preparation for surgery. "That's my Tan in a Can. You know I hate to sunbathe. It'll wash off in another week. At least, I'm *assuming* it will. What's been happening around here? You seem cheerier than I've seen you in months."

"Sit down, sit down. You want a cup of tea?"

I took a seat on his rocker. "This is fine," I said. "I'll only stay a minute. I took some medication for my nose and I can barely stand up. I'm thinking to crawl back in bed for the day."

Henry took out a can opener and began to crank open the two tins of crushed tomatoes, which he dumped into the kettle. "You'll never guess what happened. William's moved in with Rosie."

"You mean for good?"

"I hope. I finally understood that what he did with his life was simply none of my business. I kept thinking I had to save him. It was all so inappropriate. It's a bad match, but so what? Let him discover that for himself. In the meantime, it was making me crazy to have him underfoot. All that talk about sickness and death, depression and palpitations and his diet. My God. Let him 'share' that with her. Let them bore each other senseless."

"Sounds like the perfect attitude. When did he move out?"

"Over the weekend. I helped him pack. I even pitched in and moved some of his boxes. It's been heaven ever since." He flashed me a smile as he picked up the celery and pulled the stalks apart. He rinsed three ribs, then took a knife from the rack and began to dice them. "Go on and hit the sack. You look exhausted. Pop back over here at six and I'll feed you some soup."

"I may take a rain check," I said. "With luck, I'll sleep straight through."

I let myself into my apartment and staggered up to the loft, where I pulled my shoes off and buried myself in my quilt.

My phone rang thirty minutes later and I dragged myself up from the drug-induced depths of sleep. It was Rupert Valbusa. He'd had a brief chat with Lieutenant Whiteside, who'd impressed upon him the importance of getting the composite done. He was going out of town for the next five days, but if I was free, he'd be in his studio for another hour. Inwardly I groaned, but I really had no choice. I made a note of the address, which was not far from me in an industrial/commercial area just off the beach. A former Bekins warehouse on lower Anaconda Street had been converted to a complex of artists' studios available for lease. I put my shoes on and did what I could to make myself presentable. I grabbed my car keys, a jacket, and the photographs of Wendell.

Outside, the air was damp with the breezes coming off the ocean. As I drove along Cabana Boulevard, I could see patches of pale blue where the cloud cover was breaking up. By late afternoon we might have an hour of sunshine. I parked on a narrow tree-lined side street, locked my VW, and walked around the warehouse to the north side, entering the building through a door flanked by two impressive metal sculptures. The interior corridors had been painted stark white, hung with framed works of the artists currently in residence. The ceiling in the hallway rose three stories to the roof, where a series of slanted windows admitted broad shafts of daylight. Valbusa was on the top floor. I climbed the three flights of metal stairs at the far end of the hallway, my footsteps ringing dully against the painted cinder block walls. When I reached the landing at the top, I could hear the muffled strains of country music. I knocked on Valbusa's door and the radio was doused.

Rupert Valbusa was Hispanic, stocky, and muscular. I put him in his mid-thirties, with broad shoulders and a barrel chest. His eyes were dark under the unruly ruffle of his brows. His dark hair was thick, cut full around his face. We introduced ourselves, shaking hands at the door before I followed him in. When he turned to walk away I could see a narrow braid extending halfway down his back. He wore a white T-shirt, cutoffs, and a pair of tire-soled leather sandals. His legs were nicely shaped, the contours defined by dark, silky hairs.

His studio was vast and chilly, with a concrete floor and wide counters circling the perimeter. The air smelled of damp clay, and most surfaces seemed to be coated in the chalky residue of dried porcelain. Big blocks of malleable clay had been swaddled in plastic. He had a kick wheel and a power wheel, two kilns, and countless shelves lined with ceramic bowls that had been fired but not yet glazed. At the end of one counter he had a dry copier, an answering machine, and a light box for slides. There were also stacks of dog-eared sketchbooks, jars of drawing pens and pencils, charcoals, and watercolor brushes. Three easels had been set up, bearing abstract oil paintings in various stages of completion.

"Is there anything you don't do?"

"Not all of this is mine. I've taken on a couple of students, though I don't much like to teach. Some of this is their work. You do any art yourself?"

"I'm afraid not, but I envy those who do."

He moved to the nearest counter, where he picked up a manila envelope with a photograph inside. "Lieutenant Whiteside sent this over for you. Looks like he included an address for the guy's wife." He handed me a slip of paper, which I tucked in my pocket.

"Thanks. That's great. It'll save me some time."

"This the dude who interests you?" Rupert passed me the picture. I glanced at the grainy eight-by-eleven black-and-white head shot. "That's him. His name is Wendell Jaffe. I've got a few more here just to give you some other views."

I pulled out the collection of shots I'd been using for ID purposes and watched as Rupert sorted through them with care, arranging them according to some system of his own. "Good-looking fellow. What'd he do?"

"He and his partner were into real estate development, some of which was legitimate until the bottom dropped. In the end, they ripped off their investors in what's commonly known as a Ponzi scheme, promising big returns when they were really just paying off the old investors with the new investors' money. Jaffe must have realized the end was in sight. He disappeared off his boat in the course of a fishing trip and was never heard from again. Until now, of course. His partner served some jail time, but he's out again."

"This is ringing a bell. I think the *Dispatch* ran an article about Jaffe a couple of years ago."

"Probably. It's one of those big unsolved mysteries that capture the public imagination. An alleged suicide, but there's been a lot of speculation since."

Rupert studied the pictures. I could see his eyes trace the contours of Wendell's face, hairline, the distance between his eyes. He brought the picture up close to his face, angling it toward the window where the light was streaming in. "How tall?"

"About six four. Weight maybe two thirty. He's in his late fifties, but he's in good shape. I saw him in a bathing suit." I wiggled my eyebrows. "Not bad."

Rupert moved over to the copier and ran off two copies of the photograph on what looked like rough-textured beige watercolor paper. He dragged a stool over to the window. "Grab a seat," he said, nodding toward a cluster of unpainted wooden stools.

I hauled one over to the window and perched beside him, watching while he sorted through his drawing pens and pulled four from the jar. He leaned forward and opened a drawer, taking out a box of Prisma color pencils and a box of pastel chalks. He had an air of distraction, and the questions he began to ask me seemed almost ritualistic, his way of preparing for the task at hand. He secured a copy of the photograph to a board with a clip at the top. "Let's start at the top. How's his hair these days?"

"White. It used to be medium brown. It's thinner at the temples than in the photograph."

Rupert picked up the white pencil and masked out the dark hair. The immediate effect was to make Wendell seem twenty years older and very tanned.

I found myself smiling. "Pretty good," I said. "I think he's had his nose trimmed down. Here at the bridge and maybe some shaved along here." Where my finger touched the nubby paper, Rupert would shade and contour with fine strokes of chalk or pencil, both of which he wielded with an air of confidence. The nose on the paper became narrow and aristocratic.

Rupert began to chat idly while he worked. "It's always amazed me how many variations can be wrung from the basic components of the human face. Given that most of us come equipped with the standard-issue features . . . one nose, one mouth, two eyes, two ears. We not only look entirely different from one another, but we can usually identify each other on sight. Do portraits like I do, and you really begin to appreciate the subtleties of the process." Rupert's unhesitating pencil strokes were adding years and weight, transforming a six-year-old image to its current-day counterpart. He paused, indicating the eye socket. "What about the fold in here? Has he had his eyes done?"

"I don't think so."

"Droopiness? Bags? Five years would etch in a few lines, I should think."

"Maybe some, but not a lot. His cheeks seemed more sunken. Almost gaunt," I said.

He worked for a moment. "How about this?"

I studied the drawing. "That's pretty close."

By the time he was finished I was looking at a reasonable facsimile of the man I'd seen. "I think you got it. He looks good." I watched as he sprayed the paper with a fixative.

"I'll run off a dozen copies and get them over to Lieutenant Whiteside," he said. "You want some yourself? I can run you a dozen."

"That'd be great."

7

I had a quick bowl of soup with Henry and then downed half a pot of coffee, managing in the process to offset my lethargy and kick into high gear again. It was time to make contact with some of the principals in the cast. At 7:00 I drove south along the coastline toward Perdido/Olvidado. It wouldn't be dark for another hour yet, but the light was fading, the air saturated with an ashen wash of twilight. Billows of fog blowing in from the ocean concealed all but the most obvious aspects of the land. Steep hills, pleated with erosion, rose up on my left, while to the right, the heaving gray Pacific was pounding against the shore. The quarter moon was becoming visible in the thick haze of the sky, a pale crescent of light barely discernible in the mist. Along the horizon, the offshore oil platforms lay at anchor like a twinkling armada. The island of St. Michael, and two that are known as the Rose and the Cross, are threaded like beads along the Cross Islands Fault, the entire east-west structural zone undercut by parallel cracks. The Santa Ynez Fault, the North Channel Slope Fault, Pitas Point, Oak Ridge, the

San Cayetano, and the San Jacinto faults branch off like tributaries from the granddaddy of them all—the great San Andreas Fault, which cuts obliquely across the Transverse Range. From the air, the San Andreas Fault forms an ominous ridge, running for miles, like the track left by a giant mole tunneling underground.

There was a time, long before the earth's folding caused the mountains to buckle upward, when the Perdido basin was a hundred miles long and much of California was a lowland covered by vast Eocene seas. Back then this whole region was under water as far as the Arizona border. The petroleum deposits were actually derived from marine organisms, the sediment, in places, nearly thirteen thousand feet thick. There are times when I feel the hairs rising up along my arms at the vision of a world so wildly different from ours. I imagine the changes, millions of years speeded up like time-lapse photography, in which the land heaves and snaps, thrusting, plunging, and shifting in a thunderous convulsion.

I glanced out at the horizon. Twenty-four of the thirty-two platforms along the California coast are near Santa Teresa and Perdido counties, nine of them within three miles of shore. I'd heard the dispute about whether those old platforms could withstand a big 7.0-magnitude trembler. The experts were divided. On one side of the debate were the geologists and representatives of the state Seismic Safety Commission, who kept pointing out that the oldest offshore oil platforms were built between 1958 and 1969 before the petroleum industry adopted uniform design codes. Reassuring us of our comfort and security were spokesmen for the oil companies who owned the rigs. Gosh, it was baffling. I tried to picture the effect: all those rigs collapsing, oil spewing into the ocean in a gathering storm of black. I thought about the current contamination of beaches, raw sewage spilling into oceans and streams, the hole in the ozone, forests being stripped, the toxic-waste dumps, the merry plunder of mankind added to the drought and the famine that nature dishes up annually as a matter of course. It's hard to know what's actually going to get us first. Sometimes I think we should just blow the whole planet and get it over with. It's the suspense that's killing me.

I passed a stretch of state beach and rounded the point, sliding into the town of Perdido from its westernmost edge. I took the first Perdido off ramp, cruising through the downtown business district while I got my bearings. The wide main street was edged with diagonal head-in parking—lots of pickup trucks and recreational vehicles in evidence. A convertible proceeded slowly down the street behind me with its car radio booming. The combination of brass instruments and thunderous bass reminded me of the thumping passage of a Fourth of July parade. The windows on every other business seemed to be decked with handsome canvas awnings, and I wondered if the mayor had a brother-in-law in the business.

The housing tract where Dana Jaffe now lived was probably developed in the seventies when Perdido enjoyed a brief real estate boom. The house itself was a story and a half, charcoal-gray stucco with white wood trim. Most of the homes in the neighborhood had three and four vehicles parked in the driveways, suggesting a population more dense than the "single-family residential" zoning implied. I pulled into the drive behind a late-model Honda.

Twilight was deepening. Zinnias and marigolds had been planted in clusters along the walk. In the dim illumination from an ornamental fixture, I could see that the shrubs had been neatly trimmed, the grass mowed, and some effort made to distinguish the house from its mirror-image neighbors. Trellising had been added along the fence line. The honeysuckle vines trained up the latticework lent at least the illusion of privacy, perfuming the air with incredible sweetness. As I rang the bell, I extracted a business card from the depths of my handbag. The front porch was stacked high with moving cartons, all packed and sealed. I wondered where she was headed.

After a pause, Dana Jaffe answered the door with a telephone receiver tucked in the crook of her neck. She'd toted the instrument across the room, trailing twenty-five feet of cord. She was the kind of woman I've always found intimidating, with her honey-colored hair, her smoothly sculpted cheekbones, her gaze cool and level. She had a straight, narrow nose, a strong chin, and a slight overbite. A glint of very white teeth peeped out from full lips that, at rest, wouldn't quite close. She put the face of the receiver against her chest, muffling our conversation for the person on the other end. "Yes?"

I held out my card so she could read my name. "I'd like to talk to you."

She glanced at the card with a little frown of puzzlement before she handed it back. She held up an index finger, making an apologetic face as she gestured me in. I crossed the threshold and stepped into the living room just ahead of her, my gaze following the path of the telephone cord into a dining room that had been converted into office space. Apparently she did some kind of wedding consulting. I could see bridal magazines stacked everywhere. A bulletin board that hung above the desk was covered with photographs, sample invitations, illustrations of wedding bouquets, and articles about honeymoon cruises. A schedule with fifteen to twenty names and dates indicated upcoming nuptials that she needed to keep abreast of.

The carpeting was white shag, the couch and chairs upholstered in steel blue canvas, with throw pillows in off-white and seafoam green. Aside from a cluster of family photographs in antique silver frames, there were no knickknacks. The room was interspersed with a variety of glossy house plants, big healthy specimens that seemed to saturate the air with oxygen. This was fortunate given all the noxious cigarette smoke in the air. The furnishings were handsome, probably inexpensive knockoffs of designer brands.

Dana Jaffe was pencil thin, wearing tight, faded jeans and a plain white T-shirt, tennis shoes without socks. When I wear the same outfit, it looks like I'm all set to change the oil in my car. On her, the outfit had a careless elegance. She had her hair pulled into a knot at the nape of her neck, tied with a scarf. I could see now that the blond was laced with silver, but the effect was artless, as if she were confident the aging process would only add interest to a face already honed and chiseled. The overbite made her mouth seem pouty and probably kept her from being labeled "beautiful," whatever that consists of. She would be relegated to categories like "interesting" or "attractive," though personally I'd have killed for a face like hers, strong and arresting, with a flawless complexion.

She picked up the cigarette she'd left in the ashtray, dragging on it deeply as she went on with her conversation. "I don't think you'll be happy with that," she was saying. "Well, the style's not going to be flattering. You told me Corey's cousin was on the hefty side. . . . Okay, a blimp. That's exactly what I'm talking about. You don't want to put a peplum on a blimp. . . . A full skirt. . . . Uh-hun, right. That's going to minimize heavy legs and hips. . . . No, no, no. I'm not talking about bulky fullness. . . . I understand. Maybe something with a slightly dropped waist. I think we should find a dress with a shaped neckline, too, because that's going to pull the eye upward. Do you understand what I'm saying? . . . Uhm-hmmm. . . . Well, why don't I go through my books here and I'll come up with some suggestions. You might have Corey pick up a couple of brides magazines from the supermarket. We can talk tomorrow. . . . Okay. . . . All right, fine. I'll call you back. . . . You're entirely welcome. . . . You too."

She replaced the receiver and gave the telephone cord a little looping flap, pulling the length of it toward her. She extinguished the cigarette in an ashtray on her desk and then moved into the living room, smoke still trailing from her mouth. I took a quick moment to scan the room. In the small slice of family room that I could see, there were miscellaneous items of baby paraphernalia: a playpen, a high chair, a wind-up swing guaranteed to put an infant to sleep if it didn't generate a lot of puking first.

"You'd never guess I'm a grandma," she said with irony when she caught my eye.

I had placed my business card on the coffee table, and I saw her glance at it again with curiosity. I tucked in a hasty question before she had a chance to quiz me. "Are you moving? I saw the boxes on the porch. It looks like you're all set."

"Not me. My son and his wife. They've just bought a little house." She leaned over and picked up the card. "Excuse me. I'd like to know what this is about. If it has to do with Brian, you'll need to talk to his attorney. I'm not at liberty to discuss his situation."

"This is not about Brian. It's about Wendell."

Her gaze became fixed. "Have a seat," she said, indicating a nearby chair. She sat down on the edge of the couch, pulling an ashtray in closer to her. She lit another cigarette, her movements brisk, dragging deeply as she arranged both her lighter and the pack of Eve 100's on the table in front of her. "Were you acquainted with him?"

"Not at all," I said. I perched on a chrome-and-gray-leather director's chair that squawked beneath my weight. Sounded like I'd made a rude butt noise as a joke.

She blew two streams of smoke from her nose. "Because he's dead, you know. He's been gone for years. He got into trouble and he killed himself."

"That's why I'm here. Last week, the California Fidelity agent who sold Wendell his life insurance policy . . ."

"Dick What's-his-name . . . Mills."

"That's correct. Mr. Mills was vacationing in a little Mexican resort and spotted Wendell in a bar."

She burst out laughing. "Oh, sure, right."

I stirred uncomfortably. "It's true."

She cut the power on the smile by half. "Don't be silly. What are we talking here, a seance or something? Wendell's *dead*, my dear."

"As I understand it, Dick Mills did quite a bit of business with him. I gather he knew Wendell well enough to make the initial I.D. I'm handling the follow-up."

She continued to smile, but it was all form and no content. She blinked at me with interest. "He actually talked to him? You'll have to forgive my skepticism, but I'm having a problem with this. The two of them had a conversation?"

I shook my head. "Dick was on his way to the airport at the time, and he didn't want Wendell to catch sight of him. As soon as he got home, he called one of the CF vice-presidents, who turned around and hired me to fly down there. At this point, the identification isn't positive, but the chances are good. It looks like he's not only alive, but headed back to the area."

"I don't believe it. There's been some mistake." Her tone was emphatic, but her expression suggested she was waiting for the punch line, a half smile flickering. I wondered how many times she'd played the scene in her head. Some police detective or an FBI agent sitting in her living room, giving her the news that Wendell was alive and well . . . or that his body had finally been recovered. She'd probably lost track of what she wanted to hear. I could see her struggle with a number of conflicting attitudes, most of which were bad.

Agitated, she took a drag of her cigarette and then blew out a mouthful of smoke, her mouth curling up in a parody of mirth as she tried on a new reaction. "Let me hazard a guess here. I'll bet there's money involved. A little payoff, is that it?"

"Why would I do that?" I asked.

"What's the point, then? Why tell me about it? I couldn't care less."

"I was hoping you'd let me know if Wendell tries to get in touch."

"You think Wendell would try to get in touch with *me*? This is dumb. Don't be ridiculous."

"I don't know what to tell you, Mrs. Jaffe. I can understand how you feel. . . ."

"What are you *talking* about? The man is dead! Don't you get it? He turned out to be a con artist, a common crook. I've had trouble enough dealing with all the people he cheated. You're not going to turn around now and tell me he's still out there," she snapped.

"We think he faked his own death, probably to avoid prosecution for fraud and grand theft." I reached for my handbag. "I have a picture if you want to see him. This was done by a police artist. It's not exact, but it's close. I saw him myself." I pulled out the photocopy of the picture, unfolded the paper, and passed it over to her.

She studied it with an intensity that was almost embarrassing. "This isn't Wendell. This looks nothing like him." She tossed it back toward the table. The paper sailed off the edge like an airplane taking off. "I thought they did these with computers. What's the matter? Are the cops here too cheap?" She snatched up my business card again and read my name. I could see that her hand had begun to shake. "Look, Ms. Millhone. Maybe I should explain something. Wendell put me through hell. Whether he's dead or alive is immaterial from my perspective. You want to know why?"

I could see she was working herself into a snit. "I understand you had him declared dead," I ventured.

"That's right. You got it. Very good," she said. "I've collected his life insurance, that's how dead he is. This is over and done. Finito, you savvy? I'm getting on with my life. You understand what I'm saying? I'm not interested in Wendell one way or the other. I've got other problems I'm coping with at the moment, and as far as I'm concerned—"

The telephone began to ring and she glanced back with annoyance. "The machine will pick up."

The machine clicked in, and Dana intoned the standard advice about a name, telephone number, and a message. Without even thinking about it, we both turned to listen. "Please wait for the beep," Dana's recorded voice admonished. We paused dutifully, waiting for the beep.

I could hear a woman using the artificial message-giving voice that machines inspire. "Hello, Dana. This is Miriam Salazar. Your name was given to me by Judith Prancer as a bridal consultant. My daughter, Angela, is getting married next April, and I just thought we should have a preliminary conversation. I'd appreciate a call back. Thanks." She left her telephone number.

Dana smoothed her hair back, checking the scarf at the nape of her neck. "Jesus, this has been a crazy summer," she commented idly. "I've had two and three weddings every weekend, plus I'm getting ready for a midsummer bridal fair."

I stared at her, saying nothing. Like many people, she was capable of delivering informational asides while in the midst of a highly charged emotional conversation. I hardly knew where to take the matter next. Wait until she figured out that California Fidelity was going to reclaim the insurance money if Wendell showed up in the flesh.

I shouldn't even have allowed the thought to enter my head, because the minute it occurred to me she seemed to read my mind.

"Oh, wait. Don't tell me. I just collected half a million bucks. I hope the insurance company doesn't think I'm going to give the money *back*."

"You'd have to talk to them about that. Generally, they don't pay death benefits if a guy's not really dead. They're kind of cranky that way."

"Now just a goddamn minute. If he's alive—which I'm not buying for a minute—but if it turned out he was, it's hardly *my* responsibility."

"Well, it certainly isn't *theirs*."

"I've waited years for that money. I'd be dead broke without it. You don't understand the kind of struggle I've been through. I've had two boys to raise with no help from anyone."

"You'd probably be smart to talk to an attorney," I said.

"An attorney? What for? I didn't do anything. I've suffered enough because of Wendell goddamn Jaffe, and if you think for one minute I'm giving that money back, you're crazy. You want to collect, you'll have to get it from him."

"Mrs. Jaffe, I don't make policy decisions for California Fidelity. All I do is investigate and file reports. I have no control over what they do—"

"I didn't *cheat*," she cut in.

"No one's accusing you of cheating."

She cupped a hand around her ear. "Yet," she said. "Don't I hear a big fat 'yet' at the end of that sentence?"

"What you hear me saying is take it up with them. I'm only here because I thought you should be aware of what's going on. If Wendell tries to get in touch . . ."

"Jesus! Would you stop that? What earthly reason would he have to get in touch with me?"

"Because he probably read about Brian's escapades in all the Mexican papers."

That shut her up momentarily. She stared at me with the panicky blank look of a woman with a train bearing down the track at her and a car that won't start. Her voice dropped. "I can't deal with this. I'm sorry, but this is all nonsense as far as I'm concerned. I'll have to ask you to leave." She rose to her feet, and I rose at the same time.

"Hey, Mom?"

Dana jumped.

Her oldest son, Michael, was coming down the stairs. He caught sight of us and paused. "Oh, sorry. I didn't know you were busy down here." He was lanky and slim, with a dark mop of silky hair much in need of a cut. His face was narrow, nearly pretty, with large dark eyes and long lashes. He wore jeans, a sweatshirt emblazoned with a fake college decal, and high-top tennis shoes.

Dana flashed a bright smile at him to disguise her distress. "We're just finishing. What is it, baby? Did you guys want something to eat?"

"I thought I'd make a run. Juliet's out of cigarettes and the baby needs Pampers. I just wondered if you needed anything."

"Actually, you might pick up some milk for breakfast. We're almost out," she replied. "Get a half gallon of low-fat and a quart of orange juice, if you would. There's some money on the kitchen table."

"I got some," he said.

"You keep that, honey. I'll get it." She moved off toward the kitchen.

Michael continued to the bottom of the steps and snagged his jacket from the newel post where it was draped. He nodded at me shyly, perhaps mistaking me for one of his mother's bridal clients. Despite the fact that I'd been married twice, I've never had a formal wedding. The closest I'd ever come was a bride of Frankenstein outfit one Halloween when I was in the second grade. I had fangs and fake blood, and my aunt drew clumsy black stitches up and down my face. My bridal veil was affixed to my head with numerous bobby pins, most of which I'd lost by the time the evening came to an end. The dress itself was a cut-down version of a ballerina costume . . . some kind of *Swan Lake* number with an ankle-length skirt. My aunt had added sparkles, making squiggles with a tube of Elmer's glue that she sprinkled with dime-store glitter. I'd never felt so glamorous. I remember looking at myself solemnly in the mirror that night in a halo of netting, thinking it was probably the most beautiful dress I would ever own. Sure enough, I've never had anything quite like it since, though, in truth, it's not the dress so much as the feeling I miss.

Dana came back into the living room and pressed a twenty into Michael's hand. They had a brief chat about the errand. While I waited for them to finish their business, I picked up one of the silver-framed photos. It looked like Wendell in high school, which is to say dorky-looking with a bad haircut.

Michael left for the store, and Dana moved over to the table where I was standing. She took the picture from my hand and set it back on the tabletop. I said, "Is that Wendell in high school?"

She nodded, distracted. "Cottonwood Academy, which has gone out of business since. His was the last class to graduate. I gave his class ring to Michael. I'll give Brian his college ring when the time comes."

"When what time comes?"

"Oh, some special occasion. I tell them it's something their father and I always talked about."

"That's laying it on a bit thick, isn't it?"

Dana shrugged. "Just because I think Wendell's a schmuck doesn't mean they have to. I want them to have a man to look up to, even if he isn't real. They need a role model."

"So you give them an idealized version?"

"It might be a mistake, but what else can I do?" she said, coloring.

"Yeah, really. Especially when he pulls a deal like this."

"I know I've given him more credit than he deserves, but I don't want to bad-mouth the man to his sons."

"I understand the impulse. I'd probably do the same in your place," I said.

She reached out impulsively and touched my arm. "Please leave us alone. I don't know what's going on, but I don't want them brought into it."

"I won't bother you if I can help it, but you're still going to have to tell them."

"Why?"

"Because Wendell could beat you to it, and you might not like the effect."

8

It was nearly 10:00 P.M. by the time I hoofed it through the strip lot behind the Santa Teresa Yacht Club. After I left Dana Jaffe, I hit the 101 north, tearing back up the coast to my apartment, where I hastily tried on several hangers' worth of hand-me-downs Vera'd passed along to me. In her unbiased opinion I'm a complete fashion nerd, and she's trying to teach me the rudiments of "shiek." Vera's into these Annie Hall ensembles that look like you're preparing for a life sleeping on sewer grates. Jackets over vests over tunics over pants. The only thing I lack is a grocery cart for the rest of my possessions.

I sorted through the garments, wondering which items were supposed to go with which. I need a personal trainer when it comes to this shit, someone to explain the underlying strategy. Since Vera is twenty pounds heavier and a good five inches taller, I bypassed the slacks, imagining I'd look like Droopy of the Seven Dwarfs. She'd given me two long skirts with elasticized waists, swearing either would look great with my black leather boots.

There was also a forties-looking rayon drop-waist print dress with an ankle-length skirt. I pulled the garment over my head and regarded myself in the mirror. I'd seen Vera wear this, and she'd looked like a vamp. I looked like I was six, playing dress-up in the discards from my aunt's rag bag.

I went back to one of the long skirts, a black washable silk. I think she intended for me to hem the length, but I simply rolled it up at the waist, a little doughnut effect. She'd also given me a tunic top in a color she called taupe (a blend of gray and old cigar butts), with a long white vest that went over both. She'd told me I could dress up the outfit with accessories. Big duh. Like I really had some kind of clue how to make that work. I searched my drawers for jewelry to no avail and finally decided to wear the long crocheted runner my aunt had made for the dresser top. I gave it a little flap to get all the woofies out and then looped it around my neck with the ends hanging down the front. Looked good to me, kind of devil-may-care, like Isadora Duncan or Amelia Earhart.

The yacht club sits on stilts overlooking the beach with the harbormaster's office nearby and the long concrete arm of the breakwater curving out to the left. The sound of the surf was thunderous that night, like the rumble of cars moving over wooden trestles. The ocean was oddly agitated, the far-flung effects from some violent weather pattern that would probably never reach us. A dense haze hung in the air like a scrim through which I caught shadowy glimpses of the moon-tinted horizon. The sand glowed white, and the boulders piled up around the foundations of the building were draped with strands of kelp.

Even from the sidewalk down below, I could hear the trumpeting laughter of the heavy drinkers. I climbed the wide wooden steps to the entrance and in through the glass doors. A second set of stairs ascended to the right, and I made my way up toward the smoke and recorded music in the bar above. The room was L-shaped, diners occupying the long arm, drinkers confined to the short, which was just as well. The noise level was oppressive given the fact that most of the dinner crowd had departed and the bar was only half-filled. The floor was carpeted, the entire upper story wrapped in windows that overlooked the Pacific. By day, club members were treated to panoramic ocean views. At night, the black glass threw back smudged reflections, pointing up the need for the rigorous application of Windex. When I reached the maître d's pulpit, I paused, watching him approach me from across the room.

"Yes, ma'am," he said. I guessed he'd been recently promoted from his job as headwaiter because he held his left arm at an angle, a ready rack for some wine towel he no longer had to tote.

"I'm looking for Carl Eckert. Is he here tonight?"

I saw his gaze flick downward, taking in my scruffy boots, the long skirt, the vest, shoulder bag, and my ill-cut hair, which the sea wind had tossed into moplike perfection. "Is he expecting you?" His tone suggested he'd expect invading Martians first.

I held out a discreetly folded five-dollar bill. "Now he is," I said.

The fellow slipped the bill in his pocket without checking the denomination, which made me wish I had given him a single. He indicated a gentleman sitting at a window table by himself. I had plenty of time to study him as I crossed the room. I put him in his early fifties, still of an age where he'd be referred to as "youthful." He was silver-haired and stocky. His once handsome face had gone soft now along the jawline, though the effect was still nice. While most of the men in the bar were dressed casually, Carl Eckert wore a conservative dark gray herringbone suit, with a light gray shirt and navy wool tie with a grid of light gray. I wound my way among the tables, wondering what the hell I was going to say to him. He saw me headed in his direction and focused on me as I drew within range. "Carl?"

He smiled at me politely. "That's right."

"Kinsey Millhone. May I join you?"

I held out my hand. He half rose from his chair and leaned forward courteously, shaking hands with me. His grip was aggressive, the skin on his palm icy cold from his drink. "If you like," he said. His eyes were blue, and his gaze was unyielding. He gestured toward a chair.

I placed my handbag on the floor and eased onto the seat adjacent to his. "I hope I'm not intruding."

"That depends on what you want." His smile was pleasant but fleeting and never really reached as far as his eyes.

"It looks like Wendell Jaffe is alive."

His expression shifted into neutral and his body went still, animation suspended as if from a momentary power loss. For a split second it flashed on me that he might have been in touch with Wendell since his disappearance. He was apparently willing to take my word for it, which saved all the bullshit Dana'd put me through. He assimilated the information, sparing me additional expressions of shock or surprise. There was no hint of denial or disbelief. He seemed to shift into gear again. He reached in his jacket pocket smoothly and took out a pack of cigarettes, his way of stalling until he could figure out what I was up to. He shook several cigarettes into view and held the pack out for my selection.

I shook my head, refusing.

He put a cigarette between his lips. "Will it bother you if I smoke?"

"Not a bit. Go ahead." Actually I abhor smoking, but I wanted some information and I didn't think it was the time to voice my prejudice.

He struck a paper match and cupped his hands around the flame. He gave the match a shake and dropped it in the ashtray, easing the pack of matches back into his pocket again. I smelled sulfur and that first whiff of smoldering tobacco that to me smells like no other. Early mornings on the road, I catch the same scent drifting through the room vents in those hotels where the smokers aren't properly segregated from the rest of us.

"Would you like a drink?" he asked. "I'm about to order another round myself."

"I'd like that. Thanks."

"What'll it be?"

"Chardonnay would be fine."

He held his hand up for the waiter, who moved over to the table and took the order. Eckert was having Scotch.

Once the waiter disappeared, his attention came back to me and he focused his gaze. "Who are you? A cop? Narc? IRS, what?"

"I'm a private detective, working for California Fidelity on the life insurance claim."

"Dana just collected on it, didn't she?"

"Two months ago."

A group of guys in the bar burst into sudden harsh laughter, and it forced Eckert to lean forward to make himself heard. "How did all this business come to light?"

"A retired CF insurance agent spotted him in Mexico last week. I was hired to fly down the next day to verify the report."

"And you actually verified that it was Wendell?"

"More or less," I said. "I never met Mr. Jaffe, so it'd be hard for me to swear it was him."

"But you did see him," he said.

"Or someone damn close. He's had surgery, of course. It's probably the first thing he did."

Carl stared at me blankly and then shook his head. A brief smile appeared. "I assume you've told Dana?"

"I just talked to her. She wasn't thrilled."

"I should think not." He seemed to search my face. "What's your name again?"

I took out a business card and passed it across the table. "You knew his kid was in trouble?" I asked.

Behind us, there was another burst of laughter, this one louder than the last. The guys were apparently having another tedious bawdy joke fest.

He glanced at my name on the card and tucked it in his shirt pocket. "I read about Brian in the paper," he said. "This is curious."

"What is?"

"The notion of Wendell. I was just thinking about him. Since his body never surfaced, I guess I always had my doubts about his death. I never said much. I figured people would think I was unwilling to face the facts. 'In denial,' they call it. Where's he been all this time?"

"I didn't have a chance to ask."

"Is he still down there?"

"He checked out of the hotel in the dead of night and that's the last I've seen of him. He may be on his way back."

"Because of Brian," he said, instantly making the connection.

"That's my guess. At any rate, it's the only lead we have. Not really a lead, but at least a place to start."

"Why tell me?"

"In case he tries to make contact."

The waiter returned with our drinks and Carl looked up. "Thanks, Jimmy. Put this on my tab, if you would." He took the bill, tacked on a tip, and scrawled his name across the bottom before he handed it back.

The waiter murmured, "Thank you, Mr. Eckert. Will there be anything else?"

"We're fine."

"You have a good night."

Carl nodded absentmindedly, regarding me with speculation.

I reached in my handbag and pulled a copy from the sheaf of composites Valbusa had done. "I have a picture if you want to see it." I laid it on the table in front of him.

Carl stuck his cigarette in the corner of his mouth, squinting slightly from the smoke as he studied Wendell's face. He shook his head, his smile bitter. "What a fuck."

"I thought you might be glad to hear he was alive," I said.

"Hey, I went to jail because of him. Lot of people wanted a piece of my hide. When money goes down the toilet, someone has to take the blame. I didn't mind paying my debt, but I sure as hell hated paying his."

"Must have been hard."

"You have no idea. Once I filed bankruptcy, all the loans went into default. It was a mess. I don't want to get into that."

"If Wendell gets in touch, will you let me know?"

"Probably," he said. "I don't want to talk to him, that's for sure. He was a good friend. At least I thought he was."

There was another burst of laughter. He shifted restlessly and pushed his drink aside. "Let's go down to the boat. It's too fuckin' loud in here."

Without waiting for an answer, he got up and left the table. Startled, I grabbed my handbag and scurried after him.

The noise level dropped dramatically the minute we stepped outside. The air was cold and fresh. The wind had picked up, and the waves crashed against the seawall in a series of blasting sprays. Boom! A feathery plume, like a stalk of pampas grass, would dance along the breakwater and go down again, throwing off a splat of water that landed on the walk as if it were being thrown by the bucket.

When we reached the locked gate leading into Marina 1, he took out his card key and let us through. In a curiously gallant gesture, Carl put his hand on my elbow and guided me down the slippery wooden ramp. I could hear creaking sounds as the boats shifted in the harbor waters, bobbing and swaying with an occasional tinkling of metal on metal. Our footsteps formed an irregular rhythm as we clunked along the walkway.

The four marinas provide slips for about eleven hundred boats, protected from the open waters in an eighty-four-acre area. The wharf on one side is like the crook of a thumb with the breakwater curling toward it in a nearly completed circle in which the boats are nestled. In addition to visitors occupying temporary slips, there are usually a small number of permanent "live-aboards," using their boats as their primary residence. Key-secured restrooms provide toilets and showers, with a holding tank pump-out station located on the south side of the fuel dock. At the "J" dock we took a left, proceeding another thirty yards to the boat.

The *Captain Stanley Lord* was a thirty-five-foot Fuji ketch, derived from a John Alden–designed sailing vessel with the mainmast toward the bow. The exterior was painted an intense dark green with the trim in navy blue. Carl pulled himself up on the narrow deck and then extended a hand, pulling me up after him. In the dark I could make out the mainsheet and the mizzenmast, but not much else. He unlocked the door and slid the hatch forward. "Watch your head," he said as he moved down into the galley. "You know anything about boats?"

"Not much," I said. I eased carefully down four steep carpeted stairs into the galley behind him.

"This one has three headsails; a one fifty Genoa, a one ten working jib, and a storm jib, then the mainsail, of course, and the mizzen."

"Why is it called the *Captain Stanley Lord*? Who's he?"

"It's nautical lore. Wendell's sense of humor, such as it was. Stanley Lord was captain of the *Californian*, allegedly the only boat close enough to the *Titanic* to have helped with the rescue. Lord claimed he never picked up the distress signal, but a later investigation suggested he ignored the SOS. He was blamed for the extent of the disaster, and the scandal ruined his career. Wendell used the same name for the company: CSL Investments. I never did get it, but he thought it was amusing."

The interior had the cozy, unreal feeling of a doll's house, the kind of space I love best, compact and efficient, every square inch put to use. There was a diesel stove on my left, and on my right an assortment of seagoing equipment: radio, compass, a fire extinguisher, monitors for wind velocity and the electrical systems, the heater, main switch, and the engine start battery. I was picking up the faint smell of varnish, and I could see that one of the berth cushions still had a sales tag attached. All the upholstery was done in dark green canvas with the seams piped in white.

"Nice," I said.

He flushed with pleasure. "You like it?"

"It looks great," I said. I moved over to one of the berths and dropped my handbag, sitting down. I stretched my arm out along the cushion. "Comfortable," I remarked. "How long have you had it?"

"About a year," he said. "The IRS seized it shortly after Wendell disappeared. I was a guest of the feds for about eighteen months. After that, I was broke. Once I got a little money ahead, I had to track down the guy who'd bought it from the government. I went through an incredible rigmarole before he'd agree to sell. Not that he had much use for it. It was a mess when he finally turned it over to me. I don't know why people have to be such butts." He peeled off his suit coat and loosened his tie so he could ease the button on his shirt collar. "You want another white wine? I have some chilled."

"Half a glass," I said. He chatted about sailing for a while and then I brought the subject back to Wendell. "Where'd they find the boat?"

He opened a miniature refrigerator and took out a bottle of Chardonnay. "Off the Baja coast. There are huge shifting sand bars about six miles out. It looked like the boat had run aground and drifted loose again with the tide." He stripped the foil off the neck of the wine bottle, took an opener, and augered out the cork.

"He didn't have a crew?"

"He preferred to single-hand. I watched him sail that day. Orange sky, orange water with a slow, heaving swell. Had this weird feeling to it. Like the *Rime of the Ancient Mariner.* You study that in high school?"

I shook my head. "In high school, most of what I studied was cussin' and smokin' dope."

He smiled. "When you leave the Channel Islands, you sail out through a gap in the oil rigs. He turned and waved as he cast off. I watched until he left the harbor, and that's the last I ever saw of him." His tone was hypnotic, mild envy mixed with mild regret. He poured the wine in a stemmed glass and passed it over to me.

"Did you know what he was doing?"

"What *was* he doing? I guess I'm still not sure."

I said, "Apparently, he was skipping."

Eckert shrugged. "I knew he was feeling desperate. I didn't think he meant to pull a fast one. At the time—especially when his last note to Dana came to light—I tried to accept the idea of his suicide. It didn't seem in character, but everybody else was convinced, so who was I to argue?" He poured half a glass of wine for himself, set the bottle aside, and sat down on the banquette across from mine.

"Not everybody," I corrected. "The police didn't like it much, and neither did CF."

"Will this make you a hero?"

"Only if we get the money back."

"Doesn't seem very likely. Dana's probably got it all spent."

I didn't want to think about that. "How'd you feel about Wendell's 'death' at the time?"

"Terrible, of course. Actually, I missed him, even with the flak I took. Strange thing is, he told me some of it. I didn't believe him, but he tried to let me know."

"He told you he was leaving?"

"Well, he hinted as much. I mean, he never spelled it out. It was one of those statements you can interpret any way you want. He came to me, I think in March, maybe six or seven weeks before he sailed. Said, 'Carl, buddy, I'm bailing. This whole fuckin' gig is comin' down around our heads. I can't take it anymore. It's too much.' Or words to that effect. I thought the guy was just blowing smoke. I knew we had big problems, but we'd been up against it before and we'd always come out okay. I figured this was just one more hairy episode in the 'Carl and Wendell Show.' Next thing I know they find his boat drifting in the ocean. Looking back, you think, well . . . when he said 'bailing' did he mean he'd kill himself or cut out?"

"But you were stuck either way, yes?"

"Yes indeed. First thing they did was start checking back through the books. I guess I could have walked out the door then, with just the clothes on my back, but I couldn't see the point. I had nowhere to go. I didn't have a cent, so I was forced to ride it out. Unfortunately, I had no idea the extent of what he'd done."

"Was it actually fraud?"

"Oh, big time. It was major. The days went by and all this shit came to light. He'd been stripping the company till there was nothing left. In the letter he left, he claimed he'd been pouring every dime back in, but I didn't see any evidence to support the claim. What did I know? By the time I understood just how bad it was, there was no escape. I didn't even have a way to recoup my personal losses." He paused and shrugged. "What can I say? With Wendell gone, there was just us chickens left. I gave 'em everything. I copped a plea and took the jail time just to get it over with. Now you tell me he's alive. What a joke."

"Are you bitter?"

"Of course." He leaned his arm against the back of the banquette and rubbed his forehead idly. "I can understand his wanting out. At first I didn't realize the extent of his betrayal. I felt sorry for Dana and the kids, but I couldn't do anything about it if the guy was dead." He shrugged and sent me a rueful smile, moving with sudden energy. "What the hell. It's over with and you have to move on."

"That seems generous."

He gestured carelessly. He glanced at his watch. "I'm going to have to call this a day. I have a breakfast meeting in the morning at seven o'clock sharp. I need to get some sleep. Shall I walk you out?"

I got up and set my empty wineglass aside. "I can do it," I said. "It's just a straight shot to the gate." I reached out and shook his hand. "I appreciate your time. You'll probably hear from me again. Do you still have my card?"

He pulled a corner of it from his shirt pocket to assure me it was there.

"If Wendell gets in touch, could you let me know?"

"Absolutely," he said.

I eased my way up the galley stairs, ducking my head as I emerged on deck. Behind me, I was conscious of Eckert's continuing gaze, his smile bemused as he watched me depart. Weird, but in retrospect, Dana Jaffe's response had seemed the truer.

9

The walk back to my place took less than ten minutes. I was still wide awake, braced by the sea air. Instead of opening the gate and going into the backyard, I turned and headed down the street to Rosie's Tavern, which was located half a block away.

In the old days, Rosie's was perpetually deserted, cavernous and dimly lighted, no doubt under constant surveillance by the health police. I used to meet clients there because nobody ever bothered us. As a single woman, I could drop in anytime it suited me without attracting the unwanted attentions of bounders and cads. Rosie might harass me, but nobody else would. Recently, the place has been discovered by sports nuts, and a variety of teams seem to use it as a hangout, especially on occasions when they've just won a trophy and feel the need for a parade. Rosie, who can otherwise be unbearably disagreeable, actually seems to enjoy all the testosterone and hysteria. In an unprecedented move, she's even taken to displaying their hardware on the shelf behind the bar, which now boasts a permanent exhibit of winged silver angels holding globes above their heads. Tonight, the bowling championship. Tomorrow, the free world.

As usual, the place was jumping and my favorite table in the rear was occupied by a gang of rowdies. There was no sign of Rosie, but William was perched on a stool at the bar, surveying the premises with a look of sublime satisfaction. All the patrons seemed to know him, and there was much good-natured bantering going back and forth.

Henry was seated at a table by himself, his head bent above a pad of paper, where he was mapping out a crossword puzzle entitled "I Spy with My Little Eye." He'd been working on this one for the better part of a week, using espionage novels and old television shows as the underlying theme. He publishes regularly in the little crossword puzzle books you see in grocery store lines. Aside from the fact that he picks up some extra money, he's actually known by name among crossword puzzle buffs. He was wearing chinos and a white T-shirt, his face creased with concentration. I took the liberty of pulling out an extra chair at his table, turning it around so that the back rested against the table. I straddled the chair and rested my arms along the top rail.

Henry sent an irritated look in my direction and then relaxed when he saw it was me. "I thought you were one of 'them.' "

I looked around at the crowd. "Where'd we go wrong? A year ago there was never anybody in the place. Now it's a zoo. How's it going?"

"I need an eight-letter word that starts with 'I.' It can end in anything . . . more or less."

A word flashed through my head, and I counted on my fingers. "Impostor," I said.

He stared at me blankly, doing the mental arithmetic. "Not bad. I'll take it. How about five letters down—"

"Stop right there," I said, cutting in. "You know I'm terrible at this stuff, and it just makes me tense. I scored once by a fluke. I think I'll retire while I'm ahead."

He tossed his notepad on the table and placed his pencil behind his left ear. "You're right. It's time to pack it in for the day. What are you having? I'll buy you a drink."

"Nothing for me. I'm about partied out, but I'll keep you company if you're having one."

"I'm fine for now. How'd you do with Dana Jaffe? Did you get anyplace?"

"I didn't expect to. I was just making her acquaintance. I also had a chat with Wendell's ex-partner."

"And what did he have to say?"

As I filled him in on my conversations with Dana Jaffe and Carl Eckert, I saw Henry's gaze stray toward the kitchen and I found myself turning automatically. "Well, would you look at that," I said.

William was emerging with a tray full of food, a not inconsiderable burden for a man of eighty-six. As usual, he was decked out in a three-piece suit with a properly starched white shirt and a crisply knotted tie. He looked enough like Henry to be his twin, though in reality the two men were two years apart. At the moment, William was looking very pleased with himself, high-spirited and energetic. It was the first time I'd registered the changes in him. Seven months before, when he'd moved in with Henry, he'd been morbidly self-obsessed, continually cross-referencing his various illnesses and infirmities. He'd brought his medical records with him when he arrived from the Midwest, and he was constantly assessing the state of his health: his heart palpitations, his digestive tract, his allergies, his suspicions about diseases undiscovered yet. A favorite pastime of his was cruising local funerals, where he commiserated with the other mourners to assure himself he wasn't dead yet. After he and Rosie fell in love, he'd begun to lighten up, until now he worked a full day, side by side with her. Sensing that we were watching, he grinned happily. He set down the tray of food and began to unload plates. One of the patrons at the table made some remark to him. William crowed with delight and high-fived the guy on the spot.

"What's he so happy about?"

"He asked Rosie to marry him."

I stared at Henry, startled. "You're kidding. He did? God, that's great. What a hoot! I can't believe it!"

" 'A hoot' is not exactly how I'd refer to it. This just goes to show what happens when you 'live in sin.' "

"They've lived in sin for a *week.* Now he's making her an 'honest' woman, whatever that means. I think it's sweet." I put a hand on Henry's arm, giving it a shake. "You don't really mind, do you? I mean, way down deep."

"Let's put it this way. I'm not as appalled as I thought I'd be. I resigned myself to the possibility the day he moved in. He's too conventional a fellow to flaunt proprieties."

"So when's all this happening?"

"I have no idea. They haven't set the date. He just asked her tonight. She hasn't agreed to it yet."

"The way you were talking, I assumed she had."

"Well, no, but she's hardly going to turn down a gentleman of his caliber."

I gave his hand a smack. "Honestly, Henry. You're a bit of a snob."

He smiled at me, blue-eyed, his brows lifting quizzically. "I'm a complete snob, not a 'bit' of one. Come on. I'll walk you back."

Once home, I took a handful of medication for my assorted cold symptoms, including a hit of NyQuil that guaranteed a good night's sleep. At 6:00 I rolled out of bed groggily and pulled on my jogging clothes, filling out a mental checklist while I brushed my teeth. My chest was still congested, but my nose wasn't running and my cough no longer sounded like my lungs were on the verge of flopping out. My skin color had lightened to the mild gold of apricots and I thought, in another day or so, might revert to my natural skin tone. Never have I so yearned for my former pale complexion.

I bundled up against the early morning chill, my gray sweats nearly the same color as the ocean. The beach sand was a chalky white, speckled with foam from the outgoing tide. Seagulls, gray and white, stood and stared at the water like a flock of yard ornaments. The sky at the horizon was a perfect blend of cream and silver, the mist blocking out all but the darkened outlines of the islands in the channel. This was hurricane season in the far reaches of the Pacific, but so far we hadn't had a hint of tropical surf. The hush was profound, undercut only by the soft rustle of the waves. There was not another soul as far as I could see. The three-mile walk became a meditation, just me and my labored breathing, the feel of my leg muscles responding to the brisk pace. By the time I reached home, I was ready to face the day.

Through the front door, I caught the muffled sound of the telephone. I let myself into my apartment in haste. I caught it on the third ring, out of breath from the exertion. It was Mac. "What's up? This is awfully early for you." I buried my face in my T-shirt, suppressing a cough.

"We had a meeting last night. Gordon Titus has gotten wind of this Wendell Jaffe business and wants to meet with you."

"With me?" I squeaked.

Mac laughed. "He doesn't bite."

"He doesn't have to," I said. "Titus can't stand me, and the feeling is mutual. He treats me like a piece of—"

"Now, now," he broke in.

"I was going to say *dirt*!"

"Well, that's better."

"Human out-your-butt-type dirt," I amended.

"You better get yourself down here as soon as you can."

I sat for a moment making faces at the phone, my usual terribly mature method of dealing with the world. I did not exactly rush out the door as advised. I stripped off my sweat suit and took a hot shower, washed my hair thoroughly, and then got dressed. I had a bite to eat while I scanned the paper for news of interest. I rinsed my dish and my spoon and then took out a small load of trash, which I dumped in the bin by the street. When I ran out of ways to avoid the inevitable, I grabbed my handbag, a steno pad, and my car keys and headed out the gate. This was making my stomach hurt.

The office really hadn't changed much, though I noticed, for the first time, a certain shabbiness throughout. The wall-to-wall carpet was a quality synthetic, but the style had been chosen for its "wearability," a term synonymous with mottled, stain-mimicking patterns guaranteed not to soil. The space itself seemed crowded by the warren of "action stations," dozens of interlocking cubicles for examiners and underwriters. The perimeter was lined with glass-enclosed offices for the company executives. The walls needed fresh paint, and the trim was looking scuffed. Vera glanced up from her desk as I passed. From that angle I was the only witness to her facial antics, eyes crossed, tongue protruding slightly in comical disgust.

We met in Titus's office. I hadn't laid eyes on him since the day of our encounter. I had no idea what to expect, and I couldn't quite decide what behavior to adopt. He simplified the matter by greeting me pleasantly, as if this were our first meeting and we'd never exchanged a cross word. It was a brilliant move really because it freed me of any necessity to defend or apologize, relieving him of the burden of cross-referencing our past relationship. After the first sixty seconds, I found I had disconnected. I realized the man had no power over me at this point. Debts on both sides were paid, and both of us had ended up with exactly what we wanted. He'd removed what he'd seen as "deadwood" from the company payroll. I'd reestablished myself in a work environment I preferred.

Meanwhile, in the present, Mac Voorhies and Gordon Titus were a perfect contrast to one another. Mac's brown suit was as wrinkled as an autumn leaf, while his teeth and the flip of puffy white hair in front were discolored by the staining properties of nicotine. Gordon Titus wore an ice blue dress shirt with the sleeves rolled up. His gray pants were crisply pleated, the shade an eerie match for his prematurely gray hair. His tie formed a fierce punctuation mark emphasizing his office manner, which was terse and businesslike. Even Mac knew enough not to light a cigarette in his presence.

Titus sat down at his desk and opened the file in front of him.

Typically, he'd outlined the relevant data about Dana and Wendell Jaffe. Neatly indented paragraphs marched sideways across the page, the paper pockmarked with holes where the nib of his pen had plunged through. He spoke without looking at me, his face as empty of expression as a mannequin's. "Mac's brought me up to date, so we don't need to cover any old ground," he said. "What's the status of the case?"

I hauled out my steno pad and flipped to an empty page, reciting what I knew about Dana's current situation. I detailed as much as possible and then summarized the rest. "She's probably used part of the insurance benefits to finance Michael's house, with another hefty chunk going as a retainer for Brian's attorney."

Titus was making notes. "Have you talked to the company lawyers about our position in this?"

"What's the point?" Mac broke in. "So what if Wendell faked his own death? What crime did he commit? Is that against the law . . . what's it called, faking suicide?" He snapped his fingers, trying to jog his memory.

I said, " 'Pseudocide' is the term I've heard."

"Pseudocide, right. Is it against the law to falsify your own death?" he asked.

"It is if you do it with intent to defraud the insurance company," Titus said with acid.

Mac's expression was impatient. "Where's the fraud? What fraud? At this point, we don't know that he's collected a cent."

Titus's gaze flicked up to Mac. "You're absolutely right. To be precise about it, we're not even sure it's really Jaffe we're dealing with." And then to me, "I want concrete evidence, proof of identity, fingerprints or some damn thing."

"I'm doing what I can," I said, sounding both dubious and defensive. I made a note on a blank page, just to look industrious. The note said, "Find Wendell." Like I was unclear on the concept until Titus spelled it out. "In the meantime, what? You want to go after Mrs. Jaffe?"

Again, Mac's exasperation surfaced. I couldn't figure out what he was so upset about. "Goddamn it, what's she done? She hasn't committed a crime, as far as we know. How can she be held liable for spending money she believes she's legally entitled to?"

"What makes you think she wasn't in on this from the beginning? For all we know, the two colluded," Titus said.

"To what end?" I interjected mildly. "For the last five years the woman's been dead broke, accumulating debts by the bushel basket. Meanwhile Wendell's down in Mexico by the pool with some babe. What kind of deal is that? Even if she collects, all she ends up with is money to pay off the bill collectors."

"You only have her word for that," Titus said. "Besides which, we don't really know how Mr. and Mrs. Jaffe accommodated their relationship. Maybe the marriage was over and this was his way of negotiating spousal support."

"Some support," I said.

Titus plowed right over me. "And as you yourself pointed out, it looks like she's managed to buy one kid a house and probably retained the services of a hotshot attorney for the one who's in trouble. The bottom line is, we need to have a conversation with Wendell Jaffe. Now, how do you propose to find him?" The question was abrupt, but the tone was more curious than challenging.

"I figure Brian's the perfect bait, and if Wendell's too paranoid to approach him in jail, he can always contact Dana. Or Michael, his oldest, who has a child Wendell's never seen. Even his expartner, Carl, is a possibility." It all sounded weak, but what was I going to do? Fake it, that's what.

Mac stirred. "You can't run a twenty-four-hour surveillance on the whole lot of them. Even if we hire other ops on this, you're talking thousands of dollars going out, and in return for what?"

"True enough," I said. "Do you have a suggestion?"

Mac crossed his arms, turning his attention back to Titus. "Whatever we do, we better get a move on," he said. "My wife could go through half a million clams in a week."

Titus stood up and closed his file with a snap. "I'll call the company attorney and see if he can get us a temporary restraining order. With a TRO, we can get a lock on Mrs. Jaffe's bank accounts and prevent any more monies going out."

"She's going to love that," I said.

"Is there anything specific you want her to do in the meantime, Gordon?"

Titus sent me a chilly smile. "I'm sure she'll think of something." He looked at his watch as a signal that we were dismissed.

Mac went into his office, which was two doors down. There was no sign of Vera. I chatted briefly with Darcy Pascoe, the CF receptionist, and then I went back to Lonnie's office, where I took care of odds and ends. I picked up messages, opened mail, sat on my swivel chair, and swiveled for a while, hoping for inspiration about where I should go next. In the absence of a great idea, I tried the only other action item that occurred to me.

I put in a call to Lieutenant Whiteside at the police department, asking him if I could have the telephone number of Lieutenant Harris Brown, who'd worked on the case when Wendell first disappeared. Jonah Robb had told me Brown had since retired, but he might have information. "Do you think he'd be willing to talk to me?" I asked.

"I have no idea, but I'll tell you what," he said. "His telephone's unlisted, and I wouldn't want to give it to you unless I had his okay. When I can find a minute, I'll give him a call. If he's interested, I'll have him get in touch with you."

"Great. That'd be fine. I'd appreciate the contact."

I hung up the phone and made a note to myself. If I didn't hear in two days, I'd try calling back. I wasn't sure the man would be any help, but you never knew. Some of those old cops loved nothing better than to reminisce. He might have suggestions about places Wendell might be holing up. In the meantime, what? I went back to the Xerox machine and ran off several dozen copies of the flier with Wendell's photograph. I'd added my name and telephone number in a box at the bottom, indicating my interest in the man's whereabouts.

I filled my gas tank and hit the road again, heading back to Perdido. I cruised past Dana's house, did a U-turn at the intersection, and pulled into a parking place across the street. I began a door-to-door canvass, moving patiently from house to house. I worked my way down the block, leaving a flier in the screen door if there was no one home. On Dana's side of the street many couples apparently worked, because the houses were dark and there were no cars in the drive. When I found someone home, the conversations all seemed to share the same boring elements. "Hello," I would say, quickly trying to work in my message before I could be mistaken for a salesperson. "I wonder if you might give me some help. I'm a private investigator, working to locate a man we think might be in the area. Have you seen him recently?" I would hold up the artist's composite of Wendell Jaffe, waiting without much hope while the person's gaze moved across his features.

Much mental scratching of chins. "No, now I don't think so. No, ma'am. What was it the man did? I hope you're not telling me he's dangerous."

"Actually, he's wanted for questioning in a fraud investigation."

Hand cupped behind the ear. "What's that?"

I would raise my voice. "Do you remember a couple of real estate developers a few years back? They had a company called CSL Investments and they put together syndicates—"

"Oh, my Lord, yes. Well, of course I remember them. The one fellow killed himself and the other one went to jail."

On and on it went, with no one contributing any fresh information.

Across the street from Dana and about six doors down, I had better luck. I knocked on the door of a house identical to hers, same model, same exterior, dark gray with white trim. The man who answered was in his early sixties, wearing shorts, a flannel shirt, dark socks, and an incongruous pair of wingtips. His gray hair was all abristle, and he wore a pair of half-glasses at the midpoint on his septum, peering at me blue-eyed above the smudged surface of his lenses. A mask of white whiskers covered the lower part of his face, a possible refusal to shave more than twice a week. He was narrow through the shoulders, and his posture seemed stooped, a curious combination of elegance and defeat. Maybe the hard-soled shoes were a holdover from his former occupation. I was guessing salesman or a stockbroker, someone who spent his life in a three-piece suit.

"What can I do for you?" he said, the question intended more for efficiency than any real assistance.

"I wonder if you could help me. Are you acquainted with Mrs. Jaffe, from across the street?"

"The one whose boy's been screwing up? We know the family," he said cautiously. "What's he done now? Or what *hasn't* he done might be the better question in this case."

"This is actually about his father."

There was a silence. "I thought he was dead."

"That's what everybody thought until recently. Now we have reason to believe he's alive and possibly returning to California. This is an updated likeness along with my business number. I'd appreciate a call if you should spot him in the area." I held the flier out, and he took it.

"Well, I'll be damned. It's always something with that bunch," he said. I watched his gaze trace a triangle from the photograph of Wendell to Dana's house down the street and then back to my face. "This is probably none of my business, but what's your connection to the Jaffes? Are you a relative?"

"I'm a private investigator working for the company that wrote the policy on Wendell Jaffe's life."

"Is that right," he said. He cocked his head. "Why don't you come on in a second? I wouldn't mind hearing this."

10

I hesitated for just a second, and a smile creased his face.

"Don't worry about it. I'm not the boogeyman. My wife's on the premises, pulling weeds in the garden. Both of us work at home in one capacity or another. If anybody's going to spot Mr. Jaffe, it's most likely us. What's your name again?" He backed into the hallway, motioning for me to follow.

I moved across the threshold behind him. "Kinsey Millhone. Sorry. I should have introduced myself. That's my name there at the bottom of the flier." I held my hand out, and we shook.

"Good to meet you. Don't worry about it. Jerry Irwin. My wife's name is Lena. She saw you bumping doors across the street. I got a study in the back. She can bring us coffee, if you like."

"None for me, thanks."

"She's going to love this," he said. "Lena? Hey, Lena!"

We reached his study, a small room paneled in a light veneer, scored and pockmarked to look like knotty pine. An L-shaped desk occupied most of the space, the walls lined with floor-to-ceiling metal shelves. "Let me see if I can find her. Have a seat," he said. He headed off down the hall, moving toward the back door.

I sat down on a metal folding chair and did a quick check of my surroundings, trying to get a feel for Irwin in his absence. Computer, monitor, and keyboard. Lots of floppy disks neatly filed. Open banker's boxes filled with some kind of color illustrations, segregated by sheets of cardboard. A low metal bookshelf to the right of the desk held numerous heavy volumes with titles I couldn't read. I leaned closer, squinting. *Burke's General Armory, Armorial General Rietstap, New Dictionary of American Family Names, Dictionary of Surnames, Dictionary of Heraldry.* I could hear him hollering out into the backyard and moments later the sound of conversation as the two moved toward the study where I was waiting. I sat back in the chair, trying to look like a woman unconsumed by nosiness. I stood up as they entered, but Mrs. Irwin shooed me onto my seat again. Her husband tossed the flier on his desk and moved around to his chair.

Lena Irwin was petite and on the plump side for her height, dressed for gardening in Japanese farmer's pants and a blue chambray shirt with the sleeves rolled up. She'd pinned up her gray hair, damp tendrils escaping from various combs and barrettes. The spattering of freckles across her broad cheekbones suggested that her hair might have been red once upon a time. Her prescription sunglasses sat like a bow across her head. Having come in from digging, she had nails that looked as if she'd just had a set of French tips done in dirt. Her handshake was faintly gritty, and her eyes raked my face with interest. "I'm Lena. How're you?"

"I'm fine. Sorry to interrupt your gardening," I said.

Her wave was careless. "Garden's not going anyplace. I was glad to take a break. That sun out there is murder. Jerry mentioned this business about the Jaffes."

"Wendell Jaffe in particular. Did you know him?"

"We knew of him," Lena said.

Jerry spoke up. "We know her to speak to, though we tend to keep our distance. Perdido's a small town, but we were still surprised when we heard she'd moved in over there. She used to live in a nicer area. Nothing fancy, but better than this one by a long shot."

"Of course, we always thought she was a widow."

"So did she," I said. I gave a quick synopsis of the rumored change in Dana Jaffe's marital status. "Did Jerry show you the picture?"

"Yes, but I haven't had a chance to study it."

Jerry straightened the flier on his desk, lining up the page with the bottom edge of his blotter. "We read about Brian in the papers. What a mess that boy's made. We see police over there every time we turn around."

Lena interjected a change of subject. "Would you like a cup of coffee or some lemonade? Won't take but a minute."

"I better not," I said. "I have a lot of ground to cover yet. I'm trying to get these fliers out in case Wendell puts in an appearance."

"Well, we'll certainly keep an eye out. This close to the freeway, we get a lot of cars through here, especially during rush hour with people looking for a shortcut. The southbound off ramp's just a block in that direction. We have a little strip mall down the street, so we get foot traffic, too."

Lena added her comment, cleaning dirt away from her cuticles. "I run a little bookkeeping business from my office up front, so I'm sitting near a window several hours a day. We don't miss much, as you can probably tell. Well, now. I'm glad we had a chance to meet. I better finish up out back and get some work done since I mentioned it."

"I'll be on my way, then, but I'd sure appreciate the help."

She walked me as far as the front steps, a copy of the flier and my business card in hand. "I hope you don't mind my getting personal, but your first name's unusual. Do you know the origin?"

"Kinsey is my mother's maiden name. I guess she didn't want to lose it, so she passed it on to me."

"The reason I ask is that's what Jerry's been doing since he took early retirement. He researches names and family crests."

"I gathered as much. The name is English, I think."

"And what's the story on your parents? Do they live here in Perdido?"

"Both died years ago in an accident. They lived up in Santa Teresa, but they've been gone now since I was five."

She pulled her glasses down from her head, giving me a long look above the half-moon of bifocal lenses. "I wonder if your mother was related to Burton Kinsey's people up in Lompoc."

"Not as far as I know. I don't remember any mention of a name like that."

She studied my face. "Because you look an awful lot like a friend of mine who's a Kinsey by birth. She has a daughter just about your age, too. What are you, thirty-two?"

"Thirty-four," I said, "but I don't have any family left. My only close relative was my mother's sister, who died ten years back."

"Well, there's probably no connection, but I just thought I'd ask. You ought to have Jerry check his files. He has over six thousand names in his computer program. He could research the family crest and run off a copy for you."

"Maybe I'll do that the next time I'm down. It sounds interesting." I tried to picture the Kinsey family crest emblazoned on a royal banner. I could probably mount it near the suit of armor in the great hall antechamber. Might be the perfect touch on those special occasions when one hopes to impress.

"I'll tell Jerry to do the research," she said, having made up her mind. "This is not genealogy . . . he doesn't trace anybody's family tree. What he gives you is information about the derivation of the surname."

"Don't have him go to any trouble," I said.

"It's no trouble. He enjoys it. We work the art show up in Santa Teresa every Sunday afternoon. You ought to stop by and see us. We have a little booth near the wharf."

"Maybe I'll do that. And thanks for your time."

"Happy to be of help. We'll keep an eye out for you."

"That's great, and please don't hesitate to call if you see anything suspicious."

"We surely will."

I gave her a quick wave and then moved down the porch steps. I heard the door close behind me as she went back inside.

By the time I'd distributed fliers up and down the block, a locally owned moving company with a bright red van had arrived at Dana's house and two burly guys were in the process of angling a box spring down the stairs. The screen door was propped open, and I could see them struggle with the turn. Michael was pitching in, probably in an effort to speed the process and thus cut costs. A young woman I guessed to be Michael's wife, Juliet, wandered out of the house from time to time, the baby on her hip. She'd stand out in the grass, in a pair of white shorts, rocking and jiggling the baby while she watched the movers work. The garage doors were open, a yellow VW convertible parked on one side, the backseat piled high with the sorts of odds and ends no one wants to trust to the movers. There was no sign of Dana's car, and I had to guess she was out running errands.

I unlocked my car door and slid onto the driver's seat, where I busied myself. No one seemed to pay any attention to me, too busy loading furniture to notice what I was doing. Within an hour the truck had been packed with whatever furniture the couple was taking with them. Michael, Juliet, and the baby got into the VW and backed out of the driveway. When the van pulled away from the curb, Michael fell in behind it. I waited a few minutes and joined the motorcade myself, keeping several car lengths between us. Michael must have known a shortcut because I soon lost track of him. Fortunately, the van wasn't hard to spot on the highway up ahead. We drove north on 101, passing two off ramps. The truck took the third, turning right, and then left on Calistoga Street, proceeding into a section of Perdido known as the Boulevards. The van finally slowed, pulling into the curb just as the VW appeared from the opposite direction.

The house they were moving into looked as if it had been built in the twenties: rosy-beige stucco exterior with a tiny porch and a patchy front yard. The window trim had been done in a darker shade of rose with a tiny rim of azure. I'd been in half a dozen houses just like it. The interior couldn't have been much more than nine hundred square feet: two bedrooms, one bath, living room, kitchen, and a small utility room in the rear. There was a cracked concrete driveway to the right of the house, a two-car garage visible in the rear, with what looked like a bachelor apartment above.

The movers began to unload the truck. If they noticed my presence, they gave no indication of it. I made a note of the house number and the street before I fired up my engine and returned to Dana's. I had no compelling reason to talk to her again, but I needed her cooperation, and I was hoping to establish a rapport of some kind. I caught her just as she was turning into her drive. She parked the car in the garage, assembling some parcels before she opened the car door. The minute she spotted me, I could see the color tint her cheeks. She slammed her car door, emerged from the garage, and crossed the grass in my direction. She was wearing tight jeans, an old T-shirt, and tennis shoes, her hair held back by a blue-and-white cotton scarf that she had tied around her head. The assorted paper bags in her arms seemed to crackle with her agitation. "What are you doing back here again? I consider this harassment."

"Well, it's not," I said. "We're trying to get a line on Wendell and you're the logical place to start."

Her voice had dropped, and her eyes were glittering with rage and determination. "I will call you if I see him. In the meantime, if you don't stay away from me, I will notify my attorney."

"Dana, I'm not your enemy. I'm just trying to do a job. Why don't you help me? You're going to have to deal with the issue sometime. Tell Michael what's going on. Tell Brian, too. Otherwise I'm going to have to step in and tell them myself. We need your help on this."

Her nose suddenly reddened and a fiery triangle formed around her mouth and chin. Tears leapt into her eyes and she pressed her lips together, sealing back her rage. "Don't tell me what to do. I can handle this myself."

"Look. Can we talk about this inside?"

I saw her glance at the houses across the street. Without a word she turned and proceeded toward the front door, pulling keys from her shoulder bag. I followed her through the entrance and closed the front door behind us.

"I have work to do." She dumped her parcels and handbag on the bottom step and went up the stairs toward the second-floor bedrooms. I hesitated, watching her until she disappeared from view. She hadn't said I couldn't join her. I took the stairs two at a time, peering right at the landing until I located the empty master suite that Michael and his wife had apparently just vacated. There was a canister vaccuum cleaner outside the door, cord neatly retracted, cleaning tools still attached. My guess was that Dana had left it there as a tangible suggestion, hoping someone would vacuum once the furniture had been moved. No one seemed to have taken her up on the offer. She was standing in the middle of the bedroom, surveying the premises, trying (I imagined) to figure out where to begin the cleanup. I eased into the doorway and leaned against the frame, trying not to disturb the fragile truce between us. She glanced over at me without any evidence of her earlier hostility. "Do you have children?"

I shook my head.

"This is what it looks like when they leave you," she said.

The room was drab and empty. I could see a king-size square of clean carpet where the bed had been. There were stray coat hangers on the floor, and the wastebasket was jammed with last-minute discards. Nests of accumulated hair and fuzz rimmed the wall-to-wall carpeting. There was a broom leaning against the wall, a dustpan upright beside it. There was an ashtray on the windowsill, the brim filled with old cigarette butts, an empty, crumpled pack of Marlboro Lights balanced jauntily on top. Pictures were gone. I had to guess the young married couple was still at that stage of decorating where travel or rock posters were affixed to the walls with tape. I could see the patches left behind. The curtains were down. The windowpanes were lacquered with a gray film of cigarette smoke, and I guessed the glass hadn't been washed since the "kids" moved in. Even from a distance, Juliet didn't strike me as the sort who scrubbed the baseboards on her hands and knees.

That was Mom's job, and I suspected Dana would tackle it with a vengeance once I had finally left her in peace.

"Mind if I use the bathroom?" I asked.

"Help yourself." She grabbed the broom, attacking the corners of the room, coaxing dust away from the walls. While she exhumed the remains of Michael's presence, I moved into the bathroom. The area rug and the towels had been removed. The door to the medicine cabinet was hanging open, the interior empty except for a sticky circle of cough medicine on the bottom shelf. The glass shelves above were tacky with dust. The room echoed oddly without the softening influence of a shower curtain. I used the last scrap of toilet paper and then washed my hands without the benefit of soap, drying them on my jeans in the absence of a hand towel. Someone had even taken the bulb from the fixture.

I moved back into the bedroom, wondering if I should help. There was no sign of a dust cloth or a sponge or any other cleaning implements. Dana was going after the dust as if the process were therapeutic.

"How's Brian doing? Have you seen him yet?"

"He called me last night when he'd been through the booking process. His attorney's been in to see him, but I'm really not sure just what they discussed. I guess there was some kind of problem when they brought him in, and they've put him in isolation."

"Really," I said. I watched her sweep, the broom making a restful *skritch*ing sound against the carpet. "How'd he get into trouble, Dana? What happened to him?"

At first I thought she didn't intend to respond. Dust appeared in little puffs as she swept it away from the wall. Once she completed her circuit of the room, she set the broom aside and reached for a cigarette. She took a moment to light it, letting the question sit there between us. She smiled with bitterness. "It started with truancy. Once Wendell died . . . well, disappeared . . . and the scandal hit the news, it was Brian who reacted. We used to have huge battles every morning about his going off to school. He was twelve years old and he absolutely did not want to go. He tried everything. He'd claim he had stomachaches and headaches. He'd throw temper tantrums. Cry. He'd *beg* to stay home, and what was I going to do? He'd say, 'Mom, all the kids know what Daddy did. Everybody hates him and they all hate me, too.' I kept trying to tell him what his dad did had nothing to do with him, it was completely separate and had no bearing on him at all, but I couldn't talk him into it. He never bought it for a minute. And honestly, kids did seem to pick on him. Pretty soon he was getting into horrible fights, cutting classes, skipping school. Vandalism, petty theft. It was a nightmare." She tapped her cigarette against the already laden ashtray, flicking a quarter inch of ash into a tiny crevice between butts.

"What about Michael?"

"He was just the opposite. Sometimes I think Michael used school as a way of blotting out the truth. Brian was oversensitive where Michael made himself numb. We talked to school counselors, teachers. I don't know how many social workers we saw. Everybody had a theory, but nothing seemed to work. I didn't have the money to get us any real help. Brian was so *bright*, and he seemed so capable. It just broke my heart. Of course, in many ways Wendell was like that, too. Anyway, I didn't want the boys to believe he killed himself. He wouldn't do that. We had a good marriage, and he adored them. He was very family-oriented. You can ask anyone. I was sure he'd never deliberately do anything to hurt us. I've always believed Carl Eckert was the one who was fiddling with the books. Maybe Wendell couldn't face it. I'm not saying he didn't have his weaknesses. He wasn't perfect, but he tried."

I let that one sit there, unwilling to challenge her version of events. I could see her faltering attempt to correct the family story. The dead are always easier to characterize. You can assign them any attitude or motive without fear of contradiction.

"I take it the boys are different in more ways than one," I said.

"Well, yes. Obviously, Michael is the steadier, partly because he's older and feels protective. He's always been a very responsible kid, and thank goodness for that. He was the only one I could depend on after Wendell's . . . after what happened to Wendell. Especially with Brian so out of control. If Michael has a fault, it's being too earnest. He's always trying to do the right thing, Juliet being a case in point. He didn't have to marry her."

I kept myself still, making no response at all, because I realized she was giving me a critical piece of information about the situation. She assumed I was already in possession of the facts. Apparently, Juliet was pregnant when Michael married her. She went right on, talking as much to herself as to me.

"Lord knows she wasn't pushing for it. She wanted to have the baby, and she needed financial help, but it's not like she insisted on making things legal. That was Michael's idea. I'm not sure it was a good one, but they're doing okay."

"Has it been hard on you to have them living here?"

She shrugged. "For the most part, I've enjoyed it. Juliet gets on my nerves now and then, but mostly because she's so damned uncooperative. She has to do it her way. She's the expert on every subject. This at eighteen, of course. I know it comes out of her own insecurities, but it's irritating all the same. She can't stand my help, and she can't tolerate suggestions. She doesn't have a clue about motherhood. I mean, she's crazy about the baby, but she treats him like a toy. You ought to see her when she bathes him. It's enough to make your heart fail. She'll leave him lying on the counter while she goes off to get his diapers. It's a wonder he hasn't rolled off half a dozen times."

"What about Brian? Does he live here as well?"

"He and Michael shared an apartment until this latest incident. Once Brian was sentenced and started serving his time, Michael couldn't afford to keep it. His job didn't pay much and then with Juliet, he simply couldn't manage. She's insisted on staying home since the day he married her."

I noticed how neatly she substituted euphemisms. We were not discussing an unplanned pregnancy, a hasty wedding, and the subsequent financial muddle. Gone were the jail escape and the major shooting spree. These were episodes and incidents, inexplicable occurrences for which neither boy appeared to be responsible.

She seemed to pick up on my thought process, quickly shifting the subject. She moved out into the hall and grabbed the vacuum, hauling it in behind her on lustily squeaking casters. My aunt always said a canister vaccuum was useless compared with an upright. I wondered if this was the central metaphor in Dana's life. She found the closest electrical outlet and pulled out enough cord to plug it in. . . . "Maybe it's my fault what Brian's been through. God knows being a single parent is the hardest job I've ever faced. When you're penniless at the same time, there's no *way* you can win. Brian should have had the best. Instead, he's had nothing in the way of counseling. His problems have been compounded, which is hardly his doing."

"Will you talk to them for me? I don't want to interfere, but I'm going to have to talk to Brian."

"Why? What for? If Wendell shows up, it's got nothing to do with *him*."

"Maybe so, maybe not. The shooting in Mexicali was all over the news. I know Wendell read the papers down in Viento Negro. It seems reasonable to imagine he'd head back in this direction."

"You don't know that for a fact."

"No. But just suppose it's true. Don't you think Brian should be told what's going on? You don't want him doing something foolish."

She seemed to take that in. I could see her turning over the possibilities. She removed the upholstery attachment and clicked the rug and floor nozzle into place, adding the extension wand in preparation for vacuuming. "Hell, why not? Things couldn't get much worse. The poor kid," she said.

I thought it better not to mention that I was picturing him like a piece of bait in a trap.

In the office alcove below, the phone rang. Dana launched into a description of Brian's misfortunes, but I found myself listening to her canned message as it came wafting up the stairs. The live message followed at the sound of the beep, one of her bridal clients with the latest complaint. "Hello, Dana. This is Ruth. Listen, hon, Bethany's been having a little problem with this caterer you recommended? We've asked the woman twice for a written cost-per-person breakdown of the food and drink for the reception, and we can't seem to get a response. We thought maybe you could give her a call and light a little fire under her for answers. I'll be here in the morning and you can call me, okay? Thank you. I'll talk to you then, babe. Bye now."

I wondered idly if Dana ever told these young brides the problems they were going to run into once the wedding was over with: boredom, weight gain, irresponsibility, friction over sex, spending, family holidays, and who picks up the socks. Maybe it was just my basic cynicism rising to the surface, but cost-per-person food and drink breakdowns seemed trivial compared to the conflicts marriage generated.

". . . a real helper, generous, cooperative. Winsome and funny. He's got a very high IQ." She was talking about Brian, the alleged teen killer. Only a mother could describe as "winsome and funny" a kid who'd recently broken out of jail and gone on a killing rampage. She was looking at me expectantly. "I have to get on with this so I can reclaim my bedroom. You have any other questions before I get on with the vacuuming?"

Offhand, I couldn't think of any. "This is fine for now."

She kicked the switch and the vacuum cleaner shrilled to life, a high keening whine that drowned out any possibility of conversation. As I let myself out the front door, I could hear the droning of the motor as she hauled the suction wand across the floor.

11

My watch showed that it was nearly noon. I drove over to the Perdido County Jail.

The Perdido County Government Center was constructed in 1978, a sprawling mass of pale concrete that houses the Criminal Justice Center, the administration building, and the Hall of Justice. I parked my car in one of the spaces provided in the vast marina of asphalt that surrounds the complex. I went into the main entrance, pushing through the glass doors that opened onto the lower lobby. I hung a right. The main jail public counter was located down a short hallway. On the same floor were the Sheriff's Personnel Counter, Records and Licensing, and the West County Patrol Services counter, none of which interested me for the moment.

I identified myself to the civilian clerk and, in due course, was directed to the watch commander's office, where I introduced myself. I showed my identification, including my driver's license and my investigator's license. There was a brief delay while a second clerk picked up the phone and checked to see if the jail administrator was in. The minute I heard the guy's name, I knew my luck had improved. I had gone to high school with Tommy Ryckman. He was two years ahead of me, but we'd misbehaved together rather desperately in the days when one could do that without risking death or disease. I wasn't sure he'd remember me, but apparently he did. Sergeant Ryckman agreed to see me as soon as I'd received my clearance. I was directed down the hall to his small office on the right.

As I entered his office, he unfolded himself from his swivel chair, emerging to an impressive six feet eight, his face wreathed with a grin. "Well, it's been way too long. How the hell are you?"

"I'm great, Tommy. How are you?"

We shook hands across the desk and made effusive noises at each other, trading hasty summaries of the years since we'd met. He was now in his mid-thirties, clean-shaven with glossy brown hair parted on one side and slicked across. His hair was thinning slightly, and his forehead was scored as if by the tines of a fork. He wore glasses with wire frames, and his jaw looked like it would smell of citrus after-shave. His khaki sheriff's department uniform was starched and crisply pressed, the slacks looking like they'd been professionally tailored to fit. He had long arms and big hands, a wedding ring, of course.

He motioned me to a chair and then eased back into his own. Even seated, he had the build of a basketball player, his grasshopper knees visible above the edge of the desk. His black shoes must have been a size 13. His accent was still shaded by a touch of the Midwest, Wisconsin perhaps, and I remembered that he'd arrived at Santa Teresa High halfway through the school year. He had a studio portrait on his desk: a wifey-looking woman and three medium-aged kids, two boys and a girl, all with glossy brown hair neatly slicked down with water, all wearing glasses with clear plastic frames. Two of the kids were of an age where they had goofy teeth.

"You're here with regard to Brian Jaffe."

"More or less," I replied. "I'm actually more interested in the whereabouts of his father."

"So I understand. Lieutenant Whiteside told me what was going on."

"Are you familiar with the case? I've heard some of it, but nothing in any depth."

"A good buddy of mine worked with Lieutenant Brown on that case so I had him fill me in. Just about everybody down here knows that one. Lot of local citizens got sucked into CSL. Lost their shirts, most of them. Sometimes I think it was a textbook scam. My buddy's transferred since then, but Harris Brown's the one you want to talk to if we can't help."

"I've been trying to get in touch with him, but I was told he retired."

"He did, but I'm sure he'd be willing to help any way he can. Does the kid know there's a chance his dad's still alive?"

I shook my head. "I just talked to his mother and she hasn't told him yet. I understand he was just brought back to Perdido."

"That's right. Over the weekend we dispatched a couple of deputies to Mexicali, where the kid was handed over. He was transported by car up here to the main jail. He was booked in last night."

"Any chance I might see him?"

"Not today, I don't think. Inmate mealtime at the moment and after that he's scheduled for a medical exam. You can try tomorrow or the next day as long as he has no objections."

"How'd he manage to escape from Connaught?"

Ryckman stirred restlessly, breaking off eye contact. "We're not going to talk about that," he said. "Next thing you know the information ends up in the paper and then everybody gets it down. Let's just say the inmates discovered a little quirk in the system and took advantage of it. It won't happen again, I can tell you that."

"Will he be tried as an adult?"

Tommy Ryckman did a stretch, extending his arms above his head with a series of popping sounds. "You'd have to ask the DA, though personally, I'd sure like to see it. This kid is devious. We think he was the one who cooked up the escape plan to begin with, but who's going to contradict him at this point? Two guys are dead and the third's in critical condition. He'll claim he's the innocent victim. You know how it goes. These kids never take responsibility. His mother's already hired him a high-priced attorney, bringing some guy up from Los Angeles."

"Probably utilizing some of the benefits from his father's life insurance policy," I said. "I'd love to see Wendell Jaffe make a discreet appearance. I can't believe he'd risk it, but it would sure verify my intuitions."

"Well now, I'll tell you the problem you're going to have with that. Case like this, a lot of notoriety, courtroom's probably going to be closed and under tight security. You know how it goes. Kid's attorney's going to offer up spirited arguments, asserting his client's fitness for treatment under juvenile court law. He'll want a probation officer to investigate. He'll want reports submitted with other relevant evidence. He'll raise six kinds of hell, and until the matter's decided, he'll maintain his client is entitled to protection under juvenile statutes."

"I don't suppose there's any way I'd be given access to his juvenile criminal history," I said. I was stating the obvious, but sometimes a cop will surprise you.

Sergeant Ryckman laced his hands across his head, smiling at me with a sort of brotherly indulgence. "We wouldn't do that regardless," he said mildly. "You can always try the paper. Reporters over there can probably get you anything you want. Not sure how they do it, but they have their little ways." He sat forward on his chair. "I was just on my way to lunch. You want to join me in the cafeteria?"

"Sure, I'd like that," I said.

On his feet again, I realized how much he'd grown since I'd seen him last and he was over six feet tall then. Now he was stoop-shouldered and seemed to carry his head tilted to one side, perhaps hoping to avoid being knocked silly by the door frame when he entered or left a room. I would have bet money his wife was only five feet tall and spent her life with his belt buckle staring her in the face. On a dance floor, the two probably looked as though they were engaged in an obscene act. "If you don't mind, I got a few things to take care of on the way."

"Fine with me," I said.

We began to traverse the maze of corridors linking the various offices and departments, moving through a series of security checkpoints, like the airlocks on a spaceship. There were video cameras sweeping every corridor, and I knew we were being observed by the deputy manning level-one control. The smells changed subtly from one area to the next. Food, bleach, burning chemicals, as if someone had set fire to the plastic ring on a six-pack of canned sodas, musty blankets, floor wax, rubber tires. Sergeant Ryckman conducted a couple of administrative transactions, apparently minor matters fraught with clerical jargon. There were a surprising number of women working in the processing unit—all ages, all sizes, usually in jeans or polyester pants. There was a nice air of camaraderie among the people I observed. Lots of telephones ringing, lots of movement from department to department, as we cruised through.

Finally, he steered us toward the small employee cafeteria. The menu for the deputies that day was lasagna, grilled ham-and-cheese sandwiches, french fries, and corn. Not quite enough fat and carbs for my taste, but it was coming close. There was also a salad bar, featuring stainless-steel bins of chopped iceberg lettuce, sliced carrots, green pepper rings, and onions. For drinks, one had a choice of orange juice, lemonade, or cartons of milk. The prisoners' menu was listed on the board above the hot table: bean soup, grilled ham-and-cheese sandwiches, beef Stroganoff or lasagna, white bread, french fries, and the ubiquitous corn. Unlike the meals at the jail in Santa Teresa, which were served cafeteria style, the food here was prepared and dished out by inmates onto trays that were loaded, in turn, into big stainless-steel hot carts. I'd seen several being rolled into the industrial-size elevators en route to jail levels three and four.

Ryckman still had the unruly hunger of an adolescent. I watched him pile his tray with a serving of lasagna the size of a brick, two grilled sandwiches, a mound each of corn and french fries, and a hefty side of salad with a dipper of Thousand Island dressing poured on top. He tucked two cartons of low-fat milk into the remaining space on his tray. I followed him in the line, picking up plastic flatware from a bin. I opted for a grilled ham-and-cheese sandwich and a modest log pile of fries, hungrier than I thought possible given the institutional nature of the setting. We found a free corner table and unloaded our trays.

"Were you working in Perdido when Wendell formed CSL?" I asked.

"You bet," Ryckman said. "'Course, I never invest in deals like that myself. My dad always told me I was better off with my money stashed in a coffee can. Depression mentality, but it's not bad advice. Actually, you better hope the word on Jaffe doesn't get out. I know a couple deputies lost money on that scam. He shows his face, you're gonna have a posse of irate citizens riding down on that dude."

"What's the deal?" I asked. "I don't understand what these guys are about." He squirted ketchup on his fries and passed the dispenser to me. I could tell we shared the same intense interest in junk food.

Ryckman ate quickly, attention focused on his plate as the mountain of food diminished. "System works on trust—checks, credit cards, a contract of any kind. People perpetrating fraud feel no inner moral obligation to make good on their agreements. They operate along a continuum that runs from financial irresponsibility to civil consumer puffing to fraud to criminal lies. You see it all the time. Bankers, real estate brokers, investment counselors . . . anyone exposed to large sums of cash. After a while they can't seem to keep their hands off it."

"Too tempting," I remarked. I wiped my hands on a paper napkin, uncertain whether the grease was coming from the sandwich or the pile of french fries. Both were heaven to a person of my low appetites.

"It's more than that. Because it's not just bucks these boys are after as far as I can tell. The money's just a way of keeping score, like they say. You watch these guys operate and pretty soon you realize it's the game they get off on. Same goes for politicians. It's a power trip. Us ordinary mortals are just fuel for their egos."

"I'm surprised anyone in law enforcement fell for his scheme. You guys ought to know better. You probably see enough of it."

He shook his head, chewing on a bite of sandwich. "Always hope to make a killing. A little something for nothing, and I guess we're not above it."

"I had a conversation with Jaffe's ex-partner last night," I said. "He seemed pretty slick."

"He is. Went right back into business, and what the hell are we gonna do? Everybody around here knows the guy went to jail. Day he comes out they're ready to invest again. What makes these cases so hard to prosecute is the victims don't want to believe they've been deceived. The victims all become dependent on the crook who's cheating them. Once they invest, they *need* him to be successful to get their money back. Then, of course, the con man always has last-minute excuses, stalling repayment and dragging his feet. Case like that is a bitch to prove. Lot of time the DA can't even get corroboration."

"I really don't understand it when smart guys get into stuff like this."

"If you look back far enough, you could probably see it coming. You know, old Wendell's got a law degree, but he never passed the bar."

"Really. That's interesting."

"Yeah, he got into some trouble just out of law school and he ended up letting the whole business drop. He's just one of those guys: smart and well educated, but he had a bad streak that showed up even then."

"What kind of trouble?"

"Some prostitute died in the course of rough sex. Jaffe was the john, pleaded down on a charge of manslaughter, and got off on probation. It all got hushed up, of course, but it was ugly stuff. There's no way you practice law with that in your background. Perdido's too small."

"He could have gone somewhere else."

"He didn't seem to think so."

"Seems weird somehow. I haven't been thinking of him as the violent type. How'd he get from manslaughter to fraud?"

"Wendell Jaffe's sly in more ways than one. It's not like the guy lived in a four-thousand-square-foot house complete with swimming pool and tennis court. He bought a nice three-bedroom tract house in a good middle-class neighborhood. He and his wife drove American cars, the stripped-down economy models and not like new ones. His was six years old. Both of his sons went to public schools. Usually, with these guys, what you'll see is a pattern of conspicuous consumption, but Wendell didn't do that. No designer clothes. He and Dana didn't travel much or entertain lavishly. From the point of view of his investors—and this was something he was quick to assure them—he poured every penny right back into the business."

"What was the gimmick? How'd they pull it off?"

"Well, I did a little digging when I heard you were coming down. From what I understand, it was pretty straightforward. He and Eckert had about two hundred fifty investors, some of them putting up twenty-five to fifty thousand dollars apiece. CLS took fees and royalties off the top."

"On the basis of a prospectus?"

"That's right. First thing Jaffe did, he bought a shell of a company and renamed it CSL Inc."

"What kind of company?"

"This was trust-deed investment. Then he made headlines with the purchase of a one-hundred-two-million-dollar complex, which he announced he had sold six months later for a hundred eighty-nine million. Truth was, the deal never went through, but the public didn't know that. Wendell hands his investors this impressive-looking, unaudited financial statement showing assets in excess of twenty-five million dollars. After that, it was a piece of cake. They'd buy real estate and show a paper profit by selling it back to another of their shell companies, inflating the value of the property in the process."

"Jesus," I said.

"It was a typical Ponzi. Some of the people who came on board early were making out like bandits. Returns of twenty-eight percent on their initial investment. It wasn't unusual to see them turn around and invest twice that sum, cashing in on the bonanza of CSL's financial savvy. Who could resist? Jaffe seemed to be earnest, knowledgeable, hardworking, sincere, conservative. There was nothing flamboyant about the man. He paid good salaries and treated his employees decently. He seemed happily married, devoted to his family. He was a bit of a workaholic, but he managed to take occasional time off: two weeks in May on his annual fishing trip, another two weeks in August when he took the family camping."

"God, you really do know this stuff. What about Carl? How'd he fit into this?"

"Wendell was the front man. Carl did everything else. Wendell's talent was the hustle, which he did with the kind of low-key, drop-dead sincerity that made you want to pull your wallet out and give him everything you had. The two of them put together various real estate syndicates. Investors were told their money would be held in a separate account, devoted exclusively to a particular project. In actual fact, the funds for the various projects were commingled, and some funds intended for a new project were used to complete the old."

"And then the bottom dropped out of the market."

Tommy feigned a slam dunk and pointed a finger at me. "You got it. CSL suddenly began to have trouble finding new investors. Eventually, Jaffe must have realized the whole house of cards was collapsing. He also got a notice about an IRS audit, from what I hear tell. That's when he went off on his trip. I'll tell you one thing. This guy was so persuasive that even when it became apparent the investors had lost their shirts, a lot of people still believed in him, convinced that there was some other explanation for the missing funds, which is where Carl Eckert really ate the big one."

"Did Eckert realize what he was doing?"

"If you want my opinion, he did. He's claimed all along he had no idea what Wendell was up to, but Eckert himself did the nuts-and-bolts end of the biz, so he must have been aware. Hell, he had to know. He just maintained his innocence because there wasn't anyone to contradict him."

"Same thing the Jaffe kid is pulling now," I said.

Tommy smiled. "In matters like this, it always helps if your confederates are dead."

It was 1:15 when I left the building, zigzagging my way across the crowded lot to the far corner where I'd parked. Once I left the complex of government offices, I hung a left, heading back toward 101, managing to catch every traffic light between me and the freeway. At every stop, it amused me to watch women drivers take advantage of the moment to check their eye makeup and fluff their hair. I adjusted my rearview mirror, taking a quick look at the state of my own mop. I was nearly certain the little spiky patch near my left ear had grown some.

Almost inadvertently, I glanced at the car behind me. I got a quick hit of adrenaline, as though a hot wire had touched me. Renata was at the wheel, frowning slightly, her attention focused on her mobile phone. She was alone in the car, which didn't look like a rental, unless, of course, Avis and Hertz have taken to using Jaguars for their "full size." The light changed and I pulled away with Renata right behind me, moving at the same pace. I was in the inside lane of two moving in a southerly direction. She angled into the curb lane, her speed picking up as she passed me on the right.

I saw her right rear turn signal start to blink. I eased into the curb lane, taking my place behind her, trying to anticipate what she meant to do. A large shopping mall loomed up on our right. I saw her turn in, but before I could do likewise, someone cut in front of me. I braked abruptly, trying to avoid rear-ending the other driver while I scanned the parking lot ahead. Renata had taken a quick left and then turned down the second aisle, which seemed to extend the entire length of the mall. I turned into the entrance a full minute behind her. I sped through the parking lot on a parallel course, flying over speed bumps like a skier taking moguls. I kept thinking she would park, but she continued along the same path. There were two rows of cars between us, but in the one clear glimpse I caught, she was still on the phone. Whatever her conversation, she must have changed her mind about shopping. I saw her lean to the right, apparently replacing the handset. The next thing I knew, she reached an exit and took a left, easing into the flow of traffic again. I cut out at the exit, falling into the same lane as Renata, only two cars back. I didn't think she'd spotted me, and I wasn't sure she'd recognize me in a setting so different from the one in which she'd last seen me.

She passed the directional sign for Highway 101, cranking up her speed when she hit the on ramp. The driver in front of me began to slow. "Go on, go on," I was urging under my breath. The guy was old and cautious, swinging wide to the left for a right-hand turn into the gas station on the corner. By the time I whipped around him and up the ramp, Renata's Jaguar was no longer visible among the speeding northbound cars. She was the kind of driver who shot any gap she saw, and she'd apparently zigzagged her way out of sight. I drove the next twenty-five miles, straining for sight of her, but she was gone, gone, gone. I realized, belatedly, that I had missed the opportunity to pick off the numbers on her license plate. The only comfort I took was in the simple assumption that if Renata was in the area, Wendell Jaffe probably wasn't far away.

12

Back in Santa Teresa, I went straight to the office, where I hauled out my portable Smith-Corona and typed up my notes, recording the events of the past two days as well as names, addresses, and miscellaneous data. Then I calculated the time I'd put in and tacked on gasoline and mileage. I was probably going to bill CF at a flat rate of fifty bucks an hour, but I wanted to have an itemized accounting ready in case Gordon Titus turned all prissy and authoritarian. Down deep, I knew this rapt attention to the paperwork was only a thinly disguised cover for my mounting excitement. Wendell had to be close by, but what was he doing and what would it take to bring him into the light? At least the Renata sighting had confirmed my hunch . . . unless the two of them had split up, which didn't seem likely. He had family here. I wasn't sure she did. On an impulse, I checked the local telephone directory, but there were no Huffs listed. Hers was probably an alias just as his name was. I would have given just about anything to lay eyes on the man, but that was beginning to feel about as likely as a UFO sighting.

At this stage of any investigation, I'm inclined to impatience. It always feels the same way to me—as though this is the case that's finally going to do me in. So far, I haven't blown a gig. I don't always succeed in ways that I anticipate, but I haven't yet failed to bring a case to resolution. The problem with being a PI is there isn't any rule book. There's no set procedure, no company manual, and no prescribed strategy. Every case is different, and every investigator ends up flying by the seat of her (or his) pants. If you're doing a background check, you can always make the rounds, looking up deeds, titles, births and deaths, marriages, divorces, credit information, business and criminal records. Any competent detective quickly learns how to follow the trail of paper bread crumbs left by the private citizen wandering in the bureaucratic forest. But the success of a missing persons search depends on ingenuity, persistence, and just plain old dumb luck. The leads you develop are based on personal contact, and you better be good at reading human nature while you're at it. I sat and thought about what I'd learned so far. It really wasn't much, and I didn't feel I was any closer to homing in on Wendell Jaffe. I began to transcribe my notes onto index cards. If all else failed, maybe I could shuffle them and deal myself a game of solitaire.

The next time I looked up, it was 4:35. My Spanish class met on Tuesday afternoons from 5:00 until 7:00. I really didn't need to leave for another fifteen minutes, but I'd exhausted my little storehouse of clerical skills. I slipped the paperwork in a folder and locked the file cabinet. I locked the office door behind me, went out through the side door, and down the stairs. I had to stand on the street corner for a good sixty seconds, trying to remember where I'd parked my car. It finally occurred to me and I was just setting off when I heard Alison yoo-whooing from the window.

"Kinsey!"

I shaded my eyes against the late afternoon sun. She was on the little third-floor balcony outside John Ives's office, blond hair hanging over the railing like a latter-day Rapunzel. "Lieutenant Whiteside's on the line. You want me to take a message?"

"Yes, if you would, or he can call my machine and leave a message himself. I'm going off to class, but I'll be home by seven-thirty. If he wants me to call back, ask him to leave me a number."

She nodded and waved, disappearing from sight.

I retrieved my car and drove over to the adult ed facility, which was two miles away. Vera Lipton pulled into the parking lot, arriving shortly after I did. She turned into the first half-empty aisle on her right. I'd eased into the second aisle on the left, parking closer to the classroom. Both of us were testing theories about how to make the quickest getaway once Spanish class ended. Most of the available classrooms had been pressed into service, and there were anywhere from a hundred and fifty to two hundred students piling into cars at the same time.

I grabbed my legal pad, my pile of papers, and my copy of *501 Spanish Verbs.* I locked the car in haste and made a diagonal cut across the parking lot, intercepting Vera. We'd first met when I was still doing periodic investigations for California Fidelity Insurance, where she was employed as an adjuster, later promoted to claims manager. She's probably as close to a best friend as I'll ever have, though I don't really know what such a relationship entails. Now that we no longer have adjacent offices, our contact has taken on a "catch as catch can" quality. This was one reason taking a class together seemed so appealing. During the break, we'd do a fast personal update. Sometimes she'd invite me over for supper after class, and we'd end up laughing and chatting into the night. After thirty-seven years of dedicated singlehood, she'd married a family practice physician named Neil Hess, whom she'd tried to fix me up with the year before. What amused me at the time was that I could tell she was smitten, though she'd decided he was inappropriate for reasons I thought bogus. Specifically, she seemed to object to the fact that she was nearly six inches taller. In the end, love won out. Or maybe Neil got lifts.

They'd been married now for nine months—since the previous Halloween—and I'd never seen her looking better. She's a big gal to begin with: maybe five feet ten, a hundred and forty pounds on a good-size frame. She'd never been apologetic about her generous proportions. The truth was, men seemed to regard her as some sort of goddess, striking up conversations with her everywhere she went. Now that she and Neil were working out together—jogging and playing tennis—she'd dropped fifteen pounds. Her once dyed red hair had grown out to its natural color, a honeyed brown that she was wearing shoulder length. She still dressed like a flight instructor: jumpsuits with padded shoulders and tinted aviator glasses, sometimes with spike heels, tonight with boots.

When she caught sight of me, she whipped off her glasses and stuck them upright on her head like a prescription tiara. She waved enthusiastically. *"¡Hola!"* she called in merry Spanish tones. So far, this was the only word we'd really mastered, and we used it on each other as often as we could. Some guy clipping the hedges looked up expectantly, probably thinking that Vera was addressing him.

"¡Hola!" I replied. *"¿Dónde están los gatos?"* Still in search of those elusive black cats.

"En los árboles."

"Muy bueno," I said.

"God, doesn't that sound great?"

"Yeah, I'm almost sure that guy over there thinks we're Hispanic," I said.

Vera grinned, flashing him a thumbs-up before she turned back to me. "You're here early for a change. You usually come flying in fifteen minutes late."

"I was doing some paperwork and couldn't wait to quit. How are you? You look great."

We strolled into class, absorbed in chitchat and idle gossip until the instructor arrived. Patty Abkin-Quiroga is petite and enthusiastic, amazingly tolerant of our clumsy lurches through the language. There's nothing so humbling as being a dunce in a foreign tongue, and if it weren't for her compassion, we'd have lost heart after two weeks. As usual, she started the class by regaling us with a long tale in Spanish, something to do with her activities that day. Either she ate a tostado or her little boy, Edwardo, flushed his baby bottle down the toilet and she had to have the plumber come out and take a look.

When I got home after class and let myself into my apartment, I could see the message light blinking on my answering machine. I pressed the button and listened as I moved around my tiny living room, turning on lights.

"Hello, Kinsey. Lieutenant Whiteside over at Santa Teresa Police Department. I got a fax this afternoon from our pals in the Los Angeles Passport Office. They don't show anything on Dean DeWitt Huff, but they do have a record of a Renata Huff at the following address in Perdido." I snatched up a pen and scribbled a note on a paper napkin while he was reciting the particulars. "If I'm not mistaken, that's over in the Perdido Keys. Let me know what you find out. I'm off tomorrow, but I'll be back on Thursday."

I said, "All riiight," giving both raised fists a shake. I did a quick dance, complete with butt wiggles, thanking the universe for small favors. I dumped my plans for dinner up at Rosie's. Instead, I made myself a peanut-butter-and-pickle sandwich on whole-wheat bread, wrapping it in waxed paper and then sealing it in a plastic bag the way my aunt had taught me. In addition to the preservation of fresh sandwiches, my other notable household skill —thanks to her odd notions—is the ability to gift-wrap and tie a package of any size without the use of Scotch tape or stickers. This she considered essential preparation for life.

It was ten of eight and still light out when I hit the 101 again. I ate my laptop picnic, steering with one hand while I held my sandwich with the other, humming to myself as the flavors mingled on my tongue. My car radio had been ominously silent for days, and I suspected some relevant fuse had given up the ghost deep inside. I flipped the on button anyway, on the off chance it had somehow healed itself in my absence. No such luck. I flipped the radio off, amusing myself instead with recollections of the annual celebration of Perdido/Olvidado township history, which consisted of a dispirited parade, the erection of many food booths, and the local citizens walking listlessly about, spilling mustard and hot dog relish on their P/O T-shirts.

Father Junipero Serra, who was the first president of the Alta California Missions, established nine missions along a six-hundred-and-fifty-mile stretch of California coastland between San Diego and Sonoma. Father Fermin Lasuen, who assumed leadership in 1785, the year after Serra's death, founded nine more missions. There were other less luminous mission presidents, countless friars and padres whose names have vanished from public awareness. One of these, Father Prospero Olivarez, petitioned in early 1781 to build two small sister missions on the Santa Clara River. Father Olivarez argued that adjacent presidios, or forts, established on dual sites would not only serve as protection for the proposed mission to be built in Santa Teresa, but could simultaneously convert, shelter, and train scores of California Indians who could then serve as skilled laborers for the projected construction process. Father Junipero Serra greatly favored the idea and granted enthusiastic approval. Extensive drawings were submitted, and the site was dedicated. However, a series of frustrating and inexplicable delays resulted in postponement of the ground breaking until after Serra's death, at which point the plan was quashed. Father Olivarez's twin churches were never built. Some historians have portrayed Olivarez as both worldly and ambitious, positing that the withdrawal of support for his project was intended to subdue his unbecoming secular aspirations. Ecclesiastical documents that have since come to light suggest another possibility, that Father Lasuen, who was championing the establishment of missions at Soledad, San Jose, San Juan Bautista, and San Miguel, saw Olivarez as a threat to the achievement of his own aims and deliberately sabotaged his efforts until after Father Serra's demise. His own subsequent rise to power was the death knell of Olivarez's vision. Whatever the truth, cynical observers renamed the dual sites Perdido/Olvidado, a mongrelization of Prospero Olivarez's name. Translated from the Spanish, the names mean Lost and Forgotten.

This trip, I bypassed the main business district. The architecture in the town itself was a mix of boxy, blocky modern buildings interspersed with Victorian structures. On the far side of 101, between the freeway and the ocean, there were whole sections of the land entirely covered with blacktop, a series of interconnecting parking lots for supermarkets, gas stations, and fast-food establishments. One could drive for blocks through linked acres of asphalt without ever actually going out onto a city street. I took the Seacove off ramp, heading for the Perdido Keys.

Closer to the ocean, the houses seemed to take on the look of a little beach town—board-and-batten with big decks, painted sea blue and gray, the yards filled with impossibly bright purple, yellow, and orange flowers. I passed a house where there were so many wet suits hung to dry on a second-story balcony that it looked as if the guests from a cocktail party had wandered out on the deck for air.

Daylight had faded to indigo, and all the house lights in the neighborhood were coming on when I finally located the street I was looking for. The houses on both sides of this narrow lane backed onto the keys, long fingers of seawater stretching back from the ocean. The rear of each house seemed to boast a wide wooden deck with a short wood ramp leading down to a dock, the channel itself deep enough to admit sizable boats. I could smell the cool marina cologne, and the quiet was underscored by an occasional slap of water and the chorusing of frogs.

I cruised slowly, squinting at house numbers, finally spotting the address Whiteside had given me. Renata Huff's house was a two-story dark blue stucco with white trim. The roof was wood shake, and the rear portion of the property was shielded from the street by a white board fence. The house was dark, and a FOR SALE sign hung from a post in the front yard. I said, "Well, damn it."

I parked the car across the street and approached the house, moving up a long wooden ramp to the front door. I rang the bell as if I expected to be admitted. I didn't see a lockbox from the real estate company, which might mean that Renata was still in residence. Casually, I checked the houses on either side of hers. One was dark, and the other showed lights only at the rear. I turned then so I could scrutinize the houses across the street. As nearly as

I could tell, I wasn't under observation and there didn't seem to be any vicious dogs on the premises. Often, I consider this a tacit invitation to break and enter, but I had spied, through one of the two narrow windows flanking the front door, the telltale dot of red light denoting an alarm system, armed and ready. This was not gracious behavior on Renata's part.

Now what? I had the option to get back in my car and return to Santa Teresa, but I hated to admit I'd made the trip for naught. I glanced over at the house to the right of Renata's. Through a side window I could see a woman in her kitchen, head bent to some domestic chore. I walked down the ramp and crossed the yard, trying to avoid the flower beds as I made my way to the door. I rang the bell, staring with idle curiosity at Renata's front porch. Even as I watched, her burglar-fooling lights came on. Now it looked like an empty house filled with pointlessly burning lamps.

Somebody flipped on the porch light overhead and opened the door to the length of the chain. "Yes?" The woman was probably in her forties. All I could see of her was her long, dark, curly hair that cascaded past her shoulders, like the wig on a decadent seventeenth-century fop. She smelled like flea soap. I thought at first it was some new designer perfume until I noticed the towel-swaddled dog she was toting under her arm. It was one of those little brown-and-black jobs about the size of a loaf of bread. Muffin, Buffy, Princess.

I said, "Hi. I wonder if you can give me some information about the house for sale next door. I noticed the outside ramp. Do you happen to know if the place is equipped for the handicapped?"

"Yes, it is."

I was hoping for a little more in the way of information. "On the inside, too?"

"That's right. Her husband suffered a real bad stroke about ten years ago . . . a month before they started work on the house. She had the contractor adjust all the plans for wheelchair access, including a lift up to the second floor."

"Amazing," I murmured. "My sister's in a wheelchair, and

we've been looking for a place that would accommodate her disability." Since I couldn't see the woman's face, I found myself addressing my remarks to the dog, who really seemed quite attentive.

The woman said, "Really. What's wrong with her?"

"She was in a diving accident two years ago and she's paralyzed from the waist down."

"That's too bad," she said. Her tone suggested the sort of fake concern a stranger's story generates. I could have bet she was formulating questions she was too polite to ask.

Actually, I was beginning to feel pretty bad about Sis myself, though she sounded brave. "She's doing pretty well. She's adjusted, at any rate. We were driving around today, checking out the neighborhood. We've been house hunting now for what seems like ages, and this is the first that's really sparked her interest, so I told her I'd stop by and ask. Do you have any idea what they're asking for the place?"

"I heard four ninety-five."

"Really? Well, that's not bad. I think I'll have our real estate agent set up an appointment to show us through. Is the owner home during the day?"

"That's hard to say. Lately, she's been out of town quite a lot."

"What's her name again?" I asked as if she'd told me once.

"Renata Huff."

"What about her husband? If she's not home, could I have the agent give him a call instead?"

"Oh, sorry. Dean died, Mr. Huff. I thought I mentioned he had a heart attack." The dog began to wiggle, bored with all this talk that didn't directly relate to him.

"That's awful," I said. "How long ago was that?"

"I don't know. Probably five or six years."

"And she hasn't remarried?"

"She never seemed to have the interest, which is surprising. I mean, she is young—in her forties—and she comes from a lot of money. At least that's the story I heard." The dog began to lick upward, trying to hit the woman's mouth. This might have been some kind of doggy signal, but I wasn't sure what it meant. Kiss, eat, get down, stop.

"I wonder why she wants to sell? Is she leaving the area?"

"I really couldn't say, but if you want to leave me your number, the next time I see her, I can tell her you stopped by."

"All right. I'd appreciate that."

"Hang on. Let me get some paper."

She moved away from the door to a drop-leaf table in the foyer. When she came back, she had a pencil and a junk-mail envelope.

I gave her my number, inventing freely. As long as I was about it, I gave myself the prefix for Montebello, where all the rich people live. "Can you give me Mrs. Huff's number in case the agent doesn't have it?"

"I don't have that. I think it's unlisted."

"Oh, the agent probably has it. Let's don't worry about that," I said casually. "In the meantime, do you think she'd mind if I just peeped in a couple of windows?"

"I'm sure not. It's really a nice place."

"Sure looks like it," I remarked. "I notice there's a boat dock. Does Mrs. Huff have a boat?"

"Oh, yes, she has a nice big sailboat . . . a forty-eight-footer. But I haven't seen it out there for a while. She might be having some work done. I know she pulls it out of the water from time to time. Anyway, I better go before the dog gets cold."

"Right. Thanks very much. You've been very helpful."

"No problem," she said.

13

Two reproduction carriage lamps cast overlapping circles of light onto the front porch. The front door was flanked by two panels of glass. I put my cupped hands to the window on the right. I found myself peering past the foyer and down a short corridor, which seemed to open to a great room at the rear. The interior of the house had highly polished hardwood floors, bleached and then rubbed with a wash of pale gray. Doorjambs had been removed for easy wheelchair passage. A row of French doors along the rear wall allowed me to see all the way to the wood deck out back.

In the section of the great room defined by lamplight, I could see that the Oriental carpet had been laid flush with the pickled flooring. To my right, a stairway angled up to the second floor. The neighbor had mentioned a lift, but there was none in evidence. Maybe Renata had had the mechanism removed once Mr. Huff expired. I wondered if it was his passport Wendell Jaffe was using. I crossed the porch, moving right to left. From window to window, I could see the house unfold. The rooms were uncluttered, orderly, surfaces gleaming. There was a den at the front and what looked like a guest bedroom, probably with a bath attached.

I left the porch and moved along the left side of the house. The garage was locked, probably protected by the alarm system as well. I checked the gate into the backyard; it didn't seem to have a lock. I pulled a ring that had a length of string attached. The latch was released and I pushed my way in, holding my breath to see if the gate was tied to the security system. Dead silence, except for the squeaking of the gate as it swung on its hinges. I eased the gate shut behind me and moved down the narrow walkway between the garage and the fence. I could see the exhaust vent for a dryer, and I imagined the laundry room was located on the other side of the wall.

The deck was ablaze, two-hundred-watt floods creating a crazy daylight of sorts. I moved along the back of the house, peering in through the French doors. More views of the great room and the dining room next to that, with a slice of kitchen visible beyond. Oh, dear. I could see now that Renata had chosen the kind of wallpaper only decorators find attractive: a poisonous Chinese yellow with vines and puffballs exploding across the surface. There was expensive fabric to match, drapes and upholstery continuing the pattern. It was possible that a fungus had got lose in the room, replicating like a virus until every corner had been invaded. I'd seen pictures of something like this in a science magazine, mold spores blown up to nineteen hundred times their actual size.

I wandered across the deck and down the ramp to the darkened water in the marina. I turned and looked back at the house. There were no outside stairs and no visible way to reach the second-story bedrooms. I went back through the gate, letting the latch close behind me, making sure the street was clear of approaching cars. All I needed was Renata Huff returning home, headlights picking me out of the darkness as she turned into her driveway.

As I passed the mailbox at the curb, my bad angel tapped me on the shoulder and suggested a violation of U.S. postal regulations. "Would you quit that?" I said crossly. Of course, I'd already reached out and pulled the flap down, taking out the sheaf of mail that had been delivered that day. It was too dark on the street to sort out all the good stuff, so I was forced to shove the whole batch of envelopes in my handbag. God, I'm so rotten. Sometimes I can't believe the kind of shit I pull. Here I was, lying to the neighbor, stealing Renata's mail. Were there no depths to which I wouldn't sink? Apparently not. Dimly, I wondered if the penalties for mail tampering were per incident or per piece. If the latter, I was racking up a lot of jail time.

Before I headed home again, I made a detour past Dana Jaffe's house. I doused my headlights, cruising to a stop across the street from her place. I left my keys in the ignition, making my way silently across the street. All the ground-floor lights were on. Traffic at that hour was sparse to nonexistent. There were no neighbors in evidence, no dog walkers on the street. I angled my way across the grass through the darkness. Shrubs growing at the side of the house provided sufficient cover to allow me to spy without interruption. I thought I might as well add trespass and prowling to my other sins.

Dana was watching television, her face turned toward the console between the windows in front. Shifting lights played across her face as the program continued. She lit a cigarette. She sipped white wine from a glass on the table beside her. There was no sign of Wendell and nothing to suggest she had company in the house. Occasionally she would smile, perhaps in response to the canned laughter I could hear vibrating in the wall. I realized I'd been entertaining a suspicion that she was in league with him, that she knew where he was now and where he'd been all these years. Seeing her alone, I found myself dismissing the idea. I simply couldn't believe she'd collude in Wendell's abandonment of her sons. Both boys had suffered in the last five years.

I went back to my car and fired up my engine, making an illegal U-turn before I flipped on my headlights. Once I reached Santa Teresa, I stopped off at the McDonald's on Milagro and picked up a Quarter Pounder and an order of fries. For the remainder of the drive home, the air in the car was moist with the smell of steamed onions and hot pickles, meat patty nestled in melted cheese and condiments. I parked the car and toted my belated second supper with me through the squeaking back gate.

Henry's lights were out. I let myself into my apartment. I removed the Styrofoam box and set it on the counter. I opened the lid and used the top half of the container as a receptacle for my fries, taking a few minutes to bite open the handful of ketchup packets, which I squeezed over my shoestring potatoes. I perched on a bar stool, munching junk food while I sorted through the mail I'd stolen. It's hard to give up chronic thievery when my crimes net me such a bonanza of information. Purely on instinct, I'd managed to snag Renata's telephone bill with her unlisted number in a box at the top and a neatly ordered list of all the numbers from which she'd charged calls in the past thirty days. The Visa bill, a joint account, was like a little road map of places she and "Dean DeWitt Huff" had stayed. For a dead man, he was apparently having himself a fine old time. There were some nice samples of his handwriting on some of the credit card receipts. The charges from Viento Negro hadn't surfaced yet, but I could track the two of them backward from La Paz, to Cabo San Lucas, to a hotel in San Diego. All port towns easily accessible from the boat, I noticed.

I went to bed at 10:30 and slept solidly, waking at six o'clock, half a second before my alarm was set to go off. I pushed the covers aside and reached for my sweats. After hasty ablutions, I tinked down my spiral staircase and out to the street.

There was an early morning chill, but the air was curiously muggy, residual heat held in by the lowering cloud cover overhead. The early morning light was pearly. The beach looked as fine and as supple as gray leather, wrinkled by the night winds, smoothed by the surf. My cold was rapidly fading, but I didn't dare try jogging the full three miles yet. I alternated between walking and trotting, keeping track of my lungs and the creaking protests in my legs. At that hour, I tend to keep an uneasy eye out for the unexpected. I see the occasional homeless person, sexless and anonymous, sleeping in the grass, an old woman with a shopping cart alone at a picnic table. I'm especially alert to the odd-looking men in scruffy suits, gesturing, laughing, chatting with invisible companions. I'm wary of being incorporated in those strange and fearful dramas. Who knows what part we play in other people's dreams?

I showered, dressed, and ate a bowl of cereal while I scanned the paper. I drove into the office and spent a frustrating twenty minutes hunting for a parking space that wouldn't generate a ticket. I nearly had to break down and try the public lot, but I was saved at the last minute by a woman in a pickup who vacated a spot just across the street.

I went through the mail from the day before. Nothing much of interest, except the notification that I'd won a million dollars. Well, either me or the two other people mentioned. In fine print, it said that Minnie and Steve were actually already collecting their millions in $40,000 installments. I got busy and tore out perforated stamps, which I licked and pasted in various squares. I studied the material, seriously worried I might win the third prize jet ski. What the hell was I going to do with that? Maybe I'd give it to Henry for his birthday. I went ahead and balanced my checkbook, just to clear the decks. While I was eliminating some of those pesky excess dollars, I picked up the receiver and tried Renata Huff's unlisted number, without results.

Something was nagging at me, and it had nothing to do with Wendell Jaffe or Renata Huff. It was Lena Irwin's reference yesterday to the Burton Kinsey family up in Lompoc. Despite my denials, the name had set up a low hum in my memory, like the nearly inaudible buzz of power lines overhead. In many ways, my whole sense of myself was embedded in the fact of my parents' death in an automobile wreck when I was five. I knew my father had lost control of the car when a rock tumbled down a steep hill and crashed into the windshield. I was on the backseat, flung against the front seat on impact, wedged there for hours while the fire department worked to extract me from the wreckage. I remember my mother's hopeless crying and the silence that came afterward. I remember slipping a hand around the edge of the driver's seat, slipping a finger into my father's hand, not realizing he was dead. I remember going to live with the aunt who raised me after that, my mother's sister, whose name was Virginia. I called her Gin Gin or Aunt Gin. She had told me little, if anything, about the family history before or after that event. I knew, because the fact was embedded in the tale, that my parents were on their way up to Lompoc the day they were killed, but I never thought about the reason for the trip. My aunt had never told me the nature of the journey, and I'd never asked. Given my insatiable curiosity and my natural inclination to poke my nose in where it doesn't belong, it was odd to realize how little attention I'd paid to my own past. I'd simply accepted what I was told, constructing my personal mythology on the flimsiest of facts. Why had I never pushed aside that veil?

I thought about myself, about the kind of child I was when I was five and six, isolated, insular. After their deaths, I created a little world for myself in a cardboard box, filled with blankets and pillows, lighted by a table lamp with a sixty-watt bulb. I was very particular about what I ate. I would make sandwiches for myself, cheese and pickle, or Kraft olive pimento cheese, cut in four equal fingers, which I would arrange on a plate. I had to do everything myself, and it all had to be just so. Dimly, I remember my aunt hovering nearby. I wasn't aware of her worry at the time, but now when I see the image, I know she must have been deeply concerned about me. I would take my food and crawl into my container, where I would look at picture books and nibble, stare at the cardboard ceiling, hum to myself, and sleep. For four months, maybe five, I withdrew into that ecosphere of artificial warmth, that cocoon of grief. I taught myself how to read. I drew pictures, made shadow creatures with my fingers against the walls of my den. I taught myself how to tie my shoes. Perhaps I thought they'd come back for me, that mother, that father, whose faces I could project, home cinema for the orphaned, a girl child who until lately had been safely ensconced in that little family. I can still remember how cold the trailer felt whenever I crawled out. My aunt never interfered with me. When school started in the fall, I emerged like a little animal coming out of its lair. Kindergarten was fearful. I wasn't used to other children. I wasn't accustomed to noise or to regimentation. I didn't like Mrs. Bowman, the teacher, in whose eyes I could read both pity and disapproval, that judgment. I was an odd child. I was timid. I was anxious all the time. Nothing I've faced since has even come close to the horrors of grade school. I can see now how the story, whatever it was, must have followed me like a specter from level to level: penned in my record, appended to my file, from teacher to teacher, through conferences with the principal . . . what shall we do with her? How shall we cope with her tears and her stoniness? So bright, so fragile, stubborn, introverted, asocial, easily upset . . .

When the phone rang I jumped, adrenaline washing through me like a blast of ice water. I snatched up the receiver, my heart thudding in my throat. "Kinsey Millhone Investigations."

"Hello, Kinsey. This is Tommy down at the Perdido County Jail. Brian Jaffe's attorney just notified our office that you can talk to him if you want. He didn't sound too happy about it, but I guess Mrs. Jaffe insisted."

"She did?" I said, unable to disguise my astonishment.

He laughed. "Maybe she thinks you'll go to bat for him, clear up this misunderstanding about the jailbreak and the little gal who got shot to death."

"Yeah, right," I said. "When should I come down?"

"Any time you want."

"What's the protocol on this? Shall I ask for you?"

"Ask for the senior deputy. Name's Roger Tiller. He knew the Jaffe kid back when he was working truancy patrol. I thought you might like to pick his brain."

"That's great."

Before I could thank him properly, the phone clicked in my ear. I was smiling to myself as I snagged my handbag and headed for the door. The nice thing about cops—once they decide you're okay, there's nobody more generous.

. . .

Deputy Tiller and I traversed the corridor, our footsteps out of synch, keys jingling as he walked. The camera up in the corner was keeping track of us. He was older than I'd expected, in his late fifties and heavyset, his uniform fitting snugly on a five-foot-eight frame. I had a quick vision of him at the end of a shift, stripping off his clothes with relief, like a woman peeling off a girdle. His body probably bore the permanent marks of all the buckles and apparatus. His sandy hair was receding, and he had a sandy mustache to match, green eyes, a pug nose, the kind of face that would have seemed appropriate on a kid of twenty-two. His heavy leather belt was making creaking sounds, and I noticed that his posture and his manner changed when he got in range of an inmate. A small group of them, five, were waiting to be buzzed through a metal door with a glass window embedded with chicken wire. Latinos, in their twenties, they wore jail blues and white T-shirts, rubber sandals. In accordance with regulations, they were silent, their hands clasped behind their backs. White wristbands indicated that they were GP, general population, incarcerated because of DUIs and crimes against property.

I said, "Sergeant Ryckman says you met Brian Jaffe when you were working truancy patrol. How long ago was that?"

"Five years. Kid was twelve, ornery as hell. I remember one day I picked him up and took him back to school three different times. I can't even tell you how many meetings we scheduled with the student study team. School psychologist finally threw her hands up. I felt sorry for his mother. We all knew what she was going through. He's a bad apple. Smart, good-looking, had a mouth on him wouldn't quit." Deputy Tiller shook his head.

"Did you ever meet his father?"

"Yeah, I knew Wendell." He tended to talk without making eye contact, and the effect was curious.

Since that subject seemed to go nowhere, I tried another tack. "How'd you get from truancy patrol to this?"

"Applied for administrative position. To be eligible for promotion, everybody gets a year's tour of jail duty. It's the pits. I like the people well enough, but you spend the whole day in artificial light.

Like living in a cave. All this filtered air. I'd rather be out on the streets. Little danger never hurts. Helps keep your juices up." We paused in front of a freight-size elevator.

"I understand Brian escaped from juvenile hall. What was he in for?"

Deputy Tiller pressed a button and made a verbal request to have the elevator take us up to level two, where inmates designated as administrative segregation or medical were housed. The elevators themselves were devoid of interior controls, which effectively prevented their being commandeered by inmates. "Burglary, exhibiting or drawing a firearm, resisting arrest. He was actually being held in Connaught, which is medium security. These days, juvenile hall's maximum security."

"That's a switch, isn't it? I thought juvenile hall was for out-of-control minors."

"Not anymore. Old days, those kids were known as 'status offenders.' Parents could have 'em made wards of the court. Now, juvenile hall's turned into a junior prison. Kids are hard-core criminals. Three M's. Murder, mayhem, and manslaughter, lot of gang-related stuff."

"What about Jaffe? What's the story on him?"

"Kid's got no soul. You'll see it in his eyes. Completely empty in there. He's got brains, but no conscience. He's a sociopath. Our best information, it was him engineered the breakout, talked the gangbangers into it because he needed someone to speak Spanish. Once they crossed the border, the plan was they'd split up. I don't know where he was headed, but the others ended up dead."

"All three? I thought the one kid survived the shoot-out."

"Died last night without regaining consciousness."

"What about the girl? Who was responsible for her death?"

"You'd have to ask Jaffe about that since he's the only one left. Real convenient for him, and believe me, he'll take advantage of it." We'd reached the interview room on level two. Tiller took out a ring of keys and turned one in the lock. He pulled the door open on the empty room where I was to meet with Brian. "I used to think these kids could be salvaged if we did our job right. Now seems like we're just lucky to keep 'em off the streets." He shook his head, and his smile was bitter. "I'm getting too old for this stuff. Time to go shuffle me some paperwork. Have a seat. Your boy'll be here in just a minute."

The interview room was six feet by eight with no outside windows. The walls were unadorned, a semigloss beige. I could still smell the lingering odor of latex paint. I've heard there's a full-time crew whose sole job is to repaint. By the time they complete the work up on level four, it's time to go back to level one and start all over again. There was one small wooden table and two chairs with metal frames, the seats padded in green vinyl. The floor tiles were brown. There was nothing else in the room except the video camera mounted in one corner near the ceiling. I took the chair that faced the open door.

When Brian entered the room, I was surprised first by his size and second by his beauty. For eighteen he was small, and his manner seemed tentative. I'd seen eyes like his before, very clear, very blue, filled with an aching innocence. My ex-husband, Daniel, had a similar characteristic, some aspect of his nature that seemed unbearably sweet. Of course, Daniel was a drug addict. Also a liar and a cheat, in full possession of his faculties, and bright enough to know the differences between right and wrong. This kid was something else. Deputy Tiller claimed he was a sociopath, but I wasn't sure about that yet. He had Michael's pretty features, but he was blond where his brother was dark. Both were lean, though Michael was the taller and he seemed more substantial.

Brian sat down, slouching on his chair, hands held loosely between his knees. He seemed shy, but maybe that was just a trait he affected . . . sucking up to adults. "I talked to my mom. She said you might be in to see me."

"Did she tell you what I wanted?"

"Just something about my dad. She says he might be okay. Is that true?"

"We don't really know at this point. I was hired to find out."

"Did you know my dad? I mean, like before he disappeared?"

I shook my head. "I never met him. I was given some photographs and told where he'd been seen last. I did run into a guy who looked a lot like him, but then he disappeared again. I'm still hoping to track him down, but right now, I don't have any leads. Personally, I'm convinced it was him," I said.

"That's incredible, isn't it? To think he might be alive? I can't get over it. I mean, I don't even know what that'd be like." He had a full mouth and dimples. I found it hard to imagine he could fake such ingenuousness.

I said, "It must seem weird."

"Hey, no lie . . . with all this stuff going down? I wouldn't want him to see me like this."

I shrugged. "If he comes back to town, he'll probably be in trouble himself."

"Yeah, that's what Mom said. She didn't seem all that happy. I guess I can't blame her after what she went through. Like, if he's been alive this whole time, it means he laid a bum deal on her."

"You remember much about him?"

"Not really. Michael does, my brother. Did you meet him?"

"Briefly. At your mother's."

"Did you see my nephew, Brendan? He's really cool. I miss him, little pea-head."

Enough of this chitchat. I was getting restless. "Mind if I ask you about Mexicali?"

He shifted uncomfortably. He ran a hand through his hair. "Man, that was bad. Makes me sick to think of it. I didn't have anything to do with killing anybody, I swear. It was Julio and Ricardo had the gun," he said.

"What about the breakout? How did that come to pass?"

"Uhm, hey, you know? Like, I don't think my attorney wants me to talk about that."

"I just have a couple of questions . . . in strictest confidence. I'm trying to get a feel for what's going on here," I said. "Whatever you say goes no further."

"I better not," he murmured.

"Was it your idea?"

"Heck no, not me. You probably think I'm a jerk. I was stupid to go along with it . . . I can see that now . . . but at the time I just wanted to get out. I was desperate. You ever been in juvie?"

I shook my head.

"You're lucky."

I said, "Whose idea was it?"

He gave me a direct look, his blue eyes as clear as a swimming pool. "It was Earnesto came up with it."

"Were you pretty good friends?"

"No way! I only knew 'em because we were all in the same cottage at Connaught. That guy, Julio, said he'd kill me if I didn't help. I wasn't going to do it. I mean, I didn't want to go along with it, but he was big . . . real big guy . . . and he said he'd mess me up bad."

"He threatened you."

"Yeah, he said him and Ricardo would turn me out."

"Meaning sexual abuse."

"The worst," he said.

"Why you?"

"Why me?"

"Yeah. What made you so valuable to the enterprise? Why not another Hispanic if they were headed into Mexico?"

He shrugged. "Those guys are twisted. Who knows how they think?"

"What were you planning to do down in Mexico if you didn't speak the language?"

"Bum around. Hide. Cross back into Texas. Mostly I just wanted to get out of California. Court system here is not exactly on my side."

The jail officer knocked, indicating time was up.

Something about Brian's smile had already caused me to disconnect. I'm a liar by nature, a modest talent of mine, but one I cultivate. I probably know more about bullshit than half the people on the planet. If this kid was telling the truth, I didn't think he'd sound nearly so sincere.

14

On the way back to the office, I stopped off at the Hall of Records, which is located in one wing of the Santa Teresa Courthouse. The courthouse itself was reconstructed in the late 1920s after the 1925 earthquake destroyed the existing courthouse as well as a number of commercial buildings downtown. Hammered copper plates on the doors to the Hall of Records depict an allegorical history of the state of California. I pushed through the entrance doors into a large space, dissected by a counter. To the right, a small reception area was furnished by two heavy oak tables with matching leather chairs. The floors were tiled in polished dark red paving stones, the high ceilings painted with faded blue-and-gold designs. Thick beams bore the echo of the repetitive patterns. Graceful wooden columns were visible at intervals, topped with Ionic capitals, again painted in muted hues. The windows were arched, the leaded-glass panes pierced with rows of linked circles. The actual work of the department was accomplished with the aid of technology: action stations, telephones, computers, microfilm projectors. As a further concession to the present, sections of the walls had been paneled with the soundproofing equivalent of pegboard.

I kept my mind blank, struggling with a curious resistance to the piece of digging I was about to do. There were several people at the counter, and for one brief moment I considered postponing the chore until some other day. Then another clerk appeared, a tall, lean fellow in slacks and a short-sleeved dress shirt, wearing a pair of glasses with one opaque lens. "Help you?"

"I'd like to check your records for a marriage license issued in November of 1935."

"The name?" he asked.

"Millhone, Terrence Randall. Do you need her name as well?"

He made a note. "This will do."

He pushed a form across the counter, and I filled in the blanks, reassuring the county about my purposes in asking. It was a silly formality in my opinion since births, deaths, marriages, and property recordings are a matter of public record. The filing system in use was called Soundex, a curious process whereby the vowels in the last name are eliminated altogether and consonants are awarded various numerical values. The clerk helped me convert the name Millhone to its Soundex equivalent, and then he sent me over to an old-fashioned card catalog where I found my parents listed, along with the date of their marriage, and the book and page numbers of the volume where the license was recorded. I returned to the counter with the information in hand. The clerk made a call to some web-footed creature in the bowels of the building, whose job it was to conjure up the relevant records consigned to cassettes.

The clerk sat me down at the microfilm machine, rattling off a rapid series of instructions, half of which I missed. It didn't matter much, as he proceeded to turn the machine on and insert the cassette while he was telling me how to do it. Finally he left me to fast-forward my way through the bulk of the reel to the document in question. Suddenly, there they were—names and incidental personal data neatly entered into a record nearly fifty years old. Terrence Randall Millhone of Santa Teresa, California, and Rita Cynthia Kinsey of Lompoc, California, had married on November 18, 1935. He was thirty-three years old at the time of the wedding and listed his occupation as mail carrier. His father's name was Quillen Millhone. His mother's maiden name was Dace. Rita Kinsey was eighteen at the time of her marriage, occupation unlisted, daughter of Burton Kinsey and Cornelia Straith LaGrand. They were married by a Judge Stone of the Perdido Court of Appeal in a ceremony that took place in Santa Teresa at four in the afternoon. The witness who signed the form was Virginia Kinsey, my aunt Gin. So there they were, those three, standing together in the public register, not knowing that in twenty years husband and wife would be gone. As far as I knew there were no photographs of the wedding, no mementos of any kind. I'd seen only one or two pictures taken of them in later years. Somewhere I had a handful of snapshots of my babyhood and early childhood, but there were none of their respective families. I realized what a vacuum I'd been living in. Where other people had anecdotes, photograph albums, correspondence, family gatherings, all the trappings of family tradition, I had little or nothing to report. The notion of my mother's family, the Burton Kinseys, still residing up in Lompoc conjured up curious emotional contradictions. And what of my father's people? I'd never heard any mention of the Millhones at all.

I felt a sudden shift in my perspective. I could see in a flash what a strange pleasure I'd taken in being related to no one. I'd actually managed to feel superior about my isolation. I was subtle about it, but I could see that I'd turned it into a form of self-congratulation. *I* wasn't the common product of the middle class. I wasn't a party to any convoluted family drama—the feuds, unspoken alliances, secret agreements, and petty tyrannies. Of course, I wasn't a party to the good stuff, either, but who cared about that? I was different. I was special. At best, I was self-created; at worst, the hapless artifact of my aunt's peculiar notions about raising little girls. In either event, I regarded myself an outsider, a loner, which suited me to perfection. Now I had to consider the possibility of this unknown family unit . . . whether I would claim them or they would claim me.

I rewound the reel of film and took the cassette up to the counter. I left the building and crossed the street, heading toward the three-story parking structure where I'd left my car. On my right was the public library, where I knew I could rustle up the Lompoc phone book if I was interested. But was I? Reluctantly I paused, debating the issue. It's only information, I said to myself. You don't have to make a decision, you just need to know.

I took a right, going up the outside stairs and into the building. I turned right again, pushing through the turnstiles designed to capture book thieves. The city directories and various telephone books from towns all across the state were shelved on the first floor to the left of the reference desk. I found the telephone book for Lompoc and leafed through the pages where I stood. I didn't want to act as if I cared enough to sit.

There was only one "Kinsey" listed, not Burton but Cornelia, my mother's mother, with the telephone number but no address. I found the Polk Directory for Lompoc and Vandenberg Air Force Base, checking the section where the telephone numbers were listed in order, beginning with the prefix. Cornelia was listed with an address on Willow Avenue. I checked the Polk Directory for the year before and saw that Burton was listed with her. The obvious inference was that she'd been widowed sometime between this year's census and the last. Terrific. What a deal. First time I find out I have a grandfather, he's dead. I made a note of the address on one of the deposit slips at the back of my checkbook. Half the people I know use deposit slips in lieu of business cards. Why don't banks add a few blanks back there for memos? I shoved the checkbook in my bag again and resolutely forgot about it. Later, I'd decide what I wanted to do.

I went back to the law office and let myself in the side entrance. When I opened my door, I found the message light blinking on my answering machine. I pressed the playback button and then went about the business of opening a window while I listened.

"Miss Millhone, this is Harris Brown. I'm a retired Santa Teresa police lieutenant and I just got a call from Lieutenant Whiteside over there who tells me you're trying to locate Wendell Jaffe. As I believe he mentioned, that was one of the last cases I worked before I left the department, and I'd be happy to discuss some of the details with you if you'll give me a call. I'll be in and out this afternoon, but you can probably reach me between two and three-fifteen at . . . ."

I snatched up a pen and caught the number as he recited it. I checked my watch. Poot. It was only twelve forty-five. I tried the number anyway on the off chance he'd be there. No such luck. I tried Renata Huff again, but she wasn't home, either. I still had my hand on the receiver when the phone rang. "Kinsey Millhone Investigations," I said.

"May I speak to Mrs. Millhome?" some woman asked in a singsong voice.

"This is she," I replied with caution. This was going to be a pitch.

"Mrs. Millhome, this is Patty Kravitz with Telemarketing Incorporated? How are you today?" She'd been instructed to smile at this point so her voice would sound very warm and friendly.

I ran my tongue along the inside of my cheek. "Fine. What about yourself?"

"That's good. Mrs. Millhome, we know you're a busy person, but we're conducting a survey for an exciting new product and wonder if you could take a few minutes to answer some questions. If you're willing to assist us, we have a nice prize already set aside for you. Can we count on your help?"

I could hear the babble of other voices in the boiler room behind her. "What's the product?"

"I'm sorry, but we're not allowed to divulge that information. I *am* permitted to indicate that this is an airline-related service and within the next few months will result in the introduction of an innovative new concept in business and leisure travel. Can we take just a few minutes out of your busy schedule?"

"Sure, why not?"

"That's good. Now, Mrs. Millhome, are you single, married, divorced, or widowed?"

I was really liking her sincere, spontaneous manner as she read from the laminated card in front of her. I said, "Widowed."

"I'm sorry to hear that," she said in a perfunctory manner as she breezed right on. "Do you own your home or rent?"

"Well, I used to own two homes," I said casually. "One here in Santa Teresa and one in Fort Myers, Florida, but now that John's passed away, I've had to sell the property down there. The only place I rent is an apartment in New York City."

"Really."

"I do quite a bit of traveling. That's why I'm helping you with the research," I said. I could practically hear her making frantic flagging motions to her supervisor. She had a live one on the line, and she might need help.

We moved on to the matter of my annual income, which I knew would be substantial with that extra million coming in. I proceeded to lie, fib, and equivocate, amusing myself with the questions while I honed my prevarication skills. We quickly worked our way down to the part where I only needed to write a check for $39.99 to claim the prize I'd won: a complete nine-piece set of matching designer luggage, retailing for over $600.00 in most department stores.

My turn to be skeptical. "You're kidding," I said. "And this is not a gimmick? All I pay is thirty-nine ninety-nine? I don't believe it."

She assured me the offer was genuine. The luggage was absolutely free. All I was being asked to cover was the shipping and handling, which I could also charge to my credit card if that was more convenient. She offered to send someone over to pick up the check within the hour, but I thought it was easier to go ahead and put it on my card. I gave her the account number, inventing a nice series of digits, which she dutifully read back to me. I could tell from her tone of voice she could hardly believe her good luck. I was probably the only person that day who hadn't damaged her hearing by promptly hanging up. Before the end of the business day, she and her cronies would be trying to charge off merchandise to that account.

For lunch I ate a carton of nonfat yogurt at my desk and then took a nap, leaning back in my chair. In between car chases and gun battles, we private eye types have occasional days like this. At two I roused myself, reaching over to pluck up the phone, trying Harris Brown again.

The number rang four times and then somebody picked up. "Harris Brown," he said, sounding cranky and out of breath.

I took my feet off the desk and introduced myself.

His tone underwent a shift and his interest picked up. "I'm glad you called. I was surprised to hear the guy had surfaced."

"Well, we still don't have confirmation, but it's looking good to me. How long did you work the case?"

"Oh, geez, probably seven months. I never for a minute believed he was dead, but I had a hell of a time convincing anyone else. I never did manage it, as a matter of fact. It's nice to have an old hunch confirmed. Anyway, tell me what kind of help you need."

"I'm not sure yet. I guess I was hoping to brainstorm," I said. "I've got a line on the woman he was traveling with, a gal named Renata Huff, who has a house down on the Perdido Keys."

He seemed startled by the information. "Where'd you come up with that one?"

"Uhm, I'd prefer not to spell it out. Let's just say I have my little ways," I said.

"Sounds like you're doing pretty good."

"Working on it," I said. "The problem is she's the only lead I have, and I can't figure out who else he'd turn to for help."

"To do what?"

I could feel myself backpedal, uncomfortable articulating my theory about Wendell. "Well, I hesitate to say this, but my hit on this is he heard about Brian . . ."

"The escape and shoot-out."

"Right. I think he's coming back to help his kid."

There was a fractional silence. "Help him how?"

"I don't know yet. I just can't think of any other reason he'd risk coming back."

"I might buy that," he said after giving it some thought. "So you're figuring he'd either contact close family or old pals of his."

"Exactly. I know who his ex-wife is and I've talked to her, but she doesn't seem to have a clue."

"And you believe that."

"Actually, I'm inclined to. I think she's being straight."

"Go on. I'm sorry to interrupt."

"Anyway, when it comes to Wendell, mostly I'm sitting around hoping he'll show his face, which he doesn't seem to be doing. I thought if we could sit down together, we might come up with some other possibilities. Could I impose on your time?"

"I'm retired now, Miss Millhone. Time is all I've got. Unfortunately, I'm tied up this afternoon. Tomorrow's fine if that suits."

"Looks good to me. What about lunch? Are you free by any chance?"

"That'd be doable," he said. "Where are you?"

I gave him my office address.

He said, "I'm out here in Colgate, but I have an errand in town. Is there someplace we can meet?"

"Whatever's convenient for you."

He suggested a large coffee shop on upper State, not the best place for food, but I knew we wouldn't need reservations for lunch. I made a note on my calendar when I hung up the phone. On a whim, I tried Renata's number.

Two rings. She picked up.

Oh, shit, I thought. "May I speak to Mr. Huff?"

"He's not here at the moment. Would you care to leave a message?"

"Is this Mrs. Huff?"

"Yes."

I tried a smile. "Mrs. Huff, this is Patty Kravitz with Telemarketing Incorporated? How are you today?"

"Is this a sales pitch?"

"Absolutely not, Mrs. Huff. I can guarantee it. We're doing market research. The company I work for is interested in your leisure pursuits and discretionary spending. These forms are filed by number, so your answers are completely anonymous. In return for your cooperation, we have a nice prize already set aside."

"Oh, right. I bet."

Jesus, this lady wasn't very trusting. I said, "It will only take five minutes of your valuable time." Then I kept my mouth shut and let her work it out on her end.

"All right, but make it brief, and if it turns out you're selling something, I'm going to be annoyed."

"I understand that. Now, Mrs. Huff, are you single, married, divorced, or widowed?" I picked up a pencil and started doodling on a legal pad, thinking ahead frantically. What did I really hope to learn from her?

"Married."

"And do you own or rent your home?"

"What does this have to do with travel?"

"I'm getting to that. Is this a primary or vacation residence?"

Mollified. "Oh, I see. It's primary."

"And how many trips have you taken in the past six months? None, one to three, or more than three?"

"One to three."

"Of the trips taken in the past six months, what percentage were business?"

"Look, would you just get to the point?"

"Fine. No problem. We'll just skip some of these. Do you or your husband have plans to travel any time in the next few weeks?"

Dead silence.

I said, "Hello?"

"Why do you ask?"

"Actually, that brings us to the end of my questionnaire, Mrs. Huff," I said, speaking rapidly and smoothly. "As a special thank-you, we'd like to provide you, at no cost, two round-trip tickets to San Francisco and two nights, all expenses paid, at the Hyatt Hotel. Will your husband be home soon to accept the complimentary tickets? There's absolutely no obligation on your part, but he *will* have to sign for them since the survey was in his name. Can I indicate to my supervisor when you might like to have us drop those off?"

"This is not going to work," she said, her voice tinged with irritation. "We expect to be leaving town momentarily, as soon as . . . I'm not sure when he'll be here and we're not interested." With a click, she disconnected.

Shit! I banged the phone down on my end. Where was the man, and what was he up to that might "momentarily" motivate his departure from Perdido? Nobody'd heard from him. At least, nobody *I* knew of. I couldn't believe he'd talked to Carl Eckert, unless he'd done so within the last half day. As nearly as I could tell, he hadn't been in touch with Dana or Brian. I wasn't sure about Michael. I'd probably have to check that out.

What the hell was Wendell doing? Why would he come this close to his family without making contact? Of course, it was always possible he'd managed to talk to all three of them, and if that was the case, they were better liars than I was. Maybe it was time for the cops to put a tail on Renata Huff. And it might not hurt to run Wendell's picture in the local papers. As long as he was running, we might as well sic the dogs on him. Meanwhile, come suppertime, I was going to have to make yet another trip to Perdido.

15

I set out for Perdido again after supper that evening. The drive was pleasant, the light at that hour a tawny yellow, gilding the south-facing mountain ridges in gold leaf. As I passed Rincon Point, I could still see surfers out in the water. Most were straddling their boards, rocking in the low swell, chatting while they waited, ever hopeful, for a wave. The surf was mild for the moment, but the weather map in the morning paper had showed an eastern Pacific hurricane off the California Baja, and there was talk that the storm system was moving up the coast. I noticed then that the horizon was rimmed with black clouds like a row of brushes, sweeping a premature darkness in our direction. The Rincon, with its rocky projection and its offshore shoals, seems to act like a magnet for turbulent weather.

Rincón is the Spanish term for the cove formed by a land point projecting seaward. Here, the coastline is molded into a series of such indentations, and for a stretch, the ocean butts right up against the roadway. At high tide the waves erupt along the embankment, sending up a white wall of frustrated water. Beyond, on my left, fields of flowers had been cultivated on several terraces where the underlying earth was slumping toward the sea. The vibrant red, gold, and magenta of the zinnias glowed in the half-light as if illuminated from below.

It was just after 7:00 when I left Highway 101 at Perdido Street. I sailed through the light at the intersection and crossed Main Street on a northbound path that cut through the Boulevards. I turned left at Median and pulled over to the curb about six houses down. Michael's yellow VW bug was parked in the driveway. The windows along the front of the house were dark, but I could see lights on in the rear, where I imagined the kitchen and one of the two bedrooms.

I knocked at the front door, waiting on the small front porch until Michael responded. He'd changed from his work clothes into stone-washed denim coveralls, the sort of outfit a plumber wears when he's crawling under the house. Having so recently met Brian, I was struck by the similarities. One was blond, one brunette, but both had inherited Dana's sultry mouth and fine features. Michael must have expected me because he evidenced no surprise at my standing on his doorstep.

"Mind if I come in?"

"If you want. Place is a mess."

"That's all right," I replied.

I followed him through the house, moving toward the rear. The living room and the kitchen were still furnished with opened but largely unpacked moving cartons, clouds of crumpled newspaper boiling out of boxes onto the floor.

Michael and Juliet had taken refuge in the larger of the two small bedrooms, a nine-by-twelve space dominated by a king-size bed and a big color television set currently tuned to a baseball game that I gathered was being played in Los Angeles. Pizza boxes, take-out cartons, and soft-drink cans were crowded together on the surface of the dresser and atop the chest of drawers. The whole place had the air of a hostage situation where the cops were sending in fast food to satisfy the terrorists' demands. Everything was untidy, smelling of damp towels, french fries, cigarette smoke, and men's athletic socks. There were wads of Pampers in the trash, a flip-top plastic waste bin with used diapers bulging out.

Michael, his attention focused on the TV set, perched himself on the edge of the king-size bed, where Juliet was stretched out with a copy of *Cosmopolitan.* A half-filled ashtray rested on the spread beside her. She was barefoot, wearing short shorts and a fuchsia tank top. She couldn't have been more than eighteen or nineteen and had already dropped any excess weight she might have picked up during pregnancy. Her hair was chopped short, a crew cut cropped close around the ears in a style the average man hasn't worn for years. If I hadn't known better, I'd have assumed she'd just joined the service and was off to boot camp. Her face was freckled, her blue eyes lined darkly with black, lashes beaded with mascara. Her upper lids were two-toned, blue and green. She wore big dangle earrings, jaunty hoops of pink plastic, apparently purchased to match her tank top. She set the magazine aside, visibly irritated by the volume on the TV set. The picture switched to a cheap-looking commercial for a local car dealership. The jingle blasting out sounded like it had been especially written by the wife of the company president. "God, Michael. Could you turn that fuckin' thing down? What's the matter with you, are you deaf or what?"

Michael pushed the volume button on the remote control. The sound dropped to something slightly less than the levels required for ultrasonic brain surgery. Neither seemed to react to my arrival. I thought I could probably plop down on the bed and join them for the evening without attracting much notice. Juliet finally slid a look in my direction, and Michael made the formal introduction halfheartedly. "This is Kinsey Millhone. She's the private detective looking for my dad." With a nod at her, he added, "This's my wife, Juliet."

I gave Juliet a murmured, "Hi, how are you?"

"Nice to meet you," she said, her eyes already straying back to her magazine. I couldn't help noticing that I was competing for her attention with an article about how to be a good listener. She felt for the pack of cigarettes lying near her on the bed. She explored with her index finger, picked up the pack, and peered in. She made a moue of exasperation when she realized it was empty. I found myself transfixed by the sight of her. With that marine corps haircut, she looked like a teenaged boy in eye shadow and dangle earrings. She nudged Michael with her foot. "I thought you said you're going up to the corner for me. I'm out of cigarettes and the baby needs Pampers. Could you make a run? Please, please, please?"

On the television screen, baseball play was resuming. His sole function as a husband seemed to be fetching cigarettes and Pampers. I gave this marriage another ten months at best. By then she'd be bored with all these nights at home. Oddly enough, as young as Michael was, he struck me as the sort who could really make a go of it. Juliet was the one who'd be testy and petulant, opting out on her responsibilities until the relationship fell apart. Dana would probably end up taking care of the baby.

Michael, his attention still riveted to the set, made a vague reply unattended by any actual move to get up, a fact not lost on her. He was fiddling with the Cottonwood Academy class ring his mother had given him, turning it around and around.

"Mike-cull, if Brendan pees again, what am I supposed to do? I just used the last diaper."

"Hey, yeah, babe. Just a sec, okay?"

Juliet's face got all pouty and she rolled her eyes.

He glanced back at her, sensing her irritation with him. "I can go in a minute. Is the baby asleep? Mom wanted her to see him."

Startled, I realized the "her" referred to me.

Juliet swung her feet over to the side of the bed. "I don't know. I can check. I just put him down a little while ago. He hardly ever goes to sleep with the TV so loud." She got up and crossed the room, moving toward the narrow hallway between bedrooms. I followed, trying quickly to think of a generic baby compliment in case the kid turned out to have a pointy head.

I said, "I better keep my distance. I don't want him to catch my cold or anything." Sometimes mothers actually wanted you to *hold* the little buggers.

Juliet leaned around the door frame into the smaller of the two bedrooms. A wall of cardboard wardrobe cartons had been shoved into the room, all packed with heavily laden hangers dragging at the metal bars affixed across the tops. The baby's crib had been placed in the center of this fortress of wrinkled cottons and winter clothing. Somehow I pictured the room looking just like this many months from now. It did seem quieter in this jungle of old overcoats, and I imagined in time Brendan would get used to the smell of mothballs and matted wool. One whiff in later life and he'd feel like Marcel Proust. I lifted up on tiptoe, looking over Juliet's shoulder.

Brendan was sitting bolt upright, his gaze pinned on the doorway as if he knew she'd come to fetch him. He was one of those exquisite babies you see in magazine ads: plump and perfect with big blue eyes, two little teeth showing in his lower gum, dimples in his cheeks. He was wearing blue flannel sleepers with rubber-soled feet, his arms held out on either side of his body for balance. His hands seemed to wave randomly like little digital antennae, picking up signals from the outside world. The minute he caught sight of Juliet, his face was wreathed in smiles and his arms began an agitated pumping motion, indicating much baby joy. Juliet's face lost its sullen cast and she greeted him in some privately generated mother tongue. He blew bubbles, flirting and drooling. When she picked him up, he buried his face against her shoulder, bunching his knees up in a squirm of happiness. It was the only moment in recorded history when I found myself wishing I had a critter like that.

Juliet was beaming. "Isn't he beautiful?"

"He's pretty cute," I said.

"Michael doesn't even try to pick him up these days," she said. "This age, he's suddenly very possessive of me. I swear, it just happened a week ago. He used to go right to his daddy without a murmur. Now if I'm about to hand him to anyone else? You ought to see his face. His mouth gets all puckery and his chin starts to tremble. And the wailing, my Lord. He's so pitiful, it would break your heart. Dis little guy wuves his mudder," Juliet went on. Brendan reached a plump hand forward and stuck some fingers in her mouth. She pretended to bite, which stimulated a low throaty chuckle from the child in her arms. Her expression changed, nose wrinkling. "Oh, God, does he have a load in his drawers?" She stuck an index finger into the back rim of his diaper, peering into the gap. "Mike-cull?"

"What?"

She moved back toward the bedroom. "Would you just one time do like I ask? The baby pooped his pants and I'm out of Pampers. I told you that twice."

Michael got up obediently, his eyes still pinned to the television screen. Another commercial came on, and the shift seemed to break the spell.

"Sometime tonight, okay?" she said, hefting the baby on one hip.

Michael reached for his windbreaker, which he snatched from a pile of clothes on the floor. "I'll be right back," he said to no one in particular. As he hunched into his jacket, I realized it would be the perfect opportunity to talk to him.

"Why don't I go, too?" I said.

"Fine with me," he said with a look at Juliet. "You need anything else?"

She shook her head, watching a crew of cartoon bite-'ems demolish grunge from a dinner plate. I would have bet money she hadn't gotten the hang of washing dishes yet.

Once we were out on the street, Michael walked rapidly, head bent, hands in his jacket pockets. He was easily a foot taller, with a loose-limbed gait. The approaching storm had darkened the sky overhead, and a tropical breeze sent leaves scuttling along the gutters. The paper had warned that the system was weakening and would probably bring us little more than drizzle. The air was already turbulent, erratic, and humid, the sky charcoal blue where it should have been pale. Michael lifted his face, and the promise of rain seemed to buffet his cheeks.

I found myself trotting to keep up with him. "Could you slow down a little bit?"

"Sorry," he said, and cut his pace by a third.

The Stop 'N' Go was at the corner, maybe two blocks away. I could see the lights ahead of us, though the street itself was dark. Every third or fourth house we passed would have the porch lights on. Low-voltage lamps picked out the path of a front walk or an illuminated ornamental shrub. Supper smells still lingered in the chill night air: the aroma of baked potatoes and meat loaf with a barbecue sauce on top, oven-fried chicken, sweet-and-sour pork chops. I knew I'd already eaten supper, but I was hungry anyway. "I'm assuming you know your father might be heading back to town," I said to Michael, trying to distract myself.

"Mom told me that."

"You have any idea what you'll do if he gets in touch?"

"Talk to him, I guess. Why? What am I supposed to do?"

"There's still a warrant out for his arrest," I said.

Michael snorted. "Oh, great. Snitch on your dad. You haven't seen him for years, first thing you do is call the cops."

"It does sound shitty, doesn't it?"

"Doesn't just *sound* like that. It *is*."

"Do you remember much about him?"

Michael lifted one shoulder. "I was seventeen when he left. I remember Mom cried a lot and we got to stay home from school for two days. I try not to think about the rest of it. I tell you one thing, I used to think, 'Hey, so my old man killed himself . . . what's the big deal,' you know? Then I had *my* son, and it changed my attitude. I couldn't leave that little guy. I couldn't do that to him, and now I wonder how Dad could have done it to me. What kind of turd is he, do you know what I mean? Me and Brian both. We were good kids, I swear."

"Sounds like Brian was devastated."

"Yeah, that's true. Brian always acted like it didn't matter, but I know he took it hard. Most of it rolled right offa me."

"Your brother was twelve?"

"Right. I was a senior in high school. He was in the sixth grade. Kids are mean at that age."

"Kids are mean at any age," I said. "Your mother tells me Brian started getting into trouble about then."

"I guess."

"What sort of things did he do?"

"I don't know, petty stuff . . . . skipping school, marking on the walls with spray paint, fistfights, but he was just messing around. He didn't mean anything by it. I'm not saying it was right, but everybody made such a goddamn big deal out of it. Right away they're treating him like a criminal or something, and he's just a *kid.* Lot of boys that age get in trouble, you know what I mean? He was horsing around and he got caught. That's the only difference. I did the same thing when I was his age and nobody called me a 'juvenile delinquent.' And don't give me that junk about 'a cry for help.' "

"I never said a word. I'm just listening."

"Anyway, I feel sorry for him. Once people think you're bad, you might as well be bad. It's more fun than being good."

"I can't think Brian's having any fun where he is."

"I don't know what the story is on that. Brian's talked about that one guy, Guevara I think his name is. He's a real bad dude. They were in the same quad at one point, and Brian said he was always pulling shit, trying to get him in trouble with the deputies. He's the one talked him into busting out."

"Somebody told me yesterday he died."

"Serves him right."

"I take it you've talked to Brian since he got back. Your mother was in for a visit and so was I."

"Just on the phone, so he couldn't say much. Mostly he said don't believe nothin' until I heard it from him. He's burnt."

" 'Burnt' meaning what?"

"What? Oh. He's mad. Judge charged him with escape, robbery, grand theft auto, and felony murder. Can you believe it? What a crocka shit. Busting out of jail wasn't even his idea."

"Why'd he do it, then?"

"They threatened his life! Said if he didn't go with 'em, they were going to kill his ass. He was like a hostage, you know?"

"I didn't realize that," I said, trying to keep my tone neutral. Michael was so busy defending his brother, he didn't seem to catch the skepticism.

"It's the truth. Brian swears. He says Julio Rodriguez shot the lady on the road. He never killed anyone. Said the whole thing made him sick. He had no idea them beaners were going to pull that kind of shit. Premeditated murder. Jesus, come *on.*"

"Michael, that woman was killed in the perpetration of a felony, which automatically elevates the charge to murder one. Even if your brother never touched the gun, he's considered an accomplice."

"But that doesn't make him *guilty.* Whole time he was trying to get away."

I bit back the impulse to argue. I could tell he was getting irritated, and I knew I shouldn't push it if I wanted his cooperation. "I guess his attorney will have to sort that out." I decided I better shift the conversation onto neutral ground. "What about you? What sort of work do you do?"

"I work construction, finally making pretty good money. Mom wants me to go to college, but I can't see the point. With Brendan so little, I don't want Juliet to have to work. I don't know what kind of job she could get anyway. She finished high school, but she'd couldn't make much more than minimum wage, and with the cost of a baby-sitter, it doesn't make any sense."

We'd reached the corner market, ablaze with fluorescent lighting. We let our conversation lapse while Michael moved up and down the aisles, picking up the items he'd been sent to buy. I occupied myself at the magazine rack, scanning the latest issues of various "ladies" publications. Judging by the articles listed on the front covers, we were all obsessed with losing weight, sex, and cheap home decorating tips, in just about that order. I picked up a copy of *Home & Hearth*, leafing through until I came to one of those features called "Twenty-five Things to Do for Twenty-five Dollars or Less." One suggestion was to use old bedsheets to make little dresses with tie sashes for a set of metal folding chairs.

I glanced up and saw Michael at the front register. He'd apparently paid for his purchases, which the clerk was bagging. I'm not sure what it was, but I suddenly had the sensation that someone else was watching, too. I turned casually, doing a visual survey of the market. To my left I caught a flicker of movement, a blurred face reflected against the glass doors of the refrigerator cases that lined the wall across from the entrance. I turned to look, but the face was gone.

I moved to the entrance and pushed through the door, stepping out into the chill night air. There was no one visible in the parking lot. The street was devoid of traffic. No pedestrians, no stray dogs, no wind stirring in the shrubs. The feeling persisted, and I felt the hair rising up along my scalp. There was no reason to imagine that either Michael or I would warrant anyone's attention. Unless, of course, it was Wendell or Renata. The wind was accelerating, sending a mist across the pavement like the blow back from a hose.

"What's the matter?"

I turned to find Michael standing in the doorway with the loaded grocery bag in his arms. "I thought I saw someone standing in the doorway looking at you."

He shook his head. "I didn't see anyone."

"Maybe it's my inflamed imagination, but I don't often do that sort of thing," I said. I could feel a silver shiver wash across my frame.

"You think it might have been Dad?"

"I can't think who else would take an interest."

I saw him lift his head like an animal. "I hear a car engine running."

"You do?" I listened carefully but heard nothing except the rustle of wind in the trees. "Where's the sound coming from?"

He shook his head. "It's gone now. Over there, I think."

I peered over at the darkened side street he was pointing to, but there were no signs of life. The widely spaced streetlights created shallow pools of wan illumination that served only to heighten the deep shadows in between. A breeze was moving through the treetops like a wave. The rustling conveyed something shy and secretive. I could hear the patter of light rain in the uppermost leaves. Ever so faintly, at a distance, I thought I picked up the sharp tap of heels, someone walking purposefully away into the gloom beyond. I turned back. His smile faded slightly when he saw my face. "You're really spooked."

"I hate the idea of being watched."

Behind us, I noticed the clerk in the store was staring steadily in our direction, probably puzzled by our behavior. I flicked a look at Michael. "Anyway, we better get back. Juliet'll be wondering what's kept us."

We set off, walking rapidly. This time I made no attempt to slow Michael's pace. I found myself glancing back from time to time, but the street always appeared to be empty. In my experience, it's always easier to walk toward the darkness than away from it. It wasn't until the front door closed behind us that I allowed myself to relax. Even then, an involuntary yip seemed to escape my lips. Michael had moved into the kitchen with his grocery bag, but he peered around the doorway. "Hey, we're safe, okay?"

He came out of the kitchen carrying the Pampers and a carton of cigarettes. He headed for the bedroom, and I was not far behind him, doing a quick step to keep up. "I'd appreciate it if you'd let me know if your father tries to get in touch. I'll give you my card. You can call me anytime."

"Sure."

"You might warn Juliet, too," I said.

"Whatever."

He paused dutifully while I fumbled in my handbag for a business card. I used my raised knee as a desk, penning my telephone number on the back of the card, which I then passed to him. He glanced at it with no apparent interest and put it in his jacket pocket. "Thanks."

I could tell from his tone he had no intention of calling me for any reason. If Wendell tried to reach him, he'd probably welcome the contact.

We went into the bedroom, where the baseball game was still in progress. Juliet had moved into the bathroom with the baby, and I could hear her voice reverberating through the bathroom door as she prattled nonsense at Brendan. Michael's attention was already glued to the set again. He'd sunk down on the floor, his back against the bed, turning Wendell's ring, which he wore on his right hand. I wondered if the stone changed colors, like a mood ring, depending on his disposition in the moment. I took the box of Pampers and knocked on the bathroom door.

She peered out. "Oh, good. You got 'em. I appreciate that. Thanks. You want to help with his bath? I decided to put him in the tub, he was such a mess."

"I better go," I said. "It looks like the rain is just about to cut loose."

"Really? It's going to rain?"

"If we're lucky."

I could see her hesitation. "Can I ask about something? If Michael's dad came back, would he try to see the baby? Brendan *is* his only grandchild, and s'pose he never had another chance?"

"It wouldn't surprise me. I'd be careful if I were you."

She seemed on the verge of saying something but apparently decided against it. When I closed the bathroom door, Brendan was gnawing on the washrag.

16

Drops began to dot my windshield as I hit the 101, and by the time I found a parking space half a block from my apartment, the rain had settled into a steady patter. I locked the VW and picked my way through accumulating puddles to the front gate, splashing around to my door, which opens onto Henry's back patio. I could see lights on at his place. His kitchen door was open, and I picked up the scent of baking, some rich combination of vanilla and chocolate that blended irresistibly with the smell of rain and drenched grass. A sudden breeze tossed the treetops, sending down a quick shower of leaves and large drops. I veered off toward Henry's, head bent against the downpour.

Henry was easing a blade through a nine-by-nine pan of brownies, making parallel cuts. He was barefoot, wearing white shorts and a vivid blue T-shirt. I'd seen pictures of him in his youth—when he was fifty and sixty—but I preferred the lean good looks he'd acquired in his eighties. With his silky white hair and blue eyes, there was no reason to imagine he wouldn't simply keep on getting better as the years rolled by. I rapped on the frame of his aluminum screen door. He glanced up, smiling with pleasure when he saw that it was me. "Well, Kinsey. That was quick. I just left a message on your answering machine." He motioned me in.

I let myself in and wiped my wet shoes on the rag rug before I slipped them off and left them by the door. "I saw your light on and came over. I was down in Perdido and haven't even been home yet. Isn't this rain great? Where'd it come from?"

"The tag end of Hurricane Jackie, is what I heard. It's supposed to rain off and on for the next two days. There's a pot of tea brewed if you want to grab cups and saucers."

I did as he suggested, pausing at the refrigerator to take out the milk as well. Henry rinsed and dried his knife blade and moved to the kitchen table, brownies still resting in the pan in which they'd baked. At sundown in Santa Teresa, the temperature routinely drops into the fifties, but tonight, because of the storm, the air felt nearly tropical. The interior of the kitchen functioned like an incubator. Henry had hauled out his old black-bladed floor fan, which seemed to scan the room, droning incessantly as it created its own sirocco.

We sat down at the table across from one another, the pan of brownies between us resting on an oven mitt. The top was light brown, as fragile-looking as dried tobacco leaves. His knife had left a ragged line, a portion of brownie jutting up through the broken crust. Just under the surface, the texture was as dark and moist as soil. There were walnuts as thick as gravel, with intermittent small clusters of chocolate chips. Henry lifted out the first square with a spatula and passed it to me. After that show of gentility, we ate directly from the pan.

I poured us each a cup of tea, adding milk to mine. I broke a brownie in half and then broke it again. This was my notion of cutting calories. My mouth was flooded with warm chocolate, and if I moaned aloud, Henry was too polite to call attention. "I made an odd discovery," I said. "It's possible I have family in the area."

"What kind of family?"

I shrugged. "You know, people with the same name, claiming to be related, blood ties and like that."

His blue eyes rested on my face with interest. "Really. Well, I'll be damned. What're they like?"

"Don't know. I haven't met 'em."

"Oh. I thought you had. How do you know they exist?"

"I was doing a door-to-door canvass in Perdido yesterday. A woman said I looked familiar and asked me about my first name. Then she asked if I was related to the Burton Kinseys up in Lompoc. I said no, but then I looked up my parents' marriage license. My mother's father was Burton Kinsey. It's like, in the back of my mind somewhere I think I knew that, but I didn't want to cop to it in the moment. Weird, huh."

"What are you going to do?"

"Don't know yet. Think about it. Feels like a can of worms."

"Pandora's box."

"You got it. Big trouble."

"On the other hand, it might not be."

I made a face. "I don't want to take the chance. I never had family. What would I do with one?"

Henry smiled to himself. "What do you think you'd do?"

"I don't know. It seems creepy. It'd be a pain in the ass. Look at William. He drives you crazy."

"But I love him. That's what it's all about, isn't it?"

"It is?"

"Well, obviously, you're going to do as you see fit, but there's a lot to be said for kith and kin."

I was silent for a while. I ate a section of the brownies about the shape of Utah. "I think I'll let it sit. Once I get in touch, I'll be stuck."

"Do you know anything at all about them?"

"Nope."

Henry laughed. "At least you're enthusiastic about the possibilities."

I smiled uncomfortably. "I just found out today. Besides, the only one I really know of for sure is my mother's mother, Cornelia Kinsey. I guess my grandfather died."

"Ah, your grandmother's a widow. That's interesting. How do you know she wouldn't be perfect for me?"

"There's a thought," I said dryly.

"Oh, come on. What's your worry?"

"Who says I'm worried? I'm not worried."

"Then why don't you get in touch?"

"Suppose she's hateful and grasping?"

"Suppose she's gracious and smart?"

"Right. If she was so fu— gracious, how come she hasn't been in touch for twenty-nine years?" I said.

"Maybe she was busy."

I noticed the conversation was proceeding in fits and starts. We knew each other well enough that we could leave transitions out. Nevertheless, I felt as if my IQ were plummeting. "Anyway, how would I go about it? What would I do?"

"Call her up. Say hello. Introduce yourself."

I could feel myself squirm. "I'm not going to do that," I said. "I'm going to let it sit." "Dogged" is the word that would probably describe my tone, not that I'm bullheaded about things like this.

"Let it sit, then," he said with the slightest of shrugs.

"I am. I intend to. Anyway, look how much time has passed since my parents were killed. It'd be weird to make contact."

"You said that before."

"Well, it's the truth!"

"So don't make contact. You're absolutely right."

"I won't. I'm not going to," I said irritably. Personally, I found it irksome to be agreed with like that. He could have urged me to do otherwise. He could have suggested a plan of action. Instead he was telling me what I was telling *him.* Everything sounded so much more reasonable when I said it. What he repeated back to me seemed stubborn and argumentative. I couldn't figure out what was wrong with him unless this was some kind of weird response to all the refined sugar in the brownies.

The conversation shifted to William and Rosie. Nothing new to report. Sports and politics we reduced to one sentence each. Shortly thereafter I went home to my place, feeling out of sorts. Henry seemed fine, but it felt as though we'd had a terrible argument. I didn't sleep that well, either.

It was still raining at 5:59, and I skipped my run. My cold symptoms had improved, but it still didn't seem smart to exercise in a downpour. It was hard to realize that just a week ago I was lying by a pool down in Mexico, swabbing myself with unnatural substances. I lingered in bed, staring up at the skylight. The clouds were the color of old galvanized pipes, and the day fairly cried out for some serious reading. I extended one arm and studied the artificial tan, which had faded by now to a pale peach. I raised one bare leg, noticing for the first time all the streaking around my ankle. Jesus, I could do with a shave. It looked as if I had taken to wearing angora knee socks. Finally, bored with self-inspection, I dragged my butt out of bed. I showered, shaved my legs, and dressed, choosing fresh jeans and a cotton sweater since I'd be lunching with Harris Brown. I took myself out to breakfast, loading up on fats and carbohydrates, nature's antidepressants. Ida Ruth had told me she was coming in late, authorizing my use of her parking spot. I rolled into the office at nine on the dot.

Alison was talking on the telephone when I arrived. She held a hand up like a traffic cop, indicating some kind of message. I paused, waiting for a break in her conversation. "That's fine, no problem. Take your time," she said. She put a palm across the mouthpiece while the other party was apparently taking care of other business. "I put someone in your office. I hope you don't mind. I'll hold your calls."

"What for?"

Her attention jumped back to the telephone, and I assumed the other party had finally returned. I shrugged and walked down the interior corridor to my office, where the door was standing open. There was a woman at the window with her back to me.

I moved to my desk and slung my handbag on the chair. "Hi. Can I help you?"

She turned around and looked at me with the sort of curiosity reserved for celebrities at close range. I found myself looking at her the same way. We were enough alike to be sisters. Her face was as familiar as the faces in a dream, recognizable but not bearing up well to close scrutiny. Our features were not identical by any means. She looked not *like* me, but like the way I felt I looked to others. As I studied her, the resemblance faded. Quickly I could see that we were more dissimilar than similar. She was five feet two to my five feet six, heavier in a way that suggested rich food and no exercise. I'd been jogging for years, and I was sometimes conscious of the ways my basic build had been affected by all the miles I'd put in. She was heavy-breasted, broader in the beam. At the same time, she was better groomed. I had a glimpse of what I might have looked like if I paid the money for a decent haircut, learned the rudiments of makeup, and dressed with flair. The outfit she wore was a cream-colored washable silk: a long, gathered skirt and matching cardigan-style jacket, with a coral-colored silk tank top visible underneath. Through the magic of fashion, some of her chunkiness was hidden, the eye distracted by all the flowing lines.

She smiled and held out her hand. "Hello, Kinsey. Nice to meet you. I'm your cousin, Liza."

"How did you get here?" I asked. "I only found out yesterday I might have relatives in the area."

"That's when we heard, too. Well, that's not quite accurate. Last night Lena Irwin called my sister, Pam, and we had an instant meeting. Lena was sure you were related. Both my sisters were panting to drive down to meet you, but we finally decided it'd be too confusing for you. Besides, Tasha really had to get back to San Francisco, and Pamela's so pregnant she's about to pop."

Three girl cousins suddenly. That was a bit much. I shifted the subject. "How do you know Lena?"

Liza waved dismissively, a gesture I'd used a hundred times myself. "Her family's up in Lompoc. The minute she said she'd met you, we knew we had to come down. We haven't said a word to Grand, but I know she'll want to meet you."

"Grand?"

"Oh, sorry. That's our grandmother, Cornelia. Her maiden name was LaGrand, and we've always just shortened it. Everybody calls her Grand. It's been her nickname since childhood."

"How much does she know about me?"

"Not that much, really. We knew your name, of course, but we really weren't sure where you'd ended up. The whole family scandal was so ridiculous. I don't mean at the time. Good heavens, from what I've been told, it split the sisters down the middle. Am I interrupting your work? I should have asked before."

"Not at all," I said with a quick look at my watch. I had three hours before my lunch appointment. "Alison told me she'd hold the calls, but I couldn't think what could be so important. Tell me about the sisters."

"There were five of them altogether. I guess they had a brother, but he died in infancy. They were completely divided by the breach between Grand and Aunt Rita. You really never heard the story?"

"Not at all," I said. "I'm sitting here wondering if you really have the right person."

"Absolutely," she said. "Your mother was a Kinsey. Rita Cynthia, right? Her sister's name was Virginia. We called her Aunt Gin, or Gin Gin sometimes."

"So did I," I said faintly. I'd always thought of it as my pet name for her, one that I invented.

Liza went on. "I didn't know her that well because of the estrangement between those two and Grand, who'll be eighty-eight this year and sharp as a tack. I mean, she's virtually blind and her health's not that good, but she's great for her age. I'm not sure the two of them ever spoke to Grand again, but Aunt Gin would come back to visit and all the sisters would converge. The big horror was that somehow Grand would get wind of it, but I don't think she ever did. Anyway, our mother's name is Susanna. She's the baby in the family. Do you mind if I sit?"

"I'm sorry. Please do. You want coffee? I can get us some."

"No, no. I'm fine. I'm just sorry to barge in and bury you under all this. What was I saying? Oh, yes. Your mother was the oldest and mine's the youngest. There are only two surviving—my mother, Susanna . . . she's fifty-eight. And then the sister one up from her, Maura, who's sixty-one. Sarah died about five years ago. God, I'm sorry to spring all this on you. We just assumed you knew."

"What about Burton . . . Grandfather Kinsey?"

"He's gone, too. He only died a year ago, but of course he'd been sick for years." She said it like I should have known the nature of his illness.

I let that pass. I didn't want to focus on the fine points when I was still struggling with the overall picture. "How many cousins?"

"Well, there're the three of us, and Maura has two daughters, Delia and Eleanor. Sarah had four girls."

"And you're all up in Lompoc?"

"Not quite," she said. "Three of Sarah's four are on the East Coast. One's married, two in college, and I don't know what the other one's doing. She's sort of the black sheep of the family. Maura's kids are both in Lompoc. In fact, Maura and Mom live within five blocks of each other. Part of Grand's master plan." She laughed and I could see that we had the same teeth, very white and square. "We better do this in small doses or you'll die of the shock."

"I'm close to that as it is."

She laughed again. Something about this woman was getting on my nerves. She was having way too much fun, and I wasn't having any. I was trying to assimilate the information, trying to cope with its significance, trying to be polite and make all the right noises. But I felt foolish, in truth, and her breezy, presumptive manner wasn't helping much. I shifted on my chair and raised my hand like a kid in a classroom. "Could I ask you to stop and go back to the beginning?"

"I'm sorry. You must be so confused, you poor thing. I wish Tasha'd done this. She should have canceled her plane. I knew I'd probably botch it, but there just wasn't any other choice. You do know about Rita Cynthia's elopement. They must have told you *that* part." She made a statement of it, equating the story with the news that the world was round.

I shook my head again, beginning to feel like a bauble-head in somebody's rear car window. "I was five when my parents died in the accident. After that, Aunt Gin raised me, but she gave me no family history whatsoever. You can safely operate on the assumption that I'm dead ignorant."

"Oh, boy. I hope I can remember it all myself. I'll just launch in, and anything you don't get, please feel free to interrupt. First of all, our grandfather Kinsey had beaucoup bucks. His family ran a diatomite mining and processing operation. Diatomite is basically what they use to make diatomaceous earth. Do you know what that is?"

"Some kind of filtering medium, isn't it?"

"Right. The diatomite deposits up in Lompoc are among the biggest and purest in the world. The Kinseys have owned that company for years. Grandmother must have come from money, too, though she doesn't talk much about it so I don't really know the story on that. Her maiden name was LaGrand. She's always been called Grand, ever since I can remember. I already told you that. Anyway, she and Granddaddy had six kids—the boy who died and then the five girls. Rita Cynthia was the oldest. She was Grand's favorite, probably because they were so much alike. I guess she was spoiled . . . or so the story goes, a real hell-raiser. She *totally* refused to conform to Grand's expectations. Because of that, Aunt Rita's become like this family legend. The patron saint of liberation. The rest of us—all the nieces and nephews—took her as a symbol of independence and spirit, someone sassy and defiant, the emancipated person our mothers wished they'd been. Rita Cynthia thumbed her nose at Grand, who was a piece of work in those days. Rigid and snobbish, judgmental, controlling. She raised all the girls to be little robots of gentility. Don't get me wrong. She could be very generous, but there were usually strings attached. Like she'd give you the money for college, but you had to keep it local or go where she said. Same with a house. She'd give you the down payment and even cosign the loan, as long as you found a place within six blocks of her. It really broke her heart when Aunt Rita left."

"I don't understand what happened."

"Oh, boy. Right. Okay, let me get to the point. First of all, Rita made her debut in 1935. July fifth—"

"My mother was a debutante? She actually made a debut and you can recite the *date*? You must have quite a memory."

"No, no, no. It's all part of the story. Everybody knows that in our family. It's like *Goldilocks and the Three Bears* or *Rumpelstiltskin.* What happened was Grand had a set of twelve sterling silver napkin rings engraved with Rita Cynthia's name and the date of her debut. She was going to make it a tradition for each of the girls in turn, but it didn't really work out. She threw this big coming-out party and set it up so Rita could meet all these incredibly eligible bachelors. Real lah-de-dah social register types."

"In *Lompoc*?"

"Oh, golly, no. They came from everywhere. Marin County, Walnut Creek, San Francisco, Atherton, Los Angeles, you name it. Grand had her heart set on Rita's 'marrying well,' as they used to say in those days. Instead, Rita fell in love with your father, who was serving at the party."

"As a waiter?"

"Exactly. Some friend of his worked for the caterer and asked him to help out. Aunt Rita started seeing Randy Millhone on the sly. This was right in the middle of the Depression, and his real job was working for the post office here in Santa Teresa. It's not like he was really a waiter," she said.

"Oh, thank God," I said dryly, but the irony was lost on her. "What'd he do for the post office?"

"He was a mail carrier. 'An uncivil servant,' Grand used to say with her nose all turned up. As far as she was concerned, he was poor white trash . . . too old for Rita and way too low class. She found out they were dating and threw a pluperfect fit, but there was nothing she could do. Rita was eighteen and headstrong as they come. The more Grand protested, the more she dug her heels in. By November, she was gone. Just ran off and married him without telling a soul."

"She told Virginia."

"She did?"

"Sure. Aunt Gin was one of the witnesses at the wedding."

"Oh. I didn't know that, but it does make sense. The point is, when Grand found out, she was so furious she cut her off without a dime. She wouldn't even let her keep the silver napkin rings."

"A fate worse than death."

"Well, it must have seemed like it at the time," she said. "I don't know what Grandmother did with the rest of 'em, but there was one we all used to vie for at family gatherings. Grand had this whole collection of assorted napkin rings . . . different styles and monograms, all British silver," she said. "Before dinner, if she thought you'd been rude or disobedient or something? She'd make you use the Rita Cynthia napkin ring. She meant it to be mean. You know, like it was her way of shaming anyone who got out of line—ridiculing all the girls—but we ended up fighting to have possession. We considered it a coup to get to use that one. Rita Cynthia was the only member of the family who ever really got away, and we thought she was great. So secretly we'd all get together and have this pitched battle for which of us would get to be Rita Cynthia. Whoever won would misbehave something fierce, and sure enough, Grand would descend like a witch and make 'em use the Rita Cynthia napkin ring. Big disgrace, but we thought it was such a *hoot*."

"Didn't anyone object to your making such a big deal of it?"

"Oh, Grand didn't know. She could hardly see by then, and besides, we were very careful. That was the best part of the game. I'm not even sure our mothers noticed. Or if they did, they probably applauded secretly. Rita was their favorite, and Virginia ran a close second. That was the hardest part about Aunt Rita's defection. We not only lost her, but for the most part, we lost Gin as well."

"Really," I said, but I could barely hear myself. I felt as though I'd been struck. Liza couldn't have guessed how the story was affecting me. My mother was never even a real person to them. She was a ritual, a symbol, something to be fought over like a bunch of rowdy dogs with a bone. I paused to clear my throat. "Why were they driving up to Lompoc?"

This time Liza was puzzled. I could see it in her eyes.

"My parents were killed on the way to Lompoc," I said carefully, as if translating for a foreigner. "If they'd broken with the family, why were they going up there?"

"I hadn't thought about that. I guess it was part of the reunion Aunt Gin was setting up."

I must have stared at her in some significant way because her cheeks tinted suddenly. "Maybe we should wait until Tasha comes back. She flies down for a visit every couple of weeks. She can fill you in on this stuff much better than I can."

"But what about the years since then? Why didn't anybody get in touch?"

"Oh, I'm sure they tried. I mean, I know they wanted to. They talked back and forth with Aunt Gin on the phone, so everybody knew you were here. Anyway, what's done is done. I know Mom and Maura and Uncle Walter will be thrilled to hear we've met, and you really must come up."

I could feel something strange happening to my face. "None of you felt any reason to come down when Aunt Gin died?"

"Oh, God, you're upset. I feel awful. What's wrong?"

"Nothing. I just remembered I have an appointment," I said. It was only nine twenty-five. Liza's entire revelation had taken less than half an hour. "I guess we'll have to finish this on another occasion."

She was suddenly busy with her handbag and her map. "I better hit the road, then. I probably should have called first, but I thought it would be such a fun surprise. I hope I haven't blown it. Are you okay?"

"I'm fine."

"Please call. Or I'll call you and we'll get together again. Tasha's older. She knows the story better and maybe she can fill you in. Everyone was crazy about Rita Cynthia. Honestly."

Next thing I was aware of, cousin Liza was gone. I closed the door behind her and went over to the window. A white wall wound along the properties in the back, bougainvillea spilling across the top in a tumbling mass of magenta. In theory, I'd suddenly gained an entire family, cause for rejoicing if you happen to believe the ladies' magazines. In reality, I felt as if someone had just stolen everything I held dear, a common theme in all the books you read on burglary and theft.

17

The coffee shop Harris Brown had selected for our brainstorming session was a maze of interconnecting rooms with a huge oak tree growing up the middle. I parked in the side lot and walked into the entrance T. There were benches on either side of a corridor intended as an area where people could sit while they waited for their names to be called. Business had fallen off, and now there was just the length of empty space with potted rubber plants and what looked like a lectern at the end. A row of windows on either side of the entranceway gave an unobstructed view of patrons dining at tables in flanking wings of the restaurant.

I gave my name to the hostess. She was a black woman in her sixties, with a manner about her that suggested she was wasting her education. Jobs are hard to find in this town, and she was probably grateful to have the work. As I approached her station I could see her reach for a menu.

"My name's Kinsey Millhone. I'm having lunch with a man named Harris Brown, but I'm hoping to find the restroom first.

Could you show him to a table if he arrives before I get back? I'd appreciate it."

"Certainly," she said. "You know where the ladies' room is?"

"I can find it," I said, incorrectly as it turned out.

I should have had a little map or dropped bread crumbs behind me. First, I found myself heading into a closet full of floor mops and then through a door leading to the alleyway out back. I retraced my steps and turned myself around. I could see a sign then in the shape of an arrow pointing to the right: "Telephones. Restrooms." Ah, a clue. I found the proper door, with a ladies' high heel in silhouette. I did my business with dispatch, moving back to the entrance. I arrived as the hostess was returning to her position. She pointed to the dining area to her left, a wing of the restaurant parallel to the entrance. "Second table on the right."

Almost without thinking, I glanced through the two adjacent windows, spotting Harris Brown as he stood to remove his sport coat. Instinctively I backed up a step, obscuring myself behind a potted plant. I looked at the hostess and jerked a thumb in his direction. "*That's* Harris Brown?"

"He asked for Kinsey Millhone," she said.

I peered around the plant at him, but there was no mistake. Especially since he was the only man in there. Harris Brown, retired police lieutenant, was the "drunk" I'd seen on the Viento Negro hotel balcony less than a week ago. Now what was that about? I knew he'd worked the fraud investigation, but that was years ago. How had he picked up Wendell Jaffe's trail, and what was he doing down in Mexico? More to the point, wasn't he going to turn around and ask me the very same thing? He was bound to remember my handy-dandy hooker act, and while that in itself wasn't anything to be ashamed of, I wasn't quite sure how to explain what I'd been up to. Until I knew what was going on, it seemed less than cool to have a conversation with the man.

The hostess was watching me with bemusement. "You think he's too old for you? I could have told you that."

"You know him?"

"He used to come in here all the time when he was working for the police department. Brought his wife and kids in every Sunday after church."

"How long have you worked here?"

"Honey, I own the place. My husband, Samuel, and I bought it in 1965."

I could feel myself flush, though she couldn't have guessed the reason.

Dimples formed in her cheeks, and she flashed a smile at me. "Oh, I get it now. You thought I took this job because I'd fallen on hard times."

I laughed, embarrassed that I was so transparent. "I figured you were probably happy to have the work."

"Make no mistake about it, I am. I'd be happier still if the business picked up. At least I got old friends like Mr. Brown in there, though I sure don't see him as often as I used to. What's the deal? Somebody set you up on a blind date with him?"

I felt a momentary confusion. "You just said he was married."

"Well, he was till she died. I thought maybe somebody fixed you up and you didn't like his looks."

"It's a little trickier than that. Uhm, I wonder if you could do me a favor," I said. "I'm going out to the lot to that public telephone booth. When I call and ask for him, could you let him use this phone?"

She gave me a look. "You're not going to hurt his feelings, are you?"

"I promise I won't. This has nothing to do with dating, I assure you."

"As long as it's not a put-down. I won't participate in that."

"Scout's honor," I said, holding fingers to my temple.

She handed me a take-out menu that was printed on heavy paper. "Telephone number's at the top," she said.

"Thanks."

I kept my face turned away studiously as I left the restaurant, crossing to the pay phone in the corner of the lot. I propped the menu against the phone box and then fished out a quarter, which I put in the slot. After two rings the hostess answered.

"Hello," said I. "I'm looking for Harris Brown—"

"I'll go get him," she said, putting me on hold. In her absence, I was treated to the weather report on a local radio station.

After a pause, Brown picked up the line, sounding just as cranky and impatient as he had when I talked to him the first time. His manner would have been perfect for a bill collector. "Yes?"

"Hi, Lieutenant Brown. This is Kinsey Millhone."

"It's Harris," he said shortly.

"Oh, sorry, Harris. I thought maybe I could catch you before you left this morning, but I must have missed you. Something unavoidable has come up, and I'm going to have to give you a rain check on lunch. Can I call you later this week and maybe set something up then?"

His disposition improved, which was really worrisome when you consider I was bowing out of lunch with no advance notice whatsoever. "No problem," he said. "Just give me a call when it suits." Casual, good-natured.

A little warning bell went off, but I soldiered on. "Thanks. I really appreciate this, and I'm sorry for the inconvenience."

"Don't worry about it. Oh. Tell you what, though, I was hoping to have a quick chat with Wendell's ex-partner. I figure he might know something. Have you had any luck reaching him?"

I nearly blurted out the information, but I caught myself. Ah. Got it. This guy was hoping to jump the gun, bypassing me, so he could get to Wendell himself. I raised my voice. "Hello?" I let two seconds pass. "Hellllooo."

"Hello?" he repeated back to me.

"Are you there? Hello?"

"I'm here," he yelled.

"Could you speak up? I can't hear you. We have a terrible connection. What's wrong with this phone? Can you hear me?"

"I can hear you fine. Can you hear me?"

"What?"

"I said do you happen to know how I can contact Carl Eckert? I can't seem to find out where he's living these days."

I banged the mouthpiece on the little shelf the telephone company provides in any public booth. "Hellllooo! I can't hear you!" I sang. "Hello?" Then, as if annoyed, I said, "Well, goddamn it!" And slammed the receiver down.

I picked it up again once the connection was broken. I stayed where I was, my face averted, pretending to converse with animation while I kept an eye on the restaurant entrance. Moments later I saw him come out, cross the parking lot, and get into a battered Ford. I might have followed him, but to what end? At this point, I couldn't believe he was going any place interesting. The man wouldn't be that tough to connect with again, especially since I had a piece of information he was hoping to get.

As I opened my car door, I could see the hostess watching me through the plate glass window. I debated about going back with some cock-and-bull story, anything to forestall her tipping him off to my deception. On the other hand, I didn't want to make more of the incident than I had to. He probably went in there every two or three months. Why call attention to a matter I wanted her to forget?

I went back to my office, circling the block endlessly until I found a parking place. I'm afraid to calculate how much time I waste this way on any given day. Sometimes I pass Alison or Jim Thicket, the paralegal, driving in the other direction, as intent as I am ferreting out a space. Maybe Lonnie would win a big case and sport us all to a little lot of our own. I finally broke down and pulled into the public parking garage beside the library. I'd have to keep an eye on the clock and fetch my car again before the first free ninety minutes ran out. God forbid I should pay a buck an hour for parking if I didn't have to.

As long as I was close, I ducked into the minimart and bought myself a bag lunch. The forecast I'd picked up while on hold was full of cagey meteorological phrases, citing lows and highs and percentages. From this I gathered the weatherperson didn't know any better than I did what would happen next. I walked over to the courthouse and found an unoccupied spot under shelter. The sky was overcast, the air faintly chilly, trees still dripping with rain from the night before. For the moment it was clear, and the grass in the sunken garden smelled like a soggy bouquet garni.

A white-haired female docent led a group of tourists through the big stone-and-stucco archway toward the street beyond. I used to lunch here with Jonah in the days of our "romance." Now it was difficult to remember just what the attraction was about. I ate my lunch, then gathered up my crumpled papers and my empty Pepsi can, depositing the paper bag in the nearest waste container. As if on cue, I saw Jonah moving toward me across the saturated courthouse lawn. He looked surprisingly good for a man who probably wasn't very happy: tall and trim, with a wash of silver showing in his dark hair just above his ears. He hadn't seen me yet. He walked with his head down, a brown bag visible in one hand. Though I was tempted to flee, I found myself nearly rooted in place, wondering how long it would take for him to realize I was standing there. He lifted his face and looked at me without a hint of recognition. I waited, motionless, feeling oddly ill at ease. When he was ten feet away, he stopped in his tracks. I could see the tiny flecks of wet grass plastered to his shoes. "I don't believe it. How are you?"

I said, "Fine. How are you?"

His smile seemed pained and slightly sheepish. "I guess we just did this couple days ago on the phone."

"We're allowed," I said mildly. "What are you doing here?"

He looked down at the brown paper bag in his hand as if perplexed. "I'm supposed to meet Camilla for lunch."

"Oh, that's right. She works here. Well, that's convenient for you both with the station half a block away. You can give each other rides to work." Jonah knew me well enough to ignore my sarcasm, which in this case was automatic and didn't mean that much.

"You never met Camilla, did you? Why don't you hang around for a bit? She'll be here any minute, as soon as court's recessed."

"Thanks, but I have something to take care of," I said. "Anyway, I can't believe she'd be that interested. Maybe some other time." Jesus, Jonah, get a clue, I thought. No wonder Camilla was always mad at him. What wife wants to meet the woman her husband was boffing during past marital separations?

"Anyway, it's nice to see you. You're looking good," he said as he moved away.

"Jonah? I do have a question. Maybe this is something you can help me with."

He paused. "Fire away."

"You know much about Lieutenant Brown?"

He seemed puzzled by the subject. "Sure, I know some. What in particular?"

"Remember I told you CF hired me to check out this Wendell Jaffe sighting down in Mexico?"

"Yeah."

"Harris Brown was down there. In the room next door to Jaffe's."

Jonah's face went blank. "Are you sure?"

"Trust me, Jonah. This is not something I could be mistaken about. It was him. I was this close." I held my hand to my face, implying nose to nose. I repressed the fact that I'd kissed him right in the chops. That was still enough to make me shiver some in retrospect.

"Well, I suppose he could be investigating on his own time," he said. "I guess there's nothing wrong with that. It's been a lot of years, but he always had a reputation as a bird dog."

"In other words, he's persistent," I said.

"Oh, shit, yes. He spots a perp in the distance, he'll hold a point till he drops."

"If he's retired, can he still use the NCIC computer?"

"Technically, probably not, but I'm sure he still has friends in the department who'd help him out if he asked. Why?"

"I don't see how he could find Wendell without access to the system."

Jonah shrugged, unimpressed. "That's not information we have or we'd have pulled him in. If the guy's still alive, we'd have a lot of questions for him."

"He had to get his information somewhere," I said.

"Come on. Brown's been a detective thirty-five, forty years. He knows how to get information. The guy's got his sources. Maybe somebody tipped him off."

"But what's it to him? Why not pass the information on to someone in the department?"

He studied me, and I could see his mental gears engage. "Offhand, I can't tell you. Personally, I think you're making too much of this, but I can check it out."

"Discreetly," I cautioned.

"Absolutely," he said.

I began to walk backward at a slow pace. I finally turned and moved on. I didn't want to be caught up in Jonah's orbit again. I've never really understood the chemistry between the two of us. While the relationship seemed to be dead now, I wasn't sure what had triggered the spark in the beginning. For all I knew, mere proximity might set the whole thing off again. The man wasn't good for me, and I wanted him at a distance. When I looked back, I saw that he was staring after me.

By two-fifteen my office phone rang. "Kinsey? This is Jonah."

"That was quick," I said.

"That's because there isn't much to report. Word has it he was taken off the case because his personal involvement interfered with his work. He sank his entire pension into CSL and lost his shirt. Apparently, his kids were up in arms because he'd blown all his retirement monies. His wife left him, and then she got sick. Eventually she died of cancer. His kids still don't speak to him. It's a real mess."

"Well, that's interesting," I said. "Is it possible he's been authorized to pursue the case?"

"By who?"

"I don't know. The chief? The CIA? The FBI?"

"No way. I never heard of that. The guy's been retired for over a year. We got a budget barely pays for the paper clips. Where's he getting his funds? Believe me, Santa Teresa Police Department isn't going to spend money chasing after some guy who *might* have been guilty of a crime five or six years back. If he showed up, we'd chat with him, but nobody's going to put in a lot of time on it. Who cares about Jaffe? There was never even a warrant out for his arrest."

"Guess again. There's a warrant out now," I said tartly.

"This is probably just something Brown is doing on his own."

"You'd still have to wonder where he gets his information."

"Might have been the same guy told California Fidelity. Maybe the two of 'em know each other."

That sparked a response. "You mean Dick Mills? Well, that's true. If he knew Brown was interested, he might have mentioned it. I'll see if I can get a line on it from that end. That's a good suggestion."

"Let me know what you find out. I'd like to hear what's going on."

As soon as he hung up, I put a call through to California Fidelity and asked for Mac Voorhies. While I was waiting for him to free up from another call, I had a chance to reflect on the wickedness of my lying ways. I didn't actually repent, but I had to consider all the tricky repercussions. For example. I was going to have to tell Mac *something* about my encounter with Harris Brown down in Viento Negro, but how could I do that without confessing my sins? Mac knows me well enough to realize that I bend the rules on occasion, but he doesn't like to be confronted with any *instances* thereof. Like most of us, he enjoys the colorful aspects of other people's natures as long as he doesn't have to deal with any consequences.

"Mac Voorhies," he said.

I hadn't quite made up my cover story at that point, which meant I was going to have to fall back on that old hoary ruse of telling some, but not all, of the truth as I knew it. The best strategy here is to conjure up strong *feelings* of honesty and virtue even if you don't have the goods to back 'em up. I've noticed, too, that if you pretend to confide in others, they tend to accord great truth value to the contents of the revelation.

"Hi, Mac. This is Kinsey. We've had an interesting development

I thought you ought to be aware of. Apparently, five years ago when Wendell's disappearance first came to light, an STPD fraud detective named Harris Brown was assigned to the case."

"Name sounds familiar. I must have dealt with him once or twice," Mac put in. "You having trouble with the guy?"

"Not in the way you might think," I said. "I called him a couple days ago and he was very cooperative. We were supposed to meet for lunch today, but when I got there, I took one look at the man and realized I'd seen him in Viento Negro, staying in the same hotel as Wendell Jaffe."

"Doing what?"

"That's what I'm trying to find out," I said. "I'm not a big fan of coincidence. The minute I realized it was the same guy, I backed out of the restaurant and bagged the appointment. I managed to cover myself so I didn't blow the contact. Meantime, I asked a cop I know to check it out in the department, and he tells me Brown lost a bundle when Wendell's financial scheme collapsed."

Mac said, "Huhn."

"The cop suggested Brown and Dick Mills might have a prior relationship. If Dick knew Harris Brown had some kind of ax to grind, he might have told him about Wendell the same time he told you."

"I can ask Dick."

"Would you do that? I'd really appreciate it, if you don't mind," I said. "I really don't know the guy. He's probably more likely to 'fess up to you."

"No problem. Fine with me. What about Wendell? You got a line on him yet?"

"I'm getting closer," I said. "I know where Renata is, and he can't be that far off."

"You heard the latest on the kid, I guess."

"You mean Brian? I haven't heard a thing."

"Oh, yeah. You'll love this. I caught it in the car coming back from lunch. There was a computer glitch at the Perdido County Jail. Brian Jaffe was released this morning and nobody's seen him since."

18

I hit the road again. I was beginning to think the real definition of Hell was this endless loop between Santa Teresa and Perdido. As I came around the corner into Dana Jaffe's neighborhood, I spotted a Perdido County Sheriff's Department car parked in front of her house. I parked across the street and down a few houses, watching the front porch for signs of life. I'd probably been sitting there for ten minutes or so when I caught sight of Dana's neighbor, Jerry Irwin, returning from his afternoon jog. He ran on the balls of his feet, almost on tippy-toe, with the same stooped posture he favored in his leisure moments. He was wearing plaid Bermuda shorts and a white T-shirt, black socks, and running shoes. His color was high and his gray hair was matted with sweat, his glasses secured with a length of rubber tubing that made a circular indentation. He finished the last half a block with a little burst of speed, his gait the mincing, irregular hopping of someone running barefoot over hot concrete. I leaned over and rolled down the window on the passenger side.

"Hey, Jerry? How're you? Kinsey Millhone here."

He leaned forward, gasping, hands on his skinny knees while he caught his breath. A whiff of sweat wafted through the window. "Fine." Huff, puff. "Just a minute here." He was never going to look like an athlete doing this. He seemed like a man on the brink of a near death experience. He put his hands on his waist and leaned back, saying, "Whooo!" He was still breathing hard, but he managed to collect himself. He peered in at me, face wrinkling with the effort. His glasses were beginning to fog up. "I was going to call you. Thought I saw Wendell hanging around earlier."

"Really," I said. "Why don't you hop in?" I leaned over and popped up the lock, and he opened the car door, sliding onto the seat.

"'Course I can't be sure, but it sure looked like him, so I called the cops. Deputy's over there now. Did you see that?"

I checked Dana's porch, which was still deserted. "So I see. You heard about Brian?"

"Kid must lead a charmed life," Jerry remarked. "You think he's headed for home?"

"Hard to say. It'd be foolish . . . that's the first place the cops are going to check," I said. "But he may not have any other choice in the matter."

"I can't believe his mother would tolerate that."

We both peered at Dana's, hoping for activity. Guns going off, vases flying through the window. There was nothing. Dead silence, the facade of the dark gray house looking cold and blank. "I drove down to see her, but I thought I better wait until the deputy leaves. When did you see Wendell? Was it just recently?"

"Might have been an hour ago. Lena was the one who spotted him. She called me in quick and had me take a look. We couldn't quite agree if it was him or not, but I thought it was worthwhile to report. I didn't really think they'd send somebody out."

"They might have dispatched a deputy after Brian came up missing. I didn't hear the newscast myself. Did you happen to catch it?"

Jerry shook his head, pausing to wipe his sweaty forehead on his T-shirt. The car was beginning to smell like a locker room. "Might be why Wendell came back," he said.

"That occurred to me, too."

Jerry gave a little sniff to his armpit and had the decency to wince. "I better head for the shower before I stink up your car. You let me know if they catch him."

"Sure. I'll probably cruise by Michael's house just to make the rounds. I'm assuming the cops will advise him about aiding and abetting."

"For all the good it'll do."

I left the car windows down after Jerry got out. Another ten minutes passed and the sheriff's deputy emerged from Dana's. She followed him out, and the two of them stood on the front porch, conversing. The deputy was staring out at the street. Even at a distance, his expression seemed stony. Dana looked trim and long-legged in a short denim skirt, a navy T-shirt, and flats, her hair pulled back with a bright red scarf. The deputy's stance suggested the effect wasn't lost on him. They seemed to be winding up their conversation, body language cautious and just a shade antagonistic. Her telephone must have rung because I saw her give a quick look in that direction. He gave her a nod and moved down the steps while she banged through the screen door and into the house.

As soon as he'd pulled away from the curb, I got out of my car and crossed the street to Dana's. She'd left the front door open, the screen on the latch. I knocked on the door frame, but she didn't seem to hear me. I could see her pacing, head tilted, handset anchored in the crook of her neck. She paused to light a cigarette, drawing deeply. "You can have her take the pictures if you want," she was saying, "but a professional is going to do a better job—" She was interrupted by the party on the other end, and I could see a frown of annoyance form. She removed a fleck of tobacco from her tongue. Her other line began to ring. "Well now, that's true, and I know it seems like a lot of money. About that, yes. . . ."

Her other line rang again.

"Debbie, I understand what you're saying. . . . I understand that and I empathize, but it's the wrong place to pinch pennies.

Talk to Bob and see what he says. I've got another call coming in. . . . All right. Bye-bye. I'll call you back in a bit."

She pressed the button for the other line. "Boutique Bride," she said. Even through the screen door, I could see her manner shift. "Oh, hello." She turned her back to the door, voice dropping into a range I couldn't readily overhear. She set her half-smoked cigarette on the lip of an ashtray and checked her reflection in a wall-hung mirror near the desk. She smoothed her hair back and corrected a little smudge of eye makeup. "Don't do that," she was saying. "I really don't want you to do that. . . ."

I turned and scanned the street, debating whether I should knock on the door again. If Brian or Wendell was lurking in the bushes, I didn't see them. I peered back through the screen door as Dana wound down her conversation and replaced the phone on the desk.

When she caught sight of me through the screen, she gave a little jump, hand coming up automatically to her heart. "Oh, my God. You scared me to death," she said.

"I saw you on the phone and didn't want to interrupt. I heard about Brian. Mind if I come in?"

"Just a minute," she said. She moved to the screen and unlatched the thumb lock. She opened the screen and stepped back so I could enter. "I'm worried sick about him. I have no idea where he'd go, but he *has* to turn himself in. They're going to charge him with escape if he doesn't show up soon. A sheriff's deputy was just here, acting like I'd stashed him under the bed. He didn't say as much, but you know how they act, all puffy and officious."

"You haven't heard from Brian?"

She shook her head. "His attorney hasn't, either, which isn't good," she said. "He needs to know his legal position." She moved into the living room and took a seat on the near end of the couch. I moved to the far end, perching on the arm.

I tossed in a question just to see what she'd say. "Who was that on the phone?"

"Wendell's old partner, Carl. I guess he caught the news. Ever since this business with Brian came up, my phone's been ringing off the hook. I've heard from people I haven't talked to since grade school."

"You keep in touch with him?"

"He keeps in touch with me, though there's no love lost. I've always felt he was a terrible influence on Wendell."

"He paid a price for it," I said.

"Didn't we all?" she shot back.

"What about Brian's release? Has anybody figured out how he got out of jail? It's really hard to believe the computer made an error of that magnitude."

"This is Wendell's doing. No doubt about it," she said. I could see her look around for her cigarettes. She moved over to the desk, stubbing out the butt she'd left burning in the ashtray. She picked up a pack of cigarettes and a lighter, coming back to the couch. She tried to light one and changed her mind, her hands shaking badly.

"How would he get access to a sheriff's department computer?"

"I have no idea, but you said so yourself: Brian was his reason for returning to California. Now that Wendell's back, Brian's out of jail. How else do you figure it?"

"Those computers are bound to be well secured. How could he get an unauthorized jail release message sent through the system?"

"Maybe he took up hacking in the five years he was gone," she said sarcastically.

"Have you talked to Michael? Does he know Brian's out?"

"That's the first place I called. Michael went to work early, but I talked to Juliet and really put the fear of God in her. She's crazy about Brian, and she doesn't have a grain of sense. I made her swear she would call me if either of them heard from him."

"What about Wendell? Would he know how to reach Michael at the new address?"

"Why not? All he has to do is call Information. The new number's listed. It isn't any big secret. Why? Do you think Brian and Wendell would try to connect at Michael's?"

"I don't know. Do you?"

She thought about it for a moment. "It's possible," she said. She pressed her hands between her knees to still their shaking.

"I probably ought to go," I said.

"I'm staying close to the phone. If you learn anything, will you let me know?"

"Of course."

I left Dana's and headed over to the Perdido Keys. My prime worry at the moment was the whereabouts of Renata's boat. If Wendell had really found a way to arrange Brian's release, his next move would be getting the kid out of the country.

I pulled into a McDonald's and used the pay phone in the parking lot, dialing Renata's unlisted number without luck. I could hardly remember when I'd eaten last, so while I was on the premises I availed myself of the facilities, then picked up lunch: a QP with cheese, a Coke, and a large order of fries, which I took out to the car. At least the smell of fast food obliterated the last traces of Jerry Irwin's sweat.

When I reached Renata's, her big double garage door was wide open and there was no Jaguar in evidence. I did catch a glimpse of the boat at the dock, two wooden masts visible above the fence. The house itself showed no interior lights, and there was no indication of activity. I parked my VW about three doors away and demolished my meal, remembering as I finished that I'd already eaten lunch. I checked my watch. Ah, but that was hours ago. Well, two of them, at any rate.

I sat in my car and waited. Since my car radio wasn't working and I hadn't brought anything to read, I found myself ruminating about the sudden acquisition of family relationships. What was I going to do about them? Grandmother, aunts, cousins of every description . . . not that they'd lost any sleep over me. There was something troubling about the feelings being stirred up. Most of them were bad. I'd never devoted any thought to the fact that my father was a mail carrier. I had known, of course, but the information had no impact, and I usually had no reason to reflect on the significance. All that news being delivered . . . the good and the bad, debts and remittances, accounts payable, accounts receivable, dividend checks, canceled notes, word about babies being born and old friends dying, the Dear John letters breaking off engagements . . . that was the task he'd been charged with in this world, an occupation my grandmother apparently judged too lowly for consideration. Maybe Burton and Grand truly felt it was their responsibility to see that my mother chose well in this matter of a husband. I felt defensive of him, brooding and protective.

With Liza's revelation, I'd caught a glimpse of whole dramas that had been acted out without my knowledge: quarrels and rituals, the gentle cooing of women, raucous laughter, cozy chats in the kitchen over cups of coffee, holiday dinners, babies born, advice offered up, the hand-embroidered linens passed down from one generation to the next. It was a ladies' magazine picture of the family; abundant, cinnamon-scented, filled with pine boughs and ornaments, football games on the color TV set in the den, uncles dazed by too much to eat, children glassy-eyed and hyper from all the naps they'd skipped. My world seemed bleak by comparison, and for once the Spartan, stripped-down life-style I so cherished seemed paltry and deprived.

I stirred on my seat, nearly paralyzed with boredom. There was no reason to believe Renata Huff would show up. Surveillance is a bitch. It's tough to sit and stare at the front of a house for five or six hours at a stretch. It's hard to pay attention. It's hard to give a shit. Usually I have to think of it as a Zen meditation, imagining I'm in touch with my Higher Power instead of just my bladder.

Daylight began to fade. I watched the color of the sky shift from apricot to blush. The temperature was dropping almost palpably. Summer evenings are usually chilly, and with this storm system lurking off the coast, the days seemed as short as some premature autumn. I could see a fog bank moving in, a wall of dark clouds against the rapidly accumulating cobalt blue of the twilight sky. I crossed my arms in front of me for warmth, slouching down on my seat. Another hour must have passed.

I felt my awareness flicker, and my head jerked involuntarily as I lurched out of sleep. I sat up straight and made a conscious effort to keep myself awake. This lasted about a minute. Various body parts began to hurt, and I thought about how babies cry when they're tired. Staying awake becomes a physical agony when the body needs rest. I shifted, turning sideways. I pulled my knees up and swung my feet onto the passenger seat, resting my back against the car door where the armrest protruded. I felt like I was drunk, my eyes rolling in their sockets as I fought to keep them open. I imagined the chemicals from all that junk food coursing through my body with this narcotic effect. This was never going to do. I had to have fresh air. I had to get up and move.

I checked my glove compartment for my penlight and a set of key picks. I tucked my handbag on the floor out of sight and grabbed a jacket from the backseat. I got out, locked the car door, and crossed the street at an angle, moving toward Renata's with a devilish urge to snoop. Really, it wasn't my fault. I can't be held responsible when boredom sets in. For the sake of good manners, I rang the doorbell first, knowing in my heart that not a soul would come to answer. Sure enough, no response. What's a poor girl to do? I let myself through the side gate and moved around to the rear.

I moved down to the dock, which seemed to rock beneath me. Renata's boat, ironically, had been named the *Fugitive*, a forty-eight-foot ketch, sleek white, with an aft center cockpit and an aft cabin. The body was fiberglass, the deck oiled teak, the trim a varnished walnut, fittings of chrome and brass. The boat would probably sleep six in comfort, eight in a pinch. There were numerous vessels moored on either side of the key, lights shimmering against the black depths of the barely rippling water. What could be better for Wendell's purposes than to have ready access to the ocean through the keys? He might have been sailing in and out of here for years, wholly anonymous, wholly undetected.

I made a feeble effort to "halloo" the boat, which produced no results. This was not surprising, as the boat was dark and shrouded in canvas.

I went on board, clambering over cables. I unzipped the cover in three places, pushing sections back. The cabin was locked, but I used my penlight to peer through the hatches, sweeping my beam through the galley below. The interior was immaculate: beautiful inlaid woods, muted upholstery in soft sunset hues. Supplies had been laid in, canned goods and bottled water in neatly stacked cardboard boxes, waiting to be stowed. I lifted my head and scanned the houses on either side. I couldn't see a soul. I checked the houses across the way. There were numerous lights on, occasional glimpses of the residents, but no indication that I was being watched. I crawled along the deck toward the bow until I reached the hatch above the V-berth. The bed was neatly made, and there were personal effects visible: clothing, paperback books, framed photographs that I couldn't quite make out.

I moved back to the galley and sat on the aft deck, working at the tubular lock that was set into the wood between my knees. A lock of this type usually has seven pins and is best attacked with a commercially available pick tool, which was part of the set I had with me. This small hand-held device is the approximate size of an old-fashioned porcelain faucet handle of the sort where HOT and COLD are printed across the surface in blue. The tool contains seven thin metal fingers that adjust themselves to correspond to the cut depth of a key. An in-and-out motion is applied, while a slight turning force is applied at the same time, a rubber sleeve providing friction that holds the fingers firmly in place. Once the lock opens, the tool can be used as an actual key.

The lock finally yielded, but not without a few well-chosen curses. I tucked the tool in my jeans and slid back the hatch, easing myself down the galley steps. Sometimes I'm sorry I didn't hang in with the Girl Scouts. I might have qualified for some keen merit badges, breaking and entering being one. I moved through the cabin, using my penlight, searching every drawer and cubbyhole I could find. I'm not even sure what I was looking for. A compleat travel itinerary would have been a boon: passports, visas, charts marked with conspicuous red arrows and asterisks. Confirmation of Wendell's presence would have been lovely, too. There was nothing of interest. About the time I ran out of steam, I also ran out of luck.

I flipped off the penlight and I was just coming up the galley steps, emerging from the cabin, when Renata appeared. I found myself staring down the barrel of a .357 Magnum revolver. The damn gun was huge and looked like something an old western marshal might carry in a holster hanging halfway to his knees. I stopped in my tracks, instantly aware of the hole a gun like that can make in parts of the anatomy essential to life. I felt my hands come up, the universal gesture of goodwill and cooperation. Renata was apparently unaware of this, as her attitude was hostile and her tone of voice belligerent. "Who are you?"

"I'm a private investigator. My ID's in my handbag, which is out in the car."

"You know I could kill you for trespassing on this boat."

"I'm aware of that. I'm kind of hoping you won't."

She stared at me, perhaps trying to decipher my tone, which was probably not as respectful as she might have wished. "What were you doing back there?"

I turned my head slightly, as if looking at the "back there" might help me recall. I decided it was the wrong time to bullshit. "I was looking for Wendell Jaffe. His son was released from the Perdido County Jail this morning, and I thought the two might be planning to connect." I thought we'd have to stop and play out some kind of nonsense along the lines of "Who is Wendell Jaffe?" but she seemed willing to play the scene the way I'd set it. I didn't articulate the rest of my suspicion, which was that Wendell, Brian, and Renata probably intended to defect on this very boat. "By the way, just to satisfy my curiosity, was Wendell the one who set up that jail release?"

"Possibly."

"How'd he manage that?"

"Haven't I seen you somewhere before?"

"Viento Negro. Last week. I tracked you to the Hacienda Grande."

Even in the shadows I saw her eyebrows lift, and I decided to leave her with the impression that it was my superior detecting that unearthed them. Why mention Dick Mills when his spotting Wendell was dumb luck on his part? I wanted her to think of me as Wonder Woman, bullets ricocheting off my wristbands.

"I tell you what," I said conversationally. "You don't really need to keep that gun on me. I'm unarmed myself, and I'm not going to do anything rash." Slowly I lowered my hands. I expected her to protest, but she didn't seem to notice. She seemed undecided about what to do next. She could, of course, shoot me, but dead bodies are tricky to dispose of and, if not dispatched properly, tend to generate a lot of questions. The last thing she wanted was the sheriff's deputy at her door. "What do you want with Wendell?"

"I work for the company that insured his life. His wife just collected half a million bucks, and if Wendell's not dead, they want their money back." I could see her hand tremble slightly, not from fear, but from the weight of the gun. I thought it was time to take action.

I let out a piercing shriek and whacked her mightily across the wrist, using my arms as a sledgehammer like the guys do in the movies. I suspect it was the shriek that made her loosen her grip. The gun flipped up like a pancake and then hit the deck, clattering across the floor of the cockpit. I pushed Renata backward, knocking her off balance while I snatched it up. She went down on her backside. Now I held the gun. She scrambled to her feet, and her hands came up. I liked this better, though I was just as baffled as she had been about what to do. I'm capable of violence when I'm under attack, but I wasn't going to shoot her while she stood there, staring me in the face. I just had to hope *she* didn't know that. I assumed an aggressive stance, feet spread, gun held with both hands, my arms stiff. "Where's Wendell? I need to talk to him."

She made a little squeaking sound in her throat. A fiery patch formed around her nose, and then her whole face screwed up as she started to weep.

"Cut the crap, Renata, and give me the information or I will shoot your right foot on the count of five." I aimed at her right foot. "One. Two. Three. Four—"

"He's at Michael's!"

"Thank you. I appreciate that. You're too kind," I replied. "I'll leave the gun in your mailbox."

She shuddered involuntarily. "Keep it. I hate guns."

I tucked the gun in my waistband at the small of my back and hopped nimbly to the dock. When I looked back at her, she was clinging weakly to the mast.

I left my business card in her mailbox and tucked another one in her door. Then I drove to Michael's.

19

I could see lights on in the rear. I bypassed the doorbell and walked around to the backyard, peeking in every window I passed. The kitchen revealed nothing except counter surfaces piled with dirty dishes. Cardboard moving boxes still formed the bulk of the furnishings, the crumpled paper now massed like a cloud bank in the corner. When I reached the master bedroom, I saw that Juliet, in a grip of home decorating tips, had draped hand towels over tension rods, effectively obscuring my view. I returned to the front door, wondering if I'd be forced to knock like a mere commoner. I tried the knob and discovered to my delight that I could walk right in.

The television set in the living room had gone on the blink. In lieu of a color picture, there was a display of dancing lights equal to an aurora borealis. The sound that accompanied this remarkable phenomenon suggested tough guys with guns and a thrilling car chase. I peered toward the bedrooms, but I couldn't hear much above the squealing of car brakes and the firing of Uzis. I took out

Renata's gun, pointing it like a flashlight as I eased my way cautiously to the back of the house.

The baby's bedroom was dark, but the door to the master bedroom was open a crack and light slanted into the hall. I gave the door a little push with the barrel of my gun. It swung back with a creak, the hinge singing on its pin. Before me, on a rocking chair, Wendell Jaffe was sitting with his grandson in his lap. He made a sharp, startled sound. "Don't shoot the baby!"

"I'm not going to shoot the baby. What's the matter with you?"

Brendan was grinning at the sight of me, flailing his arms in a vigorous nonverbal greeting. He wore a flannel sleeper with blue bunnies, and his back end was bulky with a disposable diaper. His blond hair was still damp from a recent bath. Juliet had brushed it up in a delicate question mark on top. I could smell the baby powder halfway across the room. I put the gun away, tucking it in my blue jeans at the small of my back. This is not a cool place to carry, and I was perfectly aware that I risked shooting myself in the butt. On the other hand, I didn't want the gun shoved down in my handbag, where it would be even less accessible than it was wedged up against my rear.

As family reunions go, this didn't seem to be that good. So far, Brendan was the only one who was having any fun. Michael stood to one side, leaning against the chest of drawers, his expression withdrawn. He studied Wendell's class ring, which he seemed to use like a meditation, turning it on his finger. I've seen professional tennis players do that, focusing on the strings of a tennis racket to maintain concentration. Michael's sweatshirt, soiled jeans, and mud-caked boots suggested that he hadn't cleaned up after work. I could still see the ridge in his hair where he'd worn his hard hat that day. Wendell must have been waiting when he walked in the door.

Juliet was huddled at the head of the bed, looking tense and small in a tank top and cutoffs. Her feet were bare, legs drawn up, her arms wrapped around her knees. She was keeping herself out of the way, letting the drama play out as it would. The only illumination in the room was a table lamp, something imported from

Juliet's childhood bedroom at home. The shade was ruffled and hot pink. At the base there was a doll with a stiff pink skirt, her body wired to the fixture, her arms extended. She had a rosebud for a mouth, and her lashes formed a thick fringe above eyes that would open and shut mechanically. The light bulb couldn't have been more than forty watts, but the room seemed warm with its ambient glow.

Juliet's features were etched in sharp contrasts, one cheek hot pink, the other cast in shadow. Wendell's face looked craggy and wooden in the light, his high cheekbones carved. He seemed haggard, and the sides of his nose were shiny from cosmetic surgery. Michael, on the other hand, had the face of a stone angel, cold and sensual. His dark eyes seemed luminous, his tall, lanky frame easily the equal to his father's, though Wendell was heavier and he lacked Michael's grace. The three of them were caught in a curious tableau, the kind of picture a psychiatrist might ask you to explain to gain insight into your mind-set.

"Hello, Wendell. Sorry to interrupt. Remember me?"

Wendell's gaze shifted to Michael's face. He cocked his head in my direction. "Who's this?"

Michael stared at the floor. "Private investigator," he said. "She talked to Mom about you a couple nights ago."

I gave Wendell a little wave. "She works for the insurance company you cheated out of half a million bucks," I inserted.

"*I* did?"

"Yes, Wendell," I said facetiously. "As odd as it sounds, that's what life insurance is about. Being dead. So far, you're not holding up your end of the bargain."

He was looking at me with a mixture of caution and confusion. "Don't I know you?"

"We crossed paths at the hotel down in Viento Negro."

His eyes locked on mine in a moment of recognition. "Were you the one who broke into our room?"

I shook my head, inventing lies on the spot. "Uhn-uhn, not me. That was an ex-cop named Harris Brown."

He shook his head at the name.

"He's a police lieutenant, or he was," I went on.

"Never heard of him."

"Well, he's heard of you. He was assigned to the case when you first disappeared. Then he was taken off for reasons unknown. I thought you might explain."

"Are you sure he was looking for me?"

"I don't think his being there was a coincidence," I said. "He stayed in three fourteen. I was in three sixteen."

"Hey, Dad? Could we finish this?"

Brendan began to fuss, and Wendell patted at him without much effect. He picked up a small stuffed puppy dog and waggled it in Brendan's face while he continued his conversation. Brendan grabbed the animal by the ears and pulled it in close. He must have been teething because he gnawed on its rubber face with all the raw enthusiasm I reserve for fried chicken. Somehow his antics became an odd counterpoint to Wendell's conversation with Michael.

He apparently picked up from a point he'd been making prior to my arrival. "I had to get out, Michael. It had nothing to do with you. It was my life. It was me. I'd just screwed up so bad there wasn't any other way to handle it. I hope you'll understand someday. There's no such thing as justice in the current legal system."

"Oh, come on. Spare me the speech. What is this, a political science class? Just cut the shit and don't talk to me about fucking *justice*, okay? You didn't hang around long enough to find out."

"Please. Michael. Let's stop this. I don't want to fight. There isn't time for that. I don't expect you to agree with my decision."

"It isn't just me, Dad. What about Brian? He's the one suffered all the damage."

"I'm aware he's off course, and I'm doing what I can," Wendell said.

"Brian needed you when he was twelve. It's too late now."

"I don't think so. Not at all. You're wrong about that, trust me."

Michael seemed to wince, and his eyes rolled toward the ceiling.

"*Trust* you? Dad, you are so full of shit! Why should I trust *you*? I'm never going to trust you."

Wendell seemed disconcerted at the harshness of Michael's tone. He didn't like being contradicted. He wasn't accustomed to having his judgment questioned, especially by a kid who was seventeen when he left. Michael had become an adult in his absence, had in fact stepped in to fill the very gap that Wendell had left. Maybe he pictured himself coming back to mend the breach, cleaning up old business, setting everything to rights. Maybe he'd thought an impassioned explanation might somehow compensate for his abandonment and neglect. "I guess there's no way we can agree," he said.

"Why didn't you come back and face what you did?"

"I couldn't come back. I didn't see a way to make it work."

"Meaning you weren't interested. Meaning you didn't want to be asked to make any sacrifices in our behalf. Thanks a bunch. We appreciate your devotion. It's typical."

"Now, son, that's not true."

"Yes, it is. You could have stayed if you wanted, if we *meant* anything to you. But here's the truth. We didn't matter to you, and that was just our tough luck, right?"

"Of course you matter. What do you think I've been talking about?"

"I don't know, Dad. As far as I can tell, you're just trying to justify your behavior."

"This is pointless. I can't undo the past. I can't change what happened back then. Brian and I are going to turn ourselves in. That's the best I can do, and if that's not good enough, then I don't know what to say."

Michael broke off eye contact, shaking his head with frustration. I watched him consider and discard a retort.

Wendell cleared his throat. "I have to go. I told Brian I'd be there." He got to his feet, shifting the baby against his shoulder. Juliet swung her legs over to the side of the bed and got up, prepared to take Brendan from his grandfather's arms. It was clear the conversation had upset her. Her nose was pink, her mouth swollen with emotion.

Michael shoved his hands down in his pockets. "You didn't do Brian any favor with that fake jail release."

"That's true, as it turned out, but there was no way we could know that. I've changed my mind about a lot of things. Anyway, this is something your brother and I have to work out between us."

"You've got Brian in worse trouble than he was in before. You don't move fast, the cops'll pick him up and throw him back in the slammer and he won't see daylight 'til he's a hundred and three. And where will you be? Off on a fuckin' boat without a care in the world. Good luck."

"Doesn't it occur to you that I'll have to pay a price, too?"

"At least you don't have a murder charge hanging over your head."

"I'm not sure there's any point in going on with this," Wendell said, ignoring the actual content of Michael's remark. The two of them seemed to be talking at cross purposes. Wendell was trying to reassert his parental authority. Michael wasn't having any of that shit. He had a son now himself, and he knew how much his father had forfeited. Wendell turned away. "I have to go," he said, holding one hand out to Juliet. "I'm glad we had a chance to meet. It's too bad the circumstances weren't happier."

"Are we going to see you again?" Juliet said. Tears were spilling down her cheeks. Mascara had formed a sprinkling of soot beneath her eyes. Michael seemed watchful, his expression haunted, while grief poured from Juliet like water bursting through a wall.

Even Wendell seemed affected by her open display of feeling. "Absolutely. Of course. That's a promise."

His gaze lingered on Michael, perhaps hoping for some sign of emotion. "I'm sorry for the pain I caused you. I mean that."

Michael's shoulders hunched slightly with the effort to stay disconnected. "Yeah. Right. Whatever," he said.

Wendell hugged the baby to him, his face buried in Brendan's neck, drinking in the sweet, milky smell of the child. "Oh, you sweet boy," he said, his voice tremulous. Brendan was staring fascinated at Wendell's hair, which he grabbed. Solemnly he tried to put a fistful in his mouth. Wendell winced, gently extracting the baby's fingers. Juliet reached for Brendan. Michael watched, his eyes pooling with silver before he looked away. Sorrow rose from his skin like steam, radiating outward.

Wendell passed the baby to Juliet and kissed her on the forehead before he turned to Michael. The two grabbed each other in a tight embrace that seemed to go on forever. "I love you, son." They rocked back and forth in an ancient dance. Michael made a small sound at the back of his throat, his eyes squeezed shut. For that one unguarded moment, he and Wendell were connected. I had to look away. I couldn't imagine what it must feel like to find yourself in the presence of a parent you thought was dead. Michael pulled back. Wendell took out a handkerchief and swiped at his eyes. "I'll be in touch," he whispered, and then let out a breath.

Without looking at them, he turned and left the room. His guilt probably felt oppressive, like a weight on his chest. He moved through the house, heading for the front door with me right behind him. If he was aware of my presence, he didn't object.

The outside air had picked up a sting of moisture, wind tossing through the trees. The streetlights were almost entirely blocked by branches, shadows blowing across the street like a pile of leaves. I intended to bid the man a fare-thee-well, get in my car, and then play tag with him, following at a discreet distance until he led me to Brian. As soon as I got a fix on the kid's location, I was calling the cops. I said good night and moved off in the opposite direction.

I'm not sure he even heard me.

Preoccupied, Wendell took out a set of car keys and crossed the grass to a little red Maserati sports car that was parked at the curb. Renata apparently had a fleet of expensive autos. He unlocked the car and let himself in, quickly sliding in under the steering wheel. He slammed the car door. I unlocked my VW and jammed my key in the ignition in concert with his. I could feel Renata's gun pressing into the small of my back. I pulled it out of my waistband. I torqued myself around to the backseat, where I snagged my handbag and deposited the gun into the depths. I heard Wendell's engine grind. I fired mine up and sat there with the lights out, waiting for his front and rear lights to come on.

The grinding continued, but his engine didn't turn over. The sound was high-pitched and unproductive. Moments later I saw him fling open his car door and emerge. Agitated, he checked under the hood. He did something to the wires, got back into the car, and started grinding again. The engine was losing hope, batteries surrendering any juice they had. I put the VW in gear and flipped my lights on, pulling forward slowly until I was next to him. I rolled my window down. He leaned over from the driver's seat and rolled his down.

I said, "Hop in. I'll take you to Renata's. You can call a tow truck from her place."

He debated for a moment, with a quick glance at Michael's. He didn't have much choice. The last thing in the world he wanted was to go back in with a chore as mundane as a call to triple A. He got out, locked his car, and came around the front, getting into mine. I turned right on Perdido Street and took a left before I reached the fairgrounds, thinking to hit the frontage road that ran along the beach. I could have hopped on the freeway. Traffic wasn't heavy. The street leading to the Keys was just one ramp away, and just as easily reached by this route.

I turned left when I reached the beach. The wind had picked up considerably, and there were massive black clouds above the pitch black of the ocean. "I had a nice chat with Carl Monday night," I said. "Have you talked to him?"

"I was supposed to meet with him later, but he had to go out of town," Wendell said, distracted.

"Really. He thought he'd be too mad to talk to you."

"We have business to settle. He has something of mine."

"You mean the boat?"

"Well, that, too, but this is something else."

The sky was charcoal gray, and I could see flashes out at sea, an electrical storm sitting maybe fifty miles out. The light flickered among the darkening cloud banks, creating the illusion of artillery too far away to hear. The air was filled with a restless energy. I glanced over at Wendell. "Aren't you even curious how we picked up your trail? I'm surprised you haven't asked."

His attention was fixed on the horizon, which was illuminated intermittently as the storm progressed. "It doesn't matter. It was bound to happen sometime."

"You mind telling me where you've been all these years?"

He stared out the side window, his face averted. "Not far. You'd be surprised how few places I've been."

"You gave up a lot to get there."

Pain flickered across his face like lightning. "Yes."

"Have you been with Renata the whole time?"

"Oh, yes," he said with just a hint of bitterness. A small silence fell, and then he stirred uneasily. "Do you think I'm wrong to come back like this?"

"Depends on what you were hoping to accomplish."

"I'd like to help them."

"Help them do what? Brian's already on his path, and so is Michael. Dana coped as well as she could, and the money's been spent. You can't just step back into the life you left and make all the stories come out differently. They're working out the consequences of your decision. You'll have to do that, too."

"I guess I can't expect to mend all my fences in the course of a few days."

"I'm not sure you can do it at all," I said. "In the meantime, I'm not going to let you out of my sight. I lost you once. I don't intend to lose you again."

"I need some time. I have business to take care of."

"You had business to take care of five years ago!"

"This is different."

"Where's Brian?"

"He's safe."

"I didn't ask you *how* he was, I said 'where.' " The car began to lose speed. I looked down with bafflement, pumping the accelerator as the car slowed. "Jesus, what's this?"

"You out of gas?"

"I just filled the tank." I steered toward the right curb as the car drifted to a halt.

He peered over at the dashboard. "Gas gauge says full."

"What'd I just tell you? Of course it's full. I just filled it!"

We had reached a full stop. The silence was profound, and then the underlying thrum of wind and surf filtered into my consciousness. Even with the moon obscured by storm clouds, I could see the whitecaps out in the water.

I hauled my handbag from the backseat and fumbled in the front pocket until I found my penlight. "Let me see what's going on," I said, as though I had a clue.

I got out of the car. Wendell got out on his side and moved around to the rear in concert with me. I was glad of his company. Maybe he knew something about cars that I didn't—no big trick. In situations like this, I always like to take action. I opened the back flap and stared at the engine. Looked like it always did, about the size and shape of a sewing machine. I expected to see sprung parts, broken doohickies, the flapping ends of a fan belt, some evidence of rogue auto parts adrift from their moorings. "What do you think?"

He took the penlight and leaned closer, squinting. Boys know about these things: guns, cars, lawn mowers, garbage disposals, electric switches, baseball statistics. I'm scared to take the lid off the toilet tank because that ball thing always looks like it's on the verge of exploding. I leaned over and peered with him. "Looks a little bit like a sewing machine, doesn't it?" he remarked.

Behind us, a car backfired and a rock slammed into my rear fender. Wendell made sense of it a split second before I did. We both hit the pavement. Wendell grabbed me, and the two of us scrambled around to the side of the car. A second shot was fired, and the bullet *ping*ed off the roof. We ducked, hunched together. Wendell's arm had gone around me protectively. He flipped the switch on the penlight, making the pitch dark complete. I had a terrible desire to lift up to window level and peek out across the street. I knew there wouldn't be much to see: dark, a dirt bank, swiftly passing cars on the freeway. Our assailant must have followed us from Michael's house, first incapacitating Wendell's car and then mine.

"This has got to be one of your pals. I'm not this unpopular in my set," I said.

Another shot was fired. My rear window turned to cracked ice, though only one chunk fell out.

Wendell said, "Jesus."

I said, "Amen." Neither of us meant it as profanity.

He looked at me. His previous lethargy had vanished. At least his attention had been sharpened by the situation. "Someone's been following me the last few days."

"You have a theory?"

He shook his head. "I made some phone calls. I needed help."

"Who knew you were going to Michael's?"

"Just Renata."

I thought about that one. I'd taken her gun, which I remembered now was in my handbag. In the car. "I have a gun in the car if you can reach it," I said. "My handbag's on the backseat."

"Won't the inside light come on?"

"In *my* car? Not a chance."

Wendell opened the door on the passenger side. Sure enough, the interior light came on. The next bullet was swift and nearly caught him in the neck. We ducked down again, silent for a moment while we thought about Wendell's carotid artery.

I said, "Carl must have known you'd be at Michael's if you told him you'd meet him afterward."

"That was before his plans changed. Anyway, he doesn't know where Michael lives."

"He says his plans changed, but you don't know that for a fact. It wouldn't take a rocket scientist to call Information. All he had to do was ask Dana. He's kept in touch with her."

"Hell, he's in love with Dana. He's always been in love with her. I'm sure he was delighted to have me out of the picture."

"What about Harris Brown? He'd have a gun."

"I told you before. I never heard of him."

"Wendell, quit bullshitting. I need some answers here."

"I'm telling you the truth!"

"Stay down. I'm going to try the car door again."

Wendell flattened himself as I gave the door a yank. The next shot *thunk*ed into the sand close by. I flipped the seat forward and grabbed my bag, hauled it out of the backseat, and slammed the door again. My heart had rocketed. Anxiety was coursing through my body as if a sluice gate had opened. I needed to pee like crazy, except for the fact that my kidneys had shriveled. All my other internal organs had circled, like wagons under serious attack. I pulled out the revolver, with its white pearlite grips. "Gimme some light over here."

Wendell flipped on the penlight, shielding it like a match.

I was looking at the sort of single-action six-shooter John Wayne might have favored. I popped open the cylinder and checked the load, which was full. I snapped the cylinder shut. The gun must have weighed three pounds.

"Where'd you get that?"

"I stole it from Renata. Wait here. I'll be back."

He said something to me, but I was already duck-walking my way out into the darkness, angling toward the beach and away from our assailant. I cut left, circling out a hundred yards around the front of the car, hoping I wasn't visible to anybody interested in target practice. My eyes were fully adjusted to the dark by now, and I felt conspicuous. I looked back, trying to measure the distance I'd come. My pale blue VW looked like some kind of ghostly igloo or a giant pup tent. I reached a left-turning curve in the road, crouched, and crossed in a flash, easing back toward the point from which I imagined our attacker was firing.

It probably took ten minutes until I reached the spot, and I realized I hadn't heard a shot fired the whole time. Even in the hazy visibility of the half-dark around me, the area felt deserted. I was now directly across from my car on the two-lane road, keeping myself low to the ground. I popped my head up like a prairie dog.

"Wendell?" I called.

No answer. No shots fired. No movement in any direction and

no more sense of jeopardy. The night felt flat and totally benign at this point. I stood upright. "Wendell?"

I did a 360 turn, sweeping my gaze across the immediate vicinity, and then sank down again. I looked both ways and crossed the street at a quick clip, keeping low. When I reached the car, I slid past the front bumper into home base. "Hey, it's me," I said.

There was only sea wind and empty beach.

Wendell Jaffe was gone again.

20

It was now ten o'clock at night, and the roadway was deserted. I could see lights from the freeway tantalizingly close, but no one in their right mind was going to pick me up at that hour. I found my handbag by the car and hefted it over my shoulder. I went around to the driver's side and opened the car door. I reached in, leaning forward to snag the keys from the ignition. I could have locked the car, but what would be the point? It wasn't running at the moment, and the rear window was shattered, open to the elements and any pint-size little car thieves.

I hiked to the nearest gas station, which was maybe a mile away. It was very dark, street lamps appearing at long intervals and even then with only dim illumination. The storm had apparently stalled off the coast, where it lingered, brooding. Lightning winked through the inky clouds like a lamp with a loose connection. The wind whuffled across the sand while dried fronds rattled in the palm trees. I did a quick self-assessment and decided I was in pretty good shape, given all the excitement. One of the virtues of physical fitness is that you can walk a mile in the dark and it's no big deal. I was wearing jeans, a short-sleeved sweatshirt, and my tenny bops, not the best shoes for walking, but not agonizing, either.

The station itself was one of those places open twenty-four hours a day, but it was run largely by computer, with only one fellow in attendance. Naturally he couldn't leave the premises. I got a handful of change and headed for the public phone booth in the corner of the parking lot. I called AAA first, gave them my number, and told them where I was. The operator advised me to wait with the car, but I assured her I had no intention of hiking back in the dark. While I waited for the tow truck, I put a call through to Renata and told her what was happening. She didn't seem to bear me any grudges after our tussle on the boat deck for possession of the gun. She said Wendell wasn't home yet, but she'd hop in the car and cruise the route between the house and the frontage road where I'd last seen him.

The tow truck finally appeared about forty-five minutes later. I hopped in with the driver and directed him to my disabled car. He was a man in his forties, apparently career tow truck, full of sniffs, tobacco chaws, and learned assessments. When we reached the vehicle, he stepped down from the truck and hiked his pants up, circling the VW with his hands on his hips. He paused and spat. "What's the deal here?" He might have been asking about the shattered rear window, but I ignored that for the moment.

"I have no idea. I was tooling along about forty miles an hour and the car suddenly lost power."

He reached toward the car roof where a large-caliber slug had punched a hole the size of a dime. "Say, what *is* this?"

"Oh. You mean *that*?" I leaned forward, squinting in the half-light.

The hole looked like a neat black polka dot against the pale blue paint. He stuck the tip of one finger into it. "This here looks like a *bullet* hole."

"Gosh, it does, doesn't it?"

We circled the car, and I echoed his consternation at all the hurt places we came across. He quizzed me at length, but I fended off his questions. The guy was a tow truck driver, not a cop, I thought. I was hardly under oath.

Finally, head shaking, he slid onto the driver's seat and tried starting the car. I suspect he would have taken great satisfaction if the engine had fired right up. He struck me as the sort of fellow who didn't mind women looking foolish. No luck. He got out, went around, and peered in the back end. He grunted to himself, fiddled with some car parts, and tried the starter again without producing results. He towed the VW to the gas station, where he left it in a service bay and then departed with sly glance backward and a shake of his head. No telling what he thought of little ladies these days. I had a chat with the attendant, who assured me the mechanic would be in by seven the next morning.

By now it was well after midnight and I was not only exhausted, but I was stranded as well. I could have called Henry. I knew he'd have hopped in his car and driven down to fetch me at any hour without complaint. The problem was I simply couldn't face the drive, yet another lap in the track I was running between Santa Teresa and Perdido. Happily, the area wasn't short of motels. I spotted one on the far side of the freeway, within easy walking distance, and hoofed it across the overpass. In preparation for such emergencies, I always carry a toothbrush, toothpaste, and clean underpants shoved down in my handbag.

The motel had one vacancy. I paid more than I wanted, but I was too tired to argue. For the extra thirty dollars I was accorded one tiny bottle each of shampoo and conditioner. A matching container held just enough "body" lotion to moisturize one limb. The problem was you couldn't get the stuff out. I finally gave up the idea of being moist and went to bed stark naked and dry as a stick. I slept like a zombie without any medication and decided, with regret, that my cold was gone.

I woke up at 6:00, wondering briefly where I was. Once I remembered, I sank down under the covers and went back to sleep, not waking again until 8:25. I showered, donned my clean underwear, and then put on yesterday's clothes again. The room was paid for until noon, so I kept my key and grabbed a quick cup of coffee from the vending machine before I hiked back across 101 to my car.

The mechanic was eighteen years old, with frizzy red hair, brown eyes, a pug nose, a gap between his front teeth, and a thick Texas accent. The coverall he was wearing looked like a romper suit. When he saw me, he beckoned me over by doing curls with his index finger. He'd put the car up on the hydraulic lift, and we peered at the underside together. I could already picture dollars flying out the window. He wiped his hands on a rag and said, "Lookit."

I looked, not understanding at first what he was pointing to. He reached up and touched a vise clamp that had been affixed to a line. "Somebody put this little dingus on your fuel line. I bet you onny got about three blocks before the engine give out."

I laughed. "And that's all it was?"

He unscrewed the clamp and dropped the little dingus in the palm of my hand. "That's all. Car should run fine now."

"Thanks. This is great. How much do I owe you?"

"Thanks is good enough where I come from," he said.

I drove back to my motel room, where I sat on the unmade bed and called Renata. Her machine picked up and I left a message, asking her to give me a call. I tried Michael's house next, surprised when he snatched up the phone after half a ring.

"Hi, Michael. This is Kinsey. I thought you'd be at work. Have you heard from your father?"

"Nuhn-uhn, and Brian hasn't, either. He's called this morning to say Dad never showed. He really sounded worried. I called in sick so I could hang by the phone."

"Where is Brian?"

"He won't tell me. I think he's afraid I'll turn him in to the cops before he and Dad connect up. You think Dad's okay?"

"That's hard to say." I filled him in on events from the night before. "I left a message for Renata, and I hope to hear back. When I talked to her last night, she said she'd see if she could find him. She may have picked him up somewhere out on the road."

There was a brief silence. "Who's Renata?"

Oops. "Ahh. Nnnn. She's a friend of your dad's. I think he's been staying at her place with her."

"She lives here in Perdido?"

"She has a house on the Keys."

Another silence. "Does my mom know?"

"I don't think so. Probably not."

"Man, oh, man. What a jerk." Silence again. "Well. I guess I better let you go. I want to keep the line free in case he tries to get in touch."

I said, "You've got my number. Will you let me know if you should hear from him?"

"Sure," he said tersely. I suspected any lingering sense of loyalty to his father had been erased with the news about Renata.

I tried calling Dana. Her machine picked up. I listened to strains of the wedding march, drumming my fingers until I heard the beep. I left word for her to call me, keeping my message brief. I was still kicking myself for mentioning Renata in my conversation with Michael. Wendell had generated enough hostility in the kid without my adding the issue of his common-law wife. I tried reaching Lieutenant Ryckman at the Perdido County Jail. He was out, but I had a quick chat with Senior Deputy Tiller, who told me there was a big department shake-up over Brian's unauthorized release. Internal Affairs was scrutinizing every employee who had access to the computer. Another call came through, and he had to ring off. I said I'd try Ryckman again when I got back to Santa Teresa.

I'd just about exhausted my list of local calls. I checked out of the motel and was on the road by 10:00. I was hoping that by the time I reached the office in Santa Teresa I'd have some return messages, but I unlocked my door to find the green light glowing blankly on my answering machine. I spent the morning with my usual office routines: business calls and mail, a few bookkeeping entries, one or two bills to pay. I made a pot of coffee and then called my insurance adjuster to report last night's incident. She told me to go ahead and get the rear window replaced at the auto glass shop I'd used before. It was clear I couldn't ride around without protection because I'd be ticketed.

In the meantime I was half tempted to leave the bullet holes where they were. Make too many claims and you get your policy canceled or your rates elevated to astronomical rates. What did I care about bullet holes? I was sporting a few of those myself. I called and made an appointment to have the window taken care of late afternoon.

Shortly after lunch, Alison buzzed me to say Renata Huff was in the reception area. I went out to the front. She was sitting on the little sofa, head back, eyes closed. She was not looking good. She wore chinos, bunched together and belted at the waist, and a black V-neck top with an orange anorak over it. Her dark curls were still damp from a recent shower, but her eyes were darkly circled and her cheeks seemed gaunt from stress. She pulled herself together with an apologetic smile at Alison, who seemed especially perky by comparison.

I took Renata back to my office, sat her on my visitor's chair, and poured us both some coffee. "Thank you," she murmured, sipping gratefully. She closed her eyes again, savoring the rich liquid on her tongue. "This is good. I need this."

"You look tired."

"I am."

It was really the first time I'd had a chance to study her closely. Her face in repose was not what I'd call pretty. Her complexion was lovely—clear olive tones without flaw or blemish—but her features seemed wrong: brows dark and untamed, dark eyes too small. Her mouth was large, and her short-cropped hair made her jaw look squared off. Her expression ordinarily had a petulant cast, but in the rare moments when she smiled, her whole face was transformed—exotic, full of light. With her coloring, she could wear hues a lot of women couldn't get away with: lime green, hot pink, royal blue, and fuchsia.

"Wendell got home about midnight last night. This morning I went out to run errands. I couldn't have been gone for more than forty minutes. When I came home, everything he owned was gone and so was he. I waited for an hour or so and then got in my car and came up here. My real inclination was to call the police, but I thought I'd try you first and see what advice you might have to give."

"About what?"

"He stole some money from me. Four thousand dollars in cash."

"What about the *Fugitive*?"

She shook her head wearily. "He knows I'd kill him if he took that boat."

"Don't you have a speedboat, too?"

"It's actually not a speedboat. It's an inflatable dinghy, but it's still at the dock. Anyway, Wendell doesn't have keys to the *Fugitive.*"

"Why not?"

Her cheeks tinted slightly. "I never trusted him."

"You've been together five years and you didn't trust him with the keys to your boat?"

"He had no business on the boat without me," she said in an irritated tone.

I had to let that one pass. "So what's your suspicion?"

"I think he went back for the *Lord.* God only knows where he means to go after that."

"Why would he steal Eckert's boat?"

"He'd steal anything. Don't you get that? The *Lord* was his boat to begin with, and he wanted it back. Besides, the *Fugitive*'s a coastal cruiser. The *Lord*'s a blue water boat, better suited to his purpose."

"Which is what?"

"Getting as far away from here as possible."

"Why come to me?"

"I thought you'd know where the *Lord* was slipped. You said you talked to Carl Eckert on the boat. I didn't want to waste a lot of time at the harbormaster's office trying to track him down."

"Wendell told me Carl Eckert was out of town last night."

"Of course he's gone. That's the point. He won't even miss the boat until he gets back." She checked her watch. "Wendell must have left Perdido about ten this morning."

"How'd he manage that? Did he get the car fixed?"

"He took the Jeep I keep parked on the street. Even if it took him forty minutes to get up here, the Coast Guard still has a chance to head him off."

"Where would he go?"

"Back to Mexico, I'd guess. He knows the waters around the Baja, and he's got a counterfeit passport that identifies him as a Mexican citizen."

"I'll get my car," I said.

"We can take mine."

We clattered down the steps together, me in front, Renata bringing up the rear. "You should notify the police about the Jeep."

"Good point. I'm hoping he left it somewhere in the marina parking lot."

"Where'd he go last night, did he say? I lost track of him around ten. If he got home at midnight, what'd he do for two hours? It doesn't take that long to walk a mile and a half."

"I'm not sure. After you called, I got in my car and went looking for him. I scoured every street between my place and the beach, and there was no sign of him. From what he said later, I got the impression somebody came and got him, but he wouldn't say who. Maybe one of his boys."

"I don't think so," I said. "I talked to Michael a little while ago. He says Brian called this morning. Wendell was supposed to be there last night, but he never showed."

"Wendell's never been good at promises."

"Do you know where Brian is?"

"I have no idea. Wendell made sure I knew as little as possible. That way if I was ever questioned by the police, I could claim ignorance."

This was apparently Wendell's standard operating procedure, but I wondered if this time keeping everybody ignorant was going to work against him.

We'd reached the street by then. Renata had defied all the parking gods and snagged a place right in front where the curb was painted red. And did she have a ticket? Of course not. She unlocked the Jag, and I let myself into the passenger seat. Renata took off with a little chirp of her tires. I found myself holding on to the chicken stick. "Wendell might have gone to the cops," I said. "From what he told Michael, he intended to turn himself in. With somebody shooting at him, he might have felt safer in the slammer."

She made a little snort of contempt, flashing me a cynical look. "He had no intention of turning himself in. That was bullshit. He mentioned he was going to see Dana, but that might have been bullshit, too."

"He went to Dana's last night? What was that about?"

"I don't know that he went, but he said he wanted to talk to her before he left. He felt guilty about her. He hoped to get things squared away before he took off. He probably wanted to have his conscience clear."

"You think he left without you?"

"I certainly think he has it in him. Spineless bastard. He never faced the consequences of his own behavior. Never. At this point, I don't care if he ends up in jail." She seemed to be catching every traffic light. If there was no cross traffic visible, she would sail through on red, skipping four-way stops altogether in her haste to reach the marina. Maybe she thought traffic laws were meant only as suggestions, or maybe the traffic laws simply didn't apply to her that day.

I studied her profile, wondering how much information I could pump her for. "Do you mind if I ask about the logistics of Wendell's disappearance?"

"Like what?"

I shrugged, not quite sure where to start. "What arrangements did he make? I don't see how he could have managed it alone." I could see her hesitate, so I tried a gentle coaxing, hoping she would open up. "I'm not just being nosy. I'm thinking whatever he did then, he might try again."

I didn't think she'd answer, but she finally slid a look in my direction. "You're right. He couldn't pull it off without help," she said. "I single-handed my ketch down along the coast of Baja and picked him up in the dinghy after he abandoned the *Lord.*"

"That was risky, wasn't it? What if you'd missed him? The ocean's a big place."

"I've sailed all my life, and I'm very good with boats. The whole plan was risky, but we pulled it off. That's the point, isn't it?"

"I guess so."

"What about you? Do you sail yourself?"

I shook my head. "Too expensive."

She smiled faintly. "Find a man with some money. That's what I've always done. I learned to ski and play golf. I learned to fly first class traveling around the world."

"What happened to your first husband, Dean?" I asked.

"He died of a heart attack. He was actually number two."

"How long has Wendell been traveling on his passport?"

"The whole five years. Ever since we took off."

"And the passport office never checked?"

"They slipped up on that, which is what gave us the idea in the first place. Dean died in Spain. Somehow the papers were never processed here. When his passport expired and the time came to renew, Wendell filled out the application and we substituted his picture. He and my husband were close enough in age to use Dean's birth certificate if the documentation was ever questioned."

We reached Cabana Boulevard and turned right, the marina visible, with its forest of naked masts, to our left. The day was thickly overcast, a mist floating on the dark green waters of the harbor. I could smell brine shrimp and diesel fuel. A strong wind was blowing off the ocean, bringing with it the smell of a distant rain. Renata turned into the marina parking area and found a space in the tiny lot just outside the kiosk. She parked the Jag and the two of us got out. I led the way since I knew where the *Captain Stanley Lord* was slipped.

We passed a funky little seafood restaurant with a few outside tables and the naval reserve building. "Then what?"

She shrugged. "After we got the passport? We took off. I would come back at intervals, usually by myself, but occasionally with Wendell. He stayed on the boat. I was free to come and go as I pleased since no one knew of our connection. I kept an eye on the boys, though they didn't seem to be aware of it."

"So when Brian first got in trouble with the law, Wendell knew all about it?"

"Oh, yes. At first he didn't worry. Brian's run-ins with the law seemed like childish pranks. Truancy and vandalism."

"Boys will be boys," I said.

She ignored that. "We were off on a round-the-world cruise when things got out of hand. By the time we came home, Brian was in bigger trouble than we knew. That's when Wendell really went to work."

We passed a yacht brokerage and a fish market. The navy pier extended to our left, a big marine travel rig in place. A boat had just been hoisted out of the water, and we had to wait impatiently while the long-legged mobile rig crept across the walkway and down the short avenue to our right. "Doing what? I still don't understand how he managed it."

"I'm not sure myself. It had something to do with the name of the boat." The breakwater was nearly deserted, the threatening weather probably driving boats into port and people under cover. "Not directly," she went on. "From what he told me, Captain Stanley Lord was always blamed for something he didn't do."

"He ignored the SOS from the *Titanic*, is what I heard," I said.

"Or so people claimed. Wendell had done a lot of research on the incident, and he felt Lord was innocent."

"I don't get the connection."

"Wendell was in trouble with the law once himself. . . ."

"Oh, that's right. I remember. Somebody mentioned that. He'd graduated from law school. He was convicted of manslaughter, wasn't he?"

She nodded. "I don't know the details."

"He told you he wasn't guilty?"

"Oh, he wasn't," she said. "He took the blame for somebody

else. That's how he was able to get Brian out of jail. By calling in his marker."

I stared at her without slowing my pace. "Did you ever hear of a guy named Harris Brown?"

She shook her head in the negative. "Who's he?"

"An ex-cop. He was originally assigned to the fraud investigation after Wendell disappeared, but then he was pulled off. Turns out he'd invested a lot of money in Wendell's company, and the scam wiped him out. I was thinking he might have used some of his old connections to help Brian. I just can't figure out why he'd do it."

The ramp for Marina 1 was another fifty yards down on the left, the gate locked as usual. Seagulls were pecking intently at a fishing net. We stood there for a moment, hoping somebody with a key card would pass through so we could slipstream in behind them.

Finally I grabbed on to the fence post and held on while I climbed around on the outside of the barrier, working my way along the fencing until I reached the other side. I opened the gate for her and let her through, and we started off down the dock. Conversation between us dwindled. I turned into the sixth line of slips on the right, marked J, counting down visually to the slot where the *Lord* was tied up.

Even from a distance, I could see the slip was empty and the boat was gone.

21

Renata's mood darkened as we moved up the ramp toward the harbormaster's office, which was located above a ship's chandler selling marine hardware and supplies. I half expected an outburst of some kind, but she was remarkably silent. She waited on a small wooden balcony outside while I went through the explanations with the clerk at the counter. Since we weren't the legal owners of the missing boat and since there was no way we could prove Eckert hadn't taken the boat himself, it soon became clear that for the time being, nothing much could be done. The clerk took the information, as much to appease me as anything else. When and if Eckert showed, he could file a report. The harbormaster would then notify the Coast Guard and the local police. I left my name and telephone number and asked if they'd have Eckert get in touch if they heard from him.

Renata followed me downstairs, declining to accompany me as I walked over to the yacht club next door. I was hoping somebody there might know where Eckert had gone. I pushed in through the glass doors and went upstairs, pausing outside the dining room. From the second-floor deck, she looked cold and tired, sitting on the low concrete wall that bordered the breakwater. At her back the ocean thundered monotonously, wind tearing at her hair. In the shallows a yellow Labrador charged through the surf, chasing pigeons off the beach while the seagulls wheeled above him and screamed with amusement.

The yacht club dining room was empty except for the bartender and a fellow with a vacuum cleaner, mowing the wall-to-wall carpeting. Again I left my name and number, asking the bartender to have Carl Eckert get in touch with me if he came in.

As we walked back to the car, Renata gave me a bitter smile. "What's so funny?" I asked.

"Nothing. I was just thinking about Wendell. He has all the luck. It'll be hours before anybody starts to look for him."

"There's nothing we can do, Renata. It's always possible he'll show up," I said. "Actually, we can't really be sure he left. Hell, we can't even prove Wendell took the boat."

"You don't know him like I do. He rips everybody off one way or another."

We cruised through the parking lot in search of her missing Jeep, but it was nowhere in sight. She drove me back to the office, where I retrieved my VW and drove out to Colgate. I spent the next two irksome hours getting the rear window replaced. While I was waiting, I sat in the chrome-and-plastic reception area, drinking free bad coffee from a foam cup while I leafed through tattered back issues of *Arizona Highways.* This lasted four minutes before I left the building. As was my habit of late, I found a public telephone booth and conducted a little business from the parking lot. Once I got the hang of it, I could probably dispense with an office altogether.

I put a call through to Lieutenant Whiteside in Fraud and brought him up to date. "I think it's time to run mug shots in the paper," he said. "I'll contact the local TV station, too, and see what they can do for us. I want the public aware these guys are out there. Maybe someone will dime 'em out."

"Let's hope."

Once my rear window had been installed, I tooled on back to the office and spent the next hour and a half at my desk. I felt I should stay near the phone in case Eckert called in. In the meantime, I gave Mac a buzz and filled him in on what was happening. I no sooner put the phone down than it rang. "Kinsey Millhone Investigations. Kinsey Millhone."

An instant of silence and then a woman said, "Oh. I thought this was an answering machine."

"No, this is me. Who is this?"

"This is your cousin Tasha Howard, up in San Francisco."

"Ah, yes. Tasha. Liza mentioned you. How are you?" I said. Mentally I'd begun to drum my fingers, hoping to get her off the line in case Wendell phoned in.

"I'm fine," she said. "Something's come up and it occurred to me you might be interested. I just had a chat with Grand's attorney down in Lompoc. The house where our mothers lived is either being moved or torn down. Grand's been fighting with the city for the last several months, and we're supposed to hear something soon about the disposition of the matter. She's trying to have the house protected under the local historical preservation act. The original structure dates back to the turn of the century. The house hasn't been lived in for years, of course, but it could be restored. She owns another lot where she can put the house if she can get the city to agree. Anyway, I thought you might want to see the place again since you were there once yourself."

"I was there?"

"Oh, sure. You don't remember? The four of you—Aunt Gin, your parents, and you—came up when Burt and Grand were off on the big cruise for their forty-second anniversary. It was really meant for their fortieth, but it took 'em two years to get organized. All the cousins got to play together, and you fell off the sliding board and cut your knee. I was seven, so you must have been about four, I'd say. Maybe a little older, but I know you weren't in school yet. I can't believe you don't remember. Aunt Rita taught us all to eat peanut-butter-and-pickle sandwiches, which I've adored ever since. You were supposed to come back in the next couple of months. It was all set up for when Burt and Grand got home."

"Only my parents never made it," I said, thinking, Jesus, the peanut-butter-and-pickle sandwiches aren't even mine anymore.

"I suppose not," she said. "Anyway, I thought if you saw the house, it might jog your memory. I have to come down on business, and I'd be happy to give you the nickel tour."

"What sort of work do you do?"

"I'm an attorney. Probate and estate administration, wills, intervivos trusts, tax planning. The firm has an office up here and another one in Lompoc, so I end up flying back and forth all the time. What's your schedule look like in the next few days? Are you free any time soon?"

"Let me think about that. I appreciate the offer, but I'm currently tied up with a case. Why don't you go ahead and give me the address? If I have a chance to get up there, I can take a look and if not, well . . . so be it."

"I suppose that would do," she said reluctantly. "I was actually hoping I could see you. Liza wasn't entirely happy with the way she handled the situation. She thought maybe I could smooth the waters a bit."

"No need for that. She did fine," I said. I was keeping my distance, and I'm sure the maneuver wasn't lost on her. She gave me the address and a sketchy set of directions, which I jotted on a sheet of scratch paper. I was already struggling with an urge to toss it in the trash. I started making good-bye noises, using that airy tone that says, Okay, thanks a lot, nice talking to you.

Tasha said, "I hope this doesn't seem too personal, but I get the impression you're really not interested in cementing any family ties."

"I don't think that's too personal," I said. "I guess I'm in the process of assimilating the information. I don't really know what I want to do about it yet."

"Are you angry with Grand?"

"Of course I am, and why wouldn't I be? She threw my mother out. That estrangement must have gone on for twenty years."

"That wasn't all Grand's doing. It takes two to make a rift."

"Right," I said. "At least my mother was on her way to make amends. What did Grand ever do? She sat back and waited, which I notice she's still doing."

"What does that mean?"

"Well, where's she been all these years? I'm thirty-four years old. Until yesterday I never even knew she existed. She could have gotten in touch."

"She didn't know where you were."

"Bullshit. Liza told me everybody knew we were down here. For the last twenty-five years I've been an hour away."

"I don't mean to argue about this, but I really don't believe Grand was aware of that."

"What did she think happened, I was eaten by bears? She could have hired a detective if she'd cared enough."

"Well. I see your point, and I'm sorry about all this. We didn't make the contact to cause you pain."

"Why did you, then?"

"We were hoping to connect. We thought enough time had passed to heal old wounds."

"Those 'old wounds' are news to me. I just heard about this shit yesterday."

"I can appreciate that, and you're entitled to feel what you feel. It's just that Grand's not going to live forever. She's eighty-seven now, and she's not in the best of health. You still have a chance to enjoy the relationship."

"Correction. *She* has a chance to enjoy the relationship. I'm not sure I would."

"Will you think about it?"

"Sure."

"Do you mind if I tell her we've spoken?"

"I don't see how I can prevent it."

There was a fractional silence. "Are you really this unforgiving?"

"Absolutely. Why not? Just like Grand," I said. "I'm sure she'll appreciate the attribute."

"I see," she said coolly.

"Look, this is not your fault, and I don't mean to take it out on you. You're just going to have to give me some time here. I've made my peace with the fact that I'm alone. I like my life as it is, and I'm not at all sure I want to change."

"We're not asking you to change."

"Then you better get used to me the way I am," I said.

She had the good grace to laugh, which in an odd way helped. Our good-byes were slightly warmer. I said all the right things, and by the time I hung up my churlishness was already fading to some extent. Content so often follows form. It's not just that we're nice to the people we like . . . we like the people we're nice to. It works both ways. I guess that's what good manners are about, or so my aunt always claimed. In the meantime, I knew I wouldn't be driving up to Lompoc any time soon. To hell with that.

I went across the hall to the restroom, and when I got back the phone was ringing. I made a lunge and snatched up the receiver from the far side of the desk, easing my way around until I reached my swivel chair. When I identified myself, I could hear breathing on the line and for one split second I thought it was Wendell. "Take your time," I said. I closed my eyes and crossed my fingers, thinking, Please, please, please.

"This is Brian Jaffe."

"Ah. I thought it might be your father. Have you heard from him?"

"Nuhn-uhn. That's why I called. Have you?"

"Not since last night."

"Michael says the car Dad came to his place in is still parked at the curb."

"He was having car trouble, which is why I gave him a lift. When did you last see him?"

"Day before yesterday. He came by in the afternoon and we talked. He said he'd be back last night, but he never showed."

"He may have tried," I said. "Someone took some shots at us and he disappeared. This morning we found out the *Lord* was gone."

"The boat?"

"Right. That's the one your father was on when he vanished."

"Dad stole a boat?"

"Well, it looks that way, but nobody really knows at this point. Maybe that's the only way he could think of to get out. He must have felt he was in real jeopardy."

"Hey, yeah, getting shot at," Brian said facetiously.

I fleshed out the story for him, hoping to ingratiate myself. I nearly mentioned Renata, but I bit the words off in time. If Michael hadn't known about her, chances were that Brian didn't, either. As usual, given my perverse nature, I was feeling protective of the "villain" of the piece. Maybe Wendell would have a change of heart and return the boat. Maybe he'd talk Brian into "coming in," and the two would turn themselves over to the cops. Maybe the Easter bunny would bring me one of those spun-sugar eggs with a hole you could peek in, revealing a world much better than this.

Brian breathed in my ear some more. I waited him out. "Michael says Dad has a girlfriend. Is that true?" he said.

"Ah, mmm. I don't know what to say about that. He was traveling with a friend, but I really don't know what their relationship consists of."

"Right." He snorted with disbelief. I'd forgotten he was eighteen years old and probably knew more about sex than I did. He certainly knew more about violence. What made me think I could fool a kid like him?

"You want Renata's number? She may have heard from him."

"I got a number to call and this machine picks up. If Dad's around, he calls back. Is this the one you have?" He recited Renata's unlisted number.

"That's it. Look, why don't you give me your current location. I'll pop over there and we can talk. Maybe between us we can figure out where he is."

He thought about that. "He told me to wait. He said don't talk to anyone until he gets here. He's probably on his way." He said this without conviction in a tone edged with uneasiness.

"That's always possible," I said. "What's the plan?" Like I really thought Brian would spill the beans to me.

"I have to go."

"Wait! Brian?"

The phone clicked down in my ear.

"Goddamn it!" I sat and stared at the receiver, willing it to ring. "Come on, come on."

I knew perfectly well the kid wasn't going to call again. I became aware of the tension rippling through my shoulders. I got up and moved around the desk, finding a bare expanse of carpeting where I could stretch out on my back. The ceiling was singularly uninformative. I hate waiting for things to happen, and I don't like being at the mercy of circumstance. Maybe I could figure out where Brian was being hidden. Wendell didn't have much in the way of personal resources. He had very few friends and no confederates that I knew of. He was also being very secretive, apparently not even trusting Renata with the information about Brian. The *Fugitive* might have been a great place for him to hole up, but she and Brian would both have to be extraordinarily talented liars to pull that one off. From what I could tell, he'd seemed genuinely ignorant of her existence, and she seemed uninterested in his. I suspected if Renata had known where Brian was, she'd have blown the whistle on him. She was certainly angry enough at Wendell's desertion.

Wendell almost had to have Brian tucked away in a motel or hotel someplace. If he was able to pop in to see Brian on a near daily basis, the place probably wasn't that far away. If Brian was left on his own for long periods, he'd have to have access to food without exposing himself to public scrutiny. Maybe a motel room with a kitchen so he could cook for himself. Big? Small? There were maybe fifteen to twenty motels in the vicinity. Was I going to have to drive down there and canvass every single one? That was an unappealing possibility. Canvassing is the equivalent of cold calls in the sales field. Once in a while you might hit pay dirt, but the process is tedious. Then again, Brian was really my only access to Wendell. So far, the *Dispatch* didn't seem to be picking up on

Brian's jail release, but once pictures of the two appeared in the papers, the situation was going to heat up. Brian might have pocket money, but he probably didn't have unlimited funds. If Wendell was determined to rescue his kid, he had better be quick about it, and I had, too.

I checked my watch. It was now 6:15. I hauled myself off the floor and made sure my answering machine was in message mode. I pulled out the newspaper clippings that detailed the original escape. The mug shot of Brian Jaffe wasn't flattering, but it would serve my purposes. I grabbed my portable Smith-Corona typewriter and my handbag and headed for the door. I clattered down the stairs, typewriter bumping against my leg, and then trotted two blocks to the spot where my car was parked. I decided at the last minute to take a quick detour along the beach. By taking the long way around to a freeway entrance, I'd end up passing the marina, where I could check up on Carl Eckert. It was entirely possible that he'd returned from out of town and nobody'd bothered to let me know. I was also thinking about the little harborside snack shack where I could pick up some killer burritos to munch on in the car. Kinsey Millhone dining al fresco again.

All the slots in the small no-pay parking lot were full, so I was forced to take a ticket and actually drive through to the pay lot. I locked my car, glancing to my left as I passed the kiosk. Carl Eckert was sitting in his car, a little red sports job of some exotic sort. He looked like a man in shock, pasty-faced and sweating, his pupils dilated. He surveyed his surroundings with an air of confusion. He was wearing a snappy dark blue business suit, but his tie had been loosened and his collar button opened. His silvery hair was unkempt, as if he'd been running his hands through it.

I slowed my pace, watching. He couldn't seem to decide what to do. I saw him reach for his car keys as if to turn the ignition. He pulled his hand back, reached into his pants pocket, and took out a handkerchief, which he used to mop at his face and neck. He shoved the handkerchief in his suit coat, then took out a pack of cigarettes and shook one into view. He pushed in his car lighter.

I crossed to his car, hunkering down on the driver's side so that my gaze would be level with his. "Carl? Kinsey Millhone."

He turned and stared at me without comprehension.

"We met at the yacht club the other night. I was looking for Wendell Jaffe."

"The private investigator," he said finally.

"That's right."

"Sorry it took me so long, but I've had some bad news."

"I heard about the *Lord.* Can I do anything?"

The lighter popped out. He lit his cigarette with hands that shook so badly he could barely make the lighter meet the tip. He sucked in smoke, choking on it in his desperation for a hit of nicotine. "Son of a bitch stole my boat," he said, coughing violently. He started to say something more, but then he stopped himself and looked off across the parking lot. I'd caught the glint of tears, but I couldn't tell if they were from the smoke or the loss of his boat.

"Are you okay?" I asked.

"I live on that boat. Everything I have is tied up in the *Lord.* It's my life. He had to have known that. He'd be a fool not to know. He loved the boat as much as I did." He shook his head in disbelief.

"That's a rough one," I said.

"How'd you hear about it?"

"Renata showed up at my office after lunch," I said. "She said he'd cleared out of her place and she was worried he'd try to make a run for it. Her boat was at the dock, so I guess she thought of yours."

"How'd he get in? That's what I can't figure out. I had all the locks changed the minute I bought that boat."

"Maybe he broke in. Or he might have picked the lock," I said. "At any rate, by the time we got here, it was gone."

He stared at me. "Is that the woman? Renata? What's her last name?"

"Why?"

"I'd like to talk to her. She might know more than she's saying."

"Yeah, she might," I said. I was thinking about the shooting the night before, wondering if Carl could account for his whereabouts. "When did you get back? I heard you were out of town last night, but no one seemed to know where you were."

"Wouldn't have done much good. I was hard to reach. I had a bunch of meetings up in SLO-town in the afternoon. I was at the Best Western overnight, checked out before eight this morning, and threw my bag in the trunk. I sat in another bunch of meetings today and started home around five."

"It must have been a shock."

"Jesus, I'll say. I can't believe it's gone."

SLO-town was the shorthand for San Luis Obispo, a small college town ninety miles north of us. It sounded like he'd been completely tied up for the last two days, or had his alibi all rehearsed. "What will you do now? Do you have a place to stay?"

"I'll try one of those places unless the tourists beat me to it," he said with a nod toward the motels that lined Cabana Boulevard. "What about you? I take it you never caught up with him."

"Actually, I ran into him at Michael's last night. I was hoping we could talk, but something else came up. We were separated inadvertently, and that's the last I saw of him. I heard he was supposed to meet you, as a matter of fact."

"I had to cancel at the last minute when this other business came up."

"You never saw him at all?"

"We only chatted by phone."

"What'd he want? Did he say?"

"No. Not a word."

"He told me you had something that belonged to him."

"He said that? Well, that's odd. I wonder what he meant." He gave his watch a glance. "Oh, shit. It's getting late. I better get a move on before all the rooms get snapped up."

I stepped away from the car. "I'll let you go, then," I said. "If you hear anything about the *Lord*, will you let me know?"

"Sure thing."

The car started with a rumble. He backed out of the slot and pulled up beside the kiosk with his ticket extended to the woman in the booth. I went on about my business, moving toward the snack shack with a quick backward glance. He'd adjusted his rear-view mirror to keep an eye on me. The last thing I saw of him was his vanity license plate, which read SAILSMN. That was cute. I thought he'd probably done a little sales job on me. He was lying about something. I just wasn't sure what it was.

22

By the time I reached the beachside neighborhood on the periphery of Perdido where all the motels are situated, the ocean was tinted by an eerie gray-green haze. As I watched, an odd refraction of fading sunlight created the fleeting mirage of an island hovering above the sea, mossy and unreachable. There was something otherworldly in its gloom. I've seen something like it in the endless passageway created when two mirrors reflect one another, shadowy rooms curving back out of sight. The moment passed, and the image turned to smoke. The air was hot and still, unusually humid for the California coast. The area residents would have to search their garages tonight, looking for last summer's electric floor fans, wide blades sueded with dust. Sleep would be a restless confection of sweat and tangled sheets without hope of refreshment.

I parked on a side street just off the main thoroughfare. All the motel lights had come on, creating an artificial daylight: neon greens and blues blinking out competing invitations to passing travelers. There were countless people milling along the sidewalks, all in shorts and tank tops, looking for relief from the heat. The Frostee Freeze would probably set a sales record. Cars cruised in an endless search for parking spaces. There wasn't actually any sand in the streets, but there was the feeling of blown sand, something scrubby and windswept, a scent in the air of salt corrosion and fishing nets. The few funky bars were crowded with college students, bass-heavy music pulsing through the open doorways.

One thing I needed to keep in mind: Brian Jaffe grew up in this town. His picture had been splashed across the local papers, and he probably wasn't free to spend a lot of time on the streets—too much risk of being recognized. I added free cable TV to my mental list of motel attributes. I didn't think Brian's father would dare leave him in a dive. The bleaker the accommodations, the more likely the kid was to seek amusement elsewhere.

I started with motels on the main drag and worked my way out into the surrounding neighborhood. I don't know how motel builders get their training, but they all seem to take the same motel-naming class. Every seaside community seems to sport the same assortment. I went in and out of the Tides, the Sun 'N' Surf, the Breakwater, the Reef, the Lagoon, the Schooner, the Beachside, the Blue Sands, the White Sands, the Sandpiper, and the Casa Del Mar. I flashed the photostat of my PI license. I flashed the grainy black-and-white newspaper photograph of Brian Jaffe. I couldn't believe he'd be registered under his own name, so I tried variations: Brian Jefferson, Jeff O'Brian, Brian Huff, Dean Huff, and Wendell's favorite, Stanley Lord. I knew the date Brian had been erroneously released from jail, and I reasoned that he'd checked into a motel the same day. He was a single, and his bill was probably paid in advance. My guess was he kept to himself and hadn't done a lot of coming and going. I was hoping someone could identify him from the picture and my description. Motel managers and desk clerks shook their heads in ignorance. I left a business card with each, extracting weighty promises that they'd get in touch if someone resembling Brian Jaffe checked into their establishments. Oh, sure. Absolutely. I wasn't all the way out the door when they dropped the cards in their respective trash baskets.

At the Lighthouse—Direct Dial Phones*Color Cable TV*Weekly & Monthly Rates*Heated Pool*Complimentary Morning Coffee—on the twelfth try, I got a nod instead of a negative. The Lighthouse was a three-story oblong of boxy cinder block with a pool in the center. The exterior was painted sky blue and had a thirty-foot stylized image of a lighthouse affixed to the front. The desk clerk was in his seventies, energetic and alert. He was as bald as a doorknob, but he seemed to have all his own teeth. He tapped the clipping with an index finger crooked with arthritis.

"Oh, yes, he's here. Michael Brendan. Room one ten. I wondered why he looked familiar. An older gentleman signed the register and paid a week in advance. To tell you the truth, I wasn't sure of the relationship."

"Father and son."

"That was their claim," the clerk said, still dubious. He scanned the details of the escape and the subsequent killing of the female motorist whose car was stolen. "I remember reading about this. Looks like that young fellow got himself in a peck of trouble and he's not out yet. You want me to call the police?"

"Make that the county sheriff's department and give me ten minutes with him first. Ask them to use restraint. I don't want this turned into some kind of bloodbath. The kid is eighteen. It's not going to look good if he's gunned down in his pajamas."

I left the lobby and moved through a passageway to the courtyard. It was fully dark by then, and the lighted swimming pool glowed aquamarine. Reflections from the water shimmered against the building, blots of light in a constantly shifting pattern of white. Brian's room was on the first floor, with sliding glass doors that opened onto a small patio, which in turn opened onto the pool. Patios were separated from each other by low-growing shrubbery. Each was numbered, so finding his wasn't difficult. I caught sight of him through mesh drapes only partially drawn. The sliding doors were closed, and I had to guess the air-conditioning was cranked up to high.

He was dressed in sweatshirt-gray gym shorts and a tank top.

He looked tanned and fit, slouched on the one upholstered chair in the room, feet propped on the bed as he watched television. I went around to the end of the building and entered the corridor, passing a door marked EMPLOYEES ONLY. On impulse, I tried the knob and found it turning in my hand. I peered in. The room was the equivalent of a huge walk-in closet, with linen shelves along three walls. Sheets, towels, and cotton bedspreads were stacked in neat packets. There were also mops, vacuums, irons, ironing boards, and miscellaneous cleaning supplies. I pulled out an armload of fresh towels and carried them with me.

I found Brian's room along the inside corridor and knocked, standing at an acute angle to the fish-eye in the door. The sound from the television set was doused. I stared off down the hall, allowing him time to cross to the door. He must have tried peering at me through the lens. A muffled "Yes?"

"Criada," I called. The word was Spanish for "maid." I learned that the first week of class because so many of the women taking Spanish were hoping to learn to speak to their Hispanic maids. Otherwise the maids did anything they felt like, and the women were reduced to following them around the house, ineffectually trying to demonstrate cleaning techniques the maids pretended not to "get."

Brian didn't get it, either. He opened the door to the width of the chain, peering through the crack. "What?"

I held a batch of towels up, concealing my face. "Towelettas," I sang in Spanglish.

"Oh." He closed the door and slid the chain off the track. He stepped back, leaving the door open between us. I moved into the room. He didn't look at me. He indicated the bathroom to the left, his attention already riveted on the screen again. The show seemed to be an old black-and-white movie: men with high cheekbones and pomaded waves, women with eyebrows plucked to the size of hairline fractures. All the facial expressions were tragic. He crossed back to the set and turned up the sound. I went into his bathroom and checked it out as long as I was there. No visible guns, claw hammers, or machetes. Lots of sun block and hair mousse, a hairbrush, a blow dryer, and a safety razor. I didn't think the kid had enough hair on his face to shave it. Maybe he was just practicing, like prepubescent girls with little training bras.

I set the towels on the counter and went out to the bedroom, where I took a seat on the bed. At first, my presence didn't seem to register. Terminal disease music was swelling, and the lovers stood together with their two perfect faces side by side. His was prettier than hers. When Brian finally saw me, he was cool enough to suppress any surprise. He picked up the remote control and muted the sound again. The scene continued in silence, many animated speeches. I've often wondered if I could learn to read lips that way. The lovers on the screen were speaking directly into each other's faces, which made me worry about bad breath. Her mouth was moving, but Brian's words came out. "How'd you find me?"

I tapped my temple, trying to divert my gaze from the television set.

"Where's Dad?"

"We don't know yet. He may be sailing down the coast to pick you up."

"I wish he'd get on with it." He leaned back in his chair and raised his arms, lacing his fingers so his hands were resting across the top of his head. The gesture made his biceps bulge. He propped a foot up on the edge of the bed, kicked his chair back an inch. The tufts of hair in his armpits seemed oddly sexual. I wondered if I was reaching an age where all young boys with hard bodies would seem sexual to me. I wondered if I'd been that age all my life. He reached over and picked up a pair of clean socks, which had been rolled and folded to form a soft wad. He threw the ball of socks against the wall and caught it on the fly when it bounced back at him.

"You haven't heard from him?"

"Nope." He flung the wad again and caught it.

"You said you saw him day before yesterday. Did he say anything to indicate he might be leaving?" I asked.

"No." He dropped the wad from his right hand, straightening his arm abruptly so that the socks bounced off the anterior aspect of his elbow. He caught it as it popped up, and he let it fall again. He had to watch very carefully so he wouldn't miss. Bounce. Catch. Bounce. Catch.

"What did he say?" I asked.

He missed.

He shot me a look, annoyed at the distraction. "Fuck, I don't know. He's selling me this whole line of horseshit about how there's no justice in the legal system. Then he turns around and tells me we have to turn ourselves in. I go, 'No way, Dad. I'm not going to do it, and there's no way you can make me.' "

"What'd he say to that?"

"He didn't say anything." He tossed the sock ball against the wall again and caught it on the fly.

"You think he might have gone ahead and taken off without you?"

"Why would he do that if he was going to turn himself in?"

"Maybe he got scared."

"So he leaves me to face all this shit by myself?" His look was incredulous.

"Brian, I hate to say this, but your father isn't exactly famous for sticking it out. He gets nervous and he bolts."

"He wouldn't leave me," he said sullenly. He tossed the socks in the air, leaned forward, and caught the wad behind his back. I could see the title of the book now: *Tricks with Socks: 101 Ways to Amuse Yourself with Underwear.*

"I think you ought to go ahead and turn yourself in."

"I will when he gets here."

"Why don't I believe that? Brian, I hate to sound pompous, but I have a responsibility here. You're wanted by the cops. I don't turn you in, that's called 'aiding and abetting.' I could lose my license."

He was on his feet in an instant, half lifting me, hauling me off the bed by my shirt, fist cocked back, ready to bust my teeth out.

Our faces were suddenly six inches apart. Like the lovers. Anything cute about this kid was gone. Someone else stared down at me, a person within a person. Who could have guessed that this vicious "other" was hidden behind Brian's blue-eyed, California perfection? The voice wasn't even his: a low-pitched gravelly whisper. "Listen, you bitch. I'll tell you about aiding and abetting. You want to take me in? Just try. I'll kill your ass before you can lay a finger on me, you got that?"

I stilled myself, scarcely daring to breathe. I made my body invisible, beaming myself into hyperspace. He was nearly cross-eyed with rage, and I knew he'd strike out if he were pressed. His chest was heaving, adrenaline pumping hard through his nervous system. He was the one who killed the woman when the four of them escaped. I'd have bet money on that. Give a kid like this a weapon, give him a victim, some subject to vent his rage on, and he'd attack in a white heat. I said, "Okay, okay. Don't hit me. Don't hit."

I thought the rush of feelings would make him extraordinarily alert. Instead, emotion seemed to slow his senses, dulling his perceptions. He pulled back slightly. He brought my face into focus, frowning. "What?" His manner seemed dazed, as if his hearing had gone out on him.

My message had finally reached him, through some impossible maze of supercharged neurons. "I just want you safe when your dad comes back."

"Safe." The very concept seemed alien. He shivered, tension rippling through his body. He released me, backed away, and sank onto the chair, breathing heavily. "God. What's the matter with me? God."

"You want me to go in with you?" My shirt was permanently pleated across the front where he'd gripped it in his fist.

He shook his head.

"I can call your mother."

He bowed his head, running his hand through his hair. "I don't want her. I want him," he said. The voice belonged to the Brian

Jaffe I knew. He wiped his face against his sleeve. I thought he was close to tears, but his eyes were dry . . . empty . . . the blue as cold as a gel pack. I sat and waited, hoping he would say something more. Gradually his breathing returned to normal and he began to look like himself again.

"It'll look better in court if you return voluntarily," I ventured.

"Why should I do that? I got a legitimate jail release." The tone was petulant. The other Brian was gone, receding into the dark recesses of his underwater hole like an eel. This Brian was just a kid who thought everything should go his way. On the playground, he was the kind of kid who'd cry, "You cheated!" any time he lost a game, but he would always be the cheater, in truth.

"Oh, come on, Brian. You know better than that. I don't know who screwed with the computer, but believe me, you're not supposed to be out on the street. You've got murder charges filed against you."

"I didn't *kill* anybody." Indignant. By that, he probably meant he didn't *mean* to kill her when he pointed the gun. And why should he feel guilty afterward when it wasn't his fault? Dumb bitch. She should have kept her mouth shut when he asked for the car keys. Had to argue with him. Women all the time argued.

"Good for you," I said. "In the meantime, the sheriff's on his way over here to pick you up."

He was astonished at the betrayal, and the look he gave me was filled with outrage. "You called the *cops*? Why'd you do that?"

"Because I didn't believe you'd turn yourself in."

"Why should I?"

"See what I mean? You got an attitude. Like somehow the rules don't apply to you. Well, guess what?"

"Guess what yourself. I don't have to take any crap from you." He got up from the chair, grabbing his wallet from the top of the TV as he passed. He reached the door and opened it. A sheriff's deputy, a white guy, was standing on the threshold, his hand raised to knock. Brian wheeled and moved rapidly toward the sliding glass door. A second deputy, black, appeared on his patio. Frustrated, Brian flung his wallet to the floor with such force that it bounced like a football. The first deputy reached for him, and Brian wrenched his arm away. *"Get the fuck off me!"*

The deputy said, "Son. Now, son. I don't want to have to hurt you."

Brian was breathing heavily again, backing up, his gaze raking the air from face to face. He was hunched over, and he had his hands out as if to ward off attacking animals. Both deputies were big, made of dense flesh and tough experience, the first in his late forties, the other maybe thirty-five. I wouldn't have wanted to truck with either one of them.

The second deputy had his hand on his gun, but he hadn't drawn it. These days a confrontation with the law ends in death, pure and simple. The two officers exchanged a look, and my heart began to bang at the specter of sudden violence. The three of us were immobilized, waiting to see what the next move might be. The first deputy went on in a low tone. "It's all right. Everything's cool. Let's just keep calm here and everything's going to be fine."

Uncertainty flickered in Brian's eyes. His breathing slowed, and he regained his composure. He straightened up. I didn't think it was over, but the tension evaporated. Brian tried a deprecating smile and allowed himself to be handcuffed without resistance. He avoided my gaze, which suited me just fine. There was something embarrassing about having to watch him submit. "Bunch of dumb fucks," he murmured, but the deputies ignored him. Everybody has to save face. No offense in that.

Dana appeared at the jail while Brian was being processed through booking. She was dressed to the teeth, in a gray rayon-linen-blend power suit, the first time I'd seen her wearing anything other than jeans. It was eleven o'clock at night, and I was standing in the hall with another cup of bad coffee when I heard the snapping of her high heels down the corridor. I took one look at her and knew she was furious, not with Brian or the cops, but with me. I had followed the sheriff's car over to the jail, parking in the lot while they drove into the sally port. I had even put the call through to Dana Jaffe myself, thinking she should be informed about her little boy's arrest. I was not in the mood to take shit from her, but it was clear she intended to spew.

"You have caused trouble since the moment I laid eyes on you," she spat. Her hair was pulled back in a shiny chignon, not a strand out of place. Snowy blouse, silver earrings, her eyes lined with black.

"Do you want to hear the story?"

"No, I don't want to hear the story. I want to tell you one," she snapped. "I have a fucking restraining order on my bank accounts. Every cent I have is inaccessible. I have no money. Do you get that? None! My kid is in trouble, and what the hell can I do? I can't even get through to his lawyer."

Her linen suit was immaculate, not a wrinkle on it anywhere; tough with linen, I've heard, even in a blend. I stared down at the contents of my cup. The coffee was cold by now, the surface bespeckled with little clots of powdered milk. I was really hoping I wouldn't fling it all in her face. I watched my hand carefully to see if it would move. So far, so good.

In the meantime, Dana was going on and on, heaping invective at me for God knew what offenses. I pushed the mute button with my internal remote. It was just like watching some silent TV show. Some part of me was listening, though I tried not to let the sound penetrate. I noticed my coffee-flinging inclination was picking up momentum. I used to be a biter in kindergarten, and the impulse was the same. When I was a cop, I'd had to arrest a woman once for flinging a drink in another woman's face, which the law regards as assault and battery. California Penal Code 242: "A battery is any willful and unlawful use of force or violence upon the person of another." Battery is a consummated assault and is a necessarily included offense where battery is charged. "The force or violence necessary to constitute a battery need not be great nor need it necessarily cause pain or bodily harm, nor leave a mark," I recited to myself. Except maybe on her suit, I added. Tee hee.

I heard footsteps approaching in the corridor behind me. I

glanced back and spotted Senior Deputy Tiller, with a file folder in his hand. He nodded at me briefly and disappeared through the doorway.

"Excuse me, Tiller?"

He stuck his head back out the door. "You call me?"

I glanced at Dana. "Sorry to interrupt, but I have to talk to him," I said, and followed him into the office. Her look of annoyance indicated she wasn't nearly done with me yet.

23

Tiller looked up quizzically from the file drawer where he was tucking the folder. "What was that all about?"

I closed the door, lifting a finger to my lips. I pointed to the back. His eyes strayed to the hallway. He closed the file drawer and jerked his head toward the rear. I followed him through a maze of desks. We reached a smaller office, which I took to be his. He closed a second door behind us and motioned me onto a chair. I tossed my empty coffee cup in the trash can and sat down with relief. "Thanks. This is great. I couldn't think how else to get away from her. She must have needed someone to crank on, and I was elected."

"Well, I'm glad to oblige. You want another cup of coffee? We got a fresh pot back here. That probably came from the vending machine."

"Thanks, but I'm coffeed out for the time being. I'd like to sleep at some point. How are you?"

"Fine. I just came on, working graveyard. I see you got our boy back in the can." He sat down on his swivel chair and leaned back with a creaking sound.

"Wasn't that hard to do. I figured Wendell had to have him somewhere close, and I did a little legwork. Boring, but not tough. What's the deal on this end? Do they know yet how he got sprung?"

Tiller shrugged, uncomfortably. "They're looking into it." He changed the subject, apparently reluctant to share the details of the in-house investigation. Under the harsh fluorescent lights, I could see that his sandy hair and his mustache were threaded with silver, his eyes wreathed in creases. The boyish contours of his face had begun to shrink, leaving puckers and wrinkles. He must have been close to Wendell's age without the youth-perpetuating benefits of Wendell's cosmetic surgery. I was staring idly at his hands when I felt a little question mark appear above my head. "What is that?"

He caught the look and held out his hand. "What, the class ring?"

I leaned forward, peering. "Isn't that Cottonwood Academy?"

"You know the school? Most people never heard of it. Went out of business, I don't know how many years back. These days you don't find many all-male institutions. Sexist, they call it, and they may be right. Mine was the last class to graduate. Only sixteen of us. After that, kapoot," he said. His smile was tinged with pride and affection. "What's your connection? You must have a good eye. Most class rings look the same."

"I just saw one recently from a Cottonwood graduate."

"Really. Who's that? We're still a real tight bunch."

"Wendell Jaffe."

His gaze stuck to mine briefly, and then he looked away. He shifted on his chair. "Yeah, I guess old Wendell did go there," he said, as if it had just occurred to him. "You sure you don't want some more coffee?"

"It was you, wasn't it?"

"Me, what?"

"Brian's jail release," I said.

Tiller laughed, jolly ho-ho, but it didn't sound sincere. "Hey, sorry. Not me. I wouldn't even know how to go about it. You put me near a computer, my IQ drops about fifteen percentage points."

"Oh, come on. What's the scoop? I'm not going to tell anyone. What do I care? The kid's back. I swear I won't say a word." I shut my mouth then and let the silence accumulate. Basically he was an honest soul, capable of an occasional unlawful act, but not comfortable about it, unable to deny his culpability when confronted. His fellow cops love guys like him because they're quick with a confession, eager for the relief. He said, "No, really. You're barking up the wrong tree here." He did a neck roll, trying to relieve the tension, but I noticed he hadn't terminated the conversation. I prodded him a bit. "Did you help Brian the first time, when he escaped from juvie?"

His expression became bland, and his tone shifted into officiousness. "I don't think this line of talk is going to be productive," he said.

"All right. Let's forget about the first escape and just talk about the second. You must have owed Wendell a big one to risk your job that way."

"I think that's enough. Let's just say we drop it."

This had to be the manslaughter charge that Wendell had pleaded to, a felony conviction that would have barred Tiller from his job in law enforcement. "Tiller, I heard the story about the manslaughter charge. You're safe with me. I promise. I just want to know what happened. Why did Wendell take the fall?"

"I don't owe you an explanation."

"I never said you did. I'm asking for myself. It isn't anything official. It's a piece of information."

He was silent for a long time, staring down at his desktop. Maybe his was one of those fairy-tale families where you have to ask three times before your wish is granted.

"Tiller, please? I don't want any details. I understand your hesitation. Just the broad strokes," I said.

He sighed deeply, and when he finally spoke, his voice was so low I had to squint to hear him. "I don't really think I can say why he did it. We were young. Best friends. Twenty-four, twenty-five, something like that. He'd already decided the law was corrupt and he wasn't going to sit for his bar exams. All I ever wanted was to be a cop. The situation came up. The girl died by accident, though it was all my fault. He happened to be there, and he took the blame. He was innocent. He knew it. I knew it. He took the rap, that's all. I thought it was an incredible gesture."

It sounded weak to me, but who knows why people do what they do? A certain earnest idealism takes hold of us when we're young. That's why so many draftees are eighteen and dead. "But surely he didn't have any real hold over you. The statutes would have run out on a charge like that years ago, and it was his word against yours. So he claims you did something. You claim you didn't. He'd already been convicted. After all this time, I don't understand what the big deal was."

"No deal. It wasn't like that. He didn't threaten me. I was paying off an obligation."

"But you didn't have to do what he asked."

"No sir, I did what I wanted, and I was happy to do it for him."

"But why take the chance?"

"You never heard about honor? I owed him. It's the least I could do. And it's not like I baked a file in a cake. Brian's a bad egg. I'll admit that. I don't like the kid, but Wendell told me he'd get him out of the state. He said he'd take full responsibility, so I figured good riddance."

"I think he had a change of heart on that score. Well, actually I've heard mixed reports," I said, correcting myself. "He told both Michael and Brian he was going to turn himself in. He was apparently trying to talk Brian into following suit. But his girlfriend claims he had no intention of going through with it."

Tiller rocked on his swivel chair, staring off in the middle distance. He shook his head, mystified. "I just don't see how he's going to pull it off. What's he doing?"

"You heard about the boat?"

"Yeah, I heard. Question is, what's he think he's going to do with it? I mean, how far can he get?"

"I guess we'll just have to wait and see about that," I said. "Anyway, I gotta go. I have a thirty-mile drive ahead of me and it's past my bedtime. Is there another way out of here? I don't want to run into Dana Jaffe again. I've about had it with that bunch."

"Through the next department. Come on. I'll show you," he said, getting to his feet. He moved around the desk and took a left through an interior corridor. I followed. I thought he'd caution me to silence, extracting a promise about the confidentiality of our conversation, but he never said a word about it.

It was nearly 1:00 A.M. by the time I rolled into Santa Teresa. There was very little traffic and few pedestrians. Streetlights drew a pattern of overlapping pale gray circles on the sidewalk. Businesses were locked, but lighted. Occasionally I spotted one of the homeless seeking out the shelter of some darkened alleyway, but for the most part the streets were deserted. The temperature was finally beginning to drop, and a mild ocean breeze was offsetting the humidity to some extent.

I was feeling itchy and restless. Nothing was really happening. With Brian in jail and Wendell still missing, what was there to investigate? The hunt for the *Captain Stanley Lord* was currently in the hands of the Harbor Patrol and the Coast Guard. Even if I could charter a plane and do an aerial search—an expense Gordon Titus was never going to authorize—I wouldn't know one boat from another at altitude. In the meantime, there had to be something I could do.

Without even meaning to, I made a detour, easing through all the motel parking lots between my place and the marina. I spotted Carl Eckert's sports car at the Beachside Inn: a one-story motel, arranged in a T-shape with the short bar along the front. The parking slots were lined up, one for each room, the numbers marked on the pavement so that no one would poach. Every room on this side of the building was dark.

I drove through to the alley and circled back to Cabana. I parked on the street, a few doors down from Eckert's motel. I slipped my penlight in my jeans pocket and returned on foot, grateful that my tennies were rubber-soled and silent. The parking area was illuminated for the safety of the occupants, the fixtures aimed so as to cast light away from the windows. I could see my own shadow, like an elongated companion, follow me across the lot. Carl had secured the tonneau cover across the open body of his car. I did a thorough visual scan, taking in the darkened windows and the dimly lighted parking area. There were no signs of movement within range of me. I didn't even see the gray flickering light against the motel drapes that would indicate a television set in use. I took a deep breath and started popping snaps on the tonneau, loosening the driver's side first. I slid my hand down along the inside, feeling through the map pockets in the door. He kept his interior immaculate, which meant he probably had a system for all the gas slips and detritus. I felt a spiral-bound notebook, a road map, and some kind of paper booklet. I brought everything to the surface like a net full of fish. I paused to check my surroundings, which seemed as benign as before. I flicked the penlight across the spiral notebook. He was keeping track of his gasoline mileage.

The booklet I found was his business log, noting odometer readings, destinations, purpose of meetings, names and titles of those in attendance. Personal and business expenses were neatly separated into columns. I had to smile to myself. This from a con artist who'd spent months in jail. Maybe prison had some rehabilitative effect. Carl Eckert was behaving like a model citizen. At least he wasn't trying to cheat the IRS, as far as I could tell. Tucked in a slot at the back of the log was his itemized Best Western hotel bill, two gasoline receipts, five credit card vouchers, and—what ho!—the speeding ticket he'd picked up last night on the outskirts of Colgate. According to the time so obligingly noted by the CHP officer who issued the citation, Carl Eckert could easily have sped the remaining distance to Perdido in plenty of time to take potshots at Wendell and me.

"You want to tell me what the fuck you're doing out here?"

I jumped, papers flying, barely managing to suppress a shriek. I put a hand to my chest, heart pounding. It was Carl in his stocking feet, his hair rumpled from sleep. God, I hate sneaks! I leaned over and started picking up papers. "Jesus! Warn a person. You nearly scared me to death. What I'm doing is blowing your alibi for last night."

"I don't need an alibi for last night. I wasn't doing anything."

"Well, somebody was. Did I mention the fact that my car engine cut out, leaving Wendell and me stranded on a very dark beach road?"

"No. You didn't mention that. Go on," he said cautiously.

"Go on. That's good. Like this is news to you. Somebody was shooting at us. Wendell disappeared shortly afterward."

"You think *I* did that?"

"I think it's possible. Why else would I be out here in the dead of night?"

He shoved his hands down in his pockets and looked around at the darkened windows, realizing that our voices would carry into every room. "Let's talk about this inside," he said, and padded off toward his room. I trotted along behind him, wondering where all this was going.

Once inside, he flipped on the bed table lamp and poured himself a tumbler full of Scotch from a bottle on the desk. He held it up, a silent query. I shook my head to decline. He lit a cigarette, this time at least remembering not to bother offering me one. He sat on the edge of the bed, and I sat on the upholstered chair. The room didn't look that different from the one Brian Jaffe had occupied. Like any other liar once confronted, Carl Eckert was probably preparing another set of lies. I settled in like a kid waiting for a bedtime story. He thought for a little while, adopting his sincere look. "Okay, I'll level with you. I did drive down from SLO-town last night, but I didn't go to Perdido. I got back to the hotel after a day of meetings and checked with my service. There was a message from Harris Brown, so I called him back."

"Well, you've got *my* attention. I've been wondering how Harris Brown fits into the picture. Fill me in. I'd love it."

"Harris Brown is an ex-cop—"

"I know that part. He was assigned to the case and taken off because he lost his life savings, investing in CSL, blah, blah, blah. What else? How'd he pick up Wendell's trail down in Viento Negro?"

Carl Eckert smiled slightly, like he thought I was cute. Sometimes I am, but I wasn't sure this was one of those occasions. "Some pal of his called. An insurance agent."

"Right. That's great. I know the guy. I wasn't sure, but that was my guess," I said. "Obviously Harris Brown knew Wendell, but did Wendell know him?"

Eckert shook his head. "I doubt it. I was the one who brought Brown in as an investor back then. They might have dealt with each other by phone, but I'm pretty sure they never met. Why?"

"Because Brown was in the room right next to his, hanging out in the bar. Wendell didn't seem aware of him, and that puzzled me. What next? Harris Brown calls you last night and you call him back. Then what?"

"I was supposed to connect up with him this afternoon on the way back from SLO-town, but he was suddenly in a hurry and said he had to see me right away. I got in the car and met him at his house in Colgate."

I stared at him, uncertain whether to believe him or not. "What's his address?"

"Why do you ask?"

"So I can verify what you're saying."

Eckert shrugged and looked it up in a small leather address book. I made a careful note. If the man was bluffing, he was good. "Why the rush?" I said.

"You'd have to ask him that. He had some bug up his butt and insisted I come down last night. I was annoyed and time was short. I had a breakfast meeting at seven, but I didn't want to argue the point. I jumped in my car and came barreling down, which is when the CHP stopped me and gave me the ticket."

"What time did you get to his place?"

"Nine. I was only there an hour. I was probably back in my hotel in SLO-town by eleven-thirty."

"By your account," I said. "Actually either one of you could have driven to Perdido in plenty of time to use Wendell and me as target practice."

"Either of us could have, but I didn't. I can't speak for him."

"You didn't see Wendell at all last night?"

"I already told you that."

"Carl, what you already did is called lying through your dentures. You swore you were out of town when you were here in Colgate. Why should I believe this?"

"I have no control over what you believe."

"What was the deal with Brown once you got there?"

"We talked and I came back."

"All you did was talk? About what? Why couldn't you talk on the phone?"

He looked away from me long enough to flick the ash off his cigarette. "He wanted his money back. I delivered it."

"His money."

"The pension monies he invested in CSL."

"How much?"

"A hundred grand."

"I don't get it," I said. "He lost that money five years ago. What made him think he could suddenly collect?"

"Because he found out Wendell was alive. Maybe he had a conversation with him. How the hell do I know?"

"During which he learned what? That there were funds available?"

He stubbed out one cigarette and lit another, squinting at me stubbornly through the smoke. "You know, this is really none of your business."

"Oh, stop that already. I'm not a threat to you. I've been hired by California Fidelity to find Wendell Jaffe so we can prove he's alive. All I care about is the half a million dollars we paid off on his life insurance. If you have a cache of money somewhere, that's really not my concern."

"Then why should I tell you anything?"

"So I can understand what's going on. That's all I care about. You had the money Harris Brown was demanding, so you drove down last night. What happened then?"

"I gave him the money and drove back to San Luis Obispo."

"You keep cash like that around?"

"Yes."

"How much? You don't have to answer. This is pure curiosity on my part."

"Altogether?"

"Just the ballpark," I said.

"About three million dollars."

I blinked. "You keep that kind of money around in *cash*?"

"What else can I do with it? I can't put it in the bank. They'd report it to the government. We've got a judgment out against us. The minute anybody finds out about it, the litigants will swoop down on it like a bunch of vultures. Anything they don't get, the IRS will come after."

I could feel indignation rising up like acid indigestion. "Of course they'd swoop down. That's the money you cheated them out of."

The look he gave me was pure cynicism. "You know why they invested in CSL? They wanted something for nothing. They expected to make a killing and got killed instead. Come on, use your head. Most of 'em knew it was a crooked deal from the get-go, including Harris. He was just hoping to collect his share before the whole scheme collapsed."

"I can see we're not talking the same language here. Let's skip past the rationale and get down to the facts. You kept three million in cash on the *Lord*?"

"You don't have to take that tone with me."

"Excuse me, right. Let me try it again." I adjusted my tone, gearing down from judgmental to neutral. "You kept three million dollars in cash hidden on the *Lord*."

"Right. Wendell and I were the only ones who knew about it. Now you," he said.

"And that's what he came back for?"

"Of course. After five years on the road, he was flat broke," Carl said. "He not only came back for it, that's what he sailed away with when he stole that boat. Half of that belonged to me, which he bloody well knew."

"Oh, wow, babe. I got news for you. You got hosed."

"You're telling me? I can't believe he'd do such a thing to me."

"Well, he did it to everyone about equally," I said. "What about his kids? Did they figure into this, or was it just the money he came back for?"

"I'm sure he was concerned about his sons," Carl said. "He was a very good father."

"The kind of parent every kid needs," I said. "I'll pass that on to them. It'll help with their therapy. What are you going to do now?" I got up from the chair.

His smile was bitter. "Get down on my knees and pray the Coast Guard catches up with him."

From the doorway, I turned. "One more thing. There was talk about Wendell turning himself in to the cops. Do you think he meant that?"

"It's hard to say. I think he was hoping to join his family again. I'm just not sure there was any room for him."

I finally crawled into bed at 2:15, brain buzzing with information. I thought what Eckert said was probably true, that there was no longer room for Wendell in the family he'd left. In some curious way we were in the same position, Wendell Jaffe and me: trying to understand what our lives might have been if we could have enjoyed the benefits of family life, looking at the mislaid years and wondering how much we'd missed. At least, I assumed that was some of what was running through his mind. There were obvious differences. He had voluntarily surrendered his family, while I'd never known mine existed. More telling was the fact that he wanted his family back and I wasn't sure I did. I couldn't understand why my aunt had never told me. Maybe she'd tried to spare me the pain of Grand's rejection, but all she'd really done was postpone the revelation. Here I was, ten years after her death, having to sort it all out for myself. Ah, well. She wasn't very good at that stuff, anyway. I drifted in and out of sleep.

My alarm went off at 6:00, but I didn't have the heart to get up and jog three miles. I turned off the buzzer and squirmed down in the sheets, sinking back into sleep. I was awakened by a phone call at 9:22. I reached for the receiver, brushing hair from my eyes. "What."

"This is Mac. Sorry if I woke you. I know it's Saturday, but I thought this was important."

His voice sounded odd, and I could feel caution flashing in me like a yellow traffic light. I pulled the sheet around me and sat up in bed. "Don't worry about it. That's okay. I was up till all hours and decided to sleep in. What's happening?"

"The *Lord* was found this morning about six miles offshore," he said. "It looks like Wendell pulled off another disappearing act. Gordon and I are down here at the office. He'd like to have you come in as soon as possible."

24

I parked in the lot behind the office and went up the back stairs to the second floor. Most of the businesses in the building were shut down, which gave the premises a curious air of abandonment. I'd brought along my steno book, hoping to impress Gordon Titus with my professionalism. The notebook was empty except for an entry that read "Find Wendell." Back to that again. I couldn't believe it. We were so close to reeling him in. What was gnawing at me was the fact that I'd seen him with his grandson. I'd heard him talk to Michael, ostensibly making amends. As big a shit as he was, I had a hard time believing it was all a front. I was willing to imagine him changing his mind about surrendering to the cops. I could picture him stealing the *Lord* so he could sail down the coast and rescue Brian from a jail sentence. What I couldn't accept was the idea that he'd betray his family all over again. Even Wendell, God bless him, wasn't that mean-spirited.

The CF offices were officially closed, but there was a big jumble of keys in the lock, visible through the glass. Darcy's desk was unoccupied, but I caught a glimpse of Gordon Titus in Mac's glass-enclosed office, which was the only one showing any lights. Mac passed with two mugs of coffee in hand. I tapped on the glass. He set the mugs on Darcy's desk and unlocked the door for me. "We're in my office."

"So I see. Let me grab a cup of coffee and I'll be right there."

He picked up the mugs and moved on without comment. He seemed depressed, not a reaction I'd anticipated. I'd half expected fireworks. He'd seen the case as his way of going out in a blaze of glory, retiring from CF with a big gold star pasted to the front of his personnel file. He wore a pair of red-and-green-plaid pants and a red golfing shirt, and I wondered if his current emotional state was generated by the forfeiture of his weekend tee time.

All the workstations were empty, phones silent. Gordon Titus sat at Mac's desk, immaculately dressed, hands folded, his facial expression bland. I have a hard time trusting anyone so unflappable. While he appeared to be levelheaded, I suspected that he truly didn't care about most things. Poise and indifference so often look the same. I poured myself a mug of coffee and added nonfat milk before I opened Mac's office door and braved the chill effect of Titus's personality.

Mac was now seated on one of his two upholstered visitors' chairs, apparently unaware of how neatly Titus had displaced him. "I tell you one thing," Mac was saying, "and Kinsey can pass this on to Mrs. Jaffe for a fact. I'll have a lock on that money till Wendell dies of old age. If she has any hopes of seeing even one red cent, she'll have to drag his dead body up the steps and lay it across my desk."

"Good morning," I murmured to Titus. I took the other chair, which at least lined me up on the same side of the desk as Mac. He shook his head and sent me a dark look. "The son of a bitch has done it to us again."

"I gathered as much. What's the story?" I asked.

"You tell her," Mac said.

Titus pulled a ledger over in front of him. He opened it and leafed through, looking for a blank page. "What do we owe you to date?"

"Twenty-five hundred. That's ten days on a flat. You're lucky I didn't charge you for the mileage. I'm making two and three trips to Perdido every day, and that adds up."

"Twenty-five hundred dollars and for what?" Mac said. "We're right back where we started. We've got nothing but air."

Titus ran his finger down a column and penciled in a figure before he turned to another part of the book. "Actually, I don't think this is as bad as it seems. We have enough witnesses who'll testify that Jaffe was alive and well as recently as this week. We'll never see a dime of the money Mrs. Jaffe's already spent—we might as well write that off—but we can settle for the balance, thus cutting our losses." He glanced up. "That should be the end of it. She's hardly going to wait five years and make another claim."

"Where'd they find the boat?"

He began to write, not looking up. "A southbound tanker saw it as a radar blip right in the middle of a shipping lane last night. The guy on watch flashed a warning light, but there was no response. The tanker notified the Coast Guard, who went out at first light."

"The *Lord* was still in the area? That's interesting."

"It looks like Wendell sailed the boat as far as Winterset and then headed out toward the islands. He left the sails up. There was no big sea running, but with the storms coming through, the normal northwesterlies were countered by the hurricane effect. The *Lord* probably has a seven-knot hull speed, and with the right puff of wind it should have gone much farther. When they found the boat, it was stalled and drifting. The jib was backwinded, sheeted to the windward side, in effect, blowing the bow down off the wind while the main and the mizzen were trying to put it up wind. The boat must have lay hove to until discovery."

"I didn't know you sailed."

"I don't anymore. I did once upon a time." Brief smile, the most I'd ever gotten from him.

"Now what?"

"They'll tow it to the closest harbor."

"Which is what, Perdido?"

"Probably. I'm not certain where jurisdiction lies. Some crime scene unit will go over it. I don't think they'll find much, and frankly, I don't see that it's any longer our concern."

I looked over at Mac. "I take it there's no trace of Wendell."

"All his personal possessions were on the boat, including four thousand in cash and a Mexican passport, which doesn't prove a thing. He could have half a dozen passports."

"So we're supposed to think, what . . . that he's dead or gone?"

Mac gestured his irritation, showing the first signs of his usual impatience. "The guy's gone. There's no suicide note, but this is exactly what he pulled last time."

"God, Mac. How can you be so sure about that? Maybe it's a cover. Something to divert our attention."

"From what?"

"From what's really going on."

"Which is what?"

"Beats me," I said. "I'm just telling you what occurs to me. Last time he did this, he abandoned the *Lord* off the coast of Baja and set off in a dinghy. Renata Huff intercepted him, and the two sailed away on the *Fugitive.* This time she was sitting in my office within an hour of his disappearance. This was noon yesterday."

Mac wasn't buying it. "She was under surveillance from the time she left your office. Lieutenant Whiteside decided it made sense to keep an eye on her. All she did was go home. She's been there, off and on, ever since."

"My point exactly. Last time he made a run for it, he had a co-conspirator. This time, assuming that's what he's up to, who's he got on his side? Carl Eckert and Dana Jaffe surely wouldn't come to his rescue, and who else is there? Actually, now that I think about it, his son, Brian, was still free yesterday, and there's always Michael. Wendell might have had other friends. It's also possible he tried the gig alone this time, but it just doesn't *feel* right."

Titus spoke up. "Kinsey thinks he's actually dead," he said to Mac, his mouth turning up with amusement. He tore along the line of perforation, removing a check from the ledger.

"We're *supposed* to think he's dead!" Mac said. "That's what he did the last time, and we fell for it like a ton of bricks. He's probably on a boat right this minute, sailing off to Fiji, laughing up his ass at us."

Gordon closed the ledger and pushed the check in my direction.

"Wait a minute, Mac. Someone took some shots at us Thursday night. Wendell made it home, but suppose they flushed him out the next day? Maybe they caught up with him and killed him." I picked up the check and glanced at it casually. The amount was twenty-five hundred dollars, made out to me. "Oh, thanks. This is nice. I usually don't bill until the end of the month."

"This is final payment," he said. He folded his hands in front of him on the desk. "I have to admit I wasn't in favor of hiring you, but you've done a very nice job. I don't imagine Mrs. Jaffe will give us any more trouble. As soon as you submit your report, we'll turn the matter over to our attorney and he can see to the affidavits. We probably won't need to take the matter to court. She can return any remaining monies and that will be the end of it. In the meantime, I see no reason we can't do business together in the future, on a case-by-case basis, of course."

I stared at him. "This can't be the end of it. We don't have any idea where Wendell is."

"Wendell's current whereabouts are immaterial. We hired you to find him and you did that . . . quite handily, I might add. All we needed to do was show that he was alive, which we've now done."

"But what if he's dead?" I said. "Dana would be entitled to the money, wouldn't she?"

"Ah, but she'd have to prove it first. And what's she have? Nothing."

I looked over at Mac, feeling dissatisfied and confused. He was avoiding my gaze. He shifted on his chair, clearly uncomfortable, probably hoping I wouldn't make a fuss. I got a quick flash of his complaints about CF in my office that first day. "Does this seem right to you? This seems weird. If it turns out something's happened to Wendell, the benefits would be hers. She wouldn't have to give back any money."

"Well, yes, but she'd have to refile," Mac said.

"But aren't we in business to see that claims are settled fairly?" I looked from one to the other. Titus's face was blank, his way of disguising his perpetual dislike, not just of me, but of the world in general. Mac's expression was tinged with guilt. He was never going to stand up to Gordon Titus. He was never going to complain. He was never going to take a stand. "Isn't anybody interested in the truth?" I asked.

Titus stood up and put on his jacket. "I'll leave this to you," he said to Mac. And to me, "We appreciate the fact that you're so conscientious, Kinsey. If we're ever interested in having someone go out and establish the company's liability to the tune of half a million dollars, you'd be the first investigator we'd think of, I'm sure. Thank you for coming in. We'll look for your report first thing Monday morning."

After he left, Mac and I sat in silence for a moment, not looking at each other. Then I got up and walked out myself.

I hopped in my car and headed for Perdido. I had to know. There was no way in the world I was going to let this one go. Maybe they were right. Maybe he'd run off. Maybe he'd been faking every shred of concern for his ex-wife and his kids, for his grandson. He was not a tower of strength. As a man, he possessed neither scruples nor a sense of moral purpose, but I couldn't make my peace with events as they stood. I had to know where he was. I had to understand what had happened to him. He was a man with far more enemies than friends, which didn't bode well for him, which seemed ominous and unsettling. Suppose somebody had killed him. Suppose the whole thing was a setup. I'd already been paid off with a check and a handshake. My time was my own, and I could do as I pleased. Before this day was over, I was going to have some answers.

Perdido's population is roughly ninety-two thousand. Happily, some small percentage of the citizens had called Dana Jaffe the minute news about the finding of the *Lord* came to light. Everybody likes to share the misery of others. There's a breathless curiosity, mixed with dread and gratitude, that allows us to experience misfortune at a satisfying distance. I gathered Dana's phone had been ringing steadily for more than an hour by the time I arrived. I hadn't wanted to be the one to tell her about Wendell's possible defection. News of his death would have cheered her no end, but I thought it unfair to share my suspicions when I had no proof. Without Wendell's body, what good would it do her? Unless she killed him herself, of course, in which case she already knew more than I did.

Michael's yellow VW was parked in the driveway. I knocked on the front door, and Juliet let me in. Brendan slept heavily against her shoulder, too tired to protest the discomfort of a vertical rest.

"They're in the kitchen. I have to get him down," she murmured.

"Thanks, Juliet."

She crossed the room and went upstairs, probably grateful for the excuse to escape. Some woman was in the process of leaving a telephone message in her most solemn tone. "Well, okay, hon. Anyway, I just wanted you to know. If there's anything we can do, you just call us now, you hear? We'll talk to you soon. Bye-bye now."

Dana was sitting at the kitchen table, looking pale and beautiful. Her silver-blond hair looked silky in the light, gathered at the nape of her neck in a careless knot. She wore pale blue jeans and a long-sleeved silk shirt in a shade of steel blue that matched her eyes. She stubbed out a cigarette, glancing up at me without comment. The smell of smoke lingered in the air, along with the faint smell of sulfur matches. Michael was pouring coffee for her from a newly made pot. Where Dana seemed numb, Michael seemed to be in pain.

I'd been around so much lately that no one questioned my unsolicited presence on the scene. He poured a mug of coffee for himself and then opened the cabinet and took out a mug for me. A carton of milk and the sugar bowl were sitting in the middle of the kitchen table. I murmured a thank-you and sat down. "Anything new?"

Dana shook her head. "I can't believe he did it."

Michael leaned against the counter. "We don't know where he is, Mom."

"And that's what drives me insane. He makes just enough of an appearance to screw us up and then he's off again."

"You talked to him?" I asked.

A pause. She dropped her gaze. "He stopped by," she said, her tone faintly defensive. She shifted on her chair, reached for the pack of cigarettes, and lit another one. She'd look old before her time if she didn't knock that off.

"When was this?"

She frowned. "I don't know, not last night, but the night before. Thursday, I guess. He went to Michael's to see the baby afterward. That's how he got the address."

"You have a long talk with him?"

"I wouldn't call it 'long.' He said he was sorry. He'd made a hideous mistake. He said he'd do anything to have the five years back. It was all bullshit, but it sounded good and I guess I needed to hear it. I was pissed, of course. I mean, I said, 'Wendell, you can't *do* this! You can't just waltz back in after everything you've put us through. What do I care if you're sorry? We're all sorry. What horseshit.' "

"You think he was sincere?"

"He was always sincere. He couldn't hold on to the same point of view from one minute to the next, but he was always sincere."

"You didn't talk to him after that?"

She shook her head. "Believe me, once was enough. That should have put an end to it, but I'm still mad," she said.

"So there was no reconciliation."

"Oh, God, no. There's absolutely no way I'd do that. Sorry doesn't cut any ice with me." Her eyes came up to mine. "What now? I guess the insurance company wants their money back."

"They won't press for what you've spent, but they really can't let you walk away with half a million bucks. Unless Wendell's dead."

She became very still, breaking off eye contact. "What makes you say that?"

"It happens to everyone eventually," I said. I pushed my coffee mug away and got up from the chair. "Call me if you hear from him. He's got a lot of people interested. One, at any rate."

"Would you walk her to the door, babe?" Dana said to Michael.

Michael moved away from the counter and walked me to the front door. Lean and brooding.

"You okay?" I asked.

"Not really. How would you feel?"

"I don't think we've gotten to the end of it yet. Your father did what he did for reasons of his own. His behavior was not about you. It was about him," I said. "I don't think you should take it personally."

Michael was shaking his head emphatically. "I never want to see him. I hope I never have to see his face again."

"I understand how you feel. I'm not trying to defend the man, but he's not all bad. You have to take what you can. One day maybe you can let the good back in. You don't know the whole story. You only know this one version. There's far more to it—events, dreams, conflicts, conversations you were never privy to. His actions are coming out of that," I said. "You have to accept the fact that there was something larger at work and you may never know what it was."

"Hey, know what? I don't care. Honest to God, I don't."

"You don't maybe, but one day Brendan might. These things tend to drift down from one generation to the next. Nobody deals well with abandonment."

"Yeah."

"There's a phrase that runs through my head in situations like this: 'the vast untidy sea of truth.' "

"Meaning what?"

"The truth isn't always nice. It isn't always small enough to absorb at once. Sometimes the truth washes over you and threatens to take you right down with it. I've seen a lot of ugly things in this world."

"Yeah, well, I haven't. This is my first and I don't like it much."

"Hey, I hear you," I said. "Take care of your kid. He's really beautiful."

"He's the only good thing that's come out of this."

I had to smile. "There's always you," I said.

His eyes were hooded and his return smile was enigmatic, but I don't think the sentiment was lost on him.

I drove from Dana's to Renata's house. Whatever the flaws in Wendell Jaffe's character, he'd managed to connect himself to two women of substance. They couldn't be more different—Dana with her cool elegance, Renata with her dark exoticism. I parked out in front and made my way up the walk. If the police were still running a surveillance, they were being damn clever. No vans, no panel trucks, no curtains moving in the houses across the way. I rang the bell and waited, staring off at the street. I turned back and cupped a hand to the glass, peering in through the front door panes. I rang the doorbell again.

Renata finally appeared from the back of the house. She was wearing a white cotton skirt and a royal blue cotton T-shirt, white sandals emphasizing the deep olive tan on her legs. She opened the door, pausing for a moment with her cheek against the wood. "Hello. I heard on the radio they found the boat. He isn't really gone, is he?"

"I don't know, Renata. Honestly. Can I come in?"

She held the door open for me. "You might as well."

I followed her down the hallway to the living room, which was built across the back of the house. French doors opened onto a view of the backyard patio, which was small, mostly concrete with a fringe of annuals. Beyond the patio, a slope led down to the water. The *Fugitive* was visible, still moored at the dock.

"Would you like a bloody Mary? I'm having one." She moved to the wet bar and opened the lid of the ice bucket. She used a pair of silver tongs to lift cubes of ice, which she dropped, clinking, into her old-fashioned glass. I always wanted to be the kind of person who did that.

"You go ahead. It's a little early for me."

She squeezed lime over the ice and added an inch of vodka. She took a jug of bloody Mary mix from the minirefrigerator, gave it a whirl to shake it, and poured it over the vodka. Her movements were listless. She looked haggard. She wore very little makeup, and it was clear she'd been crying. Maybe she'd only pulled herself together, answering the door when I rang. She gave me a pained smile. "To what do I owe the pleasure?"

"I was at Dana's. As long as I was down in Perdido anyway, I thought I'd ask if I could go through some of Wendell's belongings. I keep thinking he might have forgotten something. He might have left some piece of information. I don't know how else to get a line on him."

"There aren't any 'things,' but you're welcome to have a look around if you like. Have the police been over the boat, dusting for prints or whatever it is they do?"

"All I know is what I heard this morning from the insurance company. The boat's apparently been found, but there's no sign of Wendell. I don't know about the money yet."

She brought her drink with her, crossing to a big upholstered chair. She took a seat, gesturing for me to join her in the matching chair. "What money?"

"Wendell didn't tell you about that? Carl kept three million dollars hidden somewhere on the boat."

It took about five seconds for the information to register. Then she threw her head back and started laughing, not exactly a happy sound, but better than sobbing. She collected herself. "You are *kidding*," she said.

I shook my head.

Another brief laugh and then she shook her head. "Well, that's incredible. There was that much money on the *Lord*? I can't believe it. Actually this helps me because it all makes sense."

"What does?"

"I couldn't understand his obsession with the damn boat. The *Lord* was all he talked about."

"I don't understand what you're saying."

She stirred her drink with a swizzle stick, which she licked elaborately. "Well, he loved his kids, of course, but he'd never let that interfere with his life before. He was low on money, which was never an issue as far as I was concerned. God knows I have enough for both of us. About four months ago, he started in on this talk about coming back. He wanted to see his boys. He wanted to see his grandson. He wanted to make it up to Dana for the way he'd treated her. I think what he really wanted was to get his hands on that cash. You know what? I'll bet he did it. No wonder he was so fucking secretive. Three million dollars. I'm amazed I didn't guess."

I said, "You don't seem amazed. You seem depressed."

"I suppose I am now you mention it." She took a long swallow from her glass. I had to guess she'd had more than one drink before I showed up. Tears welled in her eyes. She shook her head.

"What?" I asked.

She leaned back, resting her head against the chair, her eyes closed. "I want to believe in him. I want to think he cares about something besides money. Because if that's really the kind of man he is, then what's that say about me?" Her dark eyes came open.

"I'm not sure what Wendell Jaffe does has anything to do with anything," I remarked. "I said the same thing to Michael. Don't take it personally."

"Will the insurance company pursue him?"

"Actually, CF has nothing at stake at this point. I mean, aside from the obvious. Dana's the one who got the insurance money, and they'll deal with her in due course. Aside from that, they're out of it."

"What about the police?"

"Well, they might go after him—frankly, I hope they do—but I don't know how much manpower they'd be willing to devote. Even if we're talking fraud and grand theft, you have to catch the guy first. Then try to prove it. After all these years? You'd have to ask yourself what's the object of the exercise."

"I'll bite. What *is* the object of the exercise? I thought you worked for the insurance company."

"I did. I don't now. Let's put it this way. I have a vested interest. This is all my life has been about for the last ten days, and I won't leave it open-ended. I have to finish it out, Renata. I have to know what happens."

"God, a zealot. Just what we need." She closed her eyes again and rolled the icy glass against her temple as if to cool a raging fever. "I'm tired," she said. "I'd like to sleep for a year."

"Do you mind if I look around?"

"Be my guest. You're welcome to look. He picked the place clean, but I really haven't bothered to check myself. You'll have to pardon my disheveled emotional state. I'm having trouble comprehending the fact that after five years he left me."

"I'm not convinced that's what's going on, but look at it this way. If he did it to Dana, why not do it to you?"

She smiled with her eyes closed, and the effect was odd. I wasn't sure she really heard me. She might have already been asleep. I lifted the glass from her hand and set it on the glass-topped table with a click.

I spent the next forty-five minutes searching every nook and cranny in the house. In situations like this, you never know what you might find: personal papers, notes, correspondence, telephone numbers, a diary, an address book. Anything might help. She was right about Wendell. He'd really picked her clean. I was forced to shrug. I might have found some fabulous secret concerning his whereabouts. You never know until you look.

I came down the stairs and moved quietly through the living room. Renata stirred, her eyes coming open as I passed the couch. "Did you have any luck?" Her voice was thick with alcohol-induced weariness.

"No. But it was worth a try. Will you be all right?"

"You mean once I recover from the humiliation? Sure, I'll be fine."

I paused. "Did a guy named Harris Brown ever call Wendell?"

"Oh, yes. Harris Brown left a message, and Wendell called him back. They had a quarrel on the phone."

"When was this?"

"I don't remember. Maybe yesterday."

"What'd they quarrel about?"

"Wendell didn't tell me that. Apparently there were a lot of things he never got around to 'sharing.' If you find him, don't tell me. I think I'll have the locks changed tomorrow."

"That's Sunday. It'll be expensive."

"Today, then. This afternoon. As soon as I get up."

"Call me if you need anything."

"I need some laughs," she said.

25

The address I had for Harris Brown was in a small Colgate housing tract, one lane of dinky cottages on the bluffs overlooking the Pacific. I counted eight houses altogether on a dirt lane lined with eucalyptus. Board-and-batten, peaked roofs with twin dormers and screened-in porches across the front. Close to shacks now, they were probably built for the domestic staff on a once grand estate, the main house long demolished by the passage of time. Unlike the neighboring exteriors, which were pale pink and green, Harris Brown's house was . . . well . . . brown, perhaps a waggish form of self-referencing. It was hard to tell if the property had been shabby to begin with or if the general state of dilapidation was the function of his being widowed. Sexist creature that I am, it was hard to imagine a woman living here without keeping it better. I went up to the porch.

The front door was standing open, the wooden screen door hooked shut. I could have popped it open with a penknife, but I knocked instead. Classical music was booming from a radio in the kitchen. I could see a section of the counter from the front doorstep, brown-and-white-checked cafe curtains above the sink. I smelled chicken being fried in bacon grease, the sizzling and popping a succulent counterpoint to the music. If Harris Brown didn't show up quickly, I'd begin to pick and whimper at the screen. "Mr. Brown?" I called.

"Hello?" he answered back. He appeared in the kitchen doorway, leaning sideways from the stove. He had a towel around his waist and a two-pronged fork in one hand. "Oh. Hang on." He disappeared, apparently adjusting the flame under the skillet. If he would just offer me some chicken, I wouldn't care what he'd done. Food first, then justice. That's the proper ordering of world events.

He must have put a lid on the skillet because the sizzling sound was abruptly dampened. He moved to the far wall and turned down the radio, and then he came toward the door, wiping his hands on the towel. I was standing against the light, so I figured he really couldn't see much of me until he got up close.

He peered at the screen. "Can I help you?"

"Hi. Remember me?" I said. I suspected he'd been a cop so long he'd never forget a face, though he probably recognized me without being able to recall the context. What added another layer of confusion was the fact we'd chatted on the phone within the last few days. If he knew my voice, I didn't think he'd attach it to the hooker on the balcony in Viento Negro, but it would nag at him.

"Refresh my memory."

"Kinsey Millhone," I said. "We were supposed to have lunch."

"Oh, right, right, right. Sorry. Come on in," he said. He unhooked the screen door and held it open, his expression attentive. "We've met, haven't we? I know your face from some place."

I laughed sheepishly. "Viento Negro. The hotel balcony. I said the boys sent me up, but I'm afraid I was fibbing. I was really looking for Wendell, the same as you."

He said, "Christ." He walked away from the door. "I got chicken on the stove. You better come on back here."

I eased the screen shut behind me, taking in the room at a

glance as I passed through. Scruffy linoleum on the floor, big overstuffed chairs from the thirties, shelves piled haphazardly with books. Not only messy, but not clean. No curtains, no table lamps, a fireplace that didn't function.

I reached the kitchen and peered in. "It looks like Wendell Jaffe's disappeared again."

Harris Brown was back at the stove, skillet lid held aloft while a cloud of steam escaped. A glass pie plate full of seasoned flour sat on the edge of the stove. The surface of the unused griddle looked as though snow had fallen on it where he'd trailed the pieces from the pie plate to the skillet. If he stuck me in the neck with the fork he held, it would look like I'd been bitten by a snake. He poked at the pieces. "Really. I hadn't heard. How'd he manage that?"

I stayed where I was, leaning against the door frame. The kitchen was the one room that seemed to get all the sunlight. It was also cleaner than the rest of the house. The sink had been scoured. The refrigerator was round-shouldered, old and yellowing, but it wasn't smudged with prints. The shelves were open, filled with mismatched crockery. "I don't know," I said. "I thought you might tell me. You talked to him the other day."

"Says who?"

"His girlfriend. She was there when he called you back."

"The infamous Mrs. Huff," he said.

"How'd you find her?"

"That was easy. You told me her name in our first telephone conversation."

"Ah, that's right. I bet I even mentioned she lived in the Keys. I'd forgotten."

"I don't forget much," he said, "though I notice age is catching up with me."

Inwardly I was gritched. The man seemed too casual. "I talked to Carl last night. He told me he paid the hundred grand he owed you."

"That's right."

"Why'd you quarrel with Wendell?"

He turned over some chicken pieces, mahogany brown with a spice-speckled crust. Looked done to me, but when he stuck it with his fork, blood-tinged liquid oozed out of the joint. He lowered the flame and replaced the lid. "I quarreled with Wendell before I got the money. That's why I laid into Eckert and made him drive down that night."

"I don't understand the connection."

"Wendell tells me he's going to blow the whistle. He wants to 'clear his conscience' before he goes to jail. What a crock of shit. I can't believe it. He's going to tell 'em about the money he and Eckert have been hoarding. The minute he says it, I know that's the end of it. I'm finished. By the time the court gets done, I'll never see a cent. I get straight on the horn to Eckert and tell him he better get himself down here with the cash in hand. I mean, *pronto.*"

"Why hadn't you pressed for the money before?"

"Because I thought it was gone. Eckert claimed the two of them had blown every penny. Once I heard Wendell was alive, I threw the whole story out the window. I put the screws to Eckert, and it turns out they had a bundle. Wendell only took a million or so when he left. Eckert had the rest. Can you believe that? He'd had it the whole time, just taking out what he needed. He was clever, I'll say that. He lived like a pauper, so who would have guessed?"

"Weren't you a party to the lawsuit?"

"Well, sure, but that kind of money won't survive intact. You know what I'd get? Maybe ten cents on the dollar, and that's if I'm lucky. You got the IRS first and two hundred fifty investors? Everybody wants a piece. I didn't give a shit if he turned in the money, as long as I got mine up front. To hell with everybody else. I earned that dough, and I went to great lengths to collect."

"And what was the deal? What did you do in exchange?"

"I didn't do anything. That's the point. Once I had the money I didn't care about those two."

"You had no further interest."

"That's right."

I shook my head, confused. "I don't get this. Why would Carl Eckert pay you that much? If you want to get right down to it, why would he pay you at all? Was it blackmail?"

"Of course it wasn't blackmail. Jesus Christ, I'm a cop. He didn't *pay* me a cent. He made good on my losses. I invested a hundred grand and that's what I got back. To the nickel," he said.

"Did you tell Carl Eckert about Wendell turning in the money?"

"Sure I did. Wendell was going to the cops that night. I'd already talked to Carl. He was supposed to stop by with the money Friday morning, so I knew he had it with him. I wanted to make sure I had the money in my pocket before old looney tunes Wendell started blabbing. What a dope he was."

"Why do you say 'was'?"

"Because he's gone again, right? You just said so yourself."

"Maybe getting your money back wasn't enough."

"What the hell does that mean?"

I shrugged. "You might have wanted him dead."

He laughed. "You're really stretching for that one. Why would I want him dead?"

"The way I heard it, he ruined your relationship with your kids. Your marriage broke up. Your wife died shortly after that."

"Oh, hell. My marriage was lousy to begin with, and she was sick for years. Losing the money was what pissed my kids off. Once I slipped 'em each twenty-five grand under the table, they warmed right up."

"Nice kids."

"At least I know where I stand," he said dryly.

"You're telling me you didn't kill him."

"I'm telling you I didn't have to. I figured Dana Jaffe would do that once she found out about this other woman. It's enough he'd abandon her and the kids, but to do it over some little piece of fluff like that? Seems a bit much."

• • •

Since my apartment is only a block from the ocean, I left my car parked in front and walked back to the marina. I loitered outside the locked gate leading down to Marina 1. I could have climbed around the outside as I'd done with Renata, but there was enough foot traffic at that hour to wait for someone with a key. The day was turning grim. I didn't think it would rain, but the clouds were a thick, brooding gray and the sea air was chilly. These Santa Teresa summers are really such a treat.

Finally a guy came along in shorts and a sweatshirt. He had his card key in hand and he unlocked the gate. He even held it for me when he saw that I was interested in sliding through.

"Thanks," I said, falling into step with him as he proceeded along the walkway. "You know Carl Eckert, by any chance? He owns the boat that was stolen Friday morning."

"I heard about that. Yeah, I know Carl by sight. I think he went down to get it, as a matter of fact. I saw him motor out in his dinghy a couple of hours ago." The guy took the second left turn onto the line of slips marked D. I continued on to J, which was on the right-hand side. Sure enough, Eckert's slip was still empty, and there was no way to predict just what time he'd get back.

It was nearly one o'clock, and I'd never had lunch. I walked back to my place and brought my typewriter in from the car. I made myself a sandwich—hot hard-boiled egg, sliced across a slathering of Best Foods mayo. Whole-wheat bread, lots of salt, a vertical cut. Rules are rules. I hummed to myself, licking my fingers as I set up my Smith-Corona. I ate at my desk, typing intermittently in between big gooey bites. I worked my way through a pack of index cards, reducing everything I knew to three-by-five notes. I sorted them into various categories and tacked them on the bulletin board hanging over my desk. I turned on my desk lamp. I got myself a diet Pepsi at one point. As if it were some kind of board game, I played and replayed the same set of cards. I didn't even know what I was doing, just looking at the information, arranging and rearranging, hoping I'd see a pattern emerge.

The next time I looked at my watch it was 6:45. I felt anxiety stir. I'd meant to spend only a couple of hours at my desk, making use of the time until Eckert got back. I shoved a few bucks in my jeans pocket and grabbed a sweatshirt, pulling it over my head as I went out the door. I half trotted back to the marina, through that artificial twilight that gloomy weather generates. I caught up with a woman going down the ramp toward Marina 1. She glanced at me idly as she unlocked the gate. "Forgot my key," I murmured as I followed her in.

The *Lord* was back in its slip, shrouded in blue canvas covers. The cabin was dark, and there was no sign of Eckert. There was an inflatable dinghy bobbing in the water behind it, attached by a line. I stared at it for a while, exploring the possibilities. I walked back to the yacht club, which was blazing with lights. I pushed in through the glass doors and went up the stairs.

I spotted him across the dining room. He was sitting at the bar, wearing jeans and a denim jacket, his silver hair ruffled from the hours on the boat. The jacket-and-tie dinner crowd was already heavy, the bar itself jammed with drinkers, air dense with cigarette smoke. The maître d' looked up at me, feigning startlement at my attire. In truth, he was probably just annoyed that I hadn't paused to genuflect as I passed. I waved toward the windows, letting my face light up as if with recognition. He glanced in that direction. There wasn't any dress code in the bar, and he knew it. Half the people in there wore polo shirts and long pants, windbreakers, deck shoes.

Carl Eckert turned, catching sight of me when I was ten feet away. He murmured something to the bartender and then picked up his drink. "Let's grab a table. I think there's one outside." I nodded and followed as we picked a path through the crush.

Both the noise and the temperature dropped considerably once the door closed behind us. We were out on the deck, where only a few hardy souls were huddled. It was getting darker by the minute, though the sun was actually setting behind clouds. Below us, the ocean bucked and heaved, waves breaking on the sand with a constant thunder and swish. I loved the smell out here, though the air was damp and uninviting. Two tall propane heaters generated a rosy, oblong glow without doing much to warm the air. We sat near one nonetheless.

Carl says, "I ordered you some wine. The guy should be out with it in a minute."

"Thanks. You got your boat back, I see. What'd they find? I'd guess nothing, but one can always hope."

"Actually, they found traces of blood. Couple of little smears on the railing, but they don't know if it's Wendell's."

"Oh, right. Like it might be yours."

"You know the police. They're not going to jump to conclusions. For all we know, Wendell did it himself, trying to create the suspicion of foul play. Did you see Renata? She just left."

I shook my head, noticing the change of subject he'd engineered. "I didn't know you two knew each other."

"I know Renata. I can't say we're friends. I met her years ago when Wendell first fell in love with her. You know how it is when a good friend has a mate you don't really get along with. I couldn't understand why he wasn't happy with Dana."

I said, "Marriage is a mystery. What's she doing up here?"

"I'm not sure. She seemed down in the mouth. She wanted to talk about Wendell, but then she got upset and walked out."

"I don't think she's handling this business well," I said. "What about the money? Is it gone?"

His laugh was a dry, flat sound. "Of course. For a while I had hopes that it might still be on the boat. I can't even call the cops. That's the irony."

"When did you last talk to Wendell?"

"Must have been Thursday. He was on his way to Dana's."

"I saw him after that at Michael's. We left together, but his car wouldn't start. I'm sure now somebody tampered with it because mine was tampered with, too. I was giving him a lift when my engine cut out. That's when somebody started shooting at us."

Behind us, the door opened with a burst of noise. The waiter came out with a glass of Chardonnay on a tray. He had another Scotch and water for Carl. He set both drinks on the table, along with a bowl of pretzels. Eckert paid in cash, tossing out an extra couple of bills as a tip. The waiter thanked him and withdrew.

When the door closed again, I shifted the conversation. "I talked to Harris Brown."

"Good for you. How is he?"

"He seems fine. For a while I thought maybe he was a likely candidate for Wendell's murder."

"Murder. Oh, right."

"It does make sense," I said.

"Why does that make sense? It makes just as much sense to think he's gone off again," Carl said. "Why not suicide? God knows the people here didn't exactly welcome him with open arms. What if he killed himself? Have you considered that?"

"What if he was taken up in a spaceship?" I countered.

"Make your point. I can feel myself getting irritated with the subject. It's been a long day. I'm bushed. I'm out at least a million bucks. Not fun, I can tell you."

"Maybe you killed him."

"Why would I kill him? The fucker stole my money. If he's dead, how am I ever going to get it back?"

I shrugged. "To begin with, it wasn't *your* money. Half of it belonged to him. I only have your word for the fact that the money's missing. How do I know you didn't take it off the boat yourself and hide it somewhere else? Now that Harris Brown knows about it, you may be worried he'll hit you up for more than the hundred thousand he's claiming."

"Take my word for it. The money's gone," he said.

"Why would I take your word for anything? You were filing bankruptcy while two hundred and fifty investors were getting a judgment against you for money they couldn't collect. Turns out you had it all the time, playing poor while you had millions stuffed under the mattress."

"I know it looks like that."

"It doesn't just *look* like that. That's how it *was*."

"You can't possibly think I had a motive for killing Wendell. You don't even know if he's dead. Chances are he's not."

"I don't know what the chances are one way or the other. Let's just look at it this way. You had the money. He came back to collect his share. You'd had the cash so long you were beginning to think you were the only one entitled to it. Wendell's been 'dead' for five years. Who's really going to care if he's 'dead' for the rest of time? You'd be doing Dana a big favor. Wendell turns up alive, she has to give the money back."

"Hey, I talked to the guy on Thursday. That's the last I ever saw of him."

"That's the last anybody ever saw of him except Renata," I said.

He got up abruptly and headed for the door. I was right on his heels, banging through the door behind him. People turned to watch as he pushed his way across the crowded bar with me in his wake. He clattered down the stairs, around the corner, and out through the front door. Oddly enough, I wasn't worried, and I didn't care if he got away. Something was stirring at the back of my mind. Something about timing, about Wendell and the sequence of events. The dinghy bobbing in the water, trailing along behind the *Lord* like a little duckling. I couldn't put my finger on it yet, but I was going to get it soon.

I could see Carl ahead of me, pausing at the locked gate. He was fumbling for his card key, and I trotted down the ramp behind him. He looked back in haste, and then his eyes flickered up toward the breakwater behind me. I glanced up. There was a woman at the railing. She was barefoot, in a trench coat, staring down at us. Her bare legs and the pale oval of her face were like punctuation against the darkness. Renata.

I said, "Hang on a minute. I want to talk to her."

Eckert ignored me, pushing on through the gate while I retraced my steps. The curving wall along the breakwater is about eighteen inches wide, a ledge of hip-high concrete. The ocean crashes perpetually against the barrier, water shooting straight up. A line of spray is forced along the wall and around the bend, which is marked by a row of flagpoles. The wind off the ocean blows a constant mist in this direction, waves splatting onto the walkway on the harbor side. Renata had hopped up on the wall and she was walking the curve, waves catching at her shoulder almost playfully. Her raincoat was getting soaked—dark tan on the ocean side, lighter tan on the left where the fabric was still dry. It was like getting rained on, that spray. I could feel it on my face.

"Renata!"

She didn't seem to hear, though she was only fifty yards ahead of me. The walk was slippery from seawater, and I had to watch my step. I broke into a trot, moving gingerly, hopping over puddles as I tracked her progress. The tide was in. I could see the ocean churning, a massive black presence disappearing into blackness. All the flags were snapping. There were lights at intervals, but the effect was ornamental.

"Renata!"

She glanced back then and saw me. She slowed her pace, waiting until I caught up with her before she started up again. She stayed one pace ahead of me. I was on the walkway below while she kept to the top of the wall so that I was forced to look up at her. I could see now that she was crying, mascara smudges below her dark eyes. Her hair was a series of dripping strands that hugged her face and clung to her neck. I tugged at her coat hem and she stopped, looking down. "Where's Wendell? You said he took off Friday morning, but you're the only one who ever claimed to have seen him after Thursday night." I needed details. I really wasn't sure how she'd managed to pull it off. I thought about how haggard she'd looked when she showed up in my office. Maybe she'd been up all night. Maybe she was making me part of her alibi. "Did you kill him?"

"Who cares?"

"I'd like to know. I really would. CF took me off the case this morning and the cops don't give a shit. Come on. Just between us. I'm the only one who believes he's dead, and nobody's listening to me."

The answer was delayed as if traveling from a distance. "Yes."

"You killed him?"

"Yes."

"How?"

"I shot him. It was quick." She made a gun barrel of her index finger, firing it at me. The recoil was minimal.

I scrambled up on the wall beside her, so that our faces were level. I liked it better that way. I didn't have to raise my voice to be heard above the surf. Was she drunk? I could smell alcohol on her person, even downwind. "Was that you shooting at us at the beach?"

"Yes."

"But I had your gun. I took it away from you on the boat."

Her smile was wan. "I had a collection to choose from. Dean kept six or eight. He was very paranoid about burglars. The one I used on Wendell was a little semiautomatic with a suppressor. The shot didn't even make as much noise as a hardcover book falling on the floor."

"When did you do it?"

"That same night, Thursday. He walked home from the beach. I had my car. I got home first, so I was there to meet him when he got in. He was exhausted and his feet hurt. I made him a vodka tonic and took it out to him on the deck. He took a long swallow. I put the gun against his neck and fired. He barely jumped, and I was quick enough to keep the drink from spilling. I dragged him down the dock to the dinghy and hauled him in. I covered him with a tarp and putt-putted out of the Keys. I took my time about it so I wouldn't attract attention."

"Then what?"

"Once I was out about a quarter mile, I weighted his body down with an old twenty-five-horsepower motor I was getting rid of anyway. I kissed him on the mouth. He was already cold and he tasted like salt. I heaved him overboard and he sank."

"Along with the gun."

"Yes. After that I shifted into high gear and jammed it from Perdido up to Santa Teresa, where I eased into the marina, attached the dinghy to the *Lord*, and motored it out to sea. I brought the boat down along the coast and hauled the sails up. I got back in the dinghy and puttered into the Keys again while the *Lord* headed out into the ocean."

"But why, Renata? What did Wendell ever do to you?"

She turned her head, staring out at the horizon. When she looked back, I saw that she was smiling slightly. "I lived and traveled with the man for five years," she said. "I provided him money, a passport, shelter, support. And how does he repay me? By going back to his family . . . by being so ashamed of me, he wouldn't even admit my existence to his grown sons. He had a midlife crisis. That's all I was. Once it was over he was going back to his wife. I couldn't lose him to her. It was too humiliating."

"But Dana wasn't ever going to take him back."

"She would have. They all do. They say they won't, but when it comes right down to it, they can't resist. I'm not sure I blame them. They're just so bloody grateful when hubby finally comes crawling back. It doesn't matter what he's done. Just so he shows up again and says he loves her." The smile had faded, and she was starting to cry.

"Why the tears? He wasn't worth it."

"I miss him. I didn't think I would, but I do." She pulled the belt on her coat and let it slip off her shoulders. She was naked underneath, slim and white, shivering. Like an arrow of flesh.

"Renata, don't!"

I saw her turn and propel herself into the boiling ocean. I pulled my shoes off. I yanked my jeans down and pulled the sweatshirt over my head. It was cold. I was already soaked with spray, but for a moment I hesitated. Below me, out about ten yards now, I could see Renata swimming, slender white arms cutting through the water methodically. I didn't want to go into the water at all. It looked deep and cold and black and bitter. I flew forward, feeling birdlike, wondering if there was any chance of staying airborne forever.

I hit the water. It was stunning, and I gasped and then heard myself sing aloud with the surprise. The cold took my breath away. The weight of the water forced my lungs to labor. I caught my breath and started moving. Salt stung my eyes, but I could see the white of Renata's hands, face bobbing through the water a few yards in front of me. I'm an adequate swimmer, but not a strong one by any means. To swim for any length of time, I'm usually forced to shift from stroke to stroke—the crawl, the sidestroke, the breaststroke, rest. The ocean was buoyant, nearly playful by nature, a big liquid death, cold as torture, unforgiving.

"Renata, wait!"

She looked back, apparently surprised that I had braved the water. Almost as a courtesy, she seemed to slow down a bit, allowing me to catch up with her before she started off again. I was already winded from exertion. She seemed tired, too, and maybe that's why she consented to the rest. For a moment we bobbed together, water lifting us up and down like some kind of bizarre attraction at an amusement park.

I went under, coming up again face first, washing the hair back out of my eyes. I wiped my nose and mouth, tasting brine. Pickled by death, I'd become a human olive. "What happened to the money?"

I could see her arms move in the water, the motion keeping her near the surface of the water. "I didn't know about the money. That's why I laughed so hard when you told me."

"It's gone now. Somebody took it."

"Oh, who cares about that, Kinsey? Wendell taught me a lot. I hate to sound trite about it at a time like this, but money really can't buy happiness."

"Yeah, but at least you can afford to rent a little bit."

She didn't even bother to laugh politely. I could tell her energy was flagging, but not nearly to the extent mine was.

"What happens when you can't go on swimming?" I asked.

"Actually, I've done some research. Drowning isn't such a bad way to go. There's bound to be a moment of panic, but after that, it's euphoric. You simply slide into the ether. Like going to sleep, except you have nice sensations. It's the oxygen deprivation. Suffocation, in effect."

"I don't trust the reports. Gotta be from people who didn't really die, and what do they know? Besides, I'm not ready. Too many sins on my conscience," I said.

"You better save your strength then. I'm going on," she said, and moved off through the water. Was the woman a fish? I could barely move. The water did seem warmer, but that was worrisome. Maybe this was stage one, the preliminary illusion just before the final full-blown hallucination. We swam. She was stronger than I was. I went through all the strokes I knew, trying to keep up with her. For a while, I counted. One, two. Breathe. One, two. Breathe. "Oh, Jesus, Renata. Let's rest." I stopped, winded, and turned over on my back, looking up at the sky. The clouds actually seemed lighter than the night around us. Almost as a form of indulgence, she slowed again, treading water. Out there in the darkness, the waves were pitiless, inviting. The cold was numbing.

"Please come back to shore with me," I said. My chest was burning. I was panting in the water, but I couldn't get enough air. "I don't want to do this, Renata."

"I never asked you to."

She started swimming again.

I experienced a failure of will. My arms felt like lead. For a moment I thought about trying to keep up, but I was close to collapse. I was cold and tired. My arms were getting heavier, burning down the length of them from total muscle fatigue. I could barely breathe. I'd begun to miscalculate, gulping down saltwater every time I tried for air. I might have been crying, too. Hard to tell out there. I trod water for a bit. I felt like I'd been swimming forever, but when I turned and looked at the shore lights, it was clear we'd gone only half a mile, if that. I couldn't imagine what it'd be like swimming to exhaustion—in the dark, in black water, until fatigue overtook us. I couldn't save her. There was no way I was going to match her, swimming stroke for stroke. And what would I do if I caught up with her, wrestle her into submission? Not likely. I hadn't practiced any lifesaving skills since I was certified back in high school. She was on her way out. It wasn't going to make a bit of difference to her if she took me out with her. Once people get into killing mode, they don't always know how to stop. At least I understood now what had happened to Wendell and what would happen to her. I had to stop. I trod water, conserving energy. I simply couldn't go on. I couldn't even think of anything pithy or profound to say to her. Not that she was paying attention. She had her own destination, just as I had mine. I heard her briefly, but it didn't take long before the splashing sounds were swallowed up by the night. I rested for a while and then turned and started back to shore.

EPILOGUE

Wendell Jaffe's body emerged from the Pacific nine days later, washing up on Perdido Beach, trailing kelp like a net. Some peculiar combination of tides and storm surf had freed him from the ocean bottom and brought him ashore. Of the family survivors, I think Michael took it hardest. Brian had issues of his own to deal with, but he could at least take comfort in the fact that his father hadn't willfully abandoned him. Dana's financial problems were resolved by the hard proof of Wendell's death. It was Michael who was left with all the unfinished business.

As for me, having cost California Fidelity half a million dollars, I thought it was safe to assume I wouldn't be doing business with *them* anytime soon. That should have been the end of it, but a few facts began to filter in as the months went by. Renata's body never surfaced. I heard, inadvertently, that when her estate was probated, both her house and her boat were mortgaged to the hilt and all her bank accounts had been stripped. That bothered me. I found myself picking at the past, like a little knot in a piece of thread.

Here's what I think about when I wake in the dead of night. I'm not sure anybody really knows what happened to Dean DeWitt Huff. She claims he died of a heart attack in Spain, but did anyone ever check it out? And the husband before that? Whatever happened to him? I'd been viewing this as Wendell Jaffe's story, but suppose it was hers? The missing millions never showed. Suppose she knew about the money and persuaded him to come back? Suppose she had a boat anchored out there somewhere in the dark? She could have dived off her own dock if she wanted to drown. You really want to kill yourself, why drive thirty miles to do it? Unless you need a reliable witness—like me. Once I made my report to the police, the case was considered closed. But is it?

I've never believed the perfect crime was possible. Now I'm not so sure. She told me Wendell taught her a lot, but she never really said what it was. Please understand: I don't have the answers. I'm simply posing the questions. God knows I have questions about my own life to answer yet.

Respectfully submitted,
Kinsey Millhone

"K" IS FOR KILLER

For Mary Lawrence Young and crew . . .

Richard, Lori, and Taylor,
Lawrence,
and Mary Taylor,

and, of course, the dogs . . .

Sadie and Halley,

Toto and Emmy
Oz, Bob, Dee, Lily, and Tog,

and cats . . .

Yukio, Ace, Karmin, and Kit,

and beloved Charmin, much missed.

ACKNOWLEDGMENTS

The author wishes to acknowledge the invaluable assistance of the following people: Steven Humphrey; Susan Aharonian, treatment supervisor, and JoAnn Fults, Cater Water Treatment Plant; Larry Gillespie, Santa Barbara County coroner; Lieutenant Terry Bristol, Santa Barbara County Sheriff's Office; Detective Tom Miller, Santa Barbara Police Department; Jody Knoell, Wells Fargo Bank; Michael Creek, KMGQ; Hildy Hoffman, secretary to the mayor and council, city of Santa Barbara; Tokie Shynk, R.N., and the CCU nursing staff, Santa Barbara Cottage Hospital; Bobbie Kline, R.N., B.S., director of emergency room, Santa Barbara Cottage Hospital; and Craig Wertz, Kleen Pools, Santa Barbara.

1

The statutory definition of homicide is the "unlawful killing of one human being by another." Sometimes the phrase "with malice" is employed, the concept serving to distinguish murder from the numerous other occasions in which people deprive each other of life —wars and executions coming foremost to mind. "Malice" in the law doesn't necessarily convey hatred or even ill will but refers instead to a conscious desire to inflict serious injury or cause death. In the main, criminal homicide is an intimate, personal affair insofar as most homicide victims are killed by close relatives, friends, or acquaintances. Reason enough to keep your distance, if you're asking me.

In Santa Teresa, California, approximately eighty-five percent of all criminal homicides are resolved, meaning that the assailant is identified, apprehended, and the question of guilt or innocence is adjudicated by the courts. The victims of unsolved homicides I think of as the unruly dead: persons who reside in a limbo of their own, some state between life and death, restless, dissatisfied, longing for release. It's a fanciful notion for someone not generally given to flights of imagination, but I think of these souls locked in an uneasy relationship with those who have killed them. I've talked to homicide investigators who've been caught up in similar reveries, haunted by certain victims who seem to linger among us, persistent in their desire for vindication. In the hazy zone where wakefulness fades into sleep, in that leaden moment just before the mind sinks below consciousness, I can sometimes hear them murmuring. They mourn themselves. They sing a lullaby of the murdered. They whisper the names of their attackers, those men and women who still walk the earth, unidentified, unaccused, unpunished, unrepentant. On such nights, I do not sleep well. I lie awake listening, hoping to catch a syllable, a phrase, straining to discern in that roll call of conspirators the name of one killer. Lorna Kepler's murder ended up affecting me that way, though I didn't learn the facts of her death until months afterward.

It was mid-February, a Sunday, and I was working late, little Miss Virtue organizing itemized expenses and assorted business receipts for my tax return. I'd decided it was time to handle matters like a grown-up instead of shoving everything in a shoebox and delivering it to my accountant at the very last minute. Talk about cranky! Each year the man positively bellows at me, and I have to swear I'll reform, a vow I take seriously until tax time rolls around again and I realize my finances are in complete disarray.

I was sitting at my desk in the law firm where I rent office space. The night outside was chilly by the usual California definition, which is to say fifty degrees. I was the only one on the premises, ensconced in a halo of warm, sleep-inducing light while the other offices remained dark and quiet. I'd just put on a pot of coffee to counteract the narcolepsy that afflicts me at the approach to money matters. I laid my head on the desk, listening to the soothing gargle of the water as it filtered through the coffee maker. Even the smell of mocha java was not sufficient to stimulate my torpid senses. Five more minutes and I'd be out like a light, drooling on my blotter with my right cheek picking up inky messages in reverse.

I heard a tap at the side entrance and I lifted my head, tilting an ear in that direction like a dog on alert. It was nearly ten o'clock, and I wasn't expecting any visitors. I roused myself, left my desk, and moved out into the hallway. I cocked my head against the side door leading out into the hall. The tap was repeated, much louder. I said, "Yes?"

I heard a woman's muffled voice in response. "Is this Millhone Investigations?"

"We're closed."

"What?"

"Hang on." I put the chain on the door and opened it a crack, peering out at her.

She was on the far side of forty, her outfit of the urban cowgirl sort: boots, faded jeans, and a buckskin shirt. She wore enough heavy silver-and-turquoise jewelry to look like she would clank. She had dark hair nearly to her waist, worn loose, faintly frizzy and dyed the color of oxblood shoes. "Sorry to bother you, but the directory downstairs says there's a private investigator up here in this suite. Is he in, by any chance?"

"Ah. Well, more or less," I said, "but these aren't actual office hours. Is there any way you can come back tomorrow? I'll be happy to set up an appointment for you once I check my book."

"Are you his secretary?" Her tanned face was an irregular oval, lines cutting down along each side of her nose, four lines between her eyes where the brows were plucked to nothing and reframed in black. She'd used the same sharpened pencil to line her eyelids, too, though she wore no other makeup that I could see.

I tried not to sound irritated since the mistake is not uncommon. "I'm him," I said. "Millhone Investigations. The first name is Kinsey. Did you tell me yours?"

"No, I didn't, and I'm sorry. I'm Janice Kepler. You must think I'm a complete idiot."

Well, not *complete,* I thought.

She reached out to shake hands and then realized the crack in the doorway wasn't large enough to permit contact. She pulled her hand back. "It never occurred to me you'd be a woman. I've been seeing the Millhone Investigations on the board down in the stairwell. I come here for a support group once a week down a floor. I've been thinking I'd call, but I guess I never worked up my nerve. Then tonight as I was leaving, I saw the light on from the parking lot. I hope you don't mind. I'm actually on my way to work, so I don't have that long."

"What sort of work?" I asked, stalling.

"Shift manager at Frankie's Coffee Shop on upper State Street. Eleven to seven, which makes it hard to take care of any daytime appointments. I usually go to bed at eight in the morning and don't get up again until late afternoon. Even if I could just *tell* you my problem, it'd be a big relief. Then if it turns out it's not the sort of work you do, maybe you could recommend someone else. I could really use some help, but I don't know where to turn. Your being a woman might make it easier." The penciled eyebrows went up in an imploring double arch.

I hesitated. Support group, I thought. Drink? Drugs? Codependency? If the woman was looney-tunes, I'd really like to know. Behind her, the hall was empty, looking flat and faintly yellow in the overhead light. Lonnie Kingman's law firm takes up the entire third floor except for the two public restrooms: one marked *M* and one *W*. It was always possible she had a couple of *M* confederates lurking in the commode, ready at a signal to jump out and attack me. For what purpose, I couldn't think. Any money I had, I was being forced to give to the feds at pen point. "Just a minute," I said.

I closed the door and slid the chain off its track, opening the door again so I could admit her. She moved past me hesitantly, a crackling brown paper bag in her arms. Her perfume was musky, the scent reminiscent of saddle soap and sawdust. She seemed ill at ease, her manner infected by some edgy combination of apprehension and embarrassment. The brown paper bag seemed to contain papers of some sort. "This was in my car. I didn't want you to think I carried it around with me ordinarily."

"I'm in here," I said. I moved into my office with the woman close on my heels. I indicated a chair for her and watched as she sat down, placing the paper bag on the floor. I pulled up a chair for myself. I figured if we sat on opposite sides of my desk she'd check out my deductible expenses, which were none of her business. I'm the current ranking expert at reading upside down and seldom hesitate to insert myself into matters that are not my concern. "What support group?" I asked.

"It's for parents of murdered children. My daughter died here last April. Lorna Kepler. She was found in her cottage over by the mission."

I said, "Ah, yes. I remember, though I thought there was some speculation about the cause of death."

"Not in my mind," she said tartly. "I don't know *how* she died, but I know she was murdered just as sure as I'm sitting here." She reached up and tucked a long ribbon of loose hair behind her right ear. "The police never did come up with a suspect, and I don't know what kind of luck they're going to have after all this time. Somebody told me for every day that passes, the chances diminish, but I forget the percentage."

"Unfortunately, that's true."

She leaned over and rooted in the paper bag, pulling out a photograph in a bifold frame. "This is Lorna. You probably saw this in the papers at the time."

She held out the picture and I took it, staring down at the girl. Not a face I'd forget. She was in her early twenties with dark hair pulled smoothly away from her face, a long swatch of hair hanging down the middle of her back. She had clear hazel eyes with a nearly Oriental tilt; dark, cleanly arched brows; a wide mouth; straight nose. She was wearing a white blouse with a long snowy white scarf wrapped several times around her neck, a dark navy blazer, and faded blue jeans on a slender frame. She stared directly at the camera, smiling slightly, her hands tucked down in her front pockets. She was leaning against a floral-print wall, the paper showing lavish pale pink climbing roses against a white background. I returned the picture, wondering what in the world to say under the circumstances.

"She's very beautiful," I murmured. "When was that taken?"

"About a year ago. I had to bug her to get this. She's my youngest. Just turned twenty-five. She was hoping to be a model, but it didn't work out."

"You must have been young when you had her."

"Twenty-one," she said. "I was seventeen with Berlyn. I got married because of her. Five months gone and I was big as a house. I'm still with her daddy, which surprised everyone, including me, I guess. I was nineteen with my middle daughter. Her name's Trinny. She's real sweet. Lorna's the one I nearly died with, poor thing. Got up one morning, day before I was due, and started hemorrhaging. I didn't know what was happening. Blood everywhere. It was just like a river pouring out between my legs. I've never seen anything like it. Doctor didn't think he could save either one of us, but we pulled through. You have children, Ms. Millhone?"

"Make it Kinsey," I said. "I'm not married."

She smiled slightly. "Just between us, Lorna really was my favorite, probably because she was such a problem all her life. I wouldn't say that to either of the older girls, of course." She tucked the picture away. "Anyway, I know what it's like to have your heart ripped out. I probably look like an ordinary woman, but I'm a zombie, the living dead, maybe a little bit cracked. We've been going to this support group . . . somebody suggested it, and I thought it might help. I was ready to try anything to get away from the pain. Mace—that's my husband—went a few times and then quit. He couldn't stand the stories, couldn't stand all the suffering compressed in one room. He wants to shut it out, get shed of it, get clean. I don't think it's possible, but there's no arguing the point. To each his own, as they say."

"I can't even imagine what it must be like," I said.

"And I can't describe it, either. That's the hell of it. We're not like regular people anymore. You have a child murdered, and from that moment on you're from some other planet. You don't speak the same language as other folks. Even in this support group, we seem to speak different dialects. Everybody hangs on to their pain like it was some special license to suffer. You can't help it. We all think ours is the worst case we ever heard. Lorna's murder hasn't been solved, so naturally we think our anguish is more acute because of it. Some other family, maybe their child's killer got caught and he served a few years. Now he's out on the street again, and that's what they have to live with—knowing some fella's walking around smoking cigarettes, drinking beers, having himself a good old time every Saturday night while their child is dead. Or the killer's still in prison and'll be there for life, but he's warm, he's safe. He gets three meals a day and the clothes on his back. He might be on death row, but he won't actually *die.* Hardly anybody does unless they *beg* to be executed. Why should they? All those soft-hearted lawyers go to work. System's set up to keep 'em all alive while our kids are dead for the rest of time."

"Painful," I said.

"Yes, it is. I can't even tell you how much that hurts. I sit downstairs in that room and I listen to all the stories, and I don't know what to do. It's not like it makes my pain any less, but at least it makes it part of *something.* Without the support group, Lorna's death just evaporates. It's like nobody cares. It's not even something people talk about anymore. We're all of us wounded, so I don't feel so cut off. I'm not separate from them. Our emotional injuries just come in different forms." Her tone throughout was nearly matter-of-fact, and the dark-eyed look she gave me then seemed all the more painful because of it. "I'm telling you all this because I don't want you to think I'm crazy . . . at least any more than I actually am. You have a child murdered and you go berserk. Sometimes you recover and sometimes you don't. What I'm saying is, I know I'm obsessed. I think about Lorna's killer way more than I should. Whoever did this, I want him *punished.* I want this laid to rest. I want to know why he did it. I want to tell him face-to-face exactly what he did to my life the day he took hers. The psychologist who runs the group, she says I need to find a way to get my power back. She says it's better to get mad than go on feeling heartsick and defenseless. So. That's why I'm here. I guess that's the long and short of it."

"Taking action," I said.

"You bet. Not just talking. I'm sick and tired of talk. It gets nowhere."

"You're going to have to do a bit more talking if you want my help. You want some coffee?"

"I know that. I'd love some. Black is fine."

I filled two mugs and added milk to mine, saving my questions until I was seated again. I reached for the legal pad on my desk, and I picked up a pen. "I hate to make you go through the whole thing again, but I really need to have the details, at least as much as you know."

"I understand. Maybe that's why it took me so long to come up here. I've told this story probably six hundred times, but it never gets any easier." She blew on the surface of her coffee and then took a sip. "That's good coffee. Strong. I hate drinking coffee too weak. It's no taste. Anyway, let me think how to say this. I guess what you have to understand about Lorna is she was an independent little cuss. She did everything her way. She didn't care what other people thought, and she didn't feel what she did was anybody else's business. She'd been asthmatic as a child and ended up missing quite a bit of school, so she never did well in her classes. She was smart as a whip, but she was out half the time. Poor thing was allergic to just about everything. She didn't have many friends. She couldn't spend the night at anybody else's house because other little girls always seemed to live with pets or house dust, mold, or whatnot. She outgrew a lot of that as she matured, but she was always on medication for one thing or another. I make a point of this because I think it had a profound effect on the way she turned out. She was antisocial: bullheaded and uncooperative. She had a streak of defiance, I think because she was used to being by herself, doing what *she* wanted. And I might have spoiled her some. Children sense when they have the power to cause you distress. Makes them tyrants to some extent. Lorna didn't understand about pleasing other people, ordinary give-and-take. She was a nice person and she could be generous if she wanted, but she wasn't what you'd call loving or nurturing." She paused. "I don't know how I got off on that. I meant to talk about something else, if I can think what it was."

She frowned, blinking, and I could see her consult some interior agenda. There was a moment or two of silence while I drank my coffee and she drank hers. Finally her memory clicked in and she brightened, saying, "Oh, yes. Sorry about that." She shifted on her chair and took up the narrative. "Asthma medication sometimes caused her insomnia. Everybody thinks antihistamines make you drowsy, which they can, of course, but it isn't the deep sleep you need for ordinary rest. She didn't like to sleep. Even grown, she got by on as little as three hours sometimes. I think she was afraid of lying down. Being prone always seemed to aggravate her wheezing. She got in the habit of roaming around at night when everybody else was asleep."

"Who'd she hang out with? Did she have friends or just ramble on her own?"

"Other night owls, I'd guess. An FM disc jockey for one, the guy on that all-night jazz station. I can't remember his name, but you might know if I said it. And there was a nurse on the night shift at St. Terry's. Serena Bonney. Lorna actually worked for Serena's husband at the water treatment plant."

I made a note to myself. I'd have to check on both if I decided to help. "What sort of job?"

"It was just part-time . . . one to five for the city, doing clerical work. You know, typing and filing, answering the telephone. She'd be up half the night, and then she could sleep late if she wanted."

"Twenty hours a week isn't much," I said. "How could she afford to live?"

"Well, she had her own little place. This cabin at the back of somebody's property. It wasn't anything fancy, and the rent on that was cheap. Couple of rooms, with a bath. It might have been some kind of gardener's cottage to begin with. No insulation. She had no central heating and not a lot of kitchen to speak of, just a microwave oven and a two-burner hot plate, refrigerator the size of a little cardboard box. You know the kind. She had electricity, running water, and a telephone, and that was about the extent of it.

She could have fixed it up real cute, but she didn't want to bother. She liked it simple, she said, and besides, it wasn't all that permanent. Rent was nominal, and that's all she seemed to care about. She liked her privacy, and people learned to leave her pretty much alone."

"Hardly sounds like an allergen-free environment," I remarked.

"Well, I know, and I said as much myself. Of course by then she was doing better. The allergies and asthma were more seasonal than chronic. She might have an occasional attack after exercise or if she had a cold or she was under stress. The point is she didn't want to live around other people. She liked the feel of being in the woods. The property wasn't all that big . . . six or seven acres with a little two-lane gravel road coming in along the back. I guess it gave her the sense of isolation and quiet. She didn't want to live in some apartment building with tenants on all sides, bumping and thumping and playing loud music. She wasn't friendly. She didn't even like to say 'hi' in passing. That's just how she was. She moved into the cabin, and that's where she stayed."

"You said she was found at the cabin. Do the police think she died there as well?"

"I believe so. Like I said, she wasn't found for some time. Nearly two weeks, they think, from the state she was in. I hadn't heard from her, but I didn't think much about it. I'd talked to her on a Thursday night and she told me she was taking off. I assumed she meant that night, but she didn't say as much, at least not that I remember. If you recall, spring came late last year and the pollen count was high, which meant her allergies were acting up. Anyway, she called and said she'd be out of town for two weeks. She was taking time off from work and said she was driving up to the mountains to see whatever snows were left. Ski country was the only place she found relief when she was suffering. She said she'd call when she got back, and that was the last I talked to her."

I'd begun to scribble notes. "What date was this?"

"April nineteenth. The body was discovered May fifth."

"Where was she going? Did she give you her destination?"

"She mentioned the mountains, but she never did say where. You think that makes a difference?"

"I'm just curious," I replied. "April seems late for snow. It could have been a cover story if she was going somewhere else. Did you get the impression she was concealing something?"

"Oh, Lorna's not the kind who confided details. My other two, if they're going off on vacation, we all sit around poring over the travel brochures and hotel accommodations. Like right now, Berlyn's saved her money for a trip, and we're always talking about this cruise versus that, oohing and ahhing. The fantasy's half the fun is the way I look at it. Lorna said that just set up a lot of expectations and then reality would disappoint. She didn't look at anything the way other people did. At any rate, when I didn't hear from her, I figured she was out of town. She wasn't one to call much anyway, and none of us would have any reason to go to her place if she was gone." She hesitated, embarrassed. "I can tell I feel guilty. Just listen to how much explanation I'm going into here. I just don't want it to seem like I didn't care."

"It doesn't sound like that."

"That's good, because I loved that child more than life itself." Tears rose briefly, almost like a reflex, and I could see her blink them away. "Anyway, it was someone she'd done some work for, who finally went back there."

"What was her name?"

"Oh. Serena Bonney."

I glanced at my notes. "She's the nurse?"

"That's right."

"What kind of work had Lorna done for her?"

"She house-sat. Lorna looked after Mrs. Bonney's dad sometimes. As I understand it, the old fella wasn't well, and Mrs. Bonney didn't like leaving him by himself. I guess she was trying to make arrangements to leave town and wanted to talk to Lorna before she made reservations. Lorna didn't have an answering machine. Mrs. Bonney called several times and then decided to leave a note on her front door. Once she got close, she realized something was wrong." Janice broke off, not with emotion, but with the unpleasant images that must have been conjured up. After two weeks undiscovered, the body would have been in very poor shape.

"How did Lorna die? Was there a determination as to cause of death?"

"Well, that's the point. They never did find out. She was lying facedown on the floor in her underwear, with her sweat clothes strewn nearby. I guess she'd come back from a run and stripped down for her shower, but it didn't seem like she'd been assaulted. It's always possible she suffered an asthma attack."

"But you don't believe it."

"No, I don't, and the police didn't, either."

"She was into exercise? I find that surprising from what you've told me so far."

"Oh, she liked to keep in shape. I do know there were times when a workout made her wheezy and kind of short of breath, but she had one of those inhalers and it seemed to help. If she had a bad spell, she'd cut back on exercise and then take it up again when she was feeling better. Doctors didn't want her to act like an invalid."

"What about the autopsy?"

"Report's right in here," she said, indicating the paper bag.

"There were no signs of violence?"

Janice shook her head. "I don't know how to say this. I guess because of putrefaction they weren't even sure it was her at first. It wasn't until they compared her dental records that she was identified."

"I'm assuming the case was handled as a homicide."

"Well, yes. Even with cause of death undetermined, it was considered suspicious. They investigated as a homicide, but then nothing turned up. Now it seems like they dropped it. You know how they do those things. Something else comes along, and they concentrate on that."

"Sometimes there isn't sufficient information to make a finding in a situation like that. It doesn't mean they haven't worked hard."

"Well, I understand, but I still can't accept it."

I noticed that she had ceased to make eye contact, and I could feel the whisper of intuition crawling up along my spine. I found myself focusing on her face, wondering at her apparent uneasiness. "Janice, is there something you haven't told me?"

Her cheeks began to tint as if she were being overtaken by a hot flash. "I was just getting to that."

2

She reached into the brown paper bag again and pulled out a videotape in an unmarked box that she placed on the edge of the desk. "About a month ago, someone sent us this tape," she said. "I still don't know who, and I can't think why they'd do it except to cause us distress. Mace wasn't home. I found it in the mailbox in a plain brown wrapper with no return address. I opened the package because it had both our names on it. I went ahead and stuck it in the VCR. I don't know what I thought it was. A tape of some television show or somebody's wedding. I about died when I saw. Tape was pure smut, and there was *Lorna,* big as life. I just let out this shriek. I turned it off and threw it in the trash as fast as I could. It was like I'd been burned. I felt like I should go wash my hands in the sink. But then I had second thoughts. Because this tape could be evidence. It might tie in to the reason she was killed."

I leaned forward. "Let me clarify one point before you go on. This was the first you'd heard of it? You had no idea she was involved in anything like this?"

"Absolutely not. I was floored. Pornography? There's no way. Of course, once I saw what it was, I began to wonder if somebody put her up to it."

"Like what? I don't understand," I said.

"She might have been blackmailed. She might have been coerced. For all we know, she was working undercover for the police, which they would never admit."

"What makes you say that?" For the first time, she was sounding "off," and I felt myself step back, viewing her with caution.

"Because we'd sue them, that's why. If she got killed in the line of duty? We'd go after them."

I sat and stared at her. "Janice, I worked for the Santa Teresa Police Department myself for two years. They're serious professionals. They don't enlist the services of amateurs. In a vice investigation? I find that hard to believe."

"I didn't say they *did.* I didn't accuse anyone because that would be slander or libel or one of them. I'm just telling you what's possible."

"Such as?"

She seemed to hesitate, thinking about it. "Well. Maybe she was about to blow the whistle on whoever made the film."

"To what end? It's not against the law to make a pornographic film these days."

"But couldn't it be a cover for something else? Some other kind of crime?"

"Sure, it *could,* but let's back up a minute and let me play devil's advocate here. You told me the cause of death was undetermined, which means the coroner's office couldn't say with any certainty what she died of, right?"

Reluctantly. "That's right."

"How do you know she didn't have an aneurysm or a stroke or a heart attack? With all the allergies she suffered, she might have died from anaphylactic shock. I'm not saying you're wrong, but you're making a big leap here without a shred of proof."

"I understand. I guess it sounds crazy to you, but I know what I know. She was murdered. I'm absolutely sure of it, but I can't get anyone to listen, and what am I supposed to do? I'll tell you something else. She had quite a lot of money at the time she died."

"How much?"

"Close to five hundred thousand dollars' worth of stocks and bonds. She had some money in CDs, but the bulk was in securities. She had five or six different savings accounts, too. Now where'd she get that?"

"How do you think she acquired it?"

"Maybe somebody paid her off. To keep quiet about something."

I studied the woman, trying to assess her powers of reasoning. First, she claimed her daughter was being blackmailed or coerced. Now she was suggesting she was guilty of extortion. I set the issue aside temporarily and shifted my focus. "How did the police react to the tape?"

Dead silence.

I said, "Janice?"

Her expression was stubborn. "I didn't take it to them. I wouldn't even show it to Mace, because he'd die of embarrassment. Lorna was his angel. He'd never be the same if he knew what she'd done." She picked up the tape and put it back in the paper bag, folding the top down protectively.

"But why not show it to the cops? At least it would give them a fresh avenue . . . "

She was already shaking her head. "No, ma'am. No way. I'd never in this world turn it over to them. I know better. That's the last we'd ever see of it. I know it sounds paranoid, but I've heard of cases like this. Evidence they don't like disappears into thin air. Get to court and it's mysteriously vanished. Period, end of paragraph. I don't trust police. That's the point."

"Why trust me? How do you know I'm not in cahoots with them?"

"I have to trust someone. I want to know how she got into this . . . blue movie stuff . . . if it's why she was killed. But I'm not trained. I can't go back in time and figure out what happened. I have no way to do that." She took a deep breath and changed gears. "Anyway, I decided if I hired an investigator, that's the person I'd give the tape to. I guess now I have to ask if you're willing to help, because if you're not, I'll have to find someone else."

I thought about it briefly. Of course I was interested. I just wasn't sure about my chances of success. "An investigation like this is likely to be expensive. Are you prepared for that?"

"I wouldn't have come up if I wasn't."

"And your husband's in agreement?"

"He's not wild about the idea, but he can see I'm determined."

"All right. Let me nose around first before we sign any contracts. I want to make sure I can do you some good. Otherwise, it's a waste of my time and your money."

"Are you going to talk to the police?"

"I'll have to do that," I said. "Maybe unofficially at first. The point is, I need information, and if we can get their cooperation, it will save you some bucks."

"I understand that," she said, "but you have to understand one thing, too. I know you feel the police here are competent, and I'm sure that's true, but everybody makes an occasional mistake, and it's just human nature to want to cover it up. I don't want you to decide whether or not you can help on the basis of their attitude. They probably think I'm crazy as a loon."

"Believe me, I'm capable of making up my own mind about things." I could feel a crick in my neck, and I took a look at my watch. Time to wind it up, I thought. I asked for her home address, her home phone, and the number at the coffee shop, making notes on my legal pad. "Let me see what I can find out," I said. "In the meantime, can you leave that with me? I'd like to get myself up to speed. The meter won't actually start ticking until we have a signed contract."

She glanced down at the paper sack beside her but made no move to lift it. "I guess so. I suppose. I wouldn't want anybody else to get their hands on the tape. It'd kill Mace and the girls if they knew what was in here."

I crossed my heart and held my hand up. "I'll guard it with my life," I said. I didn't think there was any point in reminding her that pornography is a commercial venture. There were probably thousands of copies of the tape in circulation. I tucked the notes in my briefcase and snapped the lid down. She stood up when I did, hefting the bag to one hip before she passed it over to me.

"Thanks," I said. I picked up my jacket and my handbag, setting them on top of the bag, juggling the armload of items as I turned off lights. She followed me across the hall and watched me uneasily as I locked up. I glanced back at her. "You're going to have to trust me, you know. Without that, there's no point doing business together."

She nodded, and I caught a glimpse of tears in her eyes. "I hope you remember Lorna really wasn't like what you see."

"I'll remember," I said. "I'll get back to you as soon as I know anything, and we'll work out a game plan."

"All right."

"One more thing. You're going to have to tell Mace about the tape. He doesn't have to see it, but he should know it exists. I want complete honesty among the three of us."

"All right. Anyway, I've never been good at keeping secrets from him."

We parted company in the little twelve-car parking lot behind the building, after which I drove home.

Once in my neighborhood, I had to circle the block before I snagged a semilegal spot half a block away. I locked my car and walked to my place, toting the paper sack like a load of groceries. The night was downy and soft. The street was darkened by trees, the bare branches woven overhead in a loose canopy. The few stars I saw were as bright as ice chips flung across the sky. The ocean rumbled along the winter beach half a block away. I could smell salt, like woodsmoke, on the still night air. Ahead of me, a light glowed in the window of my second-story loft, and I could see the wind-tossed pine boughs tapping at the glass. A man on a bicycle passed me, dressed in dark clothes, moving quickly, the heels of his cycling shoes marked by strips of reflector tape. He made no sound except for the soft hum of air through his spokes. I found myself staring after him, as if he were an apparition.

I pushed through the gate, which swung shut behind me with a comforting squeak. When I reached the backyard, I glanced at my landlord's kitchen window automatically, though I knew it would be dark. Henry had gone back to Michigan to see his family and wouldn't return for another couple of weeks. I was keeping an eye on his place, bringing in his newspaper and sorting through his mail, sending on anything that seemed critical.

As usual, I found myself surprised at how much I missed him. I'd first met Henry Pitts four years ago when I was looking for a studio apartment. I'd been raised primarily in trailer parks, where I lived with my maiden aunt after the death of my parents when I was five years old. In my twenties, two brief marriages did little to promote my sense of permanence. After Aunt Gin's death, I moved back into her rented trailer, retreating into the solace of that compact space. I had by then left the Santa Teresa Police Department, and I was working for the man who taught me much of what I know now about private investigation. Once I was licensed and had set up an office of my own, I occupied a series of single- and double-wides in various Santa Teresa trailer parks, the last of these being the Mountain View Mobile Home Estates out in the suburb of Colgate. I probably would have gone on living there indefinitely except that I'd been evicted along with a number of my neighbors. Several parks in the area, the Mountain View among them, had converted to "seniors, 55 and older only," and the courts were in the process of reviewing all the discrimination suits that had been filed as a result. I didn't have the patience to wait for an outcome, so I began to make the rounds of the available studio rentals.

Armed with newspaper ads and a map of the city, I drove from one sorry listing to the next. The search was discouraging. Anything in my price range (which ran all the way from very cheap to extremely modest) was either badly located, filthy dirty, or in complete disrepair. Let's don't even talk about the issues of charm or character. I chanced on Henry's ad posted at the Laundromat and checked it out only because I was in the area.

I can still remember the day I first parked my VW and pushed my way through Henry's squeaking gate. It was March, and a light rain had varnished the streets, perfuming the air with the smell of wet grass and narcissus. The flowering cherry trees were in bloom, pink blossoms littering the sidewalk out in front. The studio had been a single-car garage converted into a tiny "bachelorette," which almost exactly duplicated the kind of quarters I was used to. From the outside the place was completely nondescript. The garage had been connected to the main house by means of an open breezeway that Henry had glassed in, most days using the space to proof mammoth batches of bread dough. He's a retired commercial baker and still rises early and bakes almost daily.

His kitchen window was open, and the smells of yeast, cinnamon, and simmering spaghetti sauce wafted out across the sill into the mild spring air. Before I knocked and introduced myself, I cupped my hands against the studio window and peered in at the space. At that time, there was really only one large room seventeen feet on a side, with a narrow bump-out for a small bath and a galley-style kitchenette. The space has been enlarged now to accommodate a sleeping loft and a second bathroom above. Even then, in its original state, one glance was all it took to know that I was home.

Henry had answered the door wearing a white T-shirt and shorts, flip-flops on his feet, a rag tied around his head. His hands were powdered with flour, and he had a smudge of white on his forehead. I took in the sight of his narrow, tanned face, his white hair, and his bright blue eyes, wondering if I'd known him in a life before this one. He invited me in, and while we talked, he fed me the first of the countless homemade cinnamon rolls I've consumed in his kitchen since.

Apparently he'd interviewed just about as many applicants as I had landlords. He was looking for a tenant without kids, vile personal habits, or an affinity for loud music. I was looking for a landlord who would mind his own business. I found Henry appealing because at his eighty-some years, I figured I was safe from unwanted attentions. I probably appealed to him because I was such a misanthrope. I'd spent two years as a cop and another two years amassing the four thousand hours required to apply for my private investigator's license. I'd been duly photographed, fingerprinted, bonded, and credentialed. Since my principal means of employment involved exposure to the underside of human nature, I tended even then to keep other people at a distance. I have since learned to be polite. I can even appear friendly when it suits my purposes, but I'm not really known for my cute girlish ways. Being a loner, I'm an ideal neighbor: quiet, reclusive, unobtrusive, and gone a lot.

I unlocked my door and flipped on the downstairs lights, shed my jacket, turned on the TV, pressed the power button for the VCR, and slid Lorna Kepler's video into the machine. I don't see any point in going into excruciating detail about the contents of the tape. Suffice it to say the story line was simple and there was no character development. In addition, the acting was atrocious and there was much simulated sex of a sort more ludicrous than lewd. Maybe it was only my discomfort at the subject that made the whole enterprise seem amateurish. It surprised me to see the credits, which I rewound and read again from the beginning. There was a producer, a director, and an editor whose names sounded real: Joseph Ayers, Morton Kasselbaum, and Chester Ellis. I put the tape on hold while I jotted them down, then reactivated the play button and let the tape roll again. I expected the actors to have monikers like Biff Mandate, Cherry Ravish, and Randi Bottoms, but Lorna Kepler was listed, along with two others—Russell Turpin and Nancy Dobbs, whose quite ordinary names I made note of in passing. There didn't seem to be a writer, but then I suppose pornographic sex really doesn't require much in the way of scripting. The narrative would make bizarre reading in any event.

I wondered where the film had been shot. Given what I imagined to be a pornographic film budget, no one was going to rent the locations or apply for any permits. For the most part, scenes took place in interiors that could have been anywhere. The lead actor, Russell Turpin, must have been hired solely on the basis of certain personal attributes that he displayed fore and aft. He and Nancy, ostensibly husband and wife, were sprawled naked on their living room couch, exchanging bad dialogue and subjecting each other to various sexual indignities. Nancy was awkward, her gaze straying to a spot at the left of camera where someone was clearly mouthing the lines she was supposed to say. I've seen elementary school pageants with more talent in evidence. Whatever passion she conjured up looked like something she'd learned from watching other pornographic film clips, the chief gesture being a lascivious lip licking more likely to cause chapping than arousal, in my opinion. I suspect she was actually hired because she was the only one who owned a real garter belt in this age of panty hose.

Lorna was the prime focus, and her appearance was staged for maximum effect. She seemed oblivious of the camera, her movements fluid and unhurried, her expertise undisguised. Her looks were elegant, and in the early moments of her role it was difficult to imagine the misbehaviors that would soon emerge. At first, she was cool and seemed to be secretly amused. Later, she was shameless, controlled, and intense, totally focused on herself and whatever she was feeling.

Early in the viewing, I was inclined to fast-forward past any scene not involving her, but the effect became comical—*The Perils of Pauline* with sex parts flapping back and forth. I tried to watch with the same detachment I affect at homicide sites, but the mechanism failed and I found myself squirming. I do not take lightly the degradation of human beings, especially when it's done solely for the financial gain of others. I've heard it said that the pornography industry is larger than the record and the film industries combined, staggering sums of money changing hands in the name of sex. At least this video had little violence and no scenes involving children or animals of any kind.

While there wasn't much story to speak of, the director had made an attempt to create suspense. Lorna played a sexually demonic apparition and as such stalked both husband and wife, who ran stark naked through the house. She was also sexually abusive to a repairman named Harry, who showed up in the film during one of the parts I skipped the first time. Often Lorna's appearances were heralded by smoke and her diaphanous gown was blown skyward by a wind machine. Once the action began, there were many close shots, lovingly detailed by a cameraman with a passion for his zoom lens.

I flicked the tape off and rewound it, turning my attention to the packaging. The production company was called Cyrenaic Cinema with a San Francisco address. Cyrenaic? What did that mean? I pulled my dictionary from the shelf and checked the reference. "Cyrenaic—of the Greek school of philosophy founded by Aristippus of Cyrene, who considered individual sensual pleasure the greatest good." Well, *someone* was literate. I tried directory assistance in the 415 area code. There was no telephone number listed, but the address might be good. Even if Janice and I came to an agreement, I wasn't sure she'd want to fund a trip to San Francisco.

I sorted through the files she'd given me, separating out the news clippings from the police reports. I read the autopsy report with particular care, translating the technicalities into my sketchy layman's understanding. The basic facts were about as distasteful as the film I'd just seen, without the leavening influence of all the corny dialogue. By the time Lorna's body was discovered, the process of decomposition was virtually complete. Gross examination revealed precious little of significance, as all the soft tissue had collapsed into a greasy mass. Maggots had made hasty work of her. Internal examination confirmed the absence of all organs, with only small amounts of tissue left representing the GI tract, the liver, and the circulatory system. Brain tissue was also completely liquefied and/or absent. Osseous remains showed no evidence of blunt force trauma, no stab or gunshot wounds, no ligature, no crushed or broken bones. Two old fractures were noted, but neither apparently pertained to the manner of her death. What laboratory tests could be run showed no drugs or poisons in her system. Complete dental arches were excised and retained, along with all ten fingers. Positive identification was made through dental charts and a residual print from the right thumb. There were no photographs, but I suspected those would be attached to her department file. Postmortem glossies would hardly have been passed along to her mother.

There was no way to pinpoint date or time of death, but a rough estimate was made from several environmental factors. Countless people interviewed testified as to her night owl tendencies. It was also allegedly her habit to jog shortly after she got up. As nearly as the homicide investigators could establish, she'd slept late as usual on that Saturday, April 21. She'd then pulled on her sweats and had gone out for a jog. The Saturday morning paper was in, as was the mail that had been delivered late that morning. All the mail and newspapers after the twenty-first were piled up unopened. Idly I wondered why she hadn't left for her trip Thursday night as planned. Maybe she'd finished out the work week on Friday, intending to take off Saturday morning once she was showered and dressed.

The questions were obvious, but it was useless to speculate in the absence of concrete evidence. While the cause of death was undetermined, the police had proceeded on the assumption that she'd been struck down by a person or persons unknown. Lorna had lived alone and in singular isolation. If she'd cried out for help, there had been none within range of her. I'm single myself, and though Henry Pitts lives close by, I'm sometimes uneasy. There's a certain vulnerability attached to my work. I've been variously shot, pummeled, punched, and accosted, but I've usually found a way to outmaneuver my attackers. I didn't like the idea of Lorna's final moments.

The homicide detective who'd done all the grunt work was a guy named Cheney Phillips, whom I ran into from time to time. The last I'd heard, he'd moved from homicide to vice. I'm not really sure how law enforcement agencies in other cities work, but in the Santa Teresa Police Department, officers tend to be rotated every two to three years, exposing them to a variety of responsibilities. This not only ensures a well-balanced department, but allows the opportunity for advancement without an officer's having to wait for the death or retirement of division-entrenched colleagues.

Like many cops in town, Phillips could usually be found in a local watering hole called CC's, which was frequented by attorneys and a variety of law enforcement types. His supervisor on the case had been Lieutenant Con Dolan, whom I knew very well. I was somewhat skeptical that Lorna's role in a low-budget movie was related to her death. On the other hand, I could see why Janice Kepler wanted to believe as much. What else are you going to think when it turns out your late and favorite daughter was a pornographic film star?

I was restless, nearly itchy with an overdose of caffeine. I'd probably sucked down eight to ten cups of coffee during the day, the last two that evening while I was talking to Janice. Now I could feel stimulants, like sugarplums, dancing in my head. Sometimes anxiety and caffeine have the same effect.

I checked my watch again. It was after midnight by now and well past my bedtime. I pulled out the phone book and found the number for CC's. The call took less than fifteen seconds. The bartender told me Cheney Phillips was on the premises. I gave him my name and had him give Cheney the message that I was on my way. As I hung up the phone, I could hear him yelling to Cheney across the din. I grabbed my jacket and my keys and headed out the door.

3

I drove east along Cabana, the wide boulevard that parallels the beach. When the moon is full, the darkness has the quality of a film scene shot day for night. The landscape is so highly illuminated that the trees actually cast shadows. Tonight the moon was in its final quarter, rising low in the sky. From the road I couldn't see the ocean, but I could hear the reverberating rumble of the tide rolling in. There was just enough wind to set the palm trees in motion, shaggy heads nodding together in some secret communication. A car passed me, going in the opposite direction, but there were no pedestrians in sight. I'm not often out at such an hour, and it was curiously exhilarating.

By day, Santa Teresa seems like any small southern California town. Churches and businesses hug the ground against the threat of earthquakes. The rooflines are low, and the architectural influence is largely Spanish. There's something solid and reassuring about all the white adobe and the red tile roofs. Lawns are manicured, and the shrubs are crisply trimmed. By night the same features seem stark and dramatic, full of black-and-white contrasts that lend intensity to the hardscape. The sky at night isn't really black at all. It's a soft charcoal gray, nearly chalky with light pollution, the trees like ink stains on a darkened carpet. Even the wind has a different feel to it, as light as a feather quilt against the skin.

The real name for CC's is the Caliente Cafe, a low-rent establishment housed in an abandoned service station near the railroad tracks. The original gasoline pumps and the storage tanks below had been removed years before, and the contaminated soil had been paved over with asphalt. Now, on hot days the blacktop tends to soften and a toxic syrup seeps out, a tarry liquid quickly converted into wisps of smoke, suggesting that the tarmac is on the verge of bursting into flames. Winters, the pavement cracks from dry cold, and a sulfurous smell wafts across the parking lot. CC's is not the kind of place to encourage bare feet.

I parked out in front beneath a sizzling red neon sign. Outside, the air smelled like corn tortillas fried in lard; inside, like salsa and recirculated cigarette smoke. I could hear the high-pitched whine of a blender working overtime, whipping ice and tequila into the margarita mix. The Caliente Cafe bills itself as an "authentic" Mexican cantina, which means the "day-core" consists of Mexican sombreros tacked above the doors. Bad lighting eliminates the need for anything else. Every item on the menu has been Americanized, and all the names are cute: Ensanada Ensalada, Pasta Pequeño, Linguini Bambini. The music, all canned, is usually played way too loud, like a band of mariachis hired to hover at your table while you try to eat.

Cheney Phillips was sitting at the bar, his face tilted in my direction. My request for an audience had clearly piqued his interest. Cheney was probably in his early thirties: a white guy with a disheveled mop of dark curly hair, dark eyes, good chin, prickly two-day growth of beard. His was the sort of face you might see in a men's fashion magazine or the society section of the local papers, escorting some debutante decked out like a bride. He was slim, of medium height, wearing a tobacco-brown silk sport coat over a white dress shirt, his pants a pleated cream-colored gabardine. His air of confidence suggested money of intimidating origins. Everything about him said trust fund, private schools, and casual West Coast privilege. This is pure projection on my part, and I have no idea if it's accurate. I've never really asked him how he ended up a cop. For all I know, he's third-generation law enforcement with all the women in his family doing jail administration.

I eased up onto the bar stool next to his. "Hello, Cheney. How are you? Thanks for waiting. I appreciate it."

He shrugged. "I'm usually here until closing time anyway. Can I buy you a drink?"

"Of course. I'm so wired on coffee I may never get to sleep."

"What's your pleasure?"

"Chardonnay, if you please."

"Absolutely," he said. He smiled, revealing first-rate orthodontic work. No one could have teeth that straight without years of expensive correction. Cheney's manner was habitually seductive and never more so than in a setting such as this.

The bartender had been watching our interchange with an exaggerated late night patience. In a bar like CC's, this was the hour when the sexually desperate made their last minute appeals for company. By then enough liquor had been consumed that potential partners, who earlier had been rejected as unworthy, were now being reconsidered. The bartender apparently assumed we were negotiating a one-night relationship. Cheney ordered wine for me and another vodka tonic for himself.

He checked back over his shoulder, doing a quick visual survey of the other patrons. "You ought to keep an eye on all the off-duty police officers. Last call, we go out in the parking lot and pass around a Breathalyzer, like we're copping a joint, make sure we're still sober enough to drive ourselves home."

"I heard you left homicide."

"Right. I've been doing vice for six months."

"Well, that suits," I said. "Do you like it?" He'd probably been moved to vice because he still looked young enough to have some.

"Sure, it's great. It's a one-man department. I'm the current expert on gambling, prostitution, drugs, and organized crime, such as it is in Santa Teresa. What about you? What are you up to? You probably didn't come down here to chat about my career in law enforcement." He looked up as the bartender approached, halting further conversation until our drinks had been served.

When he looked back, I said, "Janice Kepler wants to hire me to look into her daughter's death."

"Good luck," he said.

"You handled the original investigation, yes?"

"Dolan and me, with a couple more guys thrown in. This is the long and short of it," he said, ticking the items off his fingers. "There was no way to determine cause of death. We still aren't absolutely certain what day it was, let alone what time frame. There was no significant trace evidence, no witnesses, no motive, no suspects . . ."

"And no case," I supplied.

"You got it. Either this was not a homicide to begin with or the killer led a charmed life."

"I'll say."

"You going to do it?"

"Don't know yet. Thought I'd better talk to you first."

"Have you seen a picture of her? She was beautiful. Screwed up, but gorgeous. Talk about a dark side. My God."

"Like what?"

"She had this part-time job at the water treatment plant. She's a clerk-typist. You know, she does a little phone work, a little filing, maybe four hours a day. She tells everybody she's working her way through city college, which is true in its way. She takes a class now and then, but it's only half the story. What she's really up to is a bit of high-class hooking. She's making fifteen hundred bucks a pop. We're talkin' substantial sums of money at the time of her death."

"Who'd she work for?"

"Nobody. She was independent. She started doing out-call. Exotic dance and massage. Guys phone this service listed in the classifieds, and she goes out and does some kind of bump-and-grind strip while they abuse themselves. The game is you can't make a deal for more than that up front—Undercover used to call and pull that 'til everybody wised up—but once she's on the premises, she can negotiate whatever services the client wants. It's strictly their transaction."

"For which she gets paid what?"

Cheney shrugged. "Depends on what she does. Straight sex is probably a hundred and fifty bucks, which she ends up splitting with the management. Pretty quick, she figures out she has more on the ball, so she bags the cheap gigs and moves up to the big time."

"Here in town?"

"For the most part. I understand they used to see quite a bit of her in the bar at the Edgewater Hotel. She also cruised through Bubbles in Montebello, which you probably heard was closed down last July. She had a penchant for the places where the high rollers hung out."

"Did her *mother* know this?"

"Sure she did. Absolutely. Lorna was even picked up once on a misdemeanor for soliciting an undercover vice officer at Bubbles. We didn't want to rub her mother's nose in the fact, but she was certainly informed."

"Maybe it's just beginning to sink in," I said. "Someone sent her a copy of a pornographic film in which Lorna loomed large. Apparently that's what prompted her to come see me. She thinks Lorna was either blackmailed into it or working undercover."

"Oh, yeah, right," he said.

"I'm just telling you her assumption."

Cheney snorted. "She's in denial big time. Have you actually seen this tape?"

"I just saw it tonight. It was pretty raunchy."

"Yeah, well, I'm not sure how much difference it makes. The kind of stuff she was into, it really doesn't surprise me. How's it supposed to tie in? That's the part I don't get."

"Janice thinks Lorna was about to blow the whistle on someone."

"Oh, man, that lady's seen too many bad TV movies. Blow the whistle on who, and for what? Those people are legitimate . . . in some sense of the word. They're probably scumbags, but that's not against the law in this state. Look at all the politicians."

"That's what I told her. Anyway, I'm trying to figure out if there's enough to warrant my taking on the job. If you guys couldn't come up with anything, how can I?"

"Maybe you'll get lucky. I'm one of life's eternal optimists. Case is still open, but we ain't had jackshit for months. You want to look at the files, it can probably be arranged."

"That'd be great. What I'd really like to see are the crime scene photographs."

"I'll try to clear it with Lieutenant Dolan, but I don't think he'll object. You heard he's in the hospital? He had a heart attack."

I was so startled, I put a hand to my own heart, nearly knocking my glass over in the process. I caught it before it tipped, though a little wave of wine slopped out. "Dolan had a heart attack? That's awful! When was this?"

"Yesterday, right after squad meeting, he started having chest pains. Like boom, he's in trouble. Guy looks like shit, and he's short of breath. Next thing I know he's out like a light. Everybody scrambling around, doing CPR. Paramedics pulled him back from the brink, but it was really touch-and-go."

"Is he going to be okay?"

"We hope so. He's doing fine, last I heard. He's over at St. Terry's in the cardiac care unit, raising hell, of course."

"Sounds like him. I'll try to get over there first chance I have."

"He'd like that. You should do it. I talked to him this morning, and the guy's going nuts. Claims he doesn't like to sleep because he's scared he won't wake up."

"He admitted that? I never knew Lieutenant Dolan to talk about anything personal," I said.

"He's changed. He's a new man. It's amazing," he said. "You ought to see for yourself. He'd be thrilled at the company, probably talk your ear off."

I shifted the subject back to Lorna Kepler. "What about you? Do you have a theory about Lorna's death?"

Cheney shrugged. "I think somebody killed her, if that's what you're after. Rough trade, jealous boyfriend. Maybe some other hooker thought Lorna was treading on her turf. Lorna Kepler loved risk. She's the kind who liked to teeter right out on the edge."

"She have enemies?"

"Not as far as we know. Oddly enough, people seemed to like her a lot. I say 'oddly' because she was different, really unlike other folk. It was almost admiration on their part because she was so *out* there, you know? She disregarded the rules and played the game her way."

"I take it your investigation covered a lot of ground."

"That's right, though it never came to much. Frustrating. Anyway, it's all there if you want to take a look. I can have Emerald pull the files once we get Dolan's okay."

"I'd appreciate that. Lorna's mother gave me some stuff, but she didn't have everything. Just let me know and I'll pop over to the station and take a look."

"Sure thing. We can talk afterward."

"Thanks, Cheney. You're a doll."

"I know that," he said. "Just make sure you keep us informed. And play it straight. If you come up with something, we don't want it thrown out of court because you've tainted the evidence."

"You underestimate me," I said. "Now that I'm working out of Lonnie Kingman's office, I'm an angel among women. I'm a paragon."

"I believe you," he said. His smile was lingering, and his eyes held just a hint of speculation. I thought I'd probably said enough. I backed away and then turned, giving him a wave as I departed.

Once outside, I drank in the quiet of the chill night air, picking up the faint scent of cigarette smoke trailing back at me from somewhere up ahead. I lifted my head and caught a glimpse of a man easing out of sight around a bend in the road, his footsteps growing faint. There are men who walk at night, shoulders hunched, heads bent in some solitary pursuit. I tend to think of them as harmless, but one never knows. I watched until I was certain he was gone. In the distance, low-lying heavy cloud cover had been pushed up the far side of the mountain and now spilled over the top.

All the parking spots were filled. Vehicles gleamed in the harsh overhead illumination like a high-end used-car lot. My vintage VW looked distinctly out of place, a homely pale blue hump among the sleek, low-slung sports models. I unlocked the car door and slid onto the driver's seat, then paused for a moment, hands on the steering wheel, while I contemplated my next move. The single glass of white wine had done little to temper my wired state. I knew if I drove home, I'd just end up lying on my back, staring at the skylight above my bed. I fired up the ignition and then drove along the beach as far as State Street. I hung a right, heading north.

I crossed the railroad tracks, jolting the radio to life. I didn't even realize I'd left the damn thing on. It seldom worked these days, but every now and then I could coax something out of it. Sometimes I'd bang on the dash with my fist, jarring forth news or a commercial. Other times, for no apparent reason, I'd pick up a baffling fragment of the weather. The problem was probably a loose wire or faulty fuse, which is just a guess on my part. I don't even know if radios have fuses these days. At the moment, the reception was as clear as could be.

I pressed a button, neatly switching from AM to FM. I turned the dial by degrees, sliding past station after station until I caught the strains of a tenor sax. I had no idea who it was, only that the mournful mix of horns was perfect for this hour of the night. The cut came to an end, and a man's voice eased into the space. "That was 'Gato' Barbieri on sax, a tune called 'Picture in the Rain' from the movie sound track *Last Tango in Paris.* Music was composed by 'Gato' Barbieri, recorded back in 1972. And this is Hector Moreno, here on K-SPELL, bringing you the magic of jazz on this very early Monday morning."

His voice was handsome, resonant, and well modulated, with an easygoing confidence. This was a man who made his living staying up all night, talking about artists and labels, playing CDs for insomniacs. I pictured a guy in his mid-thirties, dark, substantial, possibly with a mustache, his long hair pulled back and secured with a rubber band. He must have enjoyed all the perks of local celebrity status, acting as an MC for various charity events. Radio personalities don't need even the routine good looks of the average TV anchorperson, but he'd still have name recognition value, probably his share of groupies as well. He was taking call-in requests. I felt my thoughts jump a track. Janice Kepler had mentioned Lorna's hanging out with some DJ in her late night roamings.

I began to scan the deserted streets, looking for a pay phone. I passed a service station that was shut down for the night. At the near edge of the parking lot, I spotted what must have been one of the last real telephone booths, a regular stand-up model with a bifold door. I pulled in and left the car engine running while I flipped through my notes, looking for the phone number I'd been given for Frankie's Coffee Shop. I dropped a quarter in the slot and dialed.

When a woman at Frankie's Coffee Shop finally answered the phone, I asked for Janice Kepler. The receiver was clunked down on the counter, and I could hear her name being bellowed. In the background there was a low-level buzz of activity, probably late night pie-and-coffee types, tanking up on stimulants. Janice must have appeared because I heard her make a remark to someone in passing, the two of them exchanging brief comments before she picked up. She identified herself somewhat warily, I thought. Maybe she was worried she was getting bad news.

"Hello, Janice? Kinsey Millhone. I hope this is all right. I need some information, and it seemed simpler to call than drive all the way up there."

"Well, my goodness. What are you doing up at this hour? You looked exhausted when I left you in the parking lot. I thought you'd be sound asleep by now."

"That was my intention, but I never got that far. I was too stoked on coffee, so I thought I might as well get some work done.

I had a chat with one of the homicide detectives who worked on Lorna's case. I'm still out and about and thought I might as well cover more ground while I'm at it. Didn't you mention that Lorna used to hang out with a DJ on one of the local FM stations?"

"That's right."

"Is there any way you can find out who it was?"

"I can try. Hang on." Without covering the receiver, she consulted with one of the other waitresses. "Perry, what's the name of that all-night jazz show, what station?"

"K-SPELL, I think."

I knew that much. Thinking to save time, I said, "Janice?"

"What about the disc jockey? You know his name?"

In the background, somewhat muffled, Perry said, "Which one? There's a couple." Dishes were clattering, and the speaker system was pumping out a version of "Up, Up, and Away" with stringed instruments.

"The one Lorna hung out with. 'Member I told you about him?"

I cut in on Janice. "Hey, Janice?"

"Perry, hold on. What, hon?"

"Could it be Hector Moreno?"

She let out a little bark of recognition. "That's right. That's him. I'm almost sure he's the one. Why don't you call him up and ask if he knew her?"

"I'll do that," I said.

"You be sure and let me know. And if you're still out running around town after that, come on up and have a cup of coffee on the house."

I could feel my stomach lurch at the thought of more coffee. The cups I'd consumed were already making my brain vibrate like an out-of-balance washing machine. As soon as she hung up, I depressed the lever and released it, letting the dial tone whine on while I hauled up the phone book on its chain and flipped through. All the radio stations were listed at the front end of the K's. As it turned out, K-SPL was only six or eight blocks away. Behind me, from the car, I could hear the opening bars of the next jazz selection. I found another quarter in the bottom of my handbag and dialed the studio.

The phone rang twice. "K-SPELL. This is Hector Moreno." The tone was businesslike, but it was certainly the man I'd been listening to.

"Hello," I said. "My name is Kinsey Millhone. I'd like to talk to you about Lorna Kepler."

4

Moreno had left the heavy door to the station ajar. I let myself in and the door closed behind me, the lock sliding home. I found myself standing in a dimly lit foyer. To the right of a set of elevator doors, a sign indicated K-SPL with an arrow pointing down toward some metal stairs on the right. I went down, my rubber-soled shoes making hollow sounds on the metal treads. Below, the reception area was deserted, the walls and the narrow hallway beyond painted a dreary shade of blue and a strange algae green, like the bottom of a pond. I called, "Hello."

No answer. Jazz was being piped in, obviously the station playing back on itself.

"Hello?"

I shrugged to myself and moved down the corridor, glancing into each cubicle I passed. Moreno had told me he'd be working in the third studio on the right, but when I reached it, the room was empty. I could still hear faint strains of jazz coming in over the speakers, but he'd apparently absented himself momentarily. The studio was small, littered with empty fast-food containers and empty soda cans. A half-filled coffee cup on the console was warm to the touch. There was a wall clock the size of the full moon, its second hand ticking jerkily as it made the big sweep. Click. Click. Click. Click. The passage of time had never seemed quite so concrete or so relentless. The walls were soundproofed with sections of corrugated dark gray foam.

To my left, countless cartoons and news clippings were tacked to a corkboard. The balance of the wall space was taken up with row after row of CDs, with additional shelves devoted to albums and tape cassettes. I did a visual survey, as if in preparation for a game of Concentration. Coffee mugs. Speakers. A stapler, Scotch tape dispenser. Many empty designer water bottles: Evian, Sweet Mountain, and Perrier. On the control board, I could see the mike switch, cart machines, a rainbow of lights, one marked "two track mono." One light flashed green, and another was blinking red. A microphone suspended from a boom looked like a big snow cone of gray foam. I pictured myself leaning close enough to touch my lips to the surface, using my most seductive FM tone of voice. "Hello, all you night owls. This is Kinsey Millhone here, bringing you the best in jazz at the very worst of hours. . . ."

Behind me, I heard someone thumping down the hall in my direction, and I peered out with interest. Hector Moreno approached, a man in his early fifties, supported by two crutches. His shaggy hair was gray, his brown eyes as soft as dark caramels. His upper body was immense, his torso dwindling away to legs that were sticklike and truncated. He wore a bulky black cotton sweater, chinos, and penny loafers. Beside him was a big reddish yellow dog with a thick head, heavy chest, and powerful shoulders, probably part chow, judging by the teddy bear face and the ruff of hair around its neck.

"Hi, are you Hector? Kinsey Millhone," I said. The dog bristled visibly when I held out my hand.

Hector Moreno propped himself on one crutch long enough to

shake my hand. "Nice to meet you," he said. "This is Beauty. She'll need time to make up her mind about you."

"Fair enough," I said. She could take the rest of her life, as far as I was concerned.

The dog had begun to rumble, not a growl but a low hum, as if a machine had been activated somewhere deep in her chest. Hector snapped his fingers, and she went silent. Dogs and I have never been that fond of one another. Just a week ago I'd been introduced to a boy-pup who'd actually lifted his leg and piddled on my shoe. His owner had voiced his most vigorous disapproval, but he really didn't sound that sincere to me, and I suspected he was currently recounting, with snorts and guffaws, the tale of Bowser's misbehavior on my footwear. In the meantime I had a Reebok that smelled like dog whiz, a fact not lost on Beauty, who gave it her rapt attention.

Hector swung himself forward and moved into the studio, answering the question I was too polite to ask. "I collided with a rock pile when I was twelve. I was spelunking in Kentucky, and the tunnel caved in. People expect something different, judging from my voice on the air. Grab a seat." He flashed me a smile, and I smiled in response. I followed as he set his crutches aside and hoisted himself onto the stool. I found a second stool in the corner and pulled it close to him. I noticed that Beauty arranged herself so that she was between us.

While Hector and I exchanged pleasantries, the dog watched us with an air of nearly human intelligence, her gaze shifting constantly from his face to mine. Sometimes she panted with an expression close to a grin, dangling tongue dancing as if at some private joke. Her ears shifted as we spoke, gauging our tones. I had no doubt she was prepared to intervene if she didn't like what she heard. From time to time, in response to cues I wasn't picking up myself, she would retract her tongue and close her mouth, rising to her feet with that low rumble in her chest. All it took was a gesture from him and she'd drop to the floor again, but her look then was brooding. She probably had a tendency to sulk when she wasn't allowed to feast on human flesh. Hector, ever watchful, seemed amused at the performance. "She doesn't trust many people. I got her from the pound, but she must have been beaten when she was young."

"You keep her with you all the time?" I asked.

"Yeah. She's good company. I work late nights, and when I leave the studio, the town is deserted. Except for the crazies. They're always out. You asked about Lorna. What's your connection?"

"I'm a private investigator. Lorna's mother stopped by my office earlier this evening and asked if I'd look into her death. She wasn't particularly happy with the police investigation."

"Such as it was," he said. "Did you talk to that guy Phillips? What a prick he was."

"I just talked to him. He's out of homicide and onto vice these days. What'd he do to you?"

"He didn't *do* anything. It's his attitude. I hate guys like him. Little banty roosters who push their weight around. Hang on a sec." He slid a fat cassette into a slot and depressed a button on the soundboard, leaning forward, his voice as smooth and satiny as fudge. "We've been listening to Phineas Newborn on solo piano, playing a song called 'The Midnight Sun Will Never Set.' And this is Hector Moreno, casting a little magic here at K-SPELL. Coming up, we have thirty minutes of uninterrupted music, featuring the incomparable voice of Johnny Hartman from a legendary session with the John Coltrane Quartet. *Esquire* magazine once named this the greatest album ever made. It was recorded March 7, 1963, on the Impulse label with John Coltrane on tenor sax, McCoy Tyner on piano, Jimmy Garrison on bass, and Elvin Jones on drums." He punched a button, adjusted the studio volume downward, and turned back to me. "Whatever he said about Lorna, you can take it with a grain of salt."

"He said she had a dark side, but I knew that much. I'm not sure I have the overall picture, but I'm working on that. How long had you known her before she died?"

"Little over two years. Right after I started doing this show. I was in Seattle before that, but the damp got to me. I heard about this job through a friend of a friend."

"Is your background in broadcast?"

"Communications," he said. "Radio and TV production; video to some extent, though it never interested me much. I'm from Cincinnati originally, graduated from the university, but I've worked everywhere. Anyway, I met Lorna when I first got down here. She was a night owl by nature, and she started calling in requests. Between cuts and commercials, we'd sometimes talk for an hour. She began to drop by the studio, maybe once a week at first. Toward the end, she was here just about every night. Two-thirty, three, she'd bring doughnuts and coffee, bones for Beauty if she'd been out to dinner. Sometimes I think it was the dog she cared about. They had some kind of psychic affinity. Lorna used to claim they'd been lovers in another life. Beauty's still waiting for her to come back. Three o'clock, she goes out to the stairs and just stands there, looking up. Makes this little sound in her throat that'd break your heart." He shook his head, waving off the image with curious impatience.

"What was Lorna like?"

"Complicated. I thought she was a beautiful, tortured soul. Restless, disconnected, probably depressed. But that was just one part. She was split, a contradiction. It wasn't all the dark stuff."

"Was she into drugs or alcohol?"

"Not as far as I know. She blew hot and cold. She was nearly hyper sometimes. If you want to get analytical, I'd be tempted to label her manic-depressive, but that doesn't really capture it. It was like a battle she fought, and the down side finally won."

"I guess we all have that in us."

"I do, that's for sure."

"You knew she did a porno film?"

"I heard about that. I never saw it myself, but I guess the word was out."

"When was it shot? Any time close to her death?"

"I don't know much about that. She was out of town a lot on weekends, Los Angeles, San Francisco. Could have been one of those trips. I really couldn't say for sure."

"So it was not something you discussed."

He shook his head. "She enjoyed being tight-lipped. I think it made her feel powerful. I learned not to pry into her personal affairs."

"Any idea why she did the film? Was it money?"

"I doubt it. Producer probably cleans up, but the actors get a flat rate. At least from what I've heard," he said. "Maybe she did it for the same reason she did anything. Lorna flirted with disaster every day of her life. If you want my theory, fear was the only real sensation she felt. Danger was like a drug. She had to boost the dose. She couldn't help herself. Didn't seem to matter what anyone said. I used to talk 'til I was blue in the face. It never made any difference as far as I could see. This is just my observation, and I could be all wrong, but you asked and I'm answering. She'd act like she was listening. She'd act like she agreed with every word you said, but then it washed right over her. She went right on doing it, whatever it was. She was like an addict, a junkie. She knew the life wasn't good, but she couldn't make the break."

"Did she trust you?"

"I wouldn't say that. Not really. Lorna didn't trust anyone. She was like Beauty in that respect. She might have trusted me more than most."

"Why was that?"

"I never came on to her, so I wasn't any kind of threat. With no sexual investment, she couldn't lose with me. She couldn't win, either, but that suited us both. With Lorna, you had to keep your distance. She was the kind of woman, the minute you got involved, it was over, pal. That was the end of it. The only way you could hold on to her was to keep her at arm's length. I knew the rule, but I couldn't always manage it. I was hooked myself. I kept wanting to save her, and it couldn't be done."

"Did she tell you what was going on in her life?"

"Some things. Trivia, for the most part. Just the day-to-day stuff.

She never confided anything important. Events, but not feelings. You know what I mean? Even then, I doubt she ever really leveled with me. I knew some things, but not always because she told me."

"How'd you get your information?"

"I have buddies around town. I'd get frustrated with her behavior. She'd swear she was playing straight, but I guess she really couldn't give it up. Next thing you know, she'd be picking up guys. Twosomes, threesomes, anything you want. People would see her and make a point of telling me, worried I was getting in over my head."

"And were you?"

His smile was bitter. "I didn't think so at the time."

"Did the rumors bother you?"

"Hell, yes. What she did was dangerous, and I was worried sick. I didn't like what she was doing, and I didn't like people running in here talking about her behind her back. Tattletales. I hate that. I couldn't get them to quit. With her, I tried to keep my mouth shut. It was none of my business, but I kept getting sucked in. I'd be saying, 'Why, babe? What's the point?' And she'd shake her head. 'You don't want to know, Heck. I promise. It's got nothing to do with you.' The truth is, I don't think *she* knew. It was a compulsion, like a sneeze. It felt good to do it. If she held off, something tickled until it drove her nuts."

"You have any idea who was in her life besides you?"

"I wasn't *in* her life. I was on the fringe. Way out here. She had a day job, part-time at the water treatment plant. You might talk to them, see if they can fill you in. Most times, I never even saw her before three A.M. She might've had some other kind of life entirely when the sun was up."

"Ah. Well. Food for thought," I said. "Anything else I should know?"

"Not that I can think of offhand. If something occurs to me, I can get in touch. You have a card?"

I fished one out and placed it on the console. He looked at it briefly and left it where it was.

I said, "Thanks for your time."

"I hope I've been of help. I hate the idea someone got away with murder."

"This is a start, at any rate. I may be back at some point." I hesitated, glancing at the dog still lying there between us. The minute she sensed my look, she rose to her feet, which put her head just about level with the stool where I was perched. She kept her eyes straight ahead, gazing intently at the flesh on my hip, possibly with an eye toward a late evening snack.

"Beauty," he murmured with scarcely any change of tone.

She sank to the floor, but I could tell she was still thinking about a jaw full of gluteus maximus.

"Next time I'll bring her a bone," I said. Preferably not mine.

I headed home through the business district, following a trail of stoplights that winked from red to green. The storefronts had been secured, plate-glass windows ablaze with fluorescent lighting. The streets were bleached white with the spill of illumination. I passed a lone man on a bike, dressed in black. It was almost 1:30 A.M., traffic minimal, intersections wide and deserted. Most of the bars in town were still open, and in another half hour or so, all the drunks would emerge, heading for the various downtown parking structures. Many buildings were dark. The homeless, bundled in sleep, blocked the doorways like toppled statues. For them, the night is like a vast hotel where there's always a room available. The only price they pay, sometimes, is their lives.

At 1:45 I finally stripped off my jeans, brushed my teeth, and doused the lights, crawling into bed without bothering to remove my T-shirt, underpants, and socks. These February nights were too cold to sleep naked. As I eased toward unconsciousness, I found myself mentally replaying select portions of Lorna's tape. Ah, the life of the single woman in a world ruled by sexually transmitted diseases. I lay there, trying to think back to when I'd last had sex. I couldn't even remember, which was *really* worrisome. I fell asleep wondering if there was a cause-and-effect relationship between memory loss and abstinence. Apparently so, as that was the last thing I was aware of for the next four hours.

When the alarm went off at 6:00 A.M., I rolled out of bed before my resistance came up. I pulled on my sweats and my running shoes, then headed into the bathroom, where I brushed my teeth, avoiding the sight of myself in the mirror. One ill-advised glance had revealed a face fat with sleep and hair as stiff and matted as a derelict's. I'd snipped it off six months before with a trusty little pair of nail scissors, but I hadn't done much to it since. Now the sections that weren't sticking straight up were either flat or adrift. I was really going to have to do something about it one of these days.

Given the four hours of sleep, my run was a bit on the perfunctory side. Often I tune in to the look of the beach, letting sea birds and kelp scent carry me along. Jogging becomes a meditation, shifting time into high gear. This was one of those days when exercise simply failed to uplift. In lieu of euphoria, I had to make my peace with three hundred calories' worth of sweat, screaming thighs, and burning lungs. I tacked on an extra half mile to atone for my indifference and then did a fast walk back to my place as a way of cooling down. I showered and slipped into fresh jeans and a black turtleneck, over which I pulled a heavy gray cotton sweater.

I perched on a wooden stool at the kitchen table and ate a bowl of cereal. I scanned the local paper in haste. No surprises there. While floods threatened the Midwest, the Santa Teresa rainfall averages were down and there was already speculation of another drought in the making. January and February were usually rainy, but the weather had been capricious. Storms approached the coast and then hovered, as if flirting, refusing us the wet kiss of precipitation. High-pressure systems held all the rains at bay. The skies clouded over, brooding, but yielded nothing in the end. It was frustrating stuff.

Turning to happier items, I read that one of the big oil companies was talking about building a new refinery somewhere on the south coast. That would be a handsome addition to the local landscape. A bank robbery, a conflict between land developers and opposing members of the county board of supervisors. I scanned the funnies while I sucked down my coffee and then headed into the office, where I spent the next several hours assembling the balance of my tax receipts. Obnoxious. Having finished, I pulled out a standard boilerplate contract and typed in the details of my agreement with the Keplers. I spent the bulk of the day finishing the final report on a case I'd just done. The closing bill, with expenses, was something over two thousand bucks. It wasn't much, but it kept the rent paid and my insurance intact.

At five, I put a call through to Janice, figuring she'd be up by then. Trinny, the younger of the two daughters, answered the telephone. She was a chatty little thing. When I identified myself, she said her mother's alarm was set to go off any minute. Berlyn was making a run to the bank, and her father was on his way home from a job. That took care of just about everyone. Janice had given me the address, but Trinny filled in directions, sounding pleasant enough.

I retrieved my car from the public lot several blocks away. A steady stream of moving cars spiraled down the ramp as shoppers and office workers headed home. As I drove up Capillo Hill, the very air seemed gray, sueded with twilight. Streetlights flicked on like a series of paper lanterns strung festively from pole to pole.

Janice and Mace Kepler owned a little house on the Bluffs in a neighborhood that must have been established for merchants and tradesmen in the early fifties. Many streets overlooked the Pacific, and in theory the area should have been pricey real estate. In reality there was too much fog. Painted exteriors peeled, aluminum surfaces became pitted, and wooden roof shingles warped from the constant damp. Wind whistled off the ocean, forcing lawns into patchiness. The neighborhoods themselves were comprised almost entirely of tract housing—single-family dwellings thrown up in an era when construction was cheap and the floor plans could be purchased by mail from magazines.

The Keplers had apparently done what they could. The yellow paint on the board-and-batten siding looked as if it had been applied within the year. The shutters were white, and a white split-rail fence had been constructed to define the yard. The lawn had been replaced by dense ivy, which seemed to be growing everywhere, including halfway up the two trees in the yard.

In the driveway, there was a blue panel truck emblazoned with a large cartoon replica of a faucet. A big teardrop of water hung from the spout. MACE KEPLER'S PLUMBING • HEATING • AIR was lettered in white across the truck body. A small oblong emblem indicated that Kepler was a member of PHCC, the National Association of Plumbing, Heating, and Cooling Contractors. His state license number was listed along with the twenty-four-hour emergency repairs he provided (water leaks, sewer drains, gas leaks, and water heaters) and the credit cards he took. These days doctors don't offer services that comprehensive.

I pulled into the gravel driveway and parked my vehicle behind his. I left the car unlocked and peered briefly into the backyard before I climbed the low concrete steps to the front porch. Somebody in the family had a passion for fruit trees. A veritable orchard of citrus had been planted at the rear of the lot. At this season all the branches were bare, but come summer the dark green foliage would be lush and dense, fruit tucked among the leaves like Christmas ornaments.

I rang the bell. There were muddy work shoes by the door mat. There was only a brief pause before Mace Kepler opened the door. I had to guess he'd been alerted to watch for my arrival. Given my incurable inclination to snoop, I was happy I hadn't paused to riffle through his mailbox.

We introduced ourselves, and he stepped back to admit me. Even in his leather bedroom slippers, he was probably six feet four to my five feet six. He wore a plaid shirt and work pants. He was in his sixties, quite hefty, with a broad face and a receding hairline. His deeply cleft chin seemed to have a period buried at its center, and a vertical worry line, like a slash mark, dissected the space between his eyes. On residential jobs he probably hired younger, smaller guys to navigate the crawl space underneath the house. "Janice's in the shower, but she'll be right out. Can I offer you a beer? I'm having one myself. I just got home from a hell of a day."

"No thanks," I said. "I hope I haven't picked a bad time." I waited by the door while he lumbered toward the kitchen to fetch himself a beer.

"Don't worry about it. This is fine," he said. "I just haven't had a chance to unwind yet. This is my daughter Trinny."

Trinny glanced up with a brief smile and then went about her work, pouring a cocoa-brown batter into a nine-by-thirteen aluminum cake pan. The hand mixer, its beaters still dripping brown goo, sat on the kitchen counter beside an open box of Duncan Hines chocolate cake mix. Trinny tucked the pan in the oven and set a timer shaped like a lemon. She'd already opened a cardboard container of ready-mix fudge frosting, and I'd have bet money she'd helped herself to a fingerful. While my aunt had never really taught me to bake, she'd warned me repeatedly about the ignominy of the commercial cake mix, which she ranked right up there with instant coffee and bottled garlic salt.

Trinny was barefoot, wearing an oversize white T-shirt and a pair of ragged blue jean cutoffs. Judging from the size of her butt, she'd conjured up quite a few homemade cakes in her day. Mace opened the refrigerator door and took out a beer. He found the flip in a drawer and levered off the cap, tossing the bottle top in a brown paper trash bag as he passed it.

Trinny and I murmured a "hi" to one another. Berlyn, the older daughter, emerged from the hallway, wearing a pair of black tights with a man's white broadcloth dress shirt over them. Again, Mace introduced us, and we exchanged inconsequential greetings of the "hi, how are you" type. She was intent on rolling up her sleeves as she crossed into the open kitchen. She paused beside Trinny and held her arm out for assistance. Trinny wiped her hands and began to roll up Berlyn's sleeve.

At first glance, they were sufficiently similar to be mistaken for twins. They seemed to favor their father, both big girls and buxom with heavy legs and thighs. Berlyn was a dyed blonde, with big blue eyes framed in dark lashes. She had a clear, pale complexion and a lush full mouth, vibrant with glossy pink lipstick. Trinny had opted for her natural hair color: a double fudge brown, probably the shade Berlyn was born with. Both had bright blue eyes and dark brows. Berlyn's features were the coarser, or perhaps it was the bleached hair that gave her the appearance of tartishness. Without Lorna's delicate beauty in the family for contrast, I would have said they were pretty in a slightly vulgar way. Even knowing what I knew about Lorna's promiscuity, she seemed to have had a classiness about her that the other two lacked.

Berlyn moved over to the refrigerator and pulled out a diet Pepsi. She popped the tab and ambled out the back door onto a wooden deck that ran along the back of the house. Through the window, I watched as she settled on a chaise made of interwoven plastic strips. It seemed too chilly to be sitting out there. Her eyes caught mine briefly before she looked away.

Beer in hand, Mace moved through the kitchen toward the den, indicating that I was to follow. As he closed the door behind us, I picked up the chemical scent of baking chocolate cake.

5

The den had been added onto the house by framing in one-half of the two-car garage. Subflooring had been laid over the original concrete, and look-like-oak tongue-and-groove vinyl planks had been installed on top of that. Even with the addition of an area rug, the room smelled like motor oil and old car parts. A sofa bed, coffee table, four chairs, an ottoman, and a rolling cart for the television set had been arranged in the space. In one corner was a filing cabinet and a desk piled high with papers. All of the furniture looked like garage sale purchases: mismatched fabrics, worn upholstery, someone else's discards given another chance in life.

Mace sank onto a battered brown Naugahyde lounger, activating the mechanism that flipped the footrest into place. His mouth was crowded with bad teeth. The flesh along his jaw had softened with age, and he now had parentheses setting off the thin line of his mouth. He picked up the TV remote, punched the mute button, and then clicked his way through several channels until he found a basketball game in progress. Silently, guys bounded up and down the court, leapt, fell, and bumped one another sideways. If the sound had been turned up, I knew I'd hear the high-pitched shriek of rubber soles on the hardwood floor. The ball sailed into the basket as if magnetized, not even touching the rim half the time.

Without invitation, I perched on the nearby ottoman, arranging myself so I was in his line of sight. "I take it Janice has told you about our conversation last night." I was prepared to make soothing noises about Lorna's participation in the pornographic film. Mace made no response. A fast-food commercial came on, a fifteen-by-twenty-inch full-color burger filling the TV screen. The sesame seeds were the size of rice grains, and a slice of bright orange cheese drooped invitingly from the edge of the bun. I could see Mace's eyes fix on the picture. I'd always known I wasn't as compelling as a flame-broiled beef patty, but it was deflating nonetheless to see his attention displaced. I moved my head to the left, entering his visual frame of reference.

"She told me she wants to hire you to look into Lorna's death," he said as though prompted by someone off stage.

"How do you feel about it?"

He began to tap on the chair arm. "Up to Janice," he said. "I don't mean to sound crass, but her and me have a difference of opinion with regard to that. She believes Lorna was murdered, but I'm not convinced. It could have been a gas leak. Could have been carbon monoxide poisoning from a faulty furnace." He had a big voice and big hands.

"Lorna's cabin had a furnace? I was under the impression her living quarters were pretty crude."

A brief look of impatience flashed across his face. "Janice does the same thing. She takes everything literal. I'm just giving an *example.* Every item in that cabin was either old or broke down. You have a heater that's defective, and you can get yourself in a peck of trouble. That's the point I was trying to make. I see it all the time. Hell, that's what I do for a living."

"I assume the police looked into the possibility of a gas leak."

He shrugged that one off, hunching one beefy shoulder while he worked out a kink. "Bunged myself on the back, trying to wrench a pipe off a slab," he said. "I don't know what the police did. Point is, I think this whole business ought to be laid to rest. Seems to me this speculation about murder is just another way of keeping the subject open for discussion. I loved my daughter. She's as near perfect as you could want. She's a beautiful, sweet girl, but she's dead now, and nothing's going to change that. We got two daughters living, and we need to focus our attention on them for a change. You start hiring lawyers and detectives, all you're going to have is a lot of unnecessary expense in addition to the heartache."

I could feel my inner ears prick up. No outrage, no protest, no reference whatever to all the licking and sucking? To me, Lorna's prurient behavior left her short of "near perfect" and put her closer to "wanton." Being wild didn't make her bad, but the word *sweet* was not quite the word that leapt to *my* mind. I said, "Maybe the two of you need to have another chat about this. I told her last night you'd have to agree."

"Well, we're not *in* agreement. I think the woman's got her head up her butt, but if that's what she wants, I'm willing to go along with it. We're all of us coping any way we can. If this makes her feel good, I won't interfere, but that doesn't mean I *agree* with her on the issue."

Oh, boy. Wait until the man saw the bill for my services. I didn't want to be caught in the middle of *that* dispute. "What about Trinny and Berlyn? Have you discussed this with them?"

"It's not up to them. It's me and her make decisions. The girls live at home, but we're the ones pay the bills."

"I guess what I'm really asking is how they're coping with Lorna's death."

"Oh. I guess we don't tend to talk about that much. You'd have to ask them yourself. I'm trying to put this behind us, not keep it all stirred up."

"Some people find it helpful to talk about these things. That's how they process what they've experienced."

"I hope I don't sound like a surly so-and-so on the subject, but I'm just the opposite. I'd just as soon drop it and get on with life."

"Would you object to my talking with them?"

"That's between you and them, as far as I'm concerned. They're grown-ups. As long as they're willing, you can talk all you want."

"Maybe I'll catch them before I leave. We don't necessarily have to talk today, but I'd like to have a conversation with each of them soon. It's always possible Lorna confided something that might turn out to be significant."

"I doubt it, but you can ask."

"What hours do they work?"

"Berl mans the phone here eight to five. I got a pager, and she makes sure I know about emergencies. She keeps my books, pays the bills, and handles the deposits. Trinny's in the process of looking for work. She got laid off last month, so she's here most of the time."

"What's she do?"

The series of commercials had finally come to an end, and his attention was focused on the TV set again. Two ex-athletes in suits were discussing the game. I let the matter pass, thinking I could ask her myself.

There was a knock at the den door, and Janice peered in. "Oh, hi. Trinny said you were here. I hope I'm not interrupting." She came into the den and closed the door behind her, bringing with her the scent of shower soap, deodorant, and damp hair. She was wearing a red-and-white-checked shirt and red polyester stretch pants. "I got a regular uniform for work," she said, her glance following mine. She looked spiffier than I did, polyester or no. "Did anyone offer you a beverage?" I was surprised she didn't pull out an order pad and pen.

"Thanks, but I'm fine. Mace offered earlier." I reached into my handbag and took out the contract, which I laid on the coffee table. "I stopped by with this. I hope I'm not interrupting your supper preparations."

She waved a hand. "Don't worry about it. Trinny's taken care of that. Ever since she got laid off, it's like having live-in help. We don't eat until eight, which is hours from now anyway. Meantime, how've you been? I hope you got enough sleep. You look tired."

"I am, but I'm hoping to catch up tonight. I don't know how you work the night shift. It would kill me."

"You get used to it. Actually, I prefer it. A whole different set of people come in at night. By the way, that offer of coffee still stands if you're ever up in that area when I'm on shift." She picked up the contract, a simple one-page document spelling out the terms of our agreement. "I guess I better read this before I sign. How does this work? Is this hourly or flat fee?"

"Fifty bucks an hour plus expenses," I said. "I'll submit a written report once a week. We can touch base by phone as often as you like. The agreement authorizes my services and expenditures up to five thousand dollars. Anything beyond that, we'll discuss if the time comes. You may decide you don't want to proceed, and if so, that's the end of it."

"You'll probably need an advance. Isn't that how this is done?"

"Generally," I said. We spent a few minutes talking about the particulars while Mace watched the game.

"This looks all right to me. Honey, what do you think?"

She held out the contract for him, but he ignored her. She turned back to me. "I'll be right back. The checkbook's in the other room. Will a thousand dollars be all right?"

"That'd be fine," I said. She left the room, and I turned my attention to him. "It will save me some time if you can give me the names and addresses of Lorna's friends."

"She didn't have any friends. She didn't have enemies, either, at least as far as we know."

"What about her landlord? I'll need his address."

"Twenty-six Mission Run Road. Name is J. D. Burke. Her place was at the back of his property. I imagine he'd give you the tour if you ask him nice."

"You have any idea why she might have been killed?"

"I already told you my opinion," he said.

Janice returned to the room, catching my last remark and his response. "Ignore him. He's a pill," she said. She took a swat at his head. "You behave yourself."

She sat down on the couch with her checkbook in hand. From the glimpse I caught of the check register, it looked as though it had been a while since she'd done her subtraction. She seemed to favor rounding everything off to the nearest dollar, which made all the amounts end in zero. She wrote out the check, tore it off, and passed it over to me, making a note of the check number and the sum. Then she scribbled her name at the bottom of the contract and handed it to Mace. He took the pen and added his signature without glancing at the terms. The very gesture conveyed, not indifference, but something close to it. I've been in business long enough to smell trouble, and I made up my mind to have Janice pay me as we went along. If I waited to submit a final bill of any substance, Mace would probably get his undies in a bundle and refuse to pay.

I glanced at my watch. "I better go," I said. "I have an appointment in fifteen minutes on the other side of town." I was lying, of course, but these people were beginning to give me a stomachache. "Could you walk me out?" I asked.

Janice stood up when I did. "Be happy to," she said.

"Nice meeting you," I murmured to Mace as I departed.

"Yeah, ditto for sure."

Neither Berlyn nor Trinny was visible as we passed through the living room on our way to the door. As soon as we hit the front porch, I said, "Janice, what's going on here? Have you told him about the tape? He doesn't act like he knows, and you swore you would do that."

"Well, I know, but I haven't had a chance yet. He'd already gone to work when I got home this morning. This is the first opportunity I've had. I didn't want to mention it in front of Berlyn or Trinny. . . ."

"Why not? They have a right to know what she was up to. Suppose they have information that's relevant. Maybe they're holding something back, trying to be protective of the two of you."

"Oh. I hadn't thought of that. Do you really think so?"

"It's certainly possible," I said.

"I guess I could tell them, but I hate to tarnish her memory when it's all we have."

"My investigation may turn up worse than that."

"Oh, Lord, I hope not. What makes you say that?"

"Wait a minute. Let's stop this. I can't be effective if you keep on playing games."

"I'm not playing games," she said, her tone indignant.

"Yes, you are. You can knock off the bullshit about Lorna, for starters. The detective I talked to says you knew what she was doing because he told you himself."

"He did not!"

"I don't want to get into this 'did too, did not' stuff. I'm telling you what he said."

"Well, he's a damn liar, and you can tell him that's what *I* said."

"I'll convey your position. The *point* is, you promised to tell Mace about the video. You're lucky I didn't open my big mouth and put my foot in it. I came this close to mentioning it."

"That'd be all right," she said with caution, apparently mistaking my statement for an offer.

"I bet that'd be all right with *you.* You figure he's already hostile toward me, so what difference would it make? I can just imagine his reaction. Hey, no thanks. That's your job, and you better be quick."

"I'll raise the subject at supper."

"The sooner the better. Just don't leave me in the position of knowing more than he does. He's going to feel foolish enough as it is."

"I said I'd take care of it," she said. Her manner was frosty, but I didn't care.

We parted company on that slightly strained note.

I stopped by the bank on my way through town and deposited the check. I wasn't convinced the damn thing wouldn't bounce, and if I'd had any sense, I'd have waited until it cleared before I did any further work. I intended to head home. Under the trees, the February twilight had accumulated shadows. I was looking forward to an early supper and a good night's sleep. In the interest of efficiency, I did a detour as far as Mission Run Road in search of Lorna's former landlord. If he was home, I'd have a quick chat. If he was out, I'd leave a card with a note asking him to get in touch.

The house was a two-story Victorian structure: white frame with green shutters and a wrap-around porch. Like many such homes in Santa Teresa, this had probably been the main residence on agricultural land of considerable acreage. There was a time when this parcel would have been on the outskirts of town instead of close to its center. I could picture the orchards and fields being subdivided, other houses encroaching while owner after owner put money in the bank. Now what remained was probably less than six acres populated with old trees and the suggestion of outbuildings converted to other use.

As I moved up the walk, I could hear voices, one male, one female, raised in anger, though the subject matter wasn't audible. A door slammed. The man yelled something else, but the point was lost. I went up wooden steps that were rough with flaking gray paint. The front door was standing open, the screen on the latch. I rang the bell. I could see linoleum in the hallway and on the right, stairs going up to the second-floor landing. One portion of the hallway had been sectioned off with two accordion gates, one near the stairway, the other halfway to the kitchen. Burke had a puppy or a kid, it was hard to say. Lights were on at the back of the house. I rang the bell again. A man called out from the kitchen and then appeared, heading in my direction with a dish towel tucked in his belt. He flipped on the porch light, peering out at me.

"Are you J. D. Burke?" I asked.

"That's right." His smile was tentative. He was in his mid- to late forties, with a lean face and good teeth, though one was chipped in front. He had deep creases on either side of his mouth and a fan of wrinkles at the outer corners of his eyes.

"My name is Kinsey Millhone. I'm a private investigator. Lorna Kepler's mother hired me to look into her death. Can you spare a few minutes?"

He glanced back over his shoulder and then shrugged to himself. "Sure, as long as you don't mind watching me cook." He unlatched the screen and held it open for me. "Kitchen's back here. Watch your feet," he said. He sidestepped an array of plastic blocks as he moved down the hall. "My wife thinks playpens are too confining for kids, so she lets Jack play here, where he can see what's going on." I could see that Jack had smeared peanut butter on all the stair spindles he could reach.

I followed J.D. down a chilly hallway, made darker by mahogany woodwork and wallpaper somber with age. I wondered if the art experts could brighten the finish by cleaning away the soot, restoring all the colors to their once clear tones like an old masterpiece. On the other hand, how colorful could pale brown cabbage roses get?

The kitchen was someone's depressing attempt to "modernize" what had probably been a utility porch to begin with. The countertops were covered with linoleum, rimmed with a band of metal where a line of dark gray grunge had collected. The wooden cabinets were thick with lime-green paint. The stove and refrigerator both appeared to be new, incongruous white appliances sticking out into the room. An oak table and two chairs had been tucked into an alcove, where a bay of windows with built-in benches looked out onto a tangled yard. The room was at least warmer than the hall we'd passed through.

"Have a seat."

"I'm fine. I can't stay long," I said. Really, I was reluctant to park my rear end on seats that were sticky with little fingerprints. A short person, probably Jack, had made the rounds of the room, leaving a chair rail of grape jelly that extended as far as the back door, which opened onto a small glass-enclosed porch.

J.D. leaned toward the burner and turned the flame up under his skillet while I leaned against the doorjamb. His hair was a mild brown, thinning on top, slightly shaggy across his ears. He wore a blue denim work shirt, faded blue jeans, and dusty boots. A white paper packet marked with butcher's crayon sat on the counter, along with a pile of diced onions and garlic. He added olive oil to the skillet. I do love to watch men cook.

"J.D.?" A woman's voiced reached us from the front of the house.

"Yeah?"

"Who's at the door?"

He looked toward the corridor behind me, and I turned as she approached. "This lady's a private investigator looking into Lorna's death. This is my wife, Leda. Sorry, but your name slipped right by me." With the oil hot, he scooped up the onions and minced garlic and dropped them in the pan.

I turned and held my hand out. "Kinsey Millhone. Nice to meet you."

We shook hands. Leda was exotic, a child-woman scarcely half Burke's height and probably half his age. She couldn't have been more than twenty-two or twenty-three, small and frail with a dark pixie cut. Her proferred fingers were cold, and her handshake was passive.

Burke said, "Actually, you might know Leda's dad. He's a private investigator, too."

"Really? What's his name?"

"Kurt Selkirk. He's semiretired now, but he's been around for years. Leda's his youngest. He's got five more just like her, a whole passel of girls."

"Of course I know Kurt," I said. "Next time you talk to him, tell him I said hi." Kurt Selkirk had made his living for years doing electronic surveillance, and he had a reputation as a sleazebag. Since Public Law 90-351 was passed in June of 1968, "anyone who willfully uses, endeavors to use, or procures any other person to use or endeavor to use any electronic, mechanical, or other device to intercept any oral communication" was subject to fines of not more than $10,000 or imprisonment for not more than five years. I knew for a fact that Selkirk had risked both penalties on a regular basis. Most private investigators in his age range had made a living, once upon a time, eavesdropping on cheating spouses. Now the no-fault divorce laws had changed much of that. In his case, the decision to retire was probably the result of lawsuits and threats by the federal government. I was glad he'd left the business, but I didn't mention that. "What sort of work do you do?" I asked J.D.

"Electrician," he said.

Meanwhile Leda, smiling faintly, moved past me in a cloud of musk cologne. Any oxen in the area would have been inflamed. Her eye makeup was elaborate: smoky eye shadow, black eyeliner, brows plucked into graceful arches. Her skin was very pale, her bones as delicate as a bird's. The outfit she was wearing was a long, white sleeveless tunic, cut low on her bony chest, and gauzy white harem pants, through which her thin legs were clearly visible. I couldn't believe she wasn't freezing. Her sandals were the type that always drive me insane, with thin leather straps coming up between the toes.

She moved out onto the glassed-in porch, where she busied herself with a swaddled infant, which she lifted from a wicker carriage. She brought the infant to the kitchen table, sliding onto the bench seat. She bared her quite weensie left breast, deftly affixing the baby like some kind of milking apparatus. As far as I could tell, the child hadn't made a sound, but it may have emitted a signal audible only to its mother. Jack, the toddler, was probably off somewhere finger painting with the contents of his diaper.

"I was hoping to see Lorna's cabin, but I didn't know if you had tenants in there at this point." I noticed Leda watched me carefully while I talked to him.

"Cabin's empty. You can go on back if you want. There hasn't been a way to rent it since the body was found. Word gets out and nobody wants to touch it, especially the shape she was in." Burke held his nose with exaggerated distaste.

Embarrassed, Leda said, "J.D.!" as if he'd made a rude noise with his butt.

"It's the truth," he said. He opened the butcher's packet and took out a pillow of raw ground beef, which he plunked into the skillet on top of the sautéed onions. He began to break up the bulk meat with his spatula. I could still see the densely packed noodles of beef where the meat had emerged from the grinder. Looked like worms to me. The hot skillet was turning the bottom of the bulk ground beef from pale pink to gray. I'm giving up meat. I swear to God I am.

"Can you remodel the place?"

"Right now I don't have the bucks, and it probably wouldn't help. It's just a shack."

"What was she paying?"

"Three hundred a month. Might sound like a lot unless you compare it to other rentals in the area. It's really like a one-bedroom with a wood-burning stove I finally took out. People know a place is empty, and they'll steal you blind. They'll take all the lightbulbs if nothing else."

I noticed that in typical landlord assessment, the "shack" had been elevated to a "one-bedroom apartment." "Did someone live there before she did?"

"Nope. My parents used to own the property, and I inherited when Mom died, along with some other rentals on the far side of town. I met Lorna through some people at the plant where she worked. We got talking one afternoon, and she told me she was looking for a place with some privacy. She'd heard about the cabin and asked if she could see it. She fell in love with it. I told her, 'Look, it's a mess, but if you want to fix it up, it'd be fine with me.' She moved in two weeks later without really doing much."

"Was she a party person?"

"Not to my knowledge."

"What about friends? Did she have a lot of people back there?"

"I really couldn't say. It's way back in the back. There's like this little private dirt road going in off the side street. You want to see it, you probably ought to drive your car around and come in that way. Used to be a path between the two places, but we don't use it anymore, and it's overgrown by now. Most of the time, I didn't see if she had company or not because the foliage is so dense. Winters I might catch lights, but I never paid much attention."

"Did you know she was hustling?"

He looked at me blankly.

"Turning tricks," Leda said.

J.D. looked from her face to mine. "What she did was her business. I never considered it my concern." If he was startled by the revelation, it didn't show on his face. His mouth curved down in a display of skepticism while he poked at the cooking beef. "Where'd you hear about that?" he asked me.

"From a vice detective. Apparently, a lot of hookers work the classy hotels where the high rollers hang out. Lorna had done out-call, but she upgraded to independent."

"I guess I'll have to take your word for it."

"So as far as you knew, she didn't bring clients here."

"Why would she do that? You want to impress a fella, you'd hardly bring 'em back to some little shack in the woods. You'd be better off at the hotel. That way he'd get stuck for all the drinks and stuff."

"That makes sense," I said. "I gather she was careful to keep her private life private, so she probably didn't like to mix the two, anyway. Tell me about the day you found her."

"Wasn't me. It was someone else," he said. "I'd been out of town, up at Lake Nacimiento for a couple of weeks. I don't remember the exact timetable offhand. I got home, and I was taking care of some bills came in while I was gone and realized I didn't have her rent check. I tried calling a bunch of times and never got any answer. Anyway, couple days after that, this woman came to the door. She'd been trying to get in touch with Lorna herself, and she'd gone back there to leave her a note. Soon as she got close, she picked up the stink. She came and knocked on our door and asked us to call the police. She said she was pretty sure it was a dead body, but I felt like I ought to check it out first."

"You hadn't noticed anything before?"

"I'd been aware of something smelling bad, but I didn't think much of it. I remember the guy across the street was complaining, but it wasn't like either one of us really thought it was *human*. Possum or something. Could have been a dog or a deer. There's a surprising amount of wildlife around here."

"Did you see the body?"

"No ma'am. Not me. I got as far as the porch and turned around and came back. I didn't even knock. Man, I knew something was *wrong,* and I didn't want to be the one to find out what it was. I called 911 and they sent a cop car. Even the officer had a hard time. Had to hold a handkerchief across his mouth." J.D. crossed to the pantry, where he took out a couple of cans of tomato sauce. He took the crank-style can opener from a nearby drawer and began to remove the lid on the first can.

"You think she was murdered?"

"She was too young to die without some kind of help," he said. He dumped the contents of the first can into the skillet and then cranked open the second. The warm, garlicky smell of tomato sauce wafted up from the pan, and I was already thinking maybe meat wasn't so bad. Other people's cooking always makes me faint with hunger. Must be the equivalent of lost mothering. "Any theories?"

"Not a one."

I turned to Leda. "What about you?"

"I didn't know her that well. We put the vegetable garden back in that corner of the property, so I'd sometimes see her when I went back there to pick beans."

"No friends in common?"

"Not really. J.D. knew Lorna's supervisor out at the water treatment plant. That's how she heard we had a cabin in the first place. Other than that, we didn't socialize. J.D. doesn't like to get too chummy with the tenants."

"Yeah. First thing you know they're giving you excuses instead of the rent check," he said.

"What about Lorna? Did she pay on time?"

"She was good about that. At least until the last one. Otherwise, I wouldn't have let it ride," he said. "I kept thinking she'd bring it by."

"Did you ever meet any friends of hers?"

"Not that I remember." He turned to look at Leda, who shook her head in the negative.

"Anything else you can think of that might help?"

I got murmured denials from both.

I took out a business card and jotted my home phone on the back. "If anything occurs to you, would you give me a buzz? You can call either number. I have machines on both. I'll take a look at the cabin and get back to you if there's a question."

"Watch the bugs," he said. "There's some biggies out there."

6

I nosed the VW down the narrow dirt road that cut into the property close to the rear lot line. The lane had once been black-topped, but now the surface was cracked and graying, overgrown with crabgrass. My headlights swept along the two rows of live oaks that defined the rutted pathway. The branches, interlocking overhead, formed a tunnel of darkness through which I passed. Shrubbery that once might have been neatly trimmed and shaped now spilled in a tumble that made progress slow. Granted, my car may have seen better days, but I was reluctant to let branches snap against the pale blue paint. The potholes were already acting on my shock absorbers like a factory test.

I reached a clearing where a crude cabin loomed in the shadows. I did a three-point turn, positioning the car so I could avoid backing out. I doused the lights. The illusion of privacy was immediate and profound. I could hear crickets in the underbrush. Otherwise, there was silence. It was hard to believe there were other houses nearby, flanked by city streets. The dim illumination from streetlights didn't penetrate this far, and the sound of traffic was reduced to the mild hush of a distant tide. The area felt like a wilderness, yet my office downtown couldn't have been more than ten minutes away.

Peering toward the main house, I could see nothing but the thick growth of saplings, ancient live oaks, and a few shaggy evergreens. Even with the limbs bare on the occasional deciduous tree, the distant lights were obscured. I popped open the glove compartment and took out a flashlight. I tested the beam and found that the batteries were strong. I tucked my handbag in the backseat and locked the car as I got out. About fifty feet away, between me and the main house, I could see the skeletal tepee constructions for the pole beans in the now abandoned garden. The air smelled densely of damp moss and eucalyptus.

I moved up the steps to the wooden porch that ran along the front of the cabin. The front door had been removed from its hinges and now leaned against the wall to one side of the opening. I flipped the light switch, relieved to note the electrical power was still connected. There was only one fixture overhead, with a forty-watt bulb that bathed the rooms in drab light. There was little, if any, insulation, and the place was dead cold. While all the windowpanes were intact, a fine soot had settled in every crevice and crack. Dead insects lined the sills. In one corner of the window frame, a spider had wrapped a fly in a white silken sleeping bag. The air smelled of mold, corroded metal, and spoiled water sitting fallow in the plumbing joints. A section of the wooden floor in the main room had been sawed away by the crime scene unit, the gaping hole covered over with a sheet of warped plywood. I picked my way carefully around that. Just above my head, something thumped and scampered through the attic. I imagined squirrels squeezing into roof vents, building nests for their babies. The beam of my flashlight picked up countless artifacts of the ten months of neglect: rodent droppings, dead leaves, small pyramids of debris created by the termites.

The interior living space was arranged in an L, with a narrow bathroom built into its innermost angle. The plumbing was shared between the bathroom and the kitchenette, with a dining area that wrapped around the corner to the "living" room. I could see the metal plate in the floor to which the wood-burning stove had been affixed. The walls, painted white, were dotted with daddy longlegs, and I found myself keeping an uneasy eye on them as I toured the premises. To one side of the front door was the Belltone box for the doorbell, about the size of a cigarette pack. Someone had popped the housing away from the wall, and I could see that the interior mechanism was missing. An electrical wire, sheathed in green plastic, had been cut and now drooped sideways like a wilted flower stem with the blossom gone.

Lorna's sleeping area had probably been tucked into the short arm of the L. The kitchen cabinets were empty, linoleum-lined shelves still gritty with cornmeal and old cereal dust. Karo syrup or molasses had oozed onto the surface, and I could see circles where the bottoms of the canned goods had formed rings. I checked the bathroom, which was devoid of exterior windows. The toilet was old, the tank tall and narrow. The bowl itself protruded in front, like a porcelain Adam's apple. The brown wood seat was cracked and looked as if it would pinch you in places you cherished. The sink was the size of a dishpan, supported on two metal legs. I tried the cold-water faucet, jumping back with a shriek when a shot of brown water spurted out. The water pipes began to make a low-pitched humming sound, sirens in the underground announcing the crime of trespass. The bathtub rested on ball feet. Dead leaves had collected in a swirling pattern near the drain, while black swans glided across an opaque green plastic shower curtain that hung from an elliptical metal frame.

In the main room, despite the lack of furniture, I could surmise how the space had been used. Close to the front door, dents in the pine flooring suggested the placement of a couch and two chairs. I pictured a small wooden dinette set at the other end of the living room where it turned the corner into the kitchen. To one side of the sink, there was a small cabinet with a phone jack attached just above the baseboard. Lorna probably had a portable phone or a long extension cord, which would have allowed her to keep the phone in the kitchen by day and beside her bed at night. I turned and scanned the premises. Around me, shadows deepened and the daddy longlegs began to tiptoe down the walls, restless at my intrusion. I eased out of the cabin, keeping a close eye on them.

I picked at my dinner, sitting alone in my favorite booth at Rosie's restaurant half a block from my apartment. As usual, Rosie had bullied me into ordering according to her dictates. It's a phenomenon I don't seriously complain about. Beyond McDonald's Quarter Pounders with Cheese, I don't have strong food preferences, and I'm just as happy to have someone else steer me through the menu. Tonight she recommended the caraway seed soup with dumplings, followed by a braised pork dish, yet another Hungarian recipe involving meatstuffs overwhelmed by sour cream and paprika. Rosie's is not so much a restaurant as it is a funky neighborhood bar where exotic dishes are whipped up according to her whims. The place always feels as though it's on the verge of being raided by the food police, so narrowly does it skirt most public health regulations. The scent in the air is a blend of Hungarian spices, beer, and cigarette smoke. The tables in the center of the room are those chrome-and-Formica dinette sets left over from the 1940s. Booths hug the walls: stiff, high-backed pews sawed out of construction-grade plywood, stained dark brown to disguise all the knotholes and splinters.

It was not quite seven, and none of the habitual sports enthusiasts were in evidence. Most nights, especially in the summer months, the place is filled with noisy teams of bowlers and softball players in company uniforms. In winter, they're forced to improvise. Just this week a group of revelers had invented a game called Toss the Jockstrap, and a hapless example of this support garment was now snagged on the spike of a dusty marlin above the bar. Rosie, who is otherwise quite bossy and humorless, seemed to find this amusing and left it where it was. Apparently her impending nuptials had lowered her IQ several critical points. She was currently perched up on a bar stool, scanning the local papers while she smoked a cigarette. A small color television set was blaring at one end of the bar, but neither of us was paying much attention to the broadcast. Rosie's beloved William, Henry's older brother, had flown to Michigan with him. Rosie and William were getting married in a month, though the date seemed to drift.

The telephone rang from its place on the near end of the bar. Rosie glanced over at it with annoyance, and at first I thought she wouldn't answer it at all. She took her time about it, refolding the paper before she set it aside. She finally answered on the sixth ring, and after she'd exchanged a few brief remarks with the caller, her gaze jumped to mine. She held the receiver in my direction and then clunked it down on the bar top, probably devastating someone's eardrum.

I pushed my dinner plate aside and eased out of the booth, careful that I didn't snag a splinter in the back of my thigh. One day I'm going to rent a belt sander and give all the wooden seats a thorough scouring. I'm tired of worrying about the possibility of impaling myself on spears of cheap plywood. Rosie had moved to the far end of the bar, where she turned down the volume on the TV set. I crossed to the bar and picked up the receiver. "Hello?"

"Hey, Kinsey. Cheney Phillips. How are you?"

"How'd you know where I was?"

"I talked to Jonah Robb, and he told me you used to hang out at Rosie's. I tried your home number and your machine picked up, so I figured you might be having dinner."

"Good detective work," I said. I didn't even want to ask what had made him think to discuss me with Jonah Robb, who was working the Missing Persons detail at the Santa Teresa Police Department when I'd met him three years before. I'd had a brief affair with him during one of his wife's periodic episodes of spousal abandonment. Jonah and his wife, Camilla, had been together since seventh grade. She left him at intervals, but he always took her back again. It was love junior high school style, which became very tedious for those on the periphery. I hadn't known what the game was, and I didn't understand the role I'd been tagged to play. Once I got the message, I'd opted out of the situation, but it left me feeling bad. When you're single, you sometimes make those mistakes. Still, it's disconcerting to think your name is being bandied about. I didn't like the idea that I was the subject of conversation in the local police locker room.

"What are you up to?" I said to Cheney.

"Nothing much. I'll be going down to lower State Street later tonight, looking for a guy with some information I want. I thought you might like to ride along. An old girlfriend of Lorna's tends to hustle her butt in the same neighborhood. If we spot her, I can introduce you . . . if you're interested, of course."

My heart sank as visions of an early bedtime evaporated. "It sounds great. I appreciate the offer. How do you want to work it? Shall I meet you down there?"

"You can if you like, but it's probably better if I swing by and pick you up on the way. I'll be cruising a big area, and it's hard to know where I'll be."

"You know where I live?"

"Sure," he said, and rattled off my address. "I'll be there about eleven."

"That late?" I squeaked.

"The action doesn't even get rolling 'til after midnight," he said. "Is that a problem?"

"No, it's fine."

"See you then," he said, and hung up.

I glanced at my watch and noted with despair that I had about four hours to kill. All I really wanted was to hit the sack, but not if I was going to have to get up again. When I'm down, I like to stay down. Naps leave me feeling hungover without the few carefree moments of an intervening binge. If I was going to drive around with Cheney Phillips until all hours, I thought I'd be better off staying on my feet. I decided I might as well conjure up some work in the interim. I drank two cups of coffee and then paid Rosie for my dinner, taking my jacket and handbag as I headed out into the night.

The sun had set at 5:45, and the moon probably wouldn't be

rising until 2:00 A.M. At this hour, everybody in the neighborhood was still wide awake. In almost every house I passed, front windows glowed as if the rooms within were aflame. Night moths like soft birds batted ineffectually against the porch bulbs. February had silenced all the summer insects, but I could still hear a few hearty crickets in the dry grass and an occasional nightbird. Otherwise, the quiet was pervasive. It seemed warmer than last night, and I knew, from the evening paper, that the cloud cover was increasing. The winds were northerly, shaking through the thatch of dried palm fronds above me. I walked the half block to my apartment and let myself in briefly to check for messages.

There was nothing on my machine. I went out again before I yielded to the temptation to call Cheney and cancel tonight's big adventure. The squeak in the gate seemed like a melancholy sound, cold metal protesting my departure. I got in my car and turned the key in the ignition, cranking the lever for the heater as soon as the engine roared to life. There was no way the system could deliver hot air so soon, but I needed the illusion of coziness and warmth.

I headed out the 101 for half a mile and took the Puerta Street off-ramp. St. Terry's Hospital was only two blocks down. I found a parking space on a side street, locked the car, and walked the remaining half block to the front entrance. Technically, visiting hours didn't start until eight, but I was hoping the nursing director on the cardiac care unit would bend the rules a bit.

The glass doors slid open as I approached. I passed the hospital café to the left of the lobby, with its couches arranged in numerous conversational groupings. Several ambulatory patients, wearing robes and slippers, had elected to come down and sit with family members and friends. The area was rather like a large, comfortably furnished living room, complete with piped-in music and paintings by local artists. The scent in the lobby was not at all unpleasant but nonetheless reminded me of hard times. My aunt Gin had died here on a February night over ten years ago. I shut the door on the thought and all the memories that came with it.

The gift shop was open, and I did a quick detour. I wanted to buy something for Lieutenant Dolan, though I couldn't think quite what. Neither the teddy bears nor the peignoirs seemed appropriate. Finally I picked up an oversize candy bar and the latest issue of *People.* Entering a hospital room is always easier with an item in hand—anything to smooth your intrusion on the intimacies of illness. Ordinarily I wouldn't dream of conducting business with a man in his pajamas.

I paused at the information desk long enough to get his room number and directions to CCU, then hiked down countless corridors toward the bank of elevators in the west wing. I punched the button for three and emerged into a light, airy foyer with a glossy, snow-white floor. I turned left into a short hallway. The CCU waiting room was just to the right. I peered through the glass window set into the door. The room was empty and spare: a round table, three chairs, two love seats, a television set, pay phone, and several magazines. I moved over to the door leading into CCU. There was a phone on the wall and beside it a sign advising me to call in for permission to enter. A nurse or a ward clerk picked up the call, and I told her I wanted to see Lieutenant Dolan.

"Wait a minute and I'll check."

There was a pause, and then she told me to come on in. The curious thing about illness is that a lot of it looks just like you'd expect. We've seen it all on television: the activity at the nurses' station, the charts and the machinery designed to monitor the ailing. On the cardiac care unit, the floor nurses wore ordinary street clothes, which made the atmosphere seem more relaxed and less clinical. There were five or six of them, all young and quite friendly. Medical personnel could oversee vital signs from a central vantage point. I stood at the counter and watched eight different hearts beat, a row of green spiky hiccups on screens lined up on the desk.

The ward itself was done in southwestern colors: dusty pinks, mild sky blues, cool pale greens. The doors to each room were made of sliding glass, easily visible from the nurses' station, with draw drapes that could be pulled shut if privacy was required. The feel of the unit was as clean and quiet as a desert: no flowers, no artificial plants, all the laminate surfaces plain and spare. The paintings on the walls were of desert vistas, mountains rising in the distance.

I asked for Lieutenant Dolan, and the nurse directed me down the corridor. "Second door on the left," he said.

"Thanks."

I paused in the doorway of Lieutenant Dolan's room, which was sleek and contemporary. The bed he rested on was as narrow as a monk's. I was used to seeing him on the job, in a rumpled gray suit, grumpy, harassed, completely businesslike. Here he seemed smaller. He was wearing an unstructured, pastel cotton gown with short sleeves and a tie back. He sported a day's growth of beard, which showed prickly gray across his cheeks. I could see the tired, ropy flesh of his neck, and his once muscular arms were looking stringy and thin. A floor-to-ceiling column near the head of his bed housed the paraphernalia necessary to monitor his status. Cables pasted to his chest looped up to a plug in the column, where a screen played out his vital signs like a ticker tape. He was reading the paper, half-glasses low on his nose. He was attached to an IV. When he caught sight of me, he set the paper aside and took his glasses off. He gave the edge of the sheet a tug, pulling it across his bare feet.

He motioned me in. "Well, look who it is. What brings you down here?" He ran a hand through his hair, which was sparse at best and now looked as if it had been slicked back with sweat. He pushed himself up against the angled bed. His plastic hospital bracelet made his wrist seem vulnerable, but he didn't seem ill. It was as if I'd caught him on a Sunday morning, lounging around in his pajamas before church.

"Cheney told me you were laid up, so I thought I'd pop by. I hope I didn't interrupt your paper."

"I've read it three times. I'm so desperate I'm down to the personals. Somebody named Erroll wants Louise to call him, in case you know either one."

I smiled, wishing he looked stronger, knowing I'd look even worse if I were in his place. I held out the magazine. "For you," I said. "I figure nothing in your condition precludes an overdose of gossip. If you're really bored, you can always do the crossword puzzle in the back. How're you feeling? You look good."

"I'm not bad. I've been better. The doctor's talking about moving me off the unit tomorrow, which seems like a good sign." He scratched at the stubble on his chin. "I'm taking advantage by refusing to shave. What do you think?"

"Very devil-may-care," I said. "You can go straight from here to a life on the bum."

"Pull a chair over. Have a seat. Just move that."

The chair in the near corner had the rest of the paper and several magazines piled up on the seat. I set the whole batch aside and dragged the chair over toward the bed, aware that both Dolan and I were using chitchat and busywork to cover a basic uneasiness. "What are they telling you about going back to work?"

"They won't say at this point, but I imagine it'll be a while yet. Two, three months. I scared 'em pretty bad, from what everybody says. Hell, Tom Flowers ended up doing mouth-to-mouth, which he'll never live down. Must have been a sight for sore eyes."

"You're still with us, at any rate."

"That I am. Anyway, how are you? Cheney told me about Janice Kepler. How's it going so far?"

I shrugged. "All right, I guess. I've been on it less than a day. I'm supposed to meet Cheney later. He's going to cruise lower State, looking for a snitch, and offered to point out a chum of Lorna's while he's about it."

"Probably Danielle," Dolan said. "We talked to her at the time, but she wasn't much help. You know these little gals. The life they live is so damn dangerous. Night after night, connecting up with strangers. Get in a car and you have to be aware it might be the last ride you ever take. And they see *us* as the enemy. I don't know why they do it. They're not stupid."

"They're desperate."

"I guess that's what it is. This town is nothing compared to L.A., but it's still the pits. You take someone like Lorna, and it makes no sense whatever."

"You have a theory about who killed her?"

"I wish I did. She kept her distance. She didn't buddy up to people. Her lifestyle was too unconventional for most."

"Oh, I'll say. Has anybody told you about the video?"

"Cheney mentioned it. I gather you've seen it. I probably ought to take a look myself, see if I recognize any of the players."

"You better wait 'til you're home. It'll get your heart rate right up there. Janice Kepler gave me a copy. She's feeling very paranoid and made me swear I'd guard the damn thing with my very life. I haven't checked the dirty-book stores, but it wouldn't surprise me to see half a dozen copies in stock. From the packaging, it looks like it was manufactured up in the Bay Area someplace."

"You going up there?"

"I'd like to. Seems like it's worth a try if I can talk Janice into it."

"Cheney says you want to take a look at the crime scene photographs."

"If you don't object. I saw the cabin this afternoon, but it's been empty for months. I'd like to see what it looked like when the body was found."

Lieutenant Dolan's brow furrowed with distaste. "You're welcome to take a look, but you better brace yourself. That's the worst decomp case I ever saw. We had to do toxicology from bone marrow and whatever little bit of liver tissue we could salvage."

"There's no doubt it was her?"

"Absolutely none," he said. He lifted his eyes to the monitor, and I followed his gaze. His heartbeat had picked up, and the green line was looking like a row of ragged grass. "Amazes me how the memory of something like that can cause a physiological reaction after all these months."

"Did you ever see her in real life?"

"No, and it's probably just as well. I felt bad enough as it was. 'Dust to dust' doesn't quite cover it. Anyway, I'll call Records and get a set for you. When do you want to go over there?"

"Right now, if possible. Cheney doesn't pick me up for another three hours yet. I was up late last night, and I'm dead on my feet. My only hope is to keep moving."

"Photographs will wake you up."

Most of the departments at the police station close down at six. The crime lab was closed and the detectives gone for the day. In the bowels of the building, the 911 dispatchers would still be sitting at their consoles, fielding emergency calls. The main counter, where parking tickets are paid, was as blank as the ribs on a rolltop desk, a sign indicating that the window would open again at 8:00 A.M. The door to Records was locked, but I could tell there were a couple of people working, probably data-processing technicians entering the day's warrants into the system. The small front counter wasn't currently manned, but I managed to lean over, peering into the records department around the corner to the right.

A uniformed officer spotted me and broke away from a conversation with a civilian clerk. He moved in my direction. "Can I help you?"

"I just talked to Lieutenant Dolan over at St. Terry's. He and Detective Phillips are letting me look at some files. There should be a set of photographs he said I could take."

"The name was Kepler, right? Lieutenant just called. I have 'em right back here. You want to come on through?"

"Thanks."

The officer depressed a button, releasing the door lock. I went through into a back hallway and turned right. The officer reappeared in the doorway to Records and Identification. "We got a desk back here if you want to take a seat."

I read through the file with care, making notes as I went. Janice Kepler had given me much of the same material, but there were many interdepartmental memos and notes that hadn't been part of her packet. I found the witness interviews the police had conducted with Hector Moreno, J. D. Burke, and Serena Bonney, whose home address and phone number I jotted down. There were additional interviews with Lorna's family, her former boss, Roger Bonney, and the very Danielle Rivers I was hoping to meet on lower State Street tonight. Again, I made a note of home addresses and telephone numbers. This was information I could develop on my own, but why pass it up? Lieutenant Dolan had left word that I could photocopy anything I needed. I took copies of countless pages. I'd probably interview many of the same people, and it would be instructive to compare their current opinions and observations with those made at the time. Finally I turned my attention to the crime scene photographs.

In some ways, it's hard to know which is more sordid, the pornography of sex or the pornography of homicide. Both speak of violence, the broken and debased, the humiliations to which we subject one another in the heat of passion. Some forms of sex are as cold-blooded as murder, some kinds of murder as titillating to the perpetrator as a sexual encounter.

Decomposition had erased most of the definition from Lorna Kepler's flesh. The very enzymes embedded in her cells had caused her to disintegrate. The body had been invaded, nature's little cleaning crew busily at work—maggots as light as a snowfall and as white as thread. It took me many minutes before I could look at the photographs without revulsion. Finally I was able to detach myself. This was simply the reality of death.

I was interested in the sight of the cabin in its furnished state. I had seen it empty: sooty and forsaken, full of spiders and mildew, the fusty smell of neglect. Here, in full color and again in black and white, I could see fabric, crowded countertops in use, sofa pillows in disarray, a vase full of sagging flowers in an inch of darkened water, rag rugs, the spindle-lathed wooden chair legs. I could see a pile of mail on the sofa cushion where she'd left it. There was something distasteful about the unexpected glimpses of her living space. Like a houseguest arriving early, who sees the place before the hostess has had the chance to tidy up.

Aside from a few photographs meant to orient the viewer, Lorna's body was the prime subject of most eight-by-ten glossies. She lay on her stomach. Her posture was that of someone sleeping, her limbs arranged in the classic chalk outline that marks the position of the corpse in any TV show. No blood, no emesis. It was hard to imagine what she was doing when she went down—answering the front door, running for the telephone. She wore a bra and underpants, her jogging clothes tossed in a pile close by. Her long dark hair still carried its sheen, a tumble of glossy strands. In the light of the flashbulb, small white maggots glowed like a spray of seed pearls. I slipped the pictures back in the manila envelope and tucked them in my handbag.

7

I was leaning against my VW, parked at the curb in front of my place, when Cheney came around the corner in a VW that looked even older than mine. It was beige, very dinged up, an uncanny replica of the 1968 sedan I had run off the road nearly two years before. Cheney chugged to a stop, and I tried opening the car door on the passenger side. No deal. I finally had to put a foot up against the side of the car to get sufficient leverage to wrench the door open. The squawk it made sounded like a large, unruly beast breaking wind. I slid onto the seat and pulled futilely at the door, trying to close it. Cheney reached across me and wrenched it shut again. He threw the gears into first and took off with his engine rumbling.

"Nice car. I used to have one just like this," I said. I yanked at the seat belt, making a vain attempt to buckle it across my lap. The whole device was frozen, and I finally just had to pray he'd drive without crashing and burning. I do so hate to end an evening being flung through the windshield. At my feet I could feel a breeze blowing through a hole where the floor had rusted out. If it were daytime, I knew I'd see the road whipping past, like that small glimpse of track you see when you flush the toilet on a train. I tried to keep my feet up to avoid putting weight on the spot lest I plunge through. If the car stalled, I could push us along with one foot without leaving my seat. I started to roll down the window and discovered that the crank was gone. I opened the wing window on my side, and chilly air slanted in. So far, the wing window was the only thing on my side that functioned.

Cheney was saying, "I have a little sports car, too, but I figure there's no point in taking anything like that into the neighborhood we'll be in. Did you talk to Dolan yet?"

"I went over to St. Terry's to see him this evening. He was a doll, I must say. I went straight from the hospital to the station to look at files. He even provided me copies of the crime scene photographs."

"How'd he seem?"

"He was okay, I guess. Not as grouchy as usual. Why? What's your impression?"

"He was depressed when I talked to him, but he might have brought himself up for you."

"He has to be scared."

"I sure would be," Cheney said.

Tonight he was wearing a pair of slick Italian shoes, dark pants, a coffee-brown dress shirt, and a soft, cream suede windbreaker. I have to say he didn't look like any undercover cop I ever saw. He glanced over at me and caught the fact that I was conducting a visual survey. "What."

"Where are you from?" I asked.

"Perdido," he said, naming a little town thirty miles south of us. "What about you?"

"I'm local," I said. "Your name seems familiar."

"You've known me for years."

"Yes, but do I know you from somewhere else? Do you have family in the area?"

He made a noncommittal mouth sound that generally indicated "yes."

I looked at him closely. Being a liar myself, I can recognize other people's evasive maneuvers. "What's your family do?"

"Banks."

"What about banks? They make deposits? They do holdups?"

"They, mmm, you know, own some."

I stared at him, comprehension dawning like a big cartoon sun. "Your father is X. Phillips? As in Bank of X. Phillips?"

He nodded mutely.

"What is it, Xavier?"

"Actually, it's just X."

"What's your other car, a Jag?"

"Hey, just because he has big bucks doesn't mean I do. I have a Mazda. It's not fancy. Well, a little bit fancy, but it's paid for."

I said, "Don't get *defensive.* How'd you end up a cop?"

Cheney smiled. "When I was a kid, I watched a lot of TV. I was raised in an atmosphere of benign neglect. My mother sold high-end real estate while my father ran his banks. Cop shows made a big impression. More than financial matters, at any rate."

"Is your dad okay with that?"

"He doesn't have any choice. He knows I'm not going to follow in his footsteps. Besides, I'm dyslexic. To me, the printed page looks like gibberish. What about your parents? Are they still alive?"

"Please note. I'm aware that you're changing the subject, but I'm electing to answer the question you asked. They both died a long time ago. As it turns out, I do have family up in Lompoc, but I haven't decided what to do about them yet."

"What's to decide? I didn't know we had a choice about these things."

"Long story. They've ignored my existence now for twenty-nine years, and suddenly they want to make nice. It doesn't sit well with me. That kind of family I can do without."

Cheney smiled. "Look at it this way. I feel the same way about mine, and I've been in touch with them since birth."

I laughed. "Are we cynical or what?"

"The 'or what' part sounds right."

I turned my attention to the area we'd begun to cruise. It was not far from my place. Down along Cabana Boulevard, a left turn across the tracks. The condominiums and small houses began to give way to commercial properties: warehouses, "lite" industry, a wholesale seafood company, a moving-and-storage facility. Many buildings were long, low, and windowless. Tucked in along a side street was one of two "adult" bookstores. The other was located on the lower end of State Street, several blocks away. Here, small barren trees were spaced at long intervals. The streetlights seemed pale respite against the wide stretches of the dark. Looking off toward the mountains, I could see the smoky glow of the town washed up against the sky. The houses along the hillside were linked together in a fairyland of artificial lights. We began to pass small groups of people, five or six leaning against cars, clusters of the young whose sex was difficult to distinguish. Their eyes followed us without fail, conversations halted momentarily in the hopes that we would offer business of one sort or another. Sex or drugs, it probably didn't matter as long as money changed hands. Through the window, I could smell the dope as joints were passed from hand to hand.

The dull booming of a bass note signaled the proximity of the establishment we were looking for.

Neptune's Palace was a combination bar and pool hall with an open courtyard along one side, surrounded by a wide asphalt parking lot. Patrons had spilled out into both the courtyard and the parking lot. The yellow glow of mercury-vapor lights streamed across the gleaming tops of parked cars. Blasts of music spilled from the bar. Near the front of the place, girls were lounging against a low wall, their eyes following as a succession of vehicles cruised by in search of the night's adventure. The double doors stood open like the entrance to a cave, the rectangle of tawny light softened by a fog of cigarette smoke. We circled the block twice, Cheney peering out for sight of Danielle.

"No sign of her?" I asked.

"She'll be here someplace. For her, this is like the unemployment office."

We found a parking place around the corner, where the night air was quieter. We got out and locked the car, moving along the sidewalk past numerous same-sex couples who seemed to view us with amusement. Heterosexuals are so out of it.

Cheney and I pushed our way into the bar, merging with the shoals of inebriated patrons. Music blasted from the dance floor. The damp heat from all the bodies inside was nearly tropical in its nature. The very air smelled briny from the cheap beer on tap. The nautical theme was everywhere apparent. Big fishing nets were draped from the beams across the ceiling, where reflecting bulbs played like sunlight on surface water. Up there, a light show simulated twilight on the ocean, day fading into sunset, followed by the jet black of night. Sometimes the constellations were projected overhead, and sometimes ferocious cracks of lightning formed the apparition of a storm at sea. The walls were painted in a multitude of blues, shades graduating downward from the calm blue of a summer swell to the midnight hues of the deep. Sawdust on the concrete flooring created the illusion of the ocean's sandy bottom. The dance floor itself was defined by what looked like the prow of a sunken ship. So perfect was the fantasy of life beneath the sea that I found myself feeling grateful for every breath I took.

Tables were tucked into alcoves made to look like coral reefs. The lighting was muted, much of it emanating from massive saltwater aquariums in which large, pouty-mouthed groupers undulated endlessly in search of prey. Reproduction antique navigational charts were embedded in polyurethane on every tabletop, and the world they portrayed was one of vast unpopulated oceans with treacherous creatures lurking at the outer edges. Not so different from the patrons themselves.

In the occasional brief lull between cuts, I picked up the faint effects being played through the sound system: ship's bells, the creak of wood, sails flapping, the shriek of seagulls, the tinny warning of the buoys. Most eerie was the nearly undiscernible wails of drowning seamen, as if all of us were caught up in some maritime purgatory, in which alcohol, cigarettes, laughter, and pounding music served to ward off those faint cries creeping into the silence. All the waitresses were dressed in skintight, spangled body suits as shimmering as fish scales. I had to guess most had been hired on the basis of their androgyny: cropped hair, slim hips, and no breasts to speak of. Even the boys were wearing makeup.

Cheney stayed close behind me, his hand placed comfortably in the middle of my back. Once he leaned to say something, but the noise in the place obliterated his voice. He disappeared at one point and came back with a bottle of beer in each hand. We found an expanse of unpopulated wall with a largely unobstructed view of the place. We leaned there, people watching. The volume of the music would necessitate a hearing test later. I could picture all the cilia in my ear canal going flat. I'd once fired a gun from the depths of a garbage bin and ever since had been plagued by an intermittent hissing deep inside my head. These kids were going to need ear trumpets by the age of twenty-five.

Cheney touched my arm and then pointed across the room. His mouth formed the word "Danielle," and I followed his gaze. She was standing near the door, apparently alone, though I had to guess she wouldn't be for long. She was probably in her late teens, lying regularly about her age, else how would she get in here? She had dark hair long enough to sit on and long legs that seemed to go on forever. Even at that distance, I could see slim hips, a flat belly, and the breasts of early adolescence, a body type much admired by the postmenopausal male. She was wearing lime-green satin hot pants and a halter top with a lime-green bomber jacket over it.

We made our way across the room. At a certain point in our progress, she spotted Cheney's approach. He pointed toward the courtyard. She pivoted and went out in advance of us. Outside, the temperature dropped dramatically, and the sudden absence of cigarette smoke made the air smell like freshly cut hay. The chill felt like liquid pouring over my skin. Danielle had turned to face us, hands in her jacket pockets. Up close, I could see the skillful use of cosmetics in the battle she must have fought with her own youthful looks. She could have passed for twelve. Her eyes were the luminous green of certain tropical fish, and her look was insolent.

"We have a car parked around the corner," Cheney said without preamble.

"So?"

"So we could have a little talk. Just the three of us."

"About what?"

"Life in general, Lorna Kepler in particular."

Danielle's eyes were fixed on mine. "Who's she?"

"This is Kinsey. Lorna's mother hired her."

"This is not a bust," she said warily.

"Oh, come on, Danielle. It's not a bust. She's a private investigator looking into Lorna's death."

"Because I'm telling you, Cheney, you set me up for something, you could get me in real trouble."

"It's not a setup. It's a meeting. She'll pay your regular rates."

I gave Cheney a look. I'd have to pay the little twerp?

Danielle's gaze raked the parking lot and then strayed in my direction. "I don't do women," she said sullenly.

I leaned forward and said, "Hey, me neither. In case anybody gives a shit."

Cheney ignored me and addressed himself to her. "What are you afraid of?"

"What am I *afraid* of?" she said, finger pointing to her own chest. Her nails were bitten to the quick. "I'm afraid of Lester, for one thing. I'm afraid of losing my teeth. I'm afraid Mr. Dickhead's going to flatten my nose again. The guy's a bastard, a real prick . . ."

"You should have pressed charges. I told you that the last time," Cheney said.

"Oh, right. I should have gone ahead and checked into the morgue, saved myself that messy middle step," she snapped.

"Come on. Help us out," Cheney coaxed.

She thought about it, looking off into the dark. Finally, grudgingly, she said, "I'll talk to her, not to you."

"That's all I'm asking."

"I'm not doing it because you're *asking*. I'm doing it for Lorna. And just this once. I mean it. I don't want you to set me up like this again."

Cheney grinned seductively. "You're too perfect."

Danielle made a face, mimicking his manner, which she wasn't buying for a minute. She headed off toward the street, talking back across her shoulder. "Let's get it over with before Lester shows up."

Cheney walked us to the car, where we went through the requisite door-wrenching exercise. The ensuing squawk was so loud, a couple halfway down the block stopped necking long enough to see what kind of creature we were torturing. I took the passenger seat and let Danielle take the driver's side in case she needed to make a hasty getaway. Whoever Lester was, I was getting nervous myself.

Cheney leaned toward the wing window. "Back in a bit."

"You see Lester, don't you tell him where I'm at," she warned.

"Trust me," Cheney said.

"Trust him. What a joke," she said to no one in particular.

We watched him through the front windshield as he disappeared into the dark. I sat there hoping her Monday night rates were low. I couldn't remember how much cash I had on me, and I didn't think she'd take my Visa, which was maxed out anyway.

"You can smoke if you want," I said, thinking to ingratiate myself.

"I don't *smoke,*" she said, offended. "Smoking wrecks your health. Know how much we pay in this country for smoking-related illnesses? Fifteen billion a year. My father died of emphysema. It was like walking suffocation every day of his life. Eyes bugging out. He's breathing . . . he's like this . . ." She paused to demonstrate, hand on her chest. The sounds she made were a combination of rasping and choking. "And he can't get any air. It's a horrible way to die. Dragging around this old oxygen tank. You better quit while you're ahead."

"I don't smoke. I thought you might. I was being polite."

"Don't be polite on my account," she said. "I hate smoking. It's very bad for you, plus it stinks." Danielle looked around then, regarding the interior of the VW with distaste. "What a pigsty. You could get a disease sitting in this thing."

"At least you know he's not on the take," I said.

"Cops in this town don't take money," she said. "They have too much fun sticking people in the can. He's got a much nicer car, but he's too paranoid to bring it down here. So. Enough with the chit-chat, get-to-know-you bullshit. What do you want to know about Lorna?"

"As much as you can tell me. How long did you know her?"

Danielle's mouth pulled down in a facial shrug. "Couple of years. We met working for this escort service. She was a good person. She was like a mother to me. She was my what-do-you-call-'em . . . mentor . . . only now I see I should have listened to her more."

"How so?"

"Lorna killed me. She was great. She really blew me away. I was like totally in awe. She knew what she wanted and she went after it, and if you didn't like where she was coming from, then it was too bad for you."

"What did she want?"

"A million bucks, for starters. She wanted to retire by the time she was thirty. She could have done it, too, if she'd lived long enough."

"How'd she propose to do it?"

"How do you think?"

"That's a lot of time on your back," I said.

"Not at the rates she charged. After she left the escort service? She was making two hundred thousand dollars a year. Two hundred *thousand.* I couldn't believe it. She was smart. She invested. She didn't blow money the way I would've if I'd been in her shoes. I got no head for finance. What's in my pocket I spend, and when it's gone, I start over. At least I used to be that way until she straightened me out."

"What was she going to do when she retired?"

"Travel. Goof off. Maybe marry some guy who'd take care of her for life. Thing is . . . and here's what she kept hammering at me about . . . you got money, you're independent. You can do anything you want. Some guy mistreats you, you get the fuck out. You can walk. Know what I'm saying?"

"That's my philosophy," I said.

"Yeah, mine, too, now. After she died, I opened a little savings account, and I salt it away. It's not much, but it's enough, and I'm going to let it sit. That's what Lorna always said. You put it in the bank and you let it collect interest. She put a lot of her money in blue-chip stocks, municipal bonds, shit like that, but she did it all herself. She wasn't into this business about financial managers and people like that, because, for one thing, she said it's the perfect excuse for some asshole to come along and rip you off. You know stockbrokers? She called 'em portfolio pimps." She laughed at the phrase, apparently amused at the idea of procurers on Wall Street. "How about you? You got savings?"

"As a matter of fact, I do."

"Where is it? What'd you do with it?"

"I put it in CDs," I said, feeling faintly sensitive on the subject. It seemed strange defending my financial strategy to some girl who worked the streets.

"That's good. Lorna did some of that, too. She liked tax-free munis, and she had some of her money in Ginnie Maes, whatever they are. Listen to us. This is what I like. Talkin' about all this long-term stuff. You have money, that's power, and no guy can come along and punch your lights out, right?"

"You mentioned her making two hundred thousand. She pay taxes on the money?"

"Of course! Never fuck with the feds, was her first rule of thumb. That's the first thing she taught me. Anything you make, you declare. Know how they got Al Capone and those guys? Undeclared income. You cheat the feds, you end up in the can, like big time, and that's no lie."

"What about—"

"Just a minute," she cut in. "Let me ask you something else. How much do you earn?"

I stared at her. "How much do *I* earn?"

"Yeah, like last year. What was your annual income? What'd you pay taxes on?"

"That's getting pretty personal, isn't it?"

"You don't have to act like that. This is strictly between us. You say and then I will. We'll trade tit for tat, as it were."

"Twenty-five thousand."

Now it was her turn to stare. "That's *all?* I earned twice that. No fooling. Fifty-two thousand five hundred and change."

"You got your nose broken, too," I pointed out.

"Yeah, well, you had *your* nose broken. I can tell by looking. I'm not criticizing. No offense," she said. "You're not a bad-looking chick, but for twenty-five thousand, you get punched in the chops same as me, am I right?"

"I wouldn't look at it quite like that."

"Don't bullshit yourself. I learned that from Lorna, too. Take my word for it. Your job is dangerous the same as mine, with only half the pay. You ought to switch, in my opinion. Not that I'm promoting my line of work. I'm just telling you what I think."

"I appreciate your concern. If I decide to change careers, I'll come to you for job counseling."

She smiled, amused at the sarcasm or what she assumed was sarcasm. "I'll tell you something else she taught me. Keep your big mouth shut. You do a guy, you don't talk about it afterward. Especially in the crowd she's running in. She slipped up once and swore she'd never do it again. Some of those guys . . . whoo! You're better off forgetting you ever knew 'em."

"Do you travel in those circles? The real high-class stuff?"

"Well, not all the time. Not now. When she was alive, I did now and then. Like once in a while, she'd dress me up fancy and take me with her on a big one. Me and this other girl named Rita. What a hoot. Some guys like 'em young. You shave your pubes and act like you're about ten years old. Like this one night? I made over fifteen hundred dollars. Don't ask me doing what. That's something else you don't talk about. Lester would have killed me if he found out."

"What happened to all her money when she died?" I asked.

"Beats the hell out of me. You'd have to ask her folks about that. I bet she didn't have a will. I mean, what'd she need a will for? She was young. Well, twenty-five, which is not *that* old. I bet she thought she had years, and it turned out she had nothing."

"How old are you?"

"Twenty-three."

"You are not."

"I am *too."*

"Danielle, you're not."

She smiled slightly. "Okay, I'm nineteen, but I'm mature for my age."

I said, "Seventeen is probably closer, but we'll let that pass."

"You better ask more about Lorna. You're wasting your money when you ask about me."

"What was Lorna doing out at the water treatment plant? That doesn't sound like it was worth even the part-time pay."

"She had to do *something.* She couldn't tell her parents how she was earning her bread. They were real conservative; least her dad was. I met her mom at the funeral, and she seemed nice enough. Her old man was a butt, all the time on her case, checkin' up on her. Lorna was a wild one, and she didn't like to be controlled."

"I talked to her father earlier today, and he said Lorna didn't have many friends."

Danielle dismissed that with a toss of her head. "What does he know? Just because he never met any. Lorna liked night people. Everybody she knew came out of hiding when the sun went down. Like spiders and all those what-do-you-call-'em . . . nocturnal creatures. Owls and bats. You want to meet her friends, you better get used to staying out all night. What else? This is fun. I didn't realize I was so smart."

"What about the porno film? Why'd she do that?"

"Oh, same old, same old. You know how it is. Some guy came down from San Francisco. She met him one night in at the Edgewater and got to talking about that stuff. He thought she'd be dynamite, and I guess she was. At first she didn't want to do it, but then she figured, Hey, why not? She didn't get paid much, but she said she had a ball. What'd you hear about that?"

"I didn't hear about it. I saw it."

"You did not. You saw that?"

"Sure, I have a copy."

"Well, that's weird. That video was never released."

Now it was my turn to express skepticism. "Really? It never went into distribution? I don't believe it." We sounded like a couple of talking birds.

"That's what she said. She was pissed off about it, too. She thought it could be her big break, but there was nothing she could do."

"The cassette I saw was edited, packaged, the whole bit. They must have had a lot of money tied up in it. What's the story?"

"I just know what she said. Maybe the venture was undercapitalized, whatever the term is. How'd you get a copy?"

"Someone sent it to her mother."

Danielle barked out a laugh. "You're kidding. That's gross. What kind of jerk would do a thing like that?"

"I don't know yet. I'm hoping to find out. What else can you tell me?"

"No, no. You ask and I'll answer. I can't think of anything off the top of my head."

"Who's Lester?"

"Lester had nothing to do with Lorna."

"But who is he?"

She gave me a look. "What's it to you?"

"You're afraid of him, and I want to know why."

"Get off it. You're wasting your money."

"Maybe I can afford it."

"Oh, right. On what you make? That's bullshit."

"Actually, I don't even know what you're charging."

"Trick rates. Fifty bucks."

"An hour?" I yelped.

"Not an hour. What's the matter with you? Fifty bucks a trick. Nothing about sex takes an *hour,"* she said contemptuously. "Anybody says it's an hour is rippin' you off."

"I take it Lester's your pimp."

"Listen to her. 'Pimp.' Who taught you to talk that way? Lester Dudley—Mr. Dickhead to you—is my personal manager. He's like my professional representative."

"Did he represent Lorna?"

"Of course not. I already told you, she was smart. She declined his services."

"You think he'd have any information about her?"

"Not a chance. Don't even bother. The guy's a real piece of shit."

I thought for a moment, but I'd covered the questions that came readily to mind. "Well. This should do for now. If you think of anything else, will you get in touch?"

"Sure," she said. "As long as you got the money, I got the mouth . . . so to speak."

I picked up my handbag and took out my wallet. I gave her a business card, jotting my home address and telephone number on the back. Ordinarily I don't like to give out that information, but I wanted to make it as easy for her as possible. I reviewed my cash supply. I thought maybe she'd be magnanimous and waive her fees, but she held her hand out, watching carefully as I counted bills into her palm. I had to make up the last dollar with the loose change in the bottom of my bag. Of course, I was short.

"Don't worry about it. You can owe me the dime."

"I'll give you an IOU," I said.

She waved the offer aside. "I trust you." She tucked the money in her jacket pocket. "Men are funny, you know? Big male fantasy about hookers? I see this in all these books written by men. Some guy meets a hooker and she's gorgeous: big knockers, refined, and she's got the hots for him. Him and her end up bonking, and when he's done, she won't take his money. He's so wonderful, she doesn't want to charge him money like she does everyone else. Now that's bullshit for sure. I never knew a hooker who'd do a guy for free. Anyway, hooker sex is for shit. If he thinks that's a gift, then the joke's on him."

8

It was close to one-thirty in the morning when I parked my VW in the little parking lot outside the emergency entrance to St. Terry's Hospital. After my conversation with Danielle, Cheney had dropped me back at my place. I moved in through the squeaking gate and around to the back. I heard Cheney give his horn a short toot, and then he took off. The night sky was still clear, bright with stars, but I could see patchy clouds collecting at the western edge as predicted. An airplane moved across my field of vision, a distant dot of red winking among the pinpricks of white, the sound trailing behind it like a banner advertising flight. The final quarter of the moon had narrowed to the curved silver of a shepherd's crook, a cloud like a wisp of cotton caught in its crescent. I could have sworn I still heard the booming music that had shaken Neptune's Palace. In reality, the club was less than a mile from my apartment, and I suppose it was possible the sound might have carried. It was more likely a stereo or a car radio in much closer range. Against the drumming of the high tide at the ocean half a block away, the faint thump of bass was a muted counterpoint, brooding, silky, and indistinct.

I paused, keys in hand, and leaned my head briefly against the door to my place. I was tired, but curiously disinterested in sleep. I've always been a day person, thoroughly addicted to early rising and morning sunshine in a nine-to-five world. I might work late on occasion, but for the most part I'm home by early evening and sound asleep by eleven. Tonight, yet again, I was nudged by restlessness. Some long suppressed aspect of my personality was being activated, and I could feel myself respond. I wanted to talk to Serena Bonney, the nurse who'd discovered Lorna's body. Somewhere in the accumulating verbal portrait of Lorna Kepler was the key to her death. I went back through the gate and closed it quietly behind me.

The emergency room had an air of abandonment. The sliding glass doors opened with a hush, and I moved into the quiet of the blue-and-gray space. There were lights on in the reception area, but the patient registration windows had been closed for hours. To the left, behind a small partition with its wall-mounted pay telephones, the waiting room was empty, the TV a square of blank gray. I peered to the right, toward the examining rooms. Most were dark, with the surrounding curtains pulled back and secured on overhead tracks. I could smell freshly perked coffee wafting from a little kitchenette at the rear of the facility. A young black woman in a white lab coat came out of a doorway marked "Linens." She was small and pretty. She paused when she spotted me, flashing a smile. "Oh, I'm sorry. I didn't know anyone was here. Can I help you?"

"I'm looking for Serena Bonney. Is she working this shift?"

The woman glanced at her watch. "She should be back shortly. She's on her break. You want to have a seat? The TV's on the blink, but there's lots of reading material."

"Thanks."

For the next fifteen minutes, I read outdated issues of *Family Circle* magazine: articles about children, health and fitness, nutrition, home decorating, and inexpensive home-building projects meant for Dad in his spare time—a wooden bench, a treehouse, a rustic shelf to support Mom's picturesque garden of container herbs. To me, it was like reading about life on an alien planet. All the ads showed such perfect women. Most were thirty years old, white, and had flawless complexions. Their teeth were snowy and even. None of them had wide bottoms or kangaroo pouches that pulled their slacks out of shape. There was no sign of cellulite, spider veins, or breasts drooping down to their waists. These perfect women lived in well-ordered houses with gleaming floors, an inconceivable array of home appliances, oversize fluffy mutts, and no visible men. I guess Dad was relegated to the office between his woodworking projects. Intellectually I understood that these were all highly paid models simply *posing* as housewives for the purpose of selling Kotex, floor covering, and dog food. Their lives were probably as far removed from housewifery as mine was. But what did you do if you actually were a *housewife,* confronted with all these images of perfection on the hoof? From my perspective, I couldn't see any connection at all between my lifestyle (hookers, death, celibacy, handguns, and fast food) and the lifestyle depicted in the magazine, which was probably just as well. What would I do with a fluffy mutt and containers full of dill and marjoram?

"I'm Serena Bonney. Did you want to see me?"

I looked up. The nurse in the doorway was in her early forties, a good-size woman, maybe five feet ten. She wasn't obese by any stretch, but she carried a lot of weight on her frame. The women in her family probably described themselves as "hearty peasant stock."

I set the magazine aside and got to my feet, holding out my hand. "Kinsey Millhone," I said. "Lorna Kepler's mother hired me to look into her death."

"Again?" she remarked as she shook my hand.

"Actually, the case is still open. Can I take a few minutes of your time?"

"It's a funny hour for an investigation."

"I should apologize for that. I wouldn't ordinarily bother you at work, but I've been suffering insomnia for the last couple of nights, and I thought I might as well take advantage of the fact that you're working."

"I don't really know much, but I'll do what I can. Why don't you come on into the back? It's quiet at the moment, but that may not last long."

We moved past two examining rooms and into a small, sparsely furnished office. Like the nurses upstairs, she was dressed in ordinary street clothes: a white cotton blouse, beige gabardine pants, and a matching vest. The crepe-soled shoes marked her as someone who stood for long hours on her feet. Also her wristwatch, like a meat thermometer with a sweeping second hand. Serena paused at the door frame and leaned out into the hall. "I'll be in here if you need me, Joan."

"No problem," came the reply.

Serena left the door ajar, positioning her chair so she could keep an eye on the corridor. "Sorry you had to wait. I was up on the medical floor. My father was readmitted a couple of days ago, and I try to peek in at him every chance I get." She had a wide, unlined face and high cheekbones. Her teeth were straight and square, but slightly discolored, perhaps the result of illness or poor nutrition in her youth. Her eyes were light green, her brows pale.

"Is his illness serious?" I sat down on a chrome chair with a seat padded in blue tweed.

"He had a massive heart attack a year ago and had a pacemaker put in. He's been having problems with it, and they wanted to check it out. He tends to be a bit obstreperous. He's seventy-five, but *very* active. He practically runs the Colgate Water Board, and he hates to miss a meeting. He thrives on adrenaline."

"Your father isn't Clark Esselmann, by any chance?"

"You know him?"

"I know his reputation. I had no idea. He's always raising hell with the developers." He'd been involved in local politics for fifteen years, since he'd sold his real estate company and retired in splendor. From what I'd heard, he had a rough temper and a tongue that could shift from saltiness to eloquence depending on the subject. He was stubborn and outspoken, a respectable board member for half a dozen charities.

She smiled. "That's him," she said. She slid a hand through her hair, which was coppery, a cross between red and dark gold. It looked as though she'd had some kind of body permanent, because the curl seemed too pronounced to be entirely natural. The cut was short, the style uncomplicated. I pictured her running a brush through her hair after her morning shower. Her hands were big and her nails blunt cut but nicely manicured. She spent money on herself, but not in any way that seemed flashy. Suffering illness or injury, I'd have trusted her on sight.

I murmured something innocuous and then changed the focus of the conversation. "What can you tell me about Lorna?"

"I didn't know her well. I should probably say that up front."

"Janice mentioned that you're married to the fellow Lorna worked for at the water treatment plant."

"More or less," she said. "Roger and I have been separated for about eighteen months. I'll tell you, the last few years have been hellish, to say the least. My marriage fell apart, my father had a heart attack, and then Mother died. After that, Daddy's health problems only got worse. Lorna house-sat for me when I needed to get away."

"You met her through your husband?"

"Yes. She worked for Roger for a little over three years, so I'd run into her if I popped in at the plant. I'd see her at the employee picnics in the summer and the annual Christmas party. I thought she was fascinating. Clearly a lot smarter than the job required."

"The two of you got along?"

"We got along fine."

I paused, wondering how to phrase the question that occurred to me. "If it's not too personal, can you tell me about your divorce?"

"My divorce?" she said.

"Who filed? Was it you or your husband?"

She cocked her head. "That's a curious question. What makes you ask?"

"I was wondering if your separation from Roger had anything to do with Lorna."

Serena's laugh was quick and startled. "Oh, good heavens. Not at all," she said. "We'd been married ten years, and we both got bored. He was the one who broached the subject, but he certainly didn't get any grief from me. I understood where he was coming from. He feels he has a dead-end job. He likes what he does, but he's never going to get rich. He's one of those guys whose life hasn't quite come up to his expectations. He pictured himself retired by the age of fifty. Now he's past that, and he still hasn't got a dime. On the other hand, I not only have a career I'm passionate about, but I'll have family money coming to me one of these days. Living with that got to be too much for him. We're still on friendly terms, we're just not intimate, which you're welcome to verify with him."

"I'll take your word for it," I said, though of course I'd check. "What about the house-sitting? How'd Lorna end up doing that?"

"I don't remember exactly. I probably mentioned in passing that I needed someone. Her place was small and remarkably crude. I thought she'd enjoy spending time in a more comfortable setting."

"How often did she sit?"

"Five or six times altogether, I'd guess. She hadn't done it for a while, but Roger thought she was still willing. I could check my calendar at home if it seems relevant."

"At the moment I don't know what's relevant and what's not. Were you satisfied with the job she did?"

"Sure. She was responsible; fed and walked the dog, watered plants, brought in the newspaper and the mail. It saved me the kennel fees, and I liked having someone in the house while I was gone. After Roger and I split, I moved back in to my parents' house. I was interested in a change of scene, and Dad needed some unofficial supervision because of his health. Mother's cancer had already been diagnosed and she was doing chemo. This was an arrangement that suited all of us."

"So you were living at your father's at the time Lorna died?"

"That's right. He's been under doctor's care, but he's what they call a 'noncompliant' patient. I had plans to be out of town, and I didn't want him in the house alone. Dad was adamant. He swore he didn't need help, but I insisted. What's the point of a getaway weekend if I'm worried about him the whole time? As a matter of fact, that's what I was trying to set up when I went to her place and found her. I'd tried calling for days, and there was never any answer. Roger told me she was taking a couple of weeks' accrued vacation, but she was due back any day. I wasn't sure when she'd get in, so I thought I'd stop by and leave her a little note. I parked near the cabin, and I was just getting out of my car when I noticed the smell, not to mention the flies."

"You knew what it was?"

"Well, I didn't know it was her, but I knew it was something dead. The odor's quite distinct."

I shifted the subject slightly. "Everyone I've interviewed so far has talked about how beautiful she was. I wondered if other women regarded her as a threat."

"*I* never did. Of course, I can't speak for anyone else," she said. "Men seemed to find her more appealing than women, but I never saw her flirt. Again, I'm only talking about the occasions when I saw her."

"From what I hear, she liked living on the edge," I said. I introduced the matter without framing a question, interested in what kind of response I might get. Serena held my gaze, but she made no reply. So far she'd tended to editorialize on every question I asked. I ran the query one more round. "Were you aware that she was involved in other activities?"

"I don't understand the question. What kind of activities are you referring to?"

"Of a sexual nature."

"Ah. That. Yes. I assume you're referring to the money she made from the hotel trade. Humping for hire," she said drolly. "I didn't think it was my place to bring that up."

"Was it common knowledge?"

"I don't think Roger knew, but I certainly did."

"How did you find out?"

"I'm not sure. I really can't remember. Indirectly, I think. I ran into her at the Edgewater one night. No, wait a minute. I remember what happened. She came into the ER with a broken nose. She had some explanation, but it didn't make much sense. I've seen assault and battery often enough that I wasn't fooled. I didn't say so to her, but I knew *something* was going on."

"Could it have been a boyfriend? Someone she was living with?"

I could hear voices in the hallway.

She glanced over at the door. "I guess it could have been, but as far as I knew she was never in any kind of steady relationship. Anyway, the story she told seemed suspect. I've forgotten what it was now, but it seemed phony as hell. And it wasn't just the broken nose. It was that in conjunction with some other things."

"Such as?"

"Her wardrobe, her jewelry. She was subtle about it, but I couldn't help noticing."

"When was the incident that brought her to the emergency room?"

"I don't remember exactly. Probably two years ago. Check with Medical Records. They can give you the date."

"You don't know hospitals. I'd have better luck getting access to state secrets," I said.

A baby had begun to cry fretfully in the waiting room.

"Does it make a difference?"

"It might. Suppose the guy who punched her decided to make it permanent."

"Oh. I see your point." Serena's eyes strayed to the open door again as Joan went past.

"But she didn't confide in you when she came in?"

"Not at all. After I saw her at the Edgewater, I put two and two together."

"Seems like a bit of a leap."

"Not if you'd seen her the night I ran into her. Part of it, too, was the guy she was with. Older, very slick. Gold jewelry, gorgeous suit. Clearly a man who had money to burn. I saw them in the bar and later in the boutique where she was trying on clothes. He dropped a bundle that night. Four Escada outfits, and she was modeling a fifth."

"I assume Escada is expensive."

"Dear God." She laughed, patting herself on the chest.

Lights were going on in the examining cubicle across from us. I could hear the murmuring of voices: fussy baby, shrill mom speaking rapid-fire Spanish.

Serena went on. "It happened again within the month, as I remember. Same situation, different guy, same look. It didn't take a rocket scientist to figure it out."

"You think one of these guys knocked her around?"

"I think it's a better explanation than the one she gave. I'm not saying this is always true, but some guys in that age bracket start having trouble with impotency. They pick up high-priced call girls and spread the money around. Champagne and gifts, a gorgeous babe in tow. It looks good on the surface, and everybody thinks what a stud he is. What these men are looking for is a one-up relationship because they can't 'get it up' any other way. He's paying for the service, so if the equipment doesn't work, it's her fault, not his, and he can express his disappointment any way he likes."

"With his fist."

"If you want to look at it from his point of view, why not? He's paid for her. She's his. If he can't perform, he's got her to blame and he can paste her in the chops."

"Some deal. She keeps the cash and the clothes in exchange for the punishment."

"She doesn't always get punished. Some of these guys like to be punished themselves. Beaten, humiliated. They like to have their little fannies spanked for being bad, bad, bad."

"Did Lorna tell you this?"

"No, but I've heard it from a couple of other hookers on the local circuit. I also did some reading on the subject when I was getting my degree. I used to see them come in, and I'd be incensed at the way they were treated, furious because I didn't really understand what was going on. I'd jump to the rescue, trying to save them from the 'bad' guys. For all the good *that* did. In an odd way, I'm a better nurse if I can stay detached."

"And that's what you did with her?"

"Exactly. I felt compassion, but I didn't try to 'fix' her. It was none of my business. And she didn't see it as a problem, at least as far as I knew."

"You seem to spend a lot of time at the Edgewater. Is that where the singles hang out these days?"

"The singles in our age group, yes. I'm sure the kids would find it stuffy beyond belief and the prices astronomical. Frankly, it makes married life look pretty good."

"Do you happen to remember any dates when you saw her? If I check with the hotel, it helps to pin it down."

She thought about that briefly. "Once I was with a bunch of girlfriends. We get together to celebrate birthdays. That time it was mine, so it must have been early in March. We don't always manage to get together on the exact date, but it would have been a Friday or Saturday because that's when we play."

"That was last March?"

"Must have been."

"Was this before the broken nose or afterward?"

"I have no idea."

"Did Lorna know you knew?"

"Well, she saw me that night and maybe twice before that. Since Roger and I had separated, I was out with friends almost every weekend. Lorna and I didn't come right out and discuss her 'career,' but there were veiled references." Serena had used the fingers of both hands to form the quote marks around the word *career.*

"I'm just curious. How do you happen to remember in such detail? Most people can't recall what happened *yesterday.*"

"The police asked me most of this, and it stuck in my mind. Also, I've given it a lot of thought. I don't have a clue why she was murdered, and it bothers me."

"You believe she was murdered?"

"I think it's likely, yes."

"Were you aware that she was involved in pornography?"

Serena frowned slightly. "In what way?"

"She starred in a video. Someone sent the cassette to her parents about a month ago."

"What was it, like a snuff film? S and M?"

"No. It was fairly pedestrian in terms of the story and subject matter, but Mrs. Kepler suspects it may be linked to Lorna's death."

"Do you?"

"I'm not being paid to have opinions at this point. I like to keep my options open."

"I understand," she said. "It's like making a diagnosis. No point in ruling out the obvious."

There was a knock at the door frame and Joan peered in. "Sorry to interrupt, but we've got a baby over here I'd like you to take a look at. I've got a call in to the resident, but I think you should see him."

Serena rose to her feet. "Let me know if there's anything else," she said to me as she moved toward the door.

"I'll do that. And thanks."

I drove back to my place through deserted streets. I was beginning to feel at home in the late night world. The nature of the darkness shifts from hour to hour. Once the bars close down and traffic dissipates, what emerges is the utter stillness of three A.M. The intersections are empty. Traffic lights are bright O's of red and sea-foam green in a dazzling string that you can see for half a mile.

Clouds were pouring in. A dense ground fog, like cotton batting, was laid across the mountains, and the gray hills were pocked with streetlights against the backdrop of rolling mist. Most of the residential windows I saw were dark. Where an occasional light burned, I pictured students churning out last minute papers, the nightmares of the young. Or maybe the lights burned for recent insomniacs like me.

A police car cruised slowly along Cabana Boulevard, the uniformed officer turning to stare at me as I passed. I took a left onto my street and found a parking place. I locked the car. The sky was velvety with clouds now, the stars completely obscured. Darkness hugged the ground, while the sky was tinged with eerie light, like dark gray construction paper smudged with white chalk. Behind me, I heard the low hum of air moving swiftly through the spokes of a bike. I turned in time to see the man on the bicycle passing. From the rear, his taillight and the strips of reflecting tape on his heels made him look like someone juggling three small points of light. The effect was oddly unsettling, a circus act of the spirits performed solely for me.

I went through the gate and let myself into my apartment, flipping on the light. Everything was orderly, just as I'd left it. The quiet was profound. I could feel a little nudge of anxiety, made up of weariness, the late hour, empty rooms around me. I wasn't going to be able to sleep at this point. It was like hunger—once the peak moment passed, the appetite diminished and you could simply do without. Food, sleep . . . what difference did it make? The metabolism shifts into overdrive, calling up energy from some other source. If I'd gone to bed at nine or even ten o'clock, I could have slept through the night. But now my sleep permit had reached its expiration point. Having stayed awake this long, I was consigned to further wakefulness.

My body was both fatigued and fired up. I dropped my handbag and jacket on the chair by the door. I glanced at the answering machine: no messages. Did I have any wine on the premises? No, I did not. I checked the contents of the refrigerator, which showed nothing of culinary interest. My pantry was typically barren: a few stray cans and dried items that, singly or in combination, would never constitute anything remotely edible, unless you favored uncooked lentils with maple syrup. The peanut-butter jar had concentric swirl marks in the bottom, as if the rest of it had drained away. I found a kitchen knife and scraped the sides of the jar, eating the accumulated peanut butter off the blade as I walked around. "This is really pitiful," I said, laughing, but actually I didn't mind a bit.

Idly I flipped on the TV set. Lorna's video was still in the VCR. I touched the remote control, and the tape began to run again. I had no intention of watching any late night sex, but I went through the credits twice. The night before, I'd tried directory assistance in San Francisco, hoping for a telephone number for the production company Cyrenaic Cinema. In the credits, the producer, director, and film editor were all listed by name: Joseph Ayers, Morton Kasselbaum, and Chester Ellis respectively. What the hell, telephone operators are awake all night.

I tried the names in reverse order, bombing out on the first two. When I got to the producer, I picked up a hit. The operator sang, "Thank you for using AT and T," and a recording kicked in. A mechanical voice came on the line and recited Joseph Ayers's number for me twice.

I made a note, then picked up the phone and called directory assistance in San Francisco again, this time checking for a listing in the names of the other players, Russell Turpin and Nancy Dobbs. She wasn't listed, but there were two Turpins with the first initial *R,* one on Haight and one on Greenwich. I wrote down both numbers. At the risk of wasting my time and Janice Kepler's money, a trip north might actually be worth a shot. If the contacts didn't pan out, at least there was hope of eliminating the porno angle as a factor in her daughter's death.

I put a call through to Frankie's Coffee Shop, and Janice answered on the second ring. "Janice. This is Kinsey. I have a question for you."

She said, "Fire away. We're not busy."

I brought her up to date on my conversations with Lieutenant Dolan and Serena Bonney, and then filled her in on the minisurvey I'd done of the pornographic film crew. "I think it might be worthwhile to talk to the producer and the other actor."

"I remember him," she cut in.

"Yeah, well, between Turpin and this film producer, I'm hoping we can satisfy some questions. I'll try to contact both by phone in advance, but it looks like it'd make sense to make a quick trip. If I can set up a few appointments, I thought I'd hit the road."

"You're going to drive?"

"I'd thought to."

"Don't you have a dinky little VW? Why not fly? I would, if I were you."

"I guess I could," I said dubiously. "On a short hop like that, though, the plane fare will be outrageous. I'll have to rent a car up there, too. Motel, meals . . ."

"That sounds okay to me. Just save your receipts and we'll reimburse you when you get back."

"What about Mace? Did you tell him about the tape?"

"Well, I told you I would. He was shocked, of course, and then he got mad as hell. Not with her, but whoever put her up to it."

"What's his feeling about the investigation itself? He didn't seem that thrilled yesterday."

"He told me just what he told you," she said. "If this is what it takes to make me happy, he'll go along with it."

"Great. I'll probably fly up sometime tomorrow afternoon and talk to you as soon as I get back."

"Have a good flight," she said.

9

At 9:00 the next morning, I roused myself just long enough to call Ida Ruth, telling her I'd be in shortly in case anyone was looking for me. As I pulled the covers up, I checked the Plexiglas skylight above my bed. Clear, sunny skies, probably sixty-five degrees outside. To hell with the run. I awarded myself ten more minutes of rest. I next woke at 12:37, feeling as hungover as if I'd drunk myself insensible the night before. The tricky factor with sleep is that aside from the *number* of hours you put in, the body seems to hold you accountable for their position. Snoozing from four A.M. to eleven A.M. doesn't necessarily equate with the same number of hours logged between eleven P.M. and six. I had sketched in a full seven, but my regular metabolic rhythms were now decidedly off and required additional down time to correct themselves.

I called Ida Ruth again and was relieved to discover she was out at lunch. I left a message, indicating I'd been delayed by a meeting with a client. Don't ask why I fib to a woman who doesn't even cut my paycheck. Sometimes I lie just to keep my skills up. I staggered out of bed and into the bathroom, where I brushed my teeth. I felt as if I'd been anesthetized, and I was sure that none of my extremities would function. I propped myself against the wall in the shower, hoping the hydrotherapy would mend my skewed circuits. Once dressed, I found myself eating breakfast at one in the afternoon, wondering if I'd ever get myself back on track again. I put on a pot of coffee and dosed myself with caffeine while I made some phone calls to San Francisco.

I didn't get very far. Instead of Joseph Ayers, I got an answering machine that may or may not have been his. It was one of those carefully worded messages that bypasses confirmation of the party's name or the number called. A mechanical male voice said, "Sorry I wasn't here to take your call, but if you'll leave your name, number, and a brief message, I'll get back to you."

I left my name and office number and then left messages on answering machines for both R. Turpins. One voice was female, the other male. To both Turpins I chattered happily, "I'm not sure if this is the right Turpin or not. I'm looking for Russell. I'm a friend of Lorna Kepler's. She suggested I call if I was ever in San Francisco, and since I'm going to be up there in the next couple of days, I thought I'd say hi. Give me a call when you get this message. I'd love to meet you. She spoke so highly of you. Thanks." Through San Francisco information, I checked out the names of other members of the crew, working my way patiently down the list. Most were disconnects.

As long as I was home, I opened my desk drawer and pulled out a fresh pack of index cards, transcribing the information I'd picked up on the case to date—about four cards' worth. Over the last several years I've developed the habit of using index cards to record the facts uncovered in the course of an investigation. I pin the cards on the bulletin board that hangs above my desk, and in idle moments I arrange and rearrange the data according to no known plan. At some point I realized how different a detail can look when it's seen out of context. Like the pieces in a jigsaw puzzle, the shape of reality seems to shift according to circumstance. What seems strange or unusual can make perfect sense when it's placed in the proper setting. By the same token, what seems unremarkable can suddenly yield up precious secrets when placed against a different backdrop. The system, I confess, usually nets me absolutely nothing, but a payoff comes along just often enough to warrant continuing. Besides, it's restful, it keeps me organized, and it's a visual reminder of the job at hand.

I pinned Lorna's photograph on the board beside the cards. She looked back at me levelly with calm, hazel eyes and that enigmatic smile. Her dark hair was pulled smoothly away from her face. Slim and elegant, she leaned against the wall with her hands in her pockets. I studied her as if she might reveal what she had learned in the last minutes of her life. With the silence of a cat, she returned my gaze. Time to get in touch with Lorna's day self, I thought.

I drove along the two-lane asphalt road, past the low, rolling fields of dry grass, drab green overlaid with gold. Here and there, the live oaks appeared in dark green clumps. The day was darkly overcast, the sky a strange blend of charcoal and sulfur yellow clouds. The swell of mountains in the distance were a hazy blue, sandstone escarpments visible across the face. This section of Santa Teresa County is basically desert, the soil better suited for chaparral and sage scrub than productive crops. The early settlers in the area planted all the trees. The once sear land has now been softened and civilized, but there is still the aura of harsh sunlight on newly cultivated ground. Take away the irrigation systems, the drip hoses, and the sprinklers, and the vegetation would revert to its natural state—ceanothus, coyote brush, manzanita, and rolling grasses that in dry years yield a harvest of flames. If current predictions were correct and we were entering another drought, all the foliage would turn to tinder and the land would be cleared beneath a plow of fire.

Up ahead, on the left, was the Santa Teresa Water Treatment Plant, erected in the 1960s: red tile roof, three white stucco arches, and a few small trees. Beyond the low lines of the building, I caught sight of the maze of railings that surrounded concrete basins. To my right, a sign indicated the presence of the Largo reservoir, though the body of water wasn't visible from the road.

I parked out in front and went up the concrete stairs and through the double glass doors. The reception desk sat to the left of the front entrance, which opened into a big room that apparently doubled as class space. The clerk at the desk must have been Lorna's replacement. She looked young and capable, without a hint of Lorna's beauty. The brass plate on her desk indicated that her name was Melinda Ortiz.

I gave her my business card by way of introduction. "Could I have a few minutes with the plant supervisor?"

"That's his truck behind you. He just arrived."

I turned in time to see a county truck turn into the driveway. Roger Bonney emerged and headed in our direction with the preoccupied air of someone on his way to a meeting, focus already leapfrogging to the encounter to come.

"Can I tell him what this is in regards to?"

I looked back at her. "Lorna Kepler."

"Oh, her. That was awful."

"Did you know her?"

She shook her head. "I've heard people talk about her, but I never met her myself. I've only been here two months. She had this job before the girl I replaced. There might have been one more in between. Mr. Bonney had to go through quite a few after her."

"You're part-time?"

"Afternoons. I got little kids at home, so this is perfect for me. My husband works nights, so he can keep 'em while I'm gone."

Bonney entered the reception area, manila envelope in hand. He had a broad face, very tanned, tousled curly hair that had probably turned gray when he was twenty-five. The combination of lines and creases in his face had an appealing effect. He might have been too handsome in his youth, the kind of man whose looks make me surly and unresponsive. My second husband was beautiful, and that relationship had come to a demoralizing end . . . at least from my perspective. Daniel seemed to think everything was just swell, thanks. I was inclined now to disconnect from certain male types. I like a face marked by the softening processes of maturity. A few sags and bags are reassuring somehow. Bonney caught sight of me and paused politely at Melinda's desk lest he interrupt our conversation.

She showed him my card. "She asked to talk to you. It's about Lorna Kepler."

His gaze leapt to mine. The brown eyes were unexpected. With silver-gray hair and his fair coloring, I'd imagined blue.

"I'll be happy to make an appointment for later if this is not convenient," I said.

He looked at his watch. "I have the annual state health services inspection in about fifteen minutes, but you're welcome to come with me while I walk the plant. Shouldn't take long. I like to satisfy myself everything's in order before they come."

"That'd be great."

I followed him down a short corridor to the left, pausing while he stopped in his office and dropped the envelope on his desk. He wore a pale blue dress shirt, collar unbuttoned, tie askew, stonewashed blue jeans, and heavy work boots. With a hard hat and clipboard, you could place him at a construction site and mistake him for an engineer. He was a little under six feet tall, and he'd picked up the substantial look of a man in his mid-fifties. He wasn't fat by any means, but he was broad across the shoulders and heavy through the chest. My guess was that he controlled his weight now with constant exercise, probably tennis and golf, with an occasional fierce game of racquetball. He didn't have the lean muscle mass of a long-distance runner, and he somehow struck me as the sort who'd prefer competition while he kept himself in shape. I pictured him playing high school football, which in ten more years would inspire his joints to disintegrate.

I followed on his heels as we started off again. "I appreciate your talking to me on such short notice."

"It's no problem," he said. "Ever had a tour of the water treatment plant?"

"I never even knew it was here."

"We like to educate the public."

"In case the rates go up again, I'll bet."

He smiled good-naturedly as we pushed through a heavy door. "You want the spiel or not?"

"Absolutely."

"I was sure you would," he said. "Water from the reservoir across the road comes through the intake structure, passing under the floor of the reception area. You might have been aware of it if you'd known what to listen for. Fish screens and trash racks minimize the entry of foreign material. Water comes down through here. Big channel runs under this part of the building. We're about to shut down for a maintenance inspection in the next few days."

In the area we passed, a series of gauges and meters tracked the progress of the water, which was pouring through the facility with a low-level hum. The floors were concrete, and the pipes, in a tangled grid across the wall, were painted pink, dark green, brown, and blue, with arrows pointing in four directions. A floor panel had been removed, and Bonney pointed downward without a word. I peered into the hole. Down about four feet, I could see black water moving blindly through the channel like a mole. The hair along my arms seemed to crawl in response. There was no way to tell just how deep it was or what might be undulating in its depths. I stepped away from the hole, picturing a long suckered tentacle whipping out to grab my foot and drag me in. I'm nothing if not suggestible. A door closed behind us with a hollow clank, and I was forced to suppress a shriek. Bonney didn't seem to notice.

"When did you last talk to Lorna?" I asked.

"Friday morning, April twentieth," he said. "I remember because I had a golf tournament that weekend, and I was hoping to leave work early and get out to the driving range. She was due in at one, but she phoned and said she was suffering a real bad allergy attack. She was trying to get out of town anyway, you know, to find some relief from the pollen count, so I told her to go ahead and take the day off. There wasn't any point having her come in if she was feeling punk. According to the police, she died the next day."

"So she was supposed to be back at work May seventh?"

"I'd have to check the date. It would have been two weeks from Monday, and they'd found her by then." He reverted back to tour guide mode, talking about construction costs as we entered the next section of the plant. The low hum of rushing water and the smell of chlorine created an altered awareness. The general air of the place was of backwash valves and pressurized tanks on the verge of exploding. It looked as though one good jolt from the San Andreas fault and the whole facility would collapse, spewing forth billions of gallons of water and debris, which would kill both of us in seconds. I edged up closer to him, feigning an interest I didn't quite feel.

When I tuned in again, he was saying, "The water is prechlorinated to kill disease-causing organisms. Then we add coagulants, which cause the fine particles to clump together. Polymers are generally added in the coagulation process to improve the formation of insoluble flocs that can then be filtered out. We have a lab in the back so we can monitor the water quality."

Oh, great. Now I had to worry about disease-causing organisms on the loose in the lab. Drinking water used to be such a simple matter for me. Get a glass, turn the tap on, fill water to the brim, and gulp it down until you burped. I never thought about insoluble floc or coagulants. Barf.

Simultaneous with his explanation of the plant operation, which he must have done a hundred times in the past, I could see him scrutinize every inch of the place in preparation for the upcoming inspection. We clattered down a short flight of concrete steps and through a door to the outside. The day seemed curiously bright after the artificial light inside, and the damp air was perfumed with chemicals. Long walkways ran between blocks of open basins surrounded by metal railings, where still water sat as calm as glass, reflecting gray sky and the underside of the concrete grids.

"These are the flocculation and coagulation basins. The water's kept circulating to create a floc of good size and density for later removal in the sedimentation basins."

I was saying "Mmm"- and "Uhn-hun"-type things.

He talked on, taking the whole process for granted. What I was looking at (trying not to register my profound distaste) were still troughs where water sat with a viscous-looking liquid on its surface, bubble-coated and inky. The sludge was as black as licorice and looked as if it were made up of melted tires just coming to the boil. Perversely, I pictured a plunge into the tarry depths, wondering if you'd flail to the surface with your flesh in tatters from all the chemicals. Steven Spielberg could have a ball with this stuff.

"You're not with the police department?" he asked. He hadn't stopped walking once.

"I was, once upon a time. Temperamentally, I'm better suited to the private sector."

I was trotting at his heels like a kid on a field trip, irretrievably separated from the rest of the class. Out the backside of the plant, there was a wide, shallow reservoir of cracked black sediment, like a thawing pond of crud. Thousands of years from now, anthropologists would dig this up and imagine it was some kind of sacrificial basin.

He asked, "Are you allowed to say who you're working for? Or is that privileged information?"

"Lorna's parents," I said. "Sometimes I prefer not to give out the information, but in this case it's a straightforward matter. No big secret. I had this same conversation with Serena last night."

"My soon-to-be ex? Well, that's an interesting point of departure. Why her? Because she found the body?"

"That's right. I couldn't get to sleep. I knew she worked the night shift at St. Terry's, so I thought I might as well talk to her first. If I'd thought you were up, I'd have knocked on your door as well."

"Enterprising," he remarked.

"I'm getting paid fifty bucks an hour for this. Makes sense to work every chance I get."

"How's it going so far?"

"Right now, I'm at the information-gathering phase, trying to get a feel for what I'm dealing with. I understand Lorna worked for you for what, three years?"

"About that. Originally the job was full-time, but with the budget cuts, we decided we'd try getting by with twenty hours a week. So far it's been fine, not ideal, but doable. Lorna was taking classes over at city college, and the part-time employment really suited her schedule."

By now we'd circled back through the plant on some subterranean level. The entire underground space was dominated by massive pipes. We went up a long flight of stairs and suddenly emerged into a well-lighted corridor not that far from his office. He showed me in and indicated a chair. "Have a seat."

"You have time?"

"Let's cover what we can, and what we don't have time for, we can try another day." He leaned over and pressed the button on his intercom. "Melinda, buzz me if I'm not out there when the inspectors arrive."

I heard a muffled, "Yes, sir."

"Sorry for the interruption. Go ahead," he said.

"No problem. Was Lorna good at the job?"

"I had no complaints. The work itself didn't amount to much. She was largely a receptionist."

"Did you know much about her personal life?"

"Yes and no. Actually, in a facility like ours, where you have less than twenty employees on any given shift, we get to know each other pretty well. We're in operation twenty-four hours a day, seven days a week, so this is family to me. I have to say Lorna was a little bit standoffish. She wasn't rude or cold, but she was definitely reserved. Break time, she always seemed to have her nose in a book. Brought a sack lunch, sometimes sat out in her car to eat. She didn't volunteer a lot of information. She'd answer if you asked, but she wasn't forthcoming."

"People have described her as secretive."

He made a face at the term. "I wouldn't say that. 'Secretive' has a sinister implication to my way of thinking. She was pleasant, but somewhat aloof. The term *restrained* might be apt."

"How would you describe your relationship with her?"

"*My* relationship?"

"Yes, I'm wondering if you ever saw her outside of work."

His laugh seemed embarrassed. "If you mean what I think, I have to say I'm flattered, but she was strictly an employee. She was a good-looking girl, but she was what . . . twenty-four years old?"

"Twenty-five."

"And I'm twice that. Believe me, Lorna had no interest in a man my age."

"Why not? You're nice-looking, and you seem personable."

"I appreciate your vote, but it doesn't mean much to a girl in her position. She was probably looking for marriage and a family, last thing in the world I have any interest in. In her eyes, I'd have been a slightly overweight old turd. Besides, the women I date, I like to have shared interests and intelligent conversation. Lorna was bright, but she never even heard of the Tet offensive, and the only Kennedys she knew about were Caroline and John-John."

"Just a possibility," I remarked. "I broached the same subject with Serena, wondering if Lorna was in any way associated with your divorce."

"Not at all. My marriage to Serena simply ran out of juice. Sometimes I think dissension would have been an improvement. Conflict has some spark to it. What we had was flat."

"Serena says you wanted the divorce."

"Well, that's true," he said, "but I've bent over backward to keep things friendly. It's like I said to my attorney: I feel guilty enough as it is, so let's not make matters worse. I love Serena. She's a hell of a nice gal, and I think the world of her. I'm just not ready to live without passion. I'd have to hope she represented the situation much in the same light."

"Actually, she did," I said, "but I thought it was worth exploring in the context of Lorna's death."

"I understand. Of course, I was sorry as hell when I found out what happened to her. She was honest, she was prompt, and as far as I know, she got along with everyone." I saw him ease a look at his watch under the pretext of adjusting the band.

I stirred on my chair. "I better let you go," I said. "I can see you're distracted."

"I guess I am, now that you mention it. I hope you don't think I'm rude."

"Not at all. I appreciate your time. I have to be out of town in the next couple of days, but I may get back to you, if that's okay."

"Of course. I'm sometimes hard to reach, but you can check with Melinda. We'll be closing down for maintenance and repairs on Saturday, so I'll be here if you need me then."

"I'll keep that in mind. In the meantime, if you think of anything pertinent, could you give me a call?"

"Certainly," he said.

I left another business card. We shook hands across the desk, and then he walked me out. Two inspectors were waiting by Melinda's desk. The guy wore a dress shirt, jeans, and tennis shoes. I noticed the woman inspector was dressed a lot better. Roger greeted them pleasantly, giving me a quick wave as he ushered them down the hall.

I drove to my office. It was midafternoon and faint rays of winter sun were pushing through the overcast. The sky was white, the grass a vivid shade of lime green. February comes to Santa Teresa in a tumble of hot pink geraniums, magenta bougainvillea, and orange nasturtiums. I was accustomed to functioning in the dark by now, and the light seemed harsh, the colors too glaring. Night seemed softer, like a liquid that surrounded everything, cool and soothing. At night, all the foliage was blended by shadow, fused and simplified, where daylight divided, setting objects in sharp contrast, at war with one another.

I let myself in the side entrance and then sat at my desk, shifting papers around, trying to behave as if I had some purpose. I was too tired to socialize and the lack of sleep was re-creating the sensation of being stoned. I felt as if I'd been smoking dope for the last two days. All my energy had seeped away, like sawdust leaking out through a hole in my shoe. At the same time, the infusion of coffee was causing a crackling sound in the center of my brain, like an antenna picking up radio signals from outer space. Any minute now Venusians would send warnings of the forthcoming invasion, and I'd be too out of it to call the police. I laid my head down on my desk and sank into unconsciousness.

An hour and five minutes into the nap to end all naps, the telephone rang. The sound cut through me like a chain saw. I jumped as if goosed. I snatched up the receiver and identified myself, trying to sound as though I were wide awake.

"Miss Millhone? This is Joe Ayers. What can I do for you?"

I couldn't think who the hell he was. "Mr. Ayers, I appreciate the call," I said enthusiastically. "Hang on one second." I put my hand across the mouthpiece. Joe Ayers. Joseph Ayers. Ah. The pornographic film producer. I shifted the phone to the other ear so I could make notes as we chatted. "I understand you were the producer of an art movie in which Lorna Kepler appeared."

"That's correct."

"Can you tell me about her involvement in the project?"

"I'm not sure what you're asking."

"I guess I'm not, either. Someone sent a video to her mother, and she asked me what I could find out. I noticed your name listed as the producer—"

Ayers cut in brusquely. "Miss Millhone, you're going to have to fill me in here. We have nothing to discuss. Lorna Kepler was murdered six months ago."

"It was actually ten months. I'm aware of that. Her parents are hoping to develop additional information." I was sounding pompous even to my own ears, but his irritation was irritating.

"Well, you're not going to develop anything from me," he said. "I wish I could help, but my contact with Lorna was extremely limited. Sorry I can't help you."

I checked my notes in haste, trying to talk fast enough to snag his interest. "What about the other two actors who were in the film with her, Nancy Dobbs and Russell Turpin?"

I could hear him shift with annoyance. "What about them?"

"I'd like to talk to them."

Silence. "I can probably tell you how to get to him," he said finally.

"You have a current address and telephone number?"

"I should have it somewhere." I heard him snapping through the pages of what I guessed was his address book. I tucked the phone in the crook of my neck and uncapped my pen.

"Here we go," he said.

He rattled out the information, which I made a note of. The Haight Street address corresponded with the one I'd picked up from directory assistance. I said, "This is terrific. I appreciate this. What about Miss Dobbs?"

"Can't help you there."

"Look, can you tell me what your schedule is for the next couple of days?"

"What does my schedule have to do with it?"

"I was hoping we could meet."

Through the phone, I could hear his brain cells whirring as he processed the request. "I really don't see the point. I hardly knew Lorna. I might have been in her company four days at best."

"Can you remember when you last saw her?"

"No. I know I never saw her after the shoot, and that'd be a year ago December. That was the one and only time we ever did business together. Matter of fact, that film was never even put in release, so I had no reason to contact her afterward."

"Why wasn't the film released?"

"I don't think that's any of your concern."

"What is it, some kind of secret?"

"It's not secret. It's just none of your business."

"That's too bad. I was hoping you could give us some help."

"Miss Millhone, I don't even really know who you are. You call me up, leave a message on my machine with an area code I don't even recognize. You could be anyone. Why the hell should I help you?"

"Right. You're right. You don't know me from Adam, and there's no way I can compel you to give me information. I'm down in Santa Teresa, an hour away by plane. I don't want anything in particular from you, Mr. Ayers. I'm just doing what I can to try to figure out what happened to Lorna, and I'd appreciate some background. I can't force you to cooperate."

"It's not a question of cooperation. I have nothing to contribute. Truly."

"I probably wouldn't even take an hour of your time."

I could hear him breathing while he took this in. I half expected him to hang up. Instead his tone became wary. "You're not trying to break into the business, are you?"

"The business?" I thought he was referring to the private eye trade.

"Because if you're some kind of bullshit actress, you're wasting your time. I don't care how big your tits are."

"I assure you I'm not. This is strictly legitimate. You can verify my credentials with the Santa Teresa police."

"You couldn't have caught me at a worse time. I just flew back from six weeks in Europe. My wife's having some kind of goddamn shindig I'm supposed to attend tonight. She's shelling out a fortune, and I don't know half the people she's invited. I'm dead on my feet as it is."

"What about tomorrow?"

"That's even worse. I've got business to take care of."

"Tonight then? I can probably be there in a couple of hours."

He was silent, but his annoyance was palpable. "Oh, shit. All right. What the hell," he said. "If you actually fly up, you can give me a call. If I feel up to it, I'll see you. If not, too bad. That's the best I can do, and I'll probably regret it."

"That's great. That's fine. Can I reach you at this same number?"

He sighed, probably counting to ten. I'd irritated him so desperately, we were almost friends. "Here's the number at the house. I might as well give you the address while I'm at it. You sound like you can be very obnoxious if you don't get what you want."

"I'm terrible," I said.

He gave me his home address.

"I'm going to bed," he said. I heard the phone banged down.

I put a call through to my travel agent, Lupe, and asked for reservations on the next flight out. As it happened, everything was booked until nine o'clock. She put me on standby status and told me to get on out to the airport. I went back to my place and flung a few items in a duffel bag. At the last minute, I remembered I hadn't told Ida Ruth where I'd be. I called her at home.

Here's what she said when she heard I was flying to San Francisco: "Well, I hope you're wearing something better than jeans and a turtleneck."

"Ida Ruth, I'm insulted. This is business," I said.

"Uhn-hun. Look down and describe what you have on. On second thought, don't bother. I'm sure you look stunning. You want to give me a number where you can be reached?"

"I don't know where I'll be staying. I'll call when I get there and let you know."

"Leave it on the office machine. I'll be in bed by the time you get to San Francisco," she said. "You be careful."

"Yes, ma'am. I promise."

"Take some vitamins."

"I will. See you when I get back," I said.

I tidied my apartment in case the plane went down, taking out the trash as a parting gesture to the gods. As we all know, the day I neglect this important ritual, the plane will auger in and everyone will think what a slob I was. Besides, I like order on the premises. Coming home from a trip, I like to be greeted with serenity, not sloppiness.

10

When I got to the airport, I left the VW in long-term parking and hiked back to the terminal. Like most public buildings in Santa Teresa, the airport is vaguely Spanish in appearance: one and a half stories of white stucco with a red tile roof, arches, and a curving stairway up the side. Inside the terminal, there are only five departure gates, with a tiny newsstand on the first floor and a modest coffee shop on the second. At the United counter, I picked up my ticket and gave my name to the agent in case a seat opened up on an earlier plane. No such luck. I found a seat nearby, propped my head on my fist, and snoozed like a vagrant until my flight was called. In the time I waited, I could have driven to San Francisco.

The plane was a little putt-putt with fifteen seats, ten of which were occupied. I turned my attention to the glossy airline magazine tucked in the seat pouch in front of me. This was my complimentary copy—it said so right on the front—the term *complimentary* meaning way too boring to spend real money on. While the engines were being revved up with all the high whine of racing mopeds, the flight attendant recited last rites. We couldn't hear a word she was saying, but the way her mouth was moving we got the general idea.

We took off with the aircraft bucking and shuddering, the flight smoothing out abruptly as we reached altitude. The attendant made her way down the aisle with a tray, dispensing clear plastic cups full of orange juice or Coca-Cola and childproof packets of—choose one—pretzels or peanuts. The airlines, extremely cunning at trimming costs these days, have now reduced the serving size of these peanuts to (approximately) one tablespoon per person. I broke each of mine in half, eating one piece at a time to prolong the experience.

As we droned up the coast through the night-blackened sky, communities below us appeared as a series of patchy, disconnected lights. At that altitude the towns looked like isolated colonies on an alien planet with dark stretches between what by day would be mountains. I was disoriented by the landscape. I tried to pick out Santa Maria, Paso Robles, and King City, but I had no clear sense of size or distances. I could see the 101, but the highway looked eerie and unfamiliar at that remove.

We reached San Francisco in a little under an hour and a half. Coming in, I could see the streetlights undulate across the hills, tracing the terrain like a contour map. We touched down at a commuter terminal so remote that a progression of ground agents had to be stationed along the tarmac to point us to civilization. We went into the building, up the back stairs like immigration deportees, and finally emerged into a familiar corridor. I stopped off at a newsstand and bought myself a decent city map, then found the rental car counter, where I filled out all the paperwork. By 11:05 I was on the 101, heading north toward the city.

The night was clear and cold, the lights of Oakland and Alameda visible to my right across the bay. Traffic moved swiftly, and the city began to take shape around me like a neon confection. Half a mile past Market Street, at Golden Gate Avenue, the 101 dwindled down to a surface road. I drove the short half block to Van Ness and turned left, eventually taking another left onto Lombard. Coffee shops and motels of every size and description lined both sides of the four-lane thoroughfare. Not wanting to devote unnecessary energy to the project, I checked into the Del Rey Motel at the first "Vacant" sign. I would only be there one night. All I needed was a room clean enough that I wouldn't be forced to wear shoes at all times. I asked for accommodations away from the traffic noise and was directed to 343 at the back.

The Del Rey was one of those motels where the management assumes you're going to steal everything in sight. All the coat hangers were designed so the hooks couldn't be removed from the hanging rod. There was a notice on the television warning that removal of the cord and any movement of the set would automatically sound an alarm beyond guest control. The clock radio was bolted to the bed table. This was an establishment fully prepared to outfox thieves and scam artists. I put an ear to the wall, wondering who might be lurking in the room next to mine. I could hear snores rattle against the quiet. That was going to be restful later when I tried to sleep myself. I sat down on the edge of the bed and called the office, leaving my telephone number for Ida Ruth. While I was at it, I dialed my own answering machine, using the remote code to check for messages. None. My winsome long-distance message had netted me no response, which meant I'd have to go a-calling at some point.

It was nearly midnight by now, and I could feel energy seeping out through my pores. Since I'd given up my day life to conduct my business by night, I'd noticed it was getting harder to predict the plunges into exhaustion. I longed to fling myself backward on the bed and fall asleep in my clothes. I roused myself before the notion became too seductive. In the bathroom, a printed notice warned of lingering drought conditions and begged motel guests to use as little water as possible. I took a quick (guilt-ridden) shower, then dried myself on a towel as rough as a sidewalk. I set my duffel on the bed and pulled out clean underwear and panty hose. Then I hauled out the wonder garment, my black all-purpose dress. Not that long ago, this article had been a-fester with ditch water, smelling of mildew and assorted swamp creatures. I'd sent it to the cleaners several times in the intervening months, and by now it was as good as new . . . unless you sniffed really, really closely. The fabric represented the apex of recent scientific achievement: lightweight, wrinkle-defying, quick-drying, and indestructible. Several of my acquaintances rued this latter quality, begging me to dump the dress and add another to my wardrobe. I couldn't see the point. With its long sleeves and tucked front, the all-purpose dress was perfect (well, adequate) for all occasions. I'd worn it to weddings, funerals, cocktail parties, and court appearances. I gave it a shake and undid the zipper, managing to step into the dress and my black flats simultaneously. No one would mistake me for a fashion plate, but at least I could pass myself off as a grown-up.

According to the map and the address I'd been given, Joseph Ayers was living in Pacific Heights. I laid the map on the car seat and left on the interior light so I could see where I was going. I took a left on Divisadero and headed toward Sacramento Street. Once in the vicinity, I cruised the area. Even at this hour, the Ayers residence wasn't hard to spot. The house was ablaze with lights, and a steady stream of guests, both arriving and departing, were taking advantage of the "varlet" parking out in front. I turned my car over to one of the young men in black dress pants and white tuxedo shirts. There was a Mercedes ahead of me and a Jaguar pulling up behind.

The front gate was open, and late arrivals were being steered around the side of the house toward the garden in back. Entrance to the party was being monitored by a man in a tuxedo, who viewed my outfit with visible concern. "Good evening. May I see your invitation?"

"I'm not here for the party. I have a personal appointment with Mr. Ayers."

His look said this seemed doubtful; however, he was being paid to smile, and he gave me the minimum wage's worth. "Ring the front doorbell. One of the maids will let you in."

The house was surrounded by a narrow band of yard, generous by San Francisco standards, where houses were usually constructed smack up against each other. A high boxwood hedge had been planted just inside the wrought-iron fence to maximize privacy. I moved up the brick walk. The grass on either side was tender green and recently mowed. The house was a looming three stories of old red brick, aged to the color of ripe watermelon. All of the leaded-glass windows were framed in pale gray stone. The mansard roof was gray slate, and the entire facade was washed with indirect lighting. From the rear, I could hear the alcohol-amplified voices of numerous guests superimposed on the harmonies of a three-piece combo. Occasionally a burst of laughter shot upward like a bottle rocket, exploding softly against the quiet darkness of the neighborhood.

I rang the bell as instructed. A maid in a black uniform opened the door and stepped back to admit me. I gave her my name and told her Mr. Ayers was expecting me. She didn't seem to care one way or the other, and the black all-purpose dress apparently suited her just fine, thanks. She nodded and departed, allowing me a moment to take in my surroundings. The foyer was circular, with a black marble staircase curving up from the right. The ceiling rose a full two stories and was capped with a cascading chandelier of gilt and flashing prisms. One of these days an earthquake would send the weight of it crashing, and the maid would be flattened like a cartoon coyote.

Yet another man in a tuxedo appeared in due course and escorted me toward the back of the house. The floors were black-and-white marble squares, laid out like a gameboard. The ceilings in the rooms we passed were a good twelve feet high, rimmed with plaster garlands and strange imps peering down at us. The walls in the hallway were covered in dark red silk, padded to dampen sound. I was so intent on my survey, I nearly bumped into a door. The butler butled on, ignoring me discreetly when I yelped in surprise.

He ushered me into the library and pulled the double doors together as he left the room. A large Oriental rug spread a soft mauve pattern across the parquet floor. On the left, the room was anchored by a massive antique desk of mahogany and teak, inlaid with brass. The furniture—an oversize sofa and three solidly constructed armchairs—was upholstered in burgundy leather. The room was functional, fully used, not some tidy assemblage designed to impress. I could see file cabinets, a computer setup, a fax machine, a copier, and a four-line telephone. Mahogany shelves on three walls were lined with books, one section devoted to film scripts with titles inked across the visible end.

On the fourth wall, floor-to-ceiling windows overlooked the walled grounds in the rear, where the party was in full swing. The noise level had risen, but the brunt of it was muted by the mullioned panes. I stood at the windows and looked down at the crowd below. Sections of the immense garden had been tented for the occasion, the red canvas glowing with candlelight. Tall propane heaters had been placed along the perimeter to warm the chilly night air. Tiny bulbs had been strung through all the saplings on the property. Every branch was defined by pinpoints of illumination. Tables had been covered in red satin cloths. The centerpieces were arrangements of dark red roses and carnations. Folding chairs were swaddled in clouds of red netting. I could see the caterers were still setting up a cold midnight supper—blood sausage, no doubt.

The invitations must have specified the dress requirements. The men wore black tuxedos, and all the women wore full- or cocktail-length dresses in red or black. The women were slim, and their hair was ornamental, dyed that strange California blond affected by women over fifty. Their faces seemed perfect, though by dint of surgery they all appeared to be much the same age. I suspected that none of these people were the cream of San Francisco society. These folk were the rich milk who had risen as close to the top of the bottle as money and ambition permitted in the course of one generation. My guess was that even as they drank, eyeing the buffet tables, they were trashing the host and hostess.

"If you're hungry, I can have someone bring you something to eat."

I turned. "I'm fine," I said automatically. In truth I was starving, but I knew I'd feel disadvantaged grubbing down food in this man's presence. "Kinsey Millhone," I said as I held out my hand. "Thanks for seeing me tonight."

"Joseph Ayers," he replied. He was probably in his late forties, with the intense air of a gynecologist delivering embarrassing news. He wore glasses with large lenses and heavy tortoise-shell frames. He tended to keep his head down, dark eyes peering up somberly. His handshake was firm, and his flesh felt as slick as if he'd just donned rubber gloves. His forehead was lined, his face elongated, an effect exaggerated by the creases beside his mouth and down the length of his cheeks. His dark hair was beginning to thin on top, but I could see that he'd been vigorously handsome once upon a time. He wore the requisite tuxedo. If he was still exhausted from long hours in the air, he showed no signs of it. He gestured me onto one of the leather chairs, and I took a seat. He sat down behind the desk and placed a finger against his lips, tapping thoughtfully while he studied me. "Actually, you might look good on camera. You have an interesting face."

"No offense, Mr. Ayers, but I've seen one of your films. Faces are the least of it."

He smiled slightly. "You'd be surprised. There was a time when the audience wanted big, voluptuous women—Marilyn Monroe types—almost grotesquely well endowed. Now we're looking for something a little more realistic. Not that I'm trying to talk you into anything."

"This is good," I said.

"I have a film school background," he said as if I'd pressed for an explanation. "Like George Lucas and Oliver Stone, those guys. Not that I put myself in the same league with them. I'm an academic at heart. That's the point I was trying to make."

"Do they know what you do?"

He cocked his head toward the window. "I've always said I was in the business, which is true—or at least, it was. I sold my company a year ago to an international conglomerate. That's what I've been doing in Europe these past few weeks, tying up loose ends."

"You must have been quite successful."

"More so than the average Hollywood producer. My overhead was low, and I never had to tolerate union bosses or studio heads. If I wanted to do a project, I did it, just like that." He snapped his fingers to illustrate. "Every film I've done has been an instant hit, which is more than most Hollywood producers can say."

"What about Lorna? How'd you meet her?"

"I was down in Santa Teresa Memorial Day weekend, this would have been a couple of years ago. I spotted her in a hotel bar and asked if she was interested in an acting career. She laughed in my face. I gave her my card and a couple of my videocassettes. She called me some months later and expressed an interest. I set up the shoot. She flew up to San Francisco and did two and a half days' work, for which she was paid twenty-five hundred dollars. That's the extent of it."

"I'm still puzzled by the fact that the film never went into distribution."

"Let's just say I wasn't happy with the finished product. The film looked cheap, and the camera work was lousy. The company that bought me out ended up taking my entire library, but that one wasn't included in the deal."

"Did you know Lorna was working as a hooker on the side?"

"No, but it doesn't surprise me. Do you know what they call those people? Sex workers. A sex worker might do all manner of things: massage, exotic dance, out-call, Lesbian videos, hard-core magazines. They're like migrant pickers on the circuit. They go where the work is, sometimes city to city. Not that I'm saying she'd done related work. I'm filling you in on the big picture."

I watched his face, marveling at the matter-of-fact tone he was using. "What about you? What was your relationship with her?"

"I was in London when she was killed. I left on the twentieth."

I disregarded the nonsequitur, though it interested me. When we'd talked on the phone, he'd been vague about how long ago her death had occurred. Maybe he'd done an internal audit in anticipation of my arrival.

He opened a drawer and took out a slip of paper. "I checked the payroll roster for the film she did. These are the names and addresses of a couple of crew members I've been in touch with since. I can't guarantee they're still here in San Francisco, but it's a place to start."

I took the slip and glanced at it, recognizing the names from the list I'd checked. Both San Francisco numbers were now disconnects. "Thanks. I appreciate this." Worthless as it is, I thought.

He got up from the desk. "Now if you'll forgive me, I have to put in a quick appearance before I go to bed. Are you sure you wouldn't like a drink?"

"Thanks, but I'd better not. I have ground to cover yet, and I'm not in town that long."

"I'll walk you out," he said courteously.

I followed him down the wide white marble stairs, across the foyer, and through a vast empty room with a domed ceiling and pale, glossy, hardwood floors. At the far end, there was a small stage. "What will you do now that your business is sold?"

"This is the ballroom," he said, catching the curiosity in my look. "My wife had it refurbished. She gives charity balls for diseases only rich people get. To answer your question, I won't have to do anything."

"Lucky you."

"Not luck. This was my intention from the onset. I'm a goal-oriented person. I'd advise you to do likewise."

"Absolutely," I said.

In the foyer, we shook hands. I noticed he had the door closed before I reached the front walk. I retrieved my car, tipping the parking valet a buck. From his look of amazement, everybody else must have tipped him five.

I consulted my map. Russell Turpin's Haight Street address wasn't far. I headed south on Masonic and crossed the Panhandle section of Golden Gate Park. Haight was two blocks up, and the address I needed was only four blocks down.

The sidewalks were crowded with pedestrians. Remnants of the past glories of Haight-Ashbury were still in evidence: vintage dress shops and bookstores, funky-looking restaurants, a storefront clinic. The street was well lighted, and there was still quite a bit of traffic. The street people were decked out like the flower children of old, still wearing bell-bottoms, nose rings, dreadlocks, torn blue jeans, leather, face paints, multiple earrings, backpacks, and knee-high boots. Music tumbled out of bars. In half the doorways, kids loitered, looking stoned, though perhaps on drugs more exotic than grass or 'ludes.

I circled, driving an eight-block track—two down, two over, two up, two back—trying to find a place to tuck my car. San Francisco seems ill equipped to accommodate the number of vehicles within the city limits. Parked cars are squeezed into every available linear inch of curb, angled into hillsides, lined up on sidewalks, wedged against the buildings. Front bumpers are nosed in too close to fire hydrants. Back bumpers hang out into red-painted zones. Garage space is at a premium, and every driveway bristles with signs warding off the poachers.

By the time I found parking, it was nearly 1:00 A.M. I tucked my rental around the corner on Baker Street, whipping into a place as another vehicle pulled out. I fumbled in the bottom of my handbag until I found my penlight. I locked my car and hiked up the hill the half block to Haight. All of the buildings were close-packed, pastel, four and five stories tall. An occasional frail tree contributed a grace note of green. Many of the oversize windows were still lighted. From the street I could see, in a diminishing series of acute angles, fireplace mantels, bold, abstract paintings, white walls, bookshelves, hanging plants, and crown molding.

The address I had turned out to be a "modern" fourplex of shaggy brown shingles sandwiched between two Victorian frame houses. The streetlight was burned out, and I was left to surmise that one was painted dull red, the other an indigo blue with (perhaps) white trim. In the dark, both appeared to be shades of muddy gray. I talked to a painter once who worked on movie sets. For a film shot in black and white, he said the crew used brown paint in eleven different shades. My current surroundings had the same feel, an environment drained of color, reduced to tones of chestnut and dun. The gradations were infinite but visible only to night souls.

Turpin apparently occupied a second-floor apartment, and I was gratified to note that the hand-lettered card tucked in the slot actually specified "Russell" by name, along with a housemate named

Cherie Stanislaus. I peered through the glass door at a handsomely papered foyer with an apartment door on either side. At the rear, a stairway angled left and out of sight, probably doubling back on itself to an identical hallway above. I moved out to the street and looked up at the second-floor windows. The front rooms on both sides of the building were lighted, which suggested that the occupants were still awake.

As I moved up the stairs to the entrance, I could hear the tapping of high heels approaching from behind me. I paused, looking back. The blonde coming up the stairs wore makeup so pale, the effect was ghostly. Her eyes were elaborately done up with thick false eyelashes, two shades of eye shadow, and a black pencil line on both her upper and lower lids. Her forehead was high, and her hair was teased upward at the crown, held back with a gaudy rhinestone clip. The rest of her hair was long and straight, splitting at the shoulder so that half extended down her back. A cluster of long curls tumbled over her breasts. Her long dangle earrings were shaped like elongated question marks. She wore a dark leotard on top and a slinky black skirt that was split up one side. Her hips were narrow, her stomach flat. She took out a ring of keys and gave me a long, cool look as she unlocked the foyer door. "Looking for someone?"

"Russell Turpin."

"Well, you've come to the right place." Her smile was self-contained, not unfriendly, but less than warm I thought. "He's not here, but you can come up and wait if you want. I'm his roommate."

"Thanks. You're Cherie?"

"That's right. Who are you, pray tell?"

"Kinsey Millhone," I said. "I left a message on your machine. . . ."

"I remember that. You're Lorna's friend," she said. She pushed the door open, and I followed her in. She paused, making sure the door had latched shut again before she headed up the stairs. I trailed behind. Having lied on the phone, I now had to decide whether to play this straight.

"Actually, Lorna and I never met," I said. "I'm a private investigator looking into her death. You knew she'd been killed?"

"Yes, of course we did. I'm happy to hear you mention it. Russell wasn't looking forward to delivering the bad news about Lorna's death." Her stockings were black mesh, and her three-inch stiletto heels forced her calves into high relief. When we reached the second-floor landing, she unlocked the door to apartment C. She stepped out of her shoes with a little grimace of relief, then padded through the living room in her stocking feet. I thought she'd turn on a table lamp, but apparently she preferred the gloom. "Make yourself comfortable," she said.

"You have any idea what time he'll be home?"

"Any time, I'd imagine. He doesn't like staying out too late." She turned on a light in the kitchen, which was visible through bifold shutters resting on the countertop. She pushed the shutters open. Through the gap, I watched her take out two ice-cube trays, which she cracked and emptied into an acrylic ice bucket. "I'm having a drink. If you want one, speak up. I hate playing hostess, but I'm good for one round. I have a bottle of Chardonnay open, if you're interested. You look like a white wine kind of girl."

"I'd love some. You need help?"

"Don't we all?" she remarked. "You have offices in the city?"

"I'm from Santa Teresa."

She tilted her head, peering through the pass-through at me. "Why would you come all the way up to see Russell? He's not a suspect, I hope."

"Are you his girlfriend?" I thought it was time I posed the questions instead of her.

"I wouldn't say that. We're fond of each other, but we're not exactly an 'item.' He prefers to be thought of as footloose and fancy free. One of those types."

She plunked several ice cubes in a tall glass and splashed Scotch halfway up the side. She squirted in seltzer water, using one of those devices I'd seen in old thirties movies. She took a sip, shuddering slightly, and then set the glass aside while she found a wineglass in the cupboard. She held it up to the light and decided it wasn't clean enough. She rinsed and dried it. She took the Chardonnay out of the refrigerator and filled my glass, then put the bottle in a cooler and left it on the counter. I moved over to the pass-through and took the wineglass she handed me.

"I don't know if you're aware of this, but Russell's very screwed up," she said.

"Really. I've never met him."

"You can take my word for it. You want to know why? Because he's hung like a mule."

I said, "Ah." Having seen him in action, I could attest to that.

Cherie smiled. "I like the 'ah.' It's diplomatic. Come on back to my room and we can talk while I change. If I don't get out of this girdle, I'm going to kill myself very soon."

11

Cherie's bedroom furniture consisted of a fifties "sweet" of blond wood with curving lines. She sat down at a dressing table with a big round mirror in the center and two deep drawers on either side. She turned on a dressing table lamp, leaving the rest of the room shrouded in shadows. She had twin beds with blond-wood headboards, a blond bed table, an old forty-five record player with a fat black spindle, and a black canvas-and-wrought-iron butterfly chair covered with discarded clothing. My only choice for seating was one of the twin beds. I elected to lean against the door frame instead.

Cherie wriggled out of her girdle and panty hose and tossed them on the floor, then turned to study herself in the mirror. She leaned forward, checking the lines near her eyes with a critical gaze. She shook her head in disgust. "Isn't aging the pits? Sometimes I think I should just shoot myself and get it over with."

While I watched, she spread out a clean white towel and took out cold cream, a skin toner, cotton balls, and Q-tips, apparently in preparation for removing her makeup. I've seen dental hygienists who weren't as meticulous in assembling their instruments.

"Did you know Lorna?" I asked.

"I met her. I didn't 'know' her."

"What'd you think of her?"

"I was envious, of course. She was what they call 'a natural beauty.' All so effortless. It's enough to make you sick." Her eyes met mine in the mirror. "You don't wear a lot of makeup, so you probably can't relate to this, but I spend *hours* on myself, and to what end, I ask? Fifteen minutes on the street and it all evaporates. My lipstick's eaten off. My eye shadow ends up in this crease . . . look at this. My eyeliner gets transferred to my upper lid. Every time I blow my nose, my foundation comes off on the tissue like paint. Lorna was just the opposite. She never had to do anything at all." She peeled off a false eyelash and placed it in a small box, where it lay like a wink. She peeled off the other lash and placed it beside the first. Now it looked like two eyes closed in sleep. "What I wouldn't have given to have skin like hers," she said. "Oh, well. What's a poor girl to do?" She put a hand to her forehead and lifted off her hair. Under the wig, she wore what looked like a rubber bathing cap. She dropped her voice to its natural baritone, addressing my reflection. "Well! Here's Russell now. Nice to meet you," he said. Like a disappearing act, Cherie vanished, leaving a slightly gawky-looking man in her place. He turned and struck a pose. "Be honest. Which do you prefer?"

I smiled. "I like Cherie."

"So do I," he said. He turned and looked at himself again, squinting closely. "I can't tell you how obnoxious it is waking up every morning to a beard. And a penis? My gawd. Picture *that* in your lacy little underpants. Like a big old ugly worm. Scares me to death." He began to put cold cream on his face, wiping off foundation in swipes.

I couldn't take my eyes off him. The illusion had been perfect. "Do you do this every day? Dress up in women's clothes?"

"Most days. After work. From nine to five, I'm Russell: tie, sport coat, button-down collar, the whole bit. I don't wear wingtips, but the moral and spiritual equivalent."

"What sort of work do you do?"

"I'm the assistant manager at the local Circuit City, selling stereo systems. Nights, I can relax and do anything I want."

"You don't make a living from the acting?"

"Oh. You saw the film," he said. "I hardly made a dime, and it never went anywhere, which I must say was a relief. Think of the irony of getting famous as Russell, when I'm really Cherie at heart."

"I just talked to Joe Ayers at his place. He says he sold his company."

"Trying to turn respectable, I'd imagine." He raised his eyebrows, smiling slightly. His expression suggested there was no real chance of *that.* Foundation gone, he took a cotton ball and soaked it with skin toner. He began to wipe off the cold cream and any remaining traces of makeup.

"How many films did you make for him?"

"Just the one."

"Were you disappointed it was never released?"

"I was at the time. I've realized since then that I don't care to capitalize on my 'equipment.' I despise being male. I really hate all the macho posturing and bullshit, all the *effort* it takes. It's much more fun being female. Sometimes I'm tempted to do away with 'it,' but I can't bear to have myself surgically altered, as endowed as I am. Maybe an organ donor program would be interested," he said. He waved a hand airily. "But enough of my tacky problems. What else can I tell you about Lorna?"

"I'm not sure. I gather you really didn't know her that well."

"That depends on your frame of reference. We spent two days together while the film was being shot. We had an instant rapport and laughed our tiny asses off. She was *such* a kick. Kinky and fearless, with a wicked sense of humor. We were soul sisters. I mean that. I was heartbroken when I heard that she had *died,* of all things."

"That was the only time you saw her? During the filming?"

"No, I ran into her maybe two months later, up here shopping with that piggy-looking sister."

"Which one? She has two."

"Oh, really. I can't remember the name. Something odd, as I recall. She looked like an imitation Lorna: same face, but all porked out. Anyway, I saw them on the street down around Union Square, and we stopped to chat about nothing in particular. She looked spectacular as ever. That's the last I saw of her."

"What about the other actress, Nancy Dobbs? Was she a friend of Lorna's?"

"Oh, gawd. Wasn't she the worst? Talk about wooden."

"She was pretty bad," I admitted. "Has she done other films for Ayers?"

"I doubt it. In fact, I'm sure not. I think she just did that one as a lark. Someone else had been hired and opted out at the last minute. Lorna had *her* pegged. Nancy was terribly ambitious, without the talent or the body to get very far. She's one of those women who'd try to screw her way to the top, only no one would have her, so how far could she get? What a dog." Russell laughed. "Actually, she'd have screwed a dog if she'd thought it would help."

"How'd she get along with Lorna?"

"As far as I know, they never had any kind of *snit,* but privately each felt *in*finitely superior to the other. I know because they both took to confiding in me between takes."

"Is she still in the city? I'd like to talk to her."

Russell looked at me with surprise. "You didn't see her tonight? I thought you must have talked to her at Ayers's little soiree."

"What would she be doing there?"

"She's married to him. That's the point, isn't it? All during the shoot, she really flung herself at him. Next thing we heard . . . wahlah. She was Mrs. Joseph Ayers, noted socialite. It's probably why he dumped the porno flick. Imagine *that* getting out. He calls her 'Duchess,' by the way. Isn't that pretentious?"

"Was there ever a suggestion that Joe Ayers's relationship with Lorna was other than professional?"

"He was never involved with her sexually, if that's what you mean. It's really a bit of a cliché to imagine these guys are out 'sampling the merchandise.' Believe me, his only interest was in making a buck."

"Lorna's mother seems to think her death was related to the film somehow."

"Possible, I suppose, but why would anybody kill her for that? She might have been a star if she'd lived. As for those of us who worked on it, trust me, we got along. We were all so grateful for the opportunity, we made a point of it," he said. "How in the world did her mother find out?"

"Somebody sent her the tape."

Russell stared at my reflection in the mirror. "As an expression of condolences, that's in poor taste," he said. "You'd have to wonder at the motive."

"Ain't that the truth."

I went back to the motel, feeling wide awake. By two in the morning Santa Teresa has shut down. In San Francisco all the bars had closed, but numerous businesses were still open: gas stations, bookstores, fitness gyms, video rentals, coffee shops, even clothing stores. I changed out of my flats and the all-purpose dress, stripping off my panty hose with the same relief Cherie had expressed. Once in my jeans and turtleneck, I felt like I was back in my own skin again. I found an all-night diner two doors away from the Del Rey and ate a lavish breakfast. I returned to my room and put the chain on the track. I plunked off my Reeboks, propped all the pillows at my back, and checked Lorna's file again, leafing through the crime scene sketches and the accompanying pictures.

The photographer had shot the outside of the house, front yard and back, with views looking north, south, east, and west. There were shots of both the front and back porches, wood railings, windows. The front door had been closed, but unlocked, with no signs of forced entry. Within the cabin itself, there was no weapon visible and no evidence of a struggle. I could see colored smudges where the fingerprint technicians had been at work with their various powders. According to the report, elimination fingerprints and palm prints had been taken, and most latents on the premises had been accounted for. Many were Lorna's. Some were from family members, the landlord, her friend Danielle, a couple of acquaintances who'd been interviewed by homicide investigators. Many surfaces had been wiped clean.

The photographs of Lorna began in long shot, establishing her position relative to the front door. There were intermediate-range photos, close-ups with a six-inch ruler in evidence to indicate scale. The log showed an orderly progression through the area. I was frustrated by the flat, two-dimensional images. I wanted to crawl into the frame, examine all the items on the tabletops, open up the drawers, and pick through the contents. I found myself squinting, moving pictures closer to my face and then back again, as if the subject matter might suddenly leap into sharper focus. I would stare at the body, scanning the background, taking in items through my peripheral vision.

The cabin, when I'd seen it, had been stripped of all the furniture. Only the bare bones of Lorna's living space were left intact: empty cabinets and bathroom, plumbing, and electrical fixtures. It was good to see the pictures, to correct my mental process. In memory, I had already begun to distort the room sizes and relative distances. I went through all the pictures a second time and then a third. In the ten months since Lorna's death, the crime scene had been dismantled, and this was all that remained. If murder were ever proved and a suspect charged, the entire case could easily rest on the contents of this envelope. And what were the chances? What could I possibly hope to accomplish this late in the game? Basically, in my investigation, I was mimicking the spiral method of a crime scene search: starting at the center, moving outward and around in ever-widening circles. The problem was that I had no direction and no hard line to take. I didn't even have a theory about why she had died. I felt as though I were fishing, fly casting in the hopes that I'd somehow snag myself a killer. All *that* wily devil had to do was lie low, looking up at my lure from the bottom of the cove.

I sorted through the file while I let my mind wander. Aside from the random or the serial killer, the perpetrator of a homicide has to have a *reason,* some concrete motive for wanting the victim dead. In the case of Lorna Kepler, I was still uncertain what the reason was. Financial gain was a possibility. She'd had assets in her estate. I made a note to myself to check with Janice on that score. Given the assumption that Lorna had no living issue, Janice and Mace would be her legal heirs if she died intestate. It was hard to picture either one of them guilty of murder. For one thing, if it were Janice, she'd have to be a fool to turn around and bring me into it. Mace was a question mark. He certainly hadn't conformed to my notion of a grieving parent. Her sisters were another possibility, though neither struck me as sufficiently smart or sufficiently energetic.

I picked up the phone and dialed Frankie's Coffee Shop. This time Janice answered. I could hear jukebox music in the background, but not much else.

"Hi, Janice. This is Kinsey, up in San Francisco."

"Well, Kinsey. How are you? I'm always surprised to hear from you at such an hour. Did you find the fellow she was working for?"

"I talked to him this evening, and I also tracked down one of the other actors in the film. I haven't made up my mind about either one of them. In the meantime, something else has come up. I'm wondering if I could take a look at Lorna's financial records."

"I suppose so. Can you say why, or is that classified?"

"Nothing's classified between us. You're paying for my services. I'm trying to pin down a motive. Money's an obvious possibility."

"I guess that's true, but it's hard to see how it could apply in this case. None of us had any idea she had money until after she died and we went through her files. I'm still in shock. It was unbelievable, given *my* perception. I was forever slipping her a twenty just to make sure she'd eat right. And there she was with all those stocks and bonds and savings accounts. She must have had six. You'd think with that kind of money, she'd have lived a little better."

I wanted to tell her the money was part of Lorna's pension fund, but it seemed unkind somehow since she hadn't lived long enough to use it. "Did she have a will?"

"Well, yes. Just one sheet of paper that she'd written out herself. She left everything to Mace and me."

"I'd like to see that, if you don't object."

"You can see anything you want. When I get home from work, I'll find the box of Lorna's personal effects and leave it on Berlyn's desk. You can stop by when you get back and pick it up from her."

"I'd appreciate that. I want to talk to the two of them, in any event."

"Oh, shoot, and that reminds me. Have you talked to that woman Lorna used to house-sit for?"

"Once."

"Well, I wonder if you'd do me a favor. Last time I went through Lorna's things, I came across a set of house keys I'm sure belong to her. I've been trying to return them and haven't had a minute to take care of it."

"You want me to drop them off?"

"If you would. I feel like I should do it myself, but I just don't have time. And I'd appreciate it if you'd make sure I get everything back when you finish going through it. There's some dividend and interest statements I'm going to need to pass along to the probate attorney when he files her income taxes."

"Has the estate been settled yet?"

"It's still in the works. What I'm giving you is copies, but I'd still like to have them back."

"No problem. I can probably drop it all off to you day after tomorrow."

"That'd be fine." I could hear the swell of chatter in the background. She said, "Uh-oh. I got to go."

"See you tomorrow," I said, and hung up.

I looked around at the room, which was serviceable but glum. The mattress was as dense as mud, while the pillows were foam rubber and threatened serious neck damage. I'd made reservations for a noon flight out of San Francisco. It was now almost three A.M. I wasn't ready to sleep. If I junked my return ticket, I could drive the rental car back and drop it at the airport in Santa Teresa, where my VW was sitting in the long-term parking lot. The trip would take roughly six hours, and if I could manage to avoid dozing off at the wheel, I'd be back around nine.

I suddenly found myself energized by the notion of heading home. I swung my feet over the side of the bed, found my Reeboks, pulled them on, and left the laces dangling. I went into the bathroom, gathered up my toiletries, and shoved everything in the duffel. It took me longer to wake the night manager than it took me to check out. By 3:22 I was heading south on the 101.

There's nothing as hypnotic as a highway at night. Visual stimulation is reduced to the lines on the road, asphalt zipping past in a series of streaks. Any shrubbery at the side of the road is diminished to a blur. All the trailer trucks were in transit, semis carrying goods that ranged from new cars to furniture, from flammable liquids to flattened cardboard boxes. Off to the side, I caught sight of townlet after townlet encased in darkness, illuminated only by rows of street lamps. An occasional billboard provided visual distraction. At long intervals a truck stop appeared, like an island of light.

I had to stop twice for coffee. Having opted to head back, I now found the drive narcotic and was struggling to stay awake. The radio in the rental car was good company. I flipped from station to station, listening to a talk show host, classical and country music, and countless newscasts. Once upon a time I'd smoked cigarettes, and I could still remember the habit as a way of marking time on car trips. Now I'd rather drive off a bridge than light up. Another hour passed. It was nearly dawn and the sky was turning white, the trees along the road beginning to reclaim their color, now charcoal green and dark chartreuse. Dimly I was aware of the sun coming up like a beachball into my line of vision, the colors of the sky shading up from dark gray to mauve to peach to bright yellow. I had to flip down the visor to keep the glare out of my eyes.

By 9:14 I'd turned in the rental and picked up my VW and I was pulling into a parking place in front of my apartment. My eyes felt itchy and I ached from a weariness that felt like the flu, but at least I was home. I let myself in, checked to see that there were no messages, brushed my teeth, took my shoes off, and fell into bed.

For once, sleep descended like a blow to the head, and I went down, down, down.

I woke at 5:00 P.M. The eight hours should have been adequate, but as starved as I was for sleep, I felt I was dragging myself out of quicksand. I was still struggling to adjust to the inverted pattern my life had taken. In bed at dawn, up again in the afternoon. I was eating breakfast at lunchtime, dinner in the dead of night, though often that meal turned out to be cold cereal or scrambled eggs and toast, which meant I ate breakfast twice. I was vaguely aware of a psychological shift, a change in my perception now that I'd substituted night for day. Like a form of jet lag, my internal clock was no longer synchronized with the rest of the world's. My usual sense of myself was breaking down, and I wondered if a hidden personality might suddenly emerge as if wakened from a long sleep. My day life was calling, and I was curiously reluctant to answer.

I rolled out of bed, dumped my dirty clothes, took a shower, and got dressed. I stopped at a minimart where I grabbed a carton of yogurt and an apple, eating in my car as I headed over to the Keplers'. I could have used a couple more hours of sleep, but I was hoping to talk to Lorna's sisters before their mother woke up. Like me, her days and nights were turned around, and I felt a strange bond with her.

Mace's plumbing truck wasn't parked in the drive this time. I left my VW on the berm, by the white split-rail fence, and moved up the walk to the porch, where I knocked. Trinny answered the door, though it took her a while. "Oh, hi. Mom worked a double shift and she's not up yet."

"I figured as much. She said she'd tuck some information in a box and leave it with Berlyn."

"She's not here right now. She's running some errands. You want to come in and wait?"

"Thanks." I followed her through the small, densely furnished living room to the dining area, which was located at one end of the kitchen. Sunset wasn't far off, and the kitchen windows were getting dark, lending the lighted kitchen an artificial air of warmth. An ironing board had been set up, and the scent of freshly pressed cotton made me long for summer. "Mind if I take a look at Berlyn's desk? If the box is close to the surface, I can go ahead and get it."

Trinny took up the iron again. "It's right in there." She pointed toward the door that led into the den.

One corner of the room apparently doubled as the offices for Kepler Plumbing. I remembered seeing both the desk and the filing cabinet the night I talked to Mace. A banker's box with my name scrawled on top was sitting right in plain sight. For once I resisted any further urge to snoop. I lifted the lid to check the contents. A fragrance wafted up, some delicate combination of citrus and spice. I closed my eyes, wondering if this was Lorna's scent. I'd experienced it before—the very air saturated with someone's characteristic smell. With men it's after-shave, leather, or sweat. With women it's cologne. The house keys Janice had mentioned were sitting on top of a neatly packed collection of file folders, all in alphabetical order: bank statements, past income taxes, dividends, stocks, assorted annual reports. Tucked into one end of the box was a folded cashmere scarf. I pressed the length of it against my face, smelling cut grass, cinnamon, lemon, and clove. I hauled the box back to the kitchen and set it by one of the kitchen chairs, the scarf laid on top. "Is this Lorna's? It was in the box with her stuff."

Trinny shrugged. "I guess."

I folded it twice and tucked it back where it had been. "Mind if I sit down? I was hoping I'd have a chance to talk to you."

"Fine," she said. She slid the lever on the iron to the off position.

"I hope I'm not interrupting dinner preparations."

"I got a casserole in the oven. All I have to do is heat it and make a salad real quick."

I took a seat, wondering how to coax some information out of her. I wasn't even sure what I wanted to know, but I considered it a bonus to be alone with her. She was wearing the same cutoffs I'd seen her in before. Her legs looked solid, her bare feet tucked into rubber flip-flops. Her T-shirt this time must have been an XXL, the front emblazoned with a painted design. She moved from the ironing board to the kitchen table, where she sat down across from me and began squeezing a tube of paint in a Jackson Pollock–type design on the front of a new T-shirt. Dots and squiggles. Hanging from a knob on one of the kitchen cabinets was a completed work, its lines of paint puffed out in three dimensions. She caught my gaze. "This's puff paint," she said. "You put it on and let it dry, and when you iron it on the wrong side, it puffs out like that."

"That's cute," I said. I got up and moved closer to the kitchen cabinet, taking a moment to inspect the finished product. Looked dreadful to me, but what do I know? "You sell these?"

"Well, not yet, but I'm hoping. I made this one I got on, and whenever I go out everybody's like 'Oh, wow, cool T-shirt.' So I thought since I wasn't working I could set up my own business."

My oh my. She and her sister Lorna, both driven by the entrepreneurial spirit. "How long have you been doing this?"

"Just today."

I took my seat at the kitchen table again, watching Trinny work. I began to cast out my line. Surely there was something I could wheedle out of her. To my right was a stack of travel brochures, touting Alaskan cruises, ski holidays, and package tours to Canada and the Caribbean. I picked up a pamphlet and began to scan the copy: "The world's last unspoiled paradise . . . stunning white beaches . . . deep azure lagoons . . ."

Trinny saw what I was doing. "Those are Berlyn's."

"Where's she going?"

"She doesn't know yet. She says Alaska looks good."

"Are you going, too?"

She made a disappointed face. "I don't have the money."

"Too bad. It looks like fun," I said. "She doesn't mind traveling alone?"

"Nuh-uhn. She likes it. Not all the time, but if she has to, she says. She did the one trip already, in the fall."

"Really. Where'd she go then?"

"Acapulco. She loved it. She says she'll take me if she goes back."

"That's neat. I was in Viento Negro last summer, but that's as far south as I've been."

"I haven't even been that far. Berlyn's always liked to travel. I don't have the same bug. I mean, I like it and all, but there's stuff I'd rather do."

"Like what?"

"I don't know. Buy clothes and stuff."

I tried another tack. "Lorna's death must have been hard. Are you doing okay with that?"

"I guess so. It's been hard on them. I mean, Mom and Daddy used to be a lot closer. Once Lorna died, seems like everything changed. And now it's like Mom's the only one caught up in it. Lorna's all she talks about. Berlyn gets her feelings hurt. It really pisses her off. It's like, what about us? Don't we count for anything?"

"Were you close to Lorna?"

"Not really. Lorna wasn't close to anyone. She lived in her world and we lived in ours. She had that cabin, and she liked it private. She hated it if people stopped by without asking. A lot of times she wasn't even home. Nights especially she'd be out somewhere. She made it plain you should keep away unless you called first and got yourself invited."

"How often did you see her?"

"A lot over here, whenever she stopped by. But at the cabin, maybe once or twice in the three years she lived there. Berlyn liked to go over. She's kind of nosy by nature. Lorna was real mysterious."

"Like what?"

"I don't know. Like, why was she so picky about people dropping in? What's the big deal? She didn't have to worry about us. We're her *sisters."*

"Did you ever find out where she went at night?"

"Nuh-uhn. Probably wasn't any place special. After a while, I more or less accepted her for what she was. She wasn't sociable, like us. Berlyn and me are buddies. We like to pal around and double-date and stuff like that? Right now, like, neither of us has a boyfriend, so we see movies and go out dancing on the weekends.

Lorna never did the first nice thing for either one of us. Well, she did now and then, but you practically had to lay down and beg."

"How'd you find out about her death?"

"The police stopped by the house and asked to speak to Daddy. He was the one who told Mom, and she told us. It was kind of creepy. I mean, we thought Lorna was out of town. Off on vacation, is what Mom said. So we didn't think anything about it when we didn't hear from her. We just figured she'd give us a call when she got back. It's horrible to think she was just laying there, moldering."

"It must have been awful."

"Oh, God. I started screaming, and Berl got white as a ghost. Daddy was like in *shock.* Mother took it the worst. She still isn't over it. She was staggering around shrieking and crying, practically tearing her hair out. I've never seen her like that. She's usually the one holds the rest of us together. Like when Grandma died? This was her own *mother.* She kept real calm, made airline reservations, packed our bags so we could go back to Iowa to the funeral. We were all young kids, acting dumb, boo-hooing real pitiful. She got everything all organized, as cool as you please. When we found out about Lorna, she just fell to pieces."

"Most parents don't expect to outlive their kids," I said.

"That's what everybody says. It doesn't help that the police think she was murdered and all."

"What's your opinion?"

Trinny made a mute shrug with her mouth. "I guess she could have died from her allergies. I don't like to think about it. Too icky for my taste."

I shifted the subject. "Were you the one who went to San Francisco with Lorna last year?"

"That was Berlyn," she said. "Who told you about that?"

"I met the guy on the tape."

She glanced up from her work with interest. "Which one?"

12

She had the good grace to blush. Despite the dark brown hair, she was fair-complected, and the tint hit her cheeks like a heat rash. She dropped her gaze to the work in front of her, suddenly much busier than she'd been before. I could tell she was casting about for a way to change the subject. She bent over her work. I guess it was important to get the paint dots just right.

"Trinny?"

"What?"

"How'd you happen to see the tape? And don't say 'which tape' because you know exactly which tape I'm talking about."

"I didn't see the tape."

"Oh, come on. Of course you did. If you didn't, how'd you know there was more than one guy?"

"I don't even know what you're talking about," she said with pious irritation.

"I'm talking about the porno tape in which Lorna appeared. Remember? Your mother told you."

"Maybe Mom told us that, too. About the other guy, more than one."

I said, "Uhn-hun," in my most skeptical tone. "What happened, did Lorna give you a copy?"

"Nooo," she said, giving it two sliding syllables, high note to low, offended by the notion.

"Then how'd you know there was more than one man?"

"I *guessed.* What do you care?"

I stared at her. The obvious conclusion leapt to mind. "Were *you* the one who wrapped it and put it out in the mailbox?"

"No. And anyway, I don't have to answer." This time the tone was sullen, but the blush came up again. This was better than a polygraph.

"Who did?"

"I don't know anything about anything, so you might as well change the subject. This is not a court of law, you know. I'm not under oath."

An attorney in the making. For a moment I thought she'd put her fingers in her ears and start humming, just to shut me out. I cocked my head, trying to catch her eye. "Trinny," I sang. She was studiously engaged in the T-shirt in front of her, adding a gaudy orange spiral of puff paint. I said, "Come on. I don't *care* what you did, and I swear I will never say a word to your parents. I've been wondering who sent the tape to them, and now I know. In a way, you did us all a favor. If your mother hadn't been upset about it, she wouldn't have come to me, and the whole investigation might have died where it was." I waited and then gave her a line prompt. "Was it Berlyn's idea or yours?"

"I don't have to answer."

"How about a nod if I guess right?"

Trinny added some lime-green stars to the T-shirt. It was getting tackier by the minute, but I felt as though we were getting some-place.

"I'll bet it was Berlyn."

Silence.

"Am I right?"

Trinny lifted one shoulder, still without making eye contact.

"Ah. I'm assuming that little gesture means 'yes.' So Berlyn sent the tape. Now the question is, how'd she get it?"

More silence.

"Come on, Trinny. Please, please, please?" I learned this interrogation method back in grade school, and it's particularly effective when the subject matter is a cross-your-heart-type secret just between us girls. I could see her softening. Whatever our confidences, we're usually *dying* to tell, especially if the confession involves the condemnation of someone else.

Her tongue moved across her teeth as though she were testing for fuzz. Finally she said, "Swear you won't tell?"

I held up my hand as if taking an oath. "I won't say a word to another soul. I won't even mention that you *mentioned* it."

"We just got sick of hearing how wonderful she was. Because she wasn't all that great. She was pretty and she had a great bod, but big deal, you know?"

"Really," I said.

"Plus, she took money for *sex.* I mean, Berlyn or me would *never* have done that. So how come Lorna got elevated to the stars? She wasn't pure. She wasn't even *good.*"

"Human nature, I guess. Your mother doesn't get to have Lorna in her life, but she keeps that perfect picture in her heart," I said. "It's hard to let go when that's all you have."

Her voice had begun to rise. "But Lorna was a bitch. All she thought about was *herself.* She hardly gave Mom and Daddy the time of day. I'm the one helps out, for all the good it does. I'm as sweet as I know how, and it doesn't make any difference. Lorna's the one Mom loves. Berlyn and me are just bullshit." Emotion was causing her skin to change colors, chameleonlike. Tears rose like water suddenly coming to the boil. She put a hand to her face, which twisted as a sob broke through.

I reached out and touched her hand. "Trinny, that's just not true. Your mother loves you very much. The night she came to my office, she talked about you and Berlyn, all the fun you have, all the help around the house. You're a treasure to her. Honestly."

She was crying by then, her voice high-pitched and pinched. "Then why doesn't she tell us? She never says a word."

"Maybe she's afraid to. Or maybe she doesn't know how anymore, but that doesn't mean she isn't crazy about you."

"I can't stand it. I can't." She sobbed like a child, giving rein to her grief. I sat and let her work it through on her own. Finally the tears subsided and she sighed heavily. She fumbled in the pocket of her cutoffs, pulling out a ratty hankie, which she pressed against her eyes. "Oh, God," she said. She propped her elbows on the table and then blew her nose. She looked down, realizing she'd picked up the imprint of wet paint on her forearm. "Well, shit. Look at that," she said. A bubble of laughter came up like a burp escaping.

"What's going on?" Berlyn was standing at the front door, her expression blank with suspicion.

Both of us jumped, and Trinny let out a gasp. "Berl! You scared me half to *death,*" she said. "Where did you come from?" She wiped her eyes in haste, trying to cover up the fact that she'd been crying.

Berlyn had a plastic carryall of groceries in one hand, her key ring in the other. She fixed Trinny with a look. "Pardon me for sneaking. I didn't know I was interrupting. I parked in the driveway big as life." Her gaze jumped to mine. "What's the matter with you?"

"Nothing," I said. "We were talking about Lorna, and Trinny got upset."

"Just what I need. I've heard enough about her. Daddy's got it right. Let's just drop the subject and get on to something else. Where's Mom? Is she up yet?"

"I think she's in the shower," Trinny said.

Belatedly, I became aware of water running somewhere.

Berlyn dumped her purse on a chair and moved over to the counter, where she began to unload grocery items. Like Trinny, she wore cutoffs, a T-shirt, and flip-flops, professional attire for the working plumber's helper. The roots on her blond hair were showing through. Despite the four-year age difference, her face was a projection of Lorna's in middle age. Maybe young death isn't bad, perfect beauty suspended in the amber of time.

Berlyn turned to Trinny. "Could you give me a hand?" she said, aggrieved. "How long has she been here?"

Trinny shot me a pleading look and went over to help her sister.

"Ten minutes," I supplied, though I hadn't been asked. "I just stopped by for the stuff your mother left. Trinny was showing me how to make T-shirts, and then we got talking about Lorna's death." I reached for the box, thinking to flee the premises before Janice emerged.

Berlyn studied me with interest. "So you said."

"Ah. Well. Fun as this is, I better be on my way." I got up, slung the strap of my handbag over my shoulder, and picked up the box, ignoring Berlyn. "Thanks for the painting lesson," I said to Trinny. "I'm sorry about Lorna. I know you loved her."

Her smile was pained. She said, "Bye," and gave me a half-hearted wave. Berlyn went into the den without a backward look, closing the door behind her with a decided snap. I stuck my tongue out at her and crossed my eyes, which made Trinny laugh. I mouthed, "Thank you," to Trinny and took my leave.

It was nearly six o'clock when I unlocked my office door and put the box of Lorna's files on my desk. Everybody else in the firm was gone. Even Lonnie, who usually works late, had packed it in for the day. All my tax forms and receipts were still sitting where I'd left them. I was disappointed the elves and fairies hadn't come along to finish up my work. I gathered all the bits and pieces and tucked them in a drawer, clearing space. I doubted Lorna's papers would yield any information, but I needed to take a look. I put some coffee on and sat down, set the lid of the box aside, and began to work my way through the manila folders. It looked as if someone had lifted Lorna's files directly from a desk drawer and placed them in the banker's box. Each file was labeled neatly. Tucked in the front were copies of various probate forms that Janice must have picked up from the attorney. It looked as though she were doing the preliminary work of culling and assembling, making penciled notes. I studied each sheet, trying to form a picture of Lorna Kepler's financial status.

An accountant could probably have made quick work of this stuff. I, on the other hand, having made a C minus in high school math, had to frown and sigh and chew my pencil. Janice had filled out a schedule of Lorna's assets, listing the cash in her possession at the time of her death, uncashed checks payable to her, bank accounts, stocks, bonds, Treasury bills, mutual funds. Lorna had no pension plan and no life insurance. She did have a small insurance policy for the jewelry she'd acquired. She hadn't owned any real property, but her liquid assets came to a little under five hundred thousand dollars. Not bad for a part-time clerk-harlot. Janice had included a copy of Lorna's will, which seemed clear enough. She'd left all her valuables, including jewelry, cash, stocks, bonds, and other financial assets, to her parents. Attached to the will was a copy of the completed "Proof of Holographic Instrument" that Janice had filed. In it, she attested that she was acquainted with the decedent for twenty-five years, had personal knowledge of her handwriting, that she had "examined the will and determined that its handwritten provisions were written by and the instrument signed by the hand of the decedent."

Danielle had speculated that Lorna wouldn't have a will, but the document seemed consistent with Lorna's systematic nature. Neither Berlyn nor Trinny had been left any money, but that didn't seem unusual. Two thousand bucks apiece might have gone a long way toward softening their attitudes, but she might not have understood the animosity they harbored. Or maybe she knew and felt the same about them. At any rate, the estate wasn't complicated. I didn't think it necessitated the services of an attorney, but the Keplers might have been intimidated by all the official paperwork.

I checked back through the last few years of Lorna's income tax. Her only W-2's were from the water treatment plant. Under "Your Occupation," she had listed herself as "secretary" and "mental health consultant." I had to smile at that. She'd been meticulous in reporting income, taking only standard deductions. She'd never donated a dime to charity, but she'd been (largely) honest with the government. To the recipient, I suppose the services of a prostitute might be classified under mental health. As for the payments themselves, I guess no one at the IRS had ever wondered why the bulk of her "consulting fees" were paid to her in cash.

Janice had notified the post office to forward Lorna's mail to her, and she'd tossed in a stack of unopened statements: windowed envelopes from various sources, all of them marked "important tax information." I opened a few, just to check the year end against my list. Among them was a statement from a bank in Simi Valley that I'd seen on her tax forms for the last two years. The account had been closed out, but the bank had sent her a 1099-INT, reporting the interest accrued during the first four months of the year. I tucked that in with the other statements. All the credit cards had been canceled and notices sent to each company. I sorted through some of the files Lorna'd kept: canceled checks, receipts for utilities, various credit card slips.

I laid out the canceled checks like a hand of solitaire. At the bottom, under "Memo," she'd dutifully written in the purpose of the payment: groceries, manicure, haircut, linens, sundries. There was something touching about the care she'd taken. She hadn't known she'd be dead by the time these checks came back. She hadn't known her last meal would be her last, that every action she'd taken and each endeavor she'd engaged in were part of some finite number that would soon run out. Sometimes the hardest part of my job is the incessant reminder of the fact we're all trying so assiduously to ignore: we are here temporarily . . . life is only ours on loan.

I put down my pencil and eased my feet up on the desk, rocking back on my swivel chair. The room seemed dark, and I reached over and flipped on the lamp on the bookshelf behind me. Among Lorna's possessions, there was no address book, no calendar, no appointment book of any kind. That might have sparked my curiosity, but I wondered if it didn't speak to Lorna's caution about her clients. Danielle had told me she was very tight-lipped, and I felt this discretion might extend to the keeping of written notes as well.

I reached for the manila envelope that held the crime scene photographs. I sorted through until I found the angles that showed the papers on her table and countertop. I pulled the light over closer, but there was no way to see if there was an appointment book visible. I glanced at my watch. I was dog-tired. I was also bored and hungry, but I could feel my senses quicken as the darkness gathered depth. Maybe I was turning into a vampire or a werewolf, repelled by sunlight, seduced by the moon.

I got up and shrugged into my jacket, leaving Lorna's papers on my desk. What was bothering me? I scanned the desktop. A fact . . . something obvious . . . had passed through my hands. The problem with being tired is that your brain doesn't work so hot. Idly I paused and moved a batch of papers aside, leafing through the forms. I looked at the holographic will and Janice's supporting statement. I didn't think that was it. In theory, it would seem self-serving that Janice was in a position to attest to the legitimacy of a will from which she largely benefited. However, the truth of it was that if Lorna had died with no will at all, the result would have been the same.

I picked up the bank notices and shuffled through them again, pausing when I got to the statement from the bank in Simi. The interest was minimal since she'd closed the account in April. Before that, she'd maintained a balance of roughly twenty thousand dollars. I looked at the closing date. The zero balance showed as of Friday, April 20. The day before she died.

I pulled out the files Lieutenant Dolan had given me. The personal property inventory mentioned all manner of items found on the premises, including Lorna's handbag and her wallet, containing all her credit cards and a hundred bucks in cash. Nowhere was there mention of twenty thousand dollars. I took the notice with me to the Xerox room around the corner, made a copy of the statement, and stuck it in my handbag. Serena Bonney had been the first person on the scene. I checked my notes for her father's address, packed up Lorna's papers with the crime scene photographs, and took the banker's box with me down the stairs to my car.

. . .

The address I'd picked up for Clark Esselmann turned out to be a sizable estate, maybe seven or eight acres surrounded by a low sandstone wall, beyond which the rolling lawns had been erased by the dark. Landscaping floods washed light across the exterior of the house, which was constructed in the French country style, meaning long and low with a steeply pitched roof. Mullioned windows formed a series of staunch yellow grids along the facade, while the tall fieldstone chimneys jutted up like black towers against the charcoal sky. Low-voltage lights defined the foliage and walkways, allowing me a fair sense of what it must have looked like by day. Interior lights winking in a small structure some distance from the main house suggested a guest house or perhaps maid's quarters.

When I reached the main entrance, I could see electronic gates. A key pad and intercom were planted at expensive-car window height. Naturally my VW left me disadvantaged, and in order to buzz I had to pull on the emergency brake, open the car door, and torque my whole body, risking vicious back spasms. I pushed the button, wishing I could order a Big Mac and fries.

A disembodied voice came in response. "Yes?"

"Oh, hi. I'm Kinsey Millhone. I have some house keys that belong to Serena Bonney."

There was no reply. What did I expect, a gasp of astonishment? Half a second later the two halves of the gate began to swing back in silence. I eased my VW up the circular driveway, lined with junipers. The entry was cobblestone, with a separate lane leading to the left and on around to the rear. I caught a glimpse of garages, like a line of horse stables. Just to be contrary, I bypassed the front door and drove around the side of the house to a brightly lighted gravel parking pad in back. The four-car garage was linked to the main house by a long, covered breezeway, beyond which I could see a short stretch of lawn intersected by a man-made reflecting pond, submerged lights tucked among its rocks. All across the property, lighting picked out significant landscape features: ornamental shrubs and tree trunks appearing like oils painted on black velvet. On the clear black surface of the pond, water lilies grew in clumps, breaking up a perfect inverted image of the house.

Night-blooming jasmine filled the air with perfume. I back-tracked to the front door and rang properly. Moments later Serena answered, dressed in slacks and a white silk shirt.

"I brought your keys back," I said, holding them out to her.

"Those are my keys? Oh, so they are," she said. "Where did these come from?"

"Lorna's mother came across them. You must have given Lorna a set when she was house-sitting for you."

"Thanks. I'd forgotten. Nice of you to return them."

"I've also got a question, if you can spare me a minute."

"Sure. Come on in. Dad's out on the patio. He just got out of the hospital today. Have you met him?"

"I don't think our paths have ever crossed," I said.

I followed her through the house and into a large country kitchen. A cook was in the process of preparing the evening meal, barely glancing up from her chopping board as we passed through. An informal dining table large enough to seat eight was located in a bay of French doors on the far side of the room. The ceiling rose a story and a half, with crisscrossing wooden beams. An assortment of baskets and bunches of dried herbs hung on wooden pegs. The floor was a pale, glossy pine. The layout of the room allowed space for two separate cooking islands about ten feet apart. One was topped with dark granite with its own inlaid hardwood cutting surfaces and a butler's sink. The second housed a full-size sink, two dishwashers, and a trash compactor. A fireplace on a raised hearth held a blazing fire.

Serena opened the French doors, and I followed her out. A wide flagstone patio ran the width of the house. Outside lights seemed to create an artificial day. A black-bottomed lap pool, a good seventy-five feet by twenty, defined its outer edge. The water was clear, but the black tile seemed to erase its inner dimensions. Pool lights picked up a shifting web of emerald green that somehow made the bottom look endlessly deep. Diving into that would be like a plunge into Loch Ness. God knew what creatures might be lurking in the abyss.

Clark Esselmann, in his robe and slippers, a stick in his hand, was teasing a black Labrador retriever into the ready position. "Okay, Max. Here we go now. Here we go."

The dog was full-grown, probably the same age in dog years as the old man himself. Max nearly quivered, totally focused on the game being played. As we approached, the old man threw the stick into the lap pool. The dog flung himself into the water, moving toward the stick, which was now bobbing in the water at the far end. I recognized Serena's father from numerous pictures that had appeared in the *Santa Teresa Dispatch* over the years. White-haired, in his seventies, he carried himself with an old-fashioned ramrod-straight posture. If his heart problems had affected him, it was hard to see how.

Serena smiled, watching them. "This is the first chance he's had to connect with Max. They usually go through this first thing in the morning, and what a sight they are. Dad swims in one lane and the dog swims in the other."

Vaguely I was aware of the telephone ringing somewhere inside the house. The dog collected the stick in his teeth and swam in our direction, scrambling up the stairs at the near end of the pool. He dropped it at the old man's feet and then barked once sharply. Esselmann threw the stick again. It sailed toward the deep end of the pool, landing with a faint splash. The dog flew off the side and swam, head high. The old man laughed and clapped his hands, urging the dog on. "Come on, Max. Come on."

The retriever clamped his mouth on the stick again and turned, paddling back to the stairs, where he scrambled out, water pouring off his oily coat. Max dropped the stick at Esselmann's feet and then shook himself vigorously. Water flew out in all directions. Both Serena and her father laughed. Esselmann brushed at the polka dots of water on his cotton robe. I could have sworn Max was grinning, but I might have been mistaken.

A maid in a black uniform appeared at the French door. "Mr. Esselmann? Phone for you."

The old man turned and glanced in that direction, then headed toward the house while the dog pranced sideways and barked, hoping for one more toss. Serena caught my eye and smiled. Clearly, her father's hospital discharge had lightened her mood. "Can I offer you a glass of wine?"

"I'd better not," I said. "Wine makes me sleepy, and I have work to do yet."

We moved back through the French doors into the kitchen, where the wood fire popped cheerfully. Esselmann was standing near the planning center, on the telephone. He glanced over his shoulder and raised a hand, indicating his awareness of our presence. Beyond him, the door to the hall was open, and the dog's wet footprints led to a second door that was now closed. I had to guess Max had been relegated to the basement until he managed to dry himself. I heard a scratching noise, and then the dog issued one of those brief barks intended to make his wishes known.

"Don't be ridiculous. Of course, I'll be there. . . . Well, I'm opposed, of course. We're talking about an allotment of twelve million gallons a year. I'm absolutely adamant about this, and I don't care who knows it." His manner shifted to something slightly less gruff. "I feel fine. . . . I appreciate that, Ned, and I hope you'll tell Julia I received the flowers she sent and they were lovely. . . . Yes, I'll do that. I don't have much choice. Serena keeps me on a very tight leash." He turned and rolled his eyes at her, knowing that she was nearby. "I'll see you at the meeting Friday night. Just tell Bob and Druscilla how I'm voting on this. We can talk about it then, but I hope we're in accord. . . . Thank you. I'll do that. . . . Same to you."

He hung up the handset with a shake of his head. "Damn fools. First time my back is turned, they get sweet-talked into something. I hate the oil companies. That Stockton fellow's not going to have his way on this."

"I thought you were in his corner."

"I changed my mind," he said emphatically. He held his hand out to me. "Please excuse my bad manners. I shouldn't keep you standing while I rant and rave. Clark Esselmann. You caught me in the middle of my daily romp with the dog. I don't believe we've met."

I introduced myself. His grip was firm, but I could detect a slight tremor in his fingers. Up close, I could see that his color was poor. He looked anemic, and the flesh on the back of his right hand was bruised from some medical procedure. Still, he had a certain hardy determination that seemed to prevail in the face of his recurring health problems.

"Dad, you're not seriously thinking of trying to make it to a board meeting."

"You can bet on it," he said.

"You just got home. You're in no shape. The doctor doesn't even want you driving yet."

"I can take a taxi if need be. Or I can have Ned pick me up."

"I don't mind driving you. That's not the point," she said. "I really think you ought to take it easy for a few days."

"Nonsense! I'm not so old or infirm that I can't make decisions about what I'll do on any given day. Now if you girls will excuse me, I'm going up to take a rest before dinner. It's been a pleasure, Miss Millhone. I hope the next time we meet, you'll find me decently dressed. I don't usually meet the public in my bathrobe."

Serena touched his arm. "You need help getting up the stairs?"

"Thankfully, I don't," he said. He moved from the room with a shuffling gait that nevertheless propelled him at nearly normal speeds. As he passed the basement, he reached over and opened the door. The dog must have been lurking at the top of the stairs because he appeared at once and trotted after the old man, glancing back at us with satisfaction.

As Serena turned back to me, she sighed in exasperation. "That man is so stubborn, he drives me nuts. I've never had children, but surely parents are worse. Ah, well. Enough. I'm sure you didn't come here to listen to my gripes. You said you had a question."

"I'm looking for some money Lorna might have had when she

died. Apparently she closed out a bank account on Friday of that week. As far as I can see, there's twenty thousand dollars unaccounted for. I wondered if you'd seen any cash on the premises."

Serena put a hand to her chest in surprise. "She had *that* kind of money? That's incredible."

"She actually had quite a bit more, but this is the only money that seems to be missing."

"I can tell I'm in the wrong business. Wait till Roger hears this."

"You didn't see any sign of it the day you found the body? Might have been a cashier's check."

"Not me. Ask her landlord. I didn't even go in."

"And he did?"

"Well, it was only for a minute, but I'm sure he did."

"He told me once he caught the smell, he turned right around and went back to his place and called the cops."

"That's true, but then while we were waiting for the police to show up, he opened the door and went in."

"To do what?"

Serena shook her head. "I don't know. I guess I thought he wanted to see what it was. I'd forgotten all about it till you brought it up."

13

When I got back to my apartment, Danielle was standing on my doorstep in a shallow pool of light. Her long legs were bare, capped by the shortest pink miniskirt on record. She wore black high heels, a black tank top, and a varsity letter jacket with a big black *F* across the back. Her hair was so long that it extended below the bottom of the jacket in the back. She smiled when she caught sight of me crossing the yard. "Oh, hey. I thought you were gone. I came to get my dime. The IRS says I'm short on my estimated income tax."

"Aren't you cold? It's really freezing out here."

"You must never have lived in the East. It's probably fifty degrees. With this jacket I got on, I'm as warm as toast."

"What's the *F* stand for?"

"What do you think?" she said drolly.

I smiled as I unlocked the door and flipped the lights on. She followed me in, pausing at the threshold to assess the premises. Her eyes looked enormous, the green offset by dark liner, her lashes beaded with mascara. Under all the makeup she had a smooth, baby face: snub nose, sulky mouth. She strolled the perimeter of my living room, tottering on her high heels as she peered at all the bookshelves. She picked up the framed photograph of Robert Dietz. "Well, he's cute. Who's this?"

"A friend."

She lifted her brows and gave me a look that suggested she knew what kind of friend he was. She put the picture down again and shoved her hands in her jacket pockets. I hung my own jacket across the back of a director's chair. She sat down on my sofa and rubbed a hand across the surface of the fabric as if to test the weight. Tonight her fingernails were long and perfect, painted a vivid fire-engine red. She crossed one long, bare leg across the other and swung a foot while she completed her survey. "This is not bad. They got any other units as good as this?"

"This is the only rental. My landlord's eighty-five."

"I don't discriminate. I like old guys," she said. "Maybe I could give him a discount."

"I'll pass the word along in case he's interested. What are you doing here?"

She got up and moved over to the kitchen, where she opened my cabinets to check the contents. "I was bored. I don't go in to work until eleven. It's a problem sometimes what to do before. Mr. Dickhead's in a bad mood, so I'm avoiding him."

"What's his problem?"

"Oh, who knows? He's probably raggin' it," she said. She flapped a hand in the air, dismissing his ill temper. She pulled a couple of teabags out of her jacket pocket and dangled them in the air. "You want some peppermint tea? I got some bags if you boil the water. It's good for digestion."

"I'm not worried about digestion. I haven't had dinner yet."

"Me neither. Sometimes all I have is tea if Lester's taken my money. He doesn't want me getting fat."

"What a pal," I said.

She shrugged, unconcerned. "I look after myself. I'm into megavitamins and high colonics and like that."

"There's a treat," I said. I filled the kettle with hot water and put it on the stove. I flipped the burner on.

"Laugh all you want. I bet I'm healthier than you."

"That wouldn't take much, the way I eat," I said. "Speaking of which, you want dinner? I don't cook, but I can have a pizza delivered. I have to go out in a bit, but you're welcome to join me."

"I wouldn't mind some pizza," she said. "If you just do the veggies, without all the sausage and pepperoni, it's not even bad for you. Try that place around the corner. I bonk the owner sometimes. He gives me a big discount because I chew his bone."

"I'll mention that when I call the order in," I said.

"Here, I'll do it. Where's the phone?"

I pointed to the phone on the table beside the answering machine. We both noticed the blinking light.

"You got a message," she said. She reached down automatically and pressed the replay button before I had a chance to protest. It seemed as rude for her to listen as to open my mail. A mechanical computer voice announced that I had one message. Beep.

"Oh, hi, Kinsey. This is Roger. I just wanted to touch base and see how things were going. Anyway, you don't have to call back, but if you have any more questions, you can reach me at home. Bye. Oh, I guess I better give you the number." He recited his home phone and then hung up with a click.

"Lorna's boss," she said. "You know him?"

"Sure. Do you?"

She wrinkled her nose. "I met him once." She picked up the phone and punched in a number she seemed to know by heart. She turned and looked at me while the phone rang on the other end. "I'm going to have 'em leave the cheese off. It cuts the fat," she murmured.

I left her to the negotiations while I made us each a cup of tea. The night I'd met her, she'd seemed wary, or maybe that was just her working persona. Tonight she seemed relaxed, nearly buoyant. Her mood was probably drug-induced, but there was actually something charming about her ingenuousness. She had a natural goodwill that animated every gesture. I heard her conducting business with the kind of poise that must come from "bonking" guys from every walk of life. She put a hand over the mouthpiece. "What's the address here? I forgot."

I gave her the number, which she recited into the telephone. I could have taken her to Rosie's with me, but I didn't trust Rosie to be polite. With William gone, I was worried she might revert to her former misanthropy.

Danielle hung up the phone and took off her jacket, which she folded neatly and put on one end of the sofa. She came over to the counter, clutching her oversize shoulder bag. Somehow she seemed as graceful as a colt, all arms and long legs and bony shoulders.

I passed her a mug of tea. "I have a question for you."

"Hold on. Let me say something first. I hope this is not too personal. I wouldn't want you to take offense."

"I really hate sentences that start that way," I said.

"Me too, but this is for your own good."

"Go ahead. You're going to say it anyway."

She hesitated, and the face she made conveyed exaggerated reluctance. "Promise you won't get mad?"

"Just say it. I can't stand the suspense. I have bad breath."

"That haircut of yours is really gross."

"Oh, thanks."

"You don't have to get sarcastic. I can help. Honestly. I was working on my license as a cosmetologist when I first connected up with Lester . . ."

"Mr. Dickhead," I supplied.

"Yeah, him. Anyway, I'm a great cutter. I did Lorna's hair all the time. Give me a pair of scissors and I can turn you into a vision. I'm not fooling."

"All I have is nail scissors. Maybe after dinner."

"Come on. We got fifteen minutes until the pizza gets here. And look at this." She opened up her shoulder bag and let me peek. "Ta-da." Inside she had a brush, a little hair dryer, and a pair of shears. She placed the hair dryer on the counter and clacked the scissors like a pair of castanets.

"You came over here with that stuff?"

"I keep it with me all the time. Sometimes at the Palace I do haircuts in the ladies' room."

I ended up sitting on a kitchen stool with a hand towel pinned around my neck, my hair wet from a dousing at the kitchen sink. Danielle was chatting happily while she trimmed and clipped. Snippets of hair began to tumble around me. "Now don't get scared. I know it looks like a lot, but it's just because the whole thing's uneven. You got great hair, nice and thick, with just the tiniest touch of curl. Well, I wouldn't call it curl so much as body, which is even better."

"So why didn't you get your license?"

"I lost interest. Plus, the money's not that hot. My father always said it'd be a great fallback position if the economy went sour, but hooking's better, in my opinion. A guy might not have the bucks to get his hair blown dry, but he's always got twenty for a BJ."

I mouthed the term *BJ* silently. It took me half a second to figure that one out. "What are you going to do when you get too old to bonk?"

"I'm taking classes at city college in financial management. Money's the only other subject that really interests me."

"I'm sure you'll go far."

"You gotta start somewhere. What about you? What will you do when you're too old to bonk?"

"I don't bonk now. I'm pure as the driven snow."

"Well, no wonder you get cranky. What a drag," she said.

I laughed.

For a while we were silent as she concentrated on her work. "What's the question? You said you had something you wanted to ask."

"Maybe I better check my cash supply first."

She pulled my hair. "Now don't be like that. I bet you're the kind who kids around to keep other people at a distance, right?"

"I don't think I should respond to that."

She smiled. "See? I can surprise you. I'm a lot brighter than you think. So ask."

"Ah, yes. Did Lorna mention pulling twenty grand out of a bank account before she was supposed to go out of town?"

"Why would she do that? She always traveled with a guy. She never spent her own money when she went someplace."

"What guy?"

"Anyone who asked," she said, still clipping away.

"You know where she was headed?"

"She didn't talk about that stuff."

"What about a diary or an appointment book?"

Danielle touched her temple with the tip of her scissors. "She kept it all up here. She said otherwise her clients didn't feel safe. Cops raid your place? They got a search warrant, you're dead, and so's everybody else. Quit wiggling."

"Sorry. Where'd the money go? It looks like she closed out the whole account."

"Well, she didn't give it to me. I wish she had. I'd have opened an account of my own just like that." She snapped the scissors near my ear, and seven hairs fell to earth. "I meant to do that," she added. She set the scissors on the counter and plugged in the hair dryer, picking up locks of hair on the bristles of the hairbrush. It's incredibly restful to have someone fooling with your hair like that.

I raised my voice slightly to compete with the noise. "Could she have paid off a debt or posted bail for someone?"

"Twenty G's in bail would be a hell of a crime."

"Did she owe anybody?"

"Lorna didn't have debts. Even credit cards she paid off before finance charges went on," she said. "I bet the money was stolen."

"Yeah, that occurred to me, too."

"Must have been after she was dead," she added. "Otherwise Lorna would have fought tooth and nail." She turned the dryer off and set it aside, stepping back to scrutinize her handiwork. She took a moment to fluff and rearrange individual strands and then nodded, apparently satisfied.

The doorbell rang, Mr. Pizza Man on the doorstep. I handed Danielle twenty bucks and let her conclude the deal while I ducked into the downstairs bathroom and checked myself in the mirror. The difference was remarkable. All the choppiness was gone. All the blunt, stick-out parts that seemed to go every which way were now tamed and subdued. The hair feathered away from my face in perfect layers. It even fell into place again if I shook my head. I caught sight of Danielle reflected in the mirror behind me.

"You like it?" she asked.

"It looks great."

"Told you I was good," she said, laughing.

We ate from the box, splitting a large cheeseless veggie pizza, which was tasty without causing all my arteries to seize up. At one point she said, "This is fun, isn't it? Like girlfriends."

"You miss Lorna?"

"Yeah, I do. She was a kick. After work, her and me would pal around downtown, find a coffee shop, have breakfast. I remember once we bought a quart of orange juice and a bottle of champagne. We sat out in the grass at my place and drank mimosas until dawn."

"I'm sorry I never got to meet her. She sounds nice."

At eight we folded the box and stuck it in the trash. Danielle put her jacket on while I got mine. Once outside, she asked me to drop her off at her place. I took a left on Cabana, following her directions as she routed me down a narrow alleyway not that far from Neptune's Palace. Her "hovel," as she referred to it, was a tiny board-and-batten structure at the rear of someone else's yard. The little house had probably been a toolshed at one time. She got out of the car and leaned back in the window. "You want to come in and see my place?"

"Maybe tomorrow night," I said. "I got some stuff to do tonight."

"Pop by if you can. I got it fixed up real cute. If business is slow, I'm usually home by one . . . provided Lester isn't bugging me to score. Thanks for dinner and the ride."

"Thanks for the cut."

I watched her clop off into the night, high heels tapping on the short brick walk to her front door, dark hair trailing down her back like a veil. I fired up my car and headed for the Keplers' house.

I parked in the driveway and made my way along the flagstone path leading to the porch. The porch light was off, and the yard was dark as pitch. I picked my way up the low front stairs, which were dimly illuminated by the light from the living room windows. Janice had told me they usually ate dinner at this hour. I tapped on the front door and from the direction of the kitchen heard a chair scrape back.

Mace answered my knock, his body blocking most of the light spilling out the door. I smelled tuna casserole. He had a paper napkin in one hand, and he made a swipe at his mouth. "Oh, it's you. We're eating supper right now."

"Is Janice here?"

"She's already left. She works eleven to seven every day, but some girl got sick and she went in early. Try tomorrow," he said. He was already moving to shut the door in my face.

"Mind if I talk to you?"

His face went momentarily blank, just a tiny flick of temper that wiped out any other expression. "Pardon?"

"I wondered if you'd object to a quick chat," I said.

"Yeah, I do. I work a long, hard day, and I don't like people watching while I eat."

I felt a flash of heat, as though somebody'd taken a blow torch to the back of my neck. "Maybe later," I said. I turned and moved down the porch steps. As the door closed behind me, he muttered something obscene.

I backed out of the drive with a chirp and threw the car into first. What a turd. I did not like the man at all. He was a horse's ass and a jerk, and I hoped he had itchy hemorrhoids. I drove randomly, trying to cool down. I couldn't even think what to do with myself. I would have gone to Frankie's to talk to Janice, but I knew I'd say spiteful things about her spouse.

Instead, I went to the Caliente Cafe, looking for Cheney Phillips. It was still early for a Wednesday night, but CC's was already crowded, sound system blasting and enough cigarette smoke to make breathing unpleasant. For a place with no Happy Hour, no two-for-one deals, and no hors d'oeuvres (unless you count chips and salsa as a form of canapé), CC's does a lively business from the time it opens at five P.M. until it closes at two in the morning. Cheney was sitting at the bar in a dress shirt, faded jeans, and a pair of desert boots. He had a beer in front of him and was talking with the guy sitting next to him. When he saw me, he grinned. Lordy, I'm a sucker for good teeth. "Ms. Millhone. How are you? You got your hair cut. It looks good."

"Thanks. You got a minute?"

"Of course." He picked up his beer and eased himself off the bar stool, scanning the place for a vacant table where we could talk. The bartender was moving in our direction. "We need a glass of Chardonnay," Cheney said.

We found a table on the side wall. I spewed for a while about my dislike of Mace Kepler. Cheney wasn't all that fond of the man himself, so he enjoyed my comments.

"I don't know what it is. He just gets me."

"He hates women," Cheney said.

I looked at him with surprise. "Is that it? Maybe that's what it is."

"So what else are you up to?"

I spent a few minutes filling him in on my trip to San Francisco, my talk with Trinny, her confession about the porno tape, and finally the money missing from the account. I showed him the bank statement, watching his face. "What do you think?"

By then he was slouched down on his spine, his legs stretched out in front him. He had one elbow propped up on the table, and he held the statement by one corner. He shifted on his seat. He didn't seem impressed. "She was going out of town. She probably needed money." He sat and studied the bank statement while he sipped at his Corona.

"I asked Danielle about that. She says Lorna never paid. She only traveled with guys who sported her to everything."

"Yeah, but it still isn't necessarily significant," he said.

"Of course it isn't *necessarily* significant, but it might be. That's the point. Serena says J.D. went into the cabin briefly while they were waiting for the cops. Suppose he lifted it."

"You think it's sitting right there, this big wad of dough?"

"Well, it could be," I said.

"Yeah, right. For all you know, Lorna was involved in off-track betting or she picked up a fur coat or bought a shitload of drugs."

"Uhn-hun," I said, cutting in on his recital. "Or maybe the cash was lifted by the first officer at the scene."

"There's an idea," he said, not liking the image of police corruption. "Anyway, you don't know it was cash. It could have been a check made payable to someone else. She could have moved the money over to her checking account and paid the balance on her Visa bill. Most people don't walk around with cash like that."

"I keep picturing a wad of bills."

"Well, try to picture something else."

"Serena might have taken it. She pointed a finger at J.D., but really, all we have is her word she didn't go into the cabin herself. Or maybe Lorna's parents found the stash and kept their mouths shut, figuring they'd have to have money for the funeral. I was going to ask about that, but Kepler pissed me off."

Cheney seemed amused. "You just never give up."

"I think it's interesting, that's all. Besides, I'm desperate for a lead. Mace Kepler doesn't have a record, does he? I'd love to get him on something."

"He's clean. We checked him out."

"Doesn't mean he isn't guilty. It just means he hasn't been caught yet."

"Don't get distracted." He pushed the statement across the table. "At least you know who mailed the porno tape to Mrs. K," he said.

"It doesn't lead anywhere."

"Don't sound so depressed."

"Well, I hate these raggedy-ass investigations," I said. "Sometimes the line is so clear. You pick up the scent and you follow it. It may take time, but at least you know you're going someplace. This is driving me nuts."

Cheney shrugged. "We investigated for months and didn't get anywhere."

"Yeah, I know. I don't know what made me think I could make a difference."

"What an egotist," he said. "You work on a case three days and you think, boom, you should be solving it."

"Is that all it's been? Feels like I've been on this sucker for weeks."

"Anyway, something will break. Killer's been sitting around all this time thinking he's in the clear. He's not going to like it that you're nosing around."

"Or she."

"Right. Let's don't get sexist about homicide," he said.

Cheney's pager went off. Until that moment I hadn't even been aware that he was toting one. He checked the number and then excused himself, going into the rear of the bar to use the pay phone. When he came back, he said he had to leave. One of his informants had been arrested and was asking for him.

After he left, I hung around long enough to finish my wine. Business was picking up, and the noise level was rising, along with the toxic levels of secondhand cigarette smoke. I grabbed my jacket and my shoulder bag and headed for the parking lot. It was not even midnight, but all the parking spaces were filled and cars were beginning to line the road out in front.

The sky was overcast. The lights from the city made the cloud cover glow. Across the road, at the bird refuge, a low mist was rising from the freshwater lagoon. A faint sulfurous smell seemed to permeate the air. Crickets and frogs masked the sounds of traffic on the distant highway. Closer at hand, an approaching freight train sounded its horn like a brief organ chord. I could feel the ground rumble faintly as the searchlight swept around the bend. The man on the bike went by. I turned and stared after him. The mounting thunder of the train made his passage seem as silent as a mime's. All I was aware of was the dancing of the lights, his juggling performance, for which I was an audience of one.

In the side lot, I spotted the rounded roofline of my VW where I'd parked it in a circle of artificial light. A shiny black stretch limousine was parked across the row of cars, blocking four vehicles, including mine. I peered toward the driver's side. The window was lowered soundlessly. I paused, pointing at my car to indicate that I was hemmed in. The chauffeur touched his cap but made no move to start his engine. Little Miss Helpful, I waited for half a second and then said, "Sorry to bother you, but if you can just move up about three feet, I think I can squeeze out. I'm the VW at the back." The chauffeur's gaze moved to a point behind me, and I turned to see what he was looking at.

The two men had emerged from the bar and were heading in our direction, feet crunching on gravel, their progress leisurely. I moved on toward my car, thinking to go ahead and unlock it and get in. No point in standing in the cold, I thought. The cadence of the footsteps picked up, and I turned to see what was going on. The two men appeared on either side of me, crowding in close, each man gripping an arm. "Hey!" I said.

"Please be very quiet," one of them murmured.

They began to walk me toward the limo, virtually hoisting me off the ground so that my feet barely touched as they hurried me along. I felt like a kid being held aloft by my parents, lifted over curbs and puddles. When you're little, this is fun. When you're big, it's scary stuff. The rear door of the limo opened. I tried to dig my heels in, but I had no purchase.

By the time I gathered myself and bucked, squawking, "Help!" I was in the back of the limo with the door slammed shut.

The interior was black leather and burled walnut. I could see a compact bar, a phone, and a blank television screen. Above my head, a band of varicolored lighted buttons controlled every aspect of the passengers' comfort: air temperature, windows, reading lights, the sliding moon roof. The interior glass privacy panel was rolled up between us and the chauffeur. I sat there, squeezed in between the two guys on the back bench seat, facing a third man across a spacious length of plush black carpeting. In the interest of personal safety, I made a point of looking straight ahead. I didn't want to be able to identify the two sidekicks. The guy facing me didn't seem to care if I looked at him or not. All three men were throwing out body heat, absorbed by the silence, which ate up all but the sounds of heavy breathing, largely mine.

The only lights on in the limo were small side bars. The floods from the parking lot were cut by the heavily tinted windows, but there was still ample illumination. The atmosphere in the car was tense, as if the gravitational field were somehow different here than in the rest of the world. Maybe it was the overcoats, the conviction I had that everybody in the car was packing except me. I could feel my heart thumping in my chest and the sick thrill of sweat trickling down my side. Often fear makes me sassy, but not this time. I felt excessively respectful. These were men who operated by a set of rules different from mine. Who knew what they'd consider rude or offensive?

The limo was so long that the man across from me was probably sitting eight feet away. He appeared to be in his sixties, short and blocky, balding on top. His face was dotted with miscellaneous moles, the skin as heavily lined as a pen-and-ink sketch. His cheeks bowed out almost to a heart shape, his chin forming the point. His eyebrows were an unruly tangle of white over dark, sunken eyes. His upper lids sagged. His lower lids were pouched into smoky poufs. He had thin lips and big teeth, set slightly askew in his mouth. He had big hands, thick wrists, and heavy gold jewelry. He smelled of cigars and a spicy after-shave. There was something distinctly masculine about him: brusque, decisive, opinionated. He held a small notebook loosely in one hand, though he didn't seem to be referring to it. "I hope you'll forgive the unorthodox method of arranging a meeting. We didn't intend to alarm you." No accent. No regional inflection.

The guys on either side of me sat as still as mannequins.

"Are you sure you have the right person?"

"Yes."

"I don't know you," I said.

"I'm a Los Angeles attorney. I represent a gentleman who's currently out of the country on business. He asked me to get in touch."

"Regarding what?" My heartbeat had slowed some. These were not robbers or rapists. I didn't think they were going to shoot me and fling my body out into the parking lot. The word *M-A-F-I-A* formed at the back of my mind, but I didn't allow it to become concrete thought. I didn't want confirmation, in case I was forced to testify later. These guys were professionals. They killed for business, not pleasure. So far, I *had* no business with them, so I figured I was safe.

The *alleged* attorney was saying, "You're conducting a homicide investigation my client has been following. The dead girl is Lorna Kepler. We'd appreciate it if you'd apprise us of the information you've acquired."

"What's his interest? If you don't mind my asking."

"He was a close friend. She was a beautiful person. He doesn't want anything coming to light that might sully her reputation."

"Her reputation was sullied before she died," I pointed out.

"They were engaged."

"In what?"

"They were getting married in Las Vegas on April twenty-first, but Lorna never showed."

14

I stared across the dark of the limousine at him. The claim seemed so preposterous that it might just be true. I'd been told Lorna met some heavy hitters in the course of her work. Maybe she fell in love with some guy and he with her. Mr. and Mrs. Racketeer. "Didn't he send someone up here to find her when she didn't show?"

"He's a proud man. He assumed she'd had a change of heart. Naturally, when he heard what had happened to her, the news was bittersweet," he said. "Now, of course, he wonders if he could have saved her."

"We'll probably never have the answer to that."

"What information do you have so far?"

I was forced to shrug. "I've only been working since Monday, and I haven't come up with much."

He was silent for a moment. "You spoke to a gentleman in San Francisco with whom we've had dealings. Mr. Ayers."

"That's right."

"What did he tell you?"

I paused. I wasn't sure whether Joe Ayers's cooperation or his failure to cooperate would generate disfavor in this crowd. I pictured Ayers hanging from his chandelier by his dick. Maybe the Mob didn't really do things that way. Maybe they'd picked up a bad rep these days. Living in Santa Teresa, we didn't have a lot of experience with these things. My mouth had gone dry. I was worried about my responsibility to the people I'd spoken with. "He was courteous," I said. "He gave me a couple of names and telephone numbers, but I'd already checked them out, so the information wasn't that useful."

"Who else have you spoken to?"

It's hard to sound casual when your voice starts to quake. "Family members. Her boss. She'd done some house-sitting for the boss's wife, and I talked to her." I cleared my throat.

"This was Mrs. Bonney? The one who found her?"

"That's right. I also talked to the homicide detective who handled the case."

Silence.

"That's about it," I added, sounding lame.

His eyes drifted down to his notebook. There was a glint of light when his gaze came up again. Clearly he knew exactly whom I'd spoken to and was waiting to see how candid I intended to be. I pretended I was in a courtroom on the witness stand. He was an attorney, according to *his* claim. If he had questions, let him ask and I'd answer. In the unlikely event that I knew more than he did, I thought it was better not to volunteer information.

"Who else?" he asked.

Another trickle of sweat slid down my side. "That's all I can think of offhand," I said. The car seemed hot. I wondered if they had the heater turned on.

"What about Miss Rivers?"

I looked at him blankly. "I don't know anyone by that name."

"Danielle Rivers."

"Oooh, yeah. Right. I did speak to her. Are you guys connected to that fellow on a bike?"

He ignored that one. He said, "You talked to her twice. Most recently tonight."

"I owed her some money. She came by to collect. She gave me a haircut and we ordered a vegetarian pizza. It was no big deal. Really."

His gaze was cold. "What has she told you?"

"Nothing. You know, she said Lorna was her mentor, and she passed along some of Lorna's financial strategies. She did mention her personal manager, a guy named Lester Dudley. You know him?"

"I don't believe Mr. Dudley is relevant to our discussion," he said. "What's your theory about the murder?"

"I don't have one yet."

"You don't know who killed her?"

I shook my head.

"My client is hoping you'll pass the name along when it comes into your possession."

Oh, sure, I thought. "Why?" I tried not to sound impertinent, but it was tough. It's probably smarter not to quiz these guys, but I was curious.

"He would consider it a courtesy."

"Ah, a courtesy. Got it. Like between us professionals."

"He could also make it worth your while."

"I appreciate that, but . . . mmm, I don't mean to sound rude about this, but I don't really want anything from him. You know, that I can think of at the moment. Tell him thanks for the offer."

Dead silence.

He reached into the inside breast pocket of his coat. I flinched, but all he did was take out a retractable ballpoint pen, which he clicked. He scribbled something on a business card and held it out to me. "I can be reached at this number at any hour."

The guy on my right moved forward, took the card, and passed it to me. No name. No address. Just the handwritten number. The attorney continued, his tone pleasant. "In the meantime, we'd prefer that you'd keep this conversation confidential."

"Sure."

"No exceptions."

"Okay."

"Including Mr. Phillips."

Cheney Phillips, undercover vice cop. I said, "Got it."

I felt cool air on my face and realized the limo door had been opened. The guy on my right got out, extending a hand to me. I appreciated the assist. It's hard to hump your way across a seat when the sweat on the back of your knees is causing you to stick to the upholstery. I hoped I hadn't wet myself. In this situation, I didn't even trust my legs to work. I emerged somewhat ungracefully, butt first, like a breech birth. To steady myself, I put a hand against the car parked next to mine.

The guy got back in the limo. The rear door closed with a click and the car eased away, gliding soundlessly out of the parking lot. I checked for the license plate, but the number had been obscured by mud. Not that I'd have had the plate run. I didn't really want to know who these guys were.

Under my jacket, the back of my turtleneck was cold and damp. An involuntary spasm scampered down my frame. I needed a hot shower and a slug of brandy, but I didn't have time for either. I unlocked my car and got in, slapping the lock down again as if pursued. I peered into the backseat to make sure I was alone. Even before I started the car, I flipped the heater on.

I sat in a back booth at Frankie's Coffee Shop, as far from the windows as I could get. I kept searching the other patrons, wondering if one of them was tailing me. The place was moderately full: older couples who'd probably been coming here for years, kids looking for some place to hang out. Janice had spotted me when I came in, and she appeared at the table with a coffeepot in hand. There was a setup in front of me: napkin, silverware, thick white ceramic cup turned upside down on a matching saucer. I turned the cup right-side up, and she filled it. I left it on the table so she couldn't see how badly my hands were shaking.

"You look like you could use this," she said. "You're white as a sheet."

"Can you talk?"

She glanced behind her. "Soon as the party at table five clears out," she said. "I'll leave you this." She put the pot down and moved back to her station, pausing to pick up an order from the kitchen pass-through.

When she returned, she was toting an oversize cinnamon roll and two pats of butter wrapped in silver paper. "I brought you a snack. You look like you could use a little jolt of sugar with your caffeine."

"Thanks. This looks great."

She sat down across from me, careful to keep an eye out in case customers came in.

I opened both pats and broke off a band of hot roll, which I buttered and ate, nearly moaning aloud. The dough was soft and moist, the glaze dripping down between the coils. Nothing like fear to generate an appetite for comfort foods. "Fantastic. I could get addicted. Is this a bad time for you?"

"Not at the moment. I may have to interrupt. Are you all right? You don't seem like yourself."

"I'm fine. I have a couple of things I need to ask." I paused to lick butter from my fingers, and then I wiped them on a paper napkin. "Did you know Lorna was supposed to get married in Las Vegas the weekend she died?"

Janice looked at me as if I had begun to speak a foreign language and she was waiting for subtitles to appear at the bottom of the screen. "Where in the world did you hear such a thing?"

"Think there's any truth to it?"

"Until this very second, I'd have said absolutely not. Now you mention it, I'm not so sure. It's possible," she said. "It might explain her attitude, which at the time I couldn't identify. She seemed excited. Truly, like she was wanting to tell me something, but was holding back. You know how kids are. . . . Well, maybe you don't. When kids have a secret, they can hardly keep it in. They want to tell so bad they can't stand it, so most of the time they just blab it right out. She was acting like that. At the time, I wasn't picking up on it consciously. I did notice, because that's what popped in my head the minute you said that, but at the time, I didn't press. Who was she going to marry? As far as I know, she didn't even date."

"I don't know the man's name. I gather it was some fellow from Los Angeles."

"But who told you? How did you find out about him?"

"His attorney got in touch with me a little while ago. Actually, it might have been the guy himself, playing games. It's hard to say."

"Why haven't we heard about him before now? She's been dead ten months and this is the first I've heard of it."

"Maybe we've finally started fishing in the right swamp," I said.

"You want me to ask the girls if she said anything to them?"

"I'm not sure it matters. I have no reason to believe the story's fabricated. It's a question of filling in some blanks."

"What else? You said there were a couple of things."

"On the twentieth of April—the day before she died—she closed out a savings account she kept down in Simi Valley. It looks like she withdrew approximately twenty thousand dollars, either in cash or check. It's also possible she moved the money to another account, but I can't find a record of it. Is this ringing any bells with you?"

She shook her head slowly. "No. I don't know anything about that. Mace or me didn't come across any substantial sums of money. I'd have turned it in, figuring it might be evidence. Besides, if it was Lorna's money, it'd be part of her estate and we might have to pay taxes on it. I don't cheat the government, not even the tiniest little bit. That's one thing I taught her. You don't fool around with the IRS."

"Could she have hidden it?" I asked.

"Why would she do that?"

"I have no idea. She might have closed out the account and then tucked the money away someplace until she needed it."

"You think someone stole it?"

"I don't even know if there was really any money in the first place. It looks like there was, but I can't be sure. It's possible her landlord might have taken it. At any rate, it's a detail I need to pin down."

"Well, I sure never saw it."

"Was she security conscious? I didn't see a lot of locks and bolts at her place."

"Oh, she was awful about that. She left the door wide open half the time. In fact, I've often thought somebody might have got in while she was jogging, which is why there wasn't any sign of forced entry. The police thought so, too, because they asked me about it more than once."

"Did she ever mention a safe in the house?"

Her tone was skeptical. "Oh, I don't think she had a safe. That doesn't seem like her at all. In that crappy little cabin? It wouldn't make any sense. She believed in banks. She had accounts everywhere."

"What about her jewelry? Where did she keep that? Did she have a safe-deposit box?"

"It was nothing like that. She kept a regular old jewelry box in her chest of drawers, but we didn't find anything expensive. Just some costume stuff."

"But she must have had good pieces if she went through all the trouble and expense to insure them. She even made a point of mentioning her jewelry in her will."

"I'll be happy to show you what we found, and you can see for yourself," Janice said.

"What about those home security devices where people hide their valuables—you know, fake rocks or Pepsi cans or phony heads of lettuce in the vegetable bin? Did she have anything like that?"

"I doubt it. The police never found anything in the house that I know of. I'm not sure about outside. I know they searched the yard around the cabin. If she had something like that, they'd have found it, wouldn't they?"

"You're probably right, but I may go back over there tomorrow and take a look. Feels like a waste of time, but I don't like loose ends. Anyway, it's not like I have any better ideas."

I went home to bed and slept fitfully, pricked by the awareness that I had work to do yet. While my body teetered toward exhaustion, my brain synapses fired at random. Ideas seemed to shoot up like rockets, exploding midair, a light show of impressions. By some curious metamorphosis, I was being drawn into the shadowy after-hours world Lorna Kepler had inhabited. Night turf, the darkness, seemed both exotic and familiar, and I felt myself waking to the possibilities. In the meantime, my system was operating on overload, and I didn't so much sleep as short myself out.

At five twenty-five in the evening, when I finally opened my eyes, I felt so anchored to the bed I could barely move. I closed my eyes again, wondering if I'd picked up a superfluous three hundred pounds in my sleep. I checked my extremities but found no evidence of massive overnight weight gain. I rolled out of bed with a whimper, pulled myself together with minimal attention to the particulars, and headed out my front door. At the first fast-food establishment I passed, I picked up an oversize container of hot coffee and sucked on it like a baby, effectively burning my lips.

By six, when ordinary folk were heading home from work, I was bumping down the narrow dirt lane that led to Lorna's cabin. I'd been driving with a constant eye on my rearview mirror, wondering if the fellows in the limousine were following. Whatever their tailing methods, they were experts. Since I'd started this case, I'd never been aware of being under surveillance. Even now I'd have been willing to swear there was no one watching.

I parked my car nose out, pausing as I had the first time to drink in the mossy perfume of the place. I set my empty cup on the floor and removed my flashlight and a screwdriver from the glove compartment. I got out of the car, pausing to assess the weather of the night. I was faintly aware of the ebb and flow of the freeway in the distance, a dull tide of passing cars. The air was soft and cold, the shadows shifting capriciously as if blown by the wind. I moved toward the cabin, stomach churning with uneasiness. It was amazing to me how much I'd learned about Lorna since I'd first seen the place. I'd reviewed the postmortem photographs so often, I could almost conjure up a vision of her as she'd been when she was discovered: softened, disintegrating, returning to the elements. If there were ghosts in this world, surely she was one.

The night was foggy, and I could hear the intermittent moaning of a foghorn sounding on the ocean. The night breeze had a saturated feel to it, rich with the scent of vegetation. I swept away the dark with the beam of my flashlight. The garden Leda'd planted was tangled and overgrown, tomato volunteers pushing up among the papery stalks of dead corn. A few onion sets had survived the last harvest. Come spring, even left to its own devices the garden might resurrect itself.

I stood in the front yard and studied the cabin, circling the outside. There was nothing to speak of: dirt, dead leaves, patches of dried grass. I went up the porch steps. The door was still off its hinges. I tapped to see if it was hollow, but it clunked back at me, dense and solid. I flipped on the overhead light. The dingy glow of a forty-watt bulb defined the interior spaces in a wash of faint yellow. I did a slow visual survey. Where would I hide twenty thousand dollars in cash? I started at the entryway and worked my way around to the right. The cabin was poorly insulated, and there didn't seem to be a lot of nooks and crannies. I tapped and poked, sticking the tip of my screwdriver in every crevice and crack. I felt like a dentist probing for cavities.

The kitchen seemed to suggest the greatest possibility for hiding places. I took drawers out, measured the depth of cabinets, looking for any discrepancies that might hint at an opening. I crawled along the floor, getting filthy in the process. Surely the cops had done exactly this . . . if they'd known what to search for.

I tried the bathroom next, shining my light up behind and inside the toilet tank, testing tiles for loose ones. I pulled out the medicine cabinet, peering down into the lathing behind it. I scrutinized the space in the alcove where she'd kept her bed, checked the metal floor plate in the living room on which the wood-burning stove had rested. There was nothing. Whatever Lorna did with her money, she didn't keep it on the premises. If she'd had jewelry or large sums of cash, she hadn't stuck it in a hidey-hole. Well, let's correct that. Whatever she'd done with her valuables, I didn't know where they were. Maybe someone else got to them first or maybe, as Cheney suggested, she'd used the money some other way. I finished up the search with a second survey, feeling dissatisfied.

By chance my gaze dropped to the Belltone box. The housing had been popped loose, and I leaned toward it, using my screwdriver to explore the space. For an instant I prayed a secret compartment would open up and a wad of bills would spill out. Optimist that I am, I always hope for things like that. There was nothing, of course, except the tag end of electrical wire. I'd never actually seen the working mechanism of a doorbell, but the wire seemed odd. I stood and stared at it for a moment and then leaned closer, squinting. What *was* that?

I went outside, down the creaking wooden steps. The front porch was hiked up on concrete supports, elevated about three feet, the space narrowing down to nothing where the ground sloped upward at the back. The intention must have been to keep moisture away from the floor joists, but the net effect was to create a cinder-strewn crawl space that had been screened with wooden lathing. I crouched beside the lathing and stuck my fingers through the holes. I gave a pull and a small section lifted away, allowing me to peer at the space underneath the cabin. It was pitch black. I raked the area with the beam of my flashlight and was treated to the bouncing of daddy longlegs as they warned me away.

There was a flat piece of plywood on the ground with a few garden tools laid on top. I stood up again, aligning my sights with the approximate location of the Belltone box. I adjusted my position and shone my flashlight up along the joists. I could see where the green wire came down through the floor. It was stapled along the joists at long intervals, running toward the edge of the porch close to me. I was going to have to inch my way under, not a happy thought given all the spiders lurking in the dark.

Gingerly I got down on my hands and the balls of my feet and duck-walked my way under. The spider kiddies viewed me with alarm, and many of them fled in what must have been spider fear and panic. Later they would have horrified conversations about the unpredictability of humans. "Eeew. All those fingers," they'd say. "And those big nasty feet. They always look like they're about to squish you." Spider mothers would console them. "Most humans are completely harmless, and they're just as scared of us as we are of them," they'd say.

I craned my head, sweeping the underside of the porch with the beam of my flashlight. Right at eye level a leather case had been stapled to the wood. I used the flat end of my screwdriver to force the staples out. The case was dusty and mealy where the leather had begun to deteriorate. I humped my way out from under the porch. I dusted my hands off, brushed gravel and dirt from my jeans, then flipped off the flashlight. I moved back into the cabin to examine my find. What I was holding looked like the carrying case for a little portable radio or tape recorder, complete with holes in the end into which an earphone or a mike could be plugged. There was a slit along one end for the volume control. It had to be a surveillance setup, not sophisticated by any means, but possibly effective. Somebody had planted something similar in my apartment a couple of years back, and I'd discovered it only by accident. In the meantime, the voice-activated recorder had captured my end of all phone calls, all incoming messages on my answering machine, both sides of any conversations I'd had on the premises.

Someone had been spying on Lorna. Of course, it was possible she'd planted the device herself, but only if she'd had a reason to keep an audible record of her conversations. If that were the case, I couldn't believe she wouldn't have planted the recorder inside the cabin, where reception would be good and the tapes easier to replace. Something like this, tacked to the underside of the cabin, was bound to pick up a lot of ambient noise.

Gosh-a-rudy, I thought, now who do I know who'd have access to all kinds of surveillance equipment? Could it be Miss Leda Selkirk, daughter of the PI who'd once had his license yanked for an illegal wiretap? I flipped my flashlight back on and turned the lights off in the cabin. I unlocked my car and turned the key in the ignition, easing the VW down the bumpy road toward the street.

I parked out in front of the Burkes' half-darkened house.

When Leda answered my knock, I was standing with the decrepit leather case dangling off the end of my screwdriver like the skin of some strange beast. Tonight, her midriff was bare. Here it was the middle of February and she was wearing an outfit that might have been suitable for a belly dancer: wrap-around sarong-style pants with wide legs in a thin floral fabric reminiscent of summer pajama bottoms. The top was a similar fabric, different print, with no sleeves and one button appearing right between her quite weensie breasts. I said, "Is J.D. here?"

She shook her head. "He's not home yet."

"Mind if I come in?" I pictured her playing dumb, a reaction ranging anywhere from denial to duh.

She looked at me and she looked at the leather case, apparently unable to think of a thing to say except, "Oh."

She stepped back from the door, and I went into the darkened hall, following as she led the way toward the kitchen at the rear. A glance to the left showed Jack, the sticky-fingered toddler, lying in a stupor on the couch, watching a cartoon video. The infant slept, slumped sideways in a well-padded portable car seat while colored images flickered across its face.

The kitchen still smelled like the sautéed onions and ground beef from dinner on Monday, which seemed like ages ago. Some of the dishes piled in the sink looked the same, too, though several other meals' worth had been piled on top. She was probably the type who waited until everything was used before she ventured into the washing process. "You want some coffee?" she asked. I could see a fresh pot on a Mr. Coffee stand, the mechanism still spitting out the last few drops.

"That'd be nice," I said. I sat down at the banquette and checked the kitchen table for sticky spots. I found a clear couple of inches and propped my elbow with care.

She took down a mug and filled it, then refilled hers before she put the pot back on the machine. In profile, her nose seemed too long for her face, but the effect in certain lights was lovely nonetheless. Her neck was long and her ears elfin, her short-cropped dark hair trimmed to wisps around her face. Her eyes were lined in smudged black, and her lip gloss was a brownish tint.

I put the leather case in the middle of the table.

She took a seat on the bench, pulling her feet up under her. She ran her hand through her hair, her expression somewhat sheepish. "I kept meaning to take that out, but I never got around to it. What a dork."

"You installed surveillance equipment?"

"Wasn't much. Just a mike and a tape recorder."

"Why?"

"I don't know. I was worried," she said. Her dark eyes seemed enormous, filled with innocence.

"I'm listening."

Color was rising in her face. "I thought J.D. and Lorna might be fooling around, but I was wrong." There was a baby bottle half-full of formula sitting on the table. She unscrewed the nipple and used the contents for cream. She offered me some, but I declined.

"What was it, voice-activated?"

"Well, yeah. I know it sounds kind of dumb in retrospect, but I'd just found out I was pregnant with the baby, and I was throwing up all day. Jack wasn't even out of diapers, and I was frantic about J.D. I knew I was being bitchy, but I couldn't help myself. I looked horrible and felt worse. And there was Lorna, slim and elegant. I'm not stupid. I figured out what she did for a living, and so did he. J.D. started finding excuses for going back there every other day. I knew if I confronted him, he'd laugh in my face, so I borrowed some of Daddy's stuff."

"*Were* they having an affair?"

Her expression was self-mocking. "He fixed her toilet. One of her screens had come loose, and he fixed that, too. The most he ever did was complain about me, and even that wasn't bad. She had a fit and chewed him out. She said he had a hell of a nerve when I was the one doing all the suffering and hard work. Also, she got on him because he didn't lift a finger with Jack. That's when he started cooking, which has been a big help. I feel bad I never thanked her, but I wasn't supposed to know she'd come to my defense."

"How'd you know how to install the bug?"

"I've watched Daddy do it. Lorna was gone a lot, so it wasn't hard. The doorbell never worked, but the box was there. I just drilled a hole in the floor and then crawled under the cabin. All I had to do was make sure the tape was close enough to the edge of the porch so I could switch it without a hassle. We kept the gardening tools under there. Any time I weeded, I would find a way to check the tape."

"How many tapes did you run?"

"I only used one tape, but the first time was a bust because the mike was defective and didn't pick up half the time. Second try was better, but the sound was distorted, so you couldn't hear too well. She had the radio on. She played this jazz station all the time. Up front there's this little fragment with her and J.D. I had to listen three times to be sure it was him. Then her drying her hair . . . that was entertaining. I got her end of a couple of phone calls, that whole business where she's cranking on J.D. Then more music, only country this time, then she's talking to some guy. That part's left over from the first round, I think."

"Did you tell the police?"

"There wasn't anything to tell. Besides, I was embarrassed," she said. "I didn't want J.D. to know I didn't trust him, especially when it turned out he's innocent. I felt like a fool. Plus, the whole thing's illegal, so why incriminate myself? I'm still worried they'll start thinking it was J.D. who killed her. It scared me silly when you started in on us, but at least this way I can prove the two of them were friends and got along okay."

I stared at her. "Are you trying to tell me you still *have* the tapes?"

"Well, sure, but there's only one," she said. "The first time was mostly static, so I went ahead and taped over it."

"You mind if I listen?"

"You mean right now?"

"If you don't mind."

15

She unfolded herself and got up from the table. She moved out into the hallway and disappeared from sight. Moments later she returned with an empty cassette box and a little tape recorder, the cassette already in place and visible through the oval window. "I guess I didn't have to keep this, but it made me feel better. Really, J.D. couldn't have killed her because he wasn't even in town. He took off Friday morning on a fishing trip. She wasn't killed until Saturday when he was miles away."

"Where were you that day?"

"I was gone too. I decided to go part of the way with him. He took me as far as Santa Maria and dropped Jack and me at my sister's on Friday. I spent a week with her and then came home on the bus."

"You have any objections to giving me her name and number?"

"You don't believe me?"

"Let's don't get into that, Leda. You're not exactly a Girl Scout," I said.

"Well, I know, but that doesn't mean I'd *kill* anyone."

"What about J.D.? Can he verify his whereabouts?"

"You can ask my sister's husband, Nick. That's who he went to Nacimiento with."

I made a note of the name and number.

Leda punched the play button on the recorder. After a brief interval of white noise, the sound seemed to jump out. The reception was dismal, filled with clunks and banging as people moved around. With the equipment so close, the knocking on the door sounded like lightning cracks. A chair scraped, and someone thunked across the floor.

"Oh, hi. Come on in. I got the check right here."

There were a couple of inaudible remarks between the two of them. The front door closed like a muffled explosion.

Footsteps clunking. *"How's Leda feeling?"*

"She's kind of down in the dumps, but she was this way last time. She gets to feeling fat and ugly. She's convinced I'm going out to screw around on her, so she busts out crying every time I leave the house."

I put out a hand. "Hold on a minute. That's J.D.'s voice?"

She pushed pause, and the recording stopped. "Yeah, I know. It's hard to recognize. I had to play it two or three times myself. You want to hear it again?"

"If you don't mind," I said. "I've never heard Lorna's voice, but I'm assuming you can identify her as well."

"Well, sure," Leda said. She punched the rewind button. When the tape stopped, she pressed play, and we listened to the opening again. *"Oh, hi. Come on in. I got the check right here."*

Again, muffled remarks between the two of them and the front door closed like a sonic boom.

Footsteps clunking. *"How's Leda feeling?"*

"She's kind of down in the dumps, but she was this way last time. She gets to feeling fat and ugly. She's convinced I'm going out to screw around on her, so she busts out crying every time I leave the house."

Lorna was saying, *"What's her problem? She looks darling."*

"Well, I think so, but she's got some girlfriend that happened to." Footsteps thunked across the floor and a chair scraped back, sounding like a lion roaring in the jungle.

"She only gained fifteen pounds with Jack. How could she feel fat? She doesn't even show. My mother gained forty-six with me. Now, that's uggers. I've seen pictures. Stomach hanging down to here. Boobs looked like footballs, and her legs looked like sticks." Laughter. Mumbles. Static.

"Yeah, well, it isn't real, so you can't talk her out of it. You know how she is. . . . [mumble, mumble] *. . . insecure."*

"That's what you get for hooking up with someone half your age."

"She's twenty-one!"

"Serves you right. She's an infant. Listen, you want me to keep Jack while you two go out to dinner?" More mumbles.

"xxxxxxx" The response here was completely missing, blotted out by static.

". . . problem. He and I get along great. In exchange, you can do me a favor and fog the place for me next time I go out of town. The spiders are getting out of control."

"Thanks. . . . ceipt in your mailbox." Chairs scraping. Clump, clump of footsteps crossing the cabin. Muffled voices. The conversation continued outside and then stopped abruptly. Silence. When the tape picked up again, there were strains of country music with the high whine of a hair dryer running over it. A phone began to ring. The hair dryer was turned off. Clump, clump, clump of footsteps like a series of gunshots. The phone was picked up, and Lorna raised her voice in greeting. After that, much of her end of the call was a series of short responses . . . *uhn-hun, sure, right, okay, that's great.* There was a fragmentary mention of the Palace that made me think she might be talking to Danielle. Hard to tell with the competing strains of country music overlaid. There was a second conversation between J.D. and Lorna, which was much as Leda indicated. J.D. complained, and Lorna chewed him out because he never helped at home.

Leda pressed the stop button impatiently. "It goes on like that. Pissed me off they were always talking about me behind my back. Lot of the rest is just mumbling, and most you can't even hear."

"Too bad," I said.

"Yeah, well, the equipment was kind of dinky. I didn't want to get into anything elaborate because it was too much trouble. The amplification was minimal. You get a lot of distortion that way."

"When was this done? Any way to pin down the date?"

"Not really. Lorna sat with Jack a couple different times, but I never wrote it down. It wasn't any special occasion. Just us popping out for a bite to eat. With a toddler at home, an hour by yourself feels like heaven."

"What about the month? It must have been early in the pregnancy because he mentions you're not showing yet. And wasn't there mention of a receipt? In that first conversation, it sounds like he's stopped by to pick up the rent."

"Oh. Maybe so. You could be right about that. I mean, Jeremy was born in September, so that must have been . . . I don't know . . . April sometime? She paid the first of the month."

"When did you start the taping?"

"Around then, I guess. Like I said, the first tape was all static. This is the second one I did. I think he actually had the exterminator out for all the spiders and bugs. He probably has a record of it if you want me to look it up."

"What else is on here?"

"Mostly junk, like I said. The batteries went dead about halfway through, and after that all you hear is the stuff still on there from the first time I taped." She pulled the tape out and tucked it back in the empty cassette box. She got up from the table as if to leave the room.

I caught her casually by the arm. "Mind if I take that?"

She hesitated. "What for?"

"So I can hear it again."

She made a face. "Nnn, I don't know. I don't think that's a good idea. This's the only one I got."

"I'll bring it back as soon as possible."

She shook her head. "I'd rather not."

"Come on, Leda. What are you so worried about?"

"How do I know you won't turn it over to the cops?"

"Oh, right. So they can listen to people clump around making small talk? This is not incriminating stuff. They're talking about the fuckin' *bugs,*" I said. "Besides, you can always claim you had permission. Who's going to contradict you?"

She gave that consideration. "What's your interest?"

"I was hired to do this. This is my job," I said. "Look. From what you've said, this tape was made within a month of Lorna's death. How can you be sure it's not significant?"

"You'll bring it right back?"

"I promise."

Reluctantly she put the cassette on the table and pushed it over to me. "But I want to know where to call in case I need it back," she said.

"You're a doll," I said. I took out a business card and made a note of my home phone and my home address. "I gave you this before, but here it is again. Oh, and one more thing."

Sounding crabby, she said, "What?"

Every time I manipulate people, it seems to make them so *cross.* "Has J.D. come into any money in the last few months?"

"J.D. doesn't have money. If he does, he never told me. You want me to ask when he gets in?"

"It's not important," I said. "Anyway, if you mention it, you might have to tell him what we were talking about, and I don't think you want to do that."

From the expression on her face, I thought maybe I could trust her discretion.

I stopped at a minimart on the way back to my place. Somewhere I had a tape recorder, but the batteries were probably dead. While I was at it, I bought myself a king-size cup of coffee and a nasty-looking meat sandwich wrapped in cellophane. From the pink stuff peeking out the side, it was hard to imagine what cow part this was thin slivers of. I ate driving home, feeling too starved to wait. It was not quite eight o'clock, but this was probably lunch.

Home again, I spent some time getting organized. The tape recorder was right where it was supposed to be, in the bottom drawer of my desk. I changed the batteries and found the headphones, a pencil, and a legal pad. I played the tape through, listening with my eyes closed, the headphones pressed against my ears. I played the tape back again, taking notes this time. I transcribed what I could hear clearly and left a series of dots, dashes, and question marks where the sound was garbled or inaudible. It was slow going, but I finally reached a point where I'd gleaned as much as I could.

As Leda had indicated, toward the end of the tape, after sixty minutes of boring talk, her machine had gone dead, leaving a fragment from the first taping she'd done. The one voice was Lorna's. The other voice was male, but not J.D.'s as far as I could tell. There was a segment of country music playing on the radio. Lorna must have turned it off because the silence was abrupt and punctuated by static. The guy spoke up sharply, saying, *"Hey . . ."*

Lorna sounded annoyed. *"I hate that stuff. . . . xxxxxxx. xxxxxxxxx . . ."*

"Oh, come on. I'm just kidding. But you have to admit, it's xxxxxxxxxx. She goes in xxxxxxxxxxxxx day . . . xxxxxx . . ."

"Goddamn it! Would you stop saying that? You're really sick. . . ."

"People shouldn't xxxxxxxx . . . [clatter . . . clink] . . ."

Sound of water . . . squeaking . . .

". . . xxxxxxxx . . ."

Thump, thump . . .

"I'm serious . . . by—"

"xxxxx . . ."

Laughter . . . chair scrape . . . rustle . . . murmur . . .

There was something quarrelsome in the tone, an edginess in Lorna's voice. I played the tape twice more, writing down everything I heard clearly, but the subject of the conversation never made any sense. I took the headphones off. I pinched the bridge of my nose and rubbed my hands across my face. I wondered if the guys in the forensics lab had a way to amplify sound on a tape like this. As a private investigator, I was not exactly into high-tech equipment. A portable typewriter was about as state-of-the-art as I could boast. The problem was, I didn't see how I could ask for police assistance without an explanation of some kind. Despite my assurances to Leda, she was guilty of withholding, if not evidence, then information that might have been relevant to the police investigation. Cops get very surly when you least expect it, and I didn't want them to take an interest in something that wasn't mine to begin with.

Who else did I know? I tried the Yellow Pages in the telephone book under "Audio." The businesses listed offered laser home theaters, giant-screen TVs, custom design and installation of audio systems, and presentation graphics, followed by the ads for hearing aids, hearing evaluations, and speech therapists. I tried the section entitled "Sound," which was devoted in large part to designing wireless drive-through intercoms and residential and commercial sound systems. Oh.

I checked my watch: quarter after nine. I flipped back to the White Pages under K-SPL and called Hector Moreno at the local FM station. It was probably too early to reach him, but I could at least leave a message. The phone was picked up after three rings. "K-SPELL. This is Hector Moreno."

"Hector? I can't believe it's you. This is Kinsey Millhone. Aren't you there awfully early?"

"Well, hey. How are you? I switch shifts now and then. Keeps me from getting bored. What about you? What are you up to?"

"I have a tape recording with very poor sound quality. Would you have any way to clean it up?"

"That depends on what you got. I could try," he said. "You want to drop it off? I can leave the door unlocked."

"I'll be right there."

En route, I made a stop at Rosie's, where I told her about Beauty and begged for doggie bones. Earlier she'd boiled up two pounds of veal knuckle for the stock she makes. I had to pick through the trash to get them, but she wrapped two in paper with the usual admonishment. "You should get a dog," she said.

"I'm never home," I replied. She is always on me about this. Don't ask me why. Just a piece of aggravation, in my opinion. I took the packet of bones and began to back away, hoping to curtail discussion.

"A dog is good company, and protection, too."

"I'll think about it," I said as the kitchen door swung shut.

"Get a fella while you're at it."

At the station, I let myself in. Hector had left the door ajar and the foyer lights on. I went down into the twilight of the stairwell with my paper packet of bones. Beauty was waiting for me when I reached the bottom. She was the size of a small bear, her dark eyes bright with intelligence. Her coat was red gold, the undercoat puffy and soft. When she saw me, her fur seemed to undulate and she emitted a low, humming growl. I watched her lift her head at the scent of me. Without warning she pursed her lips and howled, a soaring note of ululation that seemed to go on for minutes. I didn't move, but I could feel my own fur bristle in response to her keening. I was rooted to the bottom step, my hand on the rail. Something primitive in her singing sent ice down along my spine. I heard Hector call her, then the quick thump of his crutches as he swung along the corridor.

"Beauty!" he snapped.

At first she refused to yield. He called her again. Her eyes rolled back at him reluctantly, and I could see her debate. She was willful, intent. As strong as her urge toward obedience, she didn't want to comply. Her complaints were sorrowful, the half-talk of dogs in which sentiment is conveyed in the insistent language of canines. She howled again, watching me.

I murmured, "What's the matter with her?"

"Beats me."

"I brought her some bones."

"It's not that." He leaned down and touched her. The howling became a low cry, filled with such misery that it broke my heart. He held his hand out. I passed him the packet of veal knuckles.

Hector looked at me oddly. "You smell like Lorna. Have you been handling something of hers?"

"I don't think so. Just some papers," I said. "There was a scarf of hers in the banker's box, but that was yesterday."

"Sit down very carefully on the steps where you are."

I eased myself down into a sitting position. He began to talk to Beauty, his tone full of comfort. She watched me with a mixture of hope and confusion, thinking I was Lorna, knowing I was not. Hector offered her the bones, which failed to interest her. Instead, carefully, she extended her blunt snout and sniffed at my fingers. I could see her nostrils work as she sifted and analyzed the components of my personal scent. He scratched her ears, massaging her meaty shoulders. Finally she seemed to accept that she had erred somehow. She hung her head, watching me with puzzlement, as if at any minute I might turn into the woman she was waiting for.

Hector straightened up. "She's okay now. Come on. Here. Why don't you take these," he said, passing the bones back to me. "She might decide she likes you yet."

I followed him into the same small studio. Beauty had resumed her wary guardianship, and she positioned herself between the two of us. She put her head down on her feet. Occasionally she gave me a look, but she was clearly depressed. Hector had made fresh coffee, which he offered from a jug thermos sitting on the counter beside a cardboard box and a leather photo album. I let him pour me a cup, figuring I couldn't feel much worse. He perched up on his stool, and I watched while he phased out the jazz number that was playing. He extemporized a commentary, feigning casual knowledge from the liner notes in the CD. His voice was deep and melodious. He slipped in another cassette, adjusted the sound levels, and then turned to me. "Let's try the bones," he said. "Beauty needs a lift, poor girl."

"I feel bad," I said. "I was wearing those jeans when I went through Lorna's files."

I opened the paper packet and hunkered next to Beauty. He coached me through the process. She finally relented, allowing me to stroke her densely furred head. She took one of the knuckle bones between her feet and licked it thoroughly before she tested with her teeth. She made no particular objection when I rose again and perched up beside Hector on a second stool. Hector, meanwhile, was sorting through a stack of old black-and-white photographs with white fluted rims. He had a box of gummed corners and was mounting selected snapshots in an album fat with photographs.

"What are those?"

"My dad's got a birthday coming up, and I thought he'd get a kick. Most of these were taken during World War Two."

He passed me a snapshot of a man in pleated pants and a white dress shirt, standing in front of a microphone. "He was forty-two. He'd tried to enlist, but Uncle Sam turned him down. Too old, bad feet, punctured eardrum. He was already working as an announcer at radio station WCPO in Cincinnati, and they told him they needed him for the war effort, keep morale up here at home. He used to take me with him. Probably how I got the bug." He set the album aside. "Let's see what you have."

I took the cassette from my bag and passed it over to him. "Someone was doing a little eavesdropping. I'd rather not say who."

He turned it over in his hand. "I probably can't do much with this. I was hoping you were talking eight- or multitrack. Know how this works?"

"Not at all," I said.

"This is Mylar ribbon, coated on one side with a bonding material containing iron oxide. Signal passes through a coil in a recording head, and that causes a magnetic field to form between the poles of the magnet. Iron particles get magnetized in something called domains. No point in boring you to death," he said. "The point is, professional recording equipment is going to give you far better fidelity than a little tape like this. What was it, some kind of little dingus running off batteries?"

"Exactly. There's a lot of ambient noise, mumbling and static. You can't hear half of it."

"Doesn't surprise me. What'd you use for playback, same thing?"

"Probably the equivalent," I said. "I gather you can't help."

"Well, I can put it on my machine at home and see if that gives you anything. If the sound wasn't laid down in the first place, there's never going to be a way to pick it up on playback, but I got good speakers and could maybe filter out some frequencies, play around with bass and treble, and see what that does."

I pulled out the notes I'd made. "This is what I picked up so far. Anything I couldn't hear, I left blank with a question mark."

"Can you leave the tape with me? I can take a crack at it when I get home tonight and call you sometime tomorrow."

"I'm not sure about that. I swore I'd guard it with my life. I'd hate having to admit I left the tape with you."

"So don't tell. Someone asks for it back, just give me a call and come pick it up."

"You're a very devious person, Hector."

"Aren't we all?"

He took the page of notes I'd made and went into the other room to make a copy while I waited. I gave him my business card with my home address and phone jotted on the back. By the time I left the studio, Beauty had apparently decided I was part of her pack, though much lower in the pecking order and therefore in need of protection. She very kindly walked me to the stairwell, matching her footsteps to mine, and watched as I went up the steps and out into the foyer. I peeked back and found her still standing there, looking up, her gaze fixed on mine. I said, "Good night, Beauty."

Pulling out of the K-SPL parking lot, I caught a glimpse of a lone man on a bike streaking across the intersection. He took the corner wide and disappeared from sight, reflectors on his spokes making circles of light. For a moment I could feel a mounting roar in my ears, darkness gathering at the edges of my vision. I rolled down the window and pulled fresh air into my lungs. A wave of clamminess climbed my frame and passed. I pulled into the empty intersection and slowed, peering right, but there was no sign of him. The street lamps receded in a series of diminishing uprights that narrowed to a point and vanished.

I headed down to lower State Street, cruising Danielle's turf. I needed company or a good night's sleep, whichever came first. If I found Danielle, maybe the two of us would buy champagne and orange juice, drink a toast to Lorna just for old times' sake. Then I'd head for home. I pulled into the parking lot at Neptune's Palace and got out of my car.

From the far end of the parking lot, the noise level was considerably louder than I'd experienced before. The crowd was boisterous. The side doors were opened onto the parking lot, and a knot of revelers had spilled out. Some guy toppled sideways, taking two women with him. The three of them lay on the asphalt, laughing. This was Thursday night trade, nearly manic in its energy, everyone determined to party, gearing up for the coming weekend. Music pounded against the walls. Cigarette smoke drifted on the frigid night air in wisps and curls. I heard the shattering of glass, followed by maniacal laughter as if a genie had been released. I caught sight of a patrol car in the parking lot. The black-and-whites usually come down here every couple of hours. The beat officer parks and works his way through the place in search of liquor violations and petty criminals.

I steeled myself and pushed through the door. I traveled the length of the bar like a fish swimming upstream, scanning the assembled patrons for Danielle. She'd said she usually started work at eleven, but there was always the chance she'd stop at the bar first to have a drink. There was no sign of her at all, but I did see Berlyn on her way to the dance floor. She was wearing a short black skirt and a red satin top with spaghetti straps. Her hair was slightly too short for the topknot she affected, so that more seemed to hang down than was secured above. Her earrings were big double rhinestone hoops that glittered and bounced against her neck as she moved. At first I thought she was unaccompanied, but then I saw a fellow pushing through the crowd in front of her. The other bobbing dancers closed around her, and she was gone.

I made my way back to the front door and checked the parking lot without luck. I fired up the VW and cruised the neighborhood, pausing at all the street corners where the hookers hung out. Ten more minutes of this shit and I was heading home. Finally I pulled in at the curb, leaned over, and rolled my window down. A rail-thin brunette, wearing a T-shirt, miniskirt, and cowboy boots, separated herself from the wall she was leaning on. She ambled over and opened the door on the passenger side. I could see the puckering of goose bumps on her frail, bare arms.

"You want company?" She was strung out on something, throwing off that odd crackhead body odor. Her eyes kept sliding upward out of focus, like the roll on a TV picture.

"I'm looking for Danielle."

"Well, hon, Danielle's busy, so I'm covering her act. What you want, I can get, and that's an actual fact."

"Did she go home?"

"It's possible that Danielle has gone back to her place. Give me ten dollars more and I'll sit on your face."

I said, "Rhyming. Very nice. Meter's a little off, but otherwise you're Longfellow."

"Baby, don't be strange. You got any change?"

"I'm fresh out," I said.

"I won't pout." She pushed away from the car and sauntered back to her post. I pulled away, hoping I hadn't unleashed a fit of iambic pentameter. It hadn't occurred to me that Danielle might hang out at her place before going to work.

I headed up two blocks and hung a left, turning into the narrow alleyway where Danielle had her digs. I pulled even with the property and peered through the gap in the shrubs, my gaze moving up the brick walk that led to her door. Her curtains had been drawn, but I could see the glow of lights on inside. I really had no idea whether she brought johns back to her place or not. It was close enough to the Palace to be practical, but there were also a couple of fleabag hotels in the area, and she might have preferred to take her business there. I saw a shadow pass the window, which seemed to suggest she was on her feet. My car engine chuffed noisily, headlights slicing through the dark like blades. I could feel myself vacillate. She might be alone and glad of company. On the other hand, she might be occupied. I really didn't want to see her in a business context.

While I debated, I killed the engine and flicked out my headlights. The alley disappeared in pitch blackness, night insects chirring in the heavy silence. Within a minute my eyes were accustomed to the dark, and the landscape began to reassemble itself in shades of charcoal. I got out of the car and locked it behind me. Maybe I'd knock once. If she was busy, so be it. I felt my way from the alley to the brick walk, holding one hand in front of me lest I stumble over trash cans.

I reached her doorstep and cocked my head, listening for the sound of voices or canned laughter from the television. I gave a tentative knock. From the other side of the door, I heard low moans, sensuous and repetitive. Uh-oh. I remembered the first trailer I'd moved into after the death of my aunt. Coming in late one summer night, I'd heard a pregnant neighbor woman making sounds like that. Ever the good citizen, I'd gone over to her window, where I'd tapped and asked if she needed help. I'd thought she was in labor, realizing too late the process I'd interrupted was the one that *made* babies, not delivered them.

Behind me, someone moved out of the shadows near the alley and eased through the shrubs. Leisurely footsteps scritched on the pavement and gradually faded. Danielle's moaning was renewed, and I backed up a step. I stared out at the alleyway with puzzlement. Was that her john I'd just seen? I leaned my head against the door. "Danielle?" No response.

I knocked again. Silence.

I tried the knob. The hinges made no sound at all as the door swung inward. At first, all I saw was the blood.

16

The emergency room at St. Terry's was bedlam, a glimpse into purgatory. There had been a six-car accident on the highway, and all of the examining rooms were filled with the injured and dying. In each cubicle, against the hot white cloth of the surrounding screens, I could see a shadow play of medical procedures against a backdrop of supply carts, wall-mounted oxygen, the hanging bags of blood and glucose, X-ray machinery. Once in a while the low hum of activity would be cut by hellish shrieks from the patient on the gurney. On one stretcher, unattended, the victim writhed as if licked by flames, crying, "Mercy . . . have mercy." An orderly came by and moved him into a newly vacated examining room.

Doctors, nurses, and med techs had been mustered from every corner of St. Terry's. I watched them work in perfect concert, actions urgent and precise. What the medical soap operas on TV conveniently omit is all the pain and the puke, body functions gone bad, needles piercing flesh, the bruises and the trembling, the low cries for help. Who wants to sit there and stare at real life? We want all the drama of hospitals without the underlying anguish.

In the waiting room, the faces of the relatives who'd been notified of the collision were gray and haggard. They spoke in hushed voices, family members huddled in small groups, their postures bent with dread. Two women clung together, weeping hopelessly. On the other side of the glass doors, at one end of the parking lot, the nicotine addicts had collected in a cloud of cigarette smoke. I'd seen Serena Bonney soon after Danielle was brought in, but she'd been swallowed up by the commotion.

When I'd first pushed open Danielle's front door, she was lying on the floor naked, her face as pink and pulpy as seedless watermelon. Blood spurted from a jagged laceration in her scalp, and she moved her limbs aimlessly as if she might crawl away from her own internal injuries. I'd disconnected my emotions, doing what I could to stem the bleeding while I grabbed the phone off her bed table. The 911 dispatcher had alerted a patrol car and an ambulance, both of which arrived within minutes. Two paramedics had gone to work, administering whatever first aid they could.

The bruises on her body formed a pattern of dark, overlapping lines that suggested she'd been pounded with a blunt instrument. The weapon turned out to be a rag-wrapped length of lead pipe that her assailant had tossed in the bushes on his way out. The patrol officer had spotted it when he arrived and left it for bagging by the crime scene investigators, who showed up shortly afterward. Once the officer secured the scene, we moved out onto the small front porch, standing in a shallow pool of light while he questioned me, taking notes.

By then the alleyway was choked with vehicles. A stutter of blue lights punctuated the darkness, the police radio contributing a deadpan staccato murmur broken up by rasping intervals of static. A clutch of neighbors had assembled in the side yard in a motley assortment of sockless jogging shoes, bedroom slippers, coats, and ski jackets pulled on over nightclothes. The patrol officer began to canvass the crowd, checking to see if there were any other witnesses aside from me.

A sporty bright red Mazda pulled up in the alley with a chirp of tires. Cheney Phillips emerged and strode up the walk. He acknowledged my presence and then exchanged brief words with the uniformed officer, identifying himself before he moved into Danielle's cottage. I saw him halt on the threshold and back up a step. From the open door he did a slow survey of the bloody scene, as if clicking off a sequence of time-lapse photographs. I imagined the view as I had seen it: the rumpled bedding, furniture knocked sideways and toppled. In the meantime, Danielle had been wrapped in blankets and shifted onto the gurney. I stepped aside for the paramedics as they brought her through the front door. I made eye contact with the older of the two. "Mind if I ride along?"

"Fine with me, as long as the detective doesn't object."

Cheney caught the exchange between us and gave a nod of assent. "Catch you later," he said.

The gurney was eased into the back of the ambulance.

I left my car where it was, parked to one side of the alley behind Danielle's house. I sat beside her blanket-covered form in the rear of the ambulance, trying to stay out of range of the young paramedic, who continued to monitor her vital signs. Her eyes were bruised and as swollen as a newly hatched bird's. From time to time I could see her stir, blind with pain and confusion. I kept saying, "You're going to be okay. You're fine. It's over." I wasn't even sure she heard me, but I had to hope the reassurances were getting through. She was barely conscious. The flashing yellow lights were reflected in the plate-glass storefronts as we sped up State Street. The siren seemed somehow disassociated from events. At that hour of the night the streets were largely empty, and the journey was accomplished with remarkable dispatch. It was not until we reached the emergency room that we heard about the multicar wreck out on 101.

I sat out in the waiting room for an hour while they worked on her. By then most of the accident victims had been tended to, and the place was clearing out. I found myself leafing through the same *Family Circle* magazine I'd read before: same perfect women with the same perfect teeth. The July issue was looking dog-eared. Certain articles had been torn out, and someone had annotated the article on male menopause, penning rude comments in the margin. I read busy-day recipes for backyard barbecues, a column of readers' suggestions for solving various parental dilemmas involving their children's lying, stealing, and their inability to read. Gave me a lot of faith in the generation coming up.

Cheney Phillips walked in. His dark hair was as curly as a standard poodle's, and I noticed that he was impeccably dressed: chinos and sport coat over an immaculate white dress shirt, dark socks, and penny loafers. He moved to the reception desk and flipped out his badge, identifying himself to the clerk, who was frantically typing up admissions forms. She made a quick phone call. I watched while he followed her into the treatment room where I'd seen them take Danielle. Moments later he stepped out into the corridor, again in conversation with one of the ER doctors. Two orderlies emerged, maneuvering a rolling gurney between them. Danielle's head was swaddled in bandages. Cheney's expression was neutral as she was rolled away. The doctor disappeared into the next cubicle.

Cheney glanced up and saw me. He came out into the waiting room and took a seat next to me on the blue tweed couch. He reached for my hand and laced his fingers through mine.

"How's she doing?" I asked.

"They're taking her up to surgery. Doctor's worried about internal bleeding. I guess the guy kicked the shit out of her as a parting gesture. She's got a broken jaw, cracked ribs, damage to her spleen, and God knows what else. Doctor says she's a mess."

"She looked awful," I said. Belatedly I could feel the blood drain away from my brain. Clamminess and nausea filled me up like a well. Ordinarily I'm not squeamish, but Danielle was a friend, and I'd seen the damage. Hearing her injuries cataloged was too vivid a reminder of the suffering I'd witnessed. I put my head down between my knees until the roaring ceased. This was the second time I'd found myself fading, and I knew I needed help.

Cheney watched with concern. "You want to go find a Coke or a cup of coffee? It'll probably be an hour before we hear anything."

"I can't leave. I want to be here when she comes out of surgery."

"Cafeteria's down the hall. I'll tell the nurse where we are, and she can come get us if we're not back by then."

"All right, but make sure Serena knows. I saw her back there a little while ago."

The cafeteria had closed at ten, but we found a row of vending machines that dispensed sandwiches, yogurts, fresh fruit, ice cream, and hot and cold drinks. Cheney bought two cans of Pepsi, two ham-and-cheese sandwiches on rye, and two pieces of cherry pie on Styrofoam plates. I sat numbly at an empty table in a little alcove off to one side. He came back with a tray loaded down with the food, straws, napkins, plastic cutlery, paper packets of salt and pepper, and pouches of pickle relish, mustard, ketchup, and mayonnaise. "I hope you're hungry," he said. He began to set the table, arranging condiments on matching paper napkins in front of us.

"Seems like I just ate, but why not?" I said.

"You can't pass this up."

"Such a feast," I said, smiling. I was too tired to lift a finger. Feeling like a kid, I watched while he unwrapped the sandwiches and began to doctor them.

"We have to make these really disgusting," he said.

"Why?"

"Because then we won't notice how bland they are." He tore at plastic packets with his teeth, squeezing gobs of bright red and yellow across the meat. Salt, pepper, and smears of mayonnaise with a scattering of relish. "You want to tell me about it?" he said idly while he worked. He popped the lid on a can of Pepsi and passed an amended sandwich to me. "Eat that. No arguments."

"Who can resist?" I bit into the sandwich, nearly weeping, it tasted so good. I moaned, shifting the bite to my cheek so I could talk while I was eating. "I saw Danielle last night. We had dinner together at my place. I told her then I might see her tonight, but I really went by on a whim," I said. I put a hand against my mouth, swallowing, and then took a sip of Pepsi. "I didn't know if she had company, so I sat there in the car with the engine running, checking it out. I could see she had her lights on, so I finally decided to go knock on her door. Worst-case scenario, she'd be with some guy and I'd tiptoe away."

"He probably saw your headlights." Cheney had eaten half his sandwich in about three bites. "Our moms would kill us if they saw us eating this fast."

I was bolting food down the same as he was. "I can't help it. It's delicious."

"Anyway, keep talking. I didn't mean to interrupt."

I paused to wipe my mouth on a paper napkin. "He must have heard me, if nothing else. That car makes a racket like a power mower half the time."

"Did you actually see him leaving her place?"

I shook my head. "I only caught a glimpse of him as he was walking away. By then I was on the porch, and I could hear her moan. I thought she was 'entertaining' from the sounds she made. Like I'd caught her in the throes of passion, maybe faking it for effect. When I saw the guy out in the alley, it occurred to me something was off. I don't know what it was. On the face of it, there was no reason to think he was connected to her, but it seemed odd somehow. That's when I tried the knob."

"He probably would have killed her if you hadn't showed."

"Oh, geez, don't say that. I was this close to leaving when I spotted him."

"What about a description? Big guy? Little?"

"Can't help you there. I only saw him for a second, and it was largely in the dark."

"You're sure it was a man?"

"Well, I couldn't swear to it in court, but if you're asking what I thought at the time, I'd say yes. A woman doesn't usually whack another woman with a lead pipe," I said. "He was white, I know that."

"What else?"

"Dark clothes, and I'm sure he was wearing hard shoes because I heard his soles scratching on the pavement as he walked away. He was cool about it, too. He didn't run. Nice, leisurely pace, like he was just out for a stroll."

"How do you know he wasn't?"

I thought about it briefly. "I think because he didn't look at me. Even in the dark, people are aware of each other. I sure spotted him. In a situation like that, someone looks at you, you turn and look at them. I notice it most when I'm out on the highway. If I stare at another driver, it seems to catch their attention and they turn and stare back. He kept his face to the front, but I'm sure he knew I was watching."

Cheney hunched over his plate and started in on his pie. "We had a couple of cars cruise the area shortly after the call came in, but there was no sign of him."

"He might live somewhere down there."

"Or had his car parked nearby," he said. "Did she say she had a date tonight?"

"She didn't mention an appointment. Could have been Lester, come to think of it. She said he'd been in a foul mood, whatever that consists of." The pie was the type I remembered from grade school: a perfect blend of cherry glue and pink, shriveled fruit, with a papery crust that nearly broke the tines off the fork. The first bite was the best, the pie point.

"Hard to picture Lester doing something like this. If she's beat up, she can't work. Mr. Dickhead's all business. He wouldn't tamper with his girls. More likely a john."

"You think she pissed some guy off?"

Cheney gave me a look. "This wasn't spur of the moment. This guy went prepared, with a pipe already wrapped to hide his fingerprints."

I finished my pie and ran the fork around the surface of the Styrofoam plate. I watched the red of the cherry pie filling ooze across the tines of the plastic fork. I was thinking about the goons in the limousine, wondering if I should mention them to Cheney. I'd been warned not to tell him, but suppose it was them? I really couldn't see the motivation from their perspective. Why would an attorney from Los Angeles want to kill a local hooker? If he was so crazy about Lorna, why beat the life out of her best friend?

Cheney said, "What."

"I'm wondering if this is related to my investigation."

"Could be, I guess. We'll never know unless we catch him."

He began to gather crumpled napkins and empty Pepsi cans, piling empty plastic packets on the tray. Distracted, I pitched in, cleaning off the tabletop.

When we got back to the emergency room, Serena called the OR and had a chat with one of the surgical nurses. Even eavesdropping, I couldn't pick up any information. "You might as well go on home," she said. "Danielle's still in surgery, and once she comes out, she'll be in the recovery room for another hour. After that, they'll take her to intensive care."

"Will they let me see her?" I asked.

"They may, but I doubt it. You're not a relative."

"How bad is she?"

"Apparently she's stable, but they're not going to know much until the surgeon gets finished. He's the one to give you details, but it's going to be a while yet."

Cheney was watching me. "I can run you home, if you like."

"I'd rather stick around here than go home," I said. "I'll be fine if you want to go. Honest. You don't have to baby-sit."

"I don't mind. I got nothing better at this hour anyway. Maybe we can find a couch somewhere and let you grab a nap."

Serena suggested the little waiting room off ICU, which was where we ended up. Cheney sat and read a magazine while I curled up on sofa slightly shorter than I was. There was something soothing about the snap of paper as he turned the pages, the occasional clearing of his throat. Sleep came down like a weight pressing me to the couch. When I woke, the room was empty, but Cheney'd draped his sport coat across my upper body, so I didn't think he'd gone far. I could feel the silky lining on his jacket, which smelled of expensive after-shave. I checked the clock on the wall: it was 3:35. I lay there for a moment, wondering if there was some way to stay where I was, feeling warm and safe. I could learn to live on a waiting room couch, have meals brought in, tend to personal hygiene in the ladies' room down the hall. It'd be cheaper than paying rent, and if something happened to me, I'd be within range of medical assistance.

From the corridor I heard footsteps and the murmur of male voices. Cheney appeared in the doorway, leaning against the frame. "Ah. You're back. You want to see Danielle?"

I sat up. "Is she awake?"

"Not really. They just brought her down from surgery. She's still groggy, but she's been admitted to ICU. I told the charge nurse you're a vice detective and need to identify a witness."

I pressed my fingers against my eyes and rubbed my face. I ran my hands through my hair, realizing that for once—because of Danielle's cutting skills—every strand wasn't standing straight up on end. I gathered my resources and let out a big breath, willing myself back to wakefulness. I pushed myself to my feet and brushed some of the wrinkles out of my turtleneck. One thing about casual dressing, you always look about the same. Even sleeping in a pair of blue jeans doesn't have much effect. From the corridor, we used the house phone to call into the ICU nurses' station. Cheney handled the formalities and got us both buzzed in.

"Am I supposed to have a badge?" I murmured to him as we moved down the corridor.

"Don't worry about it. I told 'em you're working undercover as a bag lady."

I gave him a little push.

We waited outside Danielle's room, watching through the glass window while a nurse checked her blood pressure and adjusted the drip on her IV. Like the layout in the cardiac care unit, these rooms formed a U shape around the nurses' station, patients clearly visible for constant monitoring. Cheney had chatted with the doctor, and he conveyed the gist of her current situation. "He took her spleen out. Orthopedic surgeon did most of the work, as it turns out. Set her jaw, set her collarbone, taped her ribs. She had two broken fingers, a lot of bruising. She should be all right, but it's going to take a while. The cut on her scalp turned out to be the least of it. Mild concussion, lots of blood. I've done that myself. Bang your head on the medicine cabinet, it looks like you're bleeding to death."

The nurse straightened Danielle's covers and came out of the room. "Two minutes," she said, lifted fingers forming a V.

We stood side by side, in silence, looking down at her like parents taking in the sight of a newborn baby. Hard to believe she belonged to us. She was nearly unrecognizable: her eyes blackened, jaw puffy, her nose packed and taped. One splinted hand lay outside the covers. All of her bright red acrylic nails had popped off or broken, and it made her poor swollen fingers look bloody at the tips. The rest of her was scarcely more than a child-size mound. She was drifting in and out, never sufficiently alert to be aware of us. She seemed diminished by machinery, but there was something reassuring about all the personnel and equipment. As battered as she was, this was where she needed to be.

Leaving ICU, Cheney put his arm around my shoulders. "You okay?"

I leaned my head against him briefly. "I'm fine. How about you?"

"Doing okay," he said. He pressed the down arrow for the elevator. "I had the doctor leave orders. They won't give out any information about her condition, and no one gets in."

"You think the guy would come back?"

"It looks like he tried to kill her once. Who knows how serious he is about finishing the job?"

"I feel guilty. Like this is somehow connected to Lorna's death," I said.

"You want to fill me in?"

"On what?" The elevators opened. We stepped in and Cheney pressed 1. We began to descend.

"The piece you haven't told me. You're holding something back, are you not?" His tone was light, but his gaze was intent.

"I guess I am," I said. I gave a quick sketch of my conversation in the limousine with the Los Angeles attorney and his sidekicks. As we emerged from the elevator, I said, "You have any idea who the guy could be? He said he represented someone else, but he might have been talking about himself."

"I can ask around. I know those guys come up here for R and R. Give me the phone number and I'll check it out."

"I'd rather not," I said. "The less I know, the better. Are they running prostitutes up here?"

"Maybe something minor. Nothing big time. They probably control local action, but that may not mean much more than skimming off the profits. Leave the nuts and bolts to the guys under them."

Cheney had parked on a side street closer to the front entrance than the emergency room. We reached the lobby. The gift shop and the coffee shop were both closed, shadowy interiors visible through plate-glass windows. At the main desk, a man was engaged in an agitated conversation with the patient information clerk. Cheney's manner underwent a change, his posture shifting into cop mode. His expression became implacable, and his walk took on a hint of swagger. In one smooth motion he'd flipped his badge toward the clerk, his gaze pinned on the fellow giving her such grief. "Hello, Lester. You want to step over here? We can have a chat," he said.

Lester Dudley modified his own behavior correspondingly. He lost his bullying manner and smiled ingratiatingly. "Hey, Phillips. Nice to see you. Thought I caught sight of you earlier, down around Danielle's place. You hear what happened?"

"That's what I'm doing here, otherwise you wouldn't see me. This's my night off. I was home watching TV when the dispatcher rang through."

"Not alone, I hope. I hate to see a guy like you lonely. Offer still stands, day or night, male or female. Anything you got a taste for, Lester Dudley provides. . . ."

"You pandering, Lester?"

"I was just teasing, Phillips. Jesus, can't a guy make a little joke? I know the law as well as you do, probably better, if it comes right down to it."

Lester Dudley didn't suit my mental image of a pimp. From a distance he had looked like a surly adolescent, too young to be admitted to an R-rated movie without a parent or guardian. Up close I had to place him in his early forties, a flyweight, maybe five four. His hair was dark and straight, slicked back away from his face. He had small eyes, a big nose, and a slightly receding chin. His neck was thin, making his head look like a turnip.

Cheney didn't bother to introduce us, but Lester seemed aware of me, blinking at me slyly like an earth-burrowing creature suddenly hauled into daylight. He wore kid's clothes: a long-sleeved cotton knit T-shirt with horizontal stripes, blue jeans, denim jacket, and Keds. He had his arms crossed, hands tucked into his armpits. His watch was a Breitling, probably a fake, riddled with dials, and far too big for his wrist. It looked more like something he might have acquired sending off box tops. "So how's Danielle doing? I couldn't get a straight answer from the broad at the desk."

Cheney's pager went off. He checked the number on the face of it. "Shit. . . . I'll be right back," he murmured.

Lester seemed to bounce on his heels, ill at ease, staring after Cheney as he moved over to the desk.

I thought I ought to break the ice. "You're Danielle's personal manager?"

"That's right. Lester Dudley," he said, holding out his hand.

I shook hands with him despite my reluctance to make physical contact. "Kinsey Millhone," I said. "I'm a friend of hers." When you need information, you can't afford to let personal repugnance stand in your way.

He was saying, "Clerk's giving me a hard time, wouldn't give me information even after I explained who I was. Probably one of those women's liberation types."

"No doubt."

"How's she doing? Poor kid. I heard she really got the shit

kicked out of her. Some crackaholic probably did it. They're mean sonsa bitches."

"The doctor left before I had a chance to talk to him," I said. "Maybe the clerk was under orders not to give out information."

"Hey, not her. She was having way too much fun. Enjoying herself at my expense. Not that it bothers me. I'm always taking flak from these women's libber types. Can you believe they're still around? I thought they gave it up by now, but no such luck. Here just last week, this bunch of ball busters? Came down on me like a ton of bricks, claimed I was engaged in white slavery. Do you believe that? What a crock. How can they be talking about white slavery when half my girls are black?"

"You're being too literal. I think you miss the point," I said.

"Here's the point," he said. "These girls make good money. We're talking big bucks, megadollars. Where these girls going to get employment opportunities like this? They got no education. Half of 'em's got IQs in double digits. You don't hear *them* whining. Do they complain? No way. They're living like queens. I'll tell you something else. This bunch of ball busters isn't offering a damn thing. No jobs, no training, not even public assistance. How concerned could they be? These girls have to earn a living. You want to hear what I told 'em? I said, 'Ladies, this is *business.* I don't create the market. It's supply and demand.' Girls provide goods and services, and that's all it is. You think they care? You know what it's about? Sexual repression. Male-bashing bunch of fuzz-bumpers. They hate guys, hate to see anyone get their jollies with the opposite sex. . . ."

"Or," said I, "they might object to the idea of anyone exploiting young girls. Just a wild guess on my part."

"Well, if that's their position, what's the beef?" he asked. "I feel the same way as them. But they treat me like the enemy, that's what I don't get. My girls are clean and well protected, and that's the truth."

"*Danielle* was well protected?"

"Of course not," he said, exasperated that I was being so dense. "She shoulda listened to me. I told her, 'Don't take guys home.' I told her, 'Don't do a guy without I'm outside the door.' That's my job. This is how I earn my percentage. I drive her when she goes on appointments. No crazy's going to lay a hand on her if she's got an escort, for cripe's sake. She don't call, I can't help. It's as simple as that."

"Maybe it's time she got out of the life," I said.

"That what she's saying, and I go, 'Hey, that's up to you.' Nobody forces my girls to stay in. She wants out, that's her business. I'd have to ask how she's going to earn a living . . ." He let that one trail, his voice tinged with skepticism.

"Meaning what? I'm not following."

"I'm just trying to picture her working in a department store, waitressing, something like that. Minimum-wage-type job. Beat-up like that, it'd be tough, of course, but as long as she don't mind coming down in the world, who am I to object? You got scars on your face, might be a trick to get employment."

"Nobody's said anything about facial scars," I said. "Where'd you get that idea?"

"Oh. Well, I just assumed. Word on the street is she got busted up bad. Naturally, I thought, you know, some unfortunate facial involvement. It's a pity, of course, but a lot of guys try to do that, interfere with a poor girl's ability to make a living, undercut their confidence, and shit like that."

Cheney reappeared, his gaze shifting with curiosity from Lester's face to mine. "Everything okay?"

"Sure, fine," I said tersely.

"We're just talking business," Lester said. "I never did hear how Danielle is. She going to be all right?"

"Time to go," Cheney said to him. "We'll walk you out to your car."

"Hey, sure thing. Where they got her, up in orthopedics? I could send some flowers'f I knew. Someone told me her jaw's broke. Probably some coked-up lunatic."

"Skip the flowers. We're not giving out information. Doctor's orders," Cheney said.

"Pretty smart. I was going to suggest that myself. Keeps her safe from the wrong types."

I said, "Too late for that," but the irony escaped him.

Once we reached the street in front of St. Terry's, we did a parting round of handshakes as though we'd just had a business meeting. The minute Lester's back was turned, I wiped my hand on my jeans. Cheney and I waited on the sidewalk until we saw him drive away.

17

It was close to four in the morning as Cheney's little red Mazda droned through the darkened streets. With the top down, the wind whipped across my face. I leaned my head back and watched the sky race by. On the mountain side of the city, the shadowy foothills were strung with necklaces of streetlights as twinkling as bulbs on a Christmas tree. In the houses we passed, I could see an occasional house light wink on as early morning workers plugged in the coffee and staggered to the shower.

"Too cold for you?"

"This is fine," I said. "Lester seemed to know a lot about Danielle's beating. You think he did it?"

"Not if he wanted her to work," Cheney said.

The sky at that hour is a plain, unbroken gray shading down to the black of trees. Dew saturates the grass. Sometimes you can hear the spritzing of the rainbirds, computers programmed to water lawns before the sun has fully risen. If the cycle of low rainfall persisted as it had in the past, water usage would be restricted and all the lush grass would die. During the last drought, many home owners had been reduced to spraying their yards with dense green paint.

On Cabana Boulevard, a kid on a skateboard careened along the darkened sidewalk. It occurred to me that I'd been waiting to see the Juggler, the man on the bike, with his taillight and pumping feet. He was beginning to represent some capricious force at work, elfin and evil, some figment of my imagination dancing along ahead of me like the answer to a riddle. Wherever I went, he'd eventually appear, always headed somewhere in a hurry, never quite arriving at his destination.

Cheney had slowed, leaning forward to check the skateboarder as we passed him. Cheney raised a hand in greeting, and the kid waved back.

"Who's that?" I asked.

"Works night maintenance at a convalescent home. He had his driver's license pulled on a DUI. Actually, he's a good kid," he said. Moments later he turned into Danielle's alley, where my car was still parked. He pulled in behind the VW, shifting into neutral to minimize the rumble of his engine. "How's your day looking? Will you have time to sleep?"

"I hope so. I'm really bushed," I said. "Are you going to work?"

"I'm going home to bed. For a couple of hours, at any rate. I'll give you a call later. If you're up for it, we can get a bite to eat someplace."

"Let me see how my day shapes up. If I'm not in, leave a number. I'll get back to you."

"You going into the office?"

"Actually, I thought I'd go over to Danielle's and clean. Last I saw, the place was covered with blood."

"You don't have to do that. The landlord said he'd have a crew come in first thing next week. He can't get 'em till Monday, but it's better than you doing it."

"I don't mind. I'd like to do something for her. Maybe pick up her robe and slippers and take 'em over to St. Terry's."

"Up to you," he said. "I'll watch 'til you take off. Make sure your car starts and the boogeyman don't get you."

I opened the car door and got out, reaching down for my handbag. "Thanks for the ride and for everything else. I mean that."

"You're welcome."

I slammed the door, moving over to my car while Cheney hovered like a guardian angel. The VW started without a murmur. I waved to demonstrate that everything was okay, but he wasn't ready to let go. He followed me home, the two of us winding up and down the darkened streets. For once, I found a parking space right in front of my place. At that point he seemed to feel I was safe. He shifted into first and took off.

I locked the car, went through the gate, and walked around to the back, where I unlocked my front door and let myself in. I scooped up the mail that had been shoved through the slot, flipped a light on, set my bag down, and locked the front door behind me. I started peeling off my clothes as I climbed the spiral stairs, littering the floor with discarded articles of clothing like those scenes in romantic comedies where the lovers can hardly wait. I felt that way about sleep. Naked, I staggered around, closing the blinds, turning off the phone, dousing lights. I crawled under the quilt with a sigh of relief. I thought I was too tired to sleep, but as it turned out I wasn't.

I didn't wake until well after five P.M. For a moment I thought I'd slept all the way around the clock until the next dawn. I stared up at the clear Plexiglas dome above my bed, trying to orient myself in the half-light. Given the early February sunsets, the day was already draining away like gray water from the bottom of a bathtub. I assessed my mental state and decided I'd probably had enough sleep, realized I was starving, and hauled myself out of bed. I brushed my teeth, showered, and shampooed my hair. Afterward I pulled on an old sweatshirt and worn jeans. Downstairs, I collected a plastic bucket full of rags and cleaning products. Now that the immediate crisis had passed, I found myself tuning into the rage I felt for her assailant. Men who beat women were almost as low as the men who beat kids.

I tried Cheney's number, but he was apparently already up and out. I left a message on his machine, indicating the time of day and the fact that I was too hungry to wait for him. When I opened my front door, a manila envelope dropped out of the frame where it had been tucked. Across the front, Hector had scrawled a note: "Friday. 5:35 p. Knocked but no answer. Amended transcript and tape enclosed. Sorry I couldn't be more help. Give me a call when you get back." He'd jotted down his home number and the number for the studio. He must have stopped by and knocked while I was in the shower. I checked the time. He'd apparently been there only fifteen minutes before, and I had to guess it was too soon to catch him at either number. I tucked both the tape and the transcript in my handbag and then took myself to a coffee shop where breakfast was served twenty-four hours a day.

I studied Hector's notations while I made a pig of myself, hastily consuming a plate full of the sorts of foodstuffs nutritionists forbid. He hadn't managed to decipher much more than I had. To my page of notes, he'd added the following:

"Hey . . . I hate that stuff. . . . myself think. You're not . . ."

"Oh, come on. I'm just kidding. . . . [laughter] *But you have to admit, it's a great idea. She goes in at the same time every day . . . deify . . ."*

"You're sick. . . ."

"People shouldn't get in my . . . [clatter . . . clink]"

Sound of water . . . squeak . . .

"If anything happens, I'll . . ."

Thump, thump . . .

"I'm serious . . . stubby—"

"No link . . ."

Laughter . . . chair scrape . . . rustle . . . murmur . . .

At the bottom of the page, he'd scrawled three big question marks. My sentiments exactly.

When I reached Danielle's cottage, I parked in the alleyway near the hedge as I had the night before. It was dark by then. At this rate I might never see full sun again. I took out my flashlight and checked the batteries, satisfied that the beam was still strong. I spent a few minutes walking along the borders of the alleyway, using the blade of light to cut through the weeds on either side. I didn't expect to find anything. I wasn't really looking for "evidence" as such. I wanted to see if I could figure out where Danielle's assailant might have gone. There were any number of places where he might have hidden, yards he could have crossed to reach the streets on either side. In the middle of the night, even a slender tree trunk can provide cover. For all I knew, he'd taken up a position within easy viewing distance, watching the ambulance and all the cop cars arrive.

I went back to Danielle's cottage, where I crossed the backyard to the main house. I climbed the back steps and knocked on the lighted kitchen window. I could see Danielle's landlord rinsing dinner dishes before he placed them in the rack. He caught sight of me at just about that time and came to the back door, drying his hands on a dish towel. I got a key from him, pausing to chat for a few minutes about the assault. He'd gone to bed at ten. He said he was a light sleeper, but his bedroom was on the second floor, the street side of the house, and he'd heard nothing. He was a man in his seventies, retired military, though he didn't say which branch. If he knew how Danielle made a living, he made no comment. He seemed as fond of her as I was, and that was all I cared about. I professed ignorance of her current status, except to indicate that she'd survived and was expected to recover. He didn't press for specifics.

I walked back along the brick path to Danielle's small porch. The crime scene tape had been removed, but I could still see traces of fingerprint powder around the doorknob and frame. The rag-wrapped length of bloody pipe would probably be tested for fingerprints, but I doubted it would yield much. I let myself into the cottage and flipped on the overhead light. The splattered blood was like a Rorschach, a dark red pattern of smears and exclamation marks where the force of the blows had flung blood in two tracks across the wall. The bloodstained rug had been removed, probably tossed in the trash can at the rear of the lot. The blood on the baseboard looked like teardrops of paint.

The entire apartment was barely a room and a half and cheaply constructed. I toured the premises, though there wasn't much to see. Like mine, Danielle's living quarters occupied a very small space. It looked as though Danielle's battle with her assailant had been confined to the front room, most of which was taken up with a sitting area and a king-size bed. The sheets and comforter were a Laura Ashley print, pink-and-white floral polished cotton with matching drapes, and a correlating pink-and-white-striped paper lined the walls. Her kitchen consisted of a hot plate and a microwave oven sitting atop a painted chest of drawers.

The bathroom was small, painted white, with tiny old-fashioned black-and-white tiles on the floor. The sink was skirted in the same Laura Ashley print she'd used in the bedroom. She'd bought a matching polished-cotton shower curtain, with a valance covering the rod. The wall opposite the john was a minigallery. A dozen framed photographs were hung close together, many sitting crooked on the hangers. Danielle must have been flung up against the connecting wall during the assault. Several had been knocked off the wall and lay facedown on the tile floor. I lifted them with care. Two of the frames had smashed on impact, and the glass in all four was either badly cracked or broken. I stacked the four damaged pictures together, tossed glass shards in the trash, and then straightened the remaining photographs, pausing to absorb the subject matter. Danielle as a baby. Danielle with Mom and Dad. Danielle at about nine, in a dance recital with her hair done up.

I went back into the front room and found a thick sheaf of brown grocery bags tucked in the slot between the wall and the chest of drawers. I put the damaged framed photographs in the bag and set them by the front door. I'd seen similar frames at the drugstore for a couple of bucks apiece. Maybe I'd stop by and pick up some replacements. I pulled all the linens off the bed and set them out on the porch. Even the dust ruffle had picked up a spray of blood posies. I'd make a trip to the cleaners in the morning. I filled my bucket with hot water, mixing a potent brew of cleaning solutions. I wiped down the walls, scrubbed the baseboards and floors until the soapy water turned a frothy pink. I dumped that lot, refilled the bucket, and started over again.

When I'd finished, I pulled out the transcript and sat down on the bed, using Danielle's phone to try Hector at his home number. He answered promptly.

"This is Kinsey here. I'm glad I caught you at home. I thought you might be on your way to the studio."

"Not this early, and today not at all. I work Saturday through Wednesday, so Thursday and Friday nights are usually my weekend. Last night was an exception, but I try to keep those to a minimum. I got hot plans tonight. I give Beauty a bath, and then she gives me one. You got the transcript, I take it."

"Yeah, and I'm sorry I missed you. I was in the shower when you dropped it off." We spent a few minutes commiserating with one another about the poor quality of the tape recording. "What'd you make of it?"

"Not much. I picked up a couple of words, but nothing that made any sense."

"You have any idea what they're talking about?"

"Nope. Lorna sounds upset with him, is mostly what I pick up."

"You're sure it's Lorna?"

"I couldn't swear, but I'm pretty sure it was her."

"What about the guy?"

"I didn't recognize his voice. Doesn't sound like anyone I'm familiar with. You ought to listen again yourself and see what you hear. Maybe we can take turns filling in the missing pieces like a jigsaw puzzle."

"We don't have to make it our life's work," I said. "I'm not even sure it's relevant, but I'll have another go at it when I get home." I glanced down at the annotated transcript. "What about this word *deify.* That seems odd, doesn't it? Deify who?"

"I wasn't real sure about that one, but it's the only word I could think of. Phrase I keep running through my head is that business about 'she goes in at the same time every day.' I don't know what the hell that's about."

"And why 'stubby'? Lorna says that, I think."

"Well, this may sound odd, but I'll tell you the hit I got on that. I don't think she's using 'stubby' as an adjective. There's a guy here in town with the nickname Stubby. She could be talking about him."

"That's an interesting possibility. This was someone she knew?"

"Presumably. His real name is John Stockton. Call him Stubby because he's a little short fat guy. He's a developer—"

"Wait a minute," I cut in. "I just heard that name. I'm almost sure Clark Esselmann referred to him . . . assuming there's only one. Is he a member of the Colgate Water Board?"

Hector laughed. "Whoa, no chance. They'd never let him on the board. Talk about a conflict of interests. He'd vote himself into half a dozen get-rich schemes."

"Oh. Then it's probably not related. Was she talking to or about him?"

"About him, I'd guess. Actually, there could be some marginal connection. Stockton would have to apply to the water board if he were trying to get a permit for some kind of development. Since Lorna 'baby-sat' with Esselmann, she might have heard about Stubby in passing."

"Yeah, but so what? In a town like this, you hear about a lot of things, but that doesn't get you killed. How hard is it to get a permit?"

"It's not hard to *apply,* but with the current water shortage, it'd take a hell of a project to get them to say yes."

I said, "Well." I ran the idea around a couple of laps, but it didn't seem to produce any insights. "I don't know how that pertains. If they're talking about water, it might tie in somehow with 'she goes in at the same time every day.' Maybe that reference is to swimming. I know Lorna jogged, but did she also swim?"

"Not that I ever heard. Besides, if the guy's talking to Lorna, why refer to her as 'she'? He's gotta be talking about someone else. And Stockton doesn't have anything to do with swimming pools. He does malls and subdivisions," he said. "With a phrase like that, they could be talking about work. She goes in 'to work' at the same time every day. Or she goes in 'to bed' at the same time every day."

"True. Oh, well. Maybe something will occur to us if we give it a rest. Anything else strike you?" I asked.

"Not really. Just that Lorna sounded pissed."

"I thought so, too, which is why I listened so carefully. Whatever the guy's saying, she didn't like it a bit."

"Ah, well. Like you say, if it's ever going to make any sense, you'll probably have to leave it alone for a while. If I have a brainstorm, I'll give you a buzz."

"Thanks, Hector."

By the time I locked up and returned the key to Danielle's landlord, it was close to 6:45 and the place was looking better. The smell of ammonia suggested an institutional setting, but at least Danielle wouldn't have to come home to a shambles. I went out to my car, arms loaded with odds and ends. I set the plastic bucket on the front seat on the passenger's side and stuck the bundle of bedclothes on the backseat, along with the paper bag holding the broken picture frames. I slid in behind the steering wheel and sat for a moment, trying to think what to do next. Hector's suggestion about Stubby Stockton as the subject of Lorna's taped conversation was mildly intriguing. From what I'd overheard of Clark Esselmann's comments on the phone, Stockton would be present at the upcoming board meeting, which was tonight by my calculations. With luck, maybe I'd run into Serena and I could quiz her again on the subject of the missing money.

I found a public phone at the nearest gas station and looked up the number for the Colgate Water District. It was way past working hours, but the message on the answering machine gave details about the meeting, which was scheduled at seven in the conference room at the district offices. I hopped in the car, fired up the engine again, and hit the highway, heading north.

Fourteen minutes later I pulled into the parking lot behind the building, uncomfortably aware of a steady stream of cars both ahead of me and behind. Like some kind of car rally, we nosed into parking slots one after the other. I shut my engine down and got out, locking the car behind me. It was easy enough to determine where the meeting was being held simply by following the other attendees. At the back end of the building, I could see lights on, and I trotted in that direction, starting to feel competitive about the available seating spaces.

The entrance to the conference room was tucked into a small enclosed patio. Through the plate-glass window, I could see the water board members already in place. I went in, anxious to get settled while there were still seats left. The meeting room was drab and functional: brown carpet, walls paneled in dark wood veneer, an L of folding tables up front, and thirty-five folding chairs for the audience. There was a big coffee urn on a table to one side, a stack of cups, sugar packets, and a big jar of Cremora. The lighting was fluorescent and made all of us look yellow.

The Colgate Water Board consisted of seven members, each with an engraved plate indicating name and title: counsel for the water district, the general manager and chief engineer, the president, and four directors, one of whom was Clark Esselmann. The board member named Ned, whom he'd talked to by phone, was apparently Theodore Ramsey, now seated two chairs away. The "Bob" and "Druscilla" he'd mentioned in passing were Robert Ennisbrook and Druscilla Chatham respectively.

Appropriately enough, the water board members had been provided big pitchers of iced water, and they poured and drank water lustily while discussing its scarcity. Some of the members I knew by name or reputation, but with the exception of Esselmann, I didn't recognize any of their faces. Serena was in the front row, fussing with her belongings and trying to act as if she weren't worried about her father. Esselmann, in a suit and tie, looked frail but determined. He was already engaged in conversation with Mrs. Chatham, the woman to his left.

Many people had already assembled, and most of the available folding chairs were filled. I spotted an empty chair and claimed it, wondering what I was doing here. Some attendees had briefcases or legal pads. The man next to me had written out a commentary in longhand, which he seemed to be refining while we waited for the meeting to begin. I turned and checked the rows behind me, all of which were occupied. Through the plate-glass window, I could see additional people seated at the picnic table or lounging against the ornamental fence. Speakers on the patio allowed the overflow crowd to hear the proceedings.

Copies of the agenda were stacked up front, and I left my seat briefly so that I could snag one for myself. I gathered that members of the audience would be free to address the board. To that end, requests were filled out and submitted. There were many consultations back and forth, people who seemed to know one another, some in small groups representing a particular petition. I wasn't even sure what the issues were, and the agenda I scanned made it all sound so tedious, I wasn't sure I cared. I wondered if I'd be able to identify Stubby Stockton on sight. A lot of us look short and fat while seated.

At 7:03 the meeting was called to order, with a roll call of board members present. Minutes of the previous meeting were read and approved without modification. Various items on the consent agenda were approved without discussion. Much rustling and coughing and throat clearing throughout. Everyone seemed to speak in a monotone, so that every subject was reduced to its most boring components. Service policies were discussed among the board members in the sort of dry style reserved for congressional filibusters. If anything was actually being accomplished, it was lost on me. What struck me as curious was that Clark Esselmann, in his telephone conversation with Ned at the house, had seemed quite passionate. Behind the scenes, feelings apparently ran high. Here, every effort was made to neutralize emotion in the interest of public service.

One by one members of the audience were able to approach the podium, addressing the board members with prepared statements. These they read aloud in their best singsong public speaking voices, managing somehow to deliver their comments without any spontaneity, humor, or warmth. As in church, the combination of body heat and hot air was bringing the surrounding air temperature up to anesthetic levels. For someone as sleep-deprived as I'd been for the last five days, it was hard to keep from toppling off my chair sideways.

I'm ashamed to confess I actually nodded off once, a sort of dip in consciousness that I became aware of only because my head dropped. It must have happened again, because just as I began to enjoy a much needed snooze, I was jerked upright by a heated verbal exchange. Belatedly, I realized I'd missed the opening round.

Clark Esselmann was on his feet, stabbing a finger at the man at the podium. "It's people like you who're ruining this county."

The man he was addressing *had* to be John "Stubby" Stockton. He was maybe five feet tall and very heavyset, with a round baby face and dark thinning hair. He was a man who perspired heavily, and throughout the interchange he mopped at his face with his handkerchief. "People like me? Oh, really, sir. Let's leave personalities out of this. This is not about me. This is not about you. This is about jobs for this community. This is about growth and progress for the citizens of this county, the—"

"Hogwash! This is about you making money, you damn son of a bitch. What do you care about the citizens of this county? By the time this . . . this abomination comes to pass, you'll be well out of it. Counting your profits while the rest of us are stuck with this eyesore for centuries to come."

Like lovers, Clark Esselmann and John Stockton, having once engaged, seemed to have eyes only for each other. The room was electrified, a ripple of excitement undulating through the audience.

Stockton's voice was syrupy with loathing. "Sir, at the risk of offending, let me ask you this. What have *you* done to generate employment or housing or financial security for the citizens of Santa Teresa County? Would you care to answer that?"

"Don't change the subject—"

"Because the answer is nothing. You haven't contributed a stick, not a nickel or a brick to the fiscal health and well-being of the community you live in."

"That is untrue . . . that is *untrue*!" Esselmann shouted.

Stockton forged on. "You've blocked economic growth, you've obstructed employment opportunities. You've denounced development, impeded all progress. And why not? You've got yours. What do you care what happens to the rest of us? We can all go jump in the ocean as far as you're concerned."

"You're damn right you can jump in the ocean! Go jump in the ocean."

"Gentlemen!" The president had risen.

"Well, let me tell you something. You'll be long gone and the opportunity for growth will be long gone, and who's going to pay the price for your failure of imagination?"

"Gentlemen! Gentlemen!"

The president was banging his gavel on the table without any particular effectiveness. Serena was on her feet, but her father was waving her aside with the kind of peremptory motion that had probably intimidated her from childhood. I saw her sink back down while he shouted, trembling, "Save your speeches for the Rotary, young man. I'm sick of listening to this self-serving poppycock. The truth is, you're in this for the almighty buck, and you know it. If you're so interested in growth and economic opportunity, then *donate* the land and all the profits you stand to make. Don't hide behind rhetoric—"

"*You* donate. Why don't *you* give something? You've got more than the rest of us put together. And don't talk to me about hiding behind rhetoric, you pompous ass. . . ."

A uniformed security guard materialized at Stockton's side and took him by the elbow. Stockton shook him off, enraged, but a business associate appeared on the other side of him, and between the two of them he was eased out of the room. Esselmann remained on his feet, his eyes glittering with anger.

In the general swell of side conversations that followed, I leaned over to the man next to me. "I hate to seem ignorant, but what was that about?"

"John Stockton's trying to get water permits for a big parcel of land he wants to turn around and sell to Marcus Petroleum."

"I thought stuff like that had to go through the county board of supervisors," I said.

"It does. It was approved last month by a five–oh vote on the condition that they use reclaimed water from the Colgate Water District. It looked like it was going to pass without opposition, but now Esselmann is mounting a counterattack."

"But why all the heat?"

"Stockton's got some land the oil companies would love to have. All worthless without water. Esselmann supported him at first, but now he's suddenly opposed. Stubby feels betrayed."

I thought back to the phone call I'd overheard. Esselmann had mentioned the board's being sweet-talked into some kind of deal while he was in the hospital. "Was Stockton working on this while Esselmann was out ill?"

"You bet. Damn near succeeded, too. Now that he's back, he's using every ounce of influence to get the application turned down."

The woman in front of us turned and gave us a look of reproach. "There's still business going on here, if you don't mind."

"Sorry."

The president of the board was trying desperately to establish order, though the audience didn't seem particularly interested.

I put my hand across my mouth. "Have they voted on this?" I said in a lower tone.

The guy shook his head. "This issue came up a year ago, and the water board set up a blue-ribbon panel to investigate and make recommendations. They had environmental impact studies done. You know how it is. Mostly a stalling technique in hopes the whole thing would go away. The matter won't actually come to a vote until next month. That's why they're still hearing testimony on the subject."

The woman in front of us raised a finger to her lips, and our conversation dwindled.

In the meantime, Esselmann sat down abruptly, his color high. Serena went around the end of the table and joined him on his side, much to his displeasure. Stubby Stockton was nowhere to be seen, but I could hear him on the patio, his voice still raised in anger. Someone was trying to calm him, but without much success. The meeting picked up again, the president moving adroitly to the next item on the agenda, a fire sprinkler system agreement that didn't upset anyone. By the time I slipped out, Stockton was gone and the patio was empty.

18

I drove over to St. Terry's, stopping to fill my car with gas on the way. I knew I'd reached the hospital after visiting hours had ended, but ICU had its own set of rules and regulations. Family members were allowed one five-minute visit out of every hour. The hospital was as brightly lit as a resort hotel, and I was forced to circle the block, looking for a parking space. I moved through the lobby and took a right turn, heading for the elevators to the intensive care unit upstairs. Once I reached the floor, I used the wall-mounted phone to call into the ward. The night shift nurse who answered was polite but didn't recognize my name. She put me on hold without actually verifying Danielle's presence on the ward. I studied the pastel seascape hanging on the wall. Moments later she was back on the phone with me, this time using a friendlier tone. Cheney had apparently left word that I was to be admitted. She probably thought I was a cop.

I stood in the hallway and watched Danielle through the window to her room. Her hospital bed had been elevated to a slight incline. She seemed to doze. Her long dark hair fanned out across the pillow and trailed over the side of the bed. The bruising on her face seemed more pronounced tonight, the white tape across her nose a stark contrast to the swollen, sooty-looking black-and-blue eye sockets. Her mouth was dark and puffy. Her jaw had probably been wired shut because there was none of the slack-jawed look of someone sleeping. Her IV was still in place, as was her catheter.

"You need to talk to her?"

I turned to find the nurse from the night before. "I don't want to bother her," I said.

"I have to wake her up anyway to take her vital signs. You might as well come in. Just don't upset her."

"I won't. How's she doing?"

"She's doing pretty well. She's on a lot of pain medication, but she's been awake off and on. In another day or two we could probably move her down to medical, but we think she's safer up here."

I stood quietly beside the bed while the nurse took Danielle's blood pressure and her pulse, adjusting the drip on her IV. Danielle's eyes came open in that groggy, confused fashion of someone who can't quite remember where she is or why. The nurse made a note in the chart and left the room. Danielle's green eyes shone stark in the cloudy mass of bruises around her eyes.

I said, "Hi. How are you?"

"I been better," she said through her teeth. "Got my jaw wired shut. That's why I'm talkin' like this."

"I figured as much. Are you in pain?"

"Naw, I'm high." She smiled briefly, not moving her head. "I never saw the guy, in case you're wondering. All I remember is opening the door."

"Not surprising," I said. "It may come back in time."

"Hope not."

"Yeah. Tell me if you get tired. I don't want to wear you down."

"I'm okay. I like the company. What've you been up to?"

"Not much. I'm on my way home from a meeting at the water board. What a zoo. The old guy Lorna used to sit for got into a big shouting match with a developer named Stubby Stockton. The rest of the meeting was such a bore until then, it nearly put me to sleep."

Danielle made a murmuring sound to show she was listening. Her lids seemed heavy, and I thought she was close to nodding off herself. I'd hoped Stubby's name would spark some recognition, but maybe Danielle didn't have a lot of spark to spare. "Did Lorna ever mention Stubby Stockton to you?" I wasn't sure she even heard me. There was quiet in the room, and then she seemed to rouse herself.

"Client," she said.

"He was a client?" I said, startled. I thought about that for a moment, trying to process the information. "That surprises me somehow. He didn't seem like her type. When was this?"

"Long time. I think she only saw him once. Other guy's the one."

"What other guy?"

"Old guy."

"The one what?"

"Lorna screwed."

"Oh, I don't think so. You must have him mixed up with somebody else. Clark Esselmann is Serena Bonney's *father*. He's the old guy she baby-sat . . ."

She moved her good hand, plucking at the bedclothes.

"You need something?"

"Water."

I looked over at the rolling bed table. On it was a Styrofoam pitcher full of water, a plastic cup, and a plastic straw with an accordion section that created a joint about halfway down. "You're okay to drink this? I don't want you cheating because I don't know any better."

She smiled. "Wouldn't cheat . . . here."

I filled the plastic cup and bent the straw, then held the cup near her head, turning the straw at an angle until it touched her lips. She took three small sips, sucking lightly. "Thanks."

"You were talking about someone Lorna was involved with."

"Esselmann."

"You're sure we're talking about the same guy?"

"Boss's father-in-law, right?"

"Well, yeah, but why didn't you tell me before? This could be important."

"Thought I did. What difference does it make?"

"Fill me in and we'll see what difference."

"He was into kinky." She winced, trying to rearrange herself slightly in the bed. A spasm of pain seemed to cross her face.

"You okay? You don't have to talk about this right now."

" 'm fine. Ribs feel like shit, is all. Rest a minute."

I waited, thinking, "Kinky"? I pictured Esselmann getting his fanny spanked while he cavorted around in a garter belt.

I could see Danielle struggle to pull herself together. "She went there after his heart attack, but he came on to her. Said she about fell over. Not that she gave a shit. Buck's a buck, and he paid her a fortune, but she didn't expect it when he seemed so . . . proper."

"I'll bet. And his daughter never knew?"

"No one did. Then later, Lorna let the information slip. She said word got back and that's the last she saw of him. She felt bad. Daughter wanted to hire her, but old guy wouldn't have it."

"What do you mean, word got back? Who'd she let the information slip to?"

"Don't know. After that she was tight-lipped. Said you only have to learn *that* lesson once."

Behind me someone said, "Excuse me."

Danielle's ICU nurse was back. "I don't mean to seem rude about this, but could you wrap it up? The doctors really don't want her having more than five-minute visits."

"I understand. That's fine." I looked back at Danielle. "We can talk about this later. You get some rest."

"Right." Danielle's eyes closed again. I stayed with her for another minute, more for my sake than hers, and then I eased out of the room. The aide at the nurses' station watched my departure.

I found myself uncomfortably trying to conjure up an image of Lorna Kepler with Clark Esselmann. And kinky? What a thought.

It wasn't his age so much as his aura of formality. I couldn't find a way to reconcile his respectability with his (alleged) sexual proclivities. He'd probably been married to Serena's mother for fifty years or more. This all must have happened before Mrs. Esselmann died.

I made a six-block detour to Short's Drugs, where I purchased four eight-by-ten picture frames to replace the broken frames I'd brought with me from Danielle's. Lorna and Clark Esselmann, what an odd combination. The drugstore seemed filled with the same conflicting images: arthritis remedies and condoms, bedpans and birth control. While I was at it, I picked up a couple of packs of index cards, and then I went back to my place, trying to think about something else.

I parked, flipped the driver's seat forward, and hauled the banker's box full of Lorna's papers from under Danielle's blood-spattered bedclothes. For someone obsessive about the tidiness in my apartment, I seem to have no compunction at all about the state of my car. I piled my purchases on the box and anchored the load with my chin while I let myself in.

I settled in at my desk. I hadn't transcribed and consolidated my notes since the second day I was on the job, and the index cards I'd filled then seemed both scanty and inept. Information accumulates and compounds, layer upon layer, each affecting perception. Using my notebook, my calendar, gas slips, receipts, and plane ticket, I began to reconstruct the events between Tuesday and today, detailing my interviews with Lorna's boss, Roger Bonney, Joseph Ayers and Russell Turpin up in San Francisco, Trinny, Serena, Clark Esselmann, and the (alleged) attorney in the limo. Now I had to add Danielle's contention about Lorna's involvement with Clark Esselmann. That one I'd have to check out if I could figure out how. I could hardly ask Serena.

Actually, it cheered me to see how much ground I'd covered. In five days I'd constructed a fairly comprehensive picture of Lorna's lifestyle. I found myself getting absorbed in my recollections. As fast as I filled cards, I'd tack them on the board, a hodgepodge of miscellaneous facts and impressions. It was when I went back through Lorna's finances, transferring data from the schedule of assets, that I caught something I'd missed. Tucked into the file with her stock certificates was the itemized list of the jewelry she'd insured. There were four pieces listed—a necklace of matched garnets, a matching garnet bracelet, a pair of earrings, and a diamond watch—the appraised value totaling twenty-eight thousand dollars. The earrings were described as graduated stones, one-half- to one-carat diamonds, set in double hoops. I'd seen them before, only Berlyn had been wearing them, and I'd assumed they were rhinestones. I checked the time. It was nearly eleven, and I was startled to discover I'd been working for almost two hours. I picked up the phone and called the Keplers' house, hoping it wasn't too late. Mace answered. What a dick. I hated talking to him. I could hear some kind of televised sporting event blasting away in the background. Probably a prizefight, from the sound of the crowd. I stuck a finger up one nostril to disguise my voice. "Hi, Mr. Kepler, is Berlyn there, please?"

"Who's this?

"Marcy. I'm a friend. I was over there last week."

"Yeah, well, she's out. Her and Trinny both."

"You know where she's at? We were supposed to meet up, but I forgot where she said."

"What'd you say your name was?"

"Marcy. Is she over at the Palace?"

There was an ominous silence from him while in the background someone was really getting pounded. "I'll tell you this, Marcy, she better not be over there. She's over at the Palace, she's in big trouble with her dad. Is that where she said to meet?"

"Uh, no." But I was willing to bet money that's where she was. I hung up. I pushed the paperwork aside, shrugged into my jacket, and found my bag, pausing only long enough to run a comb through my hair.

When I opened my front door, a man was standing just outside.

I leapt back, shrieking, before I saw who it was. "Shit J.D.! What are you doing out here? You scared the hell out of me!"

He'd jumped, too, about the same time I had, and he now sagged against the door frame. "Well, damn. You scared *me.* I was all set to knock when you came flying out." He had a hand to his chest. "Hang on. My heart's pounding. Sorry if I scared you. I know I should have called. I just took a chance you'd be here."

"How'd you find out where I live?"

"You gave Leda this card and wrote it right here on the back. You mind if I come in?"

"All right, if you can keep it brief," I said. "I was on my way out. I've got something to take care of." I moved back from the door and watched him edge his way in. I don't like the idea of just anyone waltzing through my place. If I hadn't had some questions for him, I might have left him on the doorstep. His outfit looked like the one I'd seen him in before, but then again, so did mine. Both of us wore faded jeans and blue denim jackets. He still sported cowboy boots to my running shoes. I closed the door behind him and moved to the kitchen counter, hoping to keep him away from my desk.

Like most people who see my apartment for the first time, he looked around with interest. "Pretty slick," he said.

I indicated a stool, sneaking a look at my watch. "Have a seat."

"This is okay. I can't stay long anyway."

"I'd offer you something, but about all I've got is uncooked pasta. You like rotelli, by any chance?"

"Don't worry about it. I'm fine," he said.

I perched on one stool and left the other for him, in case he changed his mind. He seemed ill at ease, standing there with both hands stuck in the back pockets of his jeans. His gaze would hit mine and then flicker off. The light in my living room wasn't as kind to his face as the light in his own kitchen. Or maybe the unfamiliar surroundings had created new lines of tension.

I got tired of waiting to hear what he had to say. "Can I help you with something?"

"Yeah, well, Leda said you stopped by. I got home around seven, and she's pretty upset."

"Really," I said, giving it no inflection. "I wonder why."

"It's this business about the tape. She'd like to have it back, if you don't mind."

"I don't mind a bit." I moved over to the desk and removed it from the manila envelope Hector had tucked it in. I passed it over to J.D., and he put it in his jacket pocket without really looking at it.

"You have a chance to listen?" he asked. He was being way too casual.

"Briefly. What about you?"

"Well, I know pretty much what's in it. I mean, I knew what she was doing."

I said, "Ah," with a noncommittal nod. Inside, a little voice was going, *Wow, what's this about? This is interesting.* "Why was she upset?"

"I guess because she doesn't want the police to find out."

"I told her I wouldn't take it to them."

"She's not very trusting. You know, she's kind of insecure."

"That much I get, J.D.," I said. "I'm just wondering what's got her so uneasy she'd send you all the way over here."

"She's not uneasy. She doesn't want you thinking it was me." He shifted his weight from one foot to the other, smiling with embarrassment, using his very best "aw, shucks" routine. "Didn't want you puttin' the hairy eyeball on me. Scrutinizing." If there'd been a little dirt on the floor, he'd have stubbed the toe of his boot in it.

"I scrutinize everyone. It's nothing personal," I said. "In fact, since you're here, I have a question for you."

"Hey, you go right ahead. I got nothing to hide."

"Someone mentioned you went into Lorna's cabin before the cops showed up."

He frowned. "Somebody said that? Wonder who?"

"I don't think it's any secret. Serena Bonney," I said.

He nodded. "Well. That's right. See, I knew Leda'd put the mike in there. I knew about the tape, and I didn't want the cops to spot it, so what I did, I opened the door, leaned down, and clipped the mike off the wire. I wasn't even in there a minute, which is why I never thought to mention it."

"Did Lorna know she was being taped?"

"I never said anything. Tell you the truth, I was embarrassed by Leda's behavior. You know, by her attitude. She treated Lorna kind of snippy. She's young and immature, and Lorna's already giving me a hard time about her. If I told her Leda was spying on us, she'd have either laughed her butt off or gotten pissed, and I didn't think it would help their relationship."

"They had a bad relationship?"

"Well, no. It wasn't *bad,* but it wasn't that good."

"Leda was jealous," I suggested.

"She might have been a little jealous, I guess."

"So what are you here to tell me? That really everything's all right between you and Leda, and neither one of you had any reason to want Lorna out of the way, right?"

"It's the truth. I know you think somehow I had something to do with Lorna's death. . . ."

"How could I think that? You told me you were out of town."

"That's right. And she was, too. I was set to go fishing with my brother-in-law, and at the last minute she decided to go up to Santa Maria with me while I picked him up. Said she'd rather hang out with her sister than stay here by herself."

"Why are you repeating all this stuff? I don't get it."

"Because you act like you don't believe us."

"Gosh, J.D., how could I fail to believe you when you provide such nice alibis for each other?"

"It's not an alibi. Now, goddamn it. How can it be an alibi when all I'm doing is telling you where we were?"

"Whose vehicle did you take to go to Lake Nacimiento?"

He hesitated. "My brother-in-law has a truck. We took that."

"Santa Maria's an hour away. How do you know Leda didn't drive back in your car?"

"I don't for sure, but you could ask her sister. She'd tell you."

"Right."

"No, she would."

"Oh, come on. If you'd lie for Leda, why wouldn't her sister lie, too?"

"Somebody else must have seen her on Saturday. I think she

said they had a makeup party that morning. You know, where some cosmetic saleslady comes and does facials on everyone so they'll buy Mary Jane products or whatever it is. You don't have to get mad."

"Mary Kay. But you're right. I shouldn't get mad. I told Leda I'd verify all of this. I haven't had a chance to do it, so it's my fault, not yours."

"Now see? I don't know how you do that. Even when you apologize, you make it sound like you don't mean it. Why are you being so cranky with me?"

"J.D., I'm cranky because I'm in a hurry and I don't understand what you're up to."

"I'm not up to anything. I just came to get the tape. I thought while I was here, I'd . . . you know, discuss it. Anyway, you're the one that asked me. I didn't volunteer. Now it seems like I made it worse."

"Okay. I accept that. Let's let it go at that. Otherwise we'll be standing around all night explaining ourselves to one another."

"Okay. As long as you're not mad."

"Not a bit."

"And you believe me."

"I never said that. I said I accept it."

"Oh. Well, okay, then. I guess that's okay."

I could feel my eyes begin to cross.

It was twenty after eleven when I pushed my way through the crowd at Neptune's Palace. The illusion of the ocean depths was profound that night. Watery blue lights shaded down to black. A pattern of light played across the dance floor like the shimmer at the bottom of a pool. I raised my gaze to the ceiling, where a storm at sea was being projected. Lightning forked in a faux sky, and an unseen wind whipped across the ocean's surface. I could hear the cracking of the ship's timbers as the rain lashed the mast, the screams of drowning men set against a rock-and-roll backdrop.

Dancers swayed back and forth, their arms undulating in the smoke-heavy air. The music was so loud, it was almost like no sound, like silence, in the same way that black is every color intensified into nothing.

I found a perch at the bar and bought myself a beer while I scanned the crowd. The boys wore mascara and black lipstick while the girls sported punk haircuts and elaborate tattoos. I kept my gaze carefully averted. The music stopped abruptly, and the dance floor began to clear. I caught a glimpse of a familiar blond head I could have sworn was Berlyn's. She disappeared from view. I eased off the bar stool and circled to the right, peering over the roiling mob to the point where I thought I'd seen her. She was nowhere in sight, but I didn't think I was mistaken.

I lingered near a massive saltwater tank where a flat eel with vicious teeth was devouring a hapless fish. Suddenly I spotted her, sitting at a table with a beefy guy in a tank top, fatigue pants, and heavy army boots. His head had been shaved bald, but his shoulders and forearms were still thick with fur. Any body part not covered with hair seemed to be adorned with some kind of tattoo, dragons and snakes. I could see the ridges in his skull and rolls of flesh along his neck. I've often thought of fat backs as the portion of the human body that aliens would most prefer to eat.

Berlyn sat in profile. She'd shrugged off her leather jacket, which was now hanging over the back of her chair, anchored by her shoulder bag. She was wearing the earrings, two diamond-encrusted hoops dangling down on either side. Her skirt was green satin and, like her black one, short and tight. While she talked, she made frequent reference to the earrings, touching first one and then the other, reassuring herself that both were still in place. She seemed self-conscious, perhaps unaccustomed to wearing such ornate jewelry. The light from the candle in the middle of her table caught the myriad facets of the stones.

Booming music broke the air, and the two got up to dance again. Berlyn wore the same high, spiky heels, perhaps in hopes of lending grace to ankles that were otherwise as shapeless as porch posts. She had a butt on her like a loaded backpack tied around her waist. The table next to theirs had emptied, and I slid onto the chair next to hers.

Trinny suddenly appeared to my right. I'd have avoided the contact, but I knew she'd already spotted me.

"Hi, Trinny. How're you? I didn't know you came here."

"Everybody comes here. This is hot." She was glancing around as she spoke, snapping her fingers while she did some kind of chin thrust in time to the music. I wondered if this was mating behavior.

"You here by yourself?"

"Nuh-uhn, I came with Berl. She has a boyfriend she meets here because Daddy dudn't like him."

"Really, Berlyn's here, too? Where'd she go?"

"Right out on the dance floor. She was sitting right here."

She pointed in the general direction of the dance floor, and I peered dutifully. Berlyn was doing a bump-and-grind number with the beefy boyfriend. I could see his shaved head towering above the other heads bobbing on the dance floor.

"That's the guy your dad dudn't like? I can't imagine."

Trinny shrugged. "It's his hair, I think. Daddy's kind of conservative. He doesn't think guys should shave their heads."

"Yeah, but what difference could it make when he's got so much hair everywhere else?" I said.

Trinny made a face. "I don't like guys with hairy backs."

"Nice earrings Berlyn's wearing. Where'd she get 'em? I wouldn't mind a pair of those myself."

"They're just rhinestones."

"Rhinestones? That's cool. They look like real diamonds from here, don't you think?"

"Oh, right. Like she's really going to wear diamonds."

"Maybe she got 'em at one of those stores that sells look-alike jewels. You know, emeralds and rubies and like that. I look at that stuff and I can't tell the difference."

"Yeah, maybe."

I looked up. A fellow doing chin thrusts and a lot of finger popping was standing near Trinny's chair. She got up and started bumping and grinding on the spot. I waved at the air, trying to watch the dance floor around their flailing arms. "Do you mind?"

The two of them began to bebop in the direction of the dance floor. I found Berlyn again with her beau. I kept my eyes pinned on their heads bobbing on the dance floor. I leaned over as if to tie my shoe and slid my hand down into her purse. I felt her wallet, cosmetic bag, hairbrush. I sat up again and then simply extracted the handbag from the back of the chair where she'd hung it, leaving mine in its place. I hefted the strap across one shoulder and moved off to the ladies' room.

There were five or six women at the basins, makeup paraphernalia scattered across the shelving provided. All were engaged in a frenzy of hair ratting, blusher brushes, and lip pencils, not even looking up as I went into a stall and slid the bolt across. I hung the bag over a hook that had been thoughtfully provided by the management and began to search in earnest.

Berlyn's wallet was not that educational: driver's license, a couple of credit cards, a few folded credit card receipts shoved down among the currency. Her checkbook showed a series of deposits at weekly intervals, which I assumed represented paychecks from Kepler Plumbing, Inc. Chick was seriously underpaid. Scanning back over the last several months, I spotted an occasional deposit of twenty-five hundred dollars, usually followed by checks made out to Holiday Travel. That was interesting. I found the small velvet jeweler's box in which the earrings were probably kept.

I tried the interior zippered compartment, sorting through old grocery lists, Thrifty drugstore receipts, deposit slips. I pulled out passbooks for two different savings accounts. The first had been opened with a nine-thousand-dollar deposit about a month after Lorna's death. I could see intermittent withdrawals of twenty-five hundred dollars, bringing the current balance down to fifteen hundred. The second account held another six thousand dollars. There was probably a third account somewhere else. Berlyn had tucked the carbons of her deposit and withdrawal slips in the back of one passbook—information she didn't dare leave at home. If Janice had discovered her cache of hidden funds, sticky questions would arise. I lifted a carboned slip from each passbook.

Someone knocked on the stall. "Are you dead in there?"

"Just a minute," I called.

I depressed the toilet handle, letting the toilet flush noisily while I shoved everything back in the handbag. I emerged from the stall with the bag over my shoulder. A black girl with a seventies Afro moved into the stall I'd vacated. I found an empty basin and gave my hands a vigorous scrub, feeling like they needed it. I left the restroom and returned to the table in haste just as the dance music came to a blasting finale. There was tumultuous applause from the dance floor, complete with piercing whistles and foot stompings. I slid onto my chair, snagged my bag from Berlyn's chair, and slipped hers into place.

Berlyn was approaching, the big guy right in her wake. Her chair tilted perilously. I grabbed for it, but not quickly enough to prevent her bag and leather jacket from tumbling on the floor in a heap.

19

I'd caught a glimpse of Berlyn's mouth, which opened with annoyance when she realized the chair had toppled over. She was looking sweaty and cross, her perpetual state, I suspected. I turned my back abruptly so I was facing the bar. I drank my beer, heart thumping. I heard her exclamation of surprise. "Look at this. Gaaaad . . ." She dragged the profanity out into three musical notes as she scooped up her belongings, apparently pausing to check the contents of her purse. "Somebody's been *in* here."

"In your bag?" the guy said.

"Yes, Gary, in my bag," she said, voice heavy with sarcasm.

"Anything missing?" He seemed concerned, but not freaked out. Maybe he was used to her tone of voice.

She said, "Hey."

I could tell she was speaking in my direction.

She poked me in the shoulder. "I'm talking to you."

I turned, feigning innocence. "Excuse me?"

"Oh, my God. What the hell are you doing here?"

"Well, hi, Berlyn. I thought it might be you," I said. "I saw Trinny a minute ago and she said you were around someplace. What's the problem?"

She gave the bag a shake as if it were a naughty pup. "Don't give me that bullshit. Have you been in here?"

I put a hand on my chest and looked around with puzzlement. "I've been in the ladies' room. I just sat down," I said.

"Ha ha. Very funny."

I looked up at the guy with her. "Is she on drugs?"

He rolled his eyes. "Come on now, Berl, settle down, okay? She wasn't bothering you. Give the chick a break."

"Shut up." Her blond hair looked nearly white in the flickering light from above. Her eyes were darkly lined, mascara separating her lashes into tiny rows of spikes. She fixed me with a look of singular intensity, swelling the way a cat does when it senses a threat.

I let my gaze roam across her face, resting on the diamond hoop earrings, which fairly quivered at her ears. I kept my smile pleasant. "Do you have something to hide, perchance?"

She leaned forward aggressively, and for a moment I thought she might snatch me up by the front of my turtleneck. She put her face so close to mine that I could smell her beery breath, which was not that big a treat. "What did you say?"

I spoke clearly, enunciating. "I said, your earrings are nice. I wonder where you got them."

Her face went blank. "I don't have to talk to you."

I shot a look at the guy just to see how he was taking this. He didn't seem all that interested. Already I found I liked him better than her. "How about this? You want to tell me how you acquired so much money in your savings accounts?"

The beefy guy looked from me to her and back, apparently confused. "You talkin' to me or her?"

"Actually, to her. I'm a private investigator, working on a job," I said. "I don't think you want to get in the middle of this, Gary. Right now we're fine, but it's going to get ugly in a minute."

He held up his hands. "Hey, you two have a beef, you can settle it without me. See you round, Berl. I'm outta here."

I said, "Bye-bye," to him and then to Berlyn, "My car's outside. You want to talk?"

We sat in my car. The parking lot outside Neptune's Palace seemed to have as much going on as the interior. Two beat cops were having a solemn chat with a kid who seemed to have trouble standing upright. In the aisle ahead of us and two cars over, a young girl was clinging to someone's fender while she emptied the contents of her stomach. The temperature was dropping, and the sky above us seemed clear as glass. Berlyn wasn't looking at me.

"You want to start with the earrings?"

"No." Sullen. Uncooperative.

"You want to start with the money you stole from Lorna?"

"You don't have to take that attitude," she said. "I didn't exactly *steal.*"

"I'm listening."

She seemed to squirm, considering how much to "share" with me. "I'm telling you this in strictest confidence, okay?" she said.

I held a hand up Scout-style. I love confidences, and the stricter the better. I'd probably rat her out, but she didn't have to know that.

She weaseled around some more, mouth working while she decided how to put it. "Lorna called and told Mom she was going out of town. Mom didn't mention it to me 'til later, right before she went to work. I was upset because I had to talk to Lorna about this cruise to Mazatlán. She said she might be able to help me out, so I went over there. Her car was there, but her lights were out, and she didn't answer my knock. I figured she was out somewhere. I went back first thing in the morning, hoping I could catch her before she left."

"What time was this?"

"Maybe nine, nine-thirty. I was supposed to take the money to the travel agent by noon or I'd lose my deposit. I'd already given them a thousand dollars, and I had to have the balance or I'd forfeit everything I'd paid."

"That was for the cruise you took last fall?"

"Uhn-hun."

"What made you think Lorna had money?"

"Lorna always had money. Everybody knew what she did. Sometimes she was generous and sometimes not. It depended on her mood. Besides, she told me she'd help. She just about *promised.*"

I started to quiz her on the subject but decided it would be better to let that pass for now. "Go on."

"Well, I knocked on the door, but she never answered. I saw her car was still there, and I thought maybe she was in the shower or something, so I opened the door and peeked in. She was on the floor. I just stood there and stared. I was so shocked I couldn't even think."

"Was the door locked or unlocked the night before?"

"I don't know. I didn't try. I didn't even think of it. Anyway, I touched her arm and she was really cold. I knew she was dead. I could tell just by looking. Her eyes were wide open, and she was staring. It was really gross."

"What next?"

"I just felt awful. It was horrible. I sat down and started crying." She blinked, staring through the windshield, which was a little dusty for my taste. I figured she was trying to conjure up a quick tear to impress me with the sincerity of her anguish.

"You didn't call the police?" I asked.

"Well, no."

"Why not? I'm just curious about your frame of mind."

"I don't know," she said grudgingly. "I was afraid they'd think I did it."

"Why would they think that?"

"I couldn't even prove where I was earlier because I was at home by myself. Mom was there, but she was sleeping, and Trinny still had a job back then. I mean, what if I was arrested? Mom and Daddy would have *died.*"

"I understand. You wanted to protect them," I said blandly.

"I tried to think what to do. I was really screwed, you know? I'd just been praying for the money, and now it was too late. And poor Lorna. I felt so sorry for her. I kept thinking about all the things she wouldn't get to do, like get married, or have a baby. She'd never get to travel to Europe—"

"So you did what?" I said, cutting in on her recital. Her voice was getting quavery.

She took out a ratty tissue and dabbed at her nose. "Well. I knew where she kept her bank books, so I borrowed her driver's license and this passbook. I was so confused and upset, I didn't know what to do."

"I can imagine. Then what?"

"I got in my car and drove down to the valley and took some money out her savings."

"How much?"

"I don't remember. Quite a bit, I guess."

"You closed the account, didn't you?"

"What else was I supposed to do?" she said. "I figured once they found out she was dead, they'd freeze all her accounts like they did with my gramma. And then what good would it do? She *promised* she'd help. I mean, it wasn't like she'd turned me down or anything like that. She wanted me to have it."

"What about her signature? How'd you manage that?"

"We write alike anyway because I taught her myself before she went to kindergarten. She'd always imitated my writing, so it wasn't that hard to imitate hers."

"Didn't they ask for identification?"

"Sure, but we look enough alike. My face is fuller, but that's about the only difference. You know, hair color, but everybody changes that. Later, when the news hit the paper, nobody seemed to put it together. I don't even think her picture ran in the paper down there."

"What about the bank? Wasn't there a closing statement sent out?"

"Sure, but all the mail comes to me at home. Everything from them I pulled out and threw away quick."

"Well, almost everything," I said. "Then what?"

"That's all."

"What about the earrings?"

"Oh, yeah. I probably shouldn't have done that." She made a face meant to signify regret and other profound emotional responses. "I've been thinking I should put the rest of it back."

"Back where?"

"We still have some of her clothes and stuff. I thought I could stick the jewelry in an old purse, like that was where she kept it. In the pocket of her winter coat or something, and then, you know, discover it and act all amazed."

"That's certainly a plan," I said. I was missing something, but I couldn't figure out what. "Could we get back to the money for just a minute here? After you drove back from Simi, you still had Lorna's driver's license along with the cash. I'm trying to understand what you did next. Just so I can get a picture."

"I don't understand. What do you mean?"

"Well, her driver's license was listed on the police report, so you must have put it back."

"Oh, sure. I put the license right back where it was. Yeah, that's right."

"Uhn-hun. Like in her wallet or something?"

"Right. Then I realized I better make it look like she'd closed the account herself, you know, like she took some money out before she left town."

"I'm with you so far," I said with caution.

"Well, everybody thought she was already gone, so all I had to do was create the impression that she was alive all day Friday."

"Wait a minute. I thought this was Saturday. This all happened Friday?"

"It had to be Friday. The bank's not even *open* on Saturday, and neither is the travel agent."

My mouth did not actually drop open, but it felt as though it did. I turned to stare at her fully, but Berlyn didn't seem to notice. She was caught up in her narrative and probably wasn't tuned to my look of astonishment. She was really the most amazing mix of cunning and stupidity, and way too old to be so unaware.

"I went on home. I was really really upset, so I told Mom I had the cramps and went to bed. Saturday afternoon, I went back to her place and brought the mail in with the morning newspaper. I couldn't see any harm. I mean, dead is dead, so what difference did it make?"

"What'd you do with the bank book?"

"Kept it. I didn't want anybody to know the money was gone."

"So you waited a month and opened a couple of savings accounts." I was monitoring myself, trying to keep from using what an English teacher would probably refer to as the screaming accusative verb tense. Berlyn must have picked up on it to some extent because she nodded, trying to look humble and repentant. Whatever she'd told herself in the ten months since Lorna died, I suspect it sounded different now that she was explaining it to me.

"Weren't you worried about your fingerprints showing up at her place?" I said.

"Not really. I wiped off everything I touched so my prints wouldn't show, but even if I slipped up, I figured I had a right to be there. I'm her sister. I've been there lots of times. Anyway, how can they prove when a fingerprint was made?"

"I'm surprised you didn't buy yourself some new clothes or a car."

"That wouldn't be right. I didn't ask her for that stuff."

"You didn't ask her for the jewelry, either," I said tartly.

"I figure Lorna wouldn't mind. I mean, why would she care? I was so heartbroke when I found her." She ceased making eye contact, and her expression took on a troubled cast. "Anyway, why would she begrudge me when there wasn't anything she could do by then?"

"You do know you broke the law."

"I did?"

"Actually, you broke quite a few laws," I said pleasantly. I could feel my temper beginning to climb. It was like being on the verge of throwing up. I should have kept my mouth shut because I could feel myself losing it. "But here's the point, Berlyn. I mean, aside from grand theft, withholding evidence, tampering with a crime scene, obstructing justice, and God knows what other laws you managed to violate, you've completely fucked up the investigation of your own sister's murder! Some asshole's out there walking around free as a bird right this minute because of you, do you get that? What kind of fuckin' twit are you?"

That's when she finally started crying in earnest.

I leaned across the car and opened the door on her side. "Get out. Go home," I said. "Better yet, go to Frankie's and tell your mother what you did before it shows up in my report."

She turned to me, nose red, mascara streaking down her cheeks, nearly breathless from my betrayal. "But I told you in strictest confidence. You said you wouldn't *tell.*"

"I didn't actually say that, but if I did, I lied. I'm really a wretched person. I'm sorry you didn't understand that. Now get out of my car."

She got out and slammed the door, her grief having turned to fury in ten seconds flat. She put her face close to the window and yelled, "Bitch!"

I started the car and backed out, so mad I nearly ran her down in the process.

I started cruising the neighborhood, hoping to run into Cheney Phillips somewhere. Maybe he was on call, doing vice rounds like a doctor. Mostly I was looking for a way to keep occupied while I sorted through the implications of what Berlyn had said. No wonder J.D. was nervous, doing everything he could to fix the day and time of his departure with Leda. If Lorna was murdered Friday night or Saturday, they were in the clear. Run it back a day and everything was up for grabs again.

I cut down along Cabana and headed toward CC's. Maybe Cheney was hanging out there. It was not quite midnight. The wind had picked up, moaning through the trees, blowing as if there were a storm in progress, though no rain fell. The surf was being churned up, a wild spray coming off the waves as they boomed against the shore. From a side street, to my left, I could hear a car alarm crying, and the sound seemed to carry like the howling of a wolf. Out of the corner of my eye, I caught the flight of a dried palm frond that hurtled down from a tree and skittered across the road in front of me.

There were very few cars in the parking lot at the Caliente Cafe. The place was quiet for a Friday night, with just a smattering of patrons and no sign of Cheney. Before I left, I used the pay phone and tried to reach Cheney at home. He was either out or not answering, and I hung up without leaving a message on his answering machine. I wasn't really sure what bothered me more, the story Berlyn had told me or Danielle's revelation about Lorna and Clark Esselmann.

I took a detour through Montebello, feeling unsettled. The Esselmann estate was on a narrow lane, without sidewalks or streetlamps. My headlights whitewashed the road ahead. The wind was still blowing. Even with my car windows up, I could hear it whuffling through the grass. A big limb was down, and I had to slow to avoid it, my eyes following the low wall that edged along the property. All the landscape lights were out, and the house sat in darkness, its angular black shape discernible against the clay-colored sky. There was no moon at all. An owl sailed across the road, touching down briefly in the grassy field on the other side, rising up again with a small dark bundle in its grip. Some death is as silent as the flight of a bird, some prey as unprotesting as a knot of rags.

The front gates were closed, and I could see little beyond the dark shapes of the junipers along the drive. I backed up and turned around, idling my engine while I debated what to do. Later, I'd wonder what might have happened if I'd actually gone ahead and pressed the intercom button and announced myself. It probably wouldn't have made a difference, but one can never be sure. Finally I put the car in gear and headed back to my place, where I crept into bed. Above me, the wind blew dry leaves across the domed skylight like the scratchings of tiny feet, something pricking at my conscience while I tossed in sleep. Once, in the dead of night, I could have sworn a cold finger touched the side of my face, and I woke with a start. The loft was empty, and the wind had died to a whisper.

My phone rang at noon. I'd been awake for an hour but unwilling to stir. Having completed my transmigration into the nocturnal realms, I found the notion of getting up any time before two repugnant. The phone rang again. It wasn't that I needed more sleep, I simply didn't want to face daylight. On the third ring, I reached for the phone and pulled it into bed with me, tucking the receiver up between my ear and pillow. "Hello."

"This is Cheney."

I propped myself on one elbow and ran a hand through my hair. "Well, hey. I tried calling you last night, but I guess you were out."

"No, no. I was here," he said. "My girlfriend was over, and we turned the phone off at ten. What's going on with you?"

"Oh, man, we gotta talk. All kinds of shit is coming down on this investigation."

"You ain't heard the half of it. I just got a call from a buddy in the sheriff's department. Clark Esselmann died this morning in a freak accident."

"He what?"

"You're never going to believe this. The guy was electrocuted in his swimming pool. Dove in to swim some laps and got fried, I guess. The gardener was killed, too. Fellow jumped in to try to save him and died the same way he did. Esselmann's daughter said she heard a scream, but by the time she got out there, they were both dead. Luckily she figured out what was going on and flipped the circuit breaker."

"That's really weird," I said. "Why didn't the breaker cut out to begin with? Isn't that what it's for?"

"Don't ask me. They've got an electrician out there now, checking all the wiring, so we'll see what he comes up with. Anyway,

Hawthorn's at the house with the crime scene boys, and I'm on my way over. Want me to swing by and pick you up?"

"Give me six minutes. I'll be waiting out in front."

"See you."

When Cheney and I reached the entrance to Clark Esselmann's estate, he pressed the button and announced our arrival to a hollow-sounding someone on the other end. "Just a minute and I'll check," the fellow said, and clicked off. During the drive, I'd told Cheney as much as I could about Esselmann's confrontation with Stubby Stockton at the meeting the night before. I'd also told him about my conversation with Berlyn and Danielle's claim about Esselmann's relationship with Lorna.

"You've been busy," he remarked.

"Not busy enough. I came over here last night thinking I should talk to him. I don't have any idea what I intended to say, but as it turned out, the place was dark, and I didn't think I should rouse the household to quiz him about his rumored kinkiness."

"Well, it's too late now."

"Yeah, isn't it," I said.

The gates swung open, and we started up the winding driveway, which was bordered with vehicles: two unmarked cars, the electrician's truck, and a county car that probably belonged to the coroner. Cheney parked the Mazda behind the last car in line, and we approached on foot. A fire department rescue vehicle and an orange-and-white ambulance were parked out front, along with a black-and-white patrol unit from the county sheriff's department. A uniformed sheriff's deputy left his post near the front door and moved to intercept us. Cheney flashed his badge, confirming his identity, and the two spoke together briefly before the deputy waved us through.

"How come you're allowed in?" I murmured as we crossed the porch.

"I told Hawthorn there might be a peripheral connection to a case we've been working. He's got no problem with it as long as we don't interfere," Cheney said. He turned and pointed a finger at my face. "You make any trouble and I'll wring your neck."

"Why would I make trouble? I'm as curious as you are."

At the front door we paused, stepping aside for the two paramedics from the fire department who were packed up and departing, presumably no longer needed.

We moved into the house and through the big country kitchen. The interior was quiet. No audible voices, no droning of the vacuum, no ringing telephones. I didn't see Serena or any of the household staff. The French doors stood open, and the patio, like a movie set, seemed crowded with people whose status and function were not immediately clear. Most loitered at a respectful distance from the pool, but the relevant members of the team were hard at work. I recognized the photographer, the coroner, and his assistant. Two plainclothes detectives were taking measurements for a sketch. Now that we'd been admitted, no one seemed to question our right to be present. From what we could ascertain, it hadn't yet been established that a crime had been committed, but the scene was being treated with meticulous attention because of Esselmann's high standing in the community.

Both Esselmann's body and that of the gardener had been removed from the water. They lay side by side, covered discreetly with tarps. Two sets of feet were visible, one bare and one shod in work boots. The bottoms of the bare feet were marked by an irregular pattern of burns, the flesh blackened in places. There was no sign of the dog, and I assumed he'd been locked up somewhere. The second set of paramedics stood together quietly, probably waiting for the okay from the coroner to transport the bodies to the morgue. It was clear they had no further business to conduct.

Cheney left me to my own devices. He was only marginally more entitled to be there than I was, but he felt free to circulate, while I thought it was smarter to keep a low profile. I turned and looked off toward the adjacent properties. By day, the rolling lawns were patchy, the grasses interseeded with a mix of fescue and Bermuda, the latter currently dormant and forming stretches of tatty brown.

The flowering shrubs that surrounded the patio formed a waist-high wall of color. I could see exactly where the gardener had been working that morning because the hedge he'd been clipping was crisply trimmed across one section and shaggy after that. His electric clippers lay on the concrete where he must have dropped them before he jumped into the water. The lap pool looked serene, its dark surface reflecting a portion of the steeply pitched roof. Perhaps it was an artifact of my overactive imagination, but I could have sworn the faint scent of cooked flesh still lingered in the morning air.

I wandered across the patio toward the breezeway that connected the four garages to the house, and then I ambled back. I didn't see how Esselmann's death could be an accident, but neither did I understand how it could be connected to Lorna's death. It was *possible* he'd killed her, but it didn't seem likely. If he felt remorse for their relationship, or if he feared exposure, he might have elected to commit suicide, but what a bizarre way to go about it. For all he knew, Serena might have been the one who happened on the scene, and she'd have died along with him.

I noticed activity at the side of the house closest to the pool: the electrician talking with the two detectives. He gestured his explanation, and I could see all of them looking from the electrical panel to the equipment shed that housed the pump, the filter, and the big heater for the pool. The electrician moved over to the side of the pool near the far end. He hunkered, still talking, while one of the detectives peered down into the water, squinting. He got down on his hands and knees and leaned closer. He asked the electrician a question and then took off his sport coat and rolled up his sleeve, reaching into the depths. The photographer was summoned, and the detective began to detail a new set of instructions. She reloaded her camera and changed the lens.

The other detective crossed to the coroner's assistant, and they conferred. The coroner had stepped back, and the two paramedics began to prepare the bodies for removal to the ambulance. From where I was standing, I could see the news ripple across the assembled personnel. Whatever the information, it spread from twosome to twosome as the group rearranged itself. The detective moved off, and I eased my way toward the coroner's assistant, knowing if I were patient, the news train would eventually reach my little station. The electrician had left his toolbox on the patio table, and he came over to pick it up. In the meantime, the deputy was talking to the fingerprint tech, who hadn't had much work to do so far. The three of them began to chat, looking back toward the pool. I overheard the electrician use the word *deify,* and my thoughts jumped to the transcript I'd been discussing with Hector.

I laid a hand on his arm, and he glanced back at me. "Excuse me. I don't mean to butt in, but *what* did you say?"

"I said there's a problem with the GFI. Wire's come loose, which is why the circuit breaker didn't trip like it should have. One of the pool lights is busted out, and that's what sent current through the water."

"I thought the term was GFCI, ground fault circuit interrupter."

"Same thing. I use both. GFI's easier, and everybody knows what you mean." The electrician was a clean-cut kid in his twenties, one of that army of experts who make the civilized world run a little more smoothly. "Damnedest thing I ever saw," he remarked to the deputy. "Break an underwater flood like that, you'd have to take a stick and poke it out from on top. Detective's going to find out when the pool was last serviced, but somebody really blew it. We're talking a big lawsuit. And I mean big."

The fingerprint technician said, "Think the gardener could have done it?"

"Doing what? You don't punch out a pool light by accident. I told the detective, that glass is tough. It takes work. If it'd been at night with the pool lights on, somebody might have noticed. Daytime like this and all that black tile, you can hardly see the near end, let alone the far."

From the other side of the patio, the detective motioned the electrician back, and he moved in that direction. Where I was, the deputy and the fingerprint technician had shifted the discussion to somebody who'd been electrocuted by his electric lawn mower because his mother, trying to be helpful, stuck the three-pronged plug into a two-pronged extension cord. The insulation on the neutral wire was defective, which caused direct contact between the cord and the metal handle of the mower. The deputy went into quite a bit of detail about the nature of the damage, comparing it to another case he'd seen where a child bit through an electric cord while standing in a puddle of water in the bathroom.

I kept thinking about the tape recording, thinking about the phrase *she goes in at the same time every day.* Maybe Esselmann wasn't the intended victim. Maybe Serena was meant to die instead. I looked for Cheney but couldn't seem to find him. I approached the nearest of the two detectives. "Would you have any objection if I talked to Mr. Esselmann's daughter? It won't take but a minute. I'm a friend of hers," I said.

"I don't want you discussing Mr. Esselmann's death. That's my job."

"It's not about him. This is about something else."

He studied me for a moment and then glanced away. "Keep it brief," he said.

20

I went through the kitchen toward the front of the house. In the foyer, I took a right and headed up the stairs. I had no idea how the bedrooms were laid out. I moved down the hallway from room to room. At the end of the corridor, there was an intersecting T with a sitting room on the right and a bedroom on the left. I could see Serena lying on a four-poster bed, covered with a light blanket. The room was sunny and spacious, yellow-and-white paper on the walls in a tiny rosette print. There were white curtains at the window, and all the woodwork was done in white.

Serena didn't seem to be asleep. I knocked on the door frame. She turned her head and looked at me. I didn't think she'd been crying. Her face was pale, unmarked by tears, the expression in her eyes more one of resignation than sorrow, if one can make that distinction. She said, "Are they finished out there?"

I shook my head. "It'll probably be a while. You want me to call anyone?"

"Not really. I called Roger. He's coming over as soon as he can get away from the plant. Did you want something?"

"I need to ask you a question, if you can tolerate the intrusion."

"That's all right. What is it?"

"Do you use the pool on a daily basis?"

"No. I never liked swimming. That was Daddy's passion. He had the lap pool put in about five years ago."

"Does someone else here swim? One of the maids, or the cook?"

She thought about it briefly. "Occasionally a friend might call and ask to use the pool, but no one else," she said. "Why?"

"I heard a taped conversation under circumstances I'd prefer not to go into. Lorna was talking to a man who used the phrase *she goes in at the same time every day.* I thought the reference might be to swimming, but at the time it made no sense. I was just wondering if there was a 'she' on the premises who went in 'at the same time every day.' "

She smiled wanly. "Just the dog, and she only goes in when Dad does. You saw her the other night. They play fetch, and then when he does his laps, she swims alongside him."

I could feel a flicker of confusion. "I thought the dog was a male. Isn't his name Max?"

"It's Maxine. Max for short," she said. "Actually, her real name's much longer because she's pedigreed."

"Ah, Maxine. How's she doing? I didn't see her downstairs. I thought she might be up here with you."

Serena struggled into a sitting position. "Oh, heavens. Thanks for reminding me. She's still at the groomers. I took her over first thing this morning. The shop owner even came in early to accommodate the appointment. I was supposed to pick her up at eleven, but it completely slipped my mind. Ask Mrs. Holloway if she'd go over there; at least call and let them know what's happened. Poor Max, poor girl. She's going to die without Daddy. The two of them were inseparable."

"Mrs. Holloway's the housekeeper? I haven't seen her, either, but I can call if you like."

"Please. Maybe Roger can pick her up on his way over here. It's Montebello Pet Groomers in the lower village. The number's on the planning center in the kitchen. I don't want to put you to any trouble."

"It's no trouble," I said. "Are you okay?"

"Really, I'm fine. I just want some time alone, and then I'll be down. I'll probably have to talk to the detective again, anyway. I can't believe this is happening. It's all so grotesque."

"Take your time," I said. "I'll tell the pet groomers someone's picking Max up later. You want this closed? It might be quieter."

"All right. And thank you."

"That's all right. I'm sorry about your father."

"I appreciate that."

I left the room, pulling the door shut behind me. I went down to the kitchen and put a call through to the grooming shop. I identified myself as a friend of Serena's, indicating that her father had died unexpectedly. The woman was extremely gracious, expressing her condolences. The shop was closing at three, and she said she could just as easily drop Max off on her way home. I left a note to that effect, assuming that Mrs. Holloway or Serena would spot it.

By the time I returned to the patio, the bodies had been removed and the photographer had packed up and left. There was no sign of the electrician, the coroner, or his assistant. The fingerprint technician was now working over by the pool equipment. At the near end of the pool, I saw Cheney talking to the younger of the two detectives, his buddy Hawthorn, I gathered, though he never introduced us. When he spotted me, he finished up his conversation and crossed the patio to meet me. "I was wondering where you went. They're nearly done here. You want to head out?"

"We might as well," I said.

We didn't say much until we'd left the house, walking down the driveway to the spot where Cheney's car was parked. I said, "So what's the current theory? It couldn't have been an accident. That's ludicrous."

Cheney unlocked the door and held it open for me. "Doesn't look like it on the surface, but we'll see what they come up with."

He closed the door on my side, effectively cutting off communication. I leaned over and unlocked the door on his side, but I had to wait until he'd gone around and let himself in. He slid under the steering wheel.

"Quit being such a stickler and play the game," I said. "What do you think?"

"I think it's dumb to guess."

"Oh, come on, Cheney. It had to be murder. Somebody busted out the pool light and then disconnected the GFI. You don't believe it was an accident. You're the one who told Hawthorn there might be a peripheral connection between Lorna's death and Esselmann's."

"What connection?" he said perversely.

"That's what I'm asking you!" I said. "God, you're aggravating. Okay, I'll go first. Here's what I think."

He rolled his eyes, smiling, and turned the key in the ignition. He put his arm across the seat and peered out of his rear window, backing out of the gate with a breathtaking carelessness. When he reached the road, he threw the gear into first and peeled out. On the way back to my place, I told him about Leda's surreptitious tape recording. I didn't have the transcript with me, but the text was so sketchy that it wasn't difficult to recollect. "I think the guy is telling her about his scheme. He's come up with a way to kill Esselmann, and he's feeling clever. Maybe he thought she'd find it amusing, but she obviously doesn't. You ought to hear her on the tape. She's pissed off and upset, and he's trying to act like it's all a big joke. The problem is, once he's told her, he's left himself open. If he actually intends to go through with it, she'll know it was him. Given her reaction, he can't trust her to keep quiet."

"So what's your theory? Bottom line," he said.

"I think she was killed because she knew too much."

He made a face. "Yeah, but Lorna died back in April. If the guy wanted to kill Esselmann, why wait this long? If the only thing that worried him was her blowing the whistle, why not kill the old guy the minute she's dead?"

"I don't know," I said. "Maybe he had to wait until things cooled down. If he'd moved too quickly, he might have called attention to himself."

He was listening, but I could tell he wasn't convinced. "Go back to the murder scheme. What's the guy intend to do?"

"I think he's talking about a variation on what actually happened. Clark and Max go through the same routine every morning. He throws a stick into the lap pool and she fetches. She's a retriever. She was born for this stuff. After they play, the two swim. So here's the deal. Suppose the pool's been electrified. He throws the stick. She leaps in and takes a big jolt. He sees she's in trouble. He goes in after her and he dies, too. It looks like an accident, some freaky set of circumstances everyone feels bad about. Poor guy. Tried to save his doggie and died in the process. In reality, Serena took the dog to the groomer's, so Clark went in swimming by himself. Instead of Clark and the dog, you have Clark and the gardener, but the setup's the same."

Cheney was quiet for a moment. "How do you know it's Lorna on the tape?" he said. "You've never heard her voice. The guy could be talking to Serena."

"Why would she be there in the first place?" I asked promptly. I noticed it was more fun to ask questions than to have to answer them.

"Haven't made that part up yet. The point is, Serena's upset because she doesn't want the dog used as bait, so she takes Max off to the groomer's to get her out of the way."

"I've talked to Serena. The voice didn't sound like hers."

"Wait a minute. That's cheating. You told me the voices were distorted. You've talked to J.D. and you said it didn't sound like him, either."

"That's true," I said reluctantly. "But you're suggesting Serena killed her own father, and I don't believe it. Why would she do it?"

"The guy's got a lot of money. Doesn't she inherit his estate?"

"Probably, but why kill him? He'd already had a heart attack, and his health was failing. All she had to do was wait, and probably not very long at that. Besides, I've seen her with him. There was nothing but affection. An occasional complaint about his stubbornness, but you can tell she admired him. Anyway, I'll see if I can get the tape back and you can hear it for yourself."

"Who has it?"

"Leda. She sent J.D. over to pick it up last night. Or that was his claim. Actually, in the suspect department, they're not bad candidates. Both of them were nervous I'd give the tape to the police. Neither has an alibi. And you know what J.D. does for a living? He's an electrician. If anybody'd know how to hot-wire a lap pool, he would."

"The town's full of people who'd know enough to do that," he said. "Anyway, if your theory's correct, then whoever killed Esselmann had to be someone who knew the house, the pool, and the routine with the dog."

"That's right."

"Which brings us back to Serena."

"Maybe," I said slowly. "Though Roger Bonney's another one who'd know all that."

"What's his motive?"

"I have no idea, but he's certainly the link between Lorna and Esselmann."

"Well, there you have it," Cheney snorted. "Now if Roger knows Stubby, the circle will be complete, and we can charge him with murder." Cheney was being facetious, but he'd made a good point, and I could feel a ripple of uneasiness.

My thoughts veered to Danielle and the man who'd walked off into the darkness of the alleyway. "How do we know this isn't the same guy who went after Danielle? Maybe the attack on her connects up to everything else."

Cheney had reached my place, and he slowed to a stop. He pulled on the brake and put the car in neutral, turning to face me, his smile gone. "Do me a favor and think about something else. It's a fun game, but you know as well as I do it doesn't mean jack."

"I'm just trying on theories, like throwing dinner plates against the wall to see if one will stick."

He reached over and gave my hair a little tug. "Just watch yourself. Even if you're right and all these things are related, you can't go tearing off on your own," he said. "This case belongs to the county sheriff. It's got nothing to do with you."

"I know."

"Then don't give me that look. It's nothing personal."

"It is personal. Especially when it comes to Danielle," I said.

"Would you quit worrying? She's safe."

"For how long? Any day now they'll move her out of ICU. Hospitals aren't exactly high security. You ought to see the people walking in and out of there."

"You're right about that. Let me think some and see what I can do. We'll talk soon, okay?" He smiled, and I found myself smiling in return.

"Okay."

"Good. I'll give you the number for my pager. Let me know if anything turns up."

"I'll do that," I said. He recited the number and had me repeat it back to him before he put the car in gear again.

I stood at the curb and watched the Mazda pull away and then moved through the gate and went around to the rear. It was Saturday afternoon, close to three o'clock. I let myself into my apartment. I made a note of Cheney's pager number and left it on my desk. I felt I was in a state of suspended animation. The answer was hovering somewhere on the periphery, like spots in my field of vision that moved sideways every time I turned to look. There had to be some chain of events, something that linked all the pieces of the puzzle. I needed a way to distract myself, setting all the questions aside until a few answers came. I went up the spiral stairs to the loft and changed clothes, pulling on my sweatsuit and my jogging shoes. I tucked the house key in my pocket and trotted over to Cabana Boulevard.

The day was crisp and clear, the midafternoon sun pouring over the distant mountains like a golden syrup. The ocean was a dazzling carpet of diamonds, the air freshly scented with the briny smell of the sea. The run was a pleasure, bringing back in full measure the joys of physical activity. I did four miles, feeling strong, and when I came back I took a shower and started over, eating cereal and toast while I read the paper I hadn't had time for that morning. I went out and ran an errand or two, picking up groceries, stopping at a wine store. It was close to six o'clock when I finally felt relaxed enough to sit down at my desk and flip the light on.

I went back to my index cards. I was going through the motions, not really on the track of anything in particular, just trying to keep busy until I figured out what to do next. I glanced down at the sack that held the broken picture frames. Shit. Of course, I'd forgotten to take Danielle's bedding to the cleaners before it closed, but at least I could switch the frames. I moved over to the kitchen counter with the new frames I'd picked up. I put the wastebasket nearby and pulled the photographs from the paper bag. There were four eight-by-ten enlargements, all in color. I removed the frame and the matting from the first, pausing to study the image: three cats lounging on a picnic table. A sleek gray tabby was in the process of jumping down, apparently not that happy about the photographic immortality. The other two cats were long-haired, one pale cream and one black, staring at the camera with expressions of arrogance and disinterest respectively. On the back she'd written the date and the cats' names: Smokey, Tigger, and Cheshire.

As I removed the photo from the cracked frame, the glass separated into two pieces. I tucked both in the trash can and tossed the frame in after them. I pulled out a new frame and peeled off the price tag, sliding the mat and the cardboard backing out of the frame. I tucked the photo between the backing and the mat, turning it over to make sure the image was straight. I eased the three layers—mat, photo, and backing—into the space between the glass and the series of staples that were sticking out of the frame. I turned it back again. It looked good.

I picked up the second photograph and went through the same process. The glass was only cracked across one corner, but the frame itself was unsalvageable. This photograph showed two young men and a young woman on a sailboat, everyone with beer cans, sunburns, and wind-tangled hair. Danielle had probably taken the picture herself. It must have been a good day with good friends at a time in her life when she was still in possession of her innocence. I've been on outings like it. You come home dog-tired and dirty, but you never forget.

In the third picture, Danielle was posed under a white trellised arch in the company of a young clean-cut guy. From the dress she was wearing, complete with an orchid on her wrist, I guessed this was taken at her high school prom. It was nice getting a glimpse of her private life, images of her as she'd been before. She had entered the life as surely as a novice entering a convent, with a gap just as wide between past and present.

The last picture had been rematted, a wide band of gray reducing the framed image to its two central figures: Danielle and Lorna dressed up and sitting in a booth. It looked like a commercial photograph, taken by a roving photographer who made a living snapping pictures on the spot. Hard to tell where this was taken, Los Angeles or Vegas, some glitzy nightclub, with dinner and dancing. In the background, I could see a portion of a bandstand and a potted plant. Champagne glasses on the table in front of them. The frame was cheap, but the wide gray matting was a nice choice for the subject matter, isolating the two of them.

Both women were looking elegant, seated at a round table in a black leather-padded booth. Lorna was so beautiful: dark-haired, hazel-eyed, with a perfect oval face. Her expression was grave, with just the smallest hint of a smile on her lips. She wore a black satin cocktail dress, with long sleeves and a square, low-cut neckline. The diamond hoop earrings sparkled at her ears. Danielle wore kelly green, a form-fitting sequined top, probably with a miniskirt, if I knew Danielle's taste. Her long dark hair had been smoothed into a French roll. I imagined Lorna getting her all dolled up for a kind of high-class date: two call girls on the town. Along the back of the booth, I could see a man's hand and arm extending behind Lorna. I could feel my heart begin to thump.

I extracted the photograph from the frame and turned it over. With the matting removed, I could see all four people who'd been sitting at the table that night: Roger, Danielle, Lorna, and Stubby Stockton. Oh, man, this is it, I thought. This is it. Maybe not everything, but the heart of the riddle.

I carried the photo with me to the telephone and called Cheney's pager number, punching in my own telephone number and the # sign at the sound of the tone. I hung up. While I waited for him to return my call, I sat at my desk and sorted through my notes, pulling all the index cards on which Roger was mentioned. Most were from my initial interview, with additional notes from my conversation with Serena. I scanned the cards on the bulletin board, but there were no further references. I laid the cards out on my desk like a tarot reading. I found the notes I'd scribbled to myself after my meeting with him. Roger had told me Lorna called him Friday morning. I circled the day and added a question mark, affixing the card to the photograph with a paper clip.

The phone rang. "Kinsey Millhone," I said automatically.

"This is Cheney. What's up?"

"I'm not sure. Let me tell you what I came across, and you tell me." I told him briefly how I'd acquired the photographs, and then I detailed the one I was looking at. "I know you were kidding when you talked about Roger and Stubby, but they *did* know each other, and well enough to go whoring together somewhere out of town. I also went back through my notes and came across an interesting discrepancy. Roger told me Lorna called him Friday morning, but she couldn't possibly have done that. She was dead by then."

There was a brief silence. "I don't see where you're going with this."

"I have no idea. That's why I'm calling you," I said. "I mean, suppose Roger and Stubby were in business together. If Lorna told Roger about her relationship with Esselmann, they could have been using the information to pressure him. Esselmann balked. . . ."

"So Stubby killed him? That's ridiculous. Stubby's got a lot of irons in the fire. This deal doesn't work, he's got another one lined up, and if that fails, he's got more. Believe me, Stockton is in business to do business. Period. If Esselmann dies, that only sets him back because now he's gotta wait until someone's appointed to take Clark's place, yada, yada, yada . . ."

"I'm not saying Stockton. I think it's Roger. He's the one who had access to that pool equipment. He had access to Lorna. He had access to everything. Plus, he knew Danielle. Suppose he and Stockton talked business that night. Danielle's the only witness."

"How're you going to prove it? All you have is speculation. This is all air and sunshine. You've got nothing concrete. At least, nothing you could take to the DA. He'd never go for it."

"What about the tape?"

"That's not proof of anything. It's illegal for starters, and you don't even know it's Lorna. They could be talking about anything. You ever heard the concept of 'fruit of the poisonous tree'? I've been thinking about this whole business ever since I dropped you off. You got people tampering with the crime scene, tampering with evidence. Any good defense attorney would rip you to shreds."

"What about Roger's claim Lorna called him Friday morning?"

"So the guy was mistaken. She called some other day."

"What if I went in with a wire and had a talk with him. Let me ask—"

Cheney cut in, his tone a mixture of impatience and outrage. "Ask him what? We're not going to wire *you.* Don't be asinine. What are you proposing, you go knock on his door? 'Hi, Rog. It's Kinsey. Who'd you kill today? Oh, no reason, just curious. Excuse me, would you mind speaking into this artificial flower I'm wearing in my lapel?' This is not your job. Face it. There's nothing you can do."

"Bullshit. That's bullshit."

"Well, it's bullshit you're gonna have to live with. We really shouldn't even be discussing this."

"Cheney, I'm tired of the bad guys winning. I'm sick of watching people get away with murder. How come the law protects them and not us?"

"I hear you, Kinsey, but that doesn't change the facts. Even if you're right about Roger, you got no way to nail him, so you might as well drop it. Eventually he'll screw up, and we'll get him then."

"We'll see."

"Don't give me 'we'll see.' You do something stupid and it's your ass, not his. I'll talk to you later. I got another call coming in."

I hung up on him, steaming. I knew he was right, but I really hate that stuff, and his being right only made it worse. I sat for a minute and stared at the photograph of Lorna and Danielle. Was I the only one who really cared about them? I held the missing piece of the puzzle, but there were no options open to me, no means of redress. There was something humiliating about my own ineffectiveness. I crossed the room and paced back, feeling powerless. The phone rang again and I snatched up the receiver.

"This is Cheney . . ." His voice was oddly flat.

"Hey, great. I was hoping you'd call back. Surely, between us, there's a way to do this," I said. I thought he was calling to apologize for being such a hard-ass. I expected him to offer a suggestion about some action we might take, so I was completely unprepared for what came next.

"That was St. Terry's on the line. The ICU nurse. We lost Danielle. She just died," he said.

I felt myself blink, waiting for the punchline. "She died?"

"She went into cardiac arrest. I guess they coded her, but it was too late to pull her back."

"Danielle *died?* That's absurd. I just saw her last night."

"Kinsey, I'm sorry. The call just came in. I'm as surprised as you are. I hate to be the one to tell you, but I thought you should know."

"Cheney." My tone was rebuking while his had become compassionate.

"You want me to come over?"

"No, I don't want you to come over. I want you to quit fucking with my head," I snapped. "Why are you doing this?"

"I'll be there in fifteen minutes."

The line clicked out and he was gone.

Carefully, I set the receiver in the cradle. Still standing, I put a hand across my mouth. What was this? What was happening? How could Danielle be dead while Roger was beyond reach? At first, I felt nothing. My initial response was a curious blank, no sensation at all attached. I took in the truth content of what Cheney had told me, but there was no corresponding emotional reaction. Like a monkey, I plucked up this bright coin of information and turned it over in my hand. I believed in my head, but I couldn't comprehend with my heart. I remained motionless for perhaps a minute, and when feelings finally crept back, what I experienced wasn't grief, but a mounting fury. Like some ancient creature hurtling up from the deep, my rage broke the surface and I struck.

I picked up the receiver, put my hand in my jeans pocket, and pulled out the card I'd been given in the limousine. The scribbled number was there, some magical combination of digits that spelled death. I dialed, giving absolutely no thought to what I was doing. I was propelled by the hot urge to act, by the blind need to strike back at the man who had dealt me this blow.

After two rings, the phone was picked up on the other end. "Yes?"

I said, "Roger Bonney killed Lorna Kepler."

I hung up. I sat down. I felt my face twist with heat, and tears spilled briefly.

I went into the bathroom and looked out the window, but the street beyond was dark. I went back to my desk. Oh, Jesus. What had I done? I picked up the phone and dialed the number again. Endless rings. No answer. I put the phone down. Hands shaking, I pulled my gun from the bottom drawer and popped in a fresh clip. I eased the gun into the waistband at the back of my jeans and pulled on my jacket. I grabbed my handbag and car keys, turned out the lights, and locked the door behind me.

I hit the 101, heading out toward Colgate. I kept checking my rearview mirror, but there was no sign of the limousine. At Little Pony Road, I took the off-ramp and turned right, continuing past the fairgrounds until I reached the intersection at State. I stopped at the traffic light, drumming my fingers on the steering wheel in impatience, checking my rearview mirror again. Along the main thoroughfare there was only one touch of color, words written out in red neon on the drugstore I spotted. *SAV-ON,* the sign said. The shopping mall to my left was apparently having a gala all-night sale. Klieg lights pierced the sky. White plastic flags were strung from pole to pole. At the entrance to the parking lot, a clown and two mimes were motioning for passing cars to turn in. The two mimes in whiteface began a playlet between them. I couldn't tell what silent drama the two were enacting, but one turned and looked at me as I pulled away from the light. I checked back, but all I saw was the painted sorrow on his downturned mouth.

I sped past a darkened service station, the bays and gasoline pumps shut down for the night. I could hear a burglar alarm clanging, apparently in a shop close by, but there was no sign of the police and no pedestrians running to see what was wrong. If there were actually burglars in the place, they could take their sweet time. We're all so accustomed to alarms going off that we pay no attention, assuming the switches have been tripped in error and mean nothing. Six blocks beyond, I crossed a smaller intersection heading up the road that led to the water treatment plant.

The area was largely unpopulated. I could see an occasional house on my right, but the fields across the road were scruffy and dotted with boulders. Coyotes yipped and howled in the distance, driven down from the hills by the need for water. It seemed too early in the evening for predators, but the pack was obeying a law of its own. They were hunting tonight, on the scent of prey. I pictured some hapless creature flying across the ground, in fear of its life. The coyote kills quickly, a mercy for its victim, though not much consolation.

I turned into the entrance to the treatment plant. Lights were on in the building, and there were four cars out front. I left my handbag in the car, locking it behind me. There was still no sign of the limousine. Then again, the guy wouldn't use his limo to make a hit, I thought. He'd probably send his goons, and they might well check Roger's place first, wherever that might be. A county-owned truck had been parked in the drive. As I passed, I put a hand out. The hood was still warm to the touch. I went up the stairs to the lighted entry. I could feel the reassuring bulk of the handgun in the small of my back. I pushed through the glass doors.

The receptionist's desk was empty. Once upon a time Lorna Kepler had sat there. It was curious to imagine her working here day after day, greeting visitors, answering the telephone, exchanging small talk with the control technician and senior treatment mechanics. Maybe it was her last shred of pretense, the final gesture she'd made toward being an ordinary person. On the other hand, she might have found herself genuinely interested in aeration maniforms and flash mix basins.

The interior of the building seemed quiet at first. Fluorescent lights glowed against the polished tile floors. The corridor was deserted. From one of the rear offices, I picked up the strains of a country music station. I could hear someone banging on a pipe, but the sound came from deep in the bowels of the building. I moved quickly down the hallway, glancing left into Roger's office. The lights were on, but he was nowhere to be seen. I heard footsteps approaching. A fellow in coveralls and a baseball cap came around the corner, moving in my direction. He seemed to take my presence for granted, though he took his cap off politely at the sight of me. His hair was a mass of curly gray mashed into a cap-shaped line around his head. "Can I help you with something?"

"I'm looking for Roger."

The fellow pointed down. "That's him you hear whumping on the sample lines." He was in his fifties, with a wide face, and a dimple in his chin. Nice smile. He reached out a hand and introduced himself. "I'm Delbert Squalls."

"Kinsey Millhone," I said. "Could you let Roger know I'm here? It's urgent."

"Sure, no problem. Actually, I'm just on my way down. Whyn't you follow me?"

"Thanks."

Squalls retraced his steps and opened the glass-paneled door into the area I'd seen before: multicolored pipes, a wall of dials and gauges. I could see the gaping hole in the floor. Orange plastic cones had been set across one end, warning the unwary about the dangers of tumbling in.

I said, "How many guys you have working tonight?"

"Lemme see. Five, counting me. Come on this way. You're not claustrophobic, I hope."

"Not a bit," I lied, following him as he crossed to the opening. On my previous visit, I'd seen a moving river of black water down there, silent, smelling of chemicals, looking like nothing I'd ever seen before. Now I could see lights and the bleak walls of concrete, discolored in places where the water had passed. I felt the need to swallow. "Where'd all the water go?" I asked.

"We shut the sluice gates, and then we have a couple of big basins it drains into," he said conversationally. "Takes about four hours. We do this once a year. We got some postaeration sample lines in the process of repair. They'd almost completely corroded. Been clogged for months until this shutdown. We got ten hours to get the work done, and then back she comes."

A series of metal rungs affixed to the wall formed a ladder, leading down into the channel. The banging had stopped. Delbert turned around and edged his foot down into the opening and then proceeded to descend. *Tink, tink, tink* went the soles of his shoes on the metal rungs as he sank from sight. I moved forward, turning myself. Then I descended as he had to the tunnel below.

Once we reached bottom, we were twelve feet underground, standing in the influent channel through which millions of gallons of water had passed. Down here it was always night, and the only moon shone in the form of a two-hundred-watt bulb. The passage smelled damp and earthy. I could see the sluice gate at the dark end of the tunnel, streaks of sediment on the floor. This felt like spelunking, not a passion of mine. I spotted Roger, with his back to us, working on an overhead line. He was standing on a ladder about fifteen feet away, the big lightbulb, in a metal guard, hooked on the pipe near his face. He wore blue coveralls and black rubber hip boots. I could see a denim jacket tucked across the ladder's brace. It was chilly down here, and I was glad I had my jacket.

Roger didn't turn. "That you, Delbert?" he said over his shoulder.

"That's me. I brought a friend of yours. A Miss . . . what is it, Kenley?"

"It's Kinsey," I corrected.

Roger turned. The light glittered in his eyes and bleached all the color from his flesh. "Well. I was expecting you," he said.

Delbert had his hands on his hips. "You need some help with that?"

"Not really. Why don't you find Paul and give him a hand?"

"Will do."

Delbert started up the ladder again, leaving us alone. His head disappeared, back, hips, legs, boots. It was very quiet. Roger came down from the ladder he was on, wiping his hands on a rag, while I stood there trying to decide how to go about this. I saw him pick up the jacket and check a pocket in front.

"This is not what you think," I said. "Listen, Lorna was getting married the weekend she was murdered. Earlier this week a fellow picked me up in a limo with a couple of flunkies in bulging overcoats . . ." I felt my voice trail off.

He had something in his hand about the size of a walkie-talkie: black plastic housing, a couple of buttons on the front. "You know what this is?"

"Looks like a taser gun."

"That's right." He pressed a button, and two tiny probes shot out on electrical wires that carried a hundred and twenty thousand volts. The minute the probes touched me I was down, my whole body numb. Couldn't move. Couldn't breathe. After a few seconds, my brain started to work. I knew what had happened, I just didn't know what to do about it. Of all the responses I'd imagined him making, this was not on the list. I lay on my back like a stone, trying to find a way to heave oxygen into my lungs. None of my extremities responded to cues. In the meantime, Roger patted me down, coming up with my gun, which he tucked in the pocket of his coveralls.

I was making a sound, but it probably wasn't very loud. He moved to the wall and climbed the ladder. I thought he was going to leave me down there. Instead he flipped the trap door so that it came down on the hole. "Thought we might like a little privacy," he said as he descended. He found a plastic bucket that had been tossed to one side. He turned it upside down and took a seat not that far from me. He leaned close. Mildly he said, "Fuck with me, I'll smother you with this jacket. Weak as you are, it's not going to leave any marks."

That's what he did with Lorna, I thought. Shot her with a stun gun, put a pillow across her face. Wouldn't have taken long. I felt like a baby in the early stages of development, moving my limbs randomly in an attempt to turn. Grunting, I managed to roll over on my side. I lay there breathing, looking at the wet pavement from the corner of my eye. My cheek rested on something gritty: anthracite, sludge, small shells. I collected myself, inching my right arm up under me. I heard the trap door open, and Delbert Squalls called down, "Roger?"

"Yes?"

"Guy up here to see you."

"Oh, hell," he breathed. And then to Delbert, "Tell him I'll be right there."

I rolled an eye at him, unable to speak, and saw a grimace of impatience cross his face. He got his arms under me and hauled me into a sitting position, propping me against the wall. Like a rag doll, I sat with my legs straight out in front of me, feet tilted together, my shoulders slumped. At least I was breathing. Above me, I could hear someone walking around. I wanted to warn him. I wanted to tell him he was making a terrible mistake. While I made grunting noises, Roger was going up the ladder, his feet going *tink, tink, tink,* head and shoulders disappearing. I felt tears fill my eyes. My limbs were deadened from the electrical jolt. I tried moving my arms, but the result was the same ineffectual feeling as discovering your extremities "asleep." I began to flex one fist, trying to get the blood to circulate. My whole body felt oddly anesthetized. I listened, straining, but heard nothing. I struggled and finally managed to topple sideways, turning over on my hands and knees, where I remained, breathing hard, until I could gain my feet. I don't know how long it took. All was silence above. I reached for the ladder and clung to the closest rung. After a moment, I began my ascent.

By the time I climbed out, there was no sign of anyone in the corridor. I forced myself forward. I'd begun to navigate better, but my arms and legs still felt oddly disconnected. I reached his office, where I peered in the door, leaning on the frame. There was no sign of him. My gun had been placed neatly in the center of his blotter. I crossed to the desk and picked it up, tucking it into the small of my back again.

I left the office, moving into the reception area. Delbert Squalls was sitting at the desk, leafing through the telephone book, probably ordering pizzas for the night crew. He looked up as I passed.

I said, "Where'd Roger go?"

"Don't tell me he left you down there? Man's got no manners. You just missed him. He took off with that guy in the overcoat. Said he'd be right back. You want to leave him a note?"

"I don't think that's necessary."

"Oh. Well, suit yourself." He went back to his search.

"Good night, Delbert."

" 'Night. Have a good evening," he said, reaching for the phone.

I emerged from the building into the chill night air. The wind had picked up again, and the sky, though cloudless, bore the fragrance of a distant rain heading in this direction. There was no moon, and the stars looked as though they'd been blown up against the mountains.

I went down the stairs to the slot where my car was parked. I let myself into the VW and turned the key in the ignition, pulling out onto the road that led back to town. As I crossed the intersection, I thought I caught sight of a limousine slipping into the dark.

EPILOGUE

Roger Bonney hasn't been seen since that night. Only a few people understand what really happened to him. I spent a long time in conversation with Lieutenant Dolan and Cheney Phillips and, for once, I told the truth. Given the enormity of what I'd done, I felt I had to accept the responsibility. In the end, after much consideration, they decided no purpose would be served in pursuing the matter. They did go through the motions of a missing persons investigation, but nothing came of it. And so it rests.

Now, in the dead of night, I ponder the part I played in Lorna Kepler's story, in the laying to rest of those ghosts. Homicide calls up in us the primitive desire to strike a like blow, an impulse to inflict a pain commensurate with the pain we've been dealt. For the most part, we depend upon judicial process to settle our grievances. Perhaps we've even created the clumsy strictures of the courts to keep our savageries in check. The problem is that so often the law seems pale in its remedies, leaving us restless and unfulfilled in our craving for satisfaction. And then what?

As for me, the question I'm left with is simple and haunting: Having strayed into the shadows, can I find my way back?

Respectfully submitted,
Kinsey Millhone

"L"

is for

LAWLESS

For dear friends . . .
Sally and Gregory Giloth
and
Connie, Marshall, and Laura Swain
with love.

ACKNOWLEDGMENTS

The author wishes to acknowledge the invaluable assistance of the following people: Steven Humphrey; Eric S. H. Ching; Louis Skiera, Veterans Services representative; B. J. Seebol, J.D.; Carter Hicks; Carl Eckhart; Ray Connors; Captain Edward A. Aasted, Lieutenant Charlene French, and Jack Cogan, Santa Barbara Police Department; Merrill Hoffman, Santa Barbara Locksmiths; Vaughan Armstrong; Kim Oser, Hyatt Dallas/Fort Worth; Sheila Burr, California Automobile Association; A. LaMott Smith; Charles de L'Arbre, Janet Van Velsor, and Cathy Peterson, Santa Barbara Travel; and John Hunt, CompuVision, who retrieved chapter 14 from the Inky Void.

1

I don't mean to bitch, but in the future I intend to hesitate before I do a favor for the friend of a friend. Never have I taken on such a load of grief. At the outset, it all seemed so *innocent.* I swear there's no way I could have guessed what was coming down. I came *this* close to death and, perhaps worse (for my fellow dental phobics), within a hairbreadth of having my two front teeth knocked out. Currently I'm sporting a knot on my head that's the size of my fist. And all this for a job for which I didn't even get paid!

The matter came to my attention through my landlord, Henry Pitts, whom everybody knows I've been half in love with for years. The fact that he's eighty-five (a mere fifty years my senior) has never seemed to alter the basic impact of his appeal. He's a sweetheart and he seldom asks me for anything, so how could I refuse? Especially when his request seemed so harmless on the face of it, without the faintest suggestion of the troubles to come.

It was Thursday, November twenty-first, the week before Thanksgiving, and wedding festivities were just getting under way. Henry's older brother William was to marry my friend Rosie, who runs the tacky little tavern in my neighborhood. Rosie's restaurant was traditionally closed on Thanksgiving Day, and she was feeling smug that she and William could get hitched without her losing any business. With the ceremony and reception being held at the restaurant, she'd managed to eliminate the necessity for a church. She'd lined up a judge to perform the nuptials, and she apparently considered that his services were free. Henry had encouraged her to offer the judge a modest honorarium, but she'd given him a blank look, pretending she didn't speak English that well. She's Hungarian by birth and has momentary lapses when it suits her purposes.

She and William had been engaged for the better part of a year, and it was time to get on with the big event. I've never been certain of Rosie's actual age, but she has to be close to seventy. With William pushing eighty-eight, the phrase "until death do us part" was statistically more significant for them than for most.

Before I delineate the nature of the business I took on, I suppose I should fill in a few quick personal facts. My name is Kinsey Millhone. I'm a licensed investigator, female, twice divorced, without children or any other pesky dependents. For six years I'd had an informal arrangement with California Fidelity Insurance, doing arson and wrongful death claims in exchange for office space. For almost a year now, since the termination of that agreement, I'd been leasing an office from Kingman and Ives, a firm of attorneys here in Santa Teresa. Because of the wedding I was taking a week off, looking forward to rest and recreation when I wasn't helping Henry with wedding preparations. Henry, long retired from his work as a commercial baker, was making the wedding cake and would also be catering the reception.

There were eight of us in the wedding party. Rosie's sister, Klotilde, who was wheelchair bound, would be serving as the maid of honor. Henry was to be the best man, with his older brothers, Lewis and Charlie, serving as the ushers. The four of them—Henry, William, Lewis, and Charlie (also known collectively as "the boys" or "the kids")—ranged in age from Henry's eighty-five to Charlie's ninety-three. Their only sister, Nell, still vigorous at ninety-five, was one of two bridesmaids, the other being me. For the ceremony Rosie had elected to wear an off-white organza muumuu with a crown of baby's breath encircling her strangely dyed red hair. She'd found a bolt of lavish floral polished cotton on sale . . . pink and mauve cabbage roses on a background of bright green. The fabric had been shipped off to Flint, Michigan, where Nell had "run up" matching muumuus for the three of us in attendance. I couldn't wait to try mine on. I was certain that, once assembled, the three of us would resemble nothing so much as a set of ambulatory bedroom drapes. At thirty-five, I'd actually hoped to serve as the oldest living flower girl on record, but Rosie had decided to dispense with the role. This was going to be the wedding of the decade, one I wouldn't miss for all the money in the world. Which brings us back to the "precipitating events," as we refer to them in the crime trade.

I ran into Henry at nine that Thursday morning as I was leaving my apartment. I live in a converted single-car garage that's attached to Henry's house by means of an enclosed breezeway. I was heading to the supermarket, where I intended to stock up on junk food for the days ahead. When I opened my door, Henry was standing on my front step with a piece of scratch paper and a tape dispenser. Instead of his usual shorts, T-shirt, and flip-flops, he was wearing long pants and a blue dress shirt with the sleeves rolled up.

I said, "Well, don't you look terrific." His hair is stark white and he wears it brushed softly to one side. Today it was slicked down with water, and I could still smell the warm citrus of his aftershave. His blue eyes seem ablaze in his lean, tanned face. He's tall and slender, good-natured, smart, his manner a perfect blend of courtliness and nonchalance. If he wasn't old enough to be my granddaddy, I'd snap him up in a trice.

Henry smiled when he saw me. "There you are. Perfect. I was just leaving you a note. I didn't think you were home or I'd have knocked on the door instead. I'm on my way to the airport to pick up Nell and the boys, but I have a favor to ask. Do you have a minute?"

"Of course. I was on my way to the market, but that can wait," I said. "What's up?"

"Do you remember old Mr. Lee? They called him Johnny here in the neighborhood. He's the gentleman who used to live around the corner on Bay. Little white stucco house with the overgrown yard. To be accurate, Johnny lived in the garage apartment. His grandson, Bucky, and his wife have been living in the house."

The bungalow in question, which I passed in the course of my daily jog, was a run-down residence that looked as if it was buried in a field of wild grass. These were not classy folk, unless a car up on blocks is your notion of a yard ornament. Neighbors had complained for years, for all the good it did. "I know the house, but the name doesn't mean much."

"You've probably seen 'em up at Rosie's. Bucky seems to be a nice kid, though his wife is odd. Her name is Babe. She's short and plump, doesn't make a lot of eye contact. Johnny always looked like he was homeless, but he did all right."

I was beginning to remember the trio he described: old guy in a shabby jacket, the couple playing grab-ass, looking too young for marriage. I cupped a hand to my ear. "You've been using past tense. Is the old man dead?"

"I'm afraid so. Poor fellow had a heart attack and died four or five months back. I think it was sometime in July. Not that there was anything odd about it," Henry hastened to add. "He was only in his seventies, but his health had never been that good. At any rate, I ran into Bucky a little while ago and he has a problem he was asking me about. It's not urgent. It's just irksome and I thought maybe you could help."

I pictured an unmarked key to a safe-deposit box, missing heirs, missing assets, an ambiguity in the will, one of those unresolved issues that the living inherit from the newly departed. "Sure. What's the deal?"

"You want the long version or the short?"

"Make it long, but talk fast. It may save me questions."

I could see Henry warm to his subject with a quick glance at his watch. "I don't want to miss the flight, but here's the situation in a nutshell. The old guy didn't want a funeral, but he did ask to be cremated, which was done right away. Bucky was thinking about taking the ashes back to Columbus, Ohio, where his dad lives, but it occurred to him his grandfather was entitled to a military burial. I guess Johnny was a fighter pilot during World War Two, part of the American Volunteer Group under Claire Chennault. He didn't talk much about it, but now and then he'd reminisce about Burma, the air battles over Rangoon, stuff like that. Anyway, Bucky thought it'd be nicer: white marble with his name engraved, and that kind of thing. He talked to his dad about it, and Chester thought it sounded pretty good, so Bucky went out to the local Veterans Administration office and filled out a claim form. He didn't have all the information, but he did what he could. Three months went by and he didn't hear a thing. He was just getting antsy when the claim came back, marked "Cannot Identify." With a name like John Lee, that wasn't too surprising. Bucky called the VA and the guy sent him another form to complete, this one a request for military records. This time it was only three weeks and the damn thing came back with the same rubber stamp. Bucky isn't dumb, but he's probably all of twenty-three years old and doesn't have much experience with bureaucracy. He called his dad and told him what was going on. Chester got right on the horn, calling Randolph Air Force Base in Texas, which is where the Air Force keeps personnel files. I don't know how many people he must have talked to, but the upshot is the Air Force has no record of John Lee, or if they do, they won't talk. Chester is convinced he's being stonewalled, but what can he do? So that's where it stands. Bucky's frustrated and his dad's madder than a wet hen. They're absolutely determined to see Johnny get what he deserves. I told 'em you might have an idea about what to try next."

"They're sure he was really in the service?"

"As far as I know."

I felt an expression of skepticism cross my face. "I can talk to Bucky if you want, but it's not really an area I know anything about. If I'm hearing you right, the Air Force isn't really saying that he wasn't *there.* All they're saying is they can't identify him from the information Bucky's sent."

"Well, that's true," Henry said. "But until they locate his records, there isn't any way they can process the claim."

I was already beginning to pick at the problem as if it were a knot in a piece of twine. "Wasn't it called the Army Air Force back in those days?"

"What difference would that make?"

"His service records could be kept somewhere else. Maybe the army has them."

"You'd have to ask Bucky about that. I'm assuming he's already tried that line of pursuit."

"It could be something simple . . . the wrong middle initial, or the wrong date of birth."

"I said the same thing, but you know how it is. You look at something so long and you don't even really see it. It probably won't take more than fifteen or twenty minutes of your time, but I know they'd be glad to have the input. Chester's out here from Ohio, wrapping up some details on his father's probate. I didn't mean to volunteer your services, but it seems like a worthy cause."

"Well, I'll do what I can. You want me to pop over there right now? I've got the time if you think Bucky's home."

"He should be. At least he was an hour ago. I appreciate this, Kinsey. It's not like Johnny was a close friend, but he's been in the neighborhood as long as I have and I'd like to see him treated right."

"I'll give it a try, but this is not my bailiwick."

"I understand, and if it turns out to be a pain, you can dump the whole thing."

I shrugged. "I guess that's one of the advantages in not being paid. You can quit any time you want."

"Absolutely," he said.

I locked my front door while Henry headed toward the garage, and then I waited by the drive while he backed the car out. On special occasions he drives a five-window coupe, a 1932 Chevrolet with the original bright yellow paint. Today, he was taking the station wagon to the airport since he'd be returning with three passengers and countless pieces of luggage. "The sibs," as he called them, would be in town for two weeks and tended to pack for every conceivable emergency. He eased to a stop and rolled down the window. "Don't forget you're joining us for dinner."

"I didn't forget. This is Lewis's birthday, right? I even bought him a present."

"Well, you're sweet, but you didn't have to do that."

"Oh, right. Lewis always tells people not to buy a present, but if you don't, he pouts. What time's the celebration?"

"Rosie's coming over at five forty-five. You can come anytime you want. You know William. If we don't eat promptly, he gets hypoglycemic."

"He's not going with you to the airport?"

"He's being fitted for his tux. Lewis, Charlie, and I get fitted for ours this afternoon."

"Very fancy," I said. "I'll see you later."

I waved as Henry disappeared down the street and then let

myself out the gate. The walk to the Lees' took approximately thirty seconds—six doors down, turn the corner, and there it was. The style of the house was hard to classify, a vintage California cottage with a flaking stucco exterior and a faded red-tile roof. A two-car garage with dilapidated wooden doors was visible at the end of the narrow concrete drive. The scruffy backyard was now the home of a half-dismantled Ford Fairlane with a rusted-out frame. The facade of the house was barely visible, hidden behind unruly clusters of shoulder-high grass. The front walk had been obscured by two mounds of what looked like wild oats, brushy tops tilting toward each other across the path. I had to hold my arms aloft, wading through the weeds, just to reach the porch.

I rang the bell and then spent an idle moment picking burrs from my socks. I pictured microscopic pollens swarming down my gullet like a cloud of gnats, and I could feel a primitive sneeze forming at the base of my brain. I tried to think about something else. Without even entering the front door, I could have predicted small rooms with rough stucco arches between, offset perhaps by ineffectual attempts to "modernize" the place. This was going to be pointless, but I rang the bell again anyway.

The door was opened moments later by a kid I recognized. Bucky was in his early twenties. He was three or four inches taller than I am, which would have put him at five nine or five ten. He wasn't overweight, but he was as doughy as a beer pretzel. His hair was red gold, parted crookedly in the center and worn long. Most of it was pulled back and secured in some scraggly fashion at the nape of his neck. He was blue eyed, his ruddy complexion looking blotchy under a four-day growth of auburn beard. He wore blue jeans and a dark blue long-sleeved corduroy shirt with the tail hanging out. Hard to guess what he did for a living, if anything. He might have been a rock star with a six-figure bank account, but I doubted it.

"Are you Bucky?"

"Yeah."

I held my hand out. "I'm Kinsey Millhone. I'm a friend of Henry Pitts. He says you're having problems with a VA claim."

He shook my hand, but the way he was looking at me made me want to knock on his head and ask if anyone was home. I plowed on. "He thought maybe I could help. Mind if I come in?"

"Oh, sorry. I got it now. You're the private detective. At first, I thought you were someone from the VA. What's your name again?"

"Kinsey Millhone. Henry's tenant. You've probably seen me up at Rosie's. I'm there three or four nights a week."

Recognition finally flickered. "You're the one sits in that back booth."

"I'm the one."

"Sure. I remember. Come on in." He stepped back and I moved into a small entrance hall with a hardwood floor that hadn't been buffed for years. I caught a glimpse of the kitchen at the rear of the house. "My dad's not home right now, and I think Babe's in the shower. I should let her know you're here. Hey, *Babe?*"

No reply.

He tilted his head, listening. *"Hey, Babe!"*

I've never been a big fan of yelling from room to room. "You want to find her? I can wait."

"Let me do that. I'll be right back. Have a seat," he said. He moved down the hall, his hard-soled shoes clumping. He opened a door on the right and stuck his head in. There was a muffled shriek of pipes in the wall, the plumbing shuddering and thumping as the shower was turned off.

I went down a step into the living room, which was slightly bigger than the nine-by-twelve rug. At one end of the room there was a shallow brick fireplace, painted white, with a wooden mantelpiece that seemed to be littered with knickknacks. On either side of the fireplace there were built-in bookcases piled high with papers and magazines. I settled gingerly on a lumpy couch covered with a brown-and-yellow afghan. I could smell house mold or wet dog.

The coffee table was littered with empty fast-food containers, and all the seating was angled to face an ancient television set in an oversize console.

Bucky returned. "She says go ahead. We gotta be somewhere shortly and she's just now getting dressed. My dad'll be back in a little while. He went down to Perdido to look at lighting fixtures. We're trying to get Pappy's apartment fixed up to rent." He paused in the doorway, apparently seeing the room as I did. "Looks like a dump, but Pappy was real tight with a buck."

"How long have you lived here?"

"Coming up on two years, ever since Babe and me got married," he said. "I thought the old bird'd give us a break on the rent, but he made a science out of being cheap."

Being cheap myself, I was naturally curious. Maybe I could pick up some pointers, I thought. "Like what?"

Bucky's mouth pulled down. "I don't know. He didn't like to pay for trash pickup, so he'd go out early on trash days and put his garbage in the neighbors' cans. And, you know, like somebody told him once when you pay utility bills? All you have to do is use a one-cent stamp, leave off the return address, and drop it in a remote mailbox. The post office will deliver it because the city wants their money, so you can save on postage."

I said, "Hey, what a deal. What do you figure, ten bucks a year? That'd be hard to resist. He must have been quite a character."

"You never met him?"

"I used to see him up at Rosie's, but I don't think we ever met."

Bucky nodded at the fireplace. "That's him over there. One on the right."

I followed his gaze, expecting to see a photograph sitting on the mantelpiece. All I saw were three urns and a medium-size metal box. Bucky said, "That greeny marble urn is my grammaw, and right beside her is my uncle Duane. He's my daddy's only brother, killed when he's a kid. He was eight, I think. Playing on the tracks and got run over by a train. My aunt Maple's in the black urn."

For the life of me, I couldn't think of a polite response. The family fortunes must have dwindled as the years went by because it looked like less and less money had been spent with each successive death until the last one, John Lee, had been left in the box provided by the crematorium. The mantel was getting crowded. Whoever "went" next would have to be transported in a shoe box and dumped out the car window on the way home from the mortuary.

He waved the subject aside. "Anyway, forget that. I know you didn't stop by to make small talk. I got the paperwork right here." He moved over to the bookshelf and began to sort through the magazines, which were apparently interspersed with unpaid bills and other critical documents. "All we're talking is a three-hundred-dollar claim for Pappy's burial," he remarked. "Babe and me paid to have him cremated and we'd like to get reimbursed. I guess the government pays another hundred and fifty for interment. It doesn't sound like much, but we don't have a lot to spare. I don't know what Henry told you, but we can't afford to pay for your services."

"I gathered as much. I don't think there's much I can do anyway. At this point, you probably know more about VA claims than I do."

He pulled out a sheaf of papers and glanced through them briefly before he passed them over to me. I removed the paper clip and scrutinized the copy of John Lee's death certificate, the mortuary release, his birth certificate, Social Security card, and copies of the two Veterans Administration forms. The first form was the application for burial benefits, the second a request for military records. On the latter, the branch of service had been filled in, but the service number, grade, rank, and the dates the old man had served were all missing. No wonder the VA was having trouble verifying the claim. "Looks like you're missing a lot of information. I take it you don't know his serial number or the unit he served in?"

"Well, no. That's the basic problem," he said, reading over my shoulder. "It gets stupid. We can't get the records because we don't have enough information, but if we had the information we wouldn't need to make the request."

"That's called good government. Think of all the money they're saving on the unpaid claims."

"We don't want anything he's not entitled to, but what's fair is fair. Pappy served his country, and it doesn't seem like such a lot to ask. Three hundred damn dollars. The government wastes billions."

I flipped the form over and read the instructions on the back. Under "Eligibility for Basic Burial Allowance," requirements indicated that the deceased veteran must have been "discharged or released from service under conditions other than dishonorable and must have been in receipt of pension or had an original or reopened claim for pension," blah, blah, blah. "Well, here's a possibility. Was he receiving a military pension?"

"If he did, he never told us."

I looked up at Bucky. "What was he living on?"

"He had his Social Security checks, and I guess Dad pitched in. Babe and me paid rent for this place, which was six hundred bucks a month. He owned the property free and clear, so I guess he used the rent money to pay food, utilities, property taxes, and like that."

"And he lived out back?"

"That's right. Above the garage. It's just a couple little rooms, but it's real nice. We got a guy who wants to move in once the place is ready. Old friend of Pappy's. He says he'd be willing to haul out the junk if we give him a little break on the first month's rent. Most stuff is trash, but we didn't want to toss stuff until we know what's important. Right now half Pappy's things have been packed in cardboard boxes and the rest is piled up every which way."

I reread the request for military records. "What about the year his discharge certificate was issued? There's a blank here."

"Let's see." He tilted his head, reading the box where I was holding my thumb. "Oh. I must have forgot to mark that. Dad says it would've been August seventeenth of 1944 because he remembers Pappy coming home in time for his birthday party the day he turned four. He was gone two years, so he must have left sometime in 1942."

"Could he have been dishonorably discharged? From what this says, he'd be disqualified if that were the case."

"No ma'am," Bucky said emphatically.

"Just asking." I flipped the form over, scanning the small print on the back. The request for military records showed various address lists for custodians for each branch of the service, definitions, abbreviations, codes, and dates. I tried another tack. "What about medical? If he was a wartime veteran, he was probably eligible for free medical care. Maybe the local VA clinic has a file number for him somewhere."

Bucky shook his head again. "I tried that. They checked and didn't find one. Dad doesn't think he ever applied for medical benefits."

"What'd he do when he got sick?"

"He mostly doctored himself."

"Well. I'm about out of ideas," I said. I returned the papers to him. "What about his personal effects? Did he keep any letters from his Air Force days? Even an old photograph might help you figure out what fighter group he was with."

"We didn't find anything like that so far. I never even thought about pitchers. You want to take a look?"

I hesitated, trying to disguise my lack of interest. "Sure, I could do that, but frankly, if it's just a matter of three hundred dollars, you might be better off letting the whole thing drop."

"Actually, it's four hundred and fifty dollars with interment," he said.

"Even so. Do a cost/benefit analysis and you'd probably find you're already in the hole."

Bucky was nonresponsive, apparently unpersuaded by my faint-hearted counsel. The suggestion may have been intended more for me than for him. As it turned out, I should have taken my own advice. Instead I found myself dutifully trotting after Bucky as he moved through the house. What a dunce. I'm talking about me, not him.

2

I followed Bucky out the back door and down the porch steps. "Any chance your grandfather might have had a safe-deposit box?"

"Nah, it's not his style. Pappy didn't like banks and he didn't trust bankers. He had a checking account for his bills, but he didn't have stock certificates or jewelry or anything like that. He kept his savings—maybe a hundred bucks all told—in this old coffee can at the back of the refrigerator."

"Just a thought."

We crossed the patched cement parking pad to the detached garage and climbed the steep, unpainted wooden stairs to a small second-story landing just large enough to accommodate the door to Johnny Lee's apartment and a narrow sash window that looked out onto the stairs. While Bucky picked through his keys, I cupped a hand to the glass and peered into the furnished space. Didn't look like much: two rooms with a ceiling slanting down from a ridge beam. Between the two rooms there was a door frame with the door removed. There was a closet on one wall with a curtain strung across the opening.

Bucky unlocked the door and left it standing open behind him while he went in. A wall of heat seemed to block the doorway like an unseen barrier. Even in November, the sun beating down on the poorly insulated roof had heated the interior to a stuffy eighty-five degrees. I paused on the threshold, taking in the scent like an animal. The air felt close, smelling of dry wood and old wallpaper paste. Even after five months I could detect cigarette smoke and fried food. Given another minute, I probably could have determined what the old man cooked for his last meal. Bucky crossed to one of the windows and threw the sash up. The air didn't seem to move. The floor was creaking and uneven, covered with an ancient layer of cracked linoleum. The walls were papered with a pattern of tiny blue cornflowers on a cream background, the paper itself so old it looked scorched along the edges. The windows, two on the front wall and two on the rear, had yellowing shades half pulled against the flat November sunlight.

The main room had a single bed with an iron bedstead painted white. A wooden bureau was pushed against the back wall while a suite of old wicker porch furniture served as a seating area. A small wooden desk and a matching chair were tucked into one corner. There were ten to twelve cardboard boxes in a variety of sizes strewn across the floor. Some of the boxes had been packed and set aside, the flaps folded together to secure the contents. Two bookshelves had been emptied, and half the remaining books had toppled sideways.

I picked my way through the maze of boxes to the other room, which held an apartment-size stove and refrigerator, with a small microwave oven on the counter between them. A kitchen sink top had been set into a dark-stained wooden cabinet with cheap-looking hinges and pulls. The cabinet doors looked as though they'd stick when you tried to open them. Beyond the kitchen there was a small bathroom with a sink, a toilet, and a small claw-foot tub. All of the porcelain fixtures were streaked with stains. I caught sight of myself in the mirror above the sink and I could see my mouth was pulled down with distaste. Bucky had said the apartment was nice, but I'd rather shoot myself than end up in such a place.

I glanced out one of the windows. Bucky's wife, Babe, was standing at the back door across the way. She had a round face with big brown eyes and an upturned nose. Her hair was dark and straight, anchored unbecomingly behind her ears. She was wearing flip-flops, tight black pedal pushers, and a black sleeveless cotton top, stretched over drooping breasts. Her upper arms were plump and her thighs looked like they would chafe against one another when she walked. Everything about her looked unpleasantly damp. "I think your wife's calling you."

Babe's voice drifted up to us belatedly. "Bucky?"

He went to the landing. "Be right there," he yelled to her, and then in modulated tones to me: "You going to be okay if I just leave you here?" I watched him twist the apartment key from his key ring.

"I'm fine. It really sounds like you've done everything you could."

"I thought so, too. My dad's the one who's really got a bug up his butt. By the way, his name is Chester if he gets back before we do." He handed me the key. "Lock up when you're done and drop the key through the mail slot in the front door. If you find anything that looks important, you can let us know. We'll be back around one. You have a business card?"

"Sure." I took a card from my bag and handed it to him.

He tucked the card in his pocket. "Good enough."

I listened to him clatter down the outside stairs. I stood there, wondering how long I could decently wait before I locked up and fled. I could feel my stomach squeeze in the same curious twist of anxiety and excitement I experience when I've entered someone's premises illegally. My presence here was legitimate, but I felt I was engaging in an illicit act somehow. Below, I heard Babe and Bucky chatting as they locked the house and opened the garage door beneath me. I moved to the window and peered down, watching as the car emerged, seemingly from beneath my feet. The car looked like a Buick, 1955 or so, green with a big chrome grille across the front. Bucky was peering back over his shoulder as he reversed down the driveway, Babe talking at him nonstop, her hand on his knee.

I should have left as soon as the car turned out of the drive, but I thought about Henry and felt honor-bound to make at least a *pretense* of searching for something relevant. I don't mean to sound coldhearted, but Johnny Lee meant absolutely nothing to me, and the notion of mucking through his possessions was giving me the creeps. The place was depressing, airless and hot. Even the silence had a sticky feel to it.

I spent a few minutes wandering from one room to the next. The bathroom and the kitchen contained nothing of significance. I returned to the main room and scouted the periphery. I pushed aside the curtain covering the closet opening. Johnny's few clothes were hanging in a dispirited row. His shirts were soft from frequent washings, threadbare along the collar, with an occasional button missing. I checked all the pockets, peered into the shoe boxes lined up on the shelf. Not surprisingly, the shoe boxes contained old shoes.

The chest of drawers was full of underwear and socks, T-shirts, fraying handkerchiefs; nothing of interest hidden between the stacks. I sat down at his small desk and began to open drawers systematically. The contents were innocuous. Bucky had apparently removed the bulk of the old man's files: bills, receipts, canceled checks, bank statements, old income tax returns. I got up and checked some of the packed cardboard boxes, pulling back the flaps so I could poke through the contents. I found most of the relevant financial detritus in the second box I opened. A quick examination showed nothing startling. There were no personal files at all and no convenient manila envelopes filled with documents that pertained to past military service. Then again, why would he keep war-related memorabilia for forty-some-odd years? If he changed his mind about applying for VA benefits, all he had to do was supply them with the information he probably carried in his head.

The third box I looked into contained countless books about World War II, which suggested a lingering interest in the subject. Whatever his own contribution to the war, he seemed to enjoy reading other people's accounts. The titles were monotonous, except for the few punctuated with exclamation points. *Fighter! Bombs Away! Aces High! Kamakazi!* Everything was "Strategic." *Strategic Command. Strategic Air Power over Europe. Strategic Air Bombardment. Strategic Fighter Tactics.* I dragged the desk chair closer to the box and sat down, pulling out book after book, holding each by the spine while I riffled through the pages. I'm always doing silly shit like this. What did I imagine, his discharge certificate was going to drop in my lap? The truth is, most investigators have been trained to investigate. That's what we do best, even when we don't feel enthusiastic about the task at hand. Give us a room and ten minutes alone and we can't help but snoop, poking automatically into other people's business. Minding one's own business isn't half the fun. My notion of heaven is being accidentally locked in the Hall of Records overnight.

I scanned several pages of some fighter pilot's memoirs, reading about dogfights, bailouts, flames spurting from tailguns, Mustangs, P-40s, Nakajima fighters, and V formations. This war stuff was full of drama, and I could see why men got hooked on the process. I'm a bit of an adrenaline junkie myself, having picked up my "habit" during two years on the police force.

I lifted my head, hearing the chink of footsteps on the outside stairs. I checked my watch: it was only 10:35. Surely it wasn't Bucky. I rose and crossed to the doorway, peering out. A man, in his sixties, had just reached the landing.

"Can I help you?" I asked.

"Is Bucky up here?" He was balding, the white hair around his pate clipped close. Mild hazel eyes, a big nose, dimple in his chin, his face lined with soft creases.

"No, he's out at the moment. Are you Chester?"

He murmured, "No, ma'am." His manner suggested that if he'd worn a cap, he would have doffed it at that point. He smiled shyly, exposing a slight gap between his two front teeth. "My name's Ray Rawson. I'm an old friend of Johnny's . . . uh, before he passed away." He wore chinos, a clean white T-shirt, and tennis shoes with white socks.

"Kinsey Millhone," I said, introducing myself. We shook hands. "I'm a neighbor from down that way." My gesture was vague but conveyed the general direction.

Ray's gaze moved past me into the apartment. "Any idea when Bucky's due back?"

"Around one, he said."

"Are you looking to rent?"

"Oh heavens, no. Are you?"

"Well, I hope to," he said. "If I can talk Bucky into it. I put down a deposit, but he's dragging his feet on the rental agreement. I don't know what the problem is, but I'm worried he'll rent it out from under me. For a minute, when I saw all those boxes, I thought you were moving in." The guy had a southern accent I couldn't quite place. Maybe Texas or Arkansas.

"I think Bucky's trying to get the place cleared. Were you the one who offered to haul all the stuff out for a break in the rent?"

"Well, yeah, and I thought he was going to take me up on it, but now that his dad's in town, the two keep coming up with new schemes. First, Bucky and his wife decided they'd take this place and rent out the house instead. Then his dad said he wanted it for the times he comes out to visit. I don't mean to be pushy, but I was hoping to move in sometime this week. I've been staying in a hotel . . . nothing fancy, but it adds up."

"I wish I could help, but you'll have to take it up with him."

"Oh, I know it's not your problem. I was just trying to explain. Maybe I'll stop by again when he gets back. I didn't mean to interrupt."

"Not at all. Come on in, if you like. I'm just going through some boxes," I said. I moved back to my seat. I picked up a book and riffled through the pages.

Ray Rawson entered the room with all the caution of a cat. I pegged him at five ten, probably 180 pounds, with a hefty chest and biceps for a guy his age. On one arm he sported a tattoo that said "Marla"; on the other, a dragon on its hind legs with its tongue sticking out. He looked around with interest, taking in the arrangement of the furniture. "Good to see it again. Not as big as I remember. The mind plays tricks, doesn't it? I pictured . . . I don't know what . . . more wall space or something." He leaned against the bedstead and watched me work. "You looking for something?"

"More or less. Bucky's hoping to turn up some information about Johnny's military service. I'm the search-and-seizure team. Were you in the Air Force with him, by any chance?"

"Nope. We met on the job. We both worked in the shipyards in the old days—Jeffersonville Boat Works outside of Louisville, Kentucky. This was way back, just after the war started. We were building LST landing craft. I was twenty. He was ten years older and like a dad in some ways. Those were boom times. During the Depression—back in 1932—most guys weren't even pulling in a grand a year. Steelworkers made half that, less than waitresses. By the time I started working things were really looking up. Of course, everything's relative, so what did we know? Johnny did all kinds of things. He was a smart guy and taught me a lot. Can I lend you a hand?"

I shook my head. "I'm almost done," I said. "I hope you don't mind if I keep at it. I'd like to finish before I head out." I picked up the next book, leafing through the pages before I stacked it with the others. If Johnny was opposed to banks, he might have taken to hiding money between the pages.

"Any luck?"

"Nope," I said. "I'm about to tell Bucky to forget it. All he needs to know is his granddad's fighter unit. I'm a private investigator. This is my pro bono work, and it doesn't feel that productive, to tell you the truth. How well did you know Johnny?"

"Well enough, I guess. We kept in touch . . . maybe once or twice a year. I knew he had family out here, but I never met them until now."

I had a rhythm going. Pick a book up by the spine, flip the pages, set it down. Pick a book up by the spine, flip, set. I pulled the last book from the box. "I've been trying to place your accent. You mentioned Kentucky. Is that where you're from?" I stood up, tucking my fists in the small of my back to get the kinks out. I bent down and started returning books to the box.

Ray hunkered nearby and began to help. "That's right. I'm from Louisville originally, though I haven't been back for years. I've been living in Ashland, but Johnny always said if I came out to California I should look him up. What the heck. I had some time, so I hit the road. I knew the address and he told me he was living in the garage apartment out back, so I came up here first. When I didn't get an answer, I went over and knocked on Bucky's door. I had no idea Johnny'd passed on."

"Must have been a shock."

"It was. I felt awful. I didn't even call first. He'd written me a note a couple months before, so I was all set to surprise him. Joke's on me, I guess. If I'd known, I could have saved myself a trip. Even driving, it's not cheap."

"How long have you been here?"

"Little over a week. I didn't plan to stay, but I drove over two thousand miles to get here and didn't have the heart to turn around and drive back. I didn't think I'd like California, but it's nice." Ray finished packing one box and tucked the top flaps together, setting that box aside while I started work on the next.

"Lot of people feel it takes some getting used to."

"Not for me. I hope Bucky doesn't think I'm ghoulish because I want to move in. I hate to take advantage of someone else's misfortune, but what the heck," he said. "Might as well have *some* good come out of it. Seems like a nice area, and I like being near the beach. I don't think Johnny'd mind. Here, let me get these out of your way." Ray lifted one box and stacked it on top of another, pushing both to one side.

"Where are you now?"

"Couple blocks over. At the Lexington. Right near the beach and room doesn't even have a view. Up here, I notice you can see a little slice of ocean if you look through those trees."

I looked around the room with care but didn't see anything else worth examining. Johnny hadn't had that much, and what he owned was unrevealing. "Well, I think I'll give up." I dusted my jeans off, feeling grubby and hot. I went into the kitchen and washed my hands at the sink. The plumbing shrieked and the water was full of rust. "You want to check anything while you're here? Water pressure, plumbing? You could measure for cafe curtains before I lock up," I said.

He smiled. "I better wait until I sign some kind of rental agreement. I don't want to take the move for granted, the way Bucky's been acting. You want my opinion, the kid's not all that bright."

I agreed, but it seemed politic to keep my mouth shut for once. I returned to the main room, found my shoulder bag, and slung the strap across my shoulder, then dug the key from my jeans pocket. Ray moved out of the apartment just ahead of me, pausing on the stair below me while I locked up. Once the place was secured I followed him down the stairs and we walked down the driveway together toward the street. I made a quick detour, moving up onto the front porch, where I tucked the key into the mail slot in the middle of the front door. I rejoined him, and when we reached the street, he began to move in the opposite direction.

"Thanks for the help. I hope you and Bucky manage to work something out."

"Me too. See you." He gave a quick wave and moved off.

When I reached home, Henry's kitchen door was open and I could hear the babble of voices, which meant that Nell, Charlie, and Lewis were in. Before the day was over, they'd be into Scrabble and pinochle, Chinese checkers, and slapjack, squabbling like kids over the Parcheesi board.

By the time I unlocked my front door, it was almost eleven. The message light was blinking on my answering machine. I pressed the playback button. "Kinsey? This is your cousin Tasha, up in Lompoc. Could you give me a call?" She left a phone number, which I duly noted. The call had come through five minutes before.

This was not good, I thought.

At the age of eighteen, my mother had been estranged from her well-to-do family when she rebelled against my grandmother's wishes and ran off with a mailman. She and my father were married by a Santa Teresa judge with my aunt Gin in attendance, the only one of her sisters who dared to side with her. Both my mother and Aunt Gin had been banned from the family, an exile that continued until I was born some fifteen years later. My parents had given up any hope of offspring, but with my arrival tentative contact was made with the remaining sisters, who kept the renewed conversations a secret. When my grandparents left on a cruise to celebrate their anniversary, my parents drove up to Lompoc to visit. I was four at the time and remember nothing of the occasion. A year later, while we were driving north to another furtive reunion, a boulder rolled down the mountain and crashed through the car windshield, killing my father on impact. The car went off the road and my mother was critically injured. She died a short time later while the paramedics were still working to extract us from the wreckage.

After that, I was brought up by Aunt Gin, and to my knowledge, there was no further communication with the family. Aunt Gin had never married, and I was raised in accordance with her peculiar notions of what a girl-child should be. As a consequence, I turned out to be a somewhat odd human being, though not nearly as "bent" as some people might think. Since my aunt's death some ten years ago, I'd made my peace with my solitary state.

I'd learned about my "long-lost" relatives in the course of an investigation the year before, and so far, I'd managed to keep them at arm's length. Just because *they* wanted a relationship didn't obligate *me.* I'll admit I might have been a little crabby on the subject, but I couldn't help myself. I'm thirty-five years old and my orphanhood suits me. Besides, when you're "adopted" at my age, how do you know they won't become disillusioned and reject you again?

I picked up the phone and dialed Tasha's number before I had time to work myself into a snit. She answered and I identified myself.

"Thanks for calling so promptly. How are you?" she said.

"I'm fine," I said, desperately trying to figure out what she wanted from me. I'd never met her, but during our previous phone conversation, she'd told me she was an estate attorney, handling wills and probate. Did she need a private detective? Was she hoping to advise me about living trusts?

"Listen, dear. The reason I'm calling is we're hoping we can talk you into driving up to Lompoc to have Thanksgiving with us. The whole family's going to be here and we thought it'd be a nice time to get acquainted."

I felt my heart sink. I had zero interest in the family gathering, but I decided to be polite. I injected my voice with a phony touch of regret. "Oh, gee, thanks, Tasha, but I'm tied up. Some good friends are getting married that day and I'm a bridesmaid."

"On *Thanksgiving?* Well, that seems peculiar."

"It was the only time they could work out," I said, thinking ha ha tee hee.

"What about Friday or Saturday of that weekend?" she said.

"Ah." My mind went blank. "Mmm . . . I think I'm busy, but I could check," I said. I'm an excellent liar in professional matters. On the personal side I'm as lame as everybody else. I reached for my calendar, knowing it was blank. For a split second I toyed with the possibility of saying "yes," but a primitive howl of protest welled up from my gut. "Oh, gee. Nope, I'm tied up."

"Kinsey, I can sense your reluctance, and I have to tell you how sorry we all are. Whatever the quarrel between your mother and Grand had nothing to do with you. We're hoping to make up for it, if you'll let us."

I felt my eyes roll upward. Much as I'd hoped to avoid it, I was going to have to take this on. "Tasha, that's sweet and I appreciate your saying that, but this is not going to work. I don't know what else to tell you. I'm very uncomfortable with the idea of coming up there, especially on a holiday."

"Oh, really? Why is that?"

"I don't know why. I have no experience with family, so it's not anything I miss. That's just the way it is."

"Don't you want to meet the other cousins?"

"Uh, Tasha, I hope this doesn't sound rude, but we've done all right without each other so far."

"How do you know you wouldn't like us?"

"I probably would," I said. "That isn't the issue."

"Then what is?"

"For one thing, I'm not into groups and I'm not all that crazy about being pushed," I said.

There was a silence. "Does this have something to do with Aunt Gin?" she asked.

"Aunt Gin? Not at all. What makes you ask?"

"We've heard she was eccentric. I guess I'm assuming she turned you against us in some way."

"How could she do that? She never even *mentioned* you."

"Don't you think that was odd?"

"Of course it's odd. Look, Aunt Gin was big on theory, but she didn't seem to favor a lot of human contact. This is not a complaint. She taught me a lot, and many lessons I valued, but I'm not like other people. Frankly, at this point, I prefer my independence."

"That's bullshit. I don't believe you. We'd all like to think we're independent, but no one lives in isolation. This is family. You can't repudiate kinship. It's a fact of life. You're one of us whether you like it or not."

"Tasha, let's just put it out there as long as we're at it. There aren't going to be any warm, gooey family scenes. It's not in the cards. We're not going to gather around the piano for any old-fashioned sing-alongs."

"That's not what we're like. We don't do things that way."

"I'm not talking about you. I'm trying to tell you about me."

"Don't you want anything from us?"

"Like what?"

"I gather you're angry."

"Ambivalent," I corrected. "The anger's down a couple of layers. I haven't gotten to that yet."

She was silent for a moment. "All right. I accept that. I understand your reaction, but why take it out on us? If Aunt Gin was inadequate, you should have squared that with her."

I felt my defenses rise. "She wasn't 'inadequate.' That's not what I said. She had eccentric notions about child rearing, but she did what she could."

"I'm sure she loved you. I didn't mean to imply she was deficient."

"I'll tell you one thing. Whatever her failings, she did more than

Grand ever did. In fact, she probably passed along the same kind of mothering she got herself."

"So it's *Grand* you're really mad at."

"Of course! I told you *that* from the beginning," I said. "Look, I don't feel like a victim. What's done is done. It came down the way it came down, and I can live with that. It's folly to think we can go back and make it come out any different."

"Of course we can't change the past, but we can change what happens next," Tasha said. She shifted gears. "Never mind. Forget that. I'm not trying to provoke you."

"I don't want to get into a tangle any more than you do," I said.

"I'm not trying to defend Grand. I know what she did was wrong. She should have made contact. She could have done that, but she didn't, okay? It's old business. Past tense. It didn't involve any of us, so why carry it down another generation? I love her. She's a dear. She's also a bad-tempered, penny-pinching old lady, but she's not a monster."

"I never said she was a monster."

"Then why can't you just let it go and move on? You were treated unfairly. It's created some problems, but it's over and done with."

"Except that I've been marked for life and I've got two dead marriages to prove it. I'm willing to accept that. What I'm not willing to do is smooth it all over just to make her feel good."

"Kinsey, I'm uncomfortable with this . . . *grudge* you've been carrying. It's not healthy."

"Oh, come off it. Why don't you let me worry about the *grudge?*" I said. "You know what I've finally learned? I don't have to be perfect. I can feel what I feel and be who I am, and if that makes you uncomfortable, then maybe *you're* the one with the problem, not me."

"You're determined to take offense, aren't you?"

"Hey, babe, I didn't call you. You called *me,*" I said. "The point is, it's too late."

"You sound so *bitter.*"

"I'm not bitter. I'm realistic."

I could sense her debate with herself about where to go next. The attorney in her nature was probably inclined to go after me like a hostile witness. "Well, I can see there's no point in pursuing this."

"Right."

"Under the circumstances, there doesn't seem to be any reason for having lunch, either."

"Probably not."

She blew out a big breath. "Well. If there's ever anything I can do for you, I hope you'll call," she said.

"I appreciate that. I can't think what it'd be, but I'll keep that in mind."

I hung up the phone, the small of my back feeling damp from tension. I let out a bark and shook myself from head to toe. Then I fled the premises, worried Tasha would turn around and call back. I hit the supermarket, where I picked up the essentials: milk, bread, and toilet paper. I stopped by the bank and deposited a check, withdrew fifty bucks in cash, filled my VW with gas, and then came home again. I was just in the process of putting groceries away when the phone rang. I lifted the receiver with trepidation. The voice that greeted me was Bucky's.

"Hey, Kinsey? This is Bucky. I think you better get over here. Somebody broke into Pap's apartment and you might want to take a look."

3

I knocked at Bucky's front door for the second time that day. The early afternoon sun was beginning to bake the grass, and the herbal scent of dried weeds permeated the November air. To my right, through a stucco archway opening onto a short length of porch, I could see the scalloped edge of the old red-tile roof. In Santa Teresa the roof tiles used to be handmade, the C-curve shaped by laying the clay across the tile worker's thigh. Now the tiles are all S shaped, made by machine, and the old roofs are sold at a premium. The one I was looking at was probably worth ten to fifteen grand. The break-in artists should have had a go at that instead of the old man's apartment with its cracked linoleum.

Babe opened the door. She had changed clothes, discarding her black T-shirt and black pedal pushers in favor of a shapeless cotton shift. Her eyes were enormous, the color of milk chocolate, her cheeks sprinkled with freckles. Her excess weight was evenly distributed, as if she'd zipped herself into an insulated rubber wet suit.

"Hi. I'm Kinsey. Bucky called and asked if I'd stop by."

"Oh, yeah. Nice to meet you. Sorry I missed you earlier."

"I figured we'd meet eventually. Is Bucky out back?"

She ducked her head, breaking off eye contact. "Him and his dad. Chester's been screaming ever since we got home. What a butt," she murmured. "He's all the time hollering. I can't hardly stand that. I mean, we didn't make the mess, so why's he yelling at us?"

"Did they call the police?"

"Uhn-hun, and they're on their way. Supposably," she added with disdain. Maybe in her experience, the cops never showed up when they said. Her voice was breathy and soft. She was a bit of a mumbler, managing to speak without moving her lips. Maybe she was practicing to be a ventriloquist. She stepped back to let me enter, and then I followed her through the hallway as I had earlier with Bucky. Her rubber flip-flops made sucking noises on the hardwood floor.

"I take it you just got home," I said. I found myself talking to the back of her head, watching the bunch and release of her calves as she moved. Mentally, I put her on a weight program . . . something really really strict.

"Uhn-hun. Little while ago. We went out to Colgate to visit my mom. Chester got home first. He bought this ceiling light he was fixing to put in? When he went upstairs, he could see where the window was broke, all this glass laying on the steps. Somebody really tore the place up."

"Did they take anything?"

"That's what they're trying to figure out. Chester told Bucky he shouldn't have left you alone."

"Me? Well, that's dumb. Why would I tear the place apart? I'd never work that way."

"That's what Bucky said, but Chester never listens to him. By the time we got here, he was having a conniption fit. I can't wait 'til he goes back to Ohio. I'm a nervous wreck. My daddy never yelled, so I'm not used to it. My mom'd knock his block off if he ever talked to her that way. I told Bucky he better tell Chester to quit swearing at me. I don't appreciate his attitude."

"Why don't you tell him?"

"Well, I tried more'n once, but it never does any good. He's been married four times and I bet I can guess why they divorce him. Lately, his girlfriends are all twenty-four years old and even *they* get sick of him once he buys 'em a bunch of clothes."

We trooped up the steps to the garage apartment, where the door was standing open. The narrow window next to it had an irregular starburst of glass missing. The method of entry wasn't complicated. There was only one door into the place, and all the other windows were twenty feet off the ground. Most burglars aren't going to risk a ladder against the side of a building in broad daylight. It was obvious the intruder had simply come up the stairs, punched out the glass, reached around the frame, and unlocked the deadbolt from the inside. It hadn't been necessary to use a pry bar or any other tools.

Chester must have heard us because he came out to the landing, barely looking at Babe, who eased back against the wooden porch railing, trying to make herself as inconspicuous as possible. Her father-in-law had apparently dismissed her as a target . . . for the moment, at any rate.

It was easy to see where Bucky got his looks. His father was big and beefy, with wavy blond hair long enough to touch his shoulders. Was that a dye job? I tried not to stare, but I could have sworn I'd seen that color in a Clairol ad. He had small blue eyes, blond lashes, and graying sideburns. His face was big and his complexion was ruddy. He wore his shirttail out, probably to disguise the extra thirty pounds he carried. He looked like a fellow who'd played in a rock-and-roll band in his youth, writing his own excruciatingly amateurish tunes. The earring surprised me: a dangling cross of gold. I also caught a glimpse of some sort of religious medal on a gold chain that disappeared under his V-neck T-shirt. His chest hair was gray. Looking at him was like seeing previews of Bucky's coming attractions.

Might as well be direct. I held my hand out. "Kinsey Millhone, Mr. Lee. I understand you're upset."

His handshake was perfunctory. "You can knock off the 'Mr. Lee' shit and call me Chester. Might as well be on a first-name basis while I chew your ass out. You better believe I'm upset. I don't know what Bucky asked you to do, but it sure wasn't this."

I bit back a tart reply and looked past him into the apartment. The place was a shambles: boxes overturned, books flung here and there, the mattress rolled back, the sheets and pillows on the floor. Half of Johnny's clothes had been pulled from the closet and piled in a heap. In the kitchen, through the doorway, I could see cabinet doors standing open, pots and pans strewn across the floor. While the disorder was extensive, nothing appeared to be damaged or destroyed. There was no sign that anyone had taken a blade to the bedding. No graffiti, no food emptied out of canisters or pipes torn from the walls. Vandals will often festoon the walls with their own fecal paint, but there was nothing like that here. It looked more like the methods big-city cops might employ at the scene of a drug bust. But what was the object of the exercise? Fleetingly, I entertained the notion that I was being set up, called in as a witness to a phony crime scene so that Bucky and his father could claim something valuable had been taken.

Bucky appeared from the kitchen and caught sight of me. In one split second we exchanged curiously guilty looks, like co-conspirators. There's something about being accused of criminal behavior that makes you feel like you did it even if you're innocent. Bucky turned to his dad. "Toilet tank's cracked. Might have been like that before, but I never noticed."

Chester pointed a finger. "You're paying for it if it has to be replaced. Bringing her into it was your bright idea." He turned to me, jerking a thumb over his shoulder toward the bathroom. "You ought to see in there. Medicine cabinet's pulled all the way out the wall. . . ."

He droned on, pouring out the details, which seemed to give him satisfaction. He probably liked to bitch, reciting his grievances in order to justify his ill treatment of other people. His irritation was contagious, and I could feel my temper climb.

I cut into his monologue. "Hey, I didn't do this, *Chester.* You can rant and rave all you want, but the place was fine when I left. I locked up and put the key back through the mail slot like Bucky suggested. Ray Rawson was here. If you don't believe me, you can ask him."

"Everybody's innocent. Nobody did nothing. Everybody's got some kind of bullshit excuse," Chester groused.

"Dad, she didn't do it."

"You let me take care of this." He turned and looked at me narrowly. "You trying to say Ray Rawson did this?"

"Of course not. Why would he do this when he's hoping to move in?" My voice was rising in response to his, and I worked to get control.

Chester's attitude became grudging. "Well, you better have a talk with him and find out what he knows."

"Why would he know anything? He left the same time I did."

Bucky interceded, trying to introduce a note of reason. "Pappy didn't have a pot to piss in, so there's nothing here to take. Besides, he died in July. If burglars thought there was anything of value, why wait until now?"

"Maybe it was kids," I said.

"We don't have kids in this neighborhood as far as I know."

"True enough," I said. Ours was primarily a community of retirees. It was always possible, of course, that a roving band of thugs had targeted the apartment. Maybe they figured that any place this crummy looking had to be a cover for something good.

"Nuts!" Chester said with disgust. "I'm going down and wait for the police. Soon as you two crime experts finish your analysis, you can get the place cleaned up."

I gave him a look. "I'm not going to *clean* the damn place."

"I wasn't talking to you," he said. "Bucky, you and Babe get busy."

"You better wait for the cops," I said.

He swung around and stared at me. "Why is that?"

"Because this is a crime scene. The cops might want to dust for prints."

Chester's face seemed to darken. "This is bullshit. There's something not right about this." He made a motion in my direction. "You can come on down with me."

I glanced back at Bucky. "I wouldn't touch anything if I were you. You don't want to screw around with evidence."

"I hear you," he said.

Chester gestured impatiently for me to pick up the pace.

On the way down the steps, I glanced at my watch. It was 1:15 and already I was tired of taking crap from this guy. I'll take crap when I'm paid for it, but I don't like doing it without compensation.

Chester clumped into the kitchen and went straight to the refrigerator, where he jerked open the door. He took out a jar of mayonnaise, mustard, bottled hot sauce, a packet of bologna, and a loaf of Wonder white bread. Had he ordered me to come down here so I could supervise his lunch?

"I apologize if I was rough, but I don't like what's going on," he said gruffly. He wasn't looking at me, and I was tempted to do a double take to see if there was someone else in the room. He'd dropped the imperious attitude and was talking in a normal tone of voice.

"You have a theory?"

"I'll get to that in a bit. Grab a chair."

At least he had my attention. I took a seat at the kitchen table and watched in fascination as he started his preparations. Somehow in my profession I seem to spend a lot of time in kitchens looking on while men make sandwiches, and I can state categorically, they do it better than women. Men are fearless. They have no interest in nutrition and seldom study the list of chemicals provided on the package. I've never seen a man cut the crusts off the bread or worry about the aesthetics of the "presentation." Forget the sprig of parsley and the radish rosette. With men, it's strictly a grunt-and-munch operation.

Chester banged a cast-iron skillet on the burner, flipped the gas on, and tossed in a knuckle of butter, which began to sizzle within seconds. "I sent Bucky out to live with his granddad, which turned out to be a mistake. I figured the two of them could look after each other. Next thing I know, Bucky's hooked up with that gal. I got nothing against Babe . . . she's a dim-wit, but so's he . . . I just think the two of 'em got no business being married."

"Johnny didn't warn you?"

"Hell, he probably encouraged it. Anything to make trouble. He was a sneaky old coot."

I let that one pass, leaving him to tell the story his way. There was an interval of quiet while he tended to his cooking. The bologna was pale pink, the size of a bread-and-butter plate, a perfect circle of compacted piggie by-products. Chester tossed in the meat without even pausing to remove the rim of plastic casing. While the bologna was frying, he slathered mayonnaise on one slice of bread and mustard on the other. He shook hot sauce across the yellow mustard in perfect red polka dots.

As a child I was raised with the same kind of white bread, which had the following amazing properties: If you mashed it, it instantly reverted to its unbaked state. A loaf of this bread, inadvertently squished at the bottom of a grocery bag, was permanently injured and made very strange-shaped sandwiches. On the plus side, you could roll it into little pellets and flick them across the table at your aunt when she wasn't looking. If one of these bread boogers landed in her hair, she would slap at it, irritated, thinking it was a fly. I can still remember the first time I ate a piece of the neighbor's homemade white bread, which seemed as coarse and dry as a cellulose sponge. It smelled like empty beer bottles, and if you gripped it, you couldn't even see the dents your fingers made in the crust.

The air in the kitchen was now scented with browning bologna, which was curling up around the edges to form a little bowl with butter puddled in the center. I could feel myself getting dizzy from the sensory overload. I said, "I'll pay you four hundred dollars if you fix me one of those."

Chester glanced at me sharply, and for the first time, he smiled. "You want toasted?"

"You're the chef. It's your choice," I said.

While we chowed down, I decided to satisfy my curiosity as well. "What sort of work do you do back in Columbus?"

He snapped back the last of his sandwich like a starving dog, wiping his mouth on a paper napkin before he responded. "Own a little print shop in Bexley. Offset and letterpress. Cold and hot type. Brochures, flyers, business cards, custom stationery. I can collate, fold, bind, and staple. You name it. I just hired a guy looks after the place when I'm gone. He does good I'll let him buy me out. Time I did something else. I'm too young to retire, but I'm tired of working for a living."

"What would you do, come out here to live?"

Chester fired up a cigarette, a Camel, unfiltered, that smelled like burning hay. "Don't know yet. I grew up in this town, but I left as soon as I turned eighteen. Pappy came out here in 1945, which is when he bought this place. He always said he'd be in this house until the sheriff or the undertaker hauled him out by his feet. Him and me never could get along. He's rough as a cob, and talk about *child abuse.* You never heard about that in the old days. I know a lot of guys got knocked around back then. That's just what dads did. They came home from the factory, sucked down a few beers, and grabbed the first kid came handy. I been punched and kicked, flung against the wall, and called every name in the book. If I got in trouble, he'd make me pace until I dropped, and if I uttered one word of protest, he'd douse my tongue with Tabasco sauce. I hated it, hated my old man for doing it, but I just thought that's the way life was. Now all you have to do is pop a kid across the face in public, you're up on charges, buddy, looking at jail time. Foster home for the kid and the whole community up in arms."

"I guess some things change for the better," I remarked.

"You got that right. I vowed I'd never treat my kids that way, and that's a promise I kept. I never once raised a hand to 'em."

I looked at him, waiting for some rueful acknowledgment of his own abusiveness, but he didn't seem to make the connection. I moved the subject over slightly. "Your father died of a heart attack?"

Chester took a drag of his cigarette, removing a piece of tobacco from his tongue. "Keeled over in the yard. Doctor told him he better lay off the fat. He sat down one Saturday to a big plate of bacon and eggs, fried sausages, and hashed browns, four cups of coffee, and a cigarette. He pushed his chair back, said he wasn't feeling so hot, and headed out to his place. Never even reached the stairs. 'Coronary occlusion' is the term they used. Autopsy showed an opening in his artery no bigger than a thread."

"I take it you don't think his death is related to the break-in."

"I don't think he was murdered, if that's what you're getting at, but there might be some connection. Indirectly," he said. He studied the ember on the end of his cigarette. "You have to understand something about my old man. He was paranoid. He liked passwords and secret knocks, all this double-o-seven rigmarole. There were things he didn't like to talk about, the war being foremost. Once in a while, if he was tanked up on whiskey, he'd rattle off at the mouth, but you ask him a question and he'd clam right up."

"What do you think it was?"

"Well, I'm getting to that, but let me point this out first. You see, it strikes me as odd, this whole sequence of events. Old guy dies and that should have been the end of it. Except Bucky gets the bright idea of applying for these benefits, and that's what tips 'em off."

"Tips who?"

"The government."

"The government," I said.

He leaned forward, lowering his voice. "I think my old man was hiding from the feds."

I stared at him. "Why?"

"Well, I'll tell you. All the years since the war? He never once applied for benefits: no disability, no medical, no GI Bill. Now why is that?"

"I give up."

He smiled slightly, unperturbed by the fact that I wasn't buying in. "Clown around if you like, but take a look at the facts. We fill out a claim form . . . all the information's correct . . . but, first, they say they have no record of him, which is bullshit. Fabrication, pure and simple. What do you mean, they don't have a record of him? This is nonsense. Of course they do. Will they admit it? No ma'am. You following? So I get on the phone to Randolph—that's the Air Force base where all the files are kept—and I go through the whole routine again. And I get stonewalled, but good. So I call the National Personnel Records Center in St. Louis. No deal. Never heard of him. Then I call Washington, D.C. . . . we're talking the *Pentagon* here. Nothing. No record. Well, I'm being dense. I'm not getting it myself. All I know to do is raise six kinds of hell. I make it clear we're serious about this. A lousy three hundred dollars, but I don't give a good goddamn. I'm not going to let it drop.

The man served his country and he's entitled to a decent burial. What do I get? Same deal. They don't know nothin' from nothin'. Then we have this." He jerked a thumb toward the garage apartment. "See what I'm saying?"

"No."

"Well, think about it."

I waited. I didn't have the faintest idea what he was getting at.

He took a deep drag from his cigarette. "You want to know what I think?" He paused, creating drama, maximizing the effect. "I think it took 'em this long to get some boys out here to find out how much we knew."

This sentence was so loaded, I couldn't figure out which part to parse first. I tried not to sound exasperated. "About *what?*"

"About what he did during the war," he said, as though to a nitwit. "I think the old man was military intelligence."

"A lot of guys worked in military intelligence. So what?"

"That's right. But he never *admitted* it, never said a word. And you know why? I think he was a double agent."

"Oh, stop this. A spy?"

"In some capacity, yes. Information gathering. I think that's why his records are sealed."

"You think his records are sealed. And that's why you can't get verification from the VA," I said, restating his point.

"Bull's-eye." He pointed a finger at me and gave me a wink, as though I'd finally picked up the requisite IQ points.

I looked at him blankly. This was beginning to feel like one of those discussions with a UFO fanatic, where the absence of documentation is taken for proof of government suppression. "Are you saying he worked for the Germans, or spied on them for our side?"

"Not the Germans. The Japanese. I think he might have worked for 'em, but I can't be sure. He was over in Burma. He admitted that much."

"Why would that be such a big deal all these years later?"

"You tell me."

"Well, how would I know? Honestly, Chester, I can't speculate about this stuff. I never even knew your father. I have no way of guessing what he was up to. If anything."

"I'm not asking you to speculate. I'm asking you to be objective. Why else would they say he wasn't in the Air Force? Give me one good reason."

"So far you don't have any proof that he was."

"Why would he lie? The man wouldn't lie about a thing like that. You're missing the point."

"No, I'm not. The *point* is, they're not really saying he wasn't there," I said. "They're saying they can't identify him from the information you submitted. There must be a hundred John Lees. Probably more."

"With his exact date of birth and his Social Security number? Come on. You think this stuff isn't on computer? All they have to do is type it in. Press Enter. Boom, they got him. So why would they deny it?"

"What makes you think they have all this data on computer?" I said, just to be perverse. This was hardly the issue, but I was feeling argumentative.

"What makes you think they don't?"

I barely suppressed a groan. I was hating this conversation, but I couldn't find any way to get out of it. "Come on, Chester. Let's don't do this, okay?"

"You asked the question. I'm just answering."

"Oh, forget it. Have it your way. Let's say he *was* a spy, just for the sake of argument. That was forty-some-odd years ago. The man is *dead* now, so why does anybody give a shit?"

"Maybe they don't care about *him.* Maybe they care about something he has. Maybe he took something that belongs to them. Now they want it back."

"You are making me crazy. What *it?*"

"How do I know? Files. Documents. This is just a hunch."

I wanted to lay my little head on the table and weep from frustration. "Chester, this makes no sense."

"Why not?"

"Because if that's the case, why call attention to it? Why not just pay you the three hundred bucks? Then they can come out at their leisure and look for this *thing* . . . this whatever you think he has. If he's been in hiding all these years . . . if they've *really* been looking and now they know his whereabouts, why arouse your suspicions by refusing to pay some dinky little three-hundred-dollar claim?"

"Four hundred and fifty with interment thrown in," he said.

I conceded the arithmetic. "Four fifty, then," I said. "The same question applies. Why cock around?"

"Hey, I can't explain why the government does what it does. If these guys were so bright, they'd have tracked him down years ago. The VA application was the tip-off, that's all I'm saying."

I took a deep breath. "You're jumping to conclusions."

He stubbed out his cigarette. "Of course I'm jumping. The question is, am I right? The way I see it, the boys finally got a lock on him, and that's the result." He tipped his head in the direction of the garage apartment. "Here's the only question I got . . . did they find what they came for or is it still hidden somewhere? I'll tell you something else. This Rawson fellow could be part of it."

This time I groaned and put my head in my hands. This was making my neck tense, and I massaged my trapezius. "Well, look. It's an interesting hypothesis and I wish you a lot of luck. All I offered was to see if I could locate a set of dog tags or a photograph. You want to turn this into some kind of spy ring, it's not my line of work. Thanks for the sandwich. You're a genius with bologna."

Chester's gaze suddenly shifted to a spot just behind me. There was a sharp rap at the back door, and I felt myself jump.

Chester got up. "Police," he said under his breath. "Just act normal."

He moved toward the door to let the guy in while I turned and squinted at him. Act *normal.* Why wouldn't I act normal? I *am* normal.

On the back step, I could hear the uniformed police officer's murmured introduction. Chester ushered him into the kitchen. "I appreciate your coming out. This is my neighbor, Kinsey Millhone. Officer Wettig," he said, using this phony Mr. Good Citizen tone of voice.

I glanced at the officer's name tag. P. Wettig. Paul, Peter, Phillip. This was not anyone I knew from my dealings with the department. Gutierrez and Pettigrew had always handled this beat. Despite my skepticism, Chester's conspiracy theory was apparently having an effect, because I was already wondering if his 911 call had been intercepted and an impostor sent instead. Wettig was probably in his late forties, looking more like a lounge singer than a uniformed patrolman. He wore his blond hair long, pulled into a little pigtail in back; brown eyes, short blunt nose, round chin. I pegged him at six three, weighing in at 210. The uniform looked authentic, but wasn't he a little *old* to be a beat cop?

"Hi. How are you?" I said, shaking hands. "I expected to see Gerald Pettigrew and Maria Gutierrez."

Wettig's look was neutral, his tone of voice bland. "They split up. Pettigrew's on Traffic now, and Maria moved over to the county sheriff's department."

"Really. I hadn't heard that." I glanced at Chester. "You want me to stay? I can hang around if you like."

"Don't worry about it. I can call you later." He glanced at Officer Wettig. "I guess I better show you the apartment."

I watched as Chester and the officer walked down the back steps and across the concrete drive.

As soon as they were out of sight, I moved down the hallway

and peered out the front. A black-and-white patrol car was parked at the curb. I found the telephone, which was located in what looked like a little prayer niche in the hall. I pulled out the telephone directory and dialed the regular phone line for the Santa Teresa Police Department. Someone in Records answered.

I said, "Oh, hi. Can you tell me if Officer Wettig is working this shift?"

"Just a second and I'll check." She clicked off, putting me on hold. Moments later she clicked back in again. "He's on until three this afternoon. You want to leave a message?"

"No, thanks. I'll try again later," I said, and hung up. Belatedly I blushed, feeling slightly sheepish. Of course there was an Officer Wettig. What was wrong with me?

4

After I left Bucky's, I came home and took a brief but refreshing nap, which I suspected, even then, was going to be one of the highlights of my vacation. At 4:57 I ran a brush through my hair and trotted down the spiral stairs.

The lowering cloud cover was generating an aura of early twilight, and the streetlights winked on as I locked my apartment. Even with the late afternoon drop in temperature, Henry's back door was open. Raucous laughter spilled through the screen door, along with a tantalizing array of cooking smells. Henry was playing some kind of honky-tonk piano in the living room. I crossed the flagstone patio and knocked on the screen. Preparations for Lewis's birthday dinner were already under way. For his birthday, I'd bought a sterling-silver shaving set with a mug and a brush that I'd found in an antique store. It was more "collectible" than antique, but I thought it would be something he could either use or admire.

Lewis was polishing silverware, but he let me in. He'd taken off his suit coat, but he still wore dress pants, a vest, crisp white shirt with the sleeves rolled up. Charlie had one of Henry's aprons tied around his waist, and he was in the process of putting the finishing touches on Lewis's birthday cake. Henry had told me Charlie was becoming self-conscious because his hearing had deteriorated so much. He'd had his hearing officially tested about five years before. At that point, the audiologist had recommended hearing aids, for which Charlie had been fitted. He'd worn them for a week or so and then put them in a drawer. He said the ones he tried felt like someone had a thumb in each ear. Every time he flushed the toilet, it sounded like Niagara Falls. Combing his hair sounded like someone walking on gravel. He didn't see what was wrong with people talking loud enough for him to hear. Most of the time, he had a hand cupped to his right ear. He said, "What?" quite a lot. The others tended to ignore him.

The cake he was working on had listed to one side, and he was using an extra inch of white frosting to prop it up. He glanced up at me. "We don't let the birthday person bake his own birthday cake," he said. "Nell does the layers, unless it's her birthday, of course, and I do boiled frosting, which she never seems to get right."

"Everything smells great." I lifted the lid to a covered casserole. Inside, there was a mass of something lumpy and white with what looked like pimento, hard-boiled egg, and clumps of pickle relish. "What's this?"

"Say again?"

Lewis spoke up. "That started out as potato salad, but Charlie set the timer and never heard it ring, so the potatoes cooked down to mush. We decided to add all the regular ingredients and call it Charlie Pitts's Famous Mashed Potato Salad. We're also having fried chicken, baked beans, coleslaw, deviled eggs, and sliced cu-

cumbers and tomatoes with vinegar. I've had this same meal every birthday for the last eighty-six years, since I was two," he said. "We each have something special, and the rule in our family is that the siblings cook. Some are better than others, as it turns out," he added with a glance at Charlie.

I turned to Charlie. "What do you have for your birthday?"

"What's that?"

I raised my voice and repeated my question.

"Oh. Hot dogs, chili, dill pickles, and potato chips. Mother used to fuss because I refused to have a proper vegetable, but I insisted on potato chips and she finally gave in. Instead of birthday cake, I always ask for a pan of Henry's brownies, which he usually has to send halfway across the country."

"What about Henry?"

Charlie cupped a hand to his ear, and Lewis answered for him. "Country ham, biscuits with red-eye gravy, collard greens, black-eyed peas, and cheese grits. Nell, now she insists on meat loaf, mashed potatoes, green beans, and apple pie with a big wedge of cheddar cheese on top. Never varies."

William came into the kitchen in time to catch Lewis's last remark. "What doesn't?"

"I was telling Kinsey about our birthday dinners."

I smiled at William. "What's yours?"

Lewis cut in again. "William always begs for a New England boiled dinner, but we vote him down."

"Well, I like it," he said staunchly.

"Oh, you do not. Nobody could like a New England boiled dinner. You just say that because you know the rest of us would be forced to eat it as well."

"So what does he end up with?"

"Anything we feel like cooking," Lewis said with satisfaction.

We heard a tap at the back door. I turned and saw that Rosie had arrived. The minute she and William saw each other, their faces lighted up. There were seldom any public displays of affection between them, but there was no doubt about their devotion. He was undismayed by her crankiness, and she took his hypochondria in stride. As a consequence, he complained less about imaginary ailments and her sour moods had diminished.

Tonight she was decked out in a dark red muumuu with a purple-and-navy paisley shawl, the rich colors adding a note of drama to her vibrantly dyed red hair. She seemed relaxed. I'd always thought of her as someone abysmally shy, ill at ease with strangers, overbearing with friends. She tended to be quite flirtatious with men, barely tolerant of women, and oblivious of kids. At the same time, she tyrannized the restaurant staff, paying them the lowest wages she could get away with. William and I were forever trying to persuade her to loosen up the purse strings. As for me, she'd bullied me unmercifully since the day I'd moved into the neighborhood. She wasn't mean, but she was opinionated, and she never seemed to hesitate in making her views known. Since I'd begun eating most of my dinners at the restaurant, she'd routinely told me what to order, ignoring any tastes or requirements of mine. Though I like to think of myself as hard-assed, I'd never had the nerve to stand up to her. My only defense in the face of her dictatorship was passive resistance. So far, I'd refused to get a husband or a dog, two (apparently) interchangeable elements she considered essential for my safety.

Now that she was poised on the brink of matrimony, she seemed at peace with herself: playful, full of smiles. William's siblings had accepted her without a moment's hesitation . . . except for Henry, of course, who was dumbfounded when the two connected. I began to see the wedding not so much as a union between her and William, but as an official ceremony by which she'd be initiated into the tribe.

From the other room, Henry began to pound out his rendition of "Happy Birthday" to Lewis, which he belted out at top volume. We joined him in a sing-along that continued for an hour before we ate. After dinner, Henry drew me aside. "What's the story on the break-in?"

"I'm not really sure. Chester seems to think there's some nefarious plot afoot, but I have trouble buying it. Somebody broke in . . . there's no doubt about that. I'm just not sure it has anything to do with his dad."

"Chester thinks there's a link?"

"He thinks it's *all* connected. I think the guy's seen too many bad movies. He suspects Johnny was a double agent during World War Two and somehow has this stash of stolen documents in his possession. He feels the VA claim was what alerted the government, and that's who broke in."

Henry's look was confused. "Who did?"

"The CIA, I guess. Somebody who finally figured out where the old man was hiding. Anyway, that's his theory, and as they say, he's stickin' to it."

"I'm sorry I got you into it. Chester sounds like a nut."

"Don't worry about it. It's not like he actually hired me, so what difference does it make?"

"Well, it sounds like you did what you could, and I appreciate that. I owe you one."

"Oh, you do not," I said with a wave of my hand. In the years of our friendship, Henry had done so much for me, I never would catch up.

At ten, when they hauled out the Monopoly board and the popcorn paraphernalia, I excused myself and went home. I knew the game would continue until midnight or one, and I wasn't up to it. Not old enough, I guess.

I slept like a stone until 6:14 A.M., when I caught the alarm mere seconds before it was set to ring. I rolled out of bed and pulled on my sweats in preparation for my run. Through the spring and summer months, I run at six, but in winter the sun doesn't rise until nearly seven. By then I like to be out on the path. I've been jogging since I was twenty-five . . . three miles a day, usually six days a week, barring illness, injury, or an attack of laziness, which doesn't happen often. My eating patterns are erratic and my diet is appalling, so the run is my way of atoning for my sins. While I'm not crazy about the pain, I'm a sucker for the exhilaration. And I do love the air at that hour of the day. It's chilly and moist. It smells of ocean and pine and eucalyptus and mown grass. By the time I cool down, walking back to my place, the sun has streaked across the lawns, unrolling all the shadows behind the trees, turning dew to mist. There's no moment so satisfying as the last moment of a run: chest heaving, heart pounding, sweat pouring down my face. I bend from the waist and bark out a note of pure bliss, relieved of tension, stress, and the residual effects of all the Quarter Pounders with Cheese.

I finished my run and did a cool-down walking home. I let myself into the apartment, took a shower, and got dressed. I was just spooning down the last of my cold cereal when the telephone rang. I glanced at the clock. It was 7:41, not an hour at which I would ordinarily expect the world to intrude. I grabbed the phone on the second ring. "Hello?"

"Hey, it's me. Chester. Hope I'm not bothering you," he said.

"This is fine. What are you doing at this hour?"

"Was that you I seen running along Cabana a little while ago?"

"Yeeees," I said cautiously. "Is that what you called to ask, or was there something else?"

"No, no, not at all. I just wondered," he said. "I got something I want to show you. We came across it last night."

"What kind of 'it'?"

"Just come over and take a look. It's something Bucky discovered when he was cleaning out Pappy's place. I wouldn't let anyone touch nothing 'til you saw for yourself. You might have to eat crow." He sounded nearly gleeful.

"Give me five minutes."

I rinsed my dish and my spoon, put the cereal and the milk

away, and ran a damp sponge across the kitchen counter. One of the joys of living alone is the only mess you clean up is the one you just made. I tucked my keys in my jacket pocket, pulled the door shut, and took off. In the time since I'd run, the neighborhood was coming alive. I spotted Lewis halfway down the block, taking his morning constitutional. Moza Lowenstein was sweeping off her front porch, and a fellow with a parrot on his shoulder was out walking his dog.

This was one of those perfect November days with cool air, high sun, and the lingering smell of wood fires from the night before. Along our block, the palm trees and evergreens provide constants in a landscape that seems to shift subtly with the passing seasons. Even in California we experience a rendition of autumn, a sporadic mix of colors provided by the ginkgo, the sweet gum, the red oak, and white birch. An occasional maple tree might punctuate the foothills with an exclamation point of vibrant red, but the brightest hues are supplied by the blaze of forest fires that sweep through annually. This year the arsonists had struck four times across the state, leaving thousands of acres an ashen gray, as eerie and as barren as the moon.

When I got to Bucky's, I circled the main house and walked up the drive. The crudely patched concrete parking pad was littered with assorted cardboard boxes, and I assumed that progress was being made with Johnny's personal effects. I headed up the wooden stairs to the apartment above. The door was standing open, and I could hear the murmur of voices. I stepped through the doorway and paused in the entrance. Without the maze of bulky boxes, the space looked smaller and dingier. The furniture remained, but the rooms seemed almost imperceptibly diminished.

Bucky and Chester were standing near the closet, which had been emptied of the remaining clothes. Both men were wearing versions of the same short-sleeved nylon Hawaiian shirt: Bucky's in neon green, Chester's in hot blue. Nearby, Babe was folding and packing the garments into an old steamer trunk. Coat hangers were piled up to the right of her as each piece of clothing was removed. She was wearing her usual flip-flops, along with shorts and a tank top. I had to admire the comfort with which she occupied her overblown body. I'd have been cold in that outfit, but it didn't seem to bother her.

Chester smiled when he saw me. "Hey, there you are. We were just talking about you. Come over here and take a look at this. See what you think." Mr. Friendly, I thought.

Bucky stepped back, showing me a panel he'd swung away from the back wall of the closet. A small residential safe had been tucked into the space, encased in what appeared to be a block of poured concrete. The safe door was approximately sixteen inches wide and fourteen inches tall. The panel itself appeared to be carefully constructed, a flush-mounted plywood partition with inset hinges. The magnetic latch looked to be spring-loaded and probably released at a touch.

"Impressive. How'd you find that?" I asked.

Bucky smiled sheepishly, clearly pleased with himself. "We'd emptied the closet and I was sweeping it out when I bumped my broom handle up against the back wall. Sounded funny to me, so I got a flashlight and started looking at it real close, you know, knocking across the wall. Seemed like there was something goofy about this one section, so I give it a push and this panel popped open."

I hunkered down in front of the opening, peering into the cavity that had been hidden in the "found" space between the joists. The front face of the safe was imposing, but that might have been deceptive. Most home safes are not built to withstand a professional burglar with the proper tools and sufficient time to force his way in. The safe I was looking at was more likely a fire safe, in which what appears to be a solid steel wall is only a thin metal outer shell filled with insulating material. The function of such a safe is protection from a home fire of fairly short duration. Insulation in an old safe might be something as basic as natural cement. A more modern safe might rely on vermiculite mica or diatomaceous earth, particles of which can often be traced back from a burglary suspect's tools and clothing to the specific safe manufacturer.

On closer inspection, I could see the safe wasn't actually embedded in concrete. The concrete formed a sort of housing into which the safe had been shoved.

"We got a locksmith on his way," Chester said. "I couldn't stand the wait, so I called an emergency number and told 'em to send somebody out. We could have all the answers right behind this dial." He was probably picturing maps and ciphers, a small wireless radio, a Luger, and transmission schedules written in invisible ink.

"Have you looked for the combination? It's possible he wrote it down and tucked it someplace close. Most people don't trust their memories, and if he'd needed to get into it, he wouldn't want to waste time searching."

"We thought of that, but we looked every place we could think of. What about you? You searched pretty good yourself. You come across anything might be the combination to that?"

I shrugged. "I never came across any numbers, unless he was using his birthdate or Social Security."

"Can they do that?" Bucky asked. "Make up a combination to suit any set of numbers you give?"

I shrugged. "As far as I know. I'm not an expert, but I always assumed you could do that."

"What do you think, should we pull that thing out?" Chester asked.

"Couldn't hurt. The locksmith will probably have to do it anyway once he gets here," I said.

I rose to my feet and stepped out of the closet, allowing Bucky and Chester sufficient room to maneuver the safe from its resting place. It took a fair amount of huffing and puffing before they managed to set it down on the floor in the middle of the room. Once they'd eased the safe out of its concrete housing, we could take a better look. The three of us inspected the exterior surfaces as if this were some mysterious object that had appeared from outer space. The safe was maybe sixteen inches deep, with a two-tone beige-and-gray finish and rubber mounting feet. It didn't look old. The dial was calibrated with numbers from one to a hundred, which meant you could generate close to a million combinations. There wasn't any point in trying to guess the right one.

Babe had abandoned her packing and was watching the whole procedure. "Maybe it's open," she said to no one in particular.

We turned in unison and looked at her.

"Well, it *could* be," she said.

"It's worth a try," I said. I reached down and pulled the handle without success. I turned the dial a few numbers in one direction and then the other, still pulling the handle, thinking the dial might have been left close to the last digit in the combination. No such luck.

"What do we do now?" Bucky asked.

"I guess we wait," I said.

Within the hour, the safe technician arrived with a big red metal toolbox. He introduced himself as Bergan Jones from Santa Teresa Locksmiths, shaking hands first with Chester, then with Bucky and me. Babe had gone back to folding clothes, but she nodded at him shyly when he was introduced to her. Jones was tall and bony looking, sandy haired, stoop shouldered, with a high shiny forehead, sandy brows, and big glasses with tortoise-shell frames. I placed him in his middle fifties, but I could have been off five years in either direction.

"Hope you can help us out here," Chester said, waving at the safe, which Jones had already spotted.

"No problem. I probably open thirty safes a month. I know this model. Shouldn't take me long."

The four of us stood and watched in fascination as Jones opened his toolbox. There was something in his manner of an old-fashioned doctor on a house call. He'd made his initial diagnosis, the condition wasn't fatal, and we all felt relief. Now it was just a matter of the proper treatment. He took out a cone-shaped device that he attached to the dial, screwing it down tightly. Within minutes he'd popped the dial off and set it aside, then removed the two screws holding the dial ring in place, slipped off the ring and set it with the dial. Next he took out an electric drill and began to bore a hole through the metal in the area that had been covered by the dial and ring.

"You just drill right through?" Babe said. She sounded disappointed, perhaps hoping for dynamite caps or nitroglycerin.

Jones smiled. "I wouldn't put it quite like that. This is a residential fire safe. If this were a burglary safe, we'd run into hardplate: barrier material just behind this steel plating. I got a pressure bar for that, but it'd still take me thirty minutes to drill a quarter-inch hole. Lot of them have auxiliary spring-loaded relocking devices. You hit the wrong spot and you can fire the relockers. If this happens, it gets a lot worse before it gets better again. This is easy."

We were quiet while he drilled, the low-pitched whine of metal making conversation awkward. The hair on the backs of his hands was a fine gold, his fingers long, wrists narrow. He was smiling to himself, as if he knew something the rest of us hadn't considered yet. Or maybe he was just a man who enjoyed his work. As soon as a hole had been drilled, he took out another device.

"What's that?" I asked.

"Ophthalmoscope," he said. "Gadget your doctor uses to peer in your eyes. This shines light on the combination wheels so I can see what we got going." He began to peer into the newly drilled hole, moving closer while flicking an outer dial on the scope to adjust the focal length. While squinting through his ophthalmoscope, he carefully rotated the protruding spindle stub to the left. "This turns the drive wheel, which in turn picks up the third combination wheel. The third wheel moves the second wheel, which then turns the first wheel," he said. "It takes four rotations to get the first wheel moving. That's the one closest to the front of the safe. Here it comes. Perfect. The gate's exactly under the fence. Now we'll just keep reversing the direction of our rotation and lessening the number of turns. Soon as I get all three wheels lined up, the fence will be in position to drop when the lever nose hits the gate in the drive wheel. We keep turning and the lever pulls back the lock bolt and it's all over."

With that, he gave the handle a pull and the safe door opened. Chester, Bucky, and I gave out a simultaneous "Ooo" like we were watching fireworks.

Babe said, "Heck, it's empty."

"They must have got it already. God*damn,*" Chester said.

"Got what?" Babe said, but he ignored the question, shooting her a cross look.

While Bergan Jones wrote down the combination and put his tools away, Bucky peered into the safe, then got down on his back like an auto mechanic and shone a light into the interior. "Something taped up here, Dad."

I leaned over and peered with him. An item had been secured to the top of the safe: a lumpy-looking ten-inch-by-ten-inch square of beige tape.

Chester stepped over Bucky's legs and crouched by the safe, squinting at the patch. "What *is* that? Peel it off and give it here. Let me take a look at that thing."

Gingerly Bucky loosened one corner, then pulled it away like a Band-Aid from a wound. A big iron key adhered to the tape. It appeared to be an old-fashioned iron skeleton key with simple cuts in the end. He held it up. "Anybody reconnize this?"

"Beats me," I said, and then turned to Chester. "You know what it is?"

"Nope, but Pappy used to fool around with locks now I think of it. He got a kick out of it. He liked to take a lock out of a door and file a key to fit."

"I never saw him do that," Bucky said.

"This is when I was a kid. He worked for a locksmith during the Depression. I remember him telling me what a hoot it was. He had this collection of old locks—probably close to a hundred of them—but I haven't seen them for years."

I turned the key over in my hand. The design was ornate, the handle scalloped, with a hole in the other end like a skate key. Viewed straight on, the bit was shaped almost like a question mark. "The lock and keyhole would be odd looking, to say the least. You don't remember anything like it around here?"

Chester's mouth pulled down. "Not me. What about you guys? You know the place better than I do at this point."

Bucky shook his head, and Babe gave a little shrug.

I held the key out to Bergan Jones. "Any ideas?"

Jones smiled slightly, snapping down the locks on his toolbox. "Looks like a gate key. One of those big old iron jobs like they have on estates." He turned to Chester. "You want me to bill you on this?"

"I'll write you a check. Come on down to the kitchen and we'll take care of it. You probably gathered by now my pappy died a few months back. We're still trying to get his affairs sorted out. The safe came as a surprise. People ought to leave instructions. What the hell this is and who's supposed to get that. Anyways, we do appreciate your help."

"That's what I'm in business to do."

The two men departed, leaving Bucky, Babe, and me to contemplate the key. Bucky said, "Now what?"

"I have a friend who knows a lot about locks," I said. "He might have a suggestion about what kind of lock this might fit."

"Might as well. Won't do us any good otherwise."

Babe took the key and inspected it, frowning. "Maybe Pappy kept it because he liked the way it looked," she said. "It's neat. It's old-timey." She handed it to Bucky, who passed it back to me.

"Yeah, but why bother to keep it in a fireproof safe? He could have stuck it in a drawer. He could have wore it on a chain around his neck," he said.

"If you don't object, I'll see what my local expert has to say."

"Fine with me," Bucky said.

I slipped the key in my jeans pocket without mentioning the fact that my local expert was the burglar who'd also given me the set of key picks I carry in my handbag.

Walking back to my place, I found myself reviewing the entire sequence of events. I have to confess the past twenty-four hours had piqued my curiosity. It wasn't necessarily Chester's spy theory, which still seemed farfetched. What bothered me were the vague, unanswered questions surfacing in the old man's life. I like order and tidiness; no clutter and no dust bunnies hidden under the bed.

As soon as I got home, I sat down at my desk, pulled out a pack of index cards, and started making notes. It was amazing how many details I could actually recall once I began committing them to paper. When I'd exhausted the subject, I pinned the cards up on the corkboard that hangs above my desk. I put my feet up on the desk and leaned back in my swivel chair with my hands locked behind my head and studied the whole collection. Something wasn't right, but I couldn't figure out what it was. I shifted some cards around and pinned them up in a new configuration. It was something I'd read. Burma. Something about Chennault and the American Volunteer Group. For the moment the truth eluded me, but I knew it was there. I thought about nailing down the unit he'd served in. Was that really the issue here, or was there something else at stake? In scanning Johnny's books, I'd seen several AVG fighter pilots mentioned by name. One or more of those guys had to be alive today. Couldn't they provide a way to pinpoint Johnny's fighter group? It'd be a pain in the ass, and *I* sure wasn't going to do it, but I could at least steer Chester in the right direction. I'd have to check back through the books and see if I could find the reference, but what the hell, I wasn't doing anything else. Besides, once I start worrying a knot, I can't let go of it.

I put in a call to my burglar friend, whose number had been disconnected. Rats. Later in the morning I'd try the Santa Teresa Police Department. Detective Halpern in Major Crimes would probably know where he was.

5

By ten A.M. I found myself back at Bucky's. I knocked on the door, but after several minutes went by and nobody answered, I headed down the driveway toward the back. The miscellaneous collection of cardboard boxes had been shoved to one side to make the driveway passable. The garage door on the left was standing open and the Buick was missing. Maybe the three of them had gone out to breakfast. The other half of the two-car garage was piled high with junk, an impenetrable mountain of boxes, old furniture, appliances, and lawn care equipment.

The cardboard box full of World War II books was right on top. I dragged it over to the stairs and made myself comfortable while I sorted through the contents. I finally found what I was looking for at the bottom of the box in a book called *Fighter! The Story of Air Combat 1936–45* by Robert Jackson.

> On 4 July 1942 the American Volunteer Group officially ceased to be an independent fighting unit and became part of the newly-activated China Air Task Force, under command of the Tenth Air Force. Command of the CATF devolved on Claire Chennault, who exchanged his Chinese uniform for an American one and was given the rank of brigadier-general.
>
> The AVG pilots, who had held the fort in Burma for so long against impossible odds, scattered far and wide. Few of them elected to remain in China. Those who did formed the nucleus of the new 23rd Fighter Group, still flying war-weary P-40s.

A few names followed: Charles Older, "Tex" Hill, Ed Rector, and Gil Bright. What interested me was the fact that the AVG pilots were recruited by the Central Aircraft Manufacturing Company between April and July 1941. All of them were serving U.S. military personnel, bound to CAMCO by a one-year contract. But Bucky had told me Chester remembered his father arriving home after two years overseas in time for his fourth birthday party, August 17, 1944. Because he was so specific, the date had stuck in my mind and I'd jotted it down on an index card. The problem was, the AVG had already been out of business for two years at that point. So where did the truth lie? Had Johnny actually served with the AVG? More important, had he served at all? Chester would see the discrepancy in dates as confirmation of his theory. I could just imagine his response. *"Hell, the AVG was just a cover story. I could have told you that."* Chester probably envisioned his father parachuting behind enemy lines, perhaps even feigning capture so he could confer with the Japanese high command.

On the other hand, if he'd never *been* in the service, then maybe he'd only acquired the books so he could bullshit about the subject. And that might explain why he was unwilling to talk about the war. It was always going to be risky because he might well run into someone who'd been in the very unit he was claiming to have served. By creating the impression of government secrecy, he could account for his reluctance to discuss the details that might give him away.

I scanned the backyard, staring at the Ford Fairlane, sitting up on concrete blocks. Why did I care one way or the other? The old guy was dead. If it comforted his son and his grandson to believe he was a war hero (or, more grandiose yet, a spy whose cover had gone undetected now for more than forty years), what difference did it make to me? I wasn't being paid to shoot holes in Johnny's story. I wasn't being paid to do anything. So why not let it drop?

Because it's contrary to my nature said she to herself. I'm like a little terrier when it comes to the truth. I have to stick my nose down the hole and dig until I find out what's in there. Sometimes I get bitten, but that's the chance I'm usually willing to take. In some ways, I didn't care so much about the nature of the truth as knowing what it consisted of.

I became aware of the big six-inch key digging into my hip. I stretched my leg out and slid my hand into my jeans pocket. I pulled out the key and held it in my palm, hefting the weight. I rubbed my thumb along the darkened surface. I squinted at the tarnished metal just as Babe had done. The name of the lock company seemed to be faintly stamped on the shaft, but I couldn't figure out what it said in this light. It didn't appear to be any of the lock companies I knew: Schlage, Weslock, Weiser, or Yale. The safe had been an Amsec, strictly a combination lock, so I didn't think the key was in any way connected with that.

I hauled myself to my feet and slid the key back in my pocket. I was restless, trying to figure out what to do until Chester got home. It was always possible his memory was faulty. I'd only heard the story from Bucky, and he might have gotten the dates wrong. Ray Rawson had told me he worked with Johnny in the boatyards just after the war started, which had to be sometime in 1942. It struck me as odd that someone who'd known Johnny in the "olden" days had suddenly shown up on the old man's doorstep. Despite the offhand explanation, I wondered if there was something else going on.

The Lexington Hotel was located on a side street a block off lower State Street near the beach. The structure was a chunky five-story box of weary-looking yellow brick, spanning an arcade that ran across the ground floor. On one side of the building, a jagged crack, like a lightning bolt, staggered through the brick from the roof to the foundation, suggesting earthquake damage that probably dated back to 1925. The letters of the word *Lexington* descended vertically on a sign affixed to one corner of the building, a buzzing yellow band of neon with dead bugs in the loops. The marquee boasted · DAILY MAID · PHONE · COLOR TV IN EVERY ROOM. The entrance was flanked by a Mexican restaurant on one side and by a bar on the other. A blaring jukebox in each establishment competed for air space, a jarring juxtaposition of Linda Ronstadt and Helen Reddy.

I moved into a lobby that was sparsely furnished and smelled of bleach. Two rows of potted fan palms were arranged on either side of a length of trampled-looking red carpet that heralded the path to the front desk. The desk clerk was not in evidence. I picked up the house phone and asked the operator to connect me with Ray Rawson's room. He answered after two rings and I identified myself. We spoke briefly and he directed me to his fourth-floor digs. "Take the stairs. The elevator takes forever," he said as he hung up.

I took the stairs two at a time just to test my lung capacity. By the second-floor landing, I was winded and had to slow down. I clung to the stair railing while I climbed the last flight. Being fit in one sport seems to have no bearing on any other. I know joggers who wouldn't last twenty minutes on a stationary bike and swimmers who couldn't jog more than a mile without collapsing.

I composed myself slightly before I knocked at 407. Ray opened the door with a buzzing portable electric shaver in his hand. He was barefoot, in chinos and a white T-shirt, his balding head still damp from the shower. The already closely clipped fringe of gray had been trimmed since yesterday. His smile was embarrassed, and the gap between his two front teeth gave him an air of innocence. He motioned me in. "You're too quick. I was trying to get this done before you got all the way up here. Be right back."

He moved into the bathroom, the buzzing sound of the shaver fading as he closed the door.

His room was spacious and plain: white walls, white bedspread, rough white cotton curtains pulled back on fat wooden rods. There were only two windows, but both were double wide, looking out onto the backside of the building across the alleyway. The carpet was gray and seemed relatively clean. The glimpse I had of the bathroom showed glossy white ceramic tile walls and a floor of one-inch black and white hexagonals. Ray returned, smelling strongly of aftershave.

"This is not bad," I said, turning halfway around.

"Fifty bucks a night. I asked about weekly rates, just until I get a place of my own. I don't suppose Bucky's said anything about the rental."

"Not to me," I said. "Did you hear they had a break-in?"

"Who did? You mean, Bucky and them? When was this?"

I gave him the *Reader's Digest* condensed version of the story, watching as his smile was extinguished by disbelief and then concern.

"Jeez. That's terrible," he said, and then he caught my expression. "Wait a minute. Why look at me? I hope you don't think I had anything to do with it."

"It just seems odd there wasn't any problem until you showed up. Johnny died four months ago. You blow in last week and now Chester's suddenly got problems."

"Come on. Hey. I was sitting in the bar last night, watching big-screen TV. You can ask anyone."

"Mind if I sit?"

"Sure, go ahead. Take the good one. I'll take this."

There was one hard wooden chair and one upholstered chair. Ray steered me toward the latter and took the wood chair for himself. He placed his hands on his knees, rubbing the fabric as if his palms were sweating. "I'm probably the oldest and best friend Johnny ever had. I'd never do anything to mess with his son or his grandson or anything like that. You have to believe me."

"I'm not accusing you, Ray."

"Sure sounds like that to me."

"If I thought you'd broken in, I probably wouldn't have come up here. I'd have gone to the cops and had 'em dust for prints."

"They didn't do that?"

"Chester can't be sure anything was taken, which means it wasn't even a burglary as far as the cops are concerned. The techs here only lift prints at the scene of a major crime. Felonies, not misdemeanors. Malicious mischief wouldn't qualify unless thousands of dollars' worth of damage had been done, which wasn't true in this case." What I didn't bother to say was the procedure is lengthy and the department is perpetually backed up. Three weeks is standard. In a rush situation, prints could be lifted, photographed, and traced, with the resultant tracings being faxed to CAL ID in Sacramento. The turnaround time could be a day or two. In this case, we didn't even have a suspect. Except maybe him, I thought. I watched him, acutely aware of the key in my pocket. I didn't want him to know about that just yet. He seemed like a man who had something on his mind, and I wanted to hear his tale before I told him mine. "What's in Ashland?" I asked.

There was a millisecond's pause. "I got family back there."

"Was Johnny really in the service?"

"I have no idea. I already told you, I lost track of him for years."

"How'd you connect up again?"

"Johnny got in touch."

"How'd he know where to find you?"

Impatience flashed across his face as if his picture were being taken. "Because he had my address. What *is* this? I don't have to answer this stuff. It's none of your damn business."

"I'm just trying to get to the bottom of this."

"Well, try somewhere else."

"Chester thinks Johnny was a spy during World War Two, some kind of double agent for the Japanese."

Ray rolled his eyes briefly and then gave his head a quick shake. "Where'd he get that?"

"It's too complicated to explain. He says the old man was very paranoid. He thinks that's part of it."

Ray said, "The old guy *was* paranoid, but it didn't have anything to do with the Japs."

"What, then?"

"Why should I tell you? I have no reason to trust you any more than you trust me."

"And here I thought we were such pals," I said.

"Well, we're not," he said mildly.

I eased the key out of my pocket and held it up to the light. "You know anything about this?"

His gaze flicked to the key. "Where'd you get that?"

"It was in a safe Bucky found in Johnny's apartment. Have you ever seen it before?"

"No."

"What about the safe? Did you know about that?"

He shook his head slowly. This was like pulling teeth.

"I don't understand what the deal is," I said.

"There's no deal. It's nothing."

"If it's nothing, why not tell? It can't do any harm."

"Look, I might know who busted in. If it's who I think, then some guy might have followed me out here. That's all it is, and I could be wrong about that."

"What was he after?"

"Jeez. Don't you ever give up?"

"You must have *some* idea."

"Well, I don't."

"Of course you do," I said. "Why else would you drive all the way out here from Ashland?"

Agitated, he got up and crossed to the window, shoving his hands in his pockets. "Hey, come on. Enough. I'm getting tired of this. You can't force me to answer, so you might as well lay off."

I got up and followed him to the window, leaning against the wall so I could watch his face. "Here's the way my mind works. This sounds like something criminal." I tapped my temple. "I'm thinking to myself, What if Johnny never went into the Air Force? I keep having trouble with that piece of it. If he wasn't in the service, then the whole picture shifts. Because then you have to wonder where he was all that time."

Ray's gaze met mine. He started to say something, but he seemed to think better of it.

"Want to hear my theory? I just came up with this," I said. "He might have been in prison. Maybe this business about the Air Force —this AVG bullshit—was just a polite explanation for his absence. The war had started by then. It sounds a lot more patriotic to say your husband's gone overseas than he's been sent up." I waited a moment, but Ray made no response. I cupped a hand behind my ear. "Care to comment?"

He shook his head. "It's your theory. You can think anything you want."

"You're not going to help me out?"

"Not a bit," he said.

I pushed away from the wall. "Well. Maybe you'll change your mind. I live around the corner from Johnny's, five doors down on Albanil. You can stop by and chat when you're ready." I moved toward the door.

"I don't get this," he said. "I mean, what's it to you?"

I looked back at him. "I have a hunch, and I'd like to find out if I'm right. In my line of work, it's good practice."

For lunch, I treated myself to a Quarter Pounder with Cheese and then spent the afternoon curled up with the new Elmore Leonard novel. I'd been telling myself how much fun it was having nothing to do, but I noticed that I was faintly disconcerted by the idleness. Generally, I don't think of myself as compulsive, but I don't like wasting time. I tidied my apartment and cleaned out some drawers, went back to my book, and tried to concentrate. Late in the afternoon, I shrugged into my blazer and walked up to the corner for a bite to eat. I was thinking about an early movie if I could figure out what to see.

The neighborhood was quiet, half the front porches picked out in light. There was a chill in the air, and the dark seemed to be coming down earlier and earlier. I could smell somebody's supper cooking, and the images were cozy. Once in a while I find myself at loose ends, and that's when I feel the lack of a relationship. There's something about love that brings a sense of focus to life. I wouldn't complain about the sex, either, if I could remember how it went. I'd have to get out the instructor's manual if I ever managed to get laid again.

Rosie's was nearly empty, but shortly after I sat down, I spotted Babe and Bucky coming through the door. I waved and the two of them approached my back booth, walking hip to hip, their arms wound around each other's waists.

I said, "Where's your dad, Bucky? I've been hoping to run into him. We need to talk."

"He took a load over to the dump, but he should be back

shortly," Bucky said. "You want to join us? We thought we'd sit at the bar and watch the six o'clock news until Dad gets here." In the half-light of the tavern, he was looking nearly handsome. Babe was in boots, a long jeans skirt, and a blue jeans jacket.

"Thanks, but I may try to eat quick and catch an early movie."

"Well, we'll be over there if you should change your mind." They sauntered off to the bar.

Meanwhile, Rosie appeared from the kitchen and I watched her draw two beers before she came over to me. She had already pulled out her pencil and order pad and was scribbling away. "I got perfect dish for you," she said as she snatched my dinner menu. "Is slices pork liver with sausage and garlic pickles, cook with bacon. Also, I'm making you apple-and-savoy-cabbage salad with crackling biscuits."

"Sounds inspired," I said. I didn't say by what.

"You gonna have this with beer. Is better than wine, which don't mix good with garlic pickles."

"I should say not."

I ate, I must say, with a hearty appetite, though I'd probably have indigestion later. The place was beginning to fill up with the Happy Hour crowd people from the neighborhood and singles getting off work. Rosie's had become a favorite hangout among the local sporting set, thus ruining it for those of us in search of peace and quiet. If it weren't for my fondness for Rosie and the close proximity to my apartment, I might have moved on to some new eatery. I saw Bucky and Babe move over to a table. Chester came in moments later, and the three conferred before ordering supper. By then the place was so noisy that it didn't seem tactful to join them and launch into talk about Johnny's past history.

At 6:35 I paid my check and headed out the front door. I was already losing interest in the movie, but there was always a chance I could generate enthusiasm from "the sibs."

When I got home, I crossed the back patio and knocked at the frame. I heard a muffled "Yoo-hoo!" I peered in through the screen and spotted Nell sitting in a wooden kitchen chair pulled up close to the stove. She was peering in my direction, and when she saw me she motioned me in.

I opened the door and stuck my head in. "Hi, Nell. How are you?" The stove had been dismantled—the oven door open, oven racks removed—apparently in preparation for a thorough cleaning. The counter was lined with newspaper on which the oven racks were laid, still seething with oven cleaner.

"Fine and dandy. Come on in, Kinsey. It's good to see you." Ordinarily she wore her thick silver hair pulled back in an elaborate arrangement of tortoise-shell combs, but today she'd tied her hair into the folds of a scarf, which made her look like an ancient Cinderella.

"You're industrious," I said. "You just got here and already you're hard at work."

"Well, I'm not happy until I can take a stove apart and really clean in there good. Henry's extremely able when it comes to household chores, but a stove is the sort of thing needs a woman's touch. I know that sounds sexist, but it's the truth," she said.

"You need help?"

"I could sure use the company." Nell was wearing a pinafore-style apron over her cotton housedress, her long sleeves protected by cuffs of paper toweling that she'd secured with rubber bands. She was a big woman, probably close to six feet tall in her prime. Wide shouldered, heavy breasted, she had good-size feet and hands, though her knuckles were now as knotted as ropes beneath the skin. Her face was long and bony, nearly sexless in its character, sparse white brows, electric blue eyes, her skin vertically draped with seams and folds.

All the shelves had been emptied from the refrigerator, the countertops crowded with leftovers in covered bowls, olive and pickle jars, condiments, raw vegetables. The storage drawers had been removed and one was sitting in a sink full of soapy water.

She'd tossed a number of items in the kitchen wastebasket, and I could see that she'd dumped something gloppy in the disposal.

"Don't look at that. I think it's still alive," she said. She was wringing out the cloth she was using to wipe down the shelves. "Once I finish this, I intend to take a bubble bath and then I'll get into my robe and slippers. I have some reading to catch up on. I keep thinking any day now my eyes are going out on me and I want to get in as much as possible." She had unscrewed a jar lid and was peering in. She sniffed, unable to identify the contents. "What in heaven's name is this?" She held it up to the light. The liquid was bright red and syrupy.

"I think it's the glaze for the cherry tart Henry makes. You know he cleaned the refrigerator just two days ago."

She screwed the lid back on and put the jar on the counter. "That's what he said. As it happens, cleaning refrigerators is one of my specialties. I taught Henry how to do it back in 1912. His problem is he isn't sufficiently rigorous. Most of us aren't when it comes to our own trash. As long as I'm here I might as well get everything shipshape."

"Was that your lot in life, teaching all the boys how to do things around the house?"

"More or less. I helped Mother raise and educate all ten of us at home. After Father died, I felt obliged to stay on until she recovered her spirits, which took close to thirty years. She was heartsick when she lost him, though as I recollect, the two of them never got along that well. My, my. How she did grieve for the man. It occurred to me later she was putting on a bit just to keep me underfoot."

"Ten kids? I thought there were only five. You, Charlie, Lewis, William, and Henry."

She shook her head. "We were the five *surviving* children. We took after the Tilmanns, on our mother's side. In our family, there was a distinct division among the children she bore. Half took after her side of the family and the other half took after the Pitts on Father's side. Line us up for a photograph and you could see it plain as day. Now this is a fact. All Father's people up and died. It was a pitiful genetic line when you stop and calculate. They were small people with tiny heads, so they didn't have the brains our side of the family did and they had no physical stamina whatsoever. Our father's mother was a 'Mauritz' by birth. The name translates as 'Moorish,' which suggests a bunch of blackamoors somewhere up the line. They were swarthy, all of them, and just as feeble as could be. Our grandmother Mauritz died of the influenza, and so did two brothers above me. It was a mess. She went and he went and the other one went. Our sister, Alice, was another one we lost. Dark skinned, tiny head, she died of the influenza within a day of taking sick. Four cousins, an aunt. Sometimes two would go on the same day and we'd have a double funeral. That entire line was wiped out in a five-month period between November and March. Those of us who took after Mother are the only ones left, and we expect to go on for years. Mother lived to be a hundred and three. Right about the time she turned ninety, she got so crabby we threatened to withhold her sour mash whiskey if she didn't straighten up. She only required six tablespoons a day, but she believed it was absolutely essential to life. We put the bottle right up on the shelf where she could see it but couldn't reach. That settled her right down, and she went on for another thirteen years just as gentle as a lamb."

She closed the refrigerator door temporarily and returned to the sink, where the dishwater was now cool enough to allow her to wash the meat bin. She opened the cabinet under the sink, and I saw a frown cross her face.

"What's the matter?"

"Henry's out of the oven cleaner I like to use on these racks." She peered in the cabinet again. "Well, I'll just have to use a little elbow grease."

"You want me to make a quick run to the market? I can pick some up. It won't take ten minutes."

"No, that's all right. I can always use a scrub pad. It'll clean up in a jiffy. You have other things to do."

"I don't mind a bit. I was thinking about a movie, but I've lost interest, to tell the truth."

"Are you sure you don't mind?"

"Scout's honor," I said.

"I'd surely appreciate it. We're low on milk, too. Once the kids have their milk and cookies tonight, there won't be enough for breakfast. This is really awfully sweet."

"Don't even think about it. I'll be back shortly. What kind of milk? Low fat?"

"Half a gallon of skim. I'm trying to wean the kids off fat where I can."

I searched through my handbag for the car keys and then eased the strap across my shoulder as I headed out the door. My car was parked about two doors down. I fired up the ignition and pulled away from the curb. At the corner of Albanil and Bay, I turned right, passing Bucky's place, which had become my new reference point in the neighborhood. I'd probably never pass the house again without turning to look. I peered down the drive toward the garage apartment. Lights were on upstairs, and I saw a shadow move across the front windows.

I slowed to a stop, peering up at the apartment. I didn't think any of the Lees were home. The last I'd seen, the three of them were still up at Rosie's having supper. The lights went out and I saw someone emerge onto the darkened landing. Well, this was interesting. I spotted a parking place and pulled in at the curb. I turned the engine off and doused my headlights. I adjusted the rearview mirror so that it was angled on the drive and then slid down in the seat.

A man moved out of the driveway with a hefty-looking duffel bag in his right hand. He was walking in my direction, his head down, his shoulders hunched. From the dim glow of the street lamp, I could see it wasn't Bucky, Chester, or Ray. This guy had a full head of dark, curly hair. His clothing was dark, and he must have been wearing rubber-soled shoes because his footsteps made hardly any sound on the pavement as he passed. He set off across the street. I kept him in sight, watching with curiosity as he approached a white Ford Taurus parked at the far curb, facing the opposite direction. He shifted the duffel to his left hand while he took out his car keys and unlocked the door on the driver's side. Puzzled, I glanced back toward Bucky's, but the premises were still dark and there were no signs of life.

The man opened the door and shoved the duffel toward the passenger seat, slid in behind the wheel, and slammed the car door shut. I watched as he checked his reflection in the rearview mirror, smoothed his hair back, and settled a Stetson on his head. I eased out of sight while he started his ignition, flipped the lights on, and took off, his headlights raking my windshield. As soon as he turned the corner, I started my car and pulled away from the curb. I did a quick U-turn, yanked on my headlights, and took the corner maybe six seconds after he had. I caught a glimpse of his taillights as he turned right on Castle. I had to floor it to maintain visual contact. Within minutes he'd turned onto the northbound freeway off-ramp, heading toward Colgate. I eased into the line of traffic two cars behind him and kept my foot firmly pressed to the accelerator.

6

A one-car surveillance is usually a waste of time, especially at night, where a second set of headlights becomes conspicuous in a subject's rearview mirror. In this case, whatever this guy was up to, I didn't think he had any idea I was following. Coming out of Johnny's garage apartment, he'd seemed neither watchful nor cautious, and I had to believe a tail was the last thing he expected. I hadn't expected it myself, so I was at least as surprised as he was. He did nothing on the freeway—no tricky lane changes, no sudden exits—to indicate that he was aware of my presence. The Stetson, in silhouette, gave me a nice visual cue against the wash of approaching headlights. He took the off-ramp at upper State Street, and I slid into the lane behind him. While I steered with my left hand, I scrounged around in my handbag for a scrap of paper and a pen. At least I could take his license plate number while I had him in range. The nature of the plate number indicated that the car was a rental, a further clue being the Penny-Car-Rental on the license plate rim. Big duh. I made a note of the number on the back of an old grocery list. Later, I'd find someone to check the rental car records.

It was 7:17 by the time the white Taurus pulled into the gravel courtyard of the Capri, a ten-unit "motor hotel" off the frontage road. The perimeter of the parking area was delineated by a drooping strand of Christmas tree lights that had been strung from pole to pole. The motel itself was made up of two rows of small frame and clapboard cottages, each with a carport affixed to one side. The darkness had draped the exteriors in sufficient shadow to conceal the flaking paint, warping window screens, and poor construction. Most of the cottages appeared to be empty: windows unlighted, no vehicles in the carports. A pint-size U-Haul truck was parked in front of one unit. The first two cottages on the left were occupied, along with the second unit on the right, which was where the Taurus was now parked.

The driver locked his vehicle and moved up to the cottage's small concrete porch, with its light offering forty watts' worth of illumination. I waited until he'd unlocked the cottage and entered before I eased my VW along the gravel parking lot to a darkened unit across the way. I backed into the carport, doused my headlights, and rolled the window down. The stillness was punctuated by the ticking of my engine as the metal cooled. Also, by a failing green Christmas tree bulb that flickered and buzzed somewhere above my head like a jolly green bee. I sat in the dark, pondering how long I'd be willing to wait before I headed for home. Poor Nell must be wondering how far away the supermarket was. I'd promised her a quick trip—fifteen minutes max. I'd now been gone twice that long. I had a squirrelly feeling in the pit of my stomach, a strange emotional concoction of anxiety and excitement. What was in the duffel the guy had taken off the premises? Could be burglars' tools. I was operating on the assumption that this was the same guy who'd tossed the place before, though I couldn't imagine what was worth coming back for. Ray Rawson had some suspicions about who the break-in artist might have been, but he'd given no indication why anyone would bother. I wished now I'd pressed him for the information. Meanwhile, it was worth a short wait. If I ran out of patience, I'd make a note of the motel address and use a phone ruse in the morning to find out who was staying there.

I checked my watch again. It was now 7:32. The fellow had been in there fifteen minutes or so. Was he in for the night? I really couldn't sit here indefinitely, and I didn't think it made sense to go prowling around the cottage, trying to peer in the windows. The guy might be traveling with a bad-tempered mutt that would set up a stink. This was the kind of place that would *have* to accommodate kids and weird pets. How else would they get business except by accident?

Just about the time I was ready to pack it in, I saw some movement on the cottage porch. The man emerged accompanied by a woman, who now carried the duffel bag. He still wore his hat and he was toting a suitcase, which he stowed in the trunk. She handed him the duffel and he tucked it in with the suitcase. He opened the car door, giving her an assist as she got into the seat on the passenger side. I noticed they didn't bother with any checkout procedure. Either they were only leaving for a short time or they were decamping without paying. He went around to the driver's side. I started my engine at the same time he started his, using his noise as a cover for mine. His taillights came on, the two bright red spots overlaid with the white of his backup lights.

I left my headlights off, waiting until the Taurus backed out and made a right turn into the street. The Taurus took off toward the highway, and I followed at a discreet distance. I wasn't happy with the arrangement. There wasn't much other traffic on the road, and if I had to tail the guy for long, I was going to get burned. Fortunately he headed for the northbound freeway on-ramp, and by the time I eased in behind him, there were sufficient cars on the road to camouflage my presence.

The driver of the Taurus stayed in the right lane and proceeded for two off-ramps before he finally took the exit designated for the airport and the university. With two bags in the trunk, I didn't think they were on their way to a UCST night class. The ramp curved up and around to the left, widening into six lanes. A Yellow Cab merged with us from an access road, and I eased back on the accelerator, allowing the taxi to slip in between us. The Taurus stayed in the right lane and turned off at Rockpit, turning right again at the stop sign. I stayed in the slipstream as first the Taurus and then the taxi turned in at the airport.

I watched as the Taurus moved into the left lane and slowed at the ticket meter for the short-term parking lot. The ticket arm went up like an automated salute. Meanwhile, the taxi kept to the right, pulling up at the curb in the passenger loading zone, where two passengers got out with their luggage. I waited until the Taurus drove into the short-term lot before I eased the VW forward. The ticket dispenser buzzed and a parking ticket emerged from the slot like a tongue. I snagged it and rolled forward into the lot.

The Taurus had turned into the first aisle on the left and was now parked in the front row, close to the road. I caught a quick glimpse of the couple as they crossed toward the terminal. He carried both the suitcase and the duffel. She was wearing a raincoat pulled around her for warmth. I scanned the spaces available and pulled into the first empty spot. I parked, locked up, and dogtrotted after them. The two were engaged in conversation, and neither seemed aware of my company.

It was fully dark by now, the terminal building lighted up like one of those miniature cottages you put under the Christmas tree. There were two skycaps at the curb, putting tags on the suitcases of the two travelers the taxi had disgorged. The couple went into the terminal. I noticed they were bypassing the car rental offices. Were they skipping? I doubled my pace, my shoulder bag banging against one hip as I jogged down the short walk to the entrance. The terminal at the Santa Teresa Airport has only six working gates.

In the left wing, Gates 1, 2, and 3 serviced commuter airlines: the puddle-jumpers doing short runs to and from Los Angeles, San Francisco, San Jose, Fresno, Sacramento, and other points within about a four-hundred-mile radius. In the main lobby, United Airlines was sharing counter space with American. I did a quick visual survey, checking out the passengers seated in various groupings of linked upholstered chairs. The Stetson should have made the guy fairly easy to spot, but there was no sign of the pair.

Most departing passengers were processed through Gate 5, which was plainly visible across the small lobby. At this hour of the night, air traffic wasn't heavy and a check of the departures monitor indicated only two outbound flights. One was a United prop jet to Los Angeles, the other an American Airlines flight to Palm Beach with an intervening stop at Dallas/Fort Worth. Dead ahead was Gate 4, which was used as the arrival gate for United's incoming flights. Arched windows looked out onto a small grassy area, defined by outdoor lights and surrounded by a stucco wall topped with a three-foot rim of protective window glass. I could hear the high-pitched drone of a small plane approaching along the runway. I moved to the double doors and checked the courtyard. There were maybe six or eight people scattered across the area: a woman with a toddler, three college students, an older couple with a dog on a leash. No sign of the couple I was looking for.

As I passed through the main lobby toward the commuter wing, I spotted the Stetson, black felt with a broad brim and a high soft crown. The guy was in the gift shop, paying for a couple of magazines. I was catching him in profile, but the light was excellent. As if obliging me, he took off his hat and ruffled his hair before he readjusted the angle of the hat on his head. I studied him with care so that I could identify him again if it ever came to that. I put him in his late fifties, with small dark eyes in a lean, hawkish face. He had a bushy salt-and-pepper mustache. What by streetlight had appeared to be dark curly hair I could now see was heavily interwoven with strands of silver. He wore cowboy boots, jeans, and a heavy dark wool jacket. I pegged him at six feet, though the boots might have added inches, maybe 160 to 175 pounds. He tucked the magazines under his arm and crammed the change in his pocket. I backed away from the door as he turned in my direction.

Behind me was a bank of public telephones. In part as cover and in part out of desperation, I turned to the first phone and hauled up the phone book that was chained to the metal shelf below. I busied myself looking up Bucky's number while the guy came out of the gift shop behind me. Obliquely, I watched as he crossed the lobby, joining the woman, who was now standing at the ticket counter with her back to me, the duffel at her feet. Where had she come from? Probably the ladies' room. The line she was standing in was designated for the purchasing of tickets. She'd taken off her raincoat, which was now folded across one arm. The passenger in front of her finished his business and she moved to the counter, placing a big soft-sided suitcase on the weighing apparatus. She reached back with one foot, shifting the duffel forward until it rested against the counter beside her.

The ticket agent greeted her, and the two exchanged a few words. While the agent tapped on her computer keyboard, the woman reached over and picked up a cardboard identification strip from a container on the counter. She filled in the details and then gave the tag to the ticket agent, who was just in the process of assembling the ticket. The woman laid out a sheaf of bills, which the ticket agent counted and then put away. She secured the woman's identification to the suitcase, along with a claim tag, and then placed the suitcase on the conveyor belt. The moving bag was spirited through a small opening like a coffin on its way to the flames. The two finished their transaction, and the agent passed the woman's ticket envelope across the counter to her.

When the woman turned to her companion, I could see that she was six or seven months pregnant. Was this his daughter? She was much younger than the fellow who accompanied her: early to mid-thirties, gaudy auburn hair piled in a tangled knot on top. Her complexion had the pasty look of too much foundation, overlaid with a shade of powder that made her face seem faintly dirty. Her maternity outfit was one of those oversize pale blue denim dresses with short sleeves and a dropped waist, against which her belly bulged. Under the dress she wore an oversize white T-shirt with long sleeves. She also wore red-and-white-striped tights and high-topped red tennis shoes. The dress itself I'd seen in a gardening catalog, a style favored by former hippies who'd given up dope and communal sex for organic vegetables and all-natural fiber clothes.

The guy picked up the duffel and the two moved aside as the next passenger in line moved up to the counter. He put the duffel down again and they stood to one side, engaged in desultory conversation. These people were about to get on a plane, and what was I supposed to do? A citizen's arrest seemed like dicey business at best. I couldn't even swear that a crime had been committed. On the other hand, what else was this guy doing up in Johnny Lee's apartment? I'd been a cop just long enough to have a nose for these things. To all appearances, the duffel bag was about to be transported out of state. I had no idea if the pair intended to return to Santa Teresa or were engaged in unlawful flight.

I turned back to the phone book and flipped through the pages with agitation, talking to myself. Come on, come on. Lawrence. Laymon. I ran a finger down the columns. Leason. Leatherman. Leber. Ah. Fifteen listings under Lee, but only one on Bay. Bucyrus Lee. Bucky's name was Bucyrus? I found a quarter in my blazer pocket, dropped it in the slot, and dialed the number. The receiver was picked up on the second ring. "Hello, Bucky?"

"This is Chester. Who's this?"

"Kinsey . . ."

"Shit. You better get over here. All hell's broken loose."

"What's going on?"

"We came home from Rosie's to find Ray Rawson crawling

down the drive. Face all bloody, hand swoll up the size of a baseball mitt. He's got two fingers snapped sideways and God knows what else. Somebody busted in again and ripped into the space under the kitchen cabinet . . ."

Over the intercom system, an announcement was being made about an American Airlines flight. "Hang on a second," I said. I put my hand across the mouthpiece. I'd missed the specifics, but it had to be the boarding call for the flight to Palm Beach. Out of the corner of my eye, I saw the guy pick up the duffel, and together he and the pregnant woman moved out of the terminal, turning left toward the American Airlines departure gate. I could feel my heart pound. I turned my attention back to Chester. "Is Rawson okay?"

"Hey, we got cop cars all over and an ambulance on the way. He don't look so good. What's all the racket? I can hardly hear you."

"That's why I called. I'm at the airport," I said. "I saw a guy coming out of the apartment with a duffel. It looks like he and some woman are about to get on a plane. I tailed him this far, but once we lose track of that bag, it's only my word against his."

"Hang on. I'll grab Bucky and head out. Just don't let go of him until we get there."

"Chester, the plane's *boarding.* Do you know what he took?"

"I have no idea. I can't even get in until the place clears out. What about airport security? Can't they give you a hand?"

"What airport security? There's not an officer in sight. I'm here by myself."

"Well, for God's sake, do *something.*"

I flashed through the possibilities. "Authorize a ticket and I'll follow him," I said.

"To where?"

"The plane's on its way to Palm Beach with a stop in Dallas. Make up your mind because two minutes more and he's out of here."

"Do it. We'll settle later. Call me when you can."

I banged the receiver down and checked the departures monitor again in passing. Beside the posted departure time for American flight 508, the word *boarding* was blinking merrily. The terminal had emptied of waiting passengers, who were apparently assembling at the gate. I trotted across the lobby to the American Airlines ticket counter. One of the two agents was busy with a passenger, but the other caught my eye. "I can help you over here."

I moved to her station. "Are there any seats available on the flight to Palm Beach?" I had no idea if the couple were on their way to Dallas or Palm Beach, but I had to assume the latter if I intended to stick with them.

"Let me see what we have. I know the flight's not full." She began to type rapidly on the computer keyboard in front of her, pausing while her eye took in the data appearing on the screen in front of her. "We have seventeen seats . . . twelve in coach and five in first class."

"What's coach fare?"

"Four hundred and eighty-seven dollars."

That wasn't bad. "And that's round trip?"

"One way."

"Four hundred and eighty-seven dollars one way?" My voice squeaked like I had just that minute reached puberty.

"Yes, ma'am."

"I'll take it," I said. "You better leave the return open-ended. I'm not sure how long I'll be staying." The truth was, I had no idea where the couple was headed. Their real destination could be Mexico, South America, or just about anywhere. I hadn't seen any sign of passports changing hands, but I couldn't rule out the possibility. Since this wasn't the same agent who'd dealt with the pregnant woman, there wasn't any point in quizzing her. I pulled out my wallet and took out a credit card, which I placed on the counter. She didn't seem to question the wisdom of the impulse. Oh, man. Chester had better pay up or I was sunk.

"Would you prefer an aisle seat or window?"

"Aisle. Near the front." For all I knew the couple would be first off the plane, and I wanted to be ready to cut and run when they did.

She typed another entry, tapping away in a leisurely manner. "You have bags to check?"

"Just carry-on," I said. I wanted to scream at her to hurry, but there wasn't any point. The ticket machine began to rattle and hum, generating my ticket, the boarding pass, and the credit card voucher, which I signed where specified. I could feel my eyes cross slightly when I saw what I'd paid. The round-trip coach fare without benefit of upgrade certificates or advance purchase discounts had cost me $974. I did some quick arithmetic. The limit on this credit card was $2,500, and I was still paying off some purchases I'd made over the summer. By my calculations, I had about four hundred bucks left. Oh, well. It wasn't like I didn't have money in my savings account. I just couldn't get to it at this hour of the night.

I took my ticket envelope, thanked the agent, and scurried out the front of the terminal and around to Gate 6, where I placed my handbag on the conveyor moving through the X-ray machine. I removed Johnny's key from my jeans pocket and tucked it in my handbag. I walked through the metal detector without incident and reclaimed my handbag on the other side. First-class passengers and parents with small children had already passed through the gate and had left the terminal. I could see them straggling across the tarmac toward the waiting plane. General boarding was now under way, and I took my place at the rear of the slow-moving line. The man in the Stetson was clearly visible.

About six passengers ahead of me, the couple stood together, saying little or nothing. She now carried the magazines, and he toted the duffel. Their behavior with each other seemed strained, their faces devoid of animation. I saw no evidence of affection except for the belly, which suggested at least one round of intimacy six or seven months back. Maybe they'd been forced to get married because of the baby. Whatever the explanation, the emotional dynamic between them seemed dead.

When they reached the gate, the guy handed her the duffel and said something. She murmured her response without looking at him. She seemed withdrawn, decidedly chilly in her reaction to him. He put an arm around her shoulder and gave her cheek a kiss. He stepped back then and tucked his hands in his pockets, looking on while she handed her boarding pass to the gate agent and walked out with the duffel in her hand. Uh-oh, now what? He waited by the gate until she'd moved out of sight. I hesitated, considering my options. I could always follow him, but the duffel was the point, at least until I found out what was in it. Once the booty was gone, how was anyone going to trace it back to the source?

The guy turned in my direction, heading for the exit. He caught my eye briefly before I could avert my gaze. I flicked another look at him and snapped a mental photograph of his grizzled face, the scar on his chin, a deeply indented line of white that began with his lower lip and continued down along his neck. He'd either gone through a window or had his face slashed.

The gate agent took my proffered ticket, handing back the torn stub from my boarding pass. If I was going to bail out, now was the time to do it. Ahead of me, across the poorly lighted expanse of asphalt, I saw the pregnant woman reach the top of the portable staircase and pass through the door of the plane. I took a deep breath and walked out onto the tarmac, where I crossed the open space to the stairs. The air was brisk and the perpetual wind that seems to whip along the runway cut through the fabric of my tweed blazer. I climbed the portable stairs, shoes tinking on the metal treads as I ascended.

I was happier once I'd crossed the threshold of the 737 into the lighted warmth of the interior. I glanced at the three first-class passengers, but the pregnant woman wasn't among them. I checked the seat number on the stub of my boarding pass: 10D, probably over the wing on the left side of the plane. While I waited for the passengers ahead of me to stow carry-on bags and settle in their seats, I managed to skim my gaze across the first few rows of coach. She was sitting eight rows back in a window seat on the right. She'd taken out a compact and was peering into the mirror. She took out a bottle of makeup, opened it, and dotted beige across her cheeks, blending it in.

At eye level, most of the luggage bins above the seats were standing open. I moved forward, waiting for the college student ahead of me to shove a canvas bag the size of an ottoman in the overhead compartment. As I passed row eight, I saw the duffel, half concealed by the pregnant woman's folded raincoat, both items shoved in between a bulging canvas garment bag, a briefcase, and a luggage cart—the very items destined to tumble out and bonk you on the head on landing. If I'd had the nerve, I'd have simply picked up the duffel and toted it with me, shoving it under my seat until I had a moment to search the contents. The pregnant woman glanced in my direction. I turned away from her casually.

I took my seat and tucked my shoulder bag under the seat in front of me. The two seats next to me were empty, and I sent up small airline-type prayers that I'd have the row to myself. In a pinch, I could flip the arms up and stretch out for a nap. The pregnant woman got up just then and stepped out into the aisle, where she reached up into the overhead bin. She pushed the garment bag aside and wrestled a hardback book from an outer pocket of the duffel. The girl stewardperson moved down the aisle behind her, snapping the overhead bins shut with a series of small bangs.

Shortly after the doors closed, the girl stewardperson stood up in front of the assembled company and gave detailed instructions, with a practical demonstration, on how to fasten and unfasten our seat belts. I wondered if there was anybody present still befuddled by this. She also explained what to do if we were on the verge of being smashed, crushed, and burned by hurtling at high velocity from our flying altitude of twenty-six thousand feet straight down through the earth's crust. To me, the little hang-down oxygen bag seemed irrelevant, but it apparently made her feel better to pass along tips about the application of this device. To distract us from the possibility of death en route, she promised us a drink cart and a snack once we were airborne.

The plane rolled away from the terminal and taxied out onto the runway. There was a pause, and then the plane began to surge forward, picking up speed with much earnest intent. We rumbled and bumbled like the little engine that could. The plane lifted off into the night sky, the lighted buildings below becoming rapidly smaller until only a hapless grid of lights remained.

7

I checked the seat pocket in front of me: barf bag, laminated card with cartoon safety procedures, boring airline magazine, and a gift catalog in case I wanted to do my midair Christmas shopping. This was going to be a long trip, and me without my trusty Leonard novel. I felt my gaze return to the pregnant woman, who was seated across the aisle and two rows forward. At this remove, I could only see a portion of her face. The tangle of auburn hair made me long to have at her with a brush.

I still couldn't believe I was doing this. I decided I'd better do a quick inventory to assess my situation. I had the clothes on my back, which consisted of my Reeboks and socks, underwear, jeans, turtleneck, and blazer. I put my hands in my blazer pockets and came up with last week's movie receipt, two quarters, and a ballpoint pen, plus a paper clip. I felt my right-hand jeans pocket, which was empty. In the other pocket I had a wadded-up tissue, which I pulled out and used to blow my nose. One by one, I removed the items from my handbag and laid them on the seat beside me. I had my wallet with my California driver's license and my PI license; two major credit cards, one of which was good for $2,500 (less the current balance, of course), the other of which I now noticed had expired. Well, damn. I had $46.52 in cash, my telephone charge card, and an ATM card, which would be useless outside California. Where was my checkbook? Ah, sitting at home on my desk, where I'd been paying bills. Virtue is pointless in a crunch, as it turns out. If I'd neglected my debts, I'd have my checkbook with me, extending my tangible assets by three or four hundred bucks. Tucked in the inner compartment of my wallet, I had my key picks, always a handy item for the impromptu jet-setter.

Additionally, I had the toothbrush and toothpaste and the clean pair of underpants I always carry with me. I also had my Swiss Army knife, my sunglasses, a comb, a lipstick, a corkscrew, the key from Johnny's safe, two pens, the used grocery list on which I'd made a note of the Taurus's license plate number, a small bottle of aspirin, and my birth control pills. Whatever else happened, I wasn't going to get pregnant, so why fret? I was, after all, on vacation, and I had no other pressing responsibilities.

I didn't have the faintest idea what I'd do once we'd landed. Obviously, I'd wait and see what course of action my traveling companion elected. If she was leaving the country, there was nothing I could do about it, as the one thing I didn't have in my possession was my passport. I could probably travel into Mexico using my driver's license, but I didn't like to do that. I'd heard too many stories about Mexican jails. On the plus side, my return ticket was paid for, so I could always get straight back on a plane and come home. In the meantime, the worst that could happen was I'd make a fool of myself . . . not exactly unprecedented in my experience.

As soon as the seat belt sign went off, I unbuckled myself and searched through the overhead bin for a pillow and a blanket. I moved to the back of the plane and utilized the in-flight plumbing, washed my hands, checked my reflection in the lavatory mirror, and picked up a copy of *Time* magazine as I returned to my seat. The pilot came on the intercom and said some piloty things in a reassuring tone. He told us about our flying altitude, the weather, and the flight course, along with our estimated time of arrival.

The drink cart came by and I treated myself to three bucks' worth of bad wine. I could hardly wait to eat my four-hundred-and-eighty-seven-dollar snack, which turned out to be a cherry tomato, a sprig of parsley, and a "deli" bun the size of a paperweight. Dessert was a foil-wrapped chocolate wafer. Once we'd been fed, the cabin lights went down. Half the passengers opted for sleep while the other half flipped on their reading lights and either read or did paperwork. Forty-five minutes passed and I noticed the pregnant woman walking past my seat.

I turned and watched with interest as she headed toward the two lavatories at the rear of the plane. I scanned the other passengers in the immediate vicinity. Most were asleep. No one seemed to be paying any attention to me. The minute the woman closed herself into the toilet, I eased out of my seat and moved two rows forward, where I sat down in the aisle seat two over from hers. I made a brief display of checking the seat pocket, as if searching out some pertinent item therein. I wasn't going to have the time (or the audacity) to take down the duffel. The woman had apparently taken her handbag with her—not very trusting of her—so I couldn't riffle the contents. I checked her seat pocket. Nothing of interest in there. All she'd left behind was the hardback Danielle Steel novel, closed now and lying in the middle seat. I checked the inside cover, but there was no name written in the book. I noticed she was using her boarding pass as a bookmark. I plucked it out, slid the stub in my blazer pocket, and returned to my seat. No one shrieked or pointed or denounced me on sight.

Moments later, the pregnant woman passed me again, returning to her seat. I saw her pick up her book. She rose halfway and checked the seat cushion under her, then leaned down and searched in the area around her seat for the missing boarding pass. I could almost see the question mark appear, cloudlike, in the air above her head. She seemed to shrug. She got up again and took a pillow and weensy blanket from the overhead bin, flipped the light out, and settled down in her seat with the blanket across her chest.

I eased the stub of her boarding pass from my blazer pocket and took in the minimal information printed on it. Her name was Laura Huckaby, her destination Palm Beach.

Dallas/Fort Worth was in the central time zone, two hours ahead of us. After three plus hours in the air, it was 1:45 in the morning by the time we finally landed. A few minutes prior to our arrival, the flight attendant came on the intercom with the gate numbers for various connecting flights. She also advised us that the plane would be on the ground for approximately one hour and ten minutes before the continuation of flight 508 to Palm Beach. If we intended to deplane, we'd need to have our boarding passes with us for reboarding purposes. Poor Laura Huckaby was now minus her boarding pass, thanks to my chicanery. I watched her with guilt, expecting her to engage in an anxious conversation with the girl stewardperson or else remain, unhappily, in her seat until the flight took off again.

Instead, once we were parked at the gate and the seat belt sign was turned off, she got up, retrieved her raincoat and the duffel, tucked the book in the outer pocket, and joined the slowly moving line of departing passengers. I didn't know what to make of this, but I was compelled to follow. We stumped along the jetway in haphazard fashion, an irregular assortment of exhausted late night travelers. The few passengers with carry-on bags gravitated toward the exits, but most people headed toward the baggage claim area. I kept Laura Huckaby well within my sights. Her auburn hair had been flattened in sleep, and the back of her jumper was pleated with horizontal wrinkles. She still had the raincoat draped over one arm, but she had to pause twice to switch the duffel from hand to hand. Where was she going? Did she think this was Palm Beach?

The Dallas/Fort Worth Airport was done in neutrals and beiges, the floor tiles clay colored. The corridors were wide and quiet at that hour of the morning. A group of Asian businessmen was driven past us in a whirring electric cart, a repetitious tone peeping to warn unwary pedestrians. The overhead lighting made us all look jaundiced. Most concession kiosks were gated and dark. We passed a restaurant and a combination news and gift shop selling hard- and paperback books, glossy magazines, newspapers, Texas barbecue sauces, Tex-Mex cookbooks, and T-shirts with Texas logos. The baggage claim area for flight 508 appeared ahead of us beyond a revolving door. Laura Huckaby pushed through ahead of me and then hesitated on the far side, as if to get her bearings. I thought at first she might be looking for someone, but that didn't seem to be the case.

I moved past her and crossed to the carousel where the bags would be coming in. I couldn't figure out what was going on. Had she always intended to deplane at this point? Was her suitcase checked all the way through to Palm Beach or only as far as Dallas/Fort Worth? A row of linked chrome-and-faux-leather chairs was arranged to the left. A television set had been mounted up on the wall in one corner, and most of the heads were tilted in that direction. Pictured, in garish color, was the wreckage of a recent plane crash, black smoke still rising from the charred fuselage in a harshly lighted landscape. The reporter spoke directly to the camera. She wore a camel-hair overcoat, snow billowing around her. The wind whipped her hair and stung her cheeks with hot pink. The sound was barely audible, but none of us had any doubts about the subject matter. I crossed to the water fountain and took a long, noisy drink.

Out of the corner of my eye I saw Laura Huckaby approach the wall-mounted directory, where she studied a set of printed instructions about how to call the shuttle service for the numerous hotels in the vicinity. She picked up the phone receiver and punched in four numbers. A brief conversation followed. I waited until she'd hung up again and then I intersected her path, falling in behind her as she approached the escalator. We descended to street level, where we proceeded through a set of plate-glass doors.

Outside, the night air was surprisingly cold. Despite the artificial lighting, a pervasive gloom blanketed the pickup area. Landscaping had been tucked in between the sidewalk and the building. Along the buff-colored facade, the grass was planted in tufts at distinctly placed intervals like the plugs on a hair transplant. I proceeded to the area marked "Courtesy Shuttles," where I turned and waited, peering patiently along the roadway. Laura Huckaby and I made no eye contact. She seemed tired and preoccupied, exhibiting no interest in her fellow travelers. At one point she winced, pressing a fist into the small of her back. Two others joined us: a portly gentleman in a business suit, toting a briefcase and a garment bag, and a young girl in a ski parka with a bulging backpack. A few cars passed at speeds sufficient to create an exhaust-laden breeze that swirled around our feet. At this hour of the morning, air traffic had diminished, but I could still hear the dull rumble of jets taking off from time to time.

Several courtesy shuttles passed us in succession. She made no move to flag them down, nor did the other two waiting with us. Finally, a red van swung around the curve into view. On the side, in flowing gold script, *The Desert Castle* was written with a symbolic castle depicted in silhouette. Laura Huckaby raised a hand, signaling the van. The driver spotted the gesture and pulled over to the curb. He stepped out of the bus and helped the businessman with his luggage while she and I got on the bus, the businessman following. The young woman with the backpack remained where she was, her gaze still focused anxiously on approaching vehicles. I found a seat near the rear of the darkened bus. Laura Huckaby ended up near the front, her cheek propped wearily against the palm of her hand. Most of her hair was straggling out of her topknot.

The driver returned to his seat and closed the door, then picked up a clipboard and turned halfway toward us to confirm the names on his list. "Wheeler?"

"Here." The man in the business suit identified himself.

"Hudson?"

To my surprise, Laura Huckaby raised her hand. Hudson? Where did that come from? Interesting development. Not only had she deplaned in a city that was not her intended destination, but she'd apparently made hotel reservations in another name. What was she trying to pull?

"I'm meeting someone," I said, speaking up in response to his inquiring look.

The driver nodded, set the clipboard aside, put the bus in gear, and took off. We followed a complicated course of crisscrossing lanes around the terminal and finally sped through the open countryside. The land was flat and very, very dark. An occasional lighted building shot up out of the blackness like a shimmering mirage. We passed what must have been restaurant row: steak house after steak house as gaudily lighted as one of the main streets in Las Vegas. A big commercial hotel finally loomed into view, one of those tasteless facilities with the room price—$69.95 single occupancy—posted right below the name. The red neon letters of the Desert Castle appeared to empty of color and then fill up again. In subscript the sign read WHERE YOU'RE GUARANTEED A GOOD KNIGHT'S SLEEP. Oh, please. The logo consisted of the outline of two green neon palms, flanking a red neon tower with crenellated battlements.

We passed an oasis of tall palms that surrounded a mock-up of the tower depicted on the building, a structure of faux stone complete with an empty moat and drawbridge. When the shuttle pulled into the hotel's passenger loading area, I hung back until Laura

Huckaby (aka Hudson) had been assisted to the curb. There didn't seem to be any bellhumans on duty. The man in the business suit picked up his briefcase and his garment bag. The three of us moved into the lobby through revolving doors, with me bringing up the rear. Aside from the duffel, Laura Huckaby was without luggage.

Inside, the "merrie aulde England" motif had been given full play. Everything was crimson and gold, heavy velvet drapes, crenellated moldings, and tapestries hung from metal pikes sticking out of the "castle" walls. Just beyond the elevators, an arrow pointed the way to the rest rooms, which were marked Lords and Damsels. At the reception desk, I made sure I was third in line, reluctant to attract Laura Huckaby's attention. Given the hotel rates, I could afford maybe two nights' stay, but I'd have to be careful about additional charges. I had no idea how long Laura Huckaby would be here. She completed the check-in procedure and crossed to the elevators with the duffel in tow. By craning my neck slightly, I could see that the bank of elevators had a vertical strip of lights, indicating the floor each elevator was on at any given moment of operation. She entered the first elevator, and once the doors closed, I murmured, "I'll be right back," to no one in particular and sped in that direction. The red light advanced systematically from floor to floor and stopped on twelve.

I returned to the counter just as the man ahead of me finished checking in and crossed to the elevators. I moved up to the desk. Given the decor, I expected the clerk to be wearing a wimple or a corselet at the very least. Instead, she wore a regulation hotel management ensemble: white shirt, navy blazer, and a plain navy skirt. Her name tag read Vikki Biggs, Night Clerk. She was in her twenties, probably new to the staff and therefore relegated to the graveyard shift. She gave me a form to fill out. I jotted down my name and address and then watched while she ran off a credit card voucher.

She glanced at the address as she stapled the voucher to the registration form. "My goodness. Everybody's coming in from California tonight," she said. "That other woman was flying in from Santa Teresa, too."

"I know. We're together. She's my sister-in-law. Is there any way you could put me on the same floor with her?"

"We'll sure try," she said. She tapped a few lines on the ubiquitous keyboard, watching the monitor, her expression studious. Sometimes I want to lean across the desk and take a look myself. From Vikki's perspective, the news wasn't that good. "I'm sorry, but that floor's booked. I have a room on eight."

"That's fine," I said. And then as an afterthought, "What room is she in?" As if Vikki Biggs had just mentioned it and it had slipped my mind.

Ms. Biggs was no dummy. I'd apparently just crossed over into hotel management no-no land. She screwed her mouth sideways in a look of regret. "I'm not allowed to give out room numbers. I'll tell you what, though. You can give her a call as soon as you get to your room and the hotel operator will be happy to connect you."

"Oh, sure. No problem. I can always check with her later. I know she's as tired as I am. Flying the red-eye is a drag."

"I'll bet. You here for business or pleasure?"

"Little bit of both."

Ms. Biggs put my room key in a folder and slid it across the counter toward me. "Enjoy your stay."

Going up in the elevator, I was treated to symphonic music while I stared at myself in the smoky-glass mirror. "You look disgusting," I said to my reflection. Once on the eighth floor, the lighting was dim and it was dead quiet. Thieflike, I padded down the wide carpeted corridor and unlocked my door. The medieval affectations hadn't extended this far. I found myself transported from fourteenth-century England to the wild and woolly West, decor left over from some previous ownership. The room was done up in burnt orange and browns, the wallpaper textured like wood paneling. The bedspread was patterned in cactus and saddles, with a variety of cattle brands stitched across the surface. I did a quick roundup survey, circling the room to appraise the accommodations.

To the right of the door was a double closet containing four wooden hangers, an iron, and an ironing boardlet two feet long with short metal feet. Across from the closet was a dressing area with a mirrored vanity and sink, with a hair dryer affixed to the wall on the right. On the counter was a four-cup coffee maker with packets of sugar and nondairy creamer. A basket held small bottles of shampoo, conditioner, and lotion, plus a little mending kit and a shower cap in a box. In the bathroom, there was a fiberglass tub with a shower nozzle extending from the wall at about neck level. The plastic shower curtain was patterned with horseshoes and bucking broncos. There was a toilet, three bath towels, a bathmat, and one of those rubber tub mats designed to reduce the chances of a nasty spill and an even nastier lawsuit.

There was no minibar, but there was a jar of cellophane-wrapped hard candies in four gaudy flavors. Well, hey. What a treat. I'd also been blessed with a telephone, a television set, and a clock radio. In the morning, I'd call Henry and get an update on the situation in Santa Teresa. In the meantime, I closed the drapes and peeled off my clothes, which I hung neatly on my meager allotment of hangers. In the interest of sanitation, I laundered my underpants while I had the chance, using a dollop of hotel shampoo. In a pinch, I could use the hair dryer and the iron to dry them before I put them on again. A quick call to American Airlines showed no flights of any kind out of Dallas to Palm Beach until later that day, which meant Laura should be in for the night.

It was close to three-thirty A.M. when I put out the Do Not Disturb sign and slipped between the sheets buck naked. I fell almost instantly into a deep, untroubled sleep. If Laura Huckaby pulled a fast one and checked out any time within the next eight hours, then forget it. I'd put myself on a plane and head home.

I woke at noon and used my travel toothbrush to get the fur out of my mouth. I showered, shampooed my hair, and got back into yesterday's clothes, using my spare underpants since my newly laundered panties were still damp to the touch. I then enjoyed a wholesome meal of hot coffee with two packets each of sugar and whitener and four hard candies, two orange and two cherry. When I finally opened the drapes, I staggered back from the harsh Texas sun. Outside, I could see dry, flat land all the way out to the horizon, with scarcely a tree or a shrub in sight. Light blasted off the only other building in view: an office complex with a mirrored exterior on the far side of the cul-de-sac. To the right, a four-lane highway disappeared in two directions with no clear indication of the destination either way. The hotel seemed to be built in the middle of a commercial/industrial park with only one other tenant. As I watched, a group of runners appeared on my left. They looked to be kids, maybe middle school age, that stage of adolescence where body sizes and types are all over the place. Tall, short, squat, and thin as rails, knobby kneed they ran, with the slower ones bringing up the rear. They were dressed in shorts and green satin singlets, but they were too far away for me to read the school name on their uniforms.

I pulled the drapes shut and went over to the bed, where I stretched out, propping pillows behind me while I put in a call to Henry. As soon as he answered, I said, "Guess where I am."

"Jail."

I laughed. "I'm in Dallas."

"That doesn't surprise me. I talked to Chester this morning and he said you were off on some kind of wild goose chase."

"What's the latest from Bucky's? Has anybody figured out what was stolen last night?"

"Not as far as I know. Chester did tell me the kickplate at the bottom of the kitchen cabinet was pried off. It looks like the old man constructed some kind of hidden compartment when he put the sink in. The space might have been empty to begin with, but more likely somebody walked off with whatever was in there."

"A secret compartment in addition to the safe? That's interesting. Wonder what he had to hide."

"Chester thinks it was war documents."

"He told me about that. I can't believe it, but I intend to find out. The fellow I saw passed the duffel over to his wife or girlfriend, and she carried it with her on the plane last night. The guy wasn't on the flight, but he probably intends to join her. She was booked through to Palm Beach, but she got off in Dallas, so naturally I did, too."

"Oh, naturally. Why not?"

I smiled at his tone. "At any rate, you might have the police check the Capri motel. I didn't have a chance to tell Chester about that. I'm not sure about the number, but it was the second unit on the right. Her pal might still be there if he hasn't taken off by now."

"I'm making notes," Henry said. "I'll pass this along to the police, if you like."

"What about Ray? Do they think he was in on it?"

"Well, he must have had *some* connection. Police tried to question him, but he clammed right up. If he knew anything about it, he wouldn't say."

"Sounds like somebody pounded on him for the information about the kickplate."

"That'd be my guess. One of the officers took him over to the emergency room at St. Terry's, but as soon as the doctor finished treating him, he disappeared and nobody's heard from him since."

"Do me a favor. Go over to the Lexington Hotel and see if he's there. Room 407. Don't call first. He may not be answering his phone—"

Henry cut in. "Too late. He's already gone, and I don't think there's much chance of his turning up. Bucky went over there this morning and his room's been cleaned out. Not surprisingly, the police are interested in him as a material witness. What about you? You want me to tell the detective what you saw?"

"You can, but I'm not sure how much good it will do. As soon as I figure out what's going on, I'll call the Santa Teresa cops myself. The police here won't have jurisdiction, and at this point I'm not even sure what kind of crime we're discussing."

"Assault, for one thing."

"Yeah, but what if Ray Rawson doesn't show up again? Even if he surfaces, he might not know the identity of his assailant or he might refuse to press charges. As for the alleged burglary, we don't even know what was stolen, let alone who did it."

"I thought you saw the guy."

"Sure, I saw him come out of Johnny's place. I can't swear he stole anything."

"What about this gal with the duffel?"

"She might not even know the significance of the bag she's toting. She certainly wasn't involved in the assault."

"Wouldn't she be guilty of receiving stolen goods?"

"We can't even swear there was a theft," I said. "Besides, she might not have the slightest idea anything's amiss. Husband comes home. She's going off on a trip. He says, Do me a favor and take this with you when you go."

"What do you intend to do?"

"I'm not sure. I'd love to get my hands on that duffel. It might give us a feeling for what the deal is here."

"Kinsey . . . ," Henry warned.

"Henry, don't *worry.* I'm not going to take any risks."

"I hate when you say that. I know what you're like. Where are you staying? I want the telephone number."

I gave him the telephone number printed on the telephone pad. "It's a hotel called the Desert Castle, near the airport in Dallas. Room 815. The woman's up on twelve."

"What's the plan?"

"Beats me," I said. "I'm just going to have to wait and see what she does. She's ticketed on through to Palm Beach, so if she gets back on a plane, I guess I'll get on, too."

He was silent for a moment. "What about money? Do you need additional funds?"

"I got about forty bucks in cash and a plane ticket home. As long as I'm careful with my credit card, I'll do great. I hope you'll impress Chester with my professionalism. I'm really not interested in getting stiffed for expenses."

"I don't like it."

"I'm not crazy about the situation myself. I just wanted you to know where I was."

"Try not to commit a felony."

"If I knew the Texas statutes, it would help," I said.

8

I went down to the lobby. I cruised the area, trying to get a feel for the place. By day, the red velvet and gilt had all the drab ambiance of an empty movie theater. A white guy in a red uniform pushed a whining vacuum cleaner back and forth across the carpeting. The night clerk was gone and the reception desk was personed by a corps of wholesome-looking navy-suited youths. No one on duty was going to give me any help. Any odd request would be referred to the shift supervisor, the assistant manager, or the manager, all of whom would regard me with the sort of skepticism I deserved. In my quest for information, I was going to have to use ingenuity, which is to say the usual lies and deceit.

Most hotel guests tend to see a facility in terms of their own needs: the concierge's desk, restaurants, the gift shop, rest rooms, public telephones, the bell stand, conference halls, and meeting rooms. In my initial foray, I was looking for the executive offices. I skirted the perimeter and finally pushed through a glass door into a lushly carpeted corridor defined by pale wood paneling and indirect lighting. The offices of various department heads were identified in gleaming brass letters.

In this part of the hotel, there was no attempt to carry out either the medieval or the buckaroo conceit. Since this was a Saturday, the glass-fronted offices of the sales manager and the director of security were dark and the doors locked. Hours of operation were neatly lettered in gold, making it clear I would have free rein until Monday morning at nine. I assumed there were security guards on duty twenty-four hours a day, but I hadn't seen one yet. The sales manager's name was Jillian Brace. The director of security was Burnham J. Pauley. I made a note to myself and continued my swing through the administrative quarters and out a door at the far end of the empty hallway.

I returned to the front desk and waited until one of the desk clerks was free. The kid who approached me was in his mid-twenties: clean-shaven, clear complected, blue eyed, and slightly overweight. According to his name tag, he was Todd Luckenbill. Mr. and Mrs. Luckenbill had made sure his teeth were straight, his manners were impeccable, and his posture was good. No earrings, no jewels in his nose, and no visible tattoos. He said, "Yes, ma'am. May I help you?"

"Well, I hope so, Todd," I said. "I'm passing through Dallas briefly on a family matter, but it happens my boss has been looking for a hotel where we can book a big sales conference next spring. I thought I might recommend this place, but I wasn't sure what sort of group package you offered. I wonder if you could direct me to the sales manager. Is he here today?"

Todd smiled, his tone slightly chiding. "Actually, it's not a 'he.'

Jillian Brace is our sales manager, but she doesn't work on weekends. You might try her Monday morning. She's usually here by nine and I'm sure she'd be happy to talk to you."

"Gee, I'd love to do that, but I have a flight out at six. Do you think you could get me her business card? I can always give her a call when I get back to Chicago."

"Sure. If you can wait just a minute, I'll bring you one."

"Thanks. Oh, and one more thing while I'm thinking about it. My boss is concerned about conference security. We had a little problem with one of the big hotels last year, and I know he's reluctant to schedule anything until he's confident about security procedures."

"What kind of business are you in?"

"Investment banking. Very high level stuff."

"You have to talk to Mr. Pauley about that. He's the director of security. You want me to get you his card, too?"

"Sure, that'd be great. I'd really appreciate it, if it's not too much trouble."

"No problem."

While he was off on his mission, I picked up a couple of postcards from a counter display. The glossy photograph on the front showed the claret red lobby with two heralds in livery tooting on horns much longer than their arms. I checked, but they didn't seem to be on the premises this morning. Todd returned moments later with a fistful of the promised business cards. I thanked him and crossed the lobby to an alcove furnished with a mahogany table and two velvet-covered banquettes.

I found some hotel stationery in the drawer and made a few notes. Then I took a deep breath, picked up one of the house phones, and asked the hotel operator to connect me with Laura Huckaby. There was a pause, and then the operator said, "I'm sorry, but I don't show a registration for anyone by that name."

"You don't? Well, that's odd. Oh, yeah. Wait a minute. Try Hudson."

The operator made no response, but she was apparently putting me through to a guest by that name. I hoped it was the right one. I made a note of the name and circled it so I wouldn't forget.

A woman answered after one ring, sounding anxious and out of sorts. "Farley?"

Farley? What kind of name was that? I wondered if he was the guy she'd left at the airport back in Santa Teresa.

"Ms. Hudson? This is Sara Fullerton, Jillian Brace's assistant down in Sales and Marketing? How are you today?" I used that false, warm tone all telephone solicitors are taught in telephone soliciting school.

"Fine," Laura said cautiously, waiting for the punch line.

"Well, that's good. I'm glad to hear that. Ms. Hudson, we're conducting a confidential survey of certain select guests, and I wonder if I might ask you a few questions. I promise this won't take more than two minutes of your time. Can you spare us that?"

Laura didn't seem interested, but she didn't want to be rude about it. "All right, but please be quick. I'm waiting for a call, and I don't want the line tied up."

My heart began to pound. If this was not the right guest, the truth would soon surface. "I understand, and we appreciate your help. Now, according to our supplemental registration records, we show that you arrived last night from Santa Teresa, California, on American Airlines flight 508, is that correct?"

There was a silence.

"Excuse me, Ms. Hudson. Is that correct?"

Her tone was wary. "Yes."

"And your arrival time was approximately one forty-five A.M.?"

"That's right."

"Did you have any difficulty reaching the hotel shuttle service when you called from baggage claim?"

"No. I just picked up the phone and dialed."

"Was the shuttle service prompt?"

"I guess. It took about fifteen minutes, but that seemed okay."

"I see. Was the driver courteous and helpful?"

"He was fine."

"How would you rate the check-in procedure? Excellent, very good, adequate, or poor?"

"I'd say excellent. I mean, I didn't have any problems or anything." She was really getting into this now, trying to be objective but fair in her response.

"We're glad to hear that. And what is the anticipated length of your stay?"

"I don't know yet. I'll be here at least one more night, but I don't know much beyond that. You want me to notify you as soon as I find out?"

"That won't be necessary. We're happy to have you with us for as long as it suits. Now if I could just ask you to confirm your room number, that's all we'll need."

"I'm in 1236."

"Perfect—1236 corresponds with our records. And that completes the survey. We appreciate your patience, Ms. Hudson, and we hope you enjoy your stay. If we can be of any further service, please don't hesitate to get in touch."

Now all I needed was a way to get into her room.

I did a second tour of the lobby, this time looking for access to the back side of the house. I was interested in the freight elevators, service stairs, any unmarked door, or any door labeled Staff. I found one that said Employees Only. I pushed my way in and descended a short flight of concrete stairs to a door marked No Admittance. They must not have been serious because the door was unlocked and I walked right in.

Every hotel has its public face: clean, carpeted, upholstered, glossy, paneled, and polished. The actual running of a hotel is done on much less glamorous terms. The corridor I stepped into had plain concrete walls and a floor of brown vinyl tile. The air here was much warmer and smelled like machinery, cooked food, and old mops. The ceilings were high and lined with pipes, thick cables, and heating ducts. I could hear the clatter of dishes, but the acoustics made it difficult to determine the source.

I checked in both directions. To my left, wide metal doors had been rolled up and I could see the loading zone. Big trucks were backed up against the loading docks and security cameras were mounted in the corners, mechanical eyes observing anyone who passed within range. I didn't want my presence noted, so I turned around and walked the other way.

I moved on down the corridor and turned a corner into the first of several kitchens that opened off one another like a maze. Six ice machines were lined up along the wall in front of me. I counted twenty rolling metal food carts with racks for trays. The floors were freshly washed, glistening with water and smelling of disinfectant. I walked with care, passing big stainless-steel mixing bowls, soup vats, and industrial dishwashers billowing steam. Occasionally, a food service worker, in a white apron and a hairnet, would glance up at me with interest, but no one seemed to question my presence down there. A black woman was chopping green peppers. A white man was encasing one of the rolling carts with plastic sheeting to protect the food. There were big room-size ovens and stainless-steel refrigerators larger than the morgue at St. Terry's Hospital. More workers in white aprons, hairnets, and plastic gloves were washing salad greens, arranging them on plates that had been laid out on the stainless-steel counter.

I stuck my head into a big storage room the size of a National Guard armory, where there were cartons of ketchup bottles; cases of mustard, olives, pickles; shelves filled with packaged bread; racks of croissants, homemade tarts, cheesecakes, pies, rolls. Plastic bins were filled with fresh produce. The air was saturated with strong smells: cut onions, simmering tomato sauce, cabbage, celery, citrus, yeast; layer upon layer of cooking and cleaning odors. There was something unpleasant about the suffusion of scents, and I was keenly aware of my olfactory nerves conducting a confused array of data to ancient parts of my brain. It was a relief to come out on the far side of the complex. The temperature in the air dropped, and the scents were suddenly as clean as a forest's. I found the main corridor and took a right.

Ahead of me, a regular choo-choo train of linen carts was lined up against the wall. The canvas sides were yellow and bulged with the mountains of soiled sheets and towels. I set off, walking with great purpose, glancing into every room I passed. I paused in the door to the hotel laundry: a vast room filled with wall-mounted washing machines, most of which were much taller than I. A moving track was suspended from the ceiling and enormous mesh bags of linens swung around the curve on a series of hooks. Somewhere I could hear massive dryers at work. The air was dense with the smell of damp cotton and detergent. Two women in uniform were working in tandem with a machine whose function seemed to be the pressing and folding of hotel sheets. The women's motions were repetitious, taking sheets out as the machine finished its two-fold process. Each packet was refolded and stacked to one side, with no margin for error as the machine pushed the next newly pressed sheet into range.

I continued down the corridor, slowing my pace. This time I passed a little half door with a narrow shelf that formed a small counter. The sign above the door said Employee Linens. Well, well, well. I paused, looking in on what must have been the laundry facility for employee uniforms. As in a dry cleaning establishment, several hundred matching cotton uniforms had been cleaned and pressed and hung on a mechanical conveyor awaiting pickup by the staff. I leaned across the Dutch door, peering through a thick forest of cleaners' bags. There didn't appear to be anyone in attendance.

"Hello?"

No answer.

I turned the knob and opened the half door, easing in. I sorted through uniforms in rapid succession. Each uniform seemed to consist of a short red cotton skirt with a red tunic worn over it. Impossible to guess what sizes they were. A paper pinned to each hanger gave the first name of the wearer: Lucy, Guadalupe, Historia, Juanita, Lateesha, Mary, Gloria, Nettie. On and on the names went. I selected three at random and eased out again, closing the door behind me.

"Can I help you?"

I jumped, nearly bumping into the hefty white woman in a red uniform who was standing right behind me in the corridor. My mind went completely blank.

The woman's nostrils flared like she could smell deception. "What are you doing with those uniforms?" I could practically see up her nose, and it was not a pretty picture. Her name tag read Mrs. Spitz, Linen Service Supervisor.

"Ah. Good question, Mrs. Spitz. I was just looking for you. I'm Jillian Brace's assistant up in Sales and Marketing." With my free hand, I reached in my blazer pocket and pulled out a business card, which I flashed at her.

She snatched the card and studied it, squinting. "This says Burnham J. Pauley. What's going on here?" She had a big face, and every feature on it seemed to quiver with suspicion.

"Well," I said. "Gosh. I'm glad you asked. Because. As a matter of fact, Corporate is considering new uniforms. For security reasons. And Mr. Pauley told Ms. Brace to show him a sample of what we had on hand."

"That's the most ridiculous thing I ever heard," she snapped. "We just got those uniforms, as *Corporate* well knows. Besides, that's not proper procedure, and I'm sick of it. I told Mr. Tompkins at our last department meeting, this is *my* operation and I mean to keep it that way. You wait right here. I'm going to call him this minute. I will not have anyone from Corporate interfering in my business." Even her breath smelled indignant. Her eyes swung back to mine. "What's your name?"

"Vikki Biggs."

"Where's your name tag?"

"Upstairs."

She pointed a finger at me. "Don't you move. I intend to get to the bottom of this. Corporate has a nerve sending anyone down here like this. What's Miss Brace's extension?"

"It's 202," I said automatically. Now you see? This is the beauty of keeping up those skills. In a crisis situation, I had only to open my mouth and a fib flopped out. An unpracticed liar can't always rise to the occasion like I can.

She let herself in through the Dutch door, moving with surprising speed. The door snapped shut behind her. I folded the hangers across my left arm and walked on with apparent purpose, heart thumping. I rounded the corner and broke into a trot. I found the stairwell and headed up the stairs two at a time. I didn't dare risk the hotel elevators. I pictured Mrs. Spitz notifying Security, guards swarming the exits in search of me. By the third floor I was winded, but I kept right on climbing. I passed the sixth floor, gasping, thighs burning, knees feeling like my kneecaps were about to pop off. I finally staggered through the door at the landing marked "8" and found myself back on familiar turf, one bend of the corridor away from my room.

I let myself into 815. I flung the contraband uniforms across the back of a chair and collapsed on the bed, which was now neatly made. I had to laugh while I lay there, trying to catch my breath. Mrs. Spitz better have her hormone levels checked or her medication adjusted. She was going to get herself fired if she continued to mouth off at Corporate. I half expected someone to come pounding at my door with demands and accusations, an itemized accounting of the lies I'd told.

I got up and crossed to the door, where I slipped on the security chain. I spent the next few minutes trying on stolen uniforms. The first was the best fit. I looked at myself in the full-length mirror. The skirt was big in the waist, but it didn't seem to matter much with the tunic pulled over it. Pinned to each tunic was a ruffle of white, which formed a sort of collar once it was buttoned into place. The tunic itself had a little puff to the sleeve. Color wasn't bad. Worn with bare legs and my running shoes, I looked like I could clean a bathroom in nothing flat. I changed back into my jeans and hung my uniform in the closet. I wasn't sure what to do with the two remaining uniforms, so I folded them together and stuck them in the desk drawer. Before I left the hotel, I'd find a place to put them.

I ate a room service lunch, fearful of venturing out into the hotel so soon. At two o'clock, I went out into the corridor on a prospecting expedition, checking the general layout of the floor. I located the fire extinguisher, two fire exits, and the ice machine. A house phone sat on a console table across from the elevators. In the utility alcove at the end of the hall, I could see two linen carts angled into the space. I walked down there and spent a few minutes acquainting myself with available equipment. Extra irons and ironing boards, two vacuum cleaners. Beyond the alcove was a big linen closet, lined with shelves stacked nearly to the ceiling with clean sheets and towels. I could see cases of toilet paper and short towers of plastic pallets containing the miniature toiletries. Nice. I was liking this. An armload of towels usually provides good cover for getting into a room. I found a plastic door placard reading Maid in Room, which I snagged while I was at it.

Having exhausted the possibilities, I went down to the gift shop and bought a book to read. I was forced to choose among fifteen torrid romance titles, which was all the hotel stocked. I paid for a handful of miniature Peppermint Patties, pausing in the lobby only long enough to ring Laura's room. When she answered, I murmured, "Ooops, sorry," and hung up. Sounded like I'd caught her in the middle of a nap. I whiled away the afternoon, reading and napping. In a spectacular failure of imagination, I ordered a room service dinner that was a duplicate of my room service lunch: cheeseburger, fries, and diet Pepsi.

Shortly after seven o'clock, I stripped out of my jeans and donned my sassy red uniform. I wasn't crazy about the bare legs with my running shoes, but what could I do? I stocked my pockets with peppermints and took the two remaining contraband uniforms from the drawer where I'd hidden them. I tucked my room key in my pocket and headed for the fire stairs. Going up, I paused on the tenth floor long enough to hang the two stolen uniforms in the utility alcove. I didn't want the other maids inconvenienced by the theft.

The twelfth floor was laid out identically to the eighth, except that the utility room didn't seem as well stocked. I grabbed a dust rag and a vacuum cleaner, found an electrical outlet in the corridor, and began to vacuum my way toward Laura Huckaby's room. The carpet was an extravagant meadow of geometric shapes, triangles overlapping in a bright path of high-low gold and green. Vacuuming is always restful: slow, repetitive motion accompanied by a low groaning noise and that satisfying snap when something really good gets sucked up. Never had the wall-to-wall carpet been so thoroughly cleaned. I was working up a sweat, but the effort did permit me to loiter at will.

At 7:36 I heard the elevator *ping* and a room service waitcreature appeared with a dinner tray. He headed toward 1236; the tray balanced comfortably at shoulder height, he knocked on her door. I vacuumed in that direction, managing to get a glimpse of her when she let him in. She was barefoot and looking bulky in a hotel robe with a nightie hanging down below. The loungewear suggested she was in for the night, which was good from my perspective. The waiter emerged moments later. He passed me without remark and disappeared into the elevator without acknowledging my existence. On the off chance that Laura would have a visitor or head out to meet someone, I stuck to my surveillance.

When I tired of vacuuming, I took out my dust rag and got down on my hands and knees, dusting baseboards that apparently hadn't been touched for years. Sometimes it's really tough to picture the boy detectives doing this. Periodically, I tilted my head against Laura Huckaby's door without hearing a thing. Maybe if I barked and scratched, she'd let me in. Other hotel guests came and went at intervals, but no one paid me the slightest attention.

Here's what I've learned about being a maid: People seldom look you in the eye. Occasionally someone's gaze might accidentally glance off your face, but based on the interaction, no one could identify you later in a lineup. Good news for me, although even in Texas I don't think impersonating a maid would be classified as a crime.

At 8:15 I returned the vacuum cleaner to the linen room and armed myself with a supply of fresh towels. I returned to 1236 and knocked, calling out "Housekeeping" in clear, bell-like tones. Worked like a charm. Moments later, Laura Huckaby opened the door a crack with the chain in place. "Yes?"

Without eye makeup, her hazel eyes seemed soft and pale. Her complexion was made ruddy by the faint rash of freckles previously masked by foundation. She also had a dimple in her chin I hadn't noticed earlier.

I directed my comment to the doorknob so I wouldn't seem uppity. "I'm here to turn the bed down."

"This hotel offers turn-down service?" She sounded appropriately startled, as if the idea were ludicrous.

"Yes, ma'am."

She paused and then shrugged. "Just a minute," she said. She closed the door. There was a delay of some minutes and then she released the chain and stepped aside to let me enter.

I was interested to realize how much I could take in through my peripheral vision. How vain could she be? I could have sworn she'd paused to put on her makeup again. The tangled auburn hair had been freshly washed and still clung to her head. Warm, damp, shampoo-scented air wafted from the bathroom. I set the clean towels on the counter near the sink and then moved into the bedroom area and closed the drapes. The television set was turned on with the sound turned down. She'd tossed her room key on the desk. Immediately, I began to scheme to get my hands on it. I could see from the disarray that she'd been lying on the bed with the telephone pulled close. Maybe she'd received the call she'd been waiting for. There was no sign of the duffel bag as far as I could see.

She took a seat at the desk with her magazine. She crossed her legs, and I caught just a flash of bare skin. Her right ankle and shin and all the way up to her knee was a sooty mass of old bruises, turning green at the edge. Had her fifty-some companion been beating the shit out of her? It would certainly explain her icy treatment of him and her obsession with her appearance. Her dinner tray still sat on the desk in front of her, a crumpled white cloth napkin tossed carelessly across the dirty plates. Whatever she'd ordered, she hadn't eaten much. Though it was ostensibly my job, she seemed embarrassed to have me in the room, which actually worked to my advantage. She ignored me for the most part, though she would flick me an occasional self-conscious look. I was beginning to enjoy my invisibility. I could observe her at close range without any pesky personal exchanges. Was that the shadow of a bruise on the right side of her jaw, or was I imagining things? What kind of guy was she with? From all reports, he'd pounded Ray Rawson to a pulp, so he might have pounded her, too.

My uniform made an efficient little rustling sound as I folded the spread in half and then in half again. I made a hefty jelly roll of it and tucked it in one corner. I turned the sheet down halfway, plumped the pillows, and left one of the paper-wrapped Peppermint Patties on the bed table.

I returned to the vanity area and tidied up the sink, turning water off and on, though I didn't do much else. I checked her makeup supply: a concealer stick, foundation, powder, blush. In a small round container, she had a product called DermaSeal, "a waterproof cosmetic to hide facial imperfections." I peered around the corner at her briefly, only to find her peering at me. Behind me was the closet, which I longed to search. I moved into the bathroom and picked up a damp towel she'd draped across the edge of the tub. I straightened the shower curtain and flushed the toilet as if I'd just given it a scrub. I moved back into the vanity area and opened the closet door. Bingo. The duffel.

I heard her call out, "What are you doing?" She sounded annoyed, and I thought I might have overstepped my bounds.

"You need more hangers, miss?"

"What? No. I have plenty."

Just being helpful. She didn't have to sound so irritated.

I closed the closet door and retrieved the remaining clean towels. She'd crossed the room and was watching me closely as I finished my chores. I transferred my gaze to a point to the left of her. "What about the tray? I can take it if you're finished."

She flicked a look at the desk. "Please."

I set the towels aside and crossed to the desk, where I picked up the room key and tucked it on the tray, concealing it with the crumpled napkin. I went over to the door and held it open with my hip while I set the tray on the floor in the corridor. I retrieved my towel supply.

She was standing near the door with something that she held in my direction. At first, I thought she was passing me a note. Then I realized she was giving me a tip. I murmured a "Thank you" and slipped the bill in my tunic pocket without looking at the denomination. Peeking might have implied a grasping nature on my part. "You have a pleasant evening," I said.

"Thanks."

As soon as I was out the door, I pulled out the bill and checked the denomination. Oh, wow. She'd given me a five. Not bad for a simple ten-minute tidy-up. Maybe I could knock on the door across the hall. If I covered the floor, I could just about afford my room tonight. I plucked her key from the room service tray and left the tray where it was. It looked tacky sitting there, and I didn't like the effect on my newly cleaned hall, but in current job parlance, removing it was not my department.

9

By the time I got back to my room, it was 8:45. I felt grubby and half dead from the combination of manual labor, stress, greasy room-service food, and jet lag. I peeled off my uniform and hopped in the shower, letting the hot water pound down my frame like a waterfall. I dried myself off and then pulled on one of the two unisex robes provided by the hotel. My spare underpants were now dry, though a bit stiff, hanging across the towel rack like the pelt of some rare beast. Coming out of the bathroom into the dressing area, I noticed the message light on my telephone was blinking. The phone must have rung while I was in the shower—inevitably Henry, since he was the only one who knew my whereabouts. Unless the hotel management was on to me. Somewhat uneasily, I rang the hotel operator.

"This is Ms. Millhone. My message light is on."

He put me on hold and then came back on the line. "You have one message. A Mr. Pitts called at eight fifty-one. Urgent. Please call back."

"Thanks." I dialed Henry's number. Before I even heard the phone ring on his end, he picked up the receiver. I said, "That was quick. You must have been sitting right on top of the phone. What's going on?"

"I'm so glad you called. I didn't know what to do. Have you heard from Ray Rawson?"

"Why would I hear from him? I thought he was gone."

"Well, he was, but he's back and I'm afraid there's been a complication of sorts. Nell and I went shopping this morning, shortly after you rang. William and Lewis had gone over to Rosie's to help with the lunch prep, and that left Charlie here by himself. Are you there?"

"Yeah, I'm here," I said. "I can't think where this is going, but I'm listening."

"Ray Rawson showed up at Chester's and Bucky told him what was going on."

"As in what? That I'd seen the guy who beat him up?"

"I'm not sure what he was told except that you'd been hired. Bucky knew you'd left town, but he didn't know where you were. Ray must have come right over here, and since I was out, he gave Charlie some long song and dance about the danger you were in."

"Danger? That's interesting. What kind?"

"Charlie never really got that part straight. Something to do with a key, is what he said."

"Ah. Probably the one Johnny had in his safe. I was going to show it to a friend of mine who's acquainted with locks. Unfortunately, I suspect he's been incarcerated for his expertise."

"Where is it now? Bucky told Ray you had it with you last he knew," he said.

"I do. It's tucked in the bottom of my handbag," I said. "You sound worried."

"Well, yes, but it's not about that." I could hear the anxiety underlying Henry's tone. "I hate to have to say this, but Charlie told Ray your current whereabouts because Ray convinced him you needed help."

"How did Charlie know where I was?"

Henry sighed, burdened by the necessity for a full confession. "I wrote the name and number of the hotel on a pad near the phone. You know Charlie. He can barely hear under the best of circumstances. Somehow he got it in his head that Ray was a good friend and you wouldn't care if he gave out the information. Especially since you were in trouble."

"Oh, boy. The room number, too?"

"I'm afraid so," Henry said. He sounded so guilty and miserable, I couldn't protest, though I didn't like the idea of Rawson knowing where I was. Henry went on. "I can't believe the man would actually fly all the way to Dallas, but he'll probably call, and I didn't want you to be surprised or upset. I'm uneasy about this, Kinsey, but there's nothing I can do."

"Don't worry about it, Henry. I appreciate the warning."

"I could just wring Charlie's neck."

"I'm sure he was trying to be helpful," I said. "Anyway, there's probably no harm done. I don't consider Ray Rawson any kind of threat."

"I hope not. I feel terrible about leaving the information out in plain sight."

"Don't be silly. You had no reason to think anybody'd ask, and you couldn't have known Rawson was going to show up like that."

"Well, I know," he said, "but I could have said something to the sibs. I gave Charlie a fussing at, but it's myself I blame. It truly never occurred to me that he'd do such a thing."

"Hey, what's done is done. It's not your fault."

"You're sweet to say so. All I could think to do was call as soon as possible. I think you should check out or at least change rooms. I don't like the idea of his showing up on your doorstep. There's something 'off' about the whole business."

"I'd have to agree, but I'm not sure what to do. At the moment, I'm trying to keep a low profile around here," I said.

I could tell I'd put Henry on red alert. "Why is that?" he asked.

"I don't really want to go into it. Let's just say that right now I don't think it's a smart move."

"I don't want you taking any chances. You were foolish getting on that plane in the first place. It's none of your business, and the longer it goes on, the bigger mess it is."

I smiled. "Chester hired me. This is work. Besides, it's fun. I get to skulk around corridors and spy on folk."

"Don't be gone too long. We've got the wedding coming up."

"I'm not going to forget that. I'll be there. I promise."

"Call me if there's anything I can do to help."

The minute he hung up, I crossed to the door and threw on the security chain. I thought about hanging the "Do Not Disturb" on the outside knob, but that would only announce to one and all that I was actually in the room. I began to pace, giving the situation my serious consideration. I felt curiously vulnerable now that Rawson knew where I was, though why that should have made a difference I wasn't really sure. From what Chester'd said, he was in pretty bad shape, which would have made travel unpleasant to say the least. It would also cost him a bundle with no guarantee that I was still in Dallas. Of course, if he was wanted for questioning by the Santa Teresa cops, getting out of town wouldn't be a bad move on his part. I didn't really believe I was in any peril, but I wasn't unmindful of the possibility. Whatever Rawson's relationship to current events, it was clear he hadn't given me the relevant facts. I would feel a lot safer if I were in another room.

On the other hand, I didn't like the idea of asking to change.

The hotel management wasn't dumb. It wouldn't have taken Mrs. Spitz more than a minute to figure out that I was up to no good. Hotels don't take lightly to pranksters and thieves. She'd seen me at close range, and at this point, the security guards probably had a fairly accurate description of me. Notice would have gone out to all the relevant staff—the hotel equivalent of an APB. If Vikki Biggs, the night clerk, remembered my name, I'd have someone knocking at my door very soon. Conversely, if the management *hadn't* figured it out, I'd be an idiot to go down there and call attention to myself. So forget the room change.

As for vacating the premises, I'd already laid out close to a grand for plane fare and expenses. I couldn't go back and confess to Chester I'd abandoned the pursuit because Ray Rawson *might* show up at my door unannounced. My best bet was staying right where I was, especially now that I had access to Laura Huckaby's room. I put my clothes on again. If someone came banging at my door in the dead of night, I didn't like the idea of being caught unprepared. I tucked the complimentary toiletries in my handbag and added my toothpaste and my traveling toothbrush, ready to flee if necessary.

I removed the key from my bag, wondering if there might be a safer place to keep it. In the morning, I'd stick it in an envelope and mail it back to Henry. Meanwhile, I surveyed the room and the various furnishings, considering possible hiding places. I was ambivalent about the prospects. If I were compelled to depart in haste, I didn't want to have to stop and retrieve the key. I took the complimentary mending kit from my handbag. I removed my blazer and studied the construction, finally using the scissors on my Swiss Army knife to pick open a small slit on the inside seam near the shoulder pad. I eased the key in along the padding and stitched the hole shut. I'd never make it past the metal detector at an airport security check point, but I could always take the blazer off and send it through X-ray.

I slept in my clothes, shoes on, feet crossed, lying flat on my back with the spread thrown over me for warmth.

When the phone rang at 8:00 A.M., I felt like I'd been electrocuted. My heart leaped from fifty beats per minute to an astounding hundred and forty with no intervening activity except the shriek I emitted. I snatched up the receiver, pulse banging in my throat. "What."

"Oh, geez. I woke you. I feel bad. This is Ray."

I swung my feet over to the side of the bed and sat up, rubbing my face with one hand to wake myself. "So I gathered. Where are you?"

"Down in the lobby. I have to talk to you. Mind if I come up?"

"Yes, I mind," I said irritably. "What are you doing here?"

"Looking after you. I thought you should know what you're dealing with."

"I'll meet you in the coffee shop in fifteen minutes."

"I'd appreciate that."

I flung myself back on the bed and lay there for a minute, trying to compose myself. Didn't help much. My insides were churning with a low-level dread. I finally dragged myself into the dressing area, where I brushed my teeth and washed my face. I sniffed at my turtleneck, which was beginning to smell like something I'd been wearing for two days. I might have to break down and buy something new. If I sent all my clothes out to be cleaned and pressed, I'd be stuck in my red uniform until six that night. Meanwhile, if Laura Huckaby took off, I'd have to trail her across Texas looking like a parlor maid. I rubbed some hotel lotion on the relevant body parts, hoping the perfume would mask the ripe scent of unwashed garments.

I tucked the two room keys in my pocket—mine and the one I'd stolen from Laura Huckaby's desk—and peered through the spy hole. At least Rawson wasn't lurking in the corridor. I went down the fire stairs, avoiding the elevator, and found myself emerging on the far side of the lobby.

When I reached the hotel coffee shop, I paused in the doorway. Rawson wasn't hard to spot. He was the only guy in there with a swollen green-and-purple face. He had a bandage across his nose, one black eye, a split lip, assorted cuts, and three fingers on his right hand bound together with tape. He drank his coffee with a spoon, possibly to spare himself the pain from broken, cracked, or missing teeth. His white T-shirt was so new, I could still see the package creases. Either he was buying his shirts a size too small or he was built better than I remembered. At least the short sleeves allowed me to admire his dragon tattoo.

I crossed the room and slid into the booth across from him. "When'd you get here?"

There were two menus on the table, and he passed me one. "Three-thirty in the morning. The plane was delayed because of fog. I picked up a rental car at the airport. I tried calling your room as soon as I got in, but the operator wouldn't put me through, so I waited until eight." His eyes were bloodshot from the battering, which gave his otherwise mild features a demonic cast. I could see that his left earlobe had been stitched back into place.

"You're too considerate," I said. "You have a room?"

"Yeah, 1006." His smile flickered and faded. "Look, I know you got no particular reason to trust me, but it's time to deal straight."

"You might have done that two days ago before we got into this . . . whatever it is."

The waitress appeared with a coffeepot in hand. She was the motherly sort, who looked as if she'd take in stray dogs and cats. Her frizzy gray hair was held in place by a hairnet, like a spiderweb across her head, and her gravelly voice suggested a lifelong affection for unfiltered cigarettes. She flicked a speculative look at Ray. "What happened to you?"

"I was in a wreck," he said briefly. "You got any aspirin, I'll leave you money in my will."

"Let me check in the back. I can probably come up with something." She turned to me. "How about some coffee? You look like you could use some."

Mutely I held up my coffee cup, and she filled it to the brim. She set the coffeepot aside and reached for her order pad. "You ready to order or you want more time?"

"This is fine," I said, indicating that the cup of coffee would suffice.

Ray spoke up. "Have some breakfast. My treat. It's the least I can do."

I looked back at the waitress. "In that case, make it coffee, orange juice, bacon, link sausage, three scrambled eggs, and some rye toast."

He held up two fingers. "Same here."

Once she'd departed, he leaned forward on his elbows. He looked like a light-heavyweight boxer the day after the championship went back to the other guy. "I don't blame you for feeling sour, but honest . . . after the break-in at Johnny's, I didn't think he'd come back. I figured that was the end of it, so who was the wiser?"

" 'He,' who?"

"I'm getting to that," he said. "Oh, before I forget. You know the key Bucky took from Johnny's safe?"

"Yes," I said cautiously.

"You still have it?"

I hesitated for a flicker of a second, and then I lied on instinct. Why confide in him? So far he hadn't told me anything. "I don't have it with me, but I know where it is. Why?"

"I've been thinking about it. I mean, it has to be important. Why else would Johnny keep it in his safe?"

"I thought you knew. Didn't you tell Charlie I was in danger because of it?"

"Danger? Not me. I never said that. I wonder where he got that idea?"

"I talked to Henry last night. He says that's how you persuaded Charlie to tell you where I was. You said I was in danger and that's why Charlie gave you the information."

Ray shook his head, baffled. "He must have misunderstood," he said. "Sure, I was looking for you, but I never said anything about danger. That's odd. Old guy can't hear. He might have got it mixed up."

"Never mind. Just skip that. Let's talk about something else."

He glanced over toward the entrance to the restaurant, where a motley group of adolescent kids were beginning to collect. It must have been the same kids I'd seen running out on the road the day before. They must have been in town for some kind of track-and-field event. The noise level increased, and Ray's voice went up to compete with the din. "You know, you really surprised me in my hotel room the other day."

"How so?"

"You were right about Johnny. He was never in the service. He was in jail like you said."

I love being right. It always cheers me up. "What about the story about how you knew each other? Was any of that true?"

"In the main," he said. He paused and smiled, revealing a gap where a first molar should have been. He put a hand against his cheek where the bruising was deep blue with an aura of darker purple. "Don't look now, but we're surrounded."

The track team seemed to spread out and around us like a liquid, settling into booths on all sides of us. The lone waitress was passing out menus like programs for some sporting competition.

"Quit stalling," I said.

"Sorry. We did meet in Louisville, but it wasn't at the Jeffersonville Boat Works. It wasn't 1942, neither. It was earlier. Maybe '39 or '40. We were in the drunk tank together and struck up a friendship. I was nineteen at the time, and I'd been in jail a couple times. We hung out together some, you know, just messing around. Neither of us went in the army. We were both 4-F. I forget Johnny's disability. Something to do with a ruptured disk. I had two busted eardrums and a bum knee. Bad weather, that sucker's still giving me fits. Anyway, we had to do *something*—we were bored out of our gourds—so we started burglarizing joints, breaking into warehouses, stores, you know, things like that. I guess we pulled one job too many and got caught in the act. I ended up doing county time, but he got sent to state reformatory down in Lexington. He did twenty-two months of a five-year bid and moved his family out to California once he got sprung. After that, he was clean as far as I ever heard."

"What about you?"

He dropped his gaze. "Yeah, well, you know, after Johnny left, I fell into bad company. I thought I was smart, but I was just a punk like everyone else. A guy steered me wrong on another job we pulled. Cops picked us up and I got sent to the Federal Correctional Institution up in Ashland, Kentucky, where I spent another fifteen months. I was out for a year and then in again. I never had the dough for a fancy-pants attorney, so I had to take pot luck. One thing and another, I've been inside ever since."

"You've been in prison for over forty years?"

"Off and on. You think there aren't guys who've been in prison that long? I could've been out a lot sooner, but my temper got the better of me until I finally figured out how to behave," he said. "I suffered from what the docs call a 'lack of impulse control.' I learned that in prison. How to talk that way. Back then, if I thought of it, I did it. I never killed nobody," he added in haste.

"This is a big relief," I said.

"Well, later in prison, but that was self-defense."

I nodded. "Ah."

Rawson went right on. "Anyway, in the late forties, I started writing to this woman named Marla I met through a pen pal ad. I managed to escape once and I was out long enough for us to get married. She got pregnant and we had us a little girl I haven't seen in years. A lot of women fall in love with inmates. You'd be surprised."

"Nothing people do surprises me," I said.

"Another time, when I was out, I ended up breaking parole. Sometimes I think Johnny felt responsible. Like if it hadn't been for him, I might never have gotten in so tight with the criminal element. Wasn't true, but I think that's what he believed."

"You're saying Johnny kept in touch all these years because of guilt?"

"Mostly that," he said. "And maybe because I was the only one who knew he'd been in jail besides his wife. With everybody else, he was always pretending to be something he wasn't. All the tales about Burma and Claire Chennault. He got those from books. His kids thought he was a hero, but he knew he wasn't. With me, he could be himself. Meantime, I got into grand theft auto and armed robbery, which is how I finally qualified for accommodations in the penitentiary. I did time in Lewisburg and a bid in Leavenworth, but I was mostly confined in Atlanta. That's a real test of your survival skills. Atlanta's where they're housing all the Cuban criminals Castro's sending over to keep us company."

"What happened to Marla? Are you still married to her?"

"Nah. She finally divorced me because I couldn't straighten up and fly right, but that was my fault, not hers. She's a good woman."

"It must be unsettling to have freedom after forty years."

Rawson shrugged, looking off across the room. "They did what they could to prepare me for the outside. When I turned sixty, the BOP—Bureau of Prisons—started weaning me off hard time. My security level dropped to the point where I was eligible to move out of the joint. I got sent back to FCI Ashland, and what a revelation *that* was. It'd been thirty-five years since I'd seen the place. I'm looking at punks the same age as I was when I first got sent up. All of the sudden, I'm 'getting it,' you know? Like I can see the big picture. I did a complete turnaround in the space of a year, picked up my GED, and started taking college classes. I started taking care of myself, quit smoking, started lifting weights, and like that. Got myself buffed up. I went before the parole board this time and got early release."

Ray paused to look around at the kids nearby. They were crowded into booths and tables, chairs pulled up. Menus were being passed hand to hand above their heads while the rustle of restless laughter washed across them in waves. It was a sound I liked, energetic, innocent. Ray shook his head. "Kids are up on my floor, about two doors down. My God, the shrieking and pounding up and down the halls. It goes on 'til all hours."

"Are you still in touch with Marla?"

"Now and then. She remarried. Last I heard, she's still in Louisville somewhere. I'd like to go back and see her as soon as I'm done with this. I want to see my daughter, too, and make it up to her. I know I haven't been a good father—I was too busy screwing up—but I'd like to try. I want to see my mother, too."

"Your *mother's* still alive?" I asked, incredulous.

"Sure. She's eighty-five, but she's as tough as they come."

"Not that it's any of my business, but how old are you?"

"Sixty-five. Old enough to retire if I ever had a real job."

"So you were released fairly recently," I said.

"About three weeks ago. I went from Ashland to six months in a halfway house. Soon as I was sprung, I headed for the coast. I wrote to Johnny in April and gave him my release date. He said to come ahead, he'd help me out. So that's what I did. The rest is just like I told you before. I didn't know he was dead until I knocked on Bucky's door."

"What kind of help was Johnny talking about?"

Rawson shrugged. "Place to stay. A stake. He had some ideas about a little business we could run. I worked in the joint—every able-bodied inmate works—but I was only earning forty cents an hour, out of which I had to pay for my own candy bars, soda pop, and deodorant, stuff like that, so it's not like I had any kind of savings built up."

"How'd you pay for travel getting out here?"

"My mother lent me the money. I said I'd pay her back."

"Who's the guy who broke into Johnny's place?"

"His name is Gilbert Hays, a former celly of mine. He's a guy I did time with a couple of years ago. I shot off my big mouth, trying to impress the crud. Don't ask why. He's such a cocky piece of excrement, I'm still kicking myself." His grimace opened up the split in his lower lip. A line of blood welled out. He pressed a paper napkin to his mouth.

"Shot your mouth off about what?"

"Look, we're in the joint. What do any of us have to do except BS each other? He was always bragging about something, so I told him about Johnny. The guy was a miser, always squirreling cash away. Johnny didn't come right out and say so, but he used to hint he had big bucks hidden on the property."

"You were going to rip him off?"

"Not me. Hey, come on. I wouldn't do that to him. We were just telling tall tales. Later, Hays and me had a falling-out. He probably figured he could pick up a wad of cash and I'd never know the difference."

"You told him where Johnny *lived*?"

"California is all I said. He must've followed me across country, the slimy son of a bitch."

"How'd he know you'd been released?"

"Now that, I don't know. He might have talked to my PO. I seem to recall I might've threatened him once upon a time. He probably told 'em he was worried I'd come after him. Which I still might."

"How did you figure out it was him?"

"I didn't at first. Minute I heard about the break-in, I knew something was off, but I didn't think about Hays. Then I realized what happened and, like, it had to be him. Simple process of elimination because I never breathed a word about Johnny to anyone else." Ray lifted the napkin away from his bleeding lip. "How's that?"

"Well, it isn't *gushing,*" I said. "Can we back up a bit? Once you heard Johnny was dead, what made you so sure he still had money stashed somewhere?"

"I wasn't *sure,* but it just made sense. Guy drops dead of a heart attack, he doesn't have time to do anything. Talking to Bucky, I realized the kid didn't have a dime, so if there's money, it's probably still hidden somewhere on the premises. I figure if I rent his place, I can look around at my leisure."

"Meanwhile, you didn't say a word to Bucky about this."

"About the money? No way. You know why? Suppose I'm wrong? Why get their hopes up if there's nothing? If I do find some money, I can ask for a cut."

"Oh, right. This is money they don't know anything about and you're telling me you'd turn it over to them?"

He smiled sheepishly. "I might skim off a small percentage, but what harm would that do? They're still gonna come up with more than they ever had reason to expect."

"And in the meantime, this former cellmate's followed you to Johnny's door."

"That's my guess."

"How'd he know about the kickplate?"

Ray held up his battered hand. "Because I told him. Otherwise, he'd have broken every bone in my hand. He had me at a disadvantage because I wasn't expecting him. Next time I'll know, and one of us is going to end up dead."

"How did you know about the kickplate?"

Ray tapped himself on the temple. "I know how Johnny's mind worked. That day I came up there and you were looking through his books? I was doing a little survey. He'd used a kickplate before —this was way back when—so I was thinking I'd try that first." He stirred in his seat. "You don't believe me. I can tell by the look on your face."

I smiled slightly. "You're a very slick man. You lie about as well as I do, only you've had more practice."

He started to say something, but the waitress had reappeared with two steaming plates on a tray. She looked harried, to say the least. She set down juice, two side orders of buttered toast, and a variety of jams. She took a couple of small paper packets from the pocket of her uniform and put them by his plate. "I got you these," she said.

Ray picked up a packet. "What's Midol?"

"For cramps, but it'll cure anything that ails you. Just don't take too many. You might develop PMS."

"PMS?" he said blankly.

Neither of us responded. Let him figure it out. She refilled our coffee cups and moved on to another table, taking out her order pad. Ray opened a paper packet and tossed back two tablets with his orange juice. We spent a short, intense spell shoveling food down our throats.

Rawson finally dabbed a paper napkin gingerly across his lips. "You want my suggestion, I'd say let's quit hassling what's past and figure out what comes next."

"Ah. Now we're partners. The buddy system," I said.

"Sure, why not? Gilbert Hays took Johnny's money, and I want it back. This is not just for me. I'm talking about Bucky and Chester. Isn't that why they hired you? To return what Hays stole?"

"I suppose," I said.

He shrugged laconically. "So how about it, then? What's the plan?"

"How come it's up to me? You think of one," I said.

"You're the one getting paid. I'm just here to assist."

I studied him, debating the garbled tale he'd just told. I didn't really believe he was telling me the truth, but I didn't know him well enough to know what kinds of lies he told. "Actually, there is one possibility, and I could use some help," I said.

"Good. What's the deal?"

I took out Laura's room key and placed it on the table. "I have the key to Laura Huckaby's room."

His face went completely blank, and then his brow was furrowed by a squint. He leaned forward, staring. He said, "What?"

"The woman with the duffel. She's using the name Hudson, but that's the key to her room."

10

I hauled one of the linen carts out of the utility alcove on Laura Huckaby's floor. I had changed into my red uniform again, ready to go to work. I pulled a stack of clean sheets and towels from the shelf in the linen room and put them on my cart, adding boxes of tissues, toilet paper, toiletries, and the laminated Maid in Room sign I'd snitched before. I checked the clipboard attached to the cart on one end. A ballpoint pen was affixed to the clipboard with a tatty piece of string. None of the rooms had been done as far as I could see. Bernadette and Eileen were listed on the worksheet, but none of their duties had been checked off as yet. I wasn't sure what would happen if one of them showed up in the midst of my faux labors. Surely nobody would object to my pitching in . . . unless these women got territorial about toilet bowls. I pushed the linen cart ahead of me down the carpeted corridor. The wheels kept getting hung up in the high-low pile, and I struggled to keep the cart from lumbering into walls.

The plan Ray Rawson and I had worked out was this: Rawson would call Laura's room from the house phone on the far side of the lobby within view of the front desk. He'd claim to be the desk clerk, in receipt of a package that required her signature. He'd tell her he was just now going on his break, but the package would be waiting on the manager's desk. If she could come down as soon as possible, one of the other clerks would be happy to get it for her. If she asked to have it sent up, he'd inform her, regretfully, this was against hotel policy. Recently a package had been misdelivered, and the manager was now insisting the guests appear in person.

While this was going on, I was to loiter in the corridor near her room, making careful note of the time she left. As soon as the "down" elevator doors closed behind her, I would let myself into 1236 with her key. Laura would reach the lobby, where the desk clerk would search in vain for the nonexistent package. Confusion, upset, and apologies forthcoming. Everyone would profess ignorance of both package and policy. Sorry for the inconvenience. As soon as the package surfaced, it would be sent up.

Once she left the desk, on her way upstairs again, Rawson would call the room and let the phone ring once. That would be my cue to get out if I was still there. Since I knew exactly where the duffel was located, it shouldn't take more than ten seconds to snag the contents. By the time Laura emerged from the elevator on twelve, I'd be heading down the fire stairs to the eighth floor again. There I'd change into my street clothes and grab my shoulder bag. I would meet Rawson in the lobby, and before Laura even realized that she'd been ripped off, we'd be on our way to the airport, where we'd get the next flight out. I wasn't at all bothered by the ethics of stealing money from thieves. It was the notion of getting caught made my heart go pitty-pat.

I positioned my cart two rooms away from Laura's door and

checked my watch. Rawson was waiting to make his call at 10:00, allowing me time to get myself set up. It was 9:58. I occupied myself with a load of towels, which I folded and refolded, wanting to be busily engaged when Laura Huckaby came out. The corridor was dead quiet, and the acoustics were such that I could hear the telephone begin to ring when he called her room. The phone was picked up after two rings and a tidy silence ensued. I could feel my stomach churning with anticipation. Mentally I rehearsed, picturing her trip down the hall, into the elevator, over to the desk. Chat with the clerk, the search for the package, frustration and assurances, and back she'd come. I'd have at least a five-minute window of opportunity, more than ample time for the task I'd assigned myself.

I checked my watch again: 10:08. What was taking her so long? I thought she'd be wildly curious about the arrival of a package, especially one that required her signature. Whatever the delay, it was 10:17 before she emerged. I kept my face averted, avoiding her gaze as I picked up my clipboard and made random marks. She closed the door behind her and then caught sight of me. "Oh, hi. Remember me?"

I looked up at her. "Yes, ma'am. How are you?" I said. I put the clipboard down and picked up a towel, which I folded in half.

"Did you come across my key when you serviced the room last night?" She wore the usual heavy makeup, and her hair was pulled back in a ponytail, tied with a scarf of bright green chiffon.

"No, ma'am, but if it's missing, you can get a duplicate at the front desk." I folded another towel and put it on the stack.

"I guess I'll do that," she said. "Thanks. Have a good day."

"You too." I studied Laura's backside as she moved toward the elevators. She wore a white cotton turtleneck under a dark green corduroy jumper that may or may not have been designed for maternity wear. The hemline was longer in the back than it was in the front. She tugged at the garment, which was bunching up around the middle. She wore her red high-top tennis shoes, and her tights today were dark green. If my suspicions were correct and she was the victim of spousal abuse, it might explain her tendency to keep herself covered up. I slid my hand into my pocket, where her five-dollar tip was still neatly folded from the night before. That bill was the only flicker of recognition I'd netted in my guise as a char. I wished she hadn't seemed so friendly. I suddenly felt like a dog for what I was about to do.

She rounded the corner. I set the towels aside and took out the key. There was a pause. I felt like I was waiting for a starter gun to go off. I heard the indicator *ping* as the elevator reached the floor, then the muffled sound of doors sliding shut again. I was already moving toward the door to 1236. I shoved the key in the lock, turned it, opened the door, and tagged the knob with the laminated Maid in Room sign, just in case she came back without warning. 10:18. I did a quick check to verify that both the room and the bathroom were empty as expected. I flipped the light on in the dressing area.

Since last night, additional toiletries had been unpacked and arranged around the sink. I moved to the closet and opened the door. The duffel was right where I'd seen it before, with her handbag tucked beside it. I hauled the duffel out of the closet and propped it up on the counter. I did a superficial examination, making sure the bag wasn't booby-trapped in some way. The duffel was made of heavy-duty beige canvas, probably waterproof, with dark leather handles and a pocket on one side for magazines. There was a flap-closure compartment on each end of the bag, where smaller items could be tucked. I unzipped the main compartment and sorted through the contents at breakneck speed. Socks, flannel pajamas, clean underwear, panty hose. I checked the compartment on either end, but both were empty. Nothing in the outside pocket. Maybe she'd removed the cash and put it someplace else. I checked the time: 10:19. I probably still had a good three minutes to go.

I put the duffel back and picked up her handbag, riffling through the contents. Her wallet held a Kentucky driver's license, assorted credit cards, miscellaneous identification, and maybe a hundred bucks in cash. I put the handbag back beside the duffel. How much cash could we be talking about, and how much space could it occupy? Standing up on tiptoe, I checked the closet shelf, which was bare to the touch. I felt inside her raincoat pockets, then slipped a hand into the pockets of the denim dress she'd worn, now hanging beside the raincoat. I tried the cabinet under the sink, but all it contained was the water pipes and a shut-off valve. I did a quick survey of the shower surround and the toilet tank. I went into the main room, where I slid open drawer after drawer. All were empty. Nothing in the TV cabinet. Nothing in the bed table.

The phone rang suddenly. Once. Then silence.

My heart started banging. Laura Huckaby was on her way up. I was flat out of time. I moved to the desk and pulled out the pencil drawer, peering to see if there was something taped under it. I got down on my hands and knees and peered under the beds, then pulled the spread back and raised the edge of the mattress on the nearest of the two. Nope. I tried the other bed, extending my arm between the mattress and the box springs. I hauled myself up and smoothed the covers back in place. I searched the duffel again, rooting through the jumble of clothing, wondering what I'd overlooked. Maybe there was a second zippered compartment inside the first. Oh, to hell with it. I grabbed up the duffel and headed to the door. I snagged the Maid in Room sign and pulled the door shut behind me. I heard the elevator indicator *ping* and then the sound of the doors sliding open. Hastily I shoved the duffel under a pile of clean sheets and began to push the cart down the hall.

Laura Huckaby passed me, walking rapidly. She had a room key in hand, so at least her trip down hadn't been a total waste. This time she didn't even look in my direction. She let herself into her room and shut the door with a bang. I shoved the cart into the alcove at the end of the hall, pulled out the duffel, and scurried toward the fire exit. I pushed my way into the stairwell and started down at a run, skipping every other step. If Laura Huckaby was at all suspicious, it wouldn't take her long to spot the subtle disarray.

I pictured her heading straight to the closet, cursing her stupidity when she saw the duffel was missing. She'd have to know she'd been had. Whether she'd set up a stink or not would depend on how much nerve she had. If she'd been carrying a large amount of legitimate cash, why not take advantage of the hotel safe? Unless the booty itself was what Ray Rawson had lied about.

I reached the eighth floor and pushed the door open, heading for 815. I pulled up short. A man in a business suit was standing in the hall outside my room. He turned when he caught sight of me. I caught a glimpse of the name tag pinned to his suit. The duffel suddenly seemed enormous and quite conspicuous. Why would a maid be toting a canvas bag of this sort? I moved automatically toward the utility alcove. My chest felt hot and I was starting to hyperventilate. Out of the corner of my eye, I watched as he knocked on my door again. Casually, he checked the corridor in both directions, then took out a pass key and let himself into my room. Oh, God, now what?

I put the duffel on a shelf in the linen room and put a stack of clean sheets on top of it. The sheets tumbled to the floor and the duffel toppled with them. I gathered up the duffel and shoved it temporarily into an enormous laundry bag meant for dirty linen. I got down on my knees and began to refold sheets. I had to do something while I waited for the guy to get out of my room. I peered around the door. No sign of him, so I had to assume he was still in my room, nosing through my belongings. My shoulder bag was in the closet, and I didn't want him searching it, but I really didn't have a way to stop him, short of setting fire to the place. I heard the door to the fire exit open and close. Please, please, please, God, don't let it be one of the real maids, I thought. Someone stepped into view. I looked up. Well, my prayers had been answered. It wasn't the maid, it was the security guard.

I felt a flash of fear move up my frame, heat bringing color to my face. He was in his mid-forties, short hair, glasses, clean-shaven, overweight. In my opinion, he should have been doing situps for the gut he sported. He stood there, watching me fold a pillowcase. I smiled blankly. I felt like an actress in a play suffering acute stage fright. All the spit left my mouth and seeped out the other end.

"May I ask what you're doing?"

"Ah. I was just straightening these sheets. Mrs. Spitz told me to check the linen supply up here." I struggled to my feet. Even in my guise as a lowly chambermaid, I didn't want him to tower over me.

He stared at me carefully. The look in his eyes was flat, and his tone was a mix of authority and judgment. "Can I have your name?"

"Yes." I realized I'd better give him one. "Katy. I'm new. I'm in training. Eileen and Bernadette are actually working this shift. I'm supposed to help, but I dropped these sheets." I tried to smile again, but my expression came closer to a simper.

He studied me with calculation, apparently weighing the truth value of the statement I'd made. His gaze flicked down to my uniform. "Where's your name tag, Katy?"

I put my hand across my heart like the Pledge of Allegiance. I couldn't think of a response. "I lost it. I'm supposed to get another one."

"Mind if I verify that with Mrs. Spitz?"

"Sure, no problem. Go right ahead."

"What's your last name?" He'd already taken out his walkie-talkie and his thumb was moving toward the button.

"Beatty, like in Warren Beatty," I said without thinking. I realized belatedly my name was now Katy Beatty. I plowed right on. "If you came up to find the manager, he's in 815. The woman he's looking for is on her way downstairs," I said. I pointed in the direction of 815. My hand was shaking badly, but he didn't seem to notice. He'd turned to glance down the corridor behind him.

"Mr. Denton is up here?"

"Yes. At least, I think that's him. I got the impression he was looking for that woman, but she just left."

"What's the problem?"

"He didn't say."

He lowered the walkie-talkie. "How long ago was this?"

"Five minutes. I was just getting off the elevator when she got on."

He paused, staring at me as he reached back and secured his walkie-talkie on his belt. His gaze dropped to my feet and then came up again. "The shoes aren't regulation."

I looked down at my feet. "Really? Nobody ever said anything to me."

"If Mrs. Spitz sees those, you're going to get written up."

My whole face was aflame. "Thanks. I'll remember that."

He moved down the corridor. I stood there transfixed, longing to flee, reluctant to move for fear of calling attention to myself. He tapped on my door. A moment passed and the door was opened a crack. The security officer conferred with the guy in my room. Then the guy in the suit came out and pulled my door shut behind him. The two men moved quickly down the hall toward the elevators. I waited until I heard the elevator *ping* and then I retrieved the duffel from its hiding place. The elevator doors were barely closed when I double-timed down the hall, let myself into my room, and slid the chain into place. How long would it take before they figured out that Kinsey Millhone and the nonregulation maid without name tag were one and the same?

I reached down and flipped my shoes off. I pulled the red tunic over my head, unzipped the uniform skirt, and stepped out of it. I leaned against the wall while I pulled on my crew socks. I grabbed my jeans and stepped into them, hopping off-balance as I pulled them up. I tugged my turtleneck over my head, shoved my feet back in my shoes, and left the laces flopping loose. I opened the closet door. My handbag was still on the floor where I'd left it, but a glance was all it took to verify that the guy in the suit had been rooting around in it. Shit heel. I yanked the blazer off the hanger and shrugged myself into it. I did a quick survey of the room to make sure I hadn't left anything behind. I remembered the five-dollar tip in my uniform pocket and retrieved that. I picked up the duffel and started to let myself out. I went back, snatched the red uniform off the floor, and made a ball of it, shoving it into the zippered compartment of the duffel bag. If they searched again, why give them the satisfaction of finding it? I pulled the door shut behind me, then half walked, half trotted toward the fire stairs.

I went down eight flights of steps. When I reached the door to the lobby, I opened it a crack and looked out. A small group of businessmen seemed to be having an impromptu meeting in one of the conversational groupings. Papers had been spread out on the table. I peered around to the left. There was a couple conferring with the concierge, who seemed to be holding a map of the area. There was no sign of Mr. Denton or the security guard. No sign of Ray Rawson, either, for that matter. He'd said he'd meet me by the house phone, which I could plainly see across the lobby. The area was deserted, but too exposed for my taste.

I looked to my right. There was a bank of pay telephones about five feet away and, beyond that, the "Lords" and "Damsels." Across from me to the left was the entrance to the coffee shop. I left the relative safety of the stairwell and eased down the corridor and into the ladies' room. Two of the five stall doors were closed, but when I checked under the partitions, there were no feet in evidence. I locked myself in the handicapped stall, perched on the toilet seat, and tied my shoes. Then I emptied the duffel, shaking the contents out onto the floor.

First I checked the bag itself, peering into every pocket and crevice, sticking my fingers down into every corner. I'd thought I might find some kind of hidden compartment, but there didn't seem to be anything of the sort. I manipulated every seam, every brad, and every joining. I inspected each item of clothing I'd dumped out on the floor, folding and repacking the stolen uniform, a pair of cotton pajamas, two pairs of tights, T-shirts, tampons, two bras, and countless pairs of undies and socks. There was absolutely nothing there.

I could feel my anxiety begin to mount. I'd followed this pointless piece of luggage across three states, operating on the assumption that it contained something worth pursuing. Now it looked like all I was ending up with was a pile of secondhand lingerie. What was I to tell Chester? He was going to be furious when I told him I'd flown all the way to Dallas for *this.* The man didn't have the money to send me barreling across the country on the track of cotton panties. I'd broken the law. I was flirting with jail. I'd risked both my license and my livelihood. I began shoving items back into the zippered compartment. Happily, the panties looked like they'd fit, and I could use a clean pair. I hesitated. Nah, probably not a good idea. If I were arrested for theft, it might be better if I weren't wearing the evidence on my butt.

I emerged from the stall, trying to look nonchalant instead of like some big-time fugitive underwear bounty hunter. I couldn't bring myself to abandon the duffel. Basically, I was still clinging to the notion that it represented some rare and priceless artifact instead of my ticket to the joint. I glanced left across the lobby toward the house phone, but there was still no sign of Ray. I planted myself at one of the public telephones. I fumbled in my blazer pocket, emptying the contents in my search for change. On the metal shelf I laid out the movie receipt, the ball-point, my five-dollar tip, two quarters, and the paper clip. I dropped one of the quarters in the coin slot and then put a call through to Chester in California, charging it to my telephone credit card. I got my quarter back and placed it with the first, idly rearranging the items for the calming effect. I didn't think Chester would be happy. I was hoping he'd be out, but the man himself picked up on the third ring. " 'Lo."

"Hello, Chester? This is Kinsey."

"Can you speak up? I can't hear you. Who is this?"

I cupped a hand across the mouthpiece, turning my body away

so I wouldn't be shouting my name across the lobby. "It's me. Kinsey," I hissed. "I got the duffel, but there's nothing of significance in it."

Dead silence. "You're kidding."

"Uh, no, actually I'm not. Either the goods were moved or there wasn't anything stolen in the first place."

"Of course they stole *something!* They ripped the friggin' kickplate off the kitchen cabinet. Pappy probably hid cash."

"Did you ever *see* any cash?"

"No, but that doesn't mean it wasn't there."

"That's pure speculation. Maybe the guy busted in and didn't find anything. The duffel might have been empty." I began to rearrange the items on the shelf, placing one of the quarters over Lincoln's face on the five-dollar bill. On the quarter, George Washington looked naked, while on the bill, Lincoln was all dressed up in his Sunday suit. They must have caught George in the sauna with his hair pulled back.

Chester, sounding cranky, said, "I don't get this. Why call me just to lay out a line of horseshit like this?"

"I thought you should get an update. It only seemed fair."

"Fair? You think it's fair I spent all that money flying you to Dallas for nothing? I expected results."

"Wait a minute. So far you haven't spent a dime. *I've* spent the money. You're supposed to pay me back." I uncapped my ballpoint pen and gave Lincoln a mustache, which made his nose look smaller. I'd never paid attention to what a hooter he had.

"Pay you back for what? Air and sunshine? Forget it."

"Come on. We made a decision that turned out to be wrong."

"Then why should I pay? I'm not going to pay for your incompetence."

"Chester, believe me, I'm earning my keep. I could get my license yanked for half the things I've done. I'm not even allowed to do business in this state." I put the two quarters over opposite corners of the five-dollar bill to anchor it.

"That's your problem, not mine. I wouldn't have agreed if I'd known you were off on some wild goose chase."

"Well, neither would I. That's the chance we took. You knew as much as I did going in," I said. To amuse myself, I wrote a bad word on the front of the five-dollar bill. It was the only way I could think of to keep from screaming at him.

"To hell with it. You're fired!" I heard him say, "Goddamn it!" to himself just as he banged the phone down in my ear.

I made a face at the dead receiver and then rolled my eyes. I hauled up the phone book and started looking up the reservation number for American Airlines. It was embarrassing to admit this had all been for nothing, but I couldn't see what good it would do to stay in Dallas. I'd made a mistake. I'd known at the outset my actions were impulsive. I'd been operating on the best information I had, and if my judgment turned out to be misguided, there was nothing I could do about it now. I noticed I was busy defending myself, but I really couldn't help it in the wake of Chester's disgruntlement. Who could blame the man?

I picked up the five and held it closer, looking at the fine details. Paper currency has a baroque assortment of shaded names and numbers, lacy scrollwork, and official seals. Now *that* was weird. Since when was Henry Morgenthau secretary of the treasury? And who was this guy Julian, whose eensy-teensy signature was so impossible to read? Just to the right of Lincoln's portrait, it said "Series 1934 A." I dug in my handbag and pulled out my wallet, checking the few bills I carried. The only other five I had in my possession was a series 1981 Buchanan-Regan. The one-dollar bills were 1981 Buchanan-Regans and 1981-A Ortega-Regan with a couple of brand-new 1985 Ortega-Bakers thrown in. A twenty and a ten seemed to be the same vintage. If I wasn't mistaken, it meant the five-dollar tip Laura Huckaby had given me was a bill dating back to 1934. Didn't that indicate she was busy spending money from a cache of old bills? Surely she didn't simply happen to have a bill like that in her possession.

I put the phone book down, abandoning the notion of getting back on a plane. Maybe all was not lost. I picked up the duffel and moved forward, scanning the expanse of lobby within view. The five businessmen leaned toward each other, passing the pages of some report between them. As usual, in such a group, one fellow seemed to command the attention of the others. Behind me the door opened abruptly, and before I could turn around, I was snagged by the elbow and pulled into the stairwell.

11

Where the hell have you been?"

I turned, astonished. It was Ray, his badly bruised face about six inches from mine. He'd removed the tape from his nose, but it still looked like his nostrils were packed with cotton. His skin smelled medicinal, the sort of aftershave you'd sport in an emergency room, composed of equal parts rubbing alcohol, adhesive tape, and suturing material. He still clutched me with his injured hand, his splinted fingers held stiffly.

"Where have *I* been? Where have *you* been?" Our voices seemed to ricochet up the stairwell like a flock of shrieking birds. Both of us glanced upward and lowered our tones to rasping whispers. Ray urged me into the cul-de-sac formed by the final flight of steps where it dead-ended at the wall.

"Christ, those guys are on to you," he hissed. "Some yo-yo with a walkie-talkie's been giving me the third degree. I'm waiting by the house phone and he asks if I'd mind 'stepping into the office.' What was I supposed to do? He knows who you are and he wants to know what you're doing here."

"Why'd he ask you?"

"He'd been checking around. The waitress must have told him she'd seen us together. I wasn't hard to spot. With a mug like this? I told him you were a private investigator working undercover on a case I wasn't at liberty to discuss."

"Who did he think you were, a cop?"

"I told him I was part of a witness protection program, being moved to another state. I had to talk like this was all very hush-hush, life-or-death stuff."

"They couldn't have believed you. How'd you get away?"

"They don't give a shit who I am. They just want me out of here. I said I'd go up to the room and get my things. They escorted me to the elevator, and as soon as they left, I turned around and came down. Is that the duffel? Give it here."

I jerked it out of his reach. "Listen, you piker. Do you swear on a stack of Bibles you've told me the truth? This is cash we're looking for, not drugs or diamonds or stolen documents, right?"

"It's money. I swear. You didn't find it?"

"I didn't find a thing. How much are we talking about?"

"Eight thousand dollars, maybe a little less by now."

"That's *all?*"

"Come on. It's a lot when you don't have a dime, which I don't."

"Somehow I got the impression it was more," I said.

Our voices had started to reverberate again. He put a finger to his lips.

"Where'd the money come from?" I whispered hoarsely.

"I'll tell you later. Let's see if we can find a way out of here."

"There's a service corridor below this one, but you can't access it from here," I said.

"What about the floor above?"

"I don't think so." He started up the steps, but I grabbed his arm. "Wait a minute. Slow down. We need a plan."

"We need the cash," he corrected, "before hotel security catches up with us again. Maybe this Huckaby woman left the money with the manager."

"She couldn't. I was standing in the same line when she checked in. She didn't deposit any valuables. I'd have seen her do that."

"Then where is it? She's not going to let the money out of her sight. If we figure out where she's got it, you can snag it and run."

"Oh, *I* can? That's nice. What about you?"

"I'm speaking figuratively," he said.

"Well, the cash isn't in her room because I've searched."

"Then she must have it with her."

"She does *not.* I told you that. Ah!" I heard the sound an idea makes when your brain ignites, a tiny implosion, like spontaneous combustion at the base of your skull. "Wait a minute. I got it. I think I know where it is. Come with me."

I knocked on Laura Huckaby's door. There was a pause. She was probably checking through the spy hole to see who it was. Ray was standing against the wall to the left of the door, with a look of suffering on his face. "I know how Gilbert got my release date," he said dully. "I didn't want to tell you unless I had to."

"Hush," I said under my breath. I couldn't figure out what his problem was, aside from the obvious. He'd been curiously reluctant to come up here with me, suggesting all kinds of reasons I should do it myself. I'd been adamant. For one thing, if we were caught, we could act like we were just leaving. For another, now that Chester was pissed off, I didn't want to take sole responsibility.

As before, Laura opened the door a crack, leaving the chain in place.

I held up the duffel. "Hi, it's me. I'm off duty. I found this in the hall."

"Is that mine?"

"I think so. Wasn't this sitting in your closet last night?"

"How'd it get out there?"

"Beats me. I spotted it in passing and thought I'd knock," I said. "It is yours, isn't it?"

She studied it briefly. "Just a minute. I'll check." She left the door ajar, still secured by the chain, while she moved into the dressing area and opened the closet door. Ray and I exchanged a look. I knew she wasn't going to find her duffel, but I waited dutifully, playing out the charade. She returned to the door, her expression perplexed. "I guess it is mine." It was clear she didn't want to trust me, but what could she do? From her point of view, she'd been subjected to inexplicable occurrences. A lost key, a missing package, now the wandering duffel.

"I can leave it out here. You want me to do that?"

"No, that's all right." She closed the door and slipped the chain off its track. She opened the door again just wide enough for the duffel, holding her hand out as if to take it from me. I put a hand around the edge of the door, effectively preventing her from closing it.

She seemed startled by the gesture and said, "Hey!" irritably.

I hoped my smile was reassuring. "Mind if I come in? We need to talk." I pushed the door inward.

"Get away," she said, pushing back.

We grappled with the door, but Ray had moved into the picture by then, and after a mute struggle on her part, she relinquished control. She'd begun to realize that something was dreadfully wrong.

"I'm Kinsey Millhone," I said as we stepped into the room. "This is my friend Ray."

She backed up a step, taking in Ray's bruised and swollen face. "What *is* this?"

"We called a meeting about the money," I said. "Just between you, me, and him."

She pivoted, moving rapidly toward the bed table, where she snatched up the receiver. Ray intercepted her and banged down the button before she could press "0."

"Take it easy. We just want to talk to you," he said. He removed the receiver from her hand and dropped it in the cradle.

"Who are you? What is this, some kind of shake-down?"

"Not at all," I said. "We followed you from California. Your friend Gilbert stole some money, and Ray, here, wants it back."

Her eyes fixed on me and then jumped to him, comprehension dawning. "You're Ray Rawson."

"That's right."

She raised a hand rapidly as if to slap him in the face. Ray blocked the move and caught the blow on his arm. He grabbed her wrist with his good hand. "Don't do that," he said.

"Get your fuckin' hands off me!"

"Just give us the money and we'll leave you alone."

"It isn't yours. It belongs to Gilbert."

Ray shook his head. "I'm afraid not. Money belongs to me and a guy named Johnny Lee. Johnny died four months ago, so I'm passing his share along to his son and grandson. Gilbert tried to rip us off."

"You goddamn shit. That's not true! The money's his and you know it. You're the one who blew the whistle. His brother died because of you."

"That's bullshit. Is that what he said?"

"Well, yes. He told me it was some kind of sting and it was all set up. You tipped off the cops and Donnie was killed in the shoot-out," she said.

"Wait a minute, gang. What's going on?" I said.

Ray seemed unruffled, ignoring me altogether in his focus on her. "He lied to you, baby. Gilbert sold you a bill of goods. He probably had to do that to get you to participate, right? Because if you knew the truth, you wouldn't help. I hope."

"You asshole. He told me you'd try to do this, twist the truth until it suited your purposes."

"You want the truth? I'll tell you. You want to hear what went down?"

She put her hands to her ears, as if to shut him out. "I don't have to hear it from you. Gilbert told me what happened."

I raised my hand. "Would one of you stop and tell me what this is about? Do you two know each other?"

"Not exactly," Ray said. He turned to look at her, and the two of them locked eyes. Ray's gaze flicked back to mine. "This is my daughter. I haven't seen her in years."

She flung herself at him, banging with her fists on his chest. "You are such a fuck," she said, and promptly burst into tears.

I looked from one to the other. My mouth did not really fall open, but that's what it felt like.

Ray gathered her into his arms. "I know, baby, I know," he murmured, patting at her. "I feel so bad about everything."

It probably took another five or six minutes for Laura's tears to taper off. Her face was mashed against his shoulder, her bulky belly making the embrace seem awkward. Ray rested his battered cheek against her tangled hair, most of which had come loose now, hanging down in dark auburn clumps. Ray was nearly humming with unhappiness at the sound of her misery, which she managed to express with a childlike lack of inhibition. Neither was accustomed to the physical contact, and my suspicion was that the fleeting connection by no means represented resolution. If their estrangement was lifelong, it would take more than a Hallmark moment to set it right. In the meantime, I blocked any thought of my cousin Tasha and my estrangement from Grand.

I went to the window and looked out at the barren stretch of

Texas countryside. I felt about as arid. Here, as in California, the liberal application of imported water was the only means by which the land was being reclaimed from the desert. At least I understood now why he hadn't wanted to come up here. He must have dreaded the moment when the two of them would meet, especially once he understood how Gilbert Hays had used her. Why is it that life's most touching moments are so often the most depressing?

Behind me, finally, the weeping seemed to be diminishing. There was some murmuring between them that I politely tuned out. When I turned back, the two were seated side by side on one of the double beds. Laura's tears had streaked through the many layers of makeup, bringing ancient bruises to the surface. It was clear she'd recently suffered a black eye. Her jaw was tinted a drab green, washing out to yellow around the edges, colors repeated in the riper bruises of her father's face. Odd to think the same man had beaten both. He studied her face, and the effect wasn't lost on him. A look of pain filled his eyes. "He do that to you? Because if he did, I'll kill him, I swear to God."

"It wasn't like that," she said.

"It wasn't like that. *Bull*shit."

Her eyes flooded again. I moved into the dressing area and grabbed some tissues from the dispenser. When I returned to the bed, Ray took the wad and passed them over to her. She blew her nose and then looked at me with resentment. "You're not really the maid," she said resentfully. "You didn't even do the sheet corners right."

"I'm a private investigator."

"I knew this hotel wouldn't have turn-down service. I should have trusted my instincts."

"Ain't *that* the truth," I said. I sat down on the other bed. "Now would one of you fill me in?"

Ray turned to me with an expectant look. "Wait a minute. What's the deal?"

"The deal?"

"I don't know where the money is. I thought it was up here someplace."

"Ah, the money. Why don't you ask her?"

"Me? *I* don't have it. What are you talking about?"

"Yes, you do." I reached over to Laura's belly and knocked on the mound. The thudding noise was not what you'd expect of warm maternal flesh. She smacked my hand away, incensed. "Stop that!"

Ray stared. "It's in her stomach? Like, up her butt?"

"Not quite. The belly's phony."

"How'd you figure that?"

"She has tampons in the duffel. If she were pregnant, she wouldn't need 'em. It's a girl thing," I replied.

"I *am* pregnant. What's the matter with you? The baby's due in January. The sixteenth, to be exact."

"In that case, pull your dress up so we can watch it kick."

"I don't have to *do* that. I can't believe you suggested it."

"Ray, I'm telling you, she's got the money in some kind of harness. That's how she got it on the plane without it's showing up on security. Eight thousand in a duffel, they might have asked too many questions."

"That's ridiculous. There's no law that says you can't transport cash across state lines."

"There is when the money's stolen," I said in my best nanny-nanny-boo-boo tone. Really, the two of us were like sisters, squabbling over everything.

"Come on, ladies. Please."

I doubled up my fist. "You want me to punch her in the stomach? It'd be a good test."

"Oh, for God's sake! This is none of your business."

"Yes, it is. Chester hired me to find the money, and I've done just that."

"I-do-not-have-the-money," she said, enunciating every-single-word.

I pulled my fist back.

"All right! Goddamn it. It's in a canvas vest that hooks on in front. I hope you're satisfied."

I loved the indignation, like I was the one who'd been lying to her. "Well, that's great. So let's see it. I'm curious what it looks like."

"Ray, would you tell her to get away from me?"

Ray looked at me. "Just drop it. This is silly. I thought you said you wanted to hear the story."

"I do."

"Then cut the nonsense and let's get on with it." He looked back at his daughter. "You start. I'd like to hear Gilbert's version. He's saying, what, that I betrayed the others?"

"Let me wash my face first. I feel awful," she said. Her nose was red, her eyes puffy with emotion. She got up and went into the dressing area, where she ran water in the sink.

"Your daughter? You could have told me," I said.

Ray avoided my gaze like a dog that's done potty on the good rug.

When Laura returned, he let her sit on the bed while he fetched the desk chair and pulled it over closer. Her complexion, free of makeup, showed all the splotchy imperfections you'd expect. She glanced once at Ray, her expression faltering. She picked up a twist of tissue, which she wrapped around her index finger. Given center stage, she seemed oddly reluctant. "Gilbert says there was a bank robbery back in 1941."

"That's right."

I flashed a look at him. "It *is?*"

"There were five of you altogether. You, Gilbert, his brother Donnie, the guy you mentioned . . ."

"Johnny Lee," Ray supplied.

"Right. Him and a man named McDermid."

"Actually, there were six of us. Two McDermids, Frank and Darrell," Ray amended.

She shrugged, accepting the correction, which apparently didn't affect her understanding of the incident. "Gilbert says you tipped off the cops and they showed up in the middle of the robbery. There was a shoot-out and his brother Donnie was killed. So was McDermid and a policeman. The money vanished, but Gilbert was convinced you and Johnny knew where it was hidden. Johnny was in prison for two years, and when he got out, he disappeared. Gilbert had no way to trace him, so he waited 'til you got out and followed you, and sure enough, there it was. All Gilbert took was his share. Well, I guess his brother's share, too. He figures you and Johnny had the use of it for years, so whatever was left belongs to him by rights."

"Could I just clarify one thing?" I said to Laura.

"Sure."

"I take it your mother was the one who told you when Ray was getting out of prison?"

She nodded. "She mentioned it to me. Gilbert had already told me what happened, and I was furious. I mean, it was bad enough my father had been in prison all his life, but to find out he'd betrayed all his friends? That was the lowest of the low."

"Baby, I have to say this. I don't know what your relationship is with Gilbert, but hasn't it occurred to you he only got close to you so he could get to me?"

"No. Absolutely not. You don't *know* that," she said.

"Look at the facts. I mean, it only stands to reason," he said. "Didn't he ask about me early on? Maybe not by name, but just the family situation, blah, blah, blah, your dad and stepdad, things like that?"

"So what if he did? Everybody asks things like that early on."

"Well, doesn't it strike you as odd? Here, just 'coincidentally,' it turns out the two of us pulled a job together forty-some-odd years back?"

"Not really. Gilbert knew Paul from work . . . he's my stepdad," she said in an aside to me. "I guess Paul must have mentioned the name 'Rawson' in some context."

"Oh, yeah, right," Ray said with acid. "Like your stepfather sits around and bullshits about me with the guys at work."

"What difference does it make?" Laura said. "Somehow it came up. Maybe it was karma."

Ray's expression was impatient—he didn't buy that for a minute—but he made that rolling hand gesture that said "Let's get on with it."

"I'm not going to keep talking if you act like that, Ray," she said primly. "You asked for my side and that's what I'm trying to tell you, okay?"

"Okay. You're right. I'm sorry. But let me ask you this . . ."

"I'm not saying I know all the details," she interjected.

"I understand that. I'm just asking about the logic. Listen, in the gospel according to Gilbert—if what he says is true—then how come I spent forty years in prison? If I blew the whistle, I'd have made a deal. I never would have served a day. Or I'd have pled down and done county jail time just to make it look good."

Laura was silent, and I could see her struggling to come up with an explanation that made sense. "I don't really know. He never went into that."

"Well, think about it."

"I know Gilbert never served much time," she said tentatively.

"Yeah, but he was seventeen. He was still a juvenile and this was his first offense. Johnny always figured it was the younger McDermid, Darrell. Frank was too much of a stand-up guy. Darrell was the one who testified against us in court and ended up doing less than a year himself. You want to know why? Because he turned us in and in exchange they let him plead down to some lesser charge. Gilbert wants to blame me because the little fuck is greedy and wants to justify picking off all the loot for himself. By the way, you haven't said, are you two married?"

"We live together."

"You live together. That's nice. A year, couple years?"

"About that," she said.

"Don't you have any idea what he's like?"

Laura said nothing. Judging from the bruises, she knew plenty about Gilbert. "I don't believe he lied. You're the liar."

"Why don't you reserve judgment until you hear my side of it?"

I held a hand up. "Uh, Ray? Am I going to be surprised by what comes next? Is this going to be like big news and piss me off?"

His smile was sheepish. "Why?"

"Because I'm just wondering how many versions of the story you tell. This is number three, by my count."

"This is it. Last one. Swear to God."

I glanced at Laura. "The man does lie through his teeth, or what's left of them."

"I haven't *lied,*" he said. "I might have failed to mention a couple things."

"A shoot-out with the cops? What else have you failed to mention? I'd be fascinated," I said.

"I can do without the sarcasm."

"I can do without the bullshit! You said Gilbert was a former cellmate."

"I had to tell you something," he said. "Come on. This is not easy. I kept my mouth shut forty years. Johnny Lee and I swore we'd never give anything away. The problem is, he died without giving me some vital information."

"I'm going to get comfortable," I said. I leaned over and pulled the pillows out from under the bedspread and propped them up against the headboard, kicking my shoes off before I settled into place. This was like a bedtime story, and I didn't want to miss it.

"You comfy?" he said.

"I'm terrific."

"Johnny dreamed up this scheme and talked me into going in with him. You have to understand a little background on this. I hope you don't mind."

"If you're going to tell the truth for a change, take your time," I said.

Ray got to his feet and began to pace. "I'm trying to think how far back to go. Let's try this. Ohio River flooded in the winter of 1937. I guess it started raining sometime in January and the river just kept going up. Eventually, there was something like twelve thousand acres underwater all up and down the Ohio River valley. At the time, Johnny was in state reformatory down in Lexington. Well, the inmates began to riot. Sixty of them busted out of there, and Johnny Lee was one. He gets as far as Louisville and disappears in the confusion. He starts helping with flood relief." He paused, looking from Laura to me. "Just be patient," he said. "Because you have to understand how this scheme was set up in the first place."

"Fine with me," she said.

He looked at me.

"Go right ahead," I said.

"Okay. Anyway, thousands of volunteers poured into the city. And nobody asked questions. From what Johnny told me, you pitched in, nobody cared who you were or where you came from. So he's rowing through the west end, saving people off of rooftops. The water's up to the second story in most places—I've seen pictures of this—as high as traffic lights. Damnedest thing you've ever seen. Johnny made this boat out of four barrels and some crates and he's paddling right down the middle of the street. He had the time of his life. He even stuck around afterwards and helped with the cleanup, which is how he dreamed up this heist.

"Lot of buildings collapsed. I mean, the whole downtown was underwater for weeks on end, and when the river receded they put crews in there repairing anything that got broke. Johnny was smart.

He knew all kinds of things. He told them he'd done construction, so they put him to work. Anyway, while he's crawling around this basement one day, he realizes he's looking at the underside of a bank. Electrical power's been out for days, so a lot of storm sewers have broken and all this water's flowing past the foundation. There's this crack up the wall that he's supposed to fix. He puts together this patch job wouldn't fool a pro, but there's no one around. Everybody's too busy to pay attention to him. So he tells 'em it's fixed when he hasn't done a thing except cover it up. He even signs off the inspection with forged signatures. I mean, it's not like there was anyone to double-check his work.

"By the time the two of us meet up . . . this is now four years later. Back then, big vaults were poured in place, using number five rebar, which is five-eighths diameter, four inches on center, several layers offset. Understand, it's not like I'm the expert. I learned all of this from him. This particular vault was constructed during the Depression—some kind of public works project—so you can imagine how well it was put together in the first place. Vault like that, you can force entry if you got the tools and the time. He said it had always been at the back of his mind, but he knew he needed help once it came time, which is where I come in.

"Johnny starts working on the foundation with this masonry bit. Nights and weekends, he goes in through the basement of the building next door and attacks the substructure. It probably takes him a month, but he's finally right up against the floor of the vault. Nowadays, this shit is all done with high-tech equipment, but in the old days, a successful bank job was the result of pure grit and hard work. It took patience and skill. Johnny figured the alarm system was tougher than the vault. At that point, we had to bring in some other guys because we needed the help. Johnny'd apprenticed with a locksmith, so he'd studied all the manuals and knew the specs by heart, but we needed an alarm man to dismantle the alarms. I'd been in jail with a guy I thought we could trust. That was Donnie Hays, and he brought in his brother, Gilbert. Like she said, Donnie's dead now and Gilbert I got to thank for this." He held up his bruised and bandaged hand.

I saw Laura's focus shift, and she exchanged a look with me. It apparently hadn't occurred to her before that Gilbert had done the damage to Ray Rawson's face.

"Johnny pulled in another couple of guys named McDermid. I think they were cousins he'd done some time with down in Lexington. Donnie Hays defeated the alarm, and we went to work with the torches and the sledgehammers, pounding away like crazy until we finally busted through. Johnny started drilling safe-deposit boxes while the rest of us set to work, cleaning out the loot while he popped the boxes and dumped the contents."

"Wait a minute. Who's Farley? How does he fit into this?" I asked.

"Gilbert's nephew," Laura replied. "The three of us came out to the coast together."

"Oh. Sorry to interrupt. Go ahead."

"Anyway, we had us a regular bucket brigade, tossing cash and jewelry out of safe-deposit boxes, stuffing the goodies into canvas bags, then hand over hand down through the hole and out to the car waiting in the alley. We're working like dogs and everything seems to be going as planned until suddenly the cops show up and all hell breaks loose. This gun battle breaks out, in the course of which Frank McDermid and Donnie Hays were both killed, along with this cop. I was hot-blooded in those days, and I fired the shot that killed the cop. Gilbert was captured and so was Darrell McDermid. I heard later Darrell died in some accident, but I never had that confirmed."

"You and Johnny weren't captured?" I asked.

He shook his head. "Not then. Me and him escaped, but we knew it was only a matter of time before they caught us. We were desperate, sitting on this stash, anxious to find a safe place for it before the cops closed in. We decided to split up. Johnny said he had the perfect place to hide the dough, but he figured it was better if only one of us knew. I'd have trusted him with my life. He swore he wouldn't lay a hand on it until we were both free to enjoy it. We went our separate ways, and by the time we got picked up he was empty-handed. The cops beat the shit out of him, trying to find out where he'd hidden the take, but he never would say. Ended up he confessed to the crime, but he never told anyone what happened to the money. The irony was, it was the cops' beating a confession out of him that got his conviction thrown out.

"Meantime, we both suspected Darrell was the one who blew the whistle on us. Like I said, after we were picked up, he testified against us in court. He swore up and down it wasn't him turned us in, trying to lay blame off on his brother, Frank. Me and Johnny both got twenty-five years to life, but Johnny's conviction was overturned on appeal. He went home to his family while I'm sitting on my butt down in the U.S. Penitentiary in Atlanta, Georgia. Johnny went back later and removed enough from the stash to support himself and my ma, who's still back in Kentucky." He indicated her belly. "That's what's left."

"Wait a minute. What makes you so sure it's eight grand?"

"Because he told me how much he took and what he spent since then. I did the math and figured what the balance was."

"Where's the rest?"

"Well, you know. I guess it's still where it was."

I stared at him. "I hope you're not going to tell me he died without revealing where he hid it."

Ray shrugged uneasily. "That's about it."

12

Laura moaned and leaned forward as if she were on the verge of fainting. She tried to get her head down between her knees, but the bulk of her belly thwarted her. She leaned sideways against the bed pillows, pulling her knees up to her chest like a kid with a stomachache.

"What's wrong?" Ray asked.

"Oh God, I thought there'd be more. I thought you knew where it was," she whispered, beginning to weep again. I'm a hardhearted little thing. I sat there wondering why crying is occasionally referred to as boo-hooing. I've never heard weepers use syllables even remotely related.

Ray moved over and sat beside her. "Are you okay?"

She shook her head, rocking back and forth.

"Laura's fine," I said, bored. I was aware my tone was rude, but I knew what she was up to, and the girlish tears were annoying. Ray rubbed her back, patting her shoulder in a series of ineffectual moves that, nevertheless, conveyed his compassion and concern. "Hey, come on. That's okay. Just tell me what's wrong and I'll help. I promise. Don't cry."

"Excuse me, Ray, but you might want to be discreet. She's already busy double-crossing Gilbert, and she's supposedly in *love* with him. No telling what she does to people she doesn't give a shit about. Uh, such as us, in case you missed the point," I said.

He looked at her, his brow furrowing. "Is that right? Are you trying to get away from him?"

"By sticking it to *us,*" I said caustically. Neither paid attention. I could have saved my breath.

I handed her another wad of tissues, and she went through the whole nose-blowing routine again. She pressed a tissue to her eyes, damming the leak of tears. She launched into a fragmented explanation, but she couldn't quite manage it, and I was left to translate. I said, "She and Farley have joined forces. She's absconding with the money. This is just a guess on my part."

"You and Farley decided to pull a fast one?" he asked. He was trying to sound calm, but I could tell he was seriously alarmed. He knew Gilbert well enough to guess the depth of trouble she was in. She nodded, tears spilling down her cheeks.

"Oh, Jesus, baby. I wish I'd known what you were up to. That's really not a good plan."

"I can't help it. Farley loves me. He said he'd help. He knows Gilbert beats me. I have to get away before he kills me dead."

"I understand, hon, but Gilbert is a lunatic. He's not going to like that. If he finds out, I hate to think what he'll do to get even. Come on now and let's talk. Maybe we can figure out a way to get you out of this."

I loved his use of the word "we."

She sighed and sat up. Without the anchor of makeup, her eyes looked like they'd shifted upward half an inch on her face. Her nose was stopped up and her voice had dropped into a lower range. Her complexion was a mottled pink, and her hazel eyes seemed vivid against the dark red of her hair. The dark green corduroy jumper was hopelessly wrinkled, and the collar of her white turtleneck was streaked with foundation. "I don't know what I was thinking of. I just had to get away." She pulled her sleeve up. "Look at that. I'm black and blue. I look worse than you do, only this has been going on for months."

"You have to get away from him. No question about that. Why'd you put up with it?"

"Because I didn't have any choice. I've been to shelters for battered women. Twice, I've hidden out with friends. Somehow he always finds me and brings me back. Now he makes sure I don't get close to anyone. I have to account for my every minute. He won't let me work. He won't let me have a nickel of my own. When I saw this coming up, I knew it was the only chance I'd ever have. I thought if I just had money. If I just had a way to get away from him . . ."

"Then take the money," he said. "It's yours. I couldn't believe it when Kinsey mentioned your name. You can ask her. I was stunned. . . ."

"I wouldn't say 'stunned,' but he did get real quiet."

"I had no idea you were involved in this," he went on.

"What difference would that have made?" she said, blowing her nose. She seemed comforted by the fact that she'd surprised him somehow.

"I never would have come. I'd have let you have the eight grand. That's what I'm saying. It's yours. You take it. It's a gift."

"Forget that. I don't want it."

"I thought you said you didn't have any choice."

"Well, I do."

"Like what?"

"I don't know. I'll talk to Farley. We'll figure something out."

"Laura, don't be crazy. You were willing enough to take it before. Why not now?"

She turned on him harshly. "I was willing to take it because I thought you betrayed your friends to get it. I thought it served you right. I didn't think you deserved to have it after what you did."

I was getting irritated by the melodrama, wishing they'd get on with it. "Why don't you split the money and put an end to the argument?"

Ray shook his head. "We don't have to split it. She can have the whole eight grand. I can always go back to Louisville and look for the rest."

"What are your chances of finding it after forty years?" I asked.

"Probably not that good, but I'd feel better knowing she had enough to get away."

"Ray, I said I'd handle it and I will," she said.

"Why don't you let me do something?"

"It's too late."

He turned to me, his look bewildered. "You talk to her. You tell her. I don't understand where she's coming from."

I said, "Here's the deal, Ray, and you can trust me on this. She wants your love. She wants approval. She wants you to beg forgiveness for what you've put her through all her life. She doesn't want to have anything else to do with you. She certainly doesn't want your help. She'd rather die first."

"Why?"

"Because she doesn't want to *owe* you anything," I snapped.

He looked back at her. "Is that right, what she said?"

"I don't know. I guess." She paused to wipe her eyes and blow her nose again. "I thought there'd be more. I thought you'd have millions. I was counting on it."

"There never was *millions.* Is that what Gilbert said?"

"How do I know? That's what he talked about for years," she said. "Maybe, in his mind, the money grew as time passed. The point is, eight thousand dollars isn't going to get me any place. I pictured going to a foreign country, holing up someplace, but how long is eight thousand dollars going to last?"

"It'll last long enough. Go to another state. Change your name. Find work. At least the eight grand will help you get set up."

Laura's face was filled with despair. "He'll find me. I know he will. I thought I had a chance with Farley, but now I'm worried sick."

"Where's Farley all this time?" I asked.

"He's in Santa Teresa with Gilbert. We didn't want him to get suspicious."

I raised my hand. "Wait a minute. I'm confused. What was the original plan?"

"When I left Santa Teresa? I was supposed to fly to Palm Beach, Florida, where Gilbert had a buddy waiting. This is some pal he hired to keep an eye on me. Gilbert wanted to get the money out of California as soon as possible, but he thought we'd be too conspicuous if the three of us traveled together. Besides, he and Farley had to wait until their passports came through. I already had mine, so I was supposed to wait in Palm Beach and they'd join me. Later, we'd fly to Rio."

"So Farley was left to deal with Gilbert? That's a bad idea. I don't even know Farley and already I'll bet he's not smart enough to outfox Gilbert."

"That's right, doll. Gilbert's certifiable, especially when he thinks he's been betrayed," Ray said to her. "Look at what he did to me. You think that's the end of it?"

"What am I supposed to do? It's done now. It's over. I took the money and ran. The minute I got here, I counted it. I thought I'd die when I found out how little there was."

I said, "Back up a step. When was Farley supposed to join you?"

"As soon as he could. They called the passport office and the guy swore he'd put them in the mail. Farley knows where I am, and we made arrangements for him to call me from this pay phone down the street."

"He never called you at all?"

"He called me once. This morning. He had to wait 'til Gilbert went out. When I told him about the eight grand, I could tell he was scared. He said he'd think of something and call me back in an hour."

Ray said, "You haven't heard from him?"

Laura shook her head.

I said, "But Gilbert must have known you never got off the plane in Palm Beach. Didn't his buddy call him right up to say you never showed?"

"Of course he did, but Gilbert doesn't have any idea where I am."

"Well, this is a very sophisticated plan," I said. "What about Farley? I'm sure Gilbert won't suspect *him*."

"You think he's figured it out?"

"Of course he has!" Ray said. "He's waited forty years to get his hands on this dough. Gilbert's a psychopath. He's so paranoid he's almost psychic. You're an amateur. You think he can't see right through you?"

"But Dallas is huge. He'll never find me," she said. "I paid the hotel in cash and I'm using an alias."

"Farley knows where you are."

"Well, sure, but I can trust him," she said.

Ray closed his eyes. "You better hit the road."

"But where would I go?"

"Who cares? Just get out of here."

"What about Farley? He won't know where I've gone."

"That's the point," I said. "I agree with Ray. You can't worry about him. You have to put as much distance as possible between you and Gilbert."

"Well, I'm not going to do it. I told Farley I'd be here and I'm staying," she said.

I said, "Oh, boy."

"Gilbert isn't Superman. He doesn't have X-ray vision or anything like that."

"Yeah, right," I said. I searched through my handbag until I found my airline ticket. I started opening drawers in the bed table, looking for a telephone book. "Well, gang. I don't know how you're going to resolve this little conflict, but I'm getting out of here."

"You're leaving us?" Ray said, startled. "What about Chester?"

"He fired me," I said. I found the Yellow Pages in a separate book that probably weighed ten pounds. I lugged it out of the drawer and hauled it onto my lap, leafing through to the section marked "Airlines." "Look, whatever you and Laura work out, that's between the two of you. I came to help recover the cash you're so busy giving away. I'm history. It makes no sense for me to stay here. If Chester doesn't like it, he can take it up with you. He's already so frosted he probably won't pay my bill, which means I'm out of luck. I might as well go home. At least take charge of the situation to that extent." I found the number for American and put my finger on the place while I picked up the receiver.

"But you can't just abandon us," Ray said.

"I wouldn't call it that," I said.

"What would you call it?"

"Ray, we're not joined at the hip. I came here on impulse, so I thought I'd go home the same way." I tucked the phone in the crook of my neck and punched in the number for American Airlines. As soon as the number answered, I was put on terminal hold while a mechanical voice assured me my business was valued beyond rubies. "Anyway, the money's stolen," I went on conversationally, "which is just one more reason I don't want to be involved in this."

"It's been forty years since we cleaned out that vault," Ray protested. "The bank's out of business. Place went belly up back in 1949. Most customers are dead, so even if I wanted to play straight, who would I return the money to? The state of Kentucky? To what end? I spent my life in jail for that dough, and I earned every cent."

"It's still a crime," I said politely, not wanting to seem quarrelsome.

"What about the statute of limitations? Who's going to point a finger after all this time? Besides, I been tried once and I paid for my sins."

"Take it up with an attorney. You could be right. Just in case you're not, I think I'll steer clear," I said.

Laura was getting impatient. She apparently had no interest in our debate about jurisprudence. She leaned closer to me, hissing, "I wish you'd get off the phone. What if Farley's trying to get through?"

I held a hand up like a traffic cop. The American Airlines ticket agent had just come on the line and introduced himself. I said, "Oh, hi, Brad. My name is Kinsey Millhone. I have an open-ended, round-trip ticket from Santa Teresa, California, to Palm Beach, Florida, and I'd like to book the return. I'm in Dallas now, so I just need the Dallas–Santa Teresa leg."

"And what day would this be for?"

"As soon as possible. Today, if you can do it."

While agent Brad and I conducted business, Ray and Laura seemed to be negotiating some sort of father-daughter truce, a financial cease-fire of sorts. Apparently, she was allowing him to gift her with the hotly contended eight grand. Dimly, I was aware that he was telling her he had to go down to his room on the tenth floor and pick up his bags. He wanted permission to leave his bags in her room until he could figure out where to go from here.

Meanwhile she began to pace, becoming more agitated as the agent and I tried to work out my itinerary. There were some alternate routes that would get me home by way of San Francisco or Los Angeles, using short hops for the final leg. Since this was Sunday, both direct flights were completely full, and his only suggestion was that I get myself on standby and hope for the best. He went ahead and wait-listed me on two flights, one nonstop, the other with a layover. The next flight was scheduled for departure at 2:22. I checked my watch. It was just past 12:30, and with the hotel shuttle or a taxi, I could probably get over to the airport in the next thirty-five to forty minutes.

Laura had crossed back to the bed table, where she stuck her face close to mine and mouthed, "Hang *up.*" She sat down on the other bed and began to unlace her high-top tennis shoes.

I gave her a simpering smile as I began to wind up the conversation, reconfirming my notes about the flights in question. As I replaced the receiver in the cradle, I realized Ray was still in the room. "I thought you were going down to get your bags," I said.

"I was afraid if I left you'd be gone when I got back."

"That's a good bet. What's your inclination? Are you going to fly back to California?"

"Nah, I don't think so. I think I'll hang out with Laura until she hears from Farley. As soon as her situation's settled, I'll take off for Louisville. I got a rental car downstairs. Meantime, if I lay low the management will never know I'm here."

"What about Chester? I hate to spoil all the fun, but half of the money belongs to him, you know."

"Says who?"

"You did. You said you were going to turn it over to him."

"I got news for you. He's screwed. I never really meant to cut him in on the deal."

"Ah. I guess I should have known that, right?"

"You're the one who pointed out how much I lie," he said.

"So I have to be the one to break the news to him? Thanks a lot, Ray. That sucks. What am I supposed to say?"

"You'll think of something. Plead ignorance. Make it up."

"Oh, right."

"The guy's a butt, anyway. I bet you never get reimbursed."

I said, "Your confidence in him is touching."

Laura was still sulking, so we skipped the tender fare-thee-wells. I grabbed my shoulder bag, hoisted it, and backed out of the room. Then I headed for the fire stairs and made my way down twelve floors to the lobby.

I took a taxi to the airport. I could have waited for the shuttle, which was free of charge, but the truth was I didn't want to risk running into management. So far, I'd successfully outmaneuvered the hotel authorities, and I was just as happy leaving Texas without some kind of scrape with the law. I checked my wallet in the cab. Since I was on my way home, I figured I had sufficient cash for the journey . . . which is to say, plus or minus thirty-five bucks. I'd spent a little on incidentals, but in the main, I'd managed on the few resources I'd had. I'd still have to hassle with short-term parking fees when I got home—seven bucks a day for the two or three days I'd been gone—but in a pinch, I could call Henry and have him bring me the necessary cash. I hadn't formally checked out of my room, but the desk clerk had taken an impression of my credit card when I'd checked in, and I was sure the charges would appear on the next statement I received. Hotels aren't exactly dumb about these things.

The cab dropped me off at the departure gates for American Airlines. I went into the terminal and crossed the lobby, checking the monitor for the departing flight numbers I'd been given. The first was scheduled to take off at 2:22, the second not until 6:10. The later flight wasn't even listed yet, but I found the gate number for the 2:22 departure. At least traveling without luggage simplified procedures to some extent. I bypassed the ticket counter and joined the line of passengers waiting to clear security. My handbag sailed through X-ray, but when I passed through the metal detector, there was a telltale shriek. I patted my pockets, which were empty of metal except for the paper clip and random change I'd used for the pay phone. I backed up, dropped the items in a plastic dish. I tried again. The shrieking seemed to rise to an accusatory pitch. I could tell the security sorceress was about to dowse my body with her divining rod when I remembered the key I'd stitched into my shoulder pad. "Hang on a minute. I got it." To the annoyance of those behind me, I backed up again, peeled off my blazer, and laid it on the moving belt. This time, I made it through. I half expected to be quizzed about the key stitched into the shoulder seam, but no one said a word. Those people probably saw things much stranger any given day of the week. I collected my shoulder bag and the blazer and headed for the gate.

I pulled my ticket from my handbag and presented it to the gate agent, explaining my situation. The flight was completely booked and she didn't seem that optimistic about my getting a seat. I sat in the waiting area while other passengers checked in. Apparently, several of us were angling for the same flight, which I suspected was already desperately oversold. I eyed the competition, some of whom looked like those quarrelsome types who raise hell when anything goes wrong. I might have tried it myself if I'd thought it would do any good. As far as I can tell, there are only so many seats. The plane is either flightworthy or it's not. Between mechanical matters and air traffic control, you either fly or you don't. I've never heard of an airline yet that proceeded on the basis of noisy passenger complaints, so why bitch and moan?

I pulled out my paperback romance novel and began to read. As flight time approached, the passengers were boarded in orderly rows, from the rear to the front, with the privileged taking precedence. Finally, six names were called from the standby list and none of them were mine. Oh, well. The gate agent sent me an apologetic smile, but there was nothing to be done. She swore she'd put me at the head of the list for the next flight out.

In the meantime, I had close to four hours to kill. From what I gathered, the flight crews made two daily loops from Dallas to Santa Teresa, in and out of the same gate, seven days a week. All I had to do was find a way to occupy my time and then present myself back here before the boarding process began again. with luck, I'd get a seat and be homeward bound. Without luck, I'd be stuck in Dallas until two o'clock Monday afternoon.

I walked a mile in the terminal corridor, just to stretch my legs. I took advantage of the ladies' room, where I was very ladylike. As I emerged and turned right, I passed the airport equivalent of an outdoor cafe, tables separated from the terminal corridor by a low wrought-iron fence and fake plants. The small bar offered the usual wines, beers, and exotic mixed drinks while, under glass, assorted fresh seafoods were packed on a mound of crushed ice. I hadn't eaten lunch, so I ordered a beer and a plate of fresh shrimp, which came with cocktail sauce, oyster crackers, and lemon wedges. I peeled and sauced my shrimp, doing a little people watching to amuse myself while I ate. When I finished, I wandered back to the gate.

I took a seat by the window. I read my book, intermittently watching airplanes land and take off. Occasionally I nodded off, but the seats weren't really built for any serious sleep. By hook or by crook, I managed to carve the four hours down to slightly more than one. Toward the end of the time allotted, I made a trip to the newsstand and picked up the local paper. I returned to the gate at five, just as the flight from Santa Teresa was arriving. I checked with one of the gate agents and made sure my name was on the standby list.

Most seats in the waiting area were now full, so I leaned against a column and scanned the paper. The jetway door had been opened and the first-class passengers began to file out, looking ever so much fresher than the travelers behind them. The coach passengers came next, eyes straying across the crowd to find the people who'd come to meet them. Many joyous reunions. Grandmothers swept little children into their arms. A soldier hugged his sweetheart. Husbands and wives exchanged obligatory busses. Two teenagers with a cluster of helium balloons began to squeal at the sight of a sheepish-looking young guy coming down the jetway. Altogether, it was a very pleasant way to spend a few minutes, and I found myself happily distracted from the grim array of the day's news in the paper. I was just in the process of turning to the funnies when the last smattering of passengers straggled off the plane. It was the Stetson that caught my attention. I averted my gaze, glancing up only fleetingly as Gilbert walked by.

13

I glanced at my watch. My plane probably wouldn't board for another twenty to thirty minutes. The cleaning crew would have to sweep through, collecting discarded newspapers, wadded tissues, earphones, and forgotten items. I laid my paper aside and followed Gilbert, whose Stetson, pale blue denim jacket, and cowboy boots made him easy to keep an eye on. He had to be much closer to Ray's age than I'd realized on first glance. I'd pegged him in his late fifties, but he was probably sixty-two, sixty-three, somewhere in there. I couldn't figure out what Laura had seen in him in the first place, unless she was, quite literally, looking for a father. Whatever the appeal, the sexual chemistry must have been intertwined with his brutality. Too many women mistake a man's hostility for wit and his silence for depth.

He pushed through revolving doors to the same baggage claim area I'd entered early Saturday. The area was crowded and afforded me natural cover. While Gilbert waited for the bags, I scanned the area for a pay phone. There were probably some around the corner, but I didn't want to let him out of my sight. I moved over to the hotel directory and found the number for the Desert Castle. The telephone system linked all the hotels that serviced the airport but did not admit of outside calls beyond that. I pulled a pen and paper from my bag as the line was ringing. "Desert Castle," a woman said, picking up on the other end.

"Hi, I'm over at the airport. Can you give me the hotel operator?"

"No, ma'am. I'm not tied in to the hotel switchboard. This is a separate facility."

"Well, can you give me the phone number over there?"

"Yes, ma'am. You want reservations, sales, or catering?"

"Just give me the main number."

She recited the number, which I dutifully noted. I'd find a pay phone as soon as opportunity allowed.

Behind me, a bell finally sounded, mimicking a burglar alarm. The overlapping metal segments of the carousel gave a lurch and began to move in a counterclockwise direction. Two suitcases came around the bend, then a third and a fourth as the conveyor brought them up from below. The waiting passengers crowded forward, angling for position as the bags tumbled down the incline and began their slow journey on the circular metal track.

While Gilbert watched for his luggage, I retrieved the two quarters from my blazer pocket, playing with them nervously while I waited to see what he would do. He retrieved a soft-sided suitcase from the carousel and pushed through the crowd, moving toward the corridor. I turned away long before he passed, aware that any sudden movement might attract his attention. Approaching the escalator, he stepped to one side and squatted while he unzipped his suitcase and removed a sizable handgun, to which he affixed a silencer. Several people glanced down and saw what he was doing, but went about their business as though it were no big deal. Clearly, to them, he didn't look like the sort of fellow who would cut loose in a crowd, mowing down everyone within range of him. He tucked the gun in his belt and pulled his denim jacket over it.

He adjusted his Stetson, rezipped his suitcase, and proceeded in a leisurely manner to the car rental desk. He must not have had advance reservations because I saw him inquire at Budget and then move to Avis. I spotted a bank of telephones and found the only free instrument among the five. I jammed a quarter in the slot and dialed the number for the Desert Castle. I turned, checking the immediate area, but there was no sign of airport security.

"Desert Castle. How may I direct your call?"

"Could you ring Laura Hudson's room? She's in 1236," I said.

Laura's line was busy. I kept waiting for the operator to cut back in, but she had apparently quit her job and gone to work for someone in another state. I depressed the plunger and started over, using my last precious quarter to try the hotel again.

"Desert Castle. How may I direct your call?"

"Hi, I'm trying to reach Laura Hudson in 1236, but her line is busy. Can you tell me if Ray Rawson is still registered there?"

"Just a moment, please." She clicked out. Dead silence. She clicked back in. "Yes, ma'am. Would you like me to ring his room?"

"Yes, but if he doesn't answer, would you come back on the line for me?

"Certainly."

The number rang in Ray's room fifteen times, before she cut back in. "Mr. Rawson doesn't answer. Would you care to leave a message?"

"Is there any way to page him instead?"

"No, ma'am. I'm sorry. Was there anything else I could help you with?"

"I don't think so. Oh yes, wait a minute. Could you connect me with the manager?"

She'd hung up before I'd even finished the sentence.

By now, I had so much adrenaline pumping through me, I could hardly breathe. Gilbert Hays was standing at the Avis counter, filling out the paperwork. He seemed to be consulting one of those multicolored one-sheet maps of the vicinity, the desk clerk leaning over helpfully, pointing out his route. I took the escalator to the street.

Outside, lights had come on, only partially dispelling the gloom of the pickup area. A limousine pulled to the curb in front of me, the uniformed white driver coming around to the door on the passenger side to assist a silver-haired couple as they emerged. The woman wore the fur of some beast I'd never seen. She looked around uneasily, as though she were accustomed to warding off insults. The driver removed their luggage from the trunk. I searched the area, looking for airport police. Light and shadow played across the concrete in patterns as repetitious as a stencil. A wind tunnel had been created by the building's construction, and a diesel-scented gale blew through, generated by the constant rush of passing traffic. I didn't see any of the vans from the hotel. I didn't see a cab stand or any passing taxis. Gilbert had probably already been given the keys to his rental car. He'd be coming out the door behind me, searching out the waiting area for the shuttle that would take him to the slot where his vehicle was waiting. Or perhaps, far worse, the rental car had been left in the parking garage just across the way, in which case he only had to cross the street.

My gaze settled on the limousine. The driver had received his tip, touched his cap, closed the limo door on the rear passenger side. He circled the back end of the vehicle, heading for the driver's side, where he opened the door and slid behind the wheel. I began to rap frantically on the front passenger side window. The glass was tinted so darkly, I couldn't see in at all. The window was lowered with a whir. The driver looked across at me, his expression neutral. He was in his thirties, with a round face, sparsely growing red hair, combed straight back from the crown. Along the edges of his ears, I could see where his hat had rested.

I leaned in slightly, handing him my wallet, with my California driver's license and my private investigator's license showing. I said, "Please listen very carefully. I need help. I'm a private investigator from Santa Teresa, California. Somewhere behind me, there's a guy with a gun who's here in Dallas to kill a couple of friends of mine. I need to get to the Desert Castle. Do you know where that is?"

He took my wallet gingerly, like a cat who deigns to accept a treat from an unfamiliar hand. "I know the Desert Castle." He looked at the picture on my driver's license. I could see him take in the information on my private investigator's license. He began to leaf through some of my other identification cards. He handed my wallet back and then simply sat and stared at me. He popped the lock up and then reached for the keys in the ignition.

I opened the passenger door and got in.

The limo pulled away from the curb as silently as a train easing out of a station. The seats were gray leather and the dashboard was a burled walnut so shiny it looked like plastic. Just at my left knee was the handset for the car phone. "Mind if I use that to call the cops?" I asked.

"Be my guest."

I dialed 911 and explained the situation to the emergency dispatcher, who asked for my approximate location and said she'd have a county sheriff's deputy meet us at the Desert Castle. I tried the hotel again, but I couldn't get the operator to pick up at all.

We circled the airport and headed off toward open country. It was fully dark by now. The land seemed vast and flat. The headlights illuminated long stretches of green with an occasional monolithic office building jutting up on the horizon. Lighted billboards appeared like a series of flashcards. Where we crested a rise, I could see the sweep of intersecting highways defined by the lights from fast-moving traffic. Anxiety buzzed and sizzled in my gut like defective neon, outlining vital organs.

"What's your name?" I asked. If I didn't talk, I'd go mad.

"Nathaniel."

"How'd you get into this?"

"It's just a way to pick up money until I finish my novel." His tone was glum.

I said, "Ah."

"I used to live in Southern California. I was hoping to get a screenplay launched, so I moved out to Hollywood and worked for this actress who played the zany sister-in-law on a sitcom about a waitress with five adorable kids. Show only lasted couple seasons, but she was raking it in. I think most of the money went up her nose, to tell you the truth. I drove her to the studio and back every day and washed her car and things like that. Anyway, she told me if I came up with an idea for a film, she'd have me pitch it to her agent and maybe she could help me break in. So I get this idea about this wacko mother-daughter relationship where the girl dies of cancer. I tell her about it and she says she'll see what she can do. Next thing I know, I go to a movie theater on Westwood Boulevard and see this movie about some girl dies of cancer. Can you believe that? What's her name, Shirley MacLaine, and that other one, Debra Winger. There it was. I should have had it registered with the guild, only nobody mentioned that. Thanks a lot, gang."

I looked over at him. "You came up with the story line for *Terms of Endearment*?"

"Not the story line per se, but the basic concept. My chick didn't get married and have all them kids. You want my opinion, that was over the top."

"Wasn't *Terms of Endearment* a Larry McMurtry book?"

He shook his head, sighing. "My point exactly. Where do you think he got it?"

"What about the astronaut? The Jack Nicholson part?"

"I didn't fool with that and personally, I didn't think it worked all that well. Later I found out this actress had the same agent used to be partners with Shirley MacLaine's agent way back when. That's the way Hollywood works. Real incestuous. The whole deal kind of soured me, to tell you the truth. I never saw a dime, and when I asked her about it, she gives me this look like she doesn't even know what I'm talking about. I kicked the shit out of her town car and set fire to the thing."

"Really."

He slid a look in my direction. "You probably have a lot of interesting experiences in your line of work."

"I don't. It's mostly paperwork."

"Same here. People think I must know all these rock stars. Closest I ever came was once I drove Sonny Bono to his hotel. Privacy window was rolled up the whole time, which kind of pissed me off. Like I'm going to call the *National Enquirer* if he sticks his hand up some chick's skirt."

I torqued around in my seat. The privacy window was rolled down and I peered the length of the limousine's interior through the darkly tinted rear window. There was a moving stream of cars behind us, all barreling down the highway at breakneck speeds. We turned off the main highway into the commercial/industrial park. In the distance, I saw the Desert Castle appear, red neon glowing hotly against the night sky. I watched while the red drained out of the letters and filled up again. The ratio of the lighted rooms to dark created an irregular checkerboard effect, with the proliferation of black squares suggesting fifteen percent occupancy. Only a smattering of cars now followed in our wake. As this was Sunday evening, it was hard to believe that any were heading for the offices across the way. We passed the miniature oasis with its phony stone tower, the structure probably only slightly taller than I. Nathaniel swung the limo into the circular hotel entranceway, pulling to a smooth stop beneath the portico.

I felt anxiety stir, wondering if he expected payment for his services. "I don't have enough to tip you. I'm really sorry about that."

"That's cool." He handed me his business card. "You have any ideas for a female-type Sam Spade film, we could maybe collaborate. Chicks kickin' shit and stuff like that."

"I'll give it some thought. I really appreciate your help."

I got out and closed the door behind me, aware that the limo was already pulling away. There was no sign of the sheriff's deputy, but Dallas County is a big place, and it hadn't been that long since I'd called. I moved toward the revolving doors, half trotting in my haste. The lobby was crowded with the departing track team, kids in shorts, jeans, and matching satin jackets with their school mascot stitched across the back. All of them wore running shoes that made their feet look enormous and reduced their preadolescent legs to sticks. Gym bags and oversize canvas duffels had been lined up in random clusters while the kids themselves milled around, engaged in various forms of horseplay. Some of the girls sat on the floor, using the baggage for backrests. One kid had had his T-shirt peeled off against his will, and he was in the process of wrestling with two teammates to get it back. The laughter had a nervous edge to it. Really, the boys reminded me of puppies playing tug-of-war with an old sock. The supervising adults seemed to take all this energy for granted, probably hoping the kids would be exhausted by the time they got on the bus.

I moved past them to the elevators and pushed the "up" button. The elevator doors down the line opened and I got on, glancing back across the lobby to see if there was any sign of Gilbert. A silver Trailways bus was just pulling up in front, motor growling while the door opened with the sound of flatulence. I pushed twelve and the elevator doors slid shut.

Once on Laura's floor, I trotted down the hall and knocked on 1236. I was murmuring to myself, snapping my fingers rapidly. Come on, come on, come on.

Laura answered the door, slightly taken aback when she saw me. "What are you doing here? I thought you left."

"Where's Ray? I gotta talk to him."

"He's asleep. He's right here. What's wrong?"

"I saw Gilbert at the airport. He's on his way over with a gun. Get Ray, grab your things, and let's get out of here."

"Oh no." She seemed to pale at the news, one hand going to her mouth.

"What's going on?" Ray said from behind her. He was already on his feet, tucking his shirt in as he approached. I moved into the room and Laura closed the door behind me. She leaned against the wall, her eyes momentarily closing in dread. I slid the security chain across the track.

I said, "Go."

The word seemed to get her mobilized. Laura moved toward the closet, hauling out her raincoat and the duffel.

"What's happening?" Ray said, looking from one of us to the other.

"She saw Gilbert. He's got a gun and he's on his way. You should have called instead of coming all the way back," she said reprovingly. She unzipped the duffel and began to sweep cosmetics off the counter into the bag.

"I did call. The line was busy."

"I was talking to room service. We had to eat," she said.

"Ladies, would you quit bickering and let's move!"

"I am!" She began to snatch up her nightie, slippers, dirty underwear. She'd laid her denim dress across the back of the chair, and she grabbed that, holding it against her chest so she could fold it in thirds and then in half again. Ray took it, rolled it in a ball, and jammed it in the duffel, which he zipped shut.

I saw his two suitcases stacked up to the left of the door. I grabbed the smaller one and watched while he picked up the other. "Take what's essential and dump the rest," I said. "You have a car?"

"Out in the lot."

"Will Gilbert try the elevator or the stairs?"

"Who knows?"

I said, "Look. I think you two should go the back way. Gilbert's bound to waste time knocking on the door up here. He may try Ray's room, too, if it occurs to him you're here. Give me the car keys and tell me where you're parked."

"What are we supposed to do in the meantime?" Laura asked.

"Wait for me out by that fake stone tower by the drive. I'll get the car and swing around to pick you up. He doesn't know me, so if we pass in the hall, he won't think anything of it."

Ray gave me a hasty description of the car and its approximate location. The plastic tag on the key listed the license plate number, so I was reasonably certain I could find it without trouble. I handed Ray the bag while Laura did a quick survey, making sure she hadn't left anything critical. I took the chain off the hook and peered into the corridor both ways, motioning to the two of them. Ray and Laura took a right, heading for the fire stairs at the end of the hall.

I moved to the left toward the elevators.

The elevator felt like it was descending at half speed. I watched the lighted floor numbers move from right to left, counting backward in slow motion. When the elevator reached the lobby, there was the customary *ping* and then the doors slid open. Gilbert was standing two feet away, waiting to get on. For a moment, our eyes locked and held. His were bottomless dark holes. I let my gaze drift away casually as I passed, moving off to the right as if on ordinary hotel business. Behind me, the doors slid shut. I checked the lobby for some sign of the county sheriff's deputy. No sign of law enforcement. I picked up my pace, glancing back automatically at the floor indicator lights. The elevator should have been going up. Instead, the light remained frozen where it was. I heard a *ping* and the elevator doors slid open. Gilbert emerged. He stood on the wide expanse of carpeting just outside the elevators, staring in my direction. Crooks and cops often function with a heightened sense of awareness, a clarity of perception born of adrenaline. Their work, and just as often their lives, depend on acumen. Gilbert was apparently a person who registered reality with uncanny accuracy. Something in his expression told me he remembered my face from our one brief encounter at the Santa Teresa airport. How he put me together with Laura Huckaby, I'll never know. The moment was electric, recognition arcing between us like a lightning bolt.

I kept my pace at "normal" as I turned the corner. I passed the entrance to the coffee shop and turned right again into a short corridor with three doors leading off it: one blank, one marked Authorized Personnel Only, one marked Maintenance. The minute I was out of Gilbert's visual range, I broke into a run, my shoulder bag thumping against my hip. I slammed through the unmarked door and found myself in a barren back hallway I hadn't seen before. The concrete floor and bare concrete walls curved around to the left. The walls extended upward into the fading light until the upper reaches disappeared into darkness. There was no ceiling in view, but a series of thick ropes and chains hung motionless among the shadows. I passed empty racks of serving trays, wooden pallets packed with glassware, stacks of linen tablecloths, carts filled with plates in assorted sizes. Bank after bank of stacked chairs lined the walls, narrowing the passage in places.

My footsteps *chunk*ed softly, the sound blunted by the rubber tread on my Reeboks. I had to guess that this was a service corridor, bordering a banquet room, a circle within a circle with access to freight elevators and the kitchens one floor down. A short flight of stairs led upward. I grabbed the handrail and pulled myself along, skipping steps as I ran. The shoulder bag made me feel like I was dragging an anchor, but I couldn't part with it. At the top, the corridor continued. Here, stacked against the walls, were various seasonal decorations: Christmas angels, artificial spruce trees, two enormous interlocking comedy/tragedy masks, gilded wooden putti and cupids, enormous Valentine hearts pierced with golden arrows.

A grove of silk ficus suggested a small interior forest bereft of birds and other wildlife.

Behind me, I heard a door hinge squeak. I picked up my pace, following the deserted corridor. A metal ladder that looked like an interior fire escape scaled its way up the wall on my left. I let my eye take the journey first, uncertain what was up there. I glanced back, dimly aware that someone was coming along the corridor behind me. I grabbed the first rung and headed up, Reeboks *tinking* as I climbed. I paused at the top, which was some twenty feet up. A steel catwalk stretched out along the wall ahead of me. I was close enough to the ceiling to reach up and touch it. The catwalk itself was less than three feet wide. Below me, through the yawning shadows, the floor looked like a flat still river of concrete. The only thing that kept me from falling was a chain rail supported by metal uprights. As usual, when confronted with heights, my greatest fear was the irresistible urge to fling myself off.

I slowed to a creeping pace, hugging the wall. I didn't dare go any faster for fear the catwalk itself would be loosened from the wall-mounted brackets that secured it. I didn't think I could be seen, cloaked as I was by the darkness up here, but the corridor itself functioned like an echo chamber announcing my presence. Somewhere behind me, I heard hard heels on concrete, a running step that slowed suddenly to a stealthier pace. I sank to my hands and knees and crawled forward with care, the metal surface beneath me buckling and trembling. I had to hump my shoulder bag in front of me as I progressed. I was trying not to call attention to myself, but the rickety catwalk rattled and danced beneath my weight.

I spotted a small wooden door in the wall. With infinite care, I eased the latch back and opened it. Before me was a dimly lighted, musty passageway about six feet high, rimmed along the top with a continuous series of hand-cranked window panels, some of which were standing open, admitting artificial light. The floor of the passageway was carpeted and smelled of dust motes. I felt my way forward, still on hands and knees, now hauling the bag after me. The silence was punctuated only by the sound of my ragged breathing.

I turned and eased the door shut behind me, then crept over to the nearest window and lifted myself gingerly to my feet. Below was one of those vast meeting rooms meant for banquets and large assemblages. An endless pattern of fleur-de-lis proceeded across the carpeting, steel blue on a ground of gray. A series of sliding doors could be drawn across the space at the midway point, effectively dividing the one room into two. Eight evenly spaced chandeliers hung like clusters of icicles, throwing out a flat light. Around the periphery, up near the ceiling where I was, the continuous rim of mirrored-glass windows concealed the space where I hid. I peered back across my shoulder. Through the gloom now, I could see the looming apparatus for a lighting system that must have been called into play on special occasions, floods and spots with various colored gels.

By the light coming through the windows, I hunkered down and opened my bag, taking out my wallet. I removed my driver's license, PI license, and other identification, including cash and credit cards, all of which I stuffed in the pockets of my blazer in haste. I snagged Ray's car keys, my birth control pills, the key picks, and my Swiss Army knife, cursing the fact that women's suit jackets aren't constructed with an interior breast pocket. I plucked out my toothbrush and tucked it in with the other items. My blazer pockets were bulging, but I couldn't help myself. In a pinch, I'm willing to suffer tatty underpants, but not unbrushed teeth.

I became aware that the floor beneath me was vibrating ever so slightly. In California, I'd assume that a 2.2 magnitude temblor was lapping through the earth like an ocean wave. I whipped my head around toward the door. I set my bag aside, sank to a hunkering position, and duck-walked across the narrow passage. I felt the perimeter of the door, fingers searching for the latch bolt on my side. On the far side of the wall, someone was making shaky progress, just as I had, along the catwalk. I found the latch and, ever so silently, pushed the bolt through the eye.

I still had my hand on the bolt when the door gave a vicious rattle. Someone on the far side was testing the latch. A spurt of fear traveled through me, triggering tears that leapt into my eyes. I pressed my hand against my mouth to suppress a gasp. The door was chattering against the lock so hard I thought it would give way, leaving me exposed to view. Silence. Then the floor began to shake again as Gilbert moved away. I glanced to my left, following his progress as he continued down the catwalk. I prayed there wasn't another wooden doorway farther down the line.

He must have reached a dead end because a few minutes later, I felt the floor vibrate with his weight as he passed me again, this time heading toward the ladder leading down to the corridor.

I waited until I thought I was safe. It felt like an eternity but was probably close to fifteen minutes. Then I reached out carefully and pushed the bolt back. I bent my head to listen, hearing nothing. When I opened the door, the fire alarm went off.

14

My opening of the door and the clanging were so closely connected, I thought Gilbert had booby-trapped the door somehow. The overhead sprinklers came on in a torrent of internal rain. The distant scent of smoke assailed me, as unmistakable as the lingering trail of perfume when a woman passes. I moved back to the windows overlooking the banquet room. There was no sign of flames, no billowing black smoke. The room looked empty, bright and blank. Someone began to make an announcement on the public address system, giving instructions or advice about what hotel guests were supposed to do. All I could hear was the muffled urgency of the proclamation. The exact location of the fire was anybody's guess.

The lights went out, plunging me into total darkness. I felt my way over to the wooden door, crawling through unencumbered by worldly possessions. I was being stripped down to the essentials, feeling light and free and, at the same time, anxious. My handbag was a talisman, as comforting as a security blanket. Its bulk and heft were familiar, its contents assurance that certain totem items were always within reach. The bag had served as both pillow and weapon. It felt odd to be shed of it, but I knew it had to be. Blindly, I measured the width of the catwalk, sensing the cavernous abyss on my left where my hand plunged suddenly into nothingness.

The entire area was pitch black, but I could hear an ominous pop and crackling noise. A blistering wind blew, sending a shower of sparks in my direction. I could smell hot, dry wood, undercut by the acrid odor of petroleum-based products changing chemical states. I inched my way forward. Ahead, I could now discern a soft reddish glow defining the wall where the corridor curved left. A long finger of smoke curled around the corner toward me. If the fire caught me on the catwalk, it would probably sweep right past, but the rising cloud of toxic fumes would snuff me out as effectively as the flames.

While the water from the sprinkler system hissed steadily, it seemed to have no effect on the fire that I could see. The play of tawny light on the walls began to expand and dance, pushing fine ash and black smoke ahead of it, gobbling up all the available oxygen. The metal catwalk was slippery, the chain railing swinging wildly as I propelled myself onward. The public address system came to life again. The same announcement was repeated, a garbled blend of consonants. I reached the top of the ladder. I was afraid to turn my back on the encroaching fire, but I had no choice. With my right foot, I felt for the first rung, gauging the distance as I moved down from rung to rung. I began descending with care, my hands sliding on the wet metal side rail. Hanging lengths of chain turned gold in the light, sparks flying up, winking out like intermittent fireflies on a hot summer night. By now, the fire was providing sufficient illumination to see the air turn gray as smoke accumulated.

I reached the bottom of the ladder and moved to my left. The fire was heating the air to an uncomfortable degree. I could hear a snapping sound, glass shattering, the merry rustle of destruction as the flames roared toward me. Despite the liberal use of concrete, the hotel had sufficient combustible material to feed the swiftly spreading blaze. I heard the dull boom of thunder as something behind me gave way and collapsed. This entire portion of the hotel had apparently been engulfed. I spotted a door on my left. I tried the knob, which was cool to the touch. I turned it and pushed through, spilling abruptly into a second-floor hall.

Here the air was much cooler. The rain birds in the ceiling showered the deserted corridor with irregular sprays. I was getting used to the dark, which now seemed less dense, a chalky gloom instead of the impenetrable black of the inner corridor. The carpet was saturated, slapping wetly beneath my feet as I stumbled down the darkened hallway. Afraid to trust my eyes, I held my arms out stiffly, waving my hands in front of me like a game of blindman's buff. The fire alarm continued its monotonous clanging, a secondary horn bleating gutturally. In a submarine movie, we'd be diving by now. I felt my way across another door frame. Again, the knob seemed cool to the touch, suggesting that, for the time being, the fire wasn't raging on the other side. I turned the knob, pushing the door open in front of me. I found myself on the fire stairs, which I knew intimately by now. I went down through the blackness, reassured by the familiarity of the stairwell. The air was cold and smelled clean.

When I reached the main floor, the emergency generators kicked in and briefly lights flickered back to life. The corridor was deserted, doors closed. Here, there was no sign of movement, no hint of smoke, the sprinkler system muffled. Every public room I passed was empty of guests. I found a fire door marked Emergency Exit with a big flexible bar across the center, the surface posted with warnings. As I pushed through the door, yet another siren began to howl behind me. I walked rapidly, without a backward glance, until I reached the side lot where Ray's rental car was parked.

The fire engines were pulled up at the hotel entrance, where clusters of evacuated hotel guests were milling about. The night sky was a fervent yellow, choked by columns of white smoke where the fire and the water from the hoses came into contact. At the side of the building, two sprays of water crossed in midair like a pair of klieg lights. Parts of the hotel were completely engulfed by fire, glass crashing, flames curling up as a cloud of black smoke rolled out. The portion of the driveway that I could see was blocked by the fire trucks and fire hoses, emergency vehicles flashing strobes of amber light. Overhead, a helicopter hovered where a local news team was taking pictures, reporting live at the scene.

I found Ray's car keys in my blazer pocket and let myself into his rental. I started the engine and flipped the heater on. My clothes were soaked, water still trickling down my face from the hair plastered to my head. I knew I smelled of smoke, wet wool, wet denim, and damp socks. The Texas night was cold, and I could feel myself being overtaken by a bone-deep shivering. I let the engine warm up. The car was a "full-size" Ford: a four-door automatic, white with a red interior. I threw the gears into reverse and backed out of the slot, scanning the empty parking lot for signs of Gilbert.

I left my headlights off as I eased along the perimeter of the lot toward the far side. The exit was blocked by a cop with a flashlight, forcing traffic to detour. I picked a spot along a row of hedges and drove across the curb, forcing the car through the thickly growing bushes. I emerged on the access road about a hundred yards beyond the roadblock. The officer probably saw me, but there was not much that he could do. He had his hands full directing all the carloads of rubberneckers. I turned right on the road leading back to the main highway. As I passed the miniature stone castle, I slowed, giving my horn a quick beep. Ray and Laura emerged hurriedly from the shadows, Ray toting the three bags, loaded down like a pack mule. Laura still wore the phony harness in front, the eight thousand dollars borne against her belly like an infant. The illusion of pregnancy was so convincing that Ray hovered protectively. I heard the trunk pop open, followed by the thumping impact as Ray flung the bags in the back and banged the lid down. He opened the door on the passenger side front and slid onto the seat next to me while Laura let herself in the back. I put my foot on the gas and took off with a chirp, anxious to put distance between us and the enemy.

Ray said, "We didn't think you'd show. We were just about to take off on foot." He turned around, peering through the rear window at the burning hotel behind us. "Gilbert did that?"

"One assumes," I said.

"Of course he did," Laura said peevishly. "He was probably waiting out front, ready to pick us off as we came through the revolving doors."

I glanced at her in the rearview mirror. Like Ray, she had turned to peer back at the fire. The glow on the horizon varied from blood red to salmon, a white cloud billowing where the water from the fire hoses turned to steam. "It's a hell of a blaze. How'd he manage it without accelerants?"

"Give him credit. The guy's resourceful. He's quick on his feet and he's good at improvisation," she said.

Ray turned to face forward, reaching for his seat belt, which he snapped into place. I saw him glance at me again, checking my bedraggled state. I felt like a dog left in the backyard during a sudden rain. He leaned sideways on his seat, pulling out a handkerchief that he passed me. Gratefully, I mopped at the trickles of water running down my face. "Thanks."

"You going back to the airport?"

"Not looking like this. Besides, I've already missed my . . . Shit!" I realized with a jolt that I'd left my plane tickets in the shoulder bag I'd abandoned. I patted my blazer pockets, but there wasn't any point. I couldn't believe it. Of all things. In my haste, I'd simply missed the airline envelope. If I'd just grabbed the ticket or, better yet, held on to the bag itself. Now all I owned were the odds and ends I carried on my person. I was nearly sick with regret. The plane ticket represented not only my return home, but most of my liquid assets. I banged on the steering wheel. "Goddamn it," I said.

Laura leaned forward against the front seat. "What's wrong?"

"I left my plane ticket back there."

"Uh-oh. Well, it's gone now," she said, stating the obvious with what looked like a smirk. If I hadn't been at the wheel, I'd have leapt in the backseat and bitten her.

Ray must have seen the expression that crossed my face. "Where we headed?" he asked, probably hoping to avoid a rabies quarantine.

"I don't even know where we are," I groused. I pointed to the glove compartment. "You got a map in there?"

He opened the glove compartment, which was empty except for the rental car contract and a whisk broom with chewed-looking bristles. He snapped it shut and checked the passenger door pocket. I slid a hand into the pocket on my side, coming up with assorted papers, one a neatly folded map of the United States. Ray grunted with satisfaction and flipped on the overhead light. Spread out, the crackling map took up most of the available space. "Looks like you need to keep an eye out for U.S. 30 heading northeast."

"Where to?"

Laura glanced over at him. "I bet to Louisville, right?"

He turned to her. "You got a problem with that?"

"Gilbert's not a fool, Ray. Where you think he's going?"

"So the guy goes to Louisville. Who gives a shit? We're talking about a twelve-hour drive. He's never going to figure out which route we took."

"Listen, Einstein. There's only *one,*" she said.

"Can't be. That's bullshit. There must be half a dozen," he said.

She reached over and snatched the map away. "You been in prison too long." I could hear her flap the map noisily in the backseat, refolding it while she found the section showing Dallas and points east. "Look at this. There's maybe one other way to go, but 30's the obvious choice. All Gilbert has to do is drive like a maniac and get there first."

"How's he going to find us? Once we get to town, we'll take a couple motel rooms and use fictitious names. Pay cash and call ourselves anything we want. Isn't that what you did?"

"Yeah, and look what happened. Kinsey found me in no time flat. So did Gilbert, for that matter."

"It was a fluke. Finding you was pure accident. Ask her," he said.

"I wouldn't call it a *fluke,*" I said, taking offense.

"You know what I mean. The point is, it's not like you *deduced* what she was calling herself and tracked her down from that. All you did was follow her, right?"

"Yeah, but what about Gilbert? How'd he manage it?" I asked.

Ray shrugged. "He probably persuaded Farley to spill the beans."

From the backseat, Laura moaned. "Oh, jeez. Is that true? I hadn't thought about that. You think Farley's okay?"

"I can't worry about that right now," Ray said.

I glanced back at Laura, still in charge of the map. "What's the nearest big town between here and there?"

Laura checked the map again. "We get to Texarkana first and then Little Rock. After that it's Memphis, then Nashville, and straight on up. Why?"

"Because I'm heading home. We'll take a side trip to the airport in Little Rock and I'll catch a plane."

"What about your ticket?" Ray asked.

"I'll call a friend of mine. He'll help."

Laura said, "In the meantime, how about a pit stop before I wet my pants?"

"Sounds good to me," Ray said.

I watched the highway signs until I spotted an off-ramp that boasted the international symbols for food and potty chairs. Half a block off the road, we found a poorly lighted independent gas station with a cafe attached. Even Gilbert wasn't canny enough to ferret us out here. The gas tank was still very close to full, so I bypassed the pumps and parked off to one side, away from the street. Ray headed for the men's room while Laura opened the trunk and pulled out her duffel bag. "You can borrow my dress."

In the sour light of the ladies' room, I removed my Reeboks and wet socks and then peeled off my damp blazer, blue jeans, turtleneck, and soggy undergarments. I was shivering again, but Laura's dry clothes began to warm me almost as soon as I pulled them on. She still wore the dark green corduroy jumper with a white turtleneck under it while I was assigned the denim dress, a pair of tights, and slightly oversize tennis shoes. "See you in a minute," she said. She left the rest room, giving me a few minutes alone.

I ran water in the sink until the hot came through, then rinsed my face and doused my head, washing out the smell of smoke. I used the harsh paper toweling to dry my hair, then used my fingers to comb the strands into place. I felt a wave of nausea rush through me like a hot flash. I put my hands on the sink, leaning on my arms, while I composed myself. Sunday night and I was stuck in some nameless Dallas suburb with an ex-con, his daughter, and a papoose of illicit cash. I let out a big breath and stared at my reflection in the dingy mirror. I shrugged ruefully. Things could (probably) be worse. So far, no one had been hurt and I had a few bucks left. I was looking forward to a meal, though I'd have to depend on my companions to pay for it. As soon as we got to Little Rock, I'd put a call through to Henry, who would come to my rescue. He could wire me money, buy the airline ticket on his credit card, or some combination thereof. By morning I'd be safely tucked in my bed, catching up on my sleep while I counted my blessings.

I went back to the car, stuffing most of my damp belongings in the trunk beside Ray's suitcases. The blazer, though still damp, I carried with me into the cafe, unwilling to have it out of my sight. The place was largely empty and had a homely, neglected air. Even the locals must have eschewed the establishment, which had probably started as a mom-and-pop operation and been reduced some time since to its current orphaned state. I didn't see any flies, but the ghosts of Flies Past seemed to hover in the air. The front windows were swathed in dust from some half-finished construction across the street. Even the fake potted plants carried a powdering of soot.

Ray and Laura sat across from each other in a corner booth. I slid in beside Ray, not that eager to have his bruised and battered face in view while I was trying to eat. Laura didn't look much better. Like me, she wore no makeup, but while bare skin is my preferred state, she'd been carefully camouflaging the blows Gilbert had systematically administered. I had to guess that most of her bruises had been inflicted some time ago because the darkest discolorations had washed out to mild greens and yellows. Ray, by contrast, was a veritable rainbow of abuse, scabbed and cut and restitched here and there. I kept my gaze pinned to the menu, which offered all the standard items: chicken-fried steak and chicken-fried chicken, hamburgers, fries, BLTs, grilled-cheese sandwiches, and "fresh" soups probably poured from big cans in the back. We ordered cheeseburgers, fries, and large, nearly fizz-free Cokes. Without carbonation, the soft drinks tasted like the syrups once used as home remedies for ladies' maladies. The waitress had the good grace not to quiz my companions about their injuries.

While we ate, I said to Ray, "Just out of curiosity, once you get to Louisville, how will you figure out where the money's hidden?"

He finished a bite of burger and wiped his mouth with a paper napkin. "Don't know that yet. Johnny said he'd leave word with Ma in case something happened to him, but who knows if he ever got around to it. Deal was, I'd get out of prison and come find him in California. Then the two of us would go back to Louisville and pick up the money. He wanted things ceremonial, you know, celebrate all the wait and all the hard work went into it. Any rate, as near as I can tell, wherever the money's at, it takes a key to get to."

"Which I have," I said.

"What key?" Laura asked. This was apparently news to her, and she seemed to resent that I knew more than she did.

Ray ignored her. "You still got it?"

"With a little notice, I can lay hands on it," I said.

"Good. I don't want you going off without passing it over."

"You think I'm going to help you cheat Chester out of his fair share?"

"Hey, he'd do the same to me. He'll probably cheat you, too."

"I don't even want to get into that," I said. "You think Johnny really did what he said?"

"I can't believe he'd put dough like that in limbo. He'd have a backup plan, some kind of fail-safe, in case he got hit by a car, something like that. What makes you ask? You got any ideas yourself?"

I shook my head. "It's just an interesting proposition. What's your strategy?"

"My strategy is solve that problem when I come to it," he said.

Once we hit the road again, Ray crawled in the back to sleep while I drove and Laura took his place in the passenger seat. The two of us watched the silver ribbon of highway curl away beneath us. The lights on the dashboard threw off a soft illumination. In deference to Ray, we kept the radio turned down and confined our conversation to an occasional remark. Ray began to snore, a sputtering exsufflation punctuated by quiet, as if someone were holding his nose shut at intervals. When it was clear that nothing short of a four-car flame-out was going to wake him, we began to chat in low tones.

"I take it you never had a chance to spend time with him," I said.

Laura shrugged. "Not really. My mother used to make me write once a month. She was always big on taking care of those less fortunate than we were. I can remember looking around, wondering who the hell she could be talking about. Then she remarried and seemed to forget about Ray. Made me feel guilty at first 'til I forgot myself. Little kids aren't exactly famous for satisfying other people's needs."

I said, "Actually, I think kids try to satisfy everyone. What other choice do they have? When you're dependent on someone, you better hope you keep 'em happy."

"Said like a true neurotic. Are your parents still alive?"

"No. They died together in an accident when I was five."

"Yeah. Well, imagine if one of 'em suddenly showed up one day. You live your life wishing you had a father. Then suddenly you have one and you realize you don't have the vaguest idea what to do with him." She cast an uneasy look in the backseat at Ray. If he was faking sleep, he was really good at it.

I said, "Are you close to your mother?"

"I was until Gilbert. She doesn't like him much, but that's probably because he never paid her much attention. She's a bit of a southern belle. She likes guys who fawn."

"What about your stepfather? What's the story on him?"

"He and Gilbert are as thick as thieves. He never wanted to believe Gilbert's hitting me was unprovoked. It's not like he *approved.* He just always assumes there's another side to it. He's the kind who says 'Well, that's *your* story. I'm sure Gilbert would have something else to say about this.' He prides himself on being fair, not jumping to conclusions. Like a judge, you know? He wants to hear prosecution and defense arguments before he hands down his sentence. He says he doesn't want to be judgmental. What he really means is he doesn't believe a word I say. Whatever Gilbert does, I deserve, you know? He probably wishes he could take a pop at me himself."

"What about your mother? Didn't she object to Gilbert's hitting you, or didn't she know?"

"She says whatever Paul says. It's like an unspoken agreement. She doesn't want to rock the boat. She doesn't like conflicts or disagreements. All she wants is peace and quiet. She's just so thrilled to have someone taking care of her, she doesn't want to make waves. Paul always makes out like he's doing her such a big favor being married to her. I think she was twenty-four when they met. I was maybe five years old. So there she was, with an ex-husband in jail and no means of support. The only job she ever had was working as a drugstore clerk. She couldn't make enough to survive. She had to go on welfare, which she thought was the lowest of the low. Her big shame. What the hell. She needed help. It's not like I was illegitimate, but in her eyes, it was the worst. She never wants to have to sink to that again. Besides, with Paul, she doesn't have to work. He doesn't want her to. He wants her to keep house and cater to his every whim. Not a bad deal."

"Yes, it is. It sounds grim."

Laura smiled. "I guess it does, doesn't it? Anyway, when I was growing up, Paul was critical, authoritarian. He ruled the roost. He nearly broke his arm patting himself on the back for all he did for us. In his own way, he was good to her. He never gave a shit about me, but to be fair about it, I'm sure I was a pain. Probably still am, if it comes to that." She leaned her head back against the seat. "Are you married?"

"I was." I held up two fingers.

"You were married twice? Me too. Once to a guy with a 'substance abuse' problem," she said, using her fingers to mark the phrase with quotes.

"Cocaine?"

"That and heroin. Speed, grass, stuff like that. The other husband was a mama's boy. Jesus, he was weak. He got on my nerves because he was so insecure. He didn't know how to do anything.

Plus, he needed all this reassurance. Like what do I know? I'm hardly in a position to make somebody else feel good."

"What about Gilbert?"

"He was great, at first. His problem is, he doesn't trust, you know? He doesn't know how to open up. He can really be so sweet. Sometimes when he drinks, he busts out crying like a baby. Breaks my heart."

"Along with your nose," I said.

15

We passed through Greenville, Brashear, Saltillo, and Mt. Vernon, crossing sparsely wooded farmland on gently rolling hills. Laura fell asleep with her head against the window. Traffic was light and the road was hypnotic. Twice I jerked myself awake, having dropped into a moment of microsleep. To keep alert, I reviewed my intellectual *Atlas of Texarkana* facts, discovering in the process that the entire category contained only two bits of information. First, the Arkansas-Texas state line bisects the town of Texarkana, so that half the population lives in Texas and half in Arkansas. And last, the town is the site of a Federal Correctional Institution, about which I knew nothing else. So much for that form of mental stimulation.

On the outskirts of town, I pulled into an all-night filling station, where I stopped to stretch my legs. Ray was still dead to the world so Laura traded places with me and took the wheel. Laura pitched in five bucks and we bought exactly that much gas. It was close to ten-thirty when we crossed the state line, with approximately two hours to go until we reached Little Rock. I settled into the passenger seat, slouched on my spine, knees bent, my feet propped up on the dashboard. I crossed my arms for warmth. The remaining damp in my blazer enveloped me in a humid cloud of woolly smells. The drone of the engine combined with Ray's staccato snores had a tranquilizing effect. The next thing I knew I was drooling on myself. I put my feet down and sat up straight, feeling groggy and disoriented. We passed a highway sign that indicated we'd left U.S. 30 and were now heading north on U.S. 40. "How far to Little Rock?"

"We already passed Little Rock. This is Biscoe coming up."

"We *passed* Little Rock? I told you I wanted to stop," I whispered hoarsely.

"What was I supposed to do? You had the map and you were sound asleep. I had no idea where the airport was, and I didn't want to drive all over hell and gone trying to find it."

"Why not wake me?"

"I tried once. I said your name and got no response."

"Weren't there any road signs?"

"Not that I saw. Besides, they're not going to have any flights out at this hour. This is the boonies. Get a clue," she whispered back. She reverted to a normal tone, though she kept her voice down in deference to Ray. "It's time to find a motel so we can get a couple hours' sleep. I'm half dead. I about ran off the road more than once in the last hour."

I did a three-sixty scan of the terrain, spotting little in the dark beyond farms and occasional dense woods. "Take your pick," I said.

"There'll be a town coming up," she said without concern.

Sure enough, we came to a townlet with a one-story off-road motel, its vacancy sign winking. She pulled into a small gravel parking lot and got out. She turned her back to the car and reached up under her jumper, apparently removing a wad of cash from the belly harness she wore. I gave Ray a nudge and he rose from the depths like a diver in the process of decompressing.

I said, "Laura wants to stop. We're both beat."

"Fine with me," he said. He pulled himself into a sitting position, blinking with puzzlement. "We still in Texas?"

"This is Arkansas. We got Little Rock behind us and Memphis coming up."

"I thought you were leaving us."

"So did I."

He yawned, giving his face a dry rub with his hands. He squinted at his watch, trying to see the dial in the scanty light. "What time is it?"

"After one."

I could see Laura at the entrance to the motel lobby. The lights inside were dim, and the front door must have been locked because I saw her knock repeatedly, then cup her hands against the glass to peek in. Finally, some unhappy-looking soul emerged from the manager's office. Much animated conversation, hand gestures, and peering in our direction. Laura was admitted to the office, where I saw her at the counter, filling out the registration card. My guess was her being pregnant lent her an air of vulnerability, especially at this hour. A fistful of cash probably didn't hurt her cause. Moments later, she emerged from the office and returned to the car, dangling two room keys, which she handed to me as she got back behind the wheel. "Ray gets his own room. I can't sleep with that racket."

She started the car and pulled around to the rear. Ours were the last two rooms at the far end. There was only one other car and it had Iowa plates, so I figured we were temporarily safe from Gilbert. Ray hauled one of his bags from the trunk while Laura grabbed the duffel and I took the armload of damp clothes I'd dumped. Maybe hanging them up overnight would finish the drying process and render them wearable.

Ray paused at his door. "What time in the morning?"

"I think we should be on the road by six. If we're going, get on with it. No point fooling around," Laura said. "Open your drapes when you're up and we'll do likewise." She glanced at me. "Okay with you?"

"Sure, it's fine."

Ray disappeared into his room and I followed her into ours: two double beds and a drab interior complete with mustiness. If the color beige had an odor, it would smell like this. It looked like the kind of place where you wouldn't want to jump out of bed without making a noise first. Otherwise, you might inadvertently step on one of the scuttling hard-shelled bugs. The little fellow I saw had gotten trapped in the corner, where he was patiently pawing the walls like a dog wanting out. You can't squish those things without risking that sudden spurt of lemon pudding on the sole of your shoe. I hung my garments in the closet, after a gingerly inspection. No brown recluse spiders or furry rodents in evidence.

The bathroom boasted brown vinyl tile, a fiberglass shower enclosure, two plastic glasses wrapped in cellophane, and two paper-wrapped soaps the size of business cards. I pulled out my traveling toothbrush and weensy tube of toothpaste and brushed my teeth in wordless ecstasy. In the absence of a nightie, I slept in my (borrowed) underwear, folding the cotton coverlet in half for warmth. Laura went into the bathroom, piously shutting the door before she removed her belly harness. I was asleep within minutes and never heard her climb into her own creaking bed.

It was still dark when she bumped me at 5:45 A.M. "You want to shower first?" she asked.

"You go ahead."

The light blasted on in the bathroom, slanting across my face briefly before she closed the door. She'd opened the drapes, admitting illumination from the lights outside in the parking lot. Through the wall, I thought I could hear the shower next door, which meant Ray was awake. In prison, he'd probably always risen at this hour. Now a shower would be a luxury, since he'd have it to himself and wouldn't have to worry about sexual assault every time he dropped the soap. I raised up on one elbow and looked out at the auto body shop across the street. A forty-watt bulb burned above the service bay. Monday morning and where was I? I checked the printed match packet in the ashtray. Oh, yeah. Whiteley, Arkansas. I remembered the road sign outside of town claiming a population of 523. Probably an exaggeration. I felt a sudden surge of melancholy, longing for home. In the crazy days of my youth, before herpes and AIDS, I used to wake up occasionally in rooms like this one. There's a certain horror when you can't quite remember who's whistling so merrily behind the bathroom door. Often, when I found out, I couldn't help but question my taste in male companionship. It didn't take long to see morality as the quickest way to avoid self-loathing.

When Laura cleared the bathroom, fully dressed, the belly harness in place, I brushed my teeth, showered, and washed my hair with the diminishing sliver of soap. My blue jeans, while dry, were still suggestive of ashtrays and cold campfires, so I donned Laura's denim dress again. Just being clean gave me an enormous lift. I retrieved my hanging garments from the closet and took them out to the car.

The drive had been taking us on a steady line to the north. Here, the cold was more pronounced. The air felt thinner and the wind more cutting. Ray had pulled on a fleece-lined denim jacket, and as we got in the car, he tossed a sweatshirt to each of us. Gratefully, I pulled the sweatshirt over my head and wore my blazer over that. With the bulk of the sweatshirt, the fit was so tight I could hardly move my arms, but at least I was warm. Laura draped her sweatshirt across her shoulders like a shawl. I got in the backseat, waiting in the car while Laura dropped off the keys and Ray poured loose change into the vending machine around the corner from the office. They came back to the car with an assortment of snacks and soft drinks that Ray distributed among us. After Laura had pulled onto the highway, we ate a breakfast that consisted of off-brand cola, peanuts, chocolate bars, peanut-butter crackers, and cheese snacks completely devoid of nutritional value.

Laura put the heater on and the car was soon filled with the soapy scent of Ray's aftershave. Aside from the battered face and splinted fingers, both of which looked vile, he was meticulous about his grooming. He seemed to have an endless supply of plain white T-shirts and chinos. For a man in his mid-sixties, he seemed to be in good physical shape. Meanwhile, both Laura and I were looking more bedraggled by the hour. In the close quarters of the rental car, I could see that her dark auburn hair had been dyed to that flaming shade. Her part was slowly growing out, a widening margin of gray. The strands bordering her face showed a rim of white like the narrow matting on a picture frame. I wondered if premature graying was a family trait.

The sun rose from behind a mountain of early morning clouds massed on the horizon, the sky changing swiftly from apricot to butter yellow to a mild clear blue. The land around us was flat. Looking at the map, I could see this portion of the state was part of the Mississippi flood plain, all the rivers draining east and south toward the Mississippi River. Lakes and hot springs dotted the map like rain splats, the northwest corner of the state weighted down with the Boston and the Ouachita Mountains. Laura kept her foot pressed firmly to the accelerator, maintaining a steady sixty miles an hour.

We were in Memphis at seven. I kept an eye out for a pay phone, intending to call Henry, but realized California was two hours behind. He tended to rise early, but five A.M. was really pushing it. Laura, sensing my train of thought, caught my eye in the rearview mirror. "I know you want to get home, but can't you wait until Louisville?"

"What's wrong with Nashville? We'll be there by midmorning, which is perfect for me."

"You'll slow us down. Check the map if you don't believe me. We'll be coming in on 40, taking 65 North across the state line. The Nashville airport is over on the far side of town. We'll lose an hour." She passed the map back to me, folded over to the section she was talking about.

I checked the relative distances. "You won't lose an hour. You're talking twenty minutes max. I thought you didn't want to go to Louisville, so what's the big hurry now?"

"I never said I didn't want to go. That's where I *live.* I said that's where Gilbert's going. I want to get my stuff out of the apartment before he shows up."

Ray said, "Forget your stuff. Buy new. Stay away from there. You make a trip to the apartment, you run right into him."

"Not if I can get there before he does," she said. "That's why I don't want to waste time taking her to the airport. She can do that in Louisville. It isn't that much farther."

I could feel my body heat up with rising irritation. "It's another three hours."

"I'm not stopping," she said.

"Who put you in charge?"

"Who put *you?*"

"Ladies, hey! Knock it off. You're getting on my nerves. We got Gilbert to contend with. That's enough." Ray turned to look at me, his manner solicitous. "I have a suggestion. I know you're anxious to get home, but a few hours' delay isn't going to make any difference. Come to Louisville with us. We'll take you to my ma's where it's safe. You can take a hot shower and clean up while she runs your clothes through her machine." He glanced at Laura. "You come, too. She'd love to see you, I'm sure. How many years since you've visited your gramma?"

"Five or six," she said.

"See? She probably misses you like crazy. I'm sure she does," he said. "She'll fix a great home-cooked meal and then we'll take you to the airport. We'll even pay for your ticket."

Laura took her eyes off the road. "*We* will? Since when?"

"Come on. She's only in this because of us. Chester's probably never going to pay her, so now she's out the bucks. What's it going to cost us? It's the least we can do."

"You're very generous with money you don't have," she remarked.

Ray's smile faltered. Even from my position in the backseat, I could see the shift in his mood. "You saying I'm not entitled to what's in there?" he said, indicating her belly.

"Of course you're entitled. I didn't mean it that way, but this is costing us plenty as it is," she said.

"So?"

"So you could at least ask me first. I got a stake in it, too. In fact, the last I heard, you were giving me the whole eight grand."

"You turned me down."

"I did not!"

"You did when I was there," I said, practically sticking my tongue out at her.

"Would you tell her to stay out of our business! This has nothing to do with you, Kinsey, so mind your own beeswax."

I felt a laugh bubble up. "Be a sport. This is fun. I'm the adopted daughter. This is 'family dynamic.' Isn't that what it's called? I read about this stuff, but I never got to experience it. Sibling rivalry's a hoot."

"What do you know about family?"

"Not a thing. That's my point. I like all this bickering now that I've got the hang of it."

Ray said, "Is that true? You don't have family?"

"I have relatives, but no one close. Some cousins up in Lompoc, but none of this day-to-day stuff where people crank on each other and make trouble and act ugly."

"I lived a lot of years without family. It's my one regret," he said. "Anyway, will you come with us as far as Louisville? We'll get you home. I swear."

I'm a sucker when someone asks me nicely, especially an honorary father who smelled as good as he did. I said, "Sure. Why not? Your mother sounds like a trip."

"That she is," he said.

"How long since you've seen her?"

"Seventeen years. I was out on parole, but I got picked up on a violation before I got this far. She never came to see me in prison. I guess she didn't want to deal with it."

Having negotiated our agreement, we drove on in peace. We reached Nashville at 10:35, all of us hungry. Laura spotted a McDonald's, the golden arches visible off the Briley Parkway. She took the nearest off-ramp. As soon as we pulled into the parking lot, I saw her reach a hand under her jumper, where she made a discreet withdrawal from the Belly Button National Bank and Trust. Since mine was the only face unmarked by recent pounding, I was elected to go into the restaurant and purchase our lunch. To ensure variety in our diet, I bought an assortment of hamburgers, Big Macs, and Quarter Pounders with Cheese. I also bought two sizes of French fries, onion rings, and Cokes large enough to make us pee every twenty minutes. I also picked up three boxes of animal crackers, with nifty string handles, for those of us good enough to clean our plates. To show how refined we were, we ate while the car was still parked at the rear of the lot and then took advantage of the rest rooms before we hit the road again. This time Ray drove, Laura moved over to the passenger seat, and I stretched out in the back and took a nap.

When I woke, I could hear Ray and Laura talking in low tones. Somehow the murmuring took me back to the car trips of childhood, my parents in the front seat, exchanging desultory remarks. That's probably how I learned to eavesdrop originally. I kept my eyes closed and tuned in to their conversation.

Ray was saying, "I know I haven't been any kind of father to you, but I'd like to try."

"I have a father. Paul's already been a father."

"Forget him. The guy's a turd. I heard you say so."

"When?"

"Last night in the car when you were talking to Kinsey. Said he criticized the shit out of you growing up."

"Exactly. I had a father. So why do I need two?"

"Call it a relationship. I want to be a part of your life."

"What for?"

"What *for?* What kind of question is that? You're the only kid I got. We're blood kin."

"Blood kin. What bull."

"How many people can you say that about?"

"Thankfully, not many," she said with acid.

"Skip it. Have it your way. I'm not going to force myself on you. You can do what you like."

"No need to take offense. This is not about you," she said. "That's just how life is. Let's be honest. I've never gotten anything from men except grief."

"I appreciate the vote of confidence."

The conversation trailed off. I waited a suitable few minutes, then yawned audibly as if just rousing myself. I sat up in the backseat, squinting out at the countryside as it whizzed past the car windows. The sun had come out, but the light seemed pale. I could see rolling hills, carpeted in dull November green. The grass was still alive, but all the deciduous trees had dropped their leaves. The barren branches created a gray haze as far as the eye could see. In some areas we passed, I could see hemlocks and pines. In summer, I imagined the land would be intensely green, the hillsides dense with vegetation. Ray was watching me in the rearview mirror. "You ever been to Kentucky?"

"Not that I remember," I said. "Isn't this supposed to be horse country? I expected blue grass and white fences."

"That's closer to Lexington, northeast of here. The fences these days are black. Over in the far eastern part of the state, you have the coal fields of Harlan County. This is western Kentucky where most of the tobacco's grown."

"She doesn't want a travelogue, Ray."

"Yes, I do," I said. She was always taking cuts at him, which made me feel protective. If she was going to be the bad daughter, I was going to be the good. "Show me on the map."

He pointed to an area north of the Tennessee border, between the Barren River Lake and the Nolan River Lake. "We just passed through Bowling Green, and we got Mammoth Cave National Park coming up on our left. We had time, we'd do the tour. Talk about dark. You go down in the caverns, when the guide turns out the lights? You can't see for shit. It's blacker than black, and it's dead quiet. Fifty-four degrees. It's like a meat-packing plant. Three hundred miles of passageways they've found so far. Last time I went was maybe 1932. A field trip in school. Left a big impression on me. When I was in prison, I used to think about that. You know, one day I'd come back and take the tour again."

Laura was looking at him strangely. "*That's* what you thought about? Not women or whiskey or fast cars?"

"All I wanted was to get away from overhead lights and the noise. The racket's enough to drive you nuts. And the smell. That's another thing about Mammoth Cave. It smells like moss and wet rocks. Doesn't smell like sweat and testosterone. It smells like life before birth . . . what's the word, primordial."

"Geez. I'm sorry I have to go back to California so soon. You're talking me into it," I said dryly.

Ray smiled. "You joke, but you'd like it. I guarantee."

"Primordial?" Laura said with disbelief.

"What, you're surprised I know words like that? I got my GED. I even took college classes. Economics and psychology and shit like that. Just because I was in prison doesn't mean I'm a fool. Lot of smart guys in prison. You'd be surprised," he said.

"Really," she said, sounding unconvinced.

"Yeah, really. I bet I can work a sewing machine better than you, for starters."

"That wouldn't take much," she said.

"This is very uplifting sitting here talking to you. You really know how to make a guy feel good about himself."

"Fuck you."

"You're the one complains your stepdad is always putting you down. Why don't you do better, improve the situation instead of acting like him?"

Laura said nothing. Ray studied her profile and finally looked back at the road.

The silence stretched uncomfortably, and I could feel myself squirm. "How far from here?"

"About an hour and a half. How're you doing back there?"

"I'm doing good," I said.

We reached Louisville just before noon, approaching the town on Highway 65. I could see the airport on our left, and I nearly whimpered with longing. We took an intersecting highway west through an area called Shively, bypassing most of the downtown business district. To our right, I could see the clusters of tall buildings, sturdy blocks of concrete, most of them squared off on top. Ahead of us was the Ohio River, with Indiana visible on the other side.

We exited in an area called Portland, which was where Ray Rawson grew up. I could see his smile quicken as he took in the neighborhood. He turned toward me halfway, putting his arms across the seat back. "The Portland Canal's down that way. Locks were built a hundred years ago to take river traffic past the falls. My great-grandfather worked on the construction. I'll take you over there if we have time."

I was more interested in catching a plane than seeing any of the local landmarks, but I knew the offer was part of his excitement at coming home. Having been incarcerated for most of the last forty-five years, he was probably feeling like Rip van Winkle, marveling at all the changes in the world at large. It might be a comfort that his immediate neighborhood seemed untouched by the passage of time. The streets were wide, trees showing the last vestiges of autumn leaves. Most trees were bare, but down the block I could see smatterings of yellow and red leaves remaining. On the street we'd taken, coming off the freeway, many house fronts had been converted into businesses: signs for child care, a hair salon, a tackle shop selling live bait. The yards were uniformly small and flat, separated by chicken-wire fences with dilapidated gates. Dead leaves, like scraps of brown paper, choked the house gutters and littered the walks. Ten- and twelve-year-old cars were parked at the curbs. Older models were lined up in driveways, with For Sale signs painted on the windshields. Telephone poles were more plentiful than trees, and the wires cut back and forth across the streets like supports for tenting that hadn't been erected yet. Down a side street, I could see railroad cars sitting on a side track.

I would have bet money the neighborhood had looked this way since the 1940s. There was no evidence of construction, no indication of any old structures torn down or condemned to make way for the new. Shrubs were overgrown. The tree trunks were massive, obstructing windows and porches where once the overhanging branches had provided only dappled shade. Sidewalks had buckled, broken by the roots. Forty years of weather had picked at the asphalt siding on some of the houses. Here and there I could see fresh paint, but my guess was that nothing much had changed in the years since Ray had been here.

As we pulled up in front of his mother's house, I could feel a heaviness descend. It was like the low droning note in the score for a horror movie, the minor chord that betokens a dark shape in the water, or something unseen, waiting in the shadows behind the basement door. The sensation was probably simple depression, born of borrowed clothes, junk food, and erratic sleep. Whatever the genesis, I knew it was going to be hours before I could get on a plane for California.

Laura turned off the ignition on the rental car and got out. Ray emerged on his side, searching the front of the house with wonderment. I had no choice but to join them. I felt like a prisoner, suffering a temporal claustrophobia so pronounced it made my skin itch.

16

Ray's mother's house was situated on a narrow lot on a street occupied entirely by single-family dwellings. The house was a two-story red-brick structure, with a one-story red-brick extension jutting out in front. The two narrow front windows sat side by side, caged by burglar bars and capped with matching lintels. Three concrete steps led up to the door, which was set flush against the house and shaded by a small wooden roof cap. I could see a second entrance tucked around on the right side of the house down a short walk. The house next door was a fraternal twin, the only difference being the absence of the porch roof, which left its front door exposed to the elements.

Ray headed for the side entrance with Laura and me tagging along behind like baby ducklings. Between the two houses, the air seemed very chill. I crossed my arms to keep warm, shifting restlessly from foot to foot, eager to be indoors. Ray tapped on the door, which had ornamental burglar bars across the glass. Through the window I could see bright light pouring from a room on the left, but there was no sign of movement. Idly, he talked over his shoulder to me. "These are called 'shotgun' cottages, one room wide and four rooms deep so you could stand at the front door and fire a bullet all the way through." He pointed up toward the second story. "Hers is called a humpback because it's got a second bedroom above the kitchen. My great-grandfather built both these places back in 1880."

"Looks like it," Laura said.

He pointed a finger at her. "Hey, you watch it. I don't want you hurting Gramma's feelings."

"Oh, right. Like I'd really stand here and insult her house. Geez, Ray. Give me credit for *some* intelligence."

"What is it with you? You're such a fuckin' victim," he said.

Inside the house, another light came on. Laura bit back whatever tart response she'd formed to her father's chiding. The curtain was pushed aside and an elderly woman peered out. In the absence of dentures, her mouth had rolled inward in a state of collapse. She was short and heavyset, with a soft round face, her white hair pulled up tightly in a hard knot wound around with rubber bands. She squinted through wire-frame glasses, both lenses heavily magnified. "What you want?" she bellowed through the glass at us.

Ray raised his voice. "Ma, it's me. Ray."

It took her a few seconds to process the information. Her confusion cleared and she put her gnarled hands up to her mouth. She began to work the locks—deadbolt, thumb lock, and burglar chain—ending in an old-fashioned skeleton key that took some maneuvering before it yielded. The door flew open and she flung herself into his arms. "Oh, Ray," she said tremulously. "Oh, my Ray."

Ray laughed, hugging her close while she made wordless mewing sounds of joy and relief. Though plump, she was probably half his size. She had on a white pinafore-style apron over a housedress that looked hand sewn: pink cotton with an imprint of white buttons in diagonal rows, the sleeves trimmed in pink rickrack. She pulled away from him, her glasses sitting crookedly on the bridge of her nose. Her gaze shifted to Laura, who stood behind him on the walk. It was clear she had trouble distinguishing faces in the cloudy world of impaired vision. "Who's this?" she said.

"It's me, Gramma. Laura. And this is Kinsey. She hitched a ride with us from Dallas. How are you?"

"Oh, my stars, Laura! Dear love. I can't believe it. This is wonderful. I'm so happy to see you. Looka here, what a mess I'm in. Didn't nobody tell me you were coming and now you've caught me in this old thing." Laura gave her a hug and kiss, holding herself sideways to conceal the solid bulge of her belly harness.

Ray's mother didn't seem to notice one way or the other. "Let me take a look at you." She put a hand on either side of Laura's face, searching earnestly. "I wish I could see you better, child, but I believe you favor your grandfather Rawson. God love your heart. How long has it been?" Tears trickled down her cheeks, and she finally pulled her apron up over her face to hide her embarrassment. She fanned herself then, shaking off her emotions. "What's the matter with me? Get on in here, all of you. Son, I'll never forgive you for not calling first. I'm a mess. House is a mess."

We trooped into the hallway, Laura first, then Ray, with me bringing up the rear. We paused while the old woman locked the doors again. I realized no one had ever mentioned her first name. To the right was the narrow stairway leading up to the second-floor bedroom, blanketed in darkness even at this time of day. To the left was the kitchen, which seemed to be the only room with lights on. Because the houses were so close to one another, little daylight crept into this section. There was only one kitchen window, on the far left-hand wall above a porcelain-and-cast-iron sink. A big oak table with four mismatched wooden chairs took up the center of the room, a bare bulb hanging over it. The bulb itself must have been 250 watts because the light it threw off was not only dazzling, but had elevated the room temperature a good twenty degrees.

The ancient stove was green enamel, trimmed in black, with four gas burners and a lift-up stove top. To the left of the door was an Eastlake cabinet with a retractable tin counter and a built-in flour bin and sifter. I could feel a wave of memory pushing at me. Somewhere I'd seen a room like this, maybe Grand's house in Lompoc when I was four. In my mind's eye, I could still picture the goods on the shelves: the Cut-Rite waxed paper box, the cylindrical dark blue Morton salt box with the girl under her umbrella ("When It Rains, It Pours"), Sanka coffee in a short orange can, Cream of Wheat, the tin of Hershey's cocoa. Mrs. Rawson's larder was stocked with most of the same items, right down to the opaque mint-green glass jar with SUGAR printed across the front. The over-size matching screw-top salt and pepper shakers rested nearby.

Ray's mother was already busy clearing piles of newspapers from the kitchen chairs despite Ray's protests. "Now, Ma, come on. You don't have to do that. Give me that."

She smacked at his hand. "You quit. I can do this myself. If you'd told me you were coming, I'd have had the place picked up. Laura's going to think I don't know how to keep house."

He took a stack of papers from her and stuck them in a haphazard pile against the wall. Laura murmured something and excused herself, moving into the back room. I was hoping there was a bathroom close by that I could visit in due course. I pulled out a chair and sat down, doing some visual snooping while Ray and his mother tidied up.

From where I sat, I could see part of the dining room with its built-in china cupboards. The room was crammed with junk, furniture and cardboard boxes making passage difficult. I caught sight of an old brown wood radio, a Zenith with a round dial set into a round-shouldered console the size of a chest of drawers. I could see the round shape of the underlying speaker where the worn fabric was stretched over it. The wallpaper pattern was a marvel of swirling brown leaves.

The room beyond the dining room was probably the parlor with its two windows onto the street and a proper front door. The kitchen smelled like a combination of moth balls and strong coffee sitting on the stove too long. I heard the shriek of plumbing, the flush mechanism suggestive of a waterfall thundering from a great height. When Laura emerged from the back room sometime later, she'd shed her belly harness. She was probably uncomfortable with the idea of having to explain her "condition" if her grandmother took notice.

I tuned in to the old woman, who was still grumbling good-naturedly about the unexpected visit. "I don't know how you expect me to cook up any kind of supper without the fixings on hand."

"Well, I'm telling you how," Ray said patiently. "You put together a list of what you need and we'll whip over to the market and be back in two shakes."

"I have a list working if I can find it," she said, poking through loose papers in the center of the table. "Freida Green, my neighbor two doors down, she's been carrying me to the market once a week when she goes. Here now. What's that say?"

Ray took the list and read aloud in a faky tone, "Says pork chops with milk gravy, yams, fried apples and onions, corn bread . . ."

She reached for the paper, but he held it out of reach. "I never. It does not. Let me see that. Is that what you want, son?"

"Yes, ma'am." He handed her the paper.

"Well, I can do that. I have yams out yonder, and I believe I still have some of them pole beans and stewed tomatoes I put up last summer. I just baked a batch of peanut-butter cookies. We can have them for dessert if you'll pick up a quart of vanilla ice cream. I want real. I don't want iced milk." She was writing as she spoke, large, angular letters drifting across the page.

"Sounds good to me. What do you think, Kinsey?" he asked.

"Sounds great."

"Oh, forevermore. Kinsey. Shame on me for my bad manners. I forgot all about you, honey. What can I get you? I might have a can of soda pop here somewhere. Take a look in the pantry and don't mind the state it's in. I been meaning to clean that out, but hadn't got to it."

"Actually, I'd love to borrow your phone, and a pen and scratch paper, if you don't mind."

"You go and help yourself as long as you don't call Paris, France. I'm on fixed income and that telephone costs too much as it is. Here's you a piece of paper. Laura, why don't you show her where the telephone is. Right in there beside the bed. I'll get busy with this list."

Ray said, "I also promised she could throw some clothes in the washing machine. You have detergent?"

"In the utility room," she said, pointing toward the door.

I took the proffered pen and paper and moved into the bedroom, which was as stuffy as a coat closet. The only light emanated from a small bathroom that opened on the left. Heavy drapes were pinned together over windows with the shades drawn. The double-bed mattress sagged in an iron bedstead piled with hand-tied quilts. The room would have been perfect in a 1940s home furnishings diorama at the state fair. All the surfaces were coated with a fine layer of dust. In fact, nothing in the house had seemed terribly clean, probably the by-product of the old woman's poor eyesight.

The old black dial telephone sat beside a crookneck lamp on the bed table, amid large-print books, pill bottles, lotions, and ointments. I flipped the light on and dialed Information, picking up the numbers for both United and American Airlines. I called United first, listening to the usual reassurances until my "call could be answered in the order it was received." Out of deference to Ray's mom, I refrained from searching her bed table drawer while I waited for the agent to pick up on his end. I did scan the room, looking for the belly harness. Had to be around here somewhere.

The agent finally came on the line and helped me get the reservations I needed. There was a flight from Louisville to Chicago at 7:12 P.M., arriving at 7:22, which reflected the hour's time difference. After a brief layover, I then connected to a flight departing from Chicago at 8:14 P.M., arriving in Los Angeles at 10:24, California time. The flight to Santa Teresa left at 11:00 and arrived forty-five minutes later. That last connection was tight, but the agent swore the arrival and departure gates would be close to one another. Since I was traveling without luggage, he didn't think it would be a problem. He did advise me to get to the airport an hour in advance of flight time so I could pay for the ticket.

He'd just put me on hold when Ray stuck his head in the door, a clean towel in one hand. "That's for you," he said, tossing it on the bed. "When you finish your call, you can hop in the shower. There's a robe hanging on the door. Ma says she'll throw your clothes in the wash when you're ready."

I put a palm across the mouthpiece and said, "Thanks. I'll bring 'em right out. What about the stuff in the car?"

"She's got that already. I brought everything in."

He started to depart and stuck his head around the door again. "Oh. I almost forgot. Ma says there's a one-hour cleaners in the same mall as the market. You want to give me your jacket, I can drop it off before we go shopping and pick it up on the way back."

The agent had come back on the line and was already busy reconfirming the flight arrangements while I nodded enthusiastically to Ray. With the receiver still tucked in the crook of my neck, I emptied the pockets of my blazer and handed it to him. He waved and withdrew while I finished up the call.

I headed for the bathroom, where with a quick search I uncovered the belly harness tucked down in the clothes hamper. I hauled it out and inspected it, impressed by the ingenuity of the construction. The housing resembled an oversize catcher's face mask, a convex frame made of semiflexible plastic tubing, wrapped with padding, into which countless bound packets of currency had been packed. Heavy canvas straps secured the harness once in place. I checked a couple of packets, riffling through five-, ten-, twenty-, and fifty-dollar notes of varying sizes. Many bills seemed unfamiliar and I had to assume were no longer in circulation. Several packets appeared to be literally in mint condition. It grieved me to think of Laura covering day-to-day expenses with bank notes that a serious collector would have paid dearly for. Ray was a fool to stand by while his daughter threw it all away. Who knew how much money still remained to be uncovered?

I tucked the harness down in the hamper. I'm big on closure and not good at leaving so many questions unanswered. However, (she said) this was not my concern. In six hours, I'd be heading for California. If there were additional monies in a stash somewhere, that was strictly Ray's business. There was a blue chenille bathrobe hanging on a hook on the back of the door. I stripped out of the borrowed denim dress and underwear, pulled the robe on, and carried my dirty clothes out to the kitchen. Ray and Laura had apparently left on their errand. I could see yams on the stove, simmering in a dark blue-and-white-speckled enamel pan. Quart Mason jars of tomatoes and green beans had been pulled off the pantry shelves and placed on the counter. Briefly, I pondered the possibilities of botulism poisoning arising from improperly preserved foods, but what the heck, the mortality rate is only sixty-five percent. Ray's mother probably wouldn't have attained such a ripe old age if she hadn't perfected her canning skills.

The door to the utility porch was open. That room wasn't insulated and the air pouring out of it was frigid. Ray's mother went about her business as if unaware of the chill. An early-model washer and dryer were arranged against the wall to the left. Tucked between them was a battered canister-style vacuum cleaner shaped like the nose cone of a spaceship. "I'm about to hop in the shower, Mrs. Rawson. Can I give you these?" I asked.

"There you are," she said. "I was just loading the few things Laura give me. You can call me Helen if you like," she added. "My late husband used to call me Hell on Wheels."

I watched as she felt for the measuring cup, tucking her thumb over the rim so she could feel how far up the side the detergent had come. "I've been considered legally blind for years, and my eyes is getting worse. I can still make my way around as long as people don't go putting things in my path. I'm scheduled for surgery, but I had to wait until Ray come home to help out. Anyway, I'm just yammering on. I don't mean to keep you."

"This is fine," I said. "Can I help with anything?"

"Oh no, honey. Go ahead and get your shower. You can keep that robe on 'til your clothes is done. Won't take long with these old machines. My friend, Freida Green, has new and it takes her three times as long to run a load through and uses twicet the water. Soon as I'm done with this, I'm going to put some corn bread together. I hope you like to eat."

"Absolutely. I'll be out shortly and give you a hand."

The shower was a mixed blessing. The water pressure was paltry, the hot and cold fluctuating wildly in response to cycles of the washing machine. I did manage to scrub myself thoroughly, washing my hair in a cumulus cloud of soapsuds, lathering and rinsing until I felt fresh again. I dried myself off and pulled on Helen's robe. I slipped into my Reeboks, my fastidious streak preventing me from walking around barefoot on floors only marginally clean. I'm generally not vain about my appearance, but I could hardly wait to get back into my own clothes.

Before returning to the kitchen, I used my telephone credit card to put in a long-distance call to Henry. He was apparently out somewhere, but his machine picked up. I said, "Henry, this is Kinsey. I'm in Louisville, Kentucky. It's after one o'clock here and

I've got a flight out at seven. I don't know what time we'll be heading for the airport, but I should be here for the next couple of hours. If it's possible, I need to have you meet me at the airport. I'm almost out of cash and I don't have a way to get my car out of hock. I can try borrowing the money here, but these people don't seem all that dependable. If I don't hear from you before I leave, I'll call you as soon as I get to Los Angeles." I checked the telephone number written on the round cardboard disk in the middle of the dial, reciting Helen's number to him before I hung up. I ran a comb through my hair and moved back into the kitchen, where Helen put me to work setting the kitchen table.

Ray and Laura came back with my blazer, in a clear plastic cleaning bag, and an armload each of groceries, which we unpacked and put away. I hung my blazer on the knob just inside the bedroom door. Laura followed me, moving on into the bathroom to take her shower. The wash must have been done because I could hear the dryer rumbling against the wall. As soon as the load was dry, I'd pull my clothes out and get dressed.

In the meantime, Helen showed me how to peel and mash the yams while she cut apples and onions into quarters and put them in the frying pan with butter. Like a fly on the wall, I kept myself quiet, listening to Ray and his mother chat while she put supper together. "Freida Green's house got broke into here about four months ago. That's when I had all them burglar bars put on. We had a neighborhood meeting with these two police officers, told us what to do in case of attack. Freida and her friend, Minnie Paxton, took a self-defense course. Said they learned how to scream and how to kick out real hard sideways. The point is to break a fellow's kneecap and take him down. Freida was practicing and fell flat on her back. Cracked her tailbone big as life. Minnie laughed so hard she nearly peed herself 'til she saw how bad Freida was hurt. She had to set on a bag of ice for a month, poor thing."

"Well, I don't want to hear about you trying to kick some guy."

"No, no. I wouldn't do that. Makes no sense for an old woman like me. Old people can't always depend on physical strength. Even Freida said that. That's why I had all them locks put in. Summertimes, I used to leave my doors standing open to let the breeze come through. Not no more. No sir."

"Hey, Ma. Before I forget. You have any mail here for me? I think my buddy in California might have sent me a package or a letter in care of this address."

"Well, yes. Now you mention it, I did receive something and set it aside. It come quite some time ago. I believe it's here somewhere, if I can recollect where I put it. Take a look in that drawer yonder under all the junk."

Ray opened the drawer, pawing through odds and ends: lamp cords, batteries, pencils, bottle caps, coupons, hammer, screwdriver, cooking utensils. A handful of envelopes was crammed in at the back, but most were designated "Occupant." There was only one piece of personal mail, addressed to Ray Rawson with no return address. He squinted at the postmark on the envelope. "This is it," he said. He tore it open and pulled out a sympathy card with a black-and-white photograph of a graveyard pasted on the front. Inside, the message read:

> *And I will give unto thee the keys of the kingdom of heaven: and whatsoever thou shalt bind on earth shall be bound in heaven: and whatsoever thou shalt loose on earth shall be loosed in heaven. Matthew 16:19.*
>
> *Thinking of you in your hour of loss.*

On the back of the card, a small brass key was taped. Ray pulled it off, turning it over in his hand before he passed it to me. I studied first one side and then the other just as he had. It was an inch and a half long. The word *Master* was stamped on one side and the number M550 on the other. Shouldn't be hard to remember. The number was my birthdate in abbreviated form. I said, "Probably for a padlock."

"What about the key you have?"

"It's in the bedroom. I'll get it as soon as Laura's finished in there."

Supper was almost on the table when Laura finally emerged. It looked as though she'd made a special effort with her hair and makeup despite the fact her grandmother couldn't see all that well. While serving dishes were being filled at the stove, I stepped into the bedroom and picked up my Swiss Army knife from the pile of my belongings on the bed table. I slipped the jacket from the cleaners bag and used the small scissors to snip the stitches I'd put in the inside shoulder seam. I worked the key from the hole. This one was heavy, a good six inches long with an elongated round shaft. I held it closer to the table lamp, curious if this was also a Master. *Lawless* was stamped on the shaft, but there were no other identifying marks that I could see. Master padlocks I knew about. A Lawless I'd never heard of. Might be a local company or one that had since gone out of business.

I returned to the kitchen table, where I sat down and handed the key to Ray.

"What's that for?" Laura asked as she took her seat.

"I'm not sure, but I think it goes with this one," Ray said. He laid the skeleton key beside the smaller key in the middle of the table. "This one Johnny left taped to the inside of his safe. Chester found it this week when they were cleaning out the apartment."

"Those are connected to the stash?"

"I hope so. Otherwise, we're out of luck," he said.

"How come?"

"Because it's the only link we have. Unless you have an idea where to look for a pile of money forty-some years after it was hid."

"I wouldn't even know where to start," she said.

"Me neither. I was hoping Kinsey would help, but it looks like we're running out of time," he said, and then turned to his mother. "You want me to say grace, Ma?"

Why did I feel guilty? I hadn't *done* anything.

The supper was a lavish testimony to old-fashioned southern cooking. This was the first food I'd had in days that wasn't saturated with additives and preservatives. The sugar, sodium, and fat content left something to be desired, but I'm not exactly pious where food is concerned. I ate with vigor and concentration, only vaguely aware of the conversation going on around me until Ray's voice went up. He had put his fork down and was staring at his daughter with a look of horror and dismay.

"You did what?"

"What's wrong with that?"

"When did you talk to her?"

I saw the color come up in Laura's face. "When we first got here," she said defensively. "You saw me go in the other room. What did you think I was doing? I was on the phone."

"Jesus Christ. You *called* her?"

"She's my mother. Of course I called. I didn't want her to worry in case Gilbert showed up on her doorstep. So what?"

"If Gilbert shows up, she'll tell him where you are."

"She will *not.*"

"Of course she will. You think Gilbert won't charm the socks off her? Hell, forget charm. He'll beat the shit outta her. Of course she'll tell him. I did. Once he started breaking fingers, I couldn't wait to unload. Did you at least warn her?"

"Warn her of what?"

"Oh, jeez," Ray said. He rubbed his palm down his face, pulling his features out of shape.

"Look, Ray. You don't need to treat me like a nincompoop."

"You still don't get it, do you? That guy's going to kill me. He's going to kill you, too. He'll kill Kinsey, your grandmother, and anybody else who gets in his way. He wants the money. You're just the means to an end as far as he's concerned."

"How's he going to find us? He won't find us," she said.

"We gotta get out of here." Ray got up and threw his napkin down, giving me a look. I knew as well as he did that once Gilbert got confirmation of our whereabouts, he'd be here within the hour.

"I'm with you," I said as I pushed my chair back.

Laura was aghast. "We haven't even finished *eating.* What's the matter with you?"

He turned to me. "Get your clothes on. Ma, you need a coat. Turn the stove off. Just leave this. We can take care of it later."

His panic was contagious. Helen's gaze was drifting around the room, her voice was tremulous. "What's happening, son? I don't understand what's going on. Why would we leave? We haven't et our ice cream yet."

"Just do what I say and get going," he snapped, hauling her out of her chair. He started turning off burners. He turned off the oven. I was not dressed for flight. All I had on were my Reeboks and Helen's chenille bathrobe. I crossed to the utility room, nearly knocking his chair over in my haste to reach the dryer. Laura protested vigorously, but I noticed she was moving as fast as the rest of us. I pulled the dryer open, grabbed an armload of hot clothes, and headed for the bedroom. I flipped my shoes off, pulled on socks, bra, and underpants, pulled on my turtleneck and jeans, and shoved my feet back into my Reeboks, breaking down the backs. God, here I was again, going for the gold at the Throwing Clothes On Olympics. I put on my blazer and started jamming personal items in the pockets: cash, credit cards, house keys, pills, picks. From the kitchen Laura let out a shriek, followed by the sound of a bowl smashing on the floor. I moved into the kitchen while I crammed the last of the odds and ends in my jeans pockets.

The room was dead still, Helen, Ray, and Laura unmoving. The bowl of mashed yams lay on the floor in an orange splat of puree and broken china. It didn't matter at this point because Gilbert was standing in the door to the dining room with a gun aimed right at me.

17

Gilbert no longer wore the Stetson. His hair was disheveled, still bearing the faint indentation where the hat had rested. His pale blue denim jacket was lined with sheepskin, the fabric saturated in places and stiff with dark red. "Marla sends greetings. She would have come with me only she wasn't feeling that good."

At the reference to her mother, Laura started to weep. She made no sound at all, but her face got patchy and red and tears welled in her eyes. She made a barely suppressed squeaking noise at the back of her throat. She sank into a chair.

"Hey. Get up and get your hands up where I can see 'em."

The gun in his hand encouraged compliance. I certainly wasn't going to argue. Laura rose slowly, not looking at him. She let out a breath with an audible sound and tears ran down her cheeks. She'd brought this down on us with every poor choice she'd made. She'd taken the risk and now the rest of us would pay. I saw everyone in the room with such clarity: Ray had his jacket on, his car keys in hand. He'd managed to hustle his mother into her coat. She stood close to her place at the table, hands up, bundled up in her woollies like a kid on a snowy day. Five minutes more and we might have been gone. Gilbert must have been eavesdropping for some time, of course, so it probably didn't matter. The fact that all of us now had our hands in the air gave the scene a slightly comical air. It looked as if we'd been caught in the middle of a spiritual, with our hands waving toward heaven. In a western, somebody would have jumped Gilbert and grappled for the gun. Not here. I kept my gaze pinned on his face, trying to gauge his intent. Helen's gaze wandered the room, eyes unfocused, settling nowhere, roaming across the gray haze with its motionless dark shapes. I thought she'd be confused or upset, but she said nothing, sensing perhaps that the situation wouldn't be served by questions. She did quiver almost imperceptibly, the way a dog trembles standing on the groomer's table.

The air still smelled of fried pork chops and milk gravy. The remnants of the meal remained on the plates, cooking pots piled in the kitchen sink. Maybe Freida Green would come in and clean up in a few days . . . after the crime scene tape had been removed and the premises unsealed.

Gilbert held the gun in his right hand, using his left to reach into his jacket pocket. He took out a roll of duct tape. "Here's what let's do," he said conversationally. "Ray, why don't you just take a seat in that chair. Laura here is going to wrap you up in duct tape. Hey, hey, hey, babe. Goddamn it. Quit with the crying. Nothing's happened yet. I'm just trying to keep everything under control. I don't want anybody jumping out at me. Don't want this gun going off or somebody might get hurt. Grammy's not going to look so hot with a hole in her head, brains all spilling out, Ray with a big old hole in his chest. Come on, now. Help out, just to show you still care."

He tossed the roll of silver duct tape to Laura, who caught it on the fly. She seemed frozen, standing immobile as the seconds went by. "Gilbert, I beg you—"

"Tape him up!"

I flinched at his sudden screaming. Laura didn't bat an eye, but I noticed she was now in motion, crossing the room to Ray. Slowly, hands still lifted, Ray eased himself into the chair Gilbert had indicated. Laura was weeping so hard I'm not even sure she could see what she was doing. Tears washed the makeup from her cheeks, exposing the old bruises like an undercoat of paint. Tendrils of red hair had come loose, trailing around her face.

Gilbert's focus moved to Ray. "Make any trouble, I'll kill her," he said.

Ray said, "Don't do that. Be cool. I'll cooperate."

Gilbert flicked a look at me. "Why don't you pass me the keys? I'd appreciate it," he said.

I reached for the keys still sitting on the kitchen table. I hated to let go of them, but I couldn't think what else to do. I placed them in Gilbert's left palm. He glanced at them briefly and then tucked them in his jacket pocket.

Ray said, "Listen, Gilbert. This is an old score. It's got nothing to do with these three. You can do anything you want with me, but keep them out of it."

"I know I can do anything I want. I'm already doing it. I don't care about them two, the old bag and this one," he said, indicating me. "But I got accounts to settle with her. She ran out on me." He looked over at her, frowning. "Could you get busy with that tape like I said?"

"Gilbert, please don't do this. Please."

"Would you knock it off? I'm not doing anything," he said

peevishly. "What am I doing? I'm just standing here talking to your dad. Go on now and do what I told you. Ray's not going to pull any funny business."

"Can't we just leave? Get in the car and go, just the two of us?"

"You're not done. You haven't even *started,*" Gilbert said. He was beginning to sound exasperated, not a good sign.

Ray's expression was soft, looking at Laura. "It's okay, hon. Go ahead and do what he says. Let's see if we can keep everybody on an even keel here."

Gilbert smiled. "My thoughts exactly. Everybody take it easy. I want his ankles tapped to the chair legs. And let's get his hands behind him, bind 'em up nice. I'm going to check on you, so don't you be thinking you can pretend to tape him up and then not do it right. I hate when people try to fool me. You know how I am. Blow your nose and quit sniveling."

Laura fumbled in her pocket, took out a tissue, and did as he said. She tucked the tissue away and pulled out a strip of tape, the adhesive making a ripping sound as she tore it loose. She began to wrap the tape around Ray's right ankle, first folding his pant leg against his shin, then threading the tape around the chair leg in several layers.

"I want that tight. You don't get it tight enough, I'm going to shoot him in the leg."

"I am!" She flashed a look at Gilbert, and for a moment there was pure fury in her eyes instead of fear.

He seemed to like it that he'd gotten a rise out of her. A slight smile crossed his face. "What's that look for?"

"Where's Farley?" she said darkly.

"Oh, him. I left him in California. What a worthless sack of shit he turned into. All the mewling and pissing. I really hate that stuff. Here's the long and short of it: The man ratted you out. It's the truth. He gave you up. Farley told me everything, trying to save his own skin. I do not admire that. I think it sucks." He edged over to the chair where Ray was sitting. He kept a close eye on all of us, making sure no one moved while he squatted by the chair and checked the tape. He got up, apparently satisfied with the job she was doing. "When you get done with him, you can do her," he said, meaning me.

She ripped off another length of tape and began to secure Ray's left leg to the chair rung. "What'd you do to him?" she asked.

Gilbert stood upright again, backing off two steps. "What *I* did? We're not talking about what I did. I didn't do anything. It's what you did. You betrayed me, babe. How many times I told you about that? You just never learn, do you? I try—God knows I try—to let you know what I expect."

"Farley's dead?"

"Yes, he is," Gilbert said solemnly. "I'm sorry to have to be the one to tell you."

"He was your nephew. Your own flesh and blood."

"What's that got to do with it? That doesn't cut any ice. Flesh and blood don't mean bullshit. It's about loyalty. Is that simple concept so hard for you to grasp? Listen, I want to tell you something. You can't blame this on me. Anybody gets hurt, it's on your head, not mine. How many times I told you, you have to do what I say. You're not going to obey me, then I can't be responsible."

"I'm *doing* what you said. In what way am I not doing what you said?"

"I'm not talking about that. I'm talking about the money. I'm talking about Rio. Now see? Right there. You didn't fly to Rio like you were supposed to, and look what went wrong as a consequence of your behavior. Farley . . . well, never mind. I think we said enough about him."

Helen spoke up. Like me, she'd been standing there doggedly with her hands in the air. "Young man. I wonder if I could take this coat off and set down."

Gilbert frowned, irritated at the interruption. It was clear he enjoyed getting all worked up, feeling righteous, expounding on the many ways someone else was at fault. Helen wasn't looking at him.

Her gaze was fixed at a point to his right, where she was obviously mistaking the doorjamb for him. Gilbert was momentarily distracted, amused by her mistake. He waved his arms. "Hey, over here, sweetheart. You must not see all that good. You've mistook me for a coat rack."

"I see well enough. It's my feet give out," she said. "I'm eighty-five years old."

"Is that right? Arms getting tired, is that it?"

Helen said nothing. Her rheumy gaze was wandering. I kept scanning the room, looking for a weapon, trying to form a plan. I didn't want to put the others in any more jeopardy. His intentions seemed clear enough. One by one, we'd be bound and gagged, at which point he was going to kill us, and what could we do? I was closer to him than Laura was, but if I tried to jump him, he might go berserk and start shooting. I had to do something soon, but I didn't want to be foolhardy . . . acting like a heroine when it might put us in a worse situation than we were already in.

"I'm going to set. You can shoot me if you don't like it," Helen said.

Gilbert gestured with the gun. "Take a seat right where you are. You can put your hands down for now, but don't touch anything on the table."

She said, "Thank you." She braced her hands on the table and sank heavily in her chair. She shrugged out of her coat. I could see her flex her fingers gingerly, coaxing the circulation before she tucked them in her lap.

Gilbert angled himself so he could monitor Laura's progress as she bound her father's hands with tape. Ray's arms were behind him. In order to have his wrists meet behind the wooden chair back, he had to lean forward slightly and force his shoulders into a roll.

Gilbert seemed to enjoy Ray's discomfort. "Where's the harness?" he asked Laura.

"In the other room."

"When you get done with that, bring it out here and let's see what we got."

"I thought you said tape her."

"Get the harness, *then* tape her, you fuckin' idjit," he said.

"There's only eight thousand dollars. You said a million," she said irritably. She set the roll of duct tape aside and moved into the other room. Personally, I wouldn't have dared to take that tone with him. Gilbert didn't seem surprised about the money, so I had to assume Farley'd told him about the eight grand along with everything else.

Laura returned with the harness in hand. He took it from her, hefting it up onto the counter behind him. He glanced down at the contents, taking in the packets of bills. His gaze shifted to Ray. "Where's the rest of the money? Where's all the jewelry and the coin collections?"

"I don't know. I really can't swear there's anything left," Ray said.

Gilbert closed his eyes, his patience wearing thin. "Ray, I was there, remember? I helped you guys, hauling out all that cash and jewelry. What about the diamonds and the coins? There was a fortune in there, must have been two million, at least, and Johnny sure as shit didn't have it on him when he was caught."

"Hey, not to argue, but you were seventeen years old. None of us had ever seen a million bucks, let alone two. We don't really have any idea how much it was because we never had a chance to count it, and that's the truth," Ray said.

"There was a hell of a lot more than this. Seven or eight big bags. That loot didn't just disappear into thin air. The son of a bitch must have hid it. So where'd he put it?"

"Your guess is as good as mine. That's why I'm here. See if I can figure it out."

"He didn't tell you?"

"I swear to God he didn't. He knew he could trust himself, but I guess he wasn't all that sure about me."

I spoke up then, looking at Ray. "How do you know he didn't spend it?"

"It's always possible," he said. "I know he sent money to my ma. That was our agreement up front."

"He did what?" Gilbert said. He turned to Helen. "Is that right?"

"Oh my, yes," she said complacently. "I've received a money order in the amount of five hundred dollars every month since nineteen and forty-four, though it did stop some months back. July or August, as I recollect."

"Since 1944? I don't believe it. How much did he send? Five hundred a *month?* That's ridiculous," Gilbert said.

"Two hundred forty-six thousand dollars," Ray interjected. "I took high school math up at FCI Ashland. You ought to try the joint yourself, Gilbert. Improve your grasp of the basics. Vocabulary, grammar . . ."

Gilbert was still focused on Johnny's giveaway plan. "You gotta be shittin' me. Johnny Lee gave two hundred forty-six thousand dollars of my money to this old bag? I don't believe it. That's criminal."

"I kept an account if you'd care to see it. It's a little red notebook in that drawer over there," Helen said, pointing a trembling finger in the general direction of the drawer where she'd kept Ray's mail.

Gilbert moved to the drawer and jerked it open, pawing through the jumble of items with impatience. He pulled the drawer out altogether and dumped the contents on the floor. He reached down and picked up a small spiral-bound notebook, thumbing through it with his left hand, the gun still in his right. Even from where I stood, I could see column after column, dates and scratchy-looking numbers running crookedly from page to page. "Son of a bitch!" Gilbert said. "How could he do that, give the money away?" He flung the notebook on the kitchen table, where it landed in the dish of stewed tomatoes.

It was Ray's turn to enjoy. He knew better than to smile, but his tone of voice conveyed his satisfaction. "The guy kept five hundred for himself, too, so what is that? After forty-one years that brings the total up to four hundred ninety-two thousand dollars," Ray said. "Figure it out for yourself. If we netted half a million bucks from the heist, that'd leave just about eight grand."

Gilbert crossed to Ray and jammed the barrel of the gun up under his jaw, hard. "God*damn* it! *I know there was more and I want it!* I'll blow your fuckin' head off right this minute if you don't give it up."

"Killing me won't help. You kill me, you got no chance," Ray said without flinching. "Maybe I can find it, *if* there's anything left. I know how Johnny's mind worked. You don't have a clue how he went about his business."

"I found the kickplate, didn't I?"

"Only because I told you. You never would have found it without me," Ray said.

Gilbert moved the gun away, his face dark. His movements were agitated. "Here's the deal. I'm taking Laura with me. You better come up with something by tomorrow or she's dead, you got that?"

"Hey, come on. Be reasonable. I need time," Ray said.

"Tomorrow."

"I'll do what I can, but I can't promise."

"Well, I can. You get that money or she's dead meat."

"How am I going to find you?"

"Don't worry about that. I'll find you," Gilbert said.

Helen grimaced, rubbing one gnarled hand with the other.

"What's the matter with you?"

"My arthritis is acting up. I'm in pain."

"You want me to fix it? I can fix that in a jiffy with what I got in here," he said, waggling his gun. He turned back to Ray. Helen raised her hand to attract his notice.

"What?"

"Now I've set down too long. Thing about getting old is you can't do any one thing for more than about five minutes. I hope you don't mind if I stand up a bit."

"Goddamn, old woman. You're just up and down and all over the place."

Helen laughed, apparently mistaking his homicidal wrath for mere ill temper. I felt a bubble of despair rising to the surface. Maybe she was senile along with everything else. He'd kill her without hesitation—he'd kill all of us—but she didn't seem to "get" that. His threats sailed right over. Maybe it was just as well. At her age, who could tolerate fear of that magnitude? The anxiety alone could push her into heart failure. Me too, for that matter.

Gilbert pointed the gun in her direction. "You can stand up, but you behave," he said. "I don't want you running out of here, trying to flag down help." His tone shifted when he spoke to her, becoming nearly flirtatious. "Patronizing" might be another word, but Helen didn't seem to pick up on it.

She waved a hand dismissively. "I'm afraid my flagging days is over. Anyway, I'm not the one you have to worry about. It's my friend, Freida Green."

At least she'd caught his attention. I could see him suppress a smile, pretending to take her seriously. "Uh-oh. What is it, Freida some kind of hell-raiser?"

"Yes, she is. I am, too, for that matter. My late husband used to call me Hell on Wheels, get it? 'Hell on.' Helen."

"I got it, Granny. Who's Freida? She likely to be popping in here unannounced?"

"Freida's my neighbor. She lives two doors down with her friend, Minnie Paxton, but they're out of town right now. Hasn't anyone ever said, but I think them two are sweet on each other. Anyway, we had us a rash of burglaries about four months back. That's what they call them, a 'rash,' like somebody caught a disease. Two nice policemen come down to the neighborhood and told us about self-defense. Minnie learned to kick out real hard sideways, but Freida fell flat on her back when she tried it."

Ray fixed me with a look, but I couldn't read the contents. Probably simple despair at the banality of their exchange.

Gilbert laughed. "Jesus, I'd like to seen that. How old is this old bag?"

"Let's see now. I believe Freida's thirty-one. Minnie's two years younger and she's in much better shape. Freida cracked her tailbone and she got mad. Whoo! Said there had to be a better way to fight crime than tryin' to kick some fella in the kneecap."

Gilbert shook his head with skepticism. "I don't know. Bust a guy's kneecap, that can really hurt," he said.

"Well, yes," Helen said, "but first you'd have to get close enough to kick, which isn't always easy. And then my balance is not that good."

"Freida's balance ain't good, either, from what you said. So what'd she suggest?"

"She suggested she make us each a rack and bolt it onto the bottom of the table, where we could keep a loaded shotgun about like this." Helen turned slightly sideways as she rose to her feet. She took a long step away from the table, pulling up a twelve-gauge side-by-side shotgun with twenty-six-inch barrels. She pinned the butt stock between her forearm and her side, letting the butt stock rest on her right hip for support. The four of us stared at her, riveted by the sight of a gun that unwieldy in the hands of someone who, a nanosecond before, seemed so harmless and out of it. The effect, unfortunately, was undercut by the realities of age. Because of her poor eyesight, she was aiming at the window frame instead of Gilbert, a fact not lost on him. He made a face, saying, "Whoa! You better put that gun away."

"You better put *that* gun away before I blow you to kingdom come," she said. She backed up against the wall, all business, except for the problem with her aim, which was considerable. The heavy flesh on her upper arms shook, and it was clear she could barely keep the barrel up, even if it was pointed in the wrong direction. I could feel my heart begin to thump. I expected Gilbert to shoot, but he didn't seem to take her seriously.

"Gun's pretty heavy. You sure you can keep it up there?"

"Briefly," she said.

"What's that weigh, six or seven pounds? Doesn't sound like much until you have to hooolld it up for long." He dragged out the word "hold," making it sound exhausting. I got tired just hearing it, but Helen didn't seem dismayed.

"I'm going to shoot you long before my arms get tired. I feel it's only fair to warn you. The one barrel's loaded with number nine birdshot. The other's double-O buck, tear your face right off."

Gilbert laughed again. He seemed genuinely tickled by the old woman's attitude. "Jesus, Hell on. That's not nice. What about your arthritis? I thought you had arthritis so bad."

"I do. That's right. Affecting all but the one finger. Watch this." Helen shifted the gun to the left, drew a bead on him, and pulled the trigger. Ka-*blam!* I saw a few bright yellow sparks. The blast was deafening, filling the room. A shock wave of air and gas spread out from the muzzle, followed by a faint doughnut of smoke. The mass of bird shot blew by his right ear, continuing on past him at an upward angle, shattering the kitchen window. Stray pellets tore his earlobe and the top of his shoulder and the spreading fingers of the trailing shot cup raked his neck, painting it with blood. Laura screamed and hit the floor. I was down before she was. Ray's startled reaction tipped his chair over sideways. Gilbert screamed in pain and disbelief, his hands flying up. His handgun flew forward and skittered across the floor.

The muzzle jump had knocked Helen back against the wall, the butt stock slamming into her right hip as the barrels whipped upwards with the recoil. She recovered and lowered the gun again, prepared to fire. Gilbert's right cheek was already peppered with red, like a sudden rash of acne, and blood was seeping into the hair above his right ear. The air smelled acrid, and I could suddenly taste something sweet at the back of my throat.

"This time I'll blow your head off," she said.

Gilbert made a savage sound in his throat as he reached down and grabbed Laura by the hair. He hauled her to her feet, pinning her against him while he leaned down and snagged the harness with the other hand.

From the floor, Ray craned his neck, straining to see what was going on. "Ma, don't fire!"

"Pull the trigger and she's dead. I'll snap her neck," Gilbert said. He was clearly in pain, breathing heavily, no longer armed but still out of control. He had his forearm locked up under Laura's chin. She was forced to hang on to him, pulling down to keep from being strangled. Gilbert began backing out of the kitchen and into the dining room. Laura was stumbling backward, half lifted off her feet.

Helen hesitated, no doubt confused by the jumble of sounds and shapes.

Gilbert disappeared into the dining room, plowing backward through the piles of junk furniture. Laura was making a series of chuffing noises, unable to vocalize with her windpipe choked off. I could hear a crash and the sound of glass shattering as he kicked the front door open. Then silence.

I was torn between the desire to chase after Gilbert and the need to help Helen, who was trembling and deadly pale. She lowered the gun barrel and sank weakly into her chair. "What's happening? Where'd he go?"

"He's got Laura. Just be cool. Everything's going to be fine," Ray said. He was still on the floor, lying sideways in the chair, struggling to get free of his bonds. I scrambled over to him, trying to help him right himself, but with the awkwardness of the chair he was too much for me to lift. I grabbed a butcher knife off the counter and cut through the layers of duct tape that bound his hands and feet. With one hand liberated, Ray started tearing off the rest of the tape, his attention still focused on his mother. "Gimme a hand here," he grunted at me.

"What's he going to do to her?"

"Nothing 'til he gets the money. She's his insurance." I grabbed his hand and braced myself as he hauled himself up from the floor. He glanced at me briefly. "You okay?"

"I'm fine," I said. Both of us turned our attention to Helen.

The shotgun was laid across her lap. I crossed to her, took the gun, and set it on the kitchen table. Her shoulders were slumped and her hands were shaking badly, her breathing shallow and ragged. Her hip was probably bruised where the gun stock had kicked into it. She'd used up all her reserves of energy, and I worried she'd go into shock. "I should have killed him. Poor Laura. I couldn't bring myself to do it, but I should have."

Ray reached for a chair and pulled it closer to his mother's. He took her hand, patting it, his tone tender. "How you doing, Hell on Wheels?" he said.

"I'll be fine in a bit. I just need to catch my breath," she said. She patted at her chest, trying to compose herself. "I'm not as feeble-minded as I was acting."

"I couldn't figure out what you were doing," he said. "I can't believe you did that. You started talking to him, I thought it was all bullshit until you pulled out that shotgun. You were terrific. Absolutely fearless."

Helen waved him off, but she seemed pleased with herself and tickled by his praise. "Just because you get old doesn't mean you lose your nerve."

"I thought you had trouble with your eyes," I said. "How'd you know where he was?"

"He was standing up against the kitchen window, so I could make out his *shape.* I may be near blind, but my ears still work. He shouldn't have talked so much. Freida's got me into lifting weights now, and I can bench-press twenty-five pounds. Did you hear what he said? He thought I couldn't even hold up a seven-pound shotgun. I was insulted. Stereotyping the old. That's your typical macho horseshit," she said. She pressed her fingers to her lips. "I believe I'm about to get sick now. Oh, dear."

18

Ray helped his mother to the bathroom. Soon after that, I heard the toilet flush and his murmured comfort and assurances as he tucked her into bed. While I waited for him to get her settled, I returned the contents of the junk drawer and slid the drawer back into its slot. I righted Ray's chair and then got down on my hands and knees to look for Gilbert's gun. Where had the damn thing gone? I raised up like a prairie dog and surveyed the spot where he'd stood, trying to figure out what the trajectory would have been when the gun flew off across the room. Picking my way carefully through the broken glass, I crawled to the nearest corner and worked my way along the baseboard. I finally spotted the gun, a .45-caliber Colt automatic with walnut stocks, wedged behind the Eastlake cabinet. I fished it out with a fork, trying not to smudge any latent prints. If the Louisville police ran a check on him, it was possible an outstanding warrant might pop up and give them a reason to arrest him—if they could find him, of course.

I placed the gun on the kitchen table and tiptoed to the bedroom door. I tapped, and a moment later Ray opened the door a crack. "We need to call the cops," I said. I meant to slip on past, heading for the telephone, but he put his hand on my arm.

"Don't do that."

"Why not?" We were keeping our voices down in deference to his mother, who'd had enough upset for one day.

"Look, I'll be out in a minute, as soon as she's asleep. We need to talk." He began to close the door.

I put my hand on the door. "What's there to talk about? We need help."

"Please." He held a hand up, nodding to indicate that we'd discuss it momentarily. He closed the door in my face.

Reluctantly, I returned to the kitchen to wait for him. I found the broom and dustpan behind the door to the utility room, and I made a pass at the mess. Someone had tracked through the broken bowl of mashed yams. There were little yammy footprints, like dog doo, everywhere. I pulled the garbage can out from under the sink and cautiously began to pick up shards of broken glass and crockery. I used a dampened paper towel to scoop up the remaining goo.

The kitchen sink and the counter were both littered with broken glass where the window had been shattered by the shotgun blast. I couldn't believe the neighbors hadn't come running. Cold air was now blowing in, but there was nothing I could do about it. I hauled out the ancient canister vacuum cleaner and affixed the upholstery attachment to the hose. I flipped it on and spent several minutes huffing up all the glass in sight. Between chasing and being chased, all I'd done since I'd left home was dust and vacuum. I put my ear to the bedroom door at one point and could have sworn I heard Ray talking on the phone. Ah. Maybe he had paid attention to my advice after all.

Ray came back into the kitchen and closed the bedroom door behind him. He moved straight to the pantry and pulled out a bottle of bourbon, took down two small jelly glasses, and poured us both a stiff drink. He handed one glass to me and then tapped mine in a toast. While I eyed mine he tilted his head back and downed his portion. I took a deep breath and tossed mine down my throat, unprepared for the vile fire that assailed my esophagus. I could feel my face flush with heat as my stomach burst into flames. After that, I could feel all the tension drift away from me like smoke. I shook my head, shuddering, as a worm of revulsion wiggled down my frame. "Yuck. I hate that. I could never be a drunk. How can you do that, just toss it back that way?"

"Takes practice," he said. He poured himself another glass and tossed it after the first. "This is one thing I missed in prison."

He spotted the Colt where I'd laid it on the kitchen table, picked it up without comment, and tucked it in his waistband.

"Thanks, Ray. Now you've messed up any fingerprints."

"Nobody's going to run prints," he said.

"Really. What makes you say that?"

He ignored the question. He moved into the dining room and hustled up a cardboard carton, which he emptied, then flattened, and used to replace the broken window glass, securing it with Gilbert's duct tape. The outdoor light was diminished and the cold still seeped in, but at least birds and small UFOs would be prevented from flying in the gaping hole. While I looked on, he began to empty the sink of its mountain of pots and pans, stacking them neatly to one side in preparation for washing. I love watching guys help around the house.

"I heard you on the phone. Did you call 911?"

"I called Marla to see how she was. Gilbert punched her lights out. She says he broke her nose, but she doesn't want to press charges as long as he's got Laura."

"You could call 911," I said. Maybe he hadn't heard me right?

I flipped the vacuum on again and sucked up glass slivers as they came to light. I kept waiting for him to pick up the subject, but he studiously avoided it. Finally, I turned the machine off and said, "So what's the deal? Why not call the cops? Laura's been kidnapped. I hope you don't think you're going to do this on your own."

"I told you. Marla's not interested. She thinks it's premature."

"I'm not talking about Marla. I'm talking about you."

"Let's look for the money first. Nothing turns up in a day, then we can bring the cops into it."

"Ray, you're crazy. You need help."

"I can handle it."

"That's bullshit. He's going to kill her."

"Not if I can find the money."

"How're you going to do that?"

"I don't know yet."

He tied an apron around his waist. He put the stopper in the drain and turned on the hot water. He picked up the liquid detergent and squirted a solid stream into the sink, holding his injured fingers away from the water. A mountain of white suds began to pile up, into which he tucked plates and silverware. "I learned to wash dishes when I was six," he said idly, picking up a long-handled brush. "Ma stood me up on a wooden milk crate and taught me how to do it right. It was my chore from then on. In prison, they use these big industrial machines, but the principle's the same. All us old cons know how to make ourselves useful, but these new punks coming in can't do a damn thing except fight. Dopers and gang-bangers. Scary bunch."

"Ray."

"Remind me of fighting cocks . . . all puffed up and aggressive. Don't give a shit about anything. Those are kids bred to die. They have no hope, no expectations. They got attitude. It's all attitude. Insist on respect without ever doing anything to earn it. Half of 'em don't even know how to read."

"Make your point," I said.

"There's no point. I changed the subject. The point is, I don't want to call the cops."

"Is there a problem?"

"I don't like cops."

"I'm not asking you to form any kind of lasting relationship," I said. I watched him. "What is it? There's something else."

He rinsed a dinner plate and placed it in the rack, avoiding my gaze. I picked up a dish towel and began to dry while he washed. "Ray?"

He put the second dinner plate in the rack. "I'm in violation."

I'm thinking, Violation? I said, "Of what?"

He shrugged slightly.

The penny dropped. "Parole? You violated *parole?*"

"Something like that."

"But what, exactly?"

"Well, actually, 'exactly' is I walked off."

"Escaped?"

"I wouldn't call it escape. It was a halfway house."

"But you weren't supposed to *leave.* You were still an inmate. Weren't you?"

"Hey, there wasn't any fence. It's not like we were locked in our cells at night. We didn't even *have* cells. We had rooms," he said. "So it's more like I'm away without leave. Yeah, like that. AWOL."

"Oh boy," I said. I let out a big breath and considered the implications. "How'd you get a driver's license?"

"I didn't. I don't have one."

"You've been driving without? How'd you manage to rent a car without a driver's license?"

"I didn't."

I closed my eyes, wishing I could lie down on the floor and take a nap. I opened my eyes again. "You *stole* the rental car?" I couldn't help it. I know my tone was accusatory, but this was largely because I was accusing him.

Ray's mouth pulled down. "I guess you'd say that. So here's the deal. We call the cops, they'll run a check on me and back I go. Big time."

"You'd risk your daughter's life just to avoid going back to jail?"

"It's not just that."

"Then what?"

He turned and looked at me, his hazel eyes as clear as water. "How'm I going to deal with Gilbert if I got a bunch of cops on the scene?"

"Ray, you gotta trust me. It's not worth it. You'll be locked up for the rest of your life."

"What rest? I'm sixty-five years old. How much time do I have?"

"Don't be dumb. You got years. Take a look at your mom. You're going to live to be a hundred. Don't blow this."

"Kinsey, listen up. Here's the truth," he said. "We call the cops, you know what's going to happen? We go down to the jail. We fill out paperwork. They ask us a bunch of questions I don't want to answer. Either they run a check on me or they don't. If they run a check, I'm history and that's the end of her. If they don't run a check, what difference does it make? We're still fucked. Hours are going to pass, and then what? It'll turn out the cops can't do shit. Oh, too bad. So now we're out on the street again and we still don't have a clue where the money's hid. Believe me. When Gilbert catches up with us, he don't want to hear excuses. And what are we going to say? 'Sorry we didn't find the money yet. We got tied up at the precinct and time got away from us.' "

I said, "Tell him you're working on it. Tell him you have the money and want to meet him somewhere. The cops can pick him up."

Ray's expression was bored. "You been watching too much TV. Truth is, half the time when the cops get involved, they fuck it up.

Perpetrator gets caught and the victim dies. You know what happens next? Big trial. Publicity. You get a hotshot lawyer talkin' about the kidnapper's troubled youth. How he's mentally ill and how the victim was abusing him and he only did the kidnap in self-defense. Thousands and thousands of dollars get poured down the drain. The jury ends up hung and the guy takes a walk. Meanwhile, Laura's dead and I'm back in jail again. So who wins? It ain't me and it's certainly not her."

I could feel my temper climb. I tossed the dish towel aside. "You know what? You can do anything you want. This is really not my problem. You don't want to call the cops. Fine. It's up to you. I'm out of here."

"Back to California?"

"If can manage it," I said. "Of course, now that Gilbert's got the eight grand, I'm assuming you won't pay my return ticket like you promised, but that's neither here nor there. I don't have enough money for a taxi to the airport, so I'd appreciate a ride. It's the least you can do."

His temper rose in response to mine. "Sure. No problem. Let me pull the kitchen together and we're on our way. Laura dies, it's on you. You could have helped. You said 'no.' You gotta live with that same as I do."

"Me? This is *your* doing. I can't believe you'd try to lay it off on me. You sound just like Gilbert."

He put a hand out and grabbed mine. "Hey. I need help." For a moment, we locked eyes. I broke off eye contact. His tone shifted. He tried coaxing. "Let's brainstorm. The two of us. That's all I'm asking. You got hours until flight time. . . ."

"*What* flight? I've got reservations, but no ticket, and I'm flat broke."

"So how's it going to hurt you to hang out here and help?"

"Well, I'll tell you," I said. "It's two days until Thanksgiving. I'm in a wedding that day, so I have to get back. Two very dear friends are getting married and I'm a bridesmaid, okay? The airports will be jammed with all the holiday traffic. I can't just call the airlines and pick up any old flight. I was lucky to get this one."

"But you can't pay for it," Ray pointed out.

"I know that!"

He put a finger to his lips and looked significantly toward the bedroom where his mother was sleeping.

"I know I can't pay. I'm trying to figure that part out," I said in a hoarse whisper.

Ray took out his money clip. "How much?"

"Five hundred."

He put the clip back untouched. "I thought you had friends. Somebody willing to lend you the bucks."

"I do if I can get to the telephone. Your mother's asleep."

"She'll be up in a bit. She's old. She doesn't sleep much at night. She takes catnaps instead. Soon as she wakes up, you can put a call through to California. Maybe your friend can put your ticket on a credit card and you can catch that flight. Looka me. I'll peep in and see how she's doing. How's that?" He moved to the bedroom and made a big display of opening the door a crack. "She'll be out any second now. I promise. I can see her moving around."

"Oh, right."

He closed the door again. "Just help me figure out where the money's hid. Let's talk about it some. That's all I want."

He held a hand out, indicating a seat at the table.

I stared at him. Well, there it was, folks. Altruism and self-interest going head to head. Was I going to take the high road or the low? By now, did I even know which was which? So far, almost everything I'd done was illegal except the vacuuming—breaking into hotel rooms, aiding and abetting escaped felons. Probably even the vacuuming broke some union contract. Why bother to get prissy at this late date? "You are so full of shit," I said.

He pulled out a chair and I sat. I can't believe I did that. I should have walked to the corner market and found a pay phone, but what can I say? I was involved with this man, involved with his daughter and his aged, catnapping mother. As if on cue, she emerged from the bedroom, rheumy eyed and energetic. She'd hardly been down fifteen minutes and she was ready to go again. He pulled out a chair for her. "How you doing?"

"I'm fine. I feel much better," she said. "What's happening? What are we doing?"

"Trying to figure out where Johnny hid the money," Ray said. He had apparently confessed all to his mother because she didn't seem to question the subject matter or his relationship to it. At eighty-five, I guess she wasn't worried about going to jail. From somewhere, another pen and a pad of paper materialized. "We can make notes. Or I can," he said when he caught my look. "You probably want to use the phone first. It's in there."

"I *know* where the phone is. I'll be right back," I said. I used my credit card to put another call through to Henry. As luck would have it, he was still out. I left a second message on his machine, indicating that my return flight was in question because of cash shortages on my end. I repeated Helen's phone number, urging him to call me to see if he could work out some way for me to get on the plane as scheduled. While I was at it, I tried the number at Rosie's, but all that netted me was a busy signal. I went back to the kitchen.

"How'd you do?" Ray asked blandly.

"I left a message for Henry. I'm hoping he'll call back in the next hour or so."

"Too bad you didn't get through to him. I guess there's no point in going out to the airport until you talk to him."

I sat down at the table, ignoring his commiseration, which was patently insincere. I said, "Let's start with the keys."

Ray made a note on the pad. The note said "keys." He drew a circle around it, squinting thoughtfully. "What difference does it make about the keys as long as Gilbert's got 'em?"

"Because they're just about the only tangible clue we have. Let's just write down what we remember."

"Which is what? I don't remember nothing."

"Well, one was iron. About six inches long, an old-fashioned skeleton key, a Lawless. The other was a Master. . . ."

"Wait a minute. How'd you know that?"

"Because I looked," I said. I turned to Helen. "You have a telephone book? I didn't see one in there, and we're probably going to need one."

"It's in the dresser drawer. Hold on a second. I'll get it," Ray said, and got up. He disappeared into the bedroom.

I called after him, "Have you ever heard of Lawless? I thought it might be local." I looked over at Helen. "Does that ring a bell with you?"

She shook her head. "Never heard of it."

Ray came back with two books in hand, the Louisville residential listings and the Yellow Pages. "What makes you think it's local?"

I took the Yellow Pages. "I'm an optimist," I said. "In my business, I always start with the obvious." He put the residential listings on an empty chair seat. I leafed through the pages until I found the listings for locksmiths. There was no "Lawless" in evidence, but Louisville Locksmith Company looked like a promising possibility. The big display ad indicated they'd been in business since 1910. "We might want to try the public library, too. The phone books from the early forties might be informative."

"She's a private investigator," Ray said to his mother. "That's how she got into this."

"Well, I wondered who she was."

I set the phone book on the table, open to the pages where all the locksmiths were listed. I tapped the Louisville Locksmith display ad. "We'll give this place a call in a minute," I said. "Now where were we?" I glanced at his notes. "Oh yeah, the other key was a Master. I think they only make padlocks, but again, we can ask when we talk to the guy. So here's the question. Are we looking for a big door and then a smaller one? Or a door and then a cabinet or storage unit, something like that?"

Ray shrugged. "Probably the first. Back in the forties, they didn't have those self-storage places like the ones they have now. Wherever Johnny put the money, he had to be sure it wasn't going to be disturbed. Couldn't be a safe-deposit box because the key didn't look right to me. And besides, the guy hated banks. That's what got him into trouble in the first place. He's hardly going to walk into a bank with the proceeds from a bank heist, right?"

"Yeah, right. Plus, banks get torn down or remodeled or turned into other businesses. What about some other kind of public building? City Hall or the courthouse? The Board of Education, a museum?"

Ray wagged his head, not liking the idea much. "Same thing, don't you think? Some developer comes along and sees it as a prime piece of real estate. Doesn't matter what's on it."

"What about some other places around town? Historical landmarks. Wouldn't they be protected?"

"Let me think about that."

"A church," Helen said suddenly.

"That's possible," Ray said.

She pointed to the pad. "Write it down."

Ray made a note about churches. "There's the water works by the river. School buildings. Churchill Downs. They're not going to tear that place down."

"What about a big estate somewhere?"

"That's an idea. There used to be plenty around. I been gone for years, though, so I don't know what's left."

"If he was running from the cops, he had to have a place that was easily accessible," I said. "And it had to be relatively free from intrusion."

Ray wrinkled his forehead. "How could he guarantee nobody

else would find it? That's a hell of a risk. Leave big canvas bags of money somewhere. How do you know a kid won't stumble across it playing stickball?"

"Kids don't play stickball anymore. They play video games," I said.

"A construction worker, then, or a nosy neighbor? The place had to be to be dry, don't you think?"

"Probably," I said. "At least, the two keys would suggest the money isn't buried."

"I'm sorry Gilbert got his hands on those keys. Gives him the edge if we identify the place."

"Don't worry about that. I've got a set of key picks I dutifully tote with me everywhere. If we find the right locks, we're in business."

"We can always hack through the locks," Ray suggested. "I learned that in prison, among other things."

"You got quite an education."

"I'm a good student," he said modestly.

The three of us were silent for a moment, trying to get our imaginations to work.

I spoke up again. "You know, the locksmith who first saw the big key thought it might fit a gate. So how's this for a guess? Maybe Johnny had access to an old estate. The big key fit the gate and the smaller key fit the padlock on the front door."

Ray didn't seem that happy. "How'd he know the place wouldn't be sold or torn down?"

"Maybe it was a historical landmark. Protected by historical preservationists."

"Suppose they decided to restore the place and charge an entrance fee? Then everybody and his brother could walk around the place."

"Right," I said. "Anyway, once they got in, they couldn't find the money sitting out in plain sight. It'd have to be concealed."

"Which puts us right back where we were," he said.

We were silent again.

Ray said, "What gets me is we're talking big. Seven, eight big canvas bags loaded down with cash and jewelry. Those suckers were heavy. We were big strappin' guys in those days, all of us young. You should have seen us grunting and groaning, trying to get 'em stashed in the trunk of the car."

I looked at him with interest. "What was the original plan? Suppose the cops hadn't showed up when they did? What did Johnny mean to do with the money in that case?"

"Same thing, I guess. He always said the reason bank robbers got tripped up was they went out and spent the money way too fast. Started fencing silver and jewels while the cops were circulating information about what was in the heist. Made it all easy to trace."

"So whatever the plan was, he'd set it up well in advance," I said.

"He had to."

I thought about that. "Where was he caught?"

"I forget now. Outside town. On the highway, heading out in that direction somewhere."

"Ballardsville Road," Helen said. "Don't know why, but that sticks in my mind. Don't you remember?"

Ray flushed with pleasure. "She's right," he said. "How'd you remember that?"

"I heard it on the radio," she said. "I was so frightened. I thought you were with him. I didn't know the two of you had separated, and I was convinced you'd been caught."

"I was. I just happened to be somewhere else," he said.

"How soon after the robbery was Johnny picked up?"

Ray's eyes rested on mine. "You're thinking he stashed the goods somewhere between the bank downtown and the place he was caught?"

"Unless he had time to go to some other town and come back," I said. "It's like saying you always find something the last place you look. I mean, it's self-evident. Once you find what you're looking for, you don't look any place else. The last you saw him, he had the sacks full of cash. By the time he was arrested, they were gone. Therefore, the money had to have been hidden some time in that period. By the way, you never said how long it was."

"Half a day."

"So he probably didn't have time to get far."

"Yeah, that's true. I always pictured the money around town somewhere. It never occurred to me he might have left and come back. Shoot. I guess it could be anywhere in a hundred-mile radius."

"I think we should operate on the assumption that it's here in Louisville. I don't want to take on all of western Kentucky."

Ray glanced down at his notes. "So what else do we have? This don't look like much."

"Wait a minute. Try this. The little key had a number on it. I just remembered that," I said. "M550. It's close to my birthday, which is May fifth."

"What good does that do us?"

"We could go to the locksmith and have him grind one."

"To use where?"

"Well, I don't know, but at least we'll have one key in our possession. Maybe the locksmith will have some other ideas."

Ray said, "This feels lame to me. We're really grasping at straws."

"Ray, come on. You work with what you've got," I said. "Believe me, I've started with less and still pulled it off."

"All right," he said skeptically. He made a note of the locksmith's address. He reached for his jacket hanging over the chair.

I rose when he did and buttoned my blazer for warmth. "What about your mother? I don't think she should be left here alone."

She was startled by the mere suggestion. "Oh, no. I won't stay here by myself," she said emphatically. "Not with that fella on the loose. What if he come back?"

"Fine. We'll take you with us. You can wait in the car while we go about our business."

"And just set there?"

"Why not?"

"Well, I might set, but not unarmed."

"Ma, I'm not going to let you sit in the car with a loaded shotgun. Cops would come by and think we're robbing the place."

"I have a baseball bat. That was Freida's idea. She bought a Louisville Slugger and hid it under my bed."

"Jesus, this Freida's a regular artilleryman."

"Artillery*person,*" his mother corrected smartly.

"Get your coat," he said.

19

The Louisville Locksmiths shop was located on west Main Street in a three-story building of dark red brick, probably built in the 1930s. Ray found parking on a side street, and a brief argument ensued during which Helen refused to wait in the car as agreed. He finally gave in and let her accompany us, even though she insisted on bringing along her baseball bat. The storefront was narrow, flanked by dark stone columns. All the wood trim was painted mud brown, and the one street-facing window was papered over with hand-lettered signs that detailed the services offered: deadbolts installed, keys fitted, locks installed and repaired, floor and wall safes installed, combinations changed.

The interior was deep and narrow and consisted almost entirely of a long wooden counter, behind which I could see a variety of key grinding machines. Row after row of keys were hung, wall to wall, floor to ceiling, arranged according to a system known only by the owner. A sliding ladder on overhead rollers apparently supplied access to keys in the shadowy upper reaches. All available space on the scuffed wooden floor was taken up by Horizon safes being offered for sale. We were the only customers in the place, and I didn't see a bookkeeper, an assistant, or an apprentice.

The owner, Whitey Reidel, was about five feet tall and round through the middle. He wore a white dress shirt, black suspenders, and black pants. I didn't peek, but the pants looked like they'd leave a lot of ankle showing at the cuff. He had a soft, shapeless nose and big dark bags under his eyes. His hairline had receded like the tide going out, the remaining wisps of white hair sticking up in front in a curl, like a Kewpie doll's. In his habitual stance, he tended to lean forward slightly, hands on the counter, where he braced himself as if a hard wind blew. He let his eye trail across the three of us. His gaze finally settled on Helen's baseball bat.

"She coaches Little League," Ray said in response to his look.

"What can I do for you?" Reidel asked.

I stepped forward and introduced myself, explaining briefly what we needed and why we needed it. He began to shake his head, pulling his mouth down the minute I mentioned a Master padlock key with the M550 code stamped on one side.

"Can't do," he said.

"I haven't finished."

"Don't have to. Explanations won't make any difference. There's no such thing as a Master padlock key series starting with an M."

I stared at him. Ray was standing behind me, and his mother was standing next to him. I turned to Ray. "You tell him."

"You're the one saw the key. I didn't see it. I mean, I *saw* it, but I didn't pay attention to any numbers."

"I remember distinctly," I said to Reidel. "You have a piece of paper? I'll show you."

Clearly indulging me, he reached for a scratch pad and a pencil. I wrote the number down and pointed at it, as if that made my claim more legitimate. He didn't contradict me. He simply reached under the counter and pulled out the Master padlock index. "You find it, I'll grind it," he said. He rested his hands on the counter, leaning his weight on his arms.

I leafed through the index, feeling stubborn and perplexed. There were numerous series, some indicated by letters, some by numbers, none designated by the M I'd seen. "I swear it was a Master padlock key."

"I believe you."

"But how could a key show numbers that don't exist?"

His mouth pulled down again and he shrugged. "It was probably a duplicate."

"What difference would that make?"

He reached in his pocket and pulled out a loose key. "This is the key for a padlock back there. On this side is the manufacturer, a Master padlock in this case, like the key we're discussing. Did it look like this?"

"More or less," I said.

Helen had lost interest. She'd moved over to one of the free-standing safes, where she was perched wearily, leaning on her bat like a cane.

"Okay. This side says Master, right?"

"Right."

"On *this* side, you got numbers corresponding to the particular padlock the key fits. Are you following?" He looked from me to Ray, and both of us nodded like bobbleheads.

"You give me those numbers, I can look 'em up in this index and get the information I need to reproduce this key, making you a duplicate. But the duplicate isn't going to have the numbers. The duplicate's going to be a blank."

"Okay," I said, drawing the word out cautiously. I couldn't think where he meant to go with this.

"Okay. So the numbers you saw must have been stamped after the key was made."

I pointed to the scratch pad. "You're saying someone had those numbers put on this key," I said, restating it.

"Right," he said.

"But why would somebody do that?" I asked.

"Lady, you came to me. I didn't come to you," he said. When he smiled, I could see the discoloration in his teeth, dark around the gums. "Those numbers are gibberish if you're talking about a Master padlock."

"Could they be code numbers for another key manufacturer?"

"Possibly."

"So if we figured out which manufacturer, couldn't you make me this key?"

"Of course," he said. "The problem is, there's probably fifty manufacturers. You'd have to go through two, three manuals for each company, and many I don't stock. Stamped numbers or letters might also identify the key with a property or door, but there's no way to determine that from what you're telling me."

"Have you ever heard of a Lawless lock?"

He shook his head. "No such thing."

"What makes you so sure?" I said, irritated by his know-it-all attitude.

"My father owned this company and his father before him. We been in business over seventy-five years. If there'd been such a company, I'd have heard the name mentioned. It might be foreign."

I made a face, knowing there'd be no way to track *that* down. "Is there any chance whatsoever that Lawless was in business back in the forties and is now defunct?"

"Nope."

Ray put a hand on my arm. "Let's get out of here. It's okay. We're doing this by process of elimination."

"Just wait," I said.

"No way. You got a look on your face like you're about to bite the guy." He turned to his mother. "Hey, Ma. We're going now." He helped her to her feet, taking her arm on his right while he took my arm on his left. The pressure he exerted made his intentions clear. We were not going to stay and argue with a man who knew more than we did.

I felt my frustration rise. "There has to be some connection. I know I'm right."

"Don't worry about being right. Let's worry about getting Gilbert off our backs," he said. And then to Reidel, "Thanks for your help." He opened the door and ushered us out. "Besides, we don't need the key. Gilbert's got one."

"Well, he's not going to give it back."

"He might. If we can find the locks, he might cooperate. It'd be in his best interests."

"But what are the numbers for? I mean, M550 has to be a code, doesn't it? If not for a key, then something else."

"Quit worrying," he said.

"I do worry. Gilbert's going to want answers. You said so yourself."

Out on the street, it was surprisingly dark. The late afternoon wind whipped off the Ohio River, which I gathered was only three or four blocks away. A few isolated snowflakes sailed by. Streetlights had come on. Most of the businesses along Main were closing down, and building after building showed a blank face. The buildings were largely brick, five and six stories high, the ornamentation suggesting vintage architecture. Several ground-level stores had retracting metal gates now padlocked across the front. An occasional dim light might be visible deep in the interior, but for the most part, a chilling dark contributed to the overall look of abandonment along the street. Traffic in this part of town was thinning. The downtown itself, visible to the east, displayed a lighted skyline of twenty- to thirty-story office buildings.

We drove back to Helen's house, circling the block once for any sign of Gilbert. None of us knew what kind of car he was driving, but we kept an eye out, thinking we might spot him lingering in the shadows or sitting in a parked vehicle. Ray left his car in the cinder alleyway that ran behind his mother's place. We went through the backyard to the darkened rear entrance. None of us had thought about leaving lights on, so the house was pitch black. Ray went in first while Helen and I huddled on the back steps off the utility porch. Helen was still supporting herself with her baseball bat, which she'd apparently adopted as a permanent prop. All across the neighboring yards, I could see the towering shapes of winter-bare trees against the light-polluted November sky. Branches rattled in the wind. I was shivering by the time he'd turned on lamps and overhead lights and let us in. We waited in the kitchen while he checked the front rooms and the unused bedroom upstairs.

We'd been gone for less than an hour, but the house already seemed to smell dank with neglect. The bulb in the kitchen threw down a harsh, unflattering light. The patch of cardboard in the kitchen window showed a gap at one edge. Helen worked her way around the room, from the pantry to the refrigerator, taking out items for a makeshift supper. She moved with confidence, though I could see that she was counting steps. Ray and I pitched in, saying little or nothing, all of us unconsciously waiting for the phone to ring. Helen didn't have an answering machine, so there was no point in wondering if Henry or Gilbert had called in our absence.

We sat down to a meal of bacon and scrambled eggs, potatoes fried in bacon grease, leftover fried apples and onions, and homemade biscuits with homemade strawberry jam. Too bad she hadn't found a way to fry the biscuits instead of baking them. Despite the cholesterol overdose, everything we ate was exquisite. So this is what grandmothers do, I thought. I had, by then, abandoned any hope of getting home that day. It was still only Monday. I had all of Tuesday and Wednesday to catch a plane. In the meantime, I was tired of feeling stressed out about the issue. Why get my knickers in a twist? I'd do what I could here and be on my way.

After supper, Helen settled down in her bedroom with the TV on. Ray got busy with the dishes while I cleared the kitchen table. I was in the process of wiping down the surface, moving aside the sugar bowl, the salt and pepper shakers, when I noticed the sympathy card Johnny Lee had sent. Helen had apparently left it on the table, anchored by the sugar bowl. I read the greeting again, holding it slanted against the light.

Ray said, "What's that?"

"The card Johnny sent. I was just checking the message inside. The verse looks like it's been typed."

"Read it to me again," he said.

" 'And I will give unto thee the keys of the kingdom of heaven: and whatsoever thou shalt bind on earth shall be bound in heaven: and whatsoever thou shalt loose on earth shall be loosed in heaven. Matthew 16:19. Thinking of you in your hour of loss.' I think this is one of those blank cards where you write in the greeting yourself."

"That makes sense. If the verse was meant as a secret message, how's he going to find a card with that particular quote? He almost had to buy a blank and fill it in himself."

I stared at the Bible verse. "Maybe the M550 stands for Matthew chapter five, verse fifty," I suggested.

"Matthew five is the Sermon on the Mount. Doesn't have fifty verses, only forty-eight." He glanced at me, smiling self-consciously. "That's the other thing I did in prison besides boning up on crime. I was part of a Bible study group on Monday nights."

"You're a man of many surprises."

"I like to think so," he said.

I turned the card over and studied the black-and-white photograph pasted on the front. The photo showed the faded image of a graveyard in snow. I picked at the loose edge, peering at the card stock under it. The print had been glued or pasted over a standard commercial picture of the ocean at sunset. I peeled it off and checked the back, hoping for some kind of handwritten note. The print itself was four inches by six, processed on regular Kodak paper, matte finish, no border. Aside from the word *Kodak* marching across the back, the rest was blank. "You think this is a new photograph reprinted from an old neg? Or maybe a new photo reproduced from an old one?"

"What difference does it make?"

I shrugged. "Well, I don't think a picture of the ocean at sunset tells us anything. Maybe the keys aren't related. Maybe the photo is the message and the keys are a diversionary tactic."

He took the card and moved to the table, holding it to the light as I had, examining the photograph. I peeked over his shoulder. All the headstones looked old, the ornate lettering softened by rain and sanded by harsh winter snows. There were five shorter headstones and three larger monuments of the lamb and angel school. Even the smaller markers, probably granite or marble, were carved with bas-relief leaves and scrolls, crosses, doves. The dominant monument was a white marble obelisk probably twelve feet tall, mounted on a granite pedestal with the name PELISSARO visible. All of the surrounding trees were mature, though barren of leaves. A thin layer of snow covered the ground. One cluster of headstones was enclosed with iron fencing, and I could see a section of stone wall to the right.

"I don't suppose you recognize the place," I said.

Ray shook his head. "Could be a private graveyard, like a family plot on somebody's property."

"Looks too spread out for that. Seems like a private graveyard would be more compact and countrified. More homogeneous. Look at the headstones, the variation in sizes and styles."

"So what's this have to do with two keys? He didn't have time to dig up a coffin and bury the stash. It was the dead of winter. The ground was froze hard."

I looked at Ray with interest. "Really. It was winter? So this might have been taken at the time?"

"Possible, I guess, but if he buried the money, he'd have needed grave-digging machinery, which I guess he could have got hold of somehow. Seems like he told me once he'd been a groundskeeper in a cemetery. He could have put the money in a mausoleum, I suppose. Anyway, what's your thinking?"

"But why a picture of this? Maybe it's the name Pelissaro. I'm just spitballing here. He might have left the money with someone by that name. In a building or business in the general vicinity of the cemetery. The Pelissaro Building, Pelissaro Farms. The old Pelissaro estate," I said, wiggling my brows.

Ray shook his head. "You're barkin' up the wrong tree."

"Well. Maybe it's something *visible* from here. A water tower, an outbuilding, a stone quarry. Where's the phone book? Let's look. Let's dare to be stupid. We might hit pay dirt."

"Look for what?"

"The name Pelissaro. Maybe he had a confederate."

I glanced around the kitchen and spotted the residential pages sitting on the chair where he'd left them. I pulled out a chair and sat down, flipping through the White Pages to the P's. There was no Pelissaro listed. Nothing even close. I said, "Shit. Ummn. Well, maybe there was a Pelissaro back in the 1940s. We'll try the library in the morning. It can't hurt."

"We better do something fast. Gilbert's going to call any minute, and I'm not going to tell him we're off to the public *library.* I'd like to tell him we're on to something instead of sitting here daring to be stupid. That's the same as dead in his book."

"You're a pain, you know that? Here, try this." I reached for the Yellow Pages and looked up "Cemeteries." Approximately twenty were listed. "Take a look and tell me where these are located," I said. "If we got out a map and drew a big circle, we could probably narrow down the area. At the very least, we could check out all the cemeteries within a radius of the spot where Johnny was apprehended. Wouldn't that make sense? There couldn't be that many.

Judging by the photograph, this cemetery is well established. Those graves are old. They haven't gone anywhere."

"You don't know that. Around here, they move graves when they dam up a river to make a lake," he said.

"Yeah, well, if the money's underwater, we've had it," I said. "Let's operate on the assumption it's still aboveground someplace. You have a map of Louisville? You can show me what's where."

Ray went out to the car and came back with the big map of the southeastern United States, along with a set of strip maps and a map of Louisville. "Compliments of Triple A. Car I borrowed was well equipped," he said.

"You're too thoughtful," I said as I opened the city map. "Let's start with this first one. Where's Dixie Highway?"

One by one, we worked through the cemeteries listed in the Yellow Pages, marking their locations on the map of Louisville. There were four, possibly five, within reasonable driving distance of the place where Johnny Lee had been apprehended by the police. I listed each cemetery along with the address and telephone number on a separate piece of paper.

"So now what?" he asked.

"So now, first thing tomorrow morning, we'll call each of these cemeteries and find out if they have a Pelissaro buried there."

"Assuming the cemetery's in Louisville."

"Would you quit being such a butt?" I said. "We have to assume this is relevant or Johnny wouldn't have sent you the picture. His object was to give you information, not to fool you."

"Yeah, well, let's hope he didn't do too good a job. We might never decipher it."

By nine o'clock, I was exhausted and began to make mewling noises about turning in. Ray seemed restless and jumpy, worried because Gilbert hadn't been in touch.

"What are you going to tell him if he calls?" I asked.

"Don't know. I'll tell him something. I'd like to get him and

Laura over here first thing tomorrow morning so I can see she's okay. In the meantime, let's get you settled. You look beat."

He found a couple of blankets and a pillow in the top of his mother's closet. "You better make a potty stop first. There isn't a bathroom up there."

I spent a few minutes in the bathroom and then followed Ray up. As it turned out, there wasn't much of anything else up there, either: a single bed with a wood frame and a sagging spring, a bed table with one short leg, and a lamp with a forty-watt bulb and a yellowing shade. I worried briefly about bugs and then realized it was too cold up here for anything to survive.

"You got everything you need?"

"This is fine," I said.

I sat gingerly on the bed while he clumped downstairs again. I couldn't sit up straight because the eaves of the house slanted so sharply above the bed. It was bitterly cold, and the room smelled of soot. As a form of insulation, someone had layered sheets of newspaper between the mattress and the springs, and I could hear them crackle every time I moved. I lifted one corner of the mattress and did a quick check of the date: August 5, 1962.

I slept in my clothes, wrapping myself in as many layers of blanket as I could manage. By curling myself into a fetal position, I conserved whatever body heat I had left. I turned out the lamp, though I was reluctant to surrender the meager warmth thrown off by the bulb. The pillow was flat and felt faintly damp. For some time, I was aware of light coming up the stairwell. I could hear noises—Ray pacing, a chair scraping back, an occasional fragment of laughter from the TV set. I'm not sure how I managed to fall asleep under the circumstances, but I must have. I woke once and turned the light on to check my watch: 2:00 A.M., and the lights downstairs were still on. I couldn't hear the television set, but the nighttime quiet was broken by occasional unidentifiable sounds. I wakened some time later to find the house dark and completely quiet. I was acutely aware of my bladder, but there was nothing for it except mind control.

I really don't know which is worse when you sleep in someone else's house—being cold with no access to additional blankets or having to pee with no access to the indoor plumbing. I suppose I could have tiptoed downstairs on both counts, but I was afraid Helen would think I was a burglar and Ray would think I was coming on to him, trying to creep into his bed.

I woke again at first light and lay there, feeling miserable. I closed my eyes for a while. The minute I heard someone stirring, I rolled out of bed and made a beeline for the stairs. Ray and his mother were both up. I made a detour to the bathroom, where, among other things, I brushed my teeth. When I returned to the kitchen, Ray was reading the morning paper. He hadn't had a chance to shave, and his chin was prickly with white stubble and probably felt as rough as a sidewalk. I was so accustomed to his various facial bruises, I hardly noticed them. He'd covered his habitual white T-shirt with a denim workshirt that he wore loose. Despite his age he was in good shape, the definition in his upper body probably the result of hours lifting weights in prison.

"Have we heard from Gilbert?"

He shook his head.

I sat down at the kitchen table, which Helen had set at some point the night before. Ray passed me a section of the *Courier-Journal.* One more day together and we'd have our routines down pat, like an old married couple living with his mother. Helen, for her part, limped around the kitchen, using the bat as a cane.

"Is your foot bothering you?" I asked.

"My hip. I got a bruise goes from here to here," she said with satisfaction.

"Let me know if I can help."

Coffee was soon perking, and Helen began to busy herself frying sausage. This time she outdid herself, fixing each of us a dish she called a one-eyed jack, in which an egg is fried in a hole cut in the middle of a piece of fried bread. Ray put ketchup on his, but I didn't have the nerve.

After breakfast I hit the phone, making a quick call to the five cemeteries we'd put on our list. Each time I claimed I was an amateur genealogist, tracking my family history in the area. Not that anybody cared. All were nondenominational facilities with burial plots available for purchase. On the fourth call, the woman in the sales office checked her records and found a Pelissaro. I got directions to the place and then tried the last cemetery on the off chance a second Pelissaro was buried in the area. There was only the one.

Ray and I exchanged a look. He said, "I hope you're right about this."

"Look at it this way. What else do we have?"

"Yeah."

I excused myself and headed for the shower. The phone rang while I was in the process of rinsing my hair. I could hear it through the wall, a shrill counterpoint to the drumming of the water, the last of the shampoo bubbles streaming down my frame. In the bedroom, Ray answered the phone and his voice rumbled briefly. I cut my routine short, turned the water off, dried myself, and threw my clothes on. At least I had no problems deciding what to wear. By the time I reached the kitchen, Ray was in motion, putting together an assortment of tools, some of which he brought in from a small shed in the backyard. He'd found a couple of shovels, a length of rope, a pair of tin snips, pliers, a bolt cutter, a hammer, a hasp, an ancient-looking hand drill, and two wrenches. "Gilbert's on his way over with Laura. I don't know what we're up against. We may have to dig up a coffin, so I thought we'd better be prepared." The Colt was sitting on the tin pull-out counter of the Eastlake. Ray picked it up in passing and tucked it in the waistband of his pants again.

"What's that for?"

"He's not going to catch me off guard again."

I wanted to protest, but I could see his point. My anxiety was rising. My chest felt tight and something in my stomach seemed to squeeze and release, sending little ripples of fear up and down my frame. I teetered precariously between the urge to flee and an inordinate curiosity about what would happen next. What was I thinking? That I could affect the end result? Perhaps. Mostly, having come this far, I had to see it through.

20

Gilbert and Laura arrived within the hour with the canvas duffel in tow, probably packed with the eight thousand dollars in cash. Gilbert was wearing his Stetson again, perhaps hoping to enhance his tough-guy image now that he'd been bested by an eighty-five-year-old blind woman. Laura was clearly exhausted. Her skin looked bleached, residual bruises casting pale green-and-yellow shadows along her jaw. Against the pallor of her complexion, her dark auburn hair seemed harsh and artificial, too stark a contrast to the drained look of her cheeks. I could see now that her eyes were the same hazel as Ray's, the dimple in her chin a match for his. Her clothes looked slept in. She was back in the outfit I'd first seen her wearing: oversize pale blue denim dress with short sleeves, a long-sleeved white T-shirt worn under it, red-and-white-striped tights, and high-topped red tennis shoes. The belly harness was gone and the effect was odd, as if she'd suddenly dropped weight in the wake of some devastating illness.

Gilbert seemed tense. His face was still pockmarked with spots where Helen's birdshot had nicked him, and he wore a piece of adhesive tape across his earlobe. Aside from the evidence of first aid, his blue jeans looked pressed, his boots polished. He wore a clean white western-cut shirt with a leather vest and a bolo tie. The outfit was an affectation, as I guessed he'd been west of the Mississippi only once and that not much more than a week ago. At the sight of her grandmother, Laura started to cross the room, but Gilbert snapped his fingers and, like a dog, she heeled. He put his left hand on the back of her neck and murmured something in her ear. Laura looked miserable but offered no resistance. Gilbert's attention was diverted by the sight of his gun in the waistband of Ray's pants. "Hey, Ray. You want to give that back?"

"I want the keys first," Ray said.

"Let's don't get into any bullshit argument," Gilbert said.

His right hand came up to Laura's throat, and with a flick, the blade jutted out of the knife he'd palmed. The point pierced her skin, and the gasp she emitted was filled with surprise and pain. "Daddy?"

Ray saw the trickle of blood and the absolute stillness with which she stood. He glanced down at his waistband where the Colt was tucked. He took the gun out and held it toward Gilbert, butt first. "Here. Take the fuckin' thing. Get the blade off her neck."

Gilbert studied him, easing the point back almost imperceptibly. Laura didn't move. I could see the blood begin to saturate the neck of her T-shirt. Tears trickled down her cheeks.

Ray motioned impatiently. "Come on, take the gun. Just get the knife away from her throat."

Gilbert pressed a button on the knife handle, retracting the blade. Laura put her hand against the wound and looked at her bloody fingertips. She moved to a kitchen chair and sat down, her face drained of any remaining color. Gilbert switched the knife to his left hand and reached over to take the gun with his right. He checked the magazine, which was fully loaded, and then tucked the gun in his waistband, hammer cocked and safety on. He seemed to relax once the gun was back in his possession. "We gotta trust each other, right? Soon as I have my share of the money, she goes with you and we're done."

"That's the deal," Ray said. It was clear he was fuming, a response not lost on Gilbert.

"Bygones be bygones. We can shake on it," Gilbert said. He held his hand out.

Ray looked at it briefly, and then the two shook hands. "Let's get on with this, and no funny business."

Gilbert's smile was bland. "I don't need funny business as long as I have her."

Laura had watched the exchange with a mixture of horror and disbelief. "What are you doing? Why'd you give him the gun?" she said to Ray. "You really think he'll keep his word?"

Gilbert's expression never changed. "Stay out of this, babe."

Her tone was tinged with outrage, her eyes filled with betrayal. "He's not going to split the money. Are you crazy? Just tell him where it is and let's get out of here before he kills me."

"Hey!" Ray said. "This is business, okay? I spent forty years in the joint for this money, and I'm not backing off because you got problems with the guy. Where were you all these years? I know where I was. Where were you? You come along expecting me to bail you out. Well, I'm bailing, okay? So why don't you back off and let me do it my way."

"Daddy, help me. You have to help."

"I am. I'm buying your life, and it don't come cheap. My deal is with him, so butt out of this."

Laura's face took on a stony cast and she stared down at the ground, her jaw set. Gilbert seemed to enjoy the fact that she'd been rebuffed. He moved as if to touch her, but she batted his hand away. Gilbert smiled to himself and sent a wink in my direction. I didn't trust any of them, and it was making my stomach hurt.

I looked on while Ray laid out the game plan, filling Gilbert in on the calls we'd made and the reasoning behind them. I noticed he'd left out a few pertinent facts, like the name of the cemetery and the name on the monument. "We haven't found the money yet, but we're getting close. You expect to benefit, you might as well pitch in here and help," Ray said, his eyes dead with loathing. A chilly smile passed between them, full of promises. I looked from one to the other, hoping fervently I wouldn't be around if the two of them ever got into a pissing contest.

Ray said, "I assume you got the keys with you."

Gilbert pulled them from his pocket, displayed them briefly, hooked together on a ring, and then tucked them away again.

Without another word, Ray began to gather up some of the equipment he'd assembled: the rope, the two shovels, the bolt cutters. "Everybody grab something and let's go," he said. "We can stick all this stuff in the trunk."

Gilbert picked up the hand drill, taking his time about it so it wouldn't look like he was obeying orders. "One more thing. I want the old lady with us."

"I'm not going anywhere with you, bub," Helen snapped. She sat down in her chair and leaned stubbornly on her bat.

Ray paused. "What's she got to do with it?"

"We leave anyone behind, how do I know they aren't dialing the old 911?" Gilbert said to Ray, ignoring the old woman.

Ray said, "Come on. She wouldn't do that."

"Oh, yes I would," she said promptly.

Gilbert stared at Ray. "You see that? Old woman's crazy as a bed bug. She goes, too, or it's all off."

"What are you talking about? That's bullshit. You gonna forfeit the dough?"

Gilbert smiled, still gripping Laura's neck. He gave her head a shake. "I don't have to forfeit anything. You're the one going to lose."

Ray closed his eyes and then opened them. "Jesus. Get your coat, Ma. You're coming with us. I'm sorry to have to do this."

Helen's gaze moved vaguely from Gilbert to Ray. "It's all right, son. I'll go if you insist."

Since Gilbert didn't trust any of us, we took one car. Gilbert, Helen, and Laura sat together in the backseat, the old woman holding hands with her granddaughter. Helen still had her bat, which Gilbert took note of. Sensing his gaze, Helen shook the bat in his direction. "I'm not done with you, mama," Gilbert murmured.

Ray drove while I navigated from the front seat, tracing the route on the open map. He headed east on Portland Avenue, cutting back onto Market Street and from there under the bridge and up onto 71 heading north. The day was breezy, faintly warmer than it had been. The sky was a wide expanse of robin's egg blue, clouding up along the horizon. I was hoping Ray would violate some minor traffic law and get us stopped by the highway patrol, but he kept the speedometer exactly at the limit, giving hand signals I hadn't seen anyone use for years.

About a mile beyond the Watterson Expressway, he moved onto the Gene Snyder Freeway and took the first off-ramp. We exited onto 22, which we followed for some distance. The route we took was probably once a little-used dirt road, many miles out in the country. I pictured merchants and farmers in a countywide radius, traveling hours by wagon to reach the wooded area where their dead would be laid to rest. The Twelve Fountains Memorial Park was located several miles across the line into Oldham County, surrounded by limestone walls, occupying land that had once been part of a five-hundred-acre tract of woods and tangled undergrowth. Over the years, the hilly countryside had been tamed and manicured.

At the entrance, iron gates stood open, flanked by fieldstone gateposts that must have been fifteen feet tall. The road split left and right, circling an arrangement of three large stone fountains, shooting staggered columns and sprays of water into the icy November air. A discreet sign directed us to the right, where a small stone building was tucked against a backdrop of cypress and weeping willows. Ray pulled onto the gravel parking pad. I could see the woman in the office peering out at us.

Gilbert took Helen into the office with him. Laura's face was still so visibly bruised as to generate attention he didn't want. His own face was still peppered with tiny cuts, but nobody'd have the nerve to ask what happened.

While the two of them were gone, Laura caught Ray's eye in the rearview mirror. "What about her?" she said, indicating me.

"What *about* her?" Ray said, annoyed.

"Gilbert's worried about Grammy calling the cops. What makes you think *she* won't?"

I turned around in the seat to face her. "I'm not calling anyone. I'm just trying to get home," I said.

Laura ignored me. "You think she's going to sit by and watch us walk away with the money?"

"We haven't even found it yet," Ray said.

"But when we do, then what?"

Ray's expression was despairing. "Jesus, Laura. What do you want from me?"

"She's going to be trouble."

"I am not!"

Laura looked away from me and out the window, her mouth set. Gilbert and Helen were returning to the car. He ushered her unceremoniously into the backseat again and then got in on his side. Helen muttered something scathing and Ray said, "Ma, be careful." She reached forward and touched Ray's shoulder with affection.

Gilbert got in the car, slamming his door shut, handing me the pamphlet he carried with him. Since I'd called in advance, the woman in the sales office had provided us with a brochure detailing the charter and development of the memorial park. The pamphlet opened up to show a map of the cemetery with points of interest marked with an X. She'd also supplied a folded sheet of paper that showed a detailed plot map of the particular section we'd be visiting. The Pelissaro gravesite she'd circled in red.

I looked back at Gilbert. "You know, this may not lead to anything," I said.

"I hope you have a backup plan, in that case."

My backup plan was to run away real fast.

Ray fired up the engine again. I showed him the route, which the woman had marked in ballpoint pen. The cemetery was laid out in a series of interconnecting circles that from the air would have resembled the wedding ring design on a patchwork quilt. Roads encompassed each section, curving into one another like a succession of roundabouts. We took the first winding road to the left as far as the Three Maidens fountain. At the fork, we veered left, moving up past the lake, and then to the right and around to the old section of the park. The cemetery had been named for its twelve fountains, which loomed unexpectedly, wanton displays of water spewing skyward. In California, the waste of water would be subject to citation, especially in the drought years, which seemed to outnumber the rainy ones.

We passed the Soldier's Field, where the military dead were buried, their uniform white markers as neatly lined up as a newly planted orchard. The perspective shifted with us, the vanishing point sweeping across the rows of white crosses like the beam from a lighthouse. In the older sections of the cemetery, into which we drove, the mausoleums were impressive: limestone-and-granite structures complete with sloping cornices and Ionic pilasters. The larger sarcophagi were adorned with kneeling children, their heads bowed, stone lambs, urns, stone draperies, and Corinthian columns. There were pyramids, spires, and slender women in contemplative postures, cast-bronze dogs, arches, pillars, sculpted busts of stern-looking gents, and elaborate stone vases, all interspersed with inlaid granite tablets and simple headstones of more modest dimensions. We passed grave after grave, stretching away as far as the eye could see. The headstones represented so many family relationships, the endings to so many stories. The very air felt dark and the ground was saturated with sorrow. Every stone seemed to say, This is a life that mattered, this marks the passing of someone we loved and will miss deeply and forever. Even the mourners were dead now and the mourners who mourned them.

The Pelissaro plot was located in a cul-de-sac. We parked and got out. Gilbert tossed his Stetson in the backseat, and the five of us moved toward the gravesite in ragtag fashion. I held the photograph at eye level, marveling at the scene that was laid out before us exactly as it looked forty years before. The Pelissaro monument, a white marble obelisk, towered over the surrounding graves. Most of the trees in the photograph were still standing, many having grown much larger with the passage of time. As in the picture, the branches were once again barren of leaves, but this time there was no snow and the grass had gone dormant, a patchy brown mixed with dull green. I spotted the same cluster of headstones enclosed with iron fencing, the section of stone wall to the right of us.

Gilbert was already impatient. "What do we do now?" he asked Ray.

Ray and I exchanged a brief look. So far, Gilbert had honored his end of the bargain. He'd showed up with Laura, who was not only alive and well, but looked as if she hadn't been battered the night before. Ray and I stood there, stalling, knowing we really didn't have a way to hold up our end. We'd tried to indicate the limits to our understanding, but Gilbert didn't have any tolerance for ambiguity. Helen waited patiently, bundled up in her coat, attentive to a large monument she probably mistook for one of us.

Gilbert said, "I'm not going to dig up any monuments. Especially this one. Probably weighs a couple tons."

"Gimme a minute," Ray said. He surveyed the scene in front of us, his gaze taking in headstones, landscape features, valleys, trees, the ring of hills beyond. I knew what he was doing because I was doing the same thing, searching for the next move in the peculiar board game we were playing. I'd half expected a water tower looming in the distance, some pivotal word painted on its circumference. I'd hoped to see an old gardener's shed or a signpost, anything to indicate where to go from here. The Pelissaro gravesite had to be important, or why bother to send the photograph? The keys might or might not be relevant, but the monument foreshadowed *something,* if we could just figure out what.

I could see Ray doing a spot check of names on every marker within range. None of them seemed significant. I did a three-hundred-and-sixty-degree turn, scanning the cul-de-sac behind us, which was ringed by mausoleums. "I got it," I said. I put a hand on Ray's arm and pointed. There were five mausoleums in the circle, gray limestone structures sunk into the rising hill that fanned up and around the cul-de-sac like an upturned shirt collar. Each of the five facades was different. One resembled a miniature cathedral, another a scaled-down version of the Parthenon. Two looked like small bank buildings complete with colonnades and shallow steps leading up to once impressive entrances now sealed shut with blank concrete. On each, the family name was carved above the door in stone. REXROTH. BARTON. HARTFORD. WILLIAMSON. It was the fifth mausoleum that caught my attention. The name above the door was LAWLESS.

Ray snapped his fingers rapidly. "Gimme the keys," he said to Gilbert, who obliged without argument.

We scrambled down to the road, all of us intent on the sight of the mausoleum. The entrance was protected by an iron gate, with a keyhole visible even from a distance. Through the bars of the gate, a chain had been added, circling the main lock and secured with a padlock. I glanced down at the piece of paper that showed, in detail, the layout of burial plots in the area. The Lawless mausoleum was located in section M, lot 550. The message from Johnny Lee had been sent and received. I couldn't believe we'd done it, but we'd actually managed to interpret his missive.

Ray moved to the car, which we'd parked in the circle just across from the mausoleum. He opened the trunk and took out a tire iron. "Grab a tool," he said. Again, Gilbert obeyed without a murmur, arming himself with a shovel. Laura grabbed a hammer and a pickax Ray had found and tossed in the back at the last minute. The five of us crossed the pavement, Helen bringing up the rear with her bat tapping the pavement. We moved up the steps in an irregular grouping and peered through the iron bars of the gate. Inside, there was a paved foyer, maybe ten feet wide and five feet deep. On the back wall, there were spaces for sixteen vaults into which individual caskets could be placed, the vaults themselves arranged four rows high and four rows wide.

We stood back and watched as Ray inserted the small key in the Master padlock, which popped loose at a turn. The chain, once freed, clattered to the pavement. The big iron key turned in the gate lock with effort. The gate shrieked as it swung open, the shrill scraping sound of metal on metal. We went in. Of the sixteen burial slots, all seemed to be filled. Twelve bore engraved stones indicating the name of the deceased, birth and death dates, and sometimes a line of poetry. All of the birth and death dates ranged in years before the turn of the century. The four remaining slots were cemented over with plain concrete and bore no data at all.

Ray seemed reluctant to act at first. This was, after all, a family burial place. "I guess we better get a move on," he said. Tentatively, he went after the uppermost square of concrete with the tire iron. After the first blow, he began to hack in earnest at the blank face, working with concentration. Gilbert took one of the shovels and used the blade in much the same way, laboring beside Ray. The noise seemed remarkably loud to me, echoing around in the confines of the mausoleum. I'm not sure anyone outside the structure could have heard much. It certainly wouldn't be easy to pinpoint the source of all the pounding. The concrete was apparently only the barest of shells because the facing began to crack, yielding to sheer force. Once Ray had succeeded in breaking through, Gilbert chipped away at the crumbling material and widened the opening.

Meanwhile, Laura was on her knees, whacking with equal vigor at the concrete facing on the bottom vault with the pickax. Dust flew up, filling the air with a pale gritty cloud of small particles. There was something disturbing about the diligence with which they worked. All their conflicts and past quarrels had been set aside with the acceleration of the hunt. Discovery was imminent and greed had displaced their contentiousness.

Helen and I moved back against the wall, getting out of their way. Through the barred gate, looking toward the hillside, I could see the wind pushing at the tree branches. I craned my neck, looking up with uneasiness. The sky had clouded over completely, dark forms massing above us. The weather here was changeable, where in California it seemed fixed and monotonous. I couldn't imagine where this situation was heading, and I was torn between dread and some dim hope that in the end everything would turn out all right. Ray and Gilbert would split the money, shake hands, and go about their business, freeing me to go about mine. Laura would leave Gilbert. Maybe she'd spend some time with her father and her grandmother before the three parted company. Ray would probably remain with his mother while she had her eye surgery, unless he was caught and sent back to prison first.

I checked my watch. It was only 10:15 in the morning. If I managed to catch an early afternoon flight, I might get home in time for dinner. I'd missed most of the prewedding festivities. Tomorrow night, Wednesday, the night before the wedding, William and "the boys" had elected to go bowling, while Nell, Klotilde, and I would probably have supper up at Rosie's. She swore there was no need for a rehearsal dinner. "So what's to rehearse? We're going to stand side by side and repeat what the judge tells us." Nell hadn't had a chance to do the final adjustments on my bridesmaid's muumuu, but how much fitting could it need?

The pounding in the mausoleum took on a repetitious rhythm. I could hear a groundsman using a leaf blower somewhere in the distance. No cars passed along the road that rimmed us. The next thing I knew, Ray, Gilbert, and Laura were dragging canvas bags out of the building and down the steps. Helen and I followed, standing by while Ray upended one of the sacks and toppled the contents out onto the asphalt. Ray was saying, "The guy's a genius. Who the hell would have thought of this? I wish he were here. I wish he could have seen this. Look at that. Jesus, is that beautiful?"

What had tumbled onto the pavement was a hodgepodge of U.S. and foreign currency, jewelry, silver flatware and hollowware, stock certificates, coin silver, Confederate notes, bearer bonds, unidentified legal documents, coins, proof sets, stamps, and gold and silver dollars. The hillock of valuables was nearly as high as my knee, and six other canvas sacks were as crammed full as this had been. Even Helen, with her poor eyes, seemed to sense the enormity of the find. A rain spot appeared on the pavement nearby, followed by a second and a third, at wide intervals. Ray looked up with surprise, holding a hand out. "Let's get going," he said.

Laura refilled the one sack while Ray and Gilbert dragged the others to the trunk of the car and hoisted them in. When the last sack had been added, Ray slammed the trunk down. We were all in the process of getting into the car when I caught sight of Gilbert. For a moment, I thought he was pausing to tuck his shirt in, but I realized what he was reaching for was the gun. Ray saw my face and glanced back at Gilbert, who stood now, feet planted, the Colt in his hand. Laura gripped Helen's arm, the two of them immobilized. I saw Laura lean down and murmur something to her grandmother, warning her what was happening since the old woman couldn't see that well.

Gilbert was watching Ray with amusement, as if the rest of us weren't present. "I hate to tell you this, Ray babe, but your pal Johnny was a stone killer."

Ray stared at him. "Really."

"He put out a contract on Darrell McDermid and had him offed."

Ray seemed to frown. "I thought Darrell died in an accident."

"It wasn't an accident. The kid was smoked. Johnny paid a guy big money to make sure Darrell went down."

"Why? Because he ratted us out to the cops?"

"That's what Johnny said."

"So who did him?"

"Me. Kid was all tore up about his brother anyway, so I put him out of his misery."

Ray thought about it briefly and then shrugged. "So? I can live with that. Served him right. The fuck deserved what he got."

"Yeah, except Darrell wasn't guilty. Darrell never did a thing. Someone told Johnny a big fat fib," Gilbert said with mock regret. "It was me told the cops. I can't believe you guys never figured that out."

"You were the snitch?"

"I'm afraid so," he said. "I mean, let's face it. I'm a rat-fuck. I'm worthless. It's like that old joke about the guy saves a snake and then gets bit to death. He's all, 'Hey, why'd you do that when I saved your life?' And the snake goes, 'Listen, buddy, you knew I was a viper the first time you picked me up.' "

"Gilbert, I gotta tell you. I never mistook you for a nice guy. Not once." Casually Ray reached back, and when his hand came into view again, he was holding a Smith & Wesson .38 Special.

Gilbert laughed. "Fuck. A shoot-out. This should be fun."

"More for me than for you," Ray said. His eyes glittered with malice, but Gilbert only seemed amused, as if he didn't consider Ray a threat he had to take seriously.

"Daddy, don't," Laura said.

I said, "Come on, guys. You don't have to do this. There's plenty of money. . . ."

"This isn't about the money," Ray said. He wasn't looking at me. He was looking straight at Gilbert, the two of them standing no more than ten feet apart. "This is about a guy abusing my daughter, beating up my ex-wife. This is about Darrell and Farley, you asshole. Do we understand one another?"

"Absolutely," Gilbert said.

I felt myself backing up a step, so intent on the two men, I didn't see what Helen was doing. She brought up the baseball bat, flailing wildly in Gilbert's general direction, bashing Ray's arm on the back swing. She missed Gilbert altogether and nearly whacked me in the mouth. I could feel the wind against my lips as the bat whistled past. She hit the car on her follow-through, and the impact knocked the bat right out of her hand.

"Jesus, Ma! Get out of here. Get her outta here!"

Laura screamed and ducked. I hit the ground, looking up in time to see Gilbert take aim and fire at her. There was a click. He looked down at the Colt in astonishment. He recocked and pulled the trigger; the hammer clicked again. He pulled the slide back, ejecting a round, then let it slam forward again, popping another round into the chamber. He swung the gun around and aimed at Ray. He pulled the trigger. Click. He recocked and pulled the trigger again. Click. "What the fuck?" he said.

Ray smiled. "Well, shame on me. I forgot to mention I shortened the firing pin."

Ray fired and Gilbert went down with an odd sound, as if the wind had been knocked out of him. Ray moved forward easily until he was standing directly over Gilbert. He fired again.

Spellbound, I stared as he fired again.

Ray turned and looked in my direction. He said, "Don't do that."

Out of the corner of my eye, I caught a blur of motion and then

I heard the crack of the baseball bat coming down on my head. In the split second before the dark descended, I flashed on Helen with regret. Her erratic batting practice had come to an abrupt halt and she'd popped me a good one. The only problem was I could see her and her hands were empty. Laura was the one up at bat and I was gone, gone, gone.

I spent the night in a semiprivate room at a hospital called Baptist East with the worst headache I believe I've ever had in my life. Because of the concussion, the doctor wouldn't give me any pain medication and my vital signs were checked every thirty minutes or so. Since I wasn't permitted to sleep, I spent a tedious couple of hours being interrogated by two detectives from the Oldham County Sheriff's Department. The guys were nice enough, but they were naturally skeptical of the story I told. Even mildly concussed, I was lying through my teeth, cleaning up my culpability in events as I sketched them out. Finally, a call was placed to the *Courier-Journal* and some poorly paid reporter checked through the back files to find an account of the bank robbery, including names of all the suspects and a lot of colorful speculation about the missing money. As it turned out, of course, the money was still missing, as were Ray Rawson, his aged mother, and his daughter, Laura, whose common-law husband was laid out in the morgue, his body perforated with bullet holes.

I maintained stoutly that I'd been forced along at gunpoint, clobbered and abandoned when my usefulness ran out. Who was there to contradict me? It helped that when a call was placed to Lieutenant Dolan back in Santa Teresa, he spoke up in my behalf and defended my somewhat sullied honor. The investigating officer laboriously hand-printed my account of events, and I agreed to be available for testimony when (and if) Ray Rawson and his merry band were arrested and tried. I don't think the chances are all that good myself. For one thing, Ray has all that money in his possession, along with the forty years' worth of contacts and criminal cunning he picked up while he was in prison. I'm relatively certain he's managed to acquire three sets of false identification, including passports, and first-class tickets to parts unknown.

Wednesday morning, when I was released, a nurse just getting off duty offered me a ride as far as the Portland neighborhood where Helen Rawson lived. I got out at the corner and walked the remaining half block. The house was dark. The back door was standing open and I could see where miscellaneous items of clothing had been dropped in the haste of their departure. I went into the bedroom and turned on the table lamp. All the old lady's pills were gone, a sure sign she'd decamped with her son and granddaughter. I took the liberty of using her telephone, not even bothering to charge the call to my credit card. I had a dreadful time getting through to anyone. I tried Henry and got his machine again. Was the guy never home? I tried Rosie's and got no answer. I called my friend Vera, who must have gone off with her doctor-husband for the long Thanksgiving weekend. I called my old friend Jonah Robb. No answer. I even tried Darcy Pascoe, the receptionist at the company where I once worked. I was out of luck and beginning to panic, trying to figure out who in the world could help me out in a pinch. Finally, in desperation, I called the only person I could think of. The line rang four times before she picked up. I said, "Hello, Tasha? This is your cousin Kinsey. Remember you said to call if I ever needed anything?"

EPILOGUE

The wedding took place late Thanksgiving Day. Rosie's restaurant had been transformed by flowers, by candles, by room deodorants. Rosie in her white muumuu, a crown of baby's breath in her hair, and William in his tuxedo, stood before Judge Raney, holding hands with tenderness. Their faces were shining. In the candlelight they didn't look young, but they didn't look that old, either. They were glowing, intense . . . as if burning from within. Everyone seemed to be part of the promises made. Henry, Charlie, Lewis, and Nell, Klotilde in her wheelchair. The terms "for better or for worse, for richer or for poorer, in sickness and in health" pertained to all of them. They knew what loving and being loved was about. They knew about pain, infirmity, the wisdom of age.

I stood there, thinking about Ray and Laura and Helen, wondering where they'd gone. I know it's absurd, but I found it painful they hadn't cared enough to stick around and see that I was okay. In some curious way, they'd become my family. I'd seen us as a unit, facing adversity together, even if it was only for a matter of days. It's not that I thought we'd go on that way forever, but I would have liked a sense of closure—thanks, fare-thee-well, drop us a line someday.

William and Rosie were pronounced husband and wife. He took her face in his hands, and the kiss they exchanged was as light and sweet as rose petals. Trembling, he whispered, "Oh, my love. I've been waiting all of my life for you."

There wasn't a dry eye in the place, including mine.

Respectfully submitted,
Kinsey Millhone